The Mystery of Things

The Mystery of Things

A NOVEL

THE FIRST BOOK OF
THE ASHLAND GRAIL CYCLE

BY DEBRA MURPHY

Idylls Press 2005

First Edition

Published December, 2004

Idylls Press
P.O. Box 3566
Salem, OR 97302
www.idyllspress.com

Publisher's Cataloging-in-Publication
(Provided by Quality Books, Inc.)

Murphy, Debra.
    The mystery of things : a novel / by Debra Murphy. --
1st ed.
    p. cm. -- (The Ashland grail cycle ; bk. 1)
    LCCN 2004093176
    ISBN 1-59597-000-2

    1. Catholics--Fiction. 2. Milwaukee (Wis.)--Fiction.
I. Title.
PS3613.U727M97 2004   813'.6
                  QB133-2062

Grateful acknowledgment is made to Fr. Martinus Cawley of Our
Lady of Guadalupe Trappist Abbey in Lafayette, Oregon, for per-
mission to reprint an excerpt of his translation of *Nican Mopohua*,
published in his *Guadalupe from the Aztec* and available on the web at
http://www.trappistabbey.org/translations.html.

This book is a work of imagination. Though a number of scenes have
been set in real Milwaukee and Wisconsin locations, the characters
and events are wholly fictitious, and any apparent similarity to real
persons or events is unintentional.

To Daniel,

My Dragonslayer

The Mystery of Things

Prologue:
What is Already Spent

So all my best is dressing old words new,
Spending again what is already spent.

Shakespeare, *Sonnet 76*

Lenny Swiatko Jr., aged twenty-one, crouched in a broom closet of the Milwaukee City Hall, a pen in hand and a sheet of paper resting on his knee. Normally the flaccid muscles of Lenny's face molded, too readily, into the smile or frown or pucker of sympathy that best met the expectations of his interlocutor; but alone and unobserved at this moment, huddled in his little closet, Lenny permitted himself to break into a sharp-angled smile of childish vindictiveness as he signed his name with a flourish in the margin of his suicide note.

"Introibo ad altare Dei," Lenny announced to the stifling closet air as he folded the sheet of paper with a snap. A moment later he flushed with shame: he had, he realized, just committed the humiliating sin of mimesis. He couldn't remember all of a sudden which Great Author had first appropriated those ancient and sacred words, *Introibo ad altare Dei*, for the opening of his Great Play or Great Novel or whatever the devil it was — no doubt one of those incomprehensible doorstoppers he had been forced to muck through in English Lit — but whatever it was and whoever had written it, Lenny had got his inspiration from some other source than the Holy Spirit; which only proved, once again, that Lenny Swiatko Jr., whose very name had come to him second-hand, couldn't do anything, even sacrifice himself, with the originality that his ruthless and whimsical deity occasionally bestowed on more privileged others.

With great effort, Lenny pushed himself to his feet and stepped out into the bright lunchtime emptiness of the Milwaukee City Attorney's office. He walked with heavy, deliberate steps to the bank of windows on the north side of the room and looked down. The concrete heart of downtown Milwaukee shimmered beneath him, its dry soul baking in a fierce, late-summer sun that had not seen rain in sixty-six days. Only an offering in blood would lift the burning hand of God.

Lenny consulted his watch: one minute after noon. His half-time shift was over, his earthly duties done. *"Asperges me, Domine,"* he intoned as he turned away from the window toward the anteroom.

As expected—everyone else was at a lunch meeting with the Mayor—the room's sole occupant was a part-time receptionist named Nadine Jeffrey. The young woman's eyes were fixed on the computer monitor, her beaded dreadlocks occasionally clicking in rhythm with her dancing fingers as they worked the keyboard. Pausing in front of the desk, Lenny placed the sheet of paper in Jeffrey's "In" box.

"Your mom called," Jeffrey said, her distracted words underscored by the syncopated percussives of the computer keys. "You've got a doctor's appointment, you know. One o'clock."

"Mysterium Fidei," Lenny assured her with a benedictory nod.

Finally looking up, Nadine Jeffrey offered her sad-faced colleague a compassionate smile. "What was that, honey?"

Straightening the too-tight knot of his navy tie, a remnant of doubt flickered across Lenny's face, only to be dispelled by the reflexive *sotto voce* recital of more comforting old words: *"Libera nos, quaesumus, Domine, ab omnibus malis..."*

Jeffrey's eyes widened.

Giving a faint shrug—*Miserere nobis*—Lenny picked up the small armchair that squatted in front of the receptionist's desk and carried it through the open double doors that led out on to the eighth-floor gallery overlooking the rotunda. He set the chair next to the gallery railing, stepped up on the seat, and lifted one mirror-polished shoe to the brass rail.

He didn't hear Jeffrey's scream behind him as he made the sign of the cross and pushed off with his lower foot. For one swift moment between heaven and earth, Lenny balanced on the rail, his arms outstretched, the coffin-shaped rotunda opening out before him like a vast inland sea—seamless, liquid, inviting; then Lenny Swiatko Jr. pitched head-first to the rotunda floor eight stories below.

Act One:
A Bloody Field

A Gentle Knight was pricking on the plaine,
Y cladd in mightie arms and siluer shield,
Wherein old dints of deepe wounds did remaine,
The cruell marks of many a bloudy fielde.

Edmund Spenser, *The Færie Qveene*

Chapter One:
First Sight

Dead shepherd, now I find thy saw of might:
'Who ever lov'd that lov'd not at first sight?'

Shakespeare, *As You Like It*

James Ireton awoke with a shudder, his legs twitching, his heart pounding in a deep-dream adrenaline rush. Blinking against the fierce sunlight off Lake Michigan, he propped himself on his elbows, relieved to see that he was on shore, quite safe, his body sprawled on the hot, late-summer sand. There was no Crusader's cross emblazoned on his tunic, no myrtlewood Grail gleaming before him on an altar carved of cedar; no sword glistering in his hand, no iron-plated dragon rising from a blood-dark sea. Even the veiled virgin in the dark tower—he could still feel the sting of her slap on his cheek—was proving, once again, to be nothing more than a fable of his sleeping mind. Reality was the dusky water of Lake Michigan undulating at his feet, the noonday sun shattering off its tranquil surface like the white-fire of diamonds strewn across a smoky mirror.

But then the lingering images of James's dragon-dream gave way to a more immediate sensation: that he was being watched.

Raking sand from his blonde hair, James scouted his perimeter...nothing. Only the expanse of lethargic water, nibbling at the shore, and the occasional seagull winging on the scant breeze above here-and-there groupings of sunbathers, not yet ready to return to school or work after the long Labor Day weekend. To the south looped the curve of Milwaukee's modest skyline, where the distant sails of the Quadracci Pavilion shone white in the sunlight like a spectral Viking ship come ashore, and the Hoan Bridge beyond it reflected silver. Behind him, beyond the steaming traffic of Lincoln Memorial Drive, the new Heisler Institute tower rose above desiccated trees, its silhouette framed by a brooding bank of steel-dark clouds inching toward the city from the southwest.

James shook off his apprehensions with a sleepy shrug and glanced at his watch: two minutes past noon.

Bloody hell. Fr. Bricusse's class was at one, the first of the fall term, and James's briefcase was locked in his office, along with his wallet, his lunch, the class syllabus, and the one remaining set of keys he hadn't managed to lose over the summer.

Jumping up, James beat sand from the backside of his khakis and mentally rehearsed the *mea culpa* he would need to recite in order to induce the officious sixth-floor Heisler Institute janitor, for the second time in a week, to let him into his own office with the master key. Swearing under his breath, James stumbled across the sand to the pedestrian bridge spanning Memorial Drive; then up the forested path tracing the bluffs, where early-fallen leaves, dry as kindling from the summer's drought, crackled under his boots. A single match, James thought, his thighs burning with the effort of the climb, would be all that was required to set the entire lakefront ablaze.

At the top of the bluff the path opened out near the Water Tower, a city landmark in Victorian Gothic. Beyond that, rising higher still with adolescent hubris in Cream City brick and blue-green glass, stood the newly completed Heisler Institute for the Study of Western Civilization.

According to its own glossy brochure, the Heisler Institute was *a place of advanced study dedicated to the principle that Art and Idea shape the structure of our world*. Or perhaps more accurately, James thought, given the pugilistic temperament of its patron, "Mad" Max Heisler, a gauntlet thrown in the face of godless postmodernism.

Pushing through the Institute's mahogany doors, James entered the Institute's diamond-shaped atrium. Open to the full height of the tower's seven stories, the atrium's overhanging galleries met a sharply-pitched roof of turquoise glass. The tower's eastern window, which jutted out over the lake like the prow of a ship in blatant homage to the Quadracci Pavilion, flooded the atrium's white marble floor in muted, swimming light. Tiny human figures passed to and fro high above on the upper galleries, like pilgrims making their haphazard way to some empyrean blue-green heaven. The nautical motifs notwithstanding, skeptical members of the local media had already dubbed the place "St. Max's Cathedral."

"'Mad' Max Heisler," read one *Milwaukee Journal Sentinel* editorial, "Great Lakes Bank CEO and the wealthiest and most controversial businessman in town, has built his museum of antiquated ideals, his cenotaph for Dead White European Males, the way medieval kings built chantries and cathedrals—in atonement for their sins." In some circles the place was known as "Heisler's Folly."

A claustrophobe by nature, James was bypassing the sluggish elevators in favor of the moderately less objectionable stairwell when a startling flash of lightning beyond the glass ceiling whitened the air around him. The storm front he had seen approaching from the beach had apparently arrived.

A roll of thunder reverberated through the massive walls of the Milwaukee City Hall, inducing Lt. Calvin Masefield, newly arrived on the scene and dripping from the sudden cloudburst, to muse that the otherwise welcome precipitation was coming too little, or at least too late, after the record-breaking drought of the summer, to salvage that sorry looking patch of sand and weeds otherwise known as his lawn.

Masefield's wet shoes squeaked to a halt beside the hunched figure of the County Medical Examiner. The CME, who had arrived some minutes before, was kneeling beside the corpse of Milwaukee's latest case of unnatural death: a young male Caucasian, blonde and skinny, who had rushed to self-slaughter, so Masefield had been informed, with the possessed mindlessness of the Gadarene swine. The building had been evacuated, save for a handful of shaken witnesses, one of whom had been standing less than three feet from where the body had come crashing down like a random meteor. The kid's shattered arms and legs lay spread akimbo at all four points of the compass, like a fractured pinwheel, or a swastika.

The victim, Masefield thought, bending down on one knee, looked somehow familiar, though he doubted the kid's own mother could have recognized him: his forehead and facial features were caved in and pulpy from an obvious head-first impact. The lieutenant was also struck, as the CME rolled the body and began a routine check for needle tracks, by the almost military quality of the victim's conservative dress: the meticulous crease ironed into the navy slacks; the glossy polish of the black wingtips; the starched crispness of the buttoned-down shirt, bleached whiter than a celebrity's dental work. The navy tie around the kid's broken neck had been knotted so securely that it hadn't budged off-center even after an eight-story smash-up.

Feeling sweat soaking into the armpits of his shirt, and his fifty-year-old knees protesting beneath his excess poundage, Masefield struggled once again to his feet. Why, he wondered, had Ramon Cruz, the brightest if youngest detective on his swing shift, thought this open-and-shut case of self-murder required the presence — Ramon had insisted on Masefield — of the shift commander?

Hearing the swift tap of footsteps behind him, Masefield turned to see the object of his silent irritation flipping through a memobook as he stepped around a potentially slippery splatter of brain matter a few feet away from the victim's skull. With his walnut-dark hair, slicked back to frame his handsomely broken nose, all Ramon Cruz needed was a cigarette hanging out of his pouty mouth to pass as a south-of-the-border James Dean.

"So what's the deal here?" Masefield said to Cruz.

"He did a header off the eighth floor railing, just like off the high dive at the pool."

"If you could figure that out, why'd you need me?"

Cruz's erect posture seemed suddenly to lose several degrees of arrogance. "I thought you'd want to be here, Professor. The kid was Lenny Swiatko Jr."

Masefield gave a startled blink and looked down. That elusive recognition finally kicked in, and with it a stomach-punch of horror.

Every cop in Milwaukee knew the Swiatko story. The Chief of Police related it to the new recruits at every Police Academy induction ceremony as one of the city's most sterling examples of departmental loyalty and collegial self-sacrifice: Leonard Swiatko Sr., the boy's father and Calvin Masefield's first patrol partner, had been killed almost twenty years before in the line of duty, taking a bullet originally aimed at Masefield.

Masefield and Swiatko had been responding to a neighbor's report of shots fired on West Burleigh. Masefield was interviewing a witness on the sidewalk when the suspected shooter, a teenaged gangbanger just in from Chicago, suddenly emerged from behind a parked car and pointed a semiautomatic at Masefield. Swiatko, standing at the curb and radioing the dispatcher, spotted the kid and gave a warning shout. The kid whirled away from Masefield and took aim at Swiatko. Lenny reached for his weapon but hesitated to fire — *why, the boy's age?* Three shots from the sixteen-year-old assailant and Swiatko was down; two more from Masefield and the kid was on the pavement, too. First and last time Masefield had ever had to fire his weapon on duty. Lenny Jr., Swiatko's only child, had been less than a year old.

Masefield's hand ducked inside his jacket for his Marlboros. Not finding them, it took a good five seconds of fruitless scrounging in assorted garment pockets before the lieutenant remembered that he'd quit smoking some ten years before.

Masefield heaved a sigh. Truth was, he and Lenny Sr. had never gotten all that chummy. Lenny Sr., with his high school education, had been taciturn and prosaic, whereas Masefield was both ambitious and a bit of an intellectual, working with quiet determination toward a Bachelor's, then a Master's degree in Criminal Science at the University of Wisconsin-Milwaukee. Worse, Masefield had (to Lenny's mind) a weird habit of tucking books of African-American poetry into the back seat of the patrol car to scan on his breaks. Lenny had been the first in the department to pin a nickname on Masefield: *the Professor*. It hadn't been meant as a compliment. For his part, Masefield had always suspected Lenny Swiatko of residual racism; but then on the street none of it had mattered.

Masefield looked up. "Why here?" he asked Cruz. "And...why?"

Ramon Cruz thumbed a page of his memobook. "Lenny was working part-time as a clerk in the City Attorney's office. The Chief helped get him the job at the beginning of the summer. Sounds like he wasn't doing too well. You know, space cadet, high rate of absenteeism, that sort of thing. Even when he was here he'd go missing every so often, and they'd find him holed up in an eighth-floor janitor's closet, scribbling kooky letters to himself. It was common knowledge that he was institutionalized after a nervous breakdown a year or so ago." Cruz glanced up from his notes. "You hear about that?"

Masefield gave a faint shake of his head.

Cruz shook his head as well. Masefield couldn't tell if the gesture were intended as an echo of sympathy, or a thinly-veiled judgment on Masefield's guilty ignorance. "When he got out of the hospital," Cruz continued, "he went back to UWM and joined some sort of Catholic fraternity over near the campus. But I guess that didn't last long, either. You know the story. A loner. A little weird sometimes. But no one really thought it was this bad."

"No one ever does. Has anyone notified his mom?"

"We figured you'd want to do the NOD."

Masefield didn't reply right away. The last thing on earth he wanted to do was be the one to break the terrible news to Louise Swiatko. He'd hardly been able to look her in the face for twenty years as it was.

Masefield craned his neck toward the distant, vault-like ceiling of the cavernous City Hall. There was a grid of glass panels up there to let in some natural light, but the century-old Flemish Renaissance building, though recently remodeled, still seemed gloomy as hell to him, and the seven tiers of iron grillwork winding above his head evoked a Hitchcockian feeling of vertigo.

The sound of the body bag being zipped up over Lenny's pulpy head ripped up Masefield's spine like an electrical charge. He looked down again, suddenly unable to remember what he was supposed to do next. Fortunately, the CME chose that particular moment to snap off his Latex gloves and stand up.

"Not much to tell you," the CME reported, motioning for his attendants to heave the vinyl-shrouded carcass onto a cart. "Hardly an unbroken bone, but his forehead took most of the impact, lucky for him."

In his peripheral vision, Masefield saw Ramon Cruz's lips part in moist horror.

"If he'd landed feet first," the CME explained to the younger detective, "he might have survived, sort of. I've seen it happen." The CME returned his attention to Masefield. "I wouldn't expect too much from the postmortem, either, unless there's drug involvement. There were some old scrips in his wallet that he never had filled, and judging by them, I'd say we're going to get our answers from the kid's psych history. As in paranoid schiz." Clapping Masefield once on the shoulder, the CME turned in silent pity to catch up with his attendants, already on their way out of the building for the drive to the morgue.

"Did he leave any kind of note?" Masefield said to Cruz.

The young detective reached inside his jacket and pulled out a folded piece of paper. "He gave this to the receptionist. She said he was mumbling a bunch of weird stuff in what sounded like Latin, but he was climbing up on the rail before she realized what he was up to."

Masefield took the paper and unfolded it. It was a page photocopied from a Bible. Lenny had written *"Introibo ad altare Dei"* in the margin and signed his name next to a passage circled in red:

> **12** How art thou fallen from heaven, O Lucifer, son of the morning! How art thou cut down to the ground, which didst weaken the nations! **13** For thou hast said in thine heart, I will ascend into heaven, I will exalt my throne above the stars of God: I will sit also upon the mount of the congregation, in the sides of the north.

The lieutenant's eyebrows gathered in a bushy line. As a loyal son of the African Methodist Episcopal Church, Calvin Masefield instantly recognized the grand old language of the King James *Isaiah*. Only problem was, the Swiatkos were Catholics, and Masefield was pretty sure that Catholics—particularly Lithuanian Catholics like the Swiatkos—didn't use the KJV.

"Any idea what this is supposed to mean?" Masefield said, jabbing his finger at Lenny's marginal note.

Ramon Cruz shrugged. "Looks to me like something from the old Latin Mass. I can ask my mom, she loves all that stuff."

Masefield at length re-folded the paper and tucked it in his breast pocket, where his Marlboros should have been, then looked up one last time at the galleries looming oppressively above their heads. "I've always hated this place," he said. "It's like the Hoan Bridge, creepy and high up, and just begging people to come and jump off. I read somewhere that they had to put chicken wire up on the top floor during the Depression, so many people were coming downtown to jump. Nobody's done it in years."

Ramon Cruz glanced with unconcealed boredom at his watch. "Yeah, well, these whiz-bang atrium thingies are all over the city now. Lupe just gave me a tour of that spendy new Heisler Institute building above Bradford Beach. I mean, it's a lot more open, what with the windows and all, but I still felt like puking over the railing when I looked down from the top floor."

"The Heisler Institute!" Masefield was grateful for the distraction of some small-talk. "What's your sister doing in a vanilla joint like that?"

"Starting a doctoral program in English Lit." Ramon sniffed. "C'mon, Professor, you of all people, don't give me that *pochismo* crap. We've got as much right as the Anglos to get ourselves over-educated and over-qualified for cushy academic desk jobs, why the hell not?"

Masefield chuckled, but lost his smile again when he noticed the slender Hmong janitor standing a few feet away. Bucket in hand, he was obviously waiting for the two policemen to finish their conversation so that he could begin cleaning up the mess at their feet.

Masefield stepped aside.

Having paid his pound of flesh (an obsequious apology and a ten-dollar tip) to the Heisler Institute janitor, James Ireton paused, briefcase in hand, in the open doorway of seminar room 503.

The room, fitted with the same creamy plaster, mahogany trim and russet carpeting that prevailed throughout the Heisler Institute building, was narrow but deep, its northern wall turning at an oblique angle to fit itself against one side of the building's diamond-shaped atrium. Institute staff, James had heard, were already complaining that Heisler's whimsical insistence on the central rhombus had forced the building's world-famous architect to design all the atrium-adjacent offices and classrooms with compensating diagonals and acute angles, producing disorienting trapezoidal rooms.

But at least the architect had taken intelligent advantage of the lakefront location, James observed. An arched window in blue-green glass made up the whole of the east wall. A thousand slivers of silvered sunlight sparkled up from Lake Michigan below, its shimmering surface embellished here and there by the hazy smudges of white sails skimming along the horizon.

James's instinctive admiration quickly gave way to vexation, however, when he stepped into the room and took note of the four students already seated at the seminar table, three of whom were the last people in the Institute with whom he'd choose to take a class: Richard Krato, Mitch Showalter, and Bel Gunderson. Bloody hell.

His classically proportioned features hidden behind the latest edition of *The Rambler*, a right-wing Catholic weekly, Richard Krato was dressed, as ever, in the crisp white shirt, navy trousers and tie, which comprised the uniform of SANA, the Student Apostolate of North America. Sitting next to Richard and in identical clothing, but at six-foot-three packing the formidable build of a defensive lineman, Mitch Showalter frowned into a yellowed paperback edition of D. H. Lawrence's *The Plumed Serpent*. As usual, Mitch Showalter sat a little too close to Richard Krato's chair, as if he were an overgrown cyst attached to Richard's arm, or the less dominant half of a split personality. The Heisler Institute student body, which had a penchant for allotting literary nicknames to its more eccentric members, had long since dubbed the pair "Rosencrantz and Guildenstern." Or sometimes "Rosenstern and Guildencrantz." Or sometimes just "Rosenstern" for short, because (to paraphrase a famous Shakespeare critic's assessment of their namesakes), the two men, even together, did not seem to make up one whole man.

Suppressing an expletive, James took a seat at the opposite end of the table. A puff of steamy air from an open side-window brought the familiar scent of liberally applied *Narcisse* to his nostrils.

Bel. Thread-slender, flamboyant, exquisite Isabel Gunderson. She was helmeted in chin-length platinum hair, cut in an edgy bob by Erik of Norway. Her chiseled, hollow-cheeked features, recently accentuated by the extraction of her back molars, had long since earned her the journalistic appellation of "top local model." The perfection of Bel's physiognomy was marred, however, in James's view, by a pair of indifferent eyes crowned by thinly plucked eyebrows that arched sweepingly toward her temples like lopsided question marks. Right now, apparently inspired by Mitch Showalter's current reading matter, Bel was rabbiting on to the big fellow with an impromptu post-structuralist analysis of Lawrencian blood mysticism, her tinny-voiced critique ornamented like an autograph book with references to Derrida and Foucault, Artaud, and Bataille.

Eager for a distraction, any at all, James turned to scope out the fourth student, whom he did not recognize, a dark-haired, fresh-faced neophyte who, by the looks of it, was far too young to be taking an upper-level graduate seminar. With her face angled towards Bel, James couldn't make out the girl's features clearly, but her glossy black hair, streaked with coppery highlights and pulled back in some sort of complicated plait, suggested Hispanic origins, or possibly Native American.

Copping curious glances at her from time to time, James was digging in his briefcase, intending to kill a few minutes with a swift perusal of several weeks' accumulation of Institute mail, when the new girl suddenly turned his way and James noted strong but unremarkable features framing a remarkable pair of eyes: large, heavy-lidded, and as turquoise as the Caribbean reef waters in which he had immersed himself for two months of his summer holiday.

Resisting a magnetic lean toward those blue-green eyes, James fixed his startled attention on his mail: sailing magazines, literary journals, book catalogs…there was only one personal letter—not surprising perhaps for a man with so many contacts and so few friends—from the Reverend Dr. Cyril Ireton, London.

James tossed the envelope back in the briefcase. His father's jeremiads were usually little more than constipated re-workings of his latest Sunday sermon. James would gladly save this latest screed for some moment when he was feeling stronger.

At the bottom of the pile was a business envelope with no return address. Tearing it open, James extracted a single sheet of folded paper that appeared to be a photocopy of a Bible page. Much better versed in the King James Version, thanks to his father, than he had ever wanted to be, James immediately recognized the passage from the fourteenth chapter of *Isaiah*, circled in red:

> **12** How art thou fallen from heaven, O Lucifer,
> son of the morning! How art thou cut down to the
> ground, which didst weaken the nations!…

And so forth, dammit. James didn't have to finish it, he knew the passage by heart. Scripture memorization had been the preferred method of paternal punishment for Cyril Ireton's oft-transgressing son.

Looking up, James directed a blistering glance at Richard Krato, who, he had every reason to believe, was the source of this "anonymous" preachment. Time was, in fact, when Richard Krato sent him these miserable missives on a weekly basis, but not in two—or was it three?—years. Good God, why was Rich starting it up again now?

Coming up with no answer other than Richard Krato's undying sense of spiritual superiority, laced with a sizeable measure of sheer vindictiveness,

James wadded the paper into a ball, thinking to toss it in his former friend's face, then instantly reconsidered. No, Richard, like his father Peter—like all these penny-ante holy warriors—was only brazened by resistance. Better to ignore the smug little shit entirely.

James lobbed the paper into the trash can behind him.

At that moment Trisha Perl's uncombed mop of red hair bobbed through the doorway, and James's brief flare of resentment fizzled into a wash of remorse. The diminutive young woman, dressed as usual in a grotty old pair of bib overalls, pointedly ignored James's queasy smile, with which he intended to communicate a *no-hard-feelings, let-bygones-be-bygones* sort of greeting, and took the empty seat on this side of the new girl.

Trisha. Tiny, tomboyish, tough-as-an-old-boot little Trisha Perl, who seemed to have no past or future that she ever spoke of, and whose only apparent source of interior stability was a tenacious devotion to the sort of passé feminism for which good grooming and skirts represented an impossible concession to Patriarchy. Still, she had proved an efficient and hardworking stage manager for James's student production of *Othello* the previous spring, and James, drunk and in heat at the wrap party thrown by Dr. Franco Lanciano in his lakeside mansion, had been taken completely off-guard by the erotophobic young woman's unexpectedly persuasive come-hither. The epilogue of the whole tragicomic script had been a half-hour or so of perfectly ghastly sex in Trish's grungy North Farwell digs, followed three days later by the girl's public announcement, in class, that she had discovered she was lesbian.

James was relieved to see Jack Sigur's rangy figure sauntering through the doorway, his thin face newly sporting a neatly trimmed goatee over his caramello chin. James waved him over.

"Hey, congrats, Jim-bo!" Jack exclaimed in a baritone voice framed in the breezy accents of Creole Louisiana. He slid into the chair adjacent to James. "I heard you sailed through your Comps, and that the Institute Press is about to publish your Master's thesis." Before James could respond, let alone comment on the goatee, Jack had taken note of the presence of Richard and Mitch at the other end of the table and added, "But now would you loo-kee here. I cannot be*lieve* Rosenstern signed up for this class. I didn't think Mr. Peter Krato allowed his helots to get within a mile of heretics like you."

"Neither did I," James agreed sourly. "But Krato must know. I assure you, SANA members do not go to the loo without the *nihil obstat* of Peter Krato."

Jack pantomimed a stagey shudder. "Hope to hell I don't get saddled with one of 'em to write that damned research paper."

Suddenly remembering, James let out a groan. According to the syllabus for this seminar, the stated topic of which was "Shakespeare and his Precursors," students would be called upon to write research papers in tandem, ostensibly as an exercise in "cooperative scholarship," whatever the devil that was.

The sight of James's gray eyes squinting anxiously from face to face in the room elicited a chuckle of undisguised *Schadenfreude* from Jack Sigur. "Son, you *are* in the pickle barrel. But now Miss Guadalupe Cruz—" Jack nodded discreetly at the dark-haired neophyte. "—has no reason to hate your guts. Yet."

"What was her name?" The new girl was now chatting with a great deal more animation to Trisha Perl.

"Guadalupe Cruz. 'Lupe' for short. Hispanic, obviously, but I think her mother's Irish. She joined up this summer, straight out of a Master's from UW-Mad." Jack wagged a long finger in front of James's scowling face. "Not your type, *je t'assure*, so don't even think about it. Which you will, son, first time you see her standing up."

"Beg pardon?"

"I mean, Jim-bo, Lupe Cruz may have the face of a milkmaid and the morals of the Immaculate Conception, but she's also got the measurements of Miss Universe 1957."

"Jackson Sigur," James countered crossly, "*thou may find'st to be too busy is some danger.*"

Before Jack could retort in kind, Fr. Arthur Bricusse shuffled through the door. James was obliged to gather his straying thoughts.

A white-haired, spindle-shanked Oratorian priest in a rumpled black cassock, Bricusse took his place at the head of the seminar table. Looking around the room as if counting heads, Bricusse beamed openly when his eyes fell on James. James's reciprocal smile of greeting quickly gave way to a frown of worry, however, when he noticed that the fragile old man had lost more weight during the summer.

"Welcome to Western Literature 999," Bricusse began, wasting no time in calling the class to order. "As you all know, this is the infamous 'cooperative methods' seminar, required of all our doctoral candidates. The title we have given our little academic adventure this term is 'Shakespeare and his Precursors.' In the course of these next three months I hope to explore with you the impact that the works of poets and playwrights like Chaucer, Marlowe, Jonson, Sir Philip Sidney, and Edmund Spenser may have made on the altogether different literary talents and preoccupations of our greatest playwright."

Sipping from a little plastic cup of water that he carried almost everywhere, Bricusse made eye-contact with each student in turn. "The works of Shakespeare, my dear friends, like all works of genius, challenge us to look into that mirror, or *glass*, to quote Shakespeare's Cassius, which *discovers to ourselves, that of ourselves which we yet know not of.* Is it any wonder, then, that it is so easy for us to read ourselves and our own passions, prejudices, and experiences into Shakespeare's works, and draw conclusions from them which mirror our own most deeply and sometimes unconsciously held convictions? But where, we must ask, did the dramatist find *his* sources of inspiration? And how did he mold their influence to suit his own unique and extravagant imagination?"

Already tiring by the looks of it, Bricusse pulled up a chair before leading the students through the usual first-class round of introductions. This prescribed ritual took some fifteen or twenty minutes and necessitated, much to James's dismay, his own minimalist recital of biographical data. This in turn prompted a paternal sounding announcement from Bricusse that James was about to see his first book published, a revision of his Master's thesis on *Hamlet* entitled *The Conscience of the Prince.*

James managed to tune the better part of the whole embarrassing business out, until his drifting attention was snagged once again by the amusingly syncopated rhythms of the neophyte's dusky stammer, which James at first thought to be the product of nervousness, then realized, with a stab of pity, was congenital:

"I-I-I'm Lupe C-C-Cruz," the new girl finally managed to choke out after several seconds of hand-flapping semi-silence. "I g-guess I'm not really supposed to b-be in an upper-level course like this, b-b-but Father let me in because…" Cruz seemed to grope in the air for the right words. "Because I'm madly in love with Shakespeare!"

A loud snicker from Bel Gunderson brought a fierce blush to Cruz's cheeks.

"An enthusiasm we all share," Bricusse said sharply, no doubt to put a period to the eruption of chuckles at his new student's expense. "And now that we've all been properly introduced, why don't we settle the little matter of your scholarly partnerships. After assessing your enrollment sheets, which included your stated preferences for research topics, I'm delighted to report that each of you will be free to pursue at least your second choice of topic, if not your first."

Praying to God, or any other deity that might be listening, that Bricusse had had the wit to pair him with Jack Sigur, James clamped shut his eyes like a blindfolded man before a firing squad.

"First off, Jack Sigur and Trisha Perl, you'll be tackling topic number one, a comparative study of Marlovian and Shakespearean villains. Topic number four, on the treatment of Nature and Grace in Shakespeare and Spenser, goes to Richard Krato and Isabel Gunderson—"

Once more the class erupted in laughter, and even James was momentarily distracted from his own predicament. Richard Krato, after all, was an avowedly celibate disciple of SANA, the Student Apostolate of North America—a more-Catholic-than-the-Pope faction of devotees whose steel-plated leader, Peter Krato, served up new daily dogmas with the communal breakfast sausage. Bel Gunderson, on the other hand, was an intellectual dabbler whose only sustained spiritual ambition was to make her athletic way through the unexpurgated *Kama Sutra*, position by acrobatic position. The literary brainchild of such a coupling, James mused, would make for entertaining reading.

Bricusse rapped on the table top, calling the class to order. His efforts were interrupted by an even more aggressive knock on the door, followed by the entrance, without hesitation or apology, of a young man, tall and handsome in a soap opera sort of way, and dressed in an exquisite silk suit of unquestionably superior provenance. It was when the stranger bent down to whisper something in Bricusse's ear that James heard a gasp and turned just in time to see an expression of wholesale shock blossoming on Lupe Cruz's rapidly blanching face. In turn the striking interloper obviously recognized Cruz as well, for when he glanced up at the source of the noise an expression of outright hatred—or so it appeared to James—flashed briefly across the fellow's chilly green eyes.

Quickly composing himself, the stranger mumbled something further to Bricusse—James heard only the word "funds"—and shot one last swift but baleful glance at Guadalupe Cruz before striding out the door with a patently self-satisfied smirk.

Cruz slumped against the back of her chair.

James wedged himself against the back of his own chair, a spike of adrenaline shooting up his spine. *Well, now*, he thought with sudden interest, his gray eyes narrowing to focus on Cruz's stricken face, any 'milkmaid' that could put a look like that on a grown man's face had at least one good story to tell. All of a sudden he couldn't wait to see her standing up.

All in all, James thought a little over two hours later as he made for the stairwell, the first meeting of the last seminar of the last term of his five-year doctoral career had finished up in an even more ungainly fashion than was usual for such first-day-of-class ordeals. Alongside the uncomfortable presence of his old two-headed nemesis, Rosenstern, the unsettling arrival of the Bible-letter, and the curious business of Miss 1957's tantalizing interchange with Mr. Soap Opera, before the prescribed one-hundred-and-ten academic minutes had ticked to a close, James had also found himself assigned to write his research paper—his "exercise in collegial scholarship," sod all—with none other than the stuttering Miss 1957 herself. Bloody bleeding hell.

As soon as the bell rang, therefore, and the other students had begun to pair off to make preliminary plans for partnership, James put Miss Cruz off with a vague wave and a "catch you later," and made a bee-line for his mentor's new office on the seventh floor.

Stepping into the room for the first time, James looked around Fr. Arthur Bricusse's personal academic domain. Bathed in muted sunlight from one large arched window, the room seemed warmer and fitted to a more human scale than the rest of the fabulous Institute building. Furnished with wall-to-wall bookshelves and scholarly clutter, Bricusse's things were spread about in a sort of orderly disarray, as if the old man knew just where he wanted everything, but hadn't quite managed to get it there yet. James shook his head at the taped-up boxes stacked one upon the other against the walls.

"You could use an extra pair of hands in here, methinks."

"I do seem to be running out of steam these days," Bricusse admitted, reaching for a nearby cup of water and taking a thirsty drink. "And what with chaplaining that pilgrimage to Mexico last month, I just haven't found the time to cut a path through the jungle yet. But how was *your* vacation? About time you took one. Go home to England?"

James flinched at the priest's use of "home" and "England" in the same sentence. "The Caribbean, actually," he said. "I needed a rest cure. England wouldn't have been."

Bricusse raised a snowy eyebrow. "And the Caribbean was?"

James dropped into a small armchair in front of Bricusse's desk. "Very much so. I went sailing, Father, for almost two months. Quite alone."

Bricusse propped a thin hip against his desk. "Really, now, if you can make it through two months—quite alone, I mean—why don't you come back to the sacraments? Surely after so long a time you feel the need for some grace, for some sort of spiritual life. Not to mention a little, what shall I call it…divine romance?"

"I'm afraid I don't know what you mean."

Bricusse snorted. "I mean that I never knew a man as besotted as you were three years ago. Quite extraordinary. But then the Virgin gave you a rather extraordinary gift, or have you forgotten?"

James snapped one leg over the other knee. "They're lovely notions, you know, romance and grace and the Virgin and all that. I won't deny their appeal. But it turned out I wasn't up to the challenge. And those that are…" James thought of the blunt, cookie-cutter conformity of the young men of SANA. "Let's just say, in the immortal words of Frodo Baggins, that I was not made for such perilous quests."

Bricusse looked amused. "And look what happened to him! But *notions* do you call them? The Virgin a *notion*? Why, I never. God is a God of the living, James, not of the dead! My word, how a man can be so brilliant in literature and so shockingly obtuse in theology is simply beyond telling." Bricusse grew suddenly serious again. "My dear boy, I realize you've had a rough time of it, religiously speaking, but has it never occurred to you that you might be responding to the inevitable slings and arrows of the spiritual life with unconditional surrender?"

"You bet. I've walked off that bloody battlefield once and for all."

"Well I'm sorry to be the one to break the news to you, but I'm afraid you can't just 'walk off' that battlefield. Though you're hardly the first to try. Fact is, that battlefield is as wide as the wide world. Which is why St. Paul, I dare say, advised us all to *put on the whole armor of God.*"

Finally noting the brittleness of his student's expression, Bricusse abridged his homily and lifted his hands in a gesture of defeat. "You'll have to forgive a foolish fond old man," he said, "who's getting closer to heaven all the time. But you see, since heaven wouldn't be heaven for me without you, I can't help but believe that, one of these days, you and God will…sign an armistice."

"Little early for you to be talking about heaven, don't you think?" James grumbled.

"On the contrary. My heart was acting up so much over the summer that I finally decided to take Franco's advice, and step down. I've submitted my resignation as Director. Assuming the Board members second Max's and my recommendation, Franco will take over the Directorship as of January 1st."

James sat up, appalled.

"Now, I'm not giving up teaching," Bricusse added quickly, as James prepared to launch any number of objections. Shuffling around his desk to root out another stray cup of water from the nearby shelves, Bricusse proceeded to explain to James, between sips, why Dr. Franco Lanciano, in spite of his many "eccentricities"—a Traditionalist in almost every sense of the word, Lanciano had actually signed a petition calling for a constitutional amendment to restore a hereditary monarchy—would prove, in the end, a far more competent administrator than Bricusse, who by his own admission should have never been anything other than a priest and a teacher.

"But then," Bricusse concluded, "I suspect you didn't hurry in here after the seminar to air your concerns about the rise and fall of Western Civ, now did you?"

Remarking Bricusse's owlish expression, James's own face sagged: the old wizard knew.

Bricusse lifted his hand to forestall the protestations about to burst from James's lips. "I know what you're going to say: Lupe Cruz is barely out of college, struggles with a speech impediment, and probably thinks dactyls and anapests are extinct species of dinosaur from *Jurassic Park*." Bricusse laid aside his empty water cup. "That about sum up the source of your obvious discomfiture?"

"Just about," James conceded, hardly wishing to add that, as far as he could tell from Jack's report and his own limited observation of the girl from across the seminar table, Miss 1957 was also possessed of precisely the sort of feminine curvature that he had always found most difficult to resist, on the few occasions he had ever bothered to try.

He was trying now. Indeed, the last thing James Ireton wanted at this point in his already complicated life, especially after the twin disasters with Nadine Jeffrey and Trisha Perl last spring, was what his less honest contemporaries euphemized as 'a relationship.' One foot propped on his other knee, James began rapping a drumbeat of vexation on the sole of his shoe.

"In point of fact," Bricusse insisted, "your assessment is not only hasty and surprisingly shallow for a man of your intelligence and general good taste, it's just plain *wrong*. Lupe Cruz attended my Mature Tragedies course over the summer, while you were lolling about the Caribbean, and she was absolutely delightful to work with. I must say, she wrote one of the loveliest papers I've seen in my lengthy career. Yes, easily as good as any of yours, my boy, produced at a similar age. Though hardly, I might add, as belligerent in tone."

Bricusse took the opportunity of James's obstinate silence to turn once more to his bookshelves, this time to rummage through some papers until he brought forth a manuscript of some forty or fifty pages, penned, or so stated the name under the title, *Rosencrantz and Guildenstern and the Ethos of Use*, by Guadalupe Cruz. Shoving it under James's nose, Bricusse admonished his favorite student to take a good long look at it.

"You're immovable, aren't you?" James said, practically yanking the sheaf of papers from Bricusse's fingers.

Bricusse let out a huff of exasperation. "I can't do somersaults to keep you out of harm's way, you know. Besides, it seems to me that you can no longer afford to be too choosy. With whom, pray tell, might you prefer to work this term? Richard Krato, perhaps? Mitch? Isabel?"

"You left someone out."

Bricusse straightened his drooping spine. "Dear God, how in heaven's name have you succeeded in making so many enemies? All right, all right, who else is on your blacklist?"

"Trisha Perl isn't on my blacklist," James said, bracing himself for the explosion sure to come, "I am on hers."

It took a moment for the subtext to sink in, but when it did, the old priest was overcome by a rattling cough. "Patricia!" he got out finally, enunciating every syllable with breathy emphasis as he moved with surprising brusqueness towards the great arched window on the northeast wall of his office, as if desperate for a glimpse of sea or sky. "Patricia Perl! Why, if ever there was a man Patricia Perl did not need to run across, it was James Ireton! Dear God, when are you finally going to learn that you have no right to use women's bodies and affections like so much toilet paper!"

James recoiled. Feeling as if his body would freeze to the chair if he didn't move, he got to his feet, paced the carpet a bit in a back-and-forth curve, and finally came up shoulder to shoulder with the old man, whose pained glance was fixed on the dripping window. The brief cloudburst of an hour or so before had finally spent itself, giving way to a steady, soothing rain.

"I'm sorry, Father," James whispered. "It just happened. Once, last spring."

"I thought you were 'dating' Nadine Jeffrey last spring."

"I was, but, well, I think Trisha was testing her feelings towards men, and I...I happened to be the man to hand."

"James," Bricusse said in his weakest voice, "when it comes to sex, I don't think you have ever missed an opportunity. But when it comes to love, and to God, I wonder if you've ever missed an opportunity to miss an opportunity."

James stepped back, as near tears as he had been since he was a boy. "*O good old man, thou prunest a rotten tree.*"

The frangibility in James's voice seemed to startle Bricusse, for he turned suddenly and said, "Forgive me, James, that was a brutal thing for me to say."

"You needn't apologize for speaking the truth. I know how I've disappointed you."

"Nonsense, it's just—"

Suddenly there was a knock, followed by the annoying sound of the anteroom door banging open against the wall. Quickly wiping his eyes, James whirled around to see Lupe Cruz stumbling into the room, loaded to the waterline with plastic bags from the Institute bookstore.

Spotting James in turn, Cruz lost her grip on one of her packages. Books and supplies flopped out onto the carpeting.

"I'm s-s-sorry, F-Father," Cruz stammered, dropping on all fours to herd her possessions back into the sack. "Your secretary told me to go right in. I guess she didn't know you were in conference with-with-with—" She flung a wave in James's general direction.

"Not at all," Bricusse said, making haste to assist her with her vagrant packages. "James and I don't really 'conference' anymore, do we, James?"

His misery having given way to a different form of preoccupation as he stared at Miss 1957's athletic limbs and lavish curves, assembled in perfect symmetry, James finally came to himself—he felt like a novice seaman who'd lost his breath to a loose boom—and worked to frame his face for the alleged occasion: a quotidian academic conference. "I was about to leave," he volunteered robustly.

"Actually," Cruz insisted, once again on her feet and her packages safely deposited on a nearby chair, "maybe you should stay. I was going to speak to Father about our-our-our—" She swallowed. "—working together."

"An excellent idea," Bricusse agreed amiably. "Why don't you sit down. You, too, James." He shot James a meaningful look. "I'll fix us all a nice cup of tea." Not waiting for signs of acquiescence from either of his students, Bricusse hobbled over to a table behind his desk, furnished with a hot pot, Styrofoam cups, and a variety of tea bags and condiments.

James returned to his chair.

Cruz, however, stood her ground. "Father," she said, venturing a step forward, "I can guess that Mr. Ireton wasn't particularly thrilled with our being p-p-paired."

Bricusse, turning the spigot of the hot pot, chuckled softly.

"But I would just like to request tha-tha-that...I mean I think it's only fair-fair-*fair* that..." Cruz took a deep breath to support her stumbling words, before blurting out in a tumble of syllables, "Well it seems to me that if Mr. Ireton is to be allowed to choose a different partner, then I should have first dibs on the topic!"

James sat forward to rally an objection, but Bricusse waved him down. "And what was your chosen topic again?" he said to Cruz.

"A c-c-comparison of the concepts of chivalry as portrayed in Spenser's Redcrosse Knight and Shakespeare's Henry V."

Bricusse raised a finger in recognition. "Ah, yes. Well, as it happens, there was one other student who expressed an interest in that topic."

"Who was that?" James said, mentally crossing his fingers.

"Isabel Gunderson."

James deflated. He wanted the chivalry topic, too, as it fit into a knotty problem he was struggling with in the last re-write of his dissertation; but another duet with Bel Gunderson was simply out of the question, and for more than personal reasons. Bel Gunderson's literary tastes were even more grotesque to James than her sexual. He was instantly reminded of the crimson brocade bathrobe and red silk jock-strap she had given him three years before as a birthday present, and which he had straightway fobbed off on Jack Sigur as a joke. Jack, inspired by the outfit's lurid tackiness, had worn it the following year, over leotards and tights, to Lanciano's Halloween party, playing the Emperor Ming to James' perhaps all-too-appropriate Flash Gordon. James, unable in the moment to do anything but laugh, abandoned himself to a quiet expression of desperate hilarity.

Cruz regarded him crossly.

"I take it you're not eager to work with Isabel Gunderson either?" Bricusse said to Lupe, ignoring James altogether.

Finally pulling up a chair, Cruz sat down and circled her hand in the air as if groping for the right words. "Nothing personal, but ten minutes of conversation with her this afternoon convinced me that if we end up shackled together to write this p-p-paper, your vision of 'collegial scholarship' will end up looking more like the Valley of Megiddo after the Last Battle."

"Up to the horses' bridles in blood," James offered with an involuntary snort of approval.

"Nothing's sacred to her," Cruz insisted with some vehemence. "Least of all language or l-l-literature."

James all but rolled his eyes.

Tilting her head to one side, Lupe Cruz fixed her turquoise eyes on her scornful partner and said, as if it should be obvious to the merest child, "I can't possibly work with her. And I doubt, Mr. Ireton, after reading your Master's thesis over the summer, that you can, either. As the old book says, *and the Word was God.*"

James's smirk was slapped away.

It was an astonishing phenomenon, James mused, how the spark of intelligence or character could transform a face. He had seen this sort of epiphany on the stage, working with amateur actors in student productions. The gifted ones, he had noticed, had a remarkable ability to change their appearance with a mere thought; could transfigure a gangly body and adolescent demeanor into the terrible visage of a warlike king, or a debutante's complacency into the twisted determination of Lady Macbeth. Glancing up again at Lupe Cruz's turquoise eyes, showing smoky in the muted light of rainy skies filtering through tinted glass, the girl suddenly appeared to him as one of the most striking, and certainly most unusual, women he had ever met.

James shuddered. This was simply too appalling. *Even so quickly may one catch the plague?* Why, not three hours ago he had believed himself permanently inoculated against this chronic contagion.

"How do you take your tea?" he heard Bricusse asking Lupe.

All right, James conceded, arguing silently with himself as Cruz and Bricusse engaged in a bit of small-talk about sugar-to-milk ratios in a proper cup of tea, the girl could think on her feet, he would grant her that. But it was a dead cert, whatever her less objectionable qualities, that she was also an Enthusiast. Worse, one of those dreadful *poetry-can-change-lives* types who showed up in lit classes with distressing regularity to make the lives of more serious students miserable. *Madly in love with Shakespeare* was she? Such creatures were to be avoided at all costs, with or without figures o'erstepping the modesty of nature.

James risked another glance at Cruz, then at Bricusse. Not to worry, yet, nothing was settled. Bricusse was obviously still assessing the dodgy situation and if James played his part right — if he set a proper trap — he'd bet money the girl would obligingly blunder into it with that gruesome Cordelia-like honesty which she so obviously affected, and even Bricusse, fond of the girl as he so obviously was, would be forced to recognize their incompatibility.

Massaging the bridge of his nose between his thumb and forefinger, his hand half-shadowing his eyes, James cleared his throat and broke in, "I say, Miss Cruz, given our proposed topic, I'd be interested to know how you assess Shakespeare's characterization of Henry V."

James's rare and abrupt usage of the obvious Briticism, and in an exaggerated BBC accent, was so sudden and theatrical that Bricusse nearly lost hold of his teacup.

"Hero or anti-hero, what say you? My own position is that Henry is Shakespeare's portrait of the Chivalric Ideal. The glory of knighthood and all kingly grace. Perhaps even Shakespeare's semi-historical re-working of Spenser's St. George material. With the French in their usual role of the Dragon, of course."

Closing her mouth, which had slipped open somewhere in the middle of James's analysis, Lupe Cruz sat back, apparently considering the question. "I think," she said finally, "that you're going to have some problems squaring Henry's threats to b-burn, rape, and pillage Harfleurs with the, um, Chivalric Ideal. Not to mention his killing of the prisoners of war at Agincourt, in retaliation for the loss of the boys and the luggage, and his merciless treatment of his former friends. Especially Falstaff."

James's lips puckered.

"And as for St. George and the Dragon..." Cruz clucked. "If Shakespeare had really wanted to do something with that story, I think he would have expanded Redcrosse's jealousy into a fatal flaw, endowed him with a wicked uncle and a traitorous brother, had the dragon speak in iambic pentameter, and made sure they were all d-dead by the end of the fifth act. All, of course, written in the most glorious language ever uttered by anyone who was not God." Cruz turned to Bricusse and smiled sweetly. "But I'm always ready to hear a new and challenging viewpoint. Aren't you, Father?"

"Why, yes," the old priest agreed, his expression denoting a delicate poise between merriment and incredulity, "I'd love to hear James's argument to that effect."

James re-crossed his legs and occupied himself with a surveillance of the carpeting. "Just letting fly a trial balloon," he said. Several seconds passed before he was finally able to muscle his face into a civil smile and add, with a suavity that greater actors could envy, "Well, now, I think Miss Cruz and I might eventually work up something decent together after all."

Before either Bricusse or Cruz could comment on this breathtaking turn, a crackling of intercom static sounded in the room, followed by the voice of Bricusse's secretary announcing that Mr. Barry DeBrun had arrived for his four o'clock appointment.

At the news, Cruz, as white as her shirt, jerked her head toward the door, looking for all the world as if she had just seen King Hamlet's Ghost. Mr. Barry DeBrun, James concluded with newly ignited interest, was the Mr. Soap Opera who had interrupted the seminar.

Bricusse rose to press a button on the intercom. "Thank you, Christine. Please tell Barry I'll be right with him."

"Is there another way I ca-ca–can leave?"

"Why, yes. Are you all right, my dear?"

"I-I-I just don't want B-B-B...him to see me."

Eyebrow lifted, Bricusse pointed to another door on the far side of his office and explained that it led to a conference room with its own exit to the seventh floor gallery. "James can help you with your things, can't you, James?" Bricusse seized James's wayward attention with a pointed frown. "Which reminds me, you and I need to speak again before you leave for the day."

"Of course," James replied, wondering, with sudden anxiety, what the canny priest, who knew him so well, had been reading in his face for the last fifteen minutes.

Pausing at the door to the anteroom, Bricusse turned again to Lupe, his withered hand emerging from his cassock pocket with a small, foil-covered box—a token, or so he went on to explain, of his recent pilgrimage to the shrine of Our Lady of Guadalupe outside Mexico City. Inside the box was an oval-shaped silver medal of *La Guadalupana* dangling from a delicate silver chain.

Cruz seemed genuinely delighted by the gift. She clasped the chain around her neck with exclamations of thanks, and finally awarded her teacher with a warm kiss on the cheek. But before Bricusse could express his own appreciation, the anteroom door opened from the other side; James saw Cruz recoil, then break into a foolish-looking grimace when she realized that the uninvited visitor was not the mysterious Mr. Barry DeBrun, as James had hoped and she had no doubt feared, but the Heisler Institute Deputy Director, Dr. Franco Lanciano, who looked the very picture this afternoon of a titled European aristocrat in a Puccini-white summer suit and Adolph Menjou mustache. Lanciano was no aristocrat, to be sure, his fondness for the nobility to the contrary notwithstanding, but the fact took nothing away from the patrician splendor of the impression. Besides, inventing oneself was the American way—"Jay Gatsby and all that," as Lanciano insisted on reminding everyone in his *O tempora, o mores!* lectures on the postmodern decay of western culture.

"So sorry for the interruption," Lanciano addressed Bricusse with a mæstro-like flourish of one manicured hand. "I see young Barry is champing at the bit outside. But knowing how special your students are to you, I've decided, if you have no objections, to proffer an invitation to your entire Shakespeare seminar to join Adèle and me for a little *soirée* next week in our home. In celebration of the new Institute building dedication, of course. Unfortunately, we haven't room for the entire student body in our humble abode—" The place, James thought with a smirk, was huge. "—but I thought the members of your seminar might provide suitable student representation."

Not waiting for Bricusse's assent, Lanciano straightaway presented the priest with a small stack of parchment-colored envelopes as he proceeded to enumerate, in excruciating detail, his proposed celebration's guest list, wine list, and hors d'œvres menu. Bricusse made appropriate noises from time to time during the recital, but promptly palmed the invitations off to James, who with equal alacrity deposited them on Bricusse's desk. Finally, taking the still-nattering Lanciano by the elbow, Bricusse directed the Heisler Institute Deputy Director back toward the anteroom.

When the door closed behind them, Lupe Cruz rose to collect her sacks, and James decided that it was high time for his much-bruited English charm to surface. "May I call you 'Lupe'?" he said, coming over to assist her with her packages.

"Sure. Do you prefer 'James' or 'J-J-Jim'?"

"James, if you don't mind."

They crossed the floor into the adjacent conference room. At the door leading to the gallery, James paused and set down her sacks, signaling his intention to detain her further. "Well now," he said, his gentlemanly smile nailed in place, "perhaps we should set a time to get together. To discuss the paper, I mean. If you give me your address and phone number, I'll ring you."

She recited her phone number and Stowell Avenue address, and when he made no effort to retrieve pencil or paper to take note of them, offered to write it down for him.

"I think I'll remember," he assured her. Then, stepping closer, so close that there wasn't an inch of space between her round breasts and his pounding chest, he added, "What's this Barry DeBrun to you?"

Lupe's eyelids fluttered. "He's s-someone I knew y-y-years ago. In high school."

"An old boyfriend?"

"That would *not* be an accurate description of the relationship!"

James was sure she was about to add, *as if it's any of your goddamned business, Mr. Ireton*, when he forestalled any such comment with a choir-boy's grin. "I apologize," he said, capping his performance with a mockingly chivalrous sweep of one arm, "it was none of my business."

Cruz looked dubious. "I'll b-b-be hearing from you then."

"You will indeed."

James watched her as she gathered up her packages and labored along the gallery toward the elevator. When the elevator doors shut behind her, James's tattered smile disappeared entirely.

––––––––––––

Back in Bricusse's office some minutes later, James was leaning against the desk, ten pages into Cruz's annoyingly well-written paper, when Bricusse returned.

"So who is he?" James said, looking up and nodding at the door from which Bricusse had emerged.

"Hm? Oh, you mean DeBrun. Yes, well, he's one of Max Heisler's bright young men at the Great Lakes Bank. And now his son-in-law as well."

Straightening, James set aside the paper. "That man," he said with amazement, "married *Fran Heisler?*" Fran was Max Heisler's only child, and therefore an heiress of no small fortune. She was a pleasant, brainy girl, James had always thought, but also chubby and a bit wall-eyed like her father — no temptations there. Given her financial status, however, even if James had never pursued her, she had never lacked for other suitors.

As Bricusse went on to relate the few facts at his disposal about Fran Heisler's "whirlwind romance" with Barry DeBrun at Harvard Business School, James, who within seconds was no longer thinking of Fran Heisler at all, or even Barry DeBrun, contrived to strike a casual pose on the edge of Bricusse's desk. Unfortunately his foot, swinging back and forth like a metronome wound too tightly, provided the telltale sign that he was not as relaxed as he would like to appear.

"Max, as you may imagine," Bricusse concluded, "was not thrilled about the elopement. Much as he dotes on Fran, he's never had any illusions about most men's motives for pursuing her. To tell you the truth, I think he only gave DeBrun a position at the bank so he could keep an eye on him."

"Keep your friends close, but your sons-in-law closer."

"Hm, yes." Folding his hands, Bricusse looked squarely at his protégé. "Lupe Cruz, on the other hand—" James's leg stopped swinging. "—now there's a lovely young woman. No money, of course, but rich in many other, and more important, gifts. You know, after learning that Nadine Jeffrey could only deal with the disappointments of her personal life by dropping out of the Institute, not to mention what you've told me this afternoon about Trisha Perl, I would be very distressed to see anything similar happen to Lupe."

When James didn't respond at once, Bricusse rose and made a surprisingly vigorous loop around the desk. "God knows I have tried never to intrude myself into your private life, as powerful as the temptation has been these last three years of your going your own way, but in case I haven't made myself entirely clear—" The old man pressed an arthritic finger against James's chest. "—it is my firm conviction that Lupe Cruz is meant to be some fortunate man's treasured partner in life, not your next two-week affair—!" Bricusse's heated words were cut short by a labored wheeze, followed by an ugly fit of coughing.

"There, now," James soothed, taking hold of Bricusse's bony shoulders. "No need to get yourself worked up. I know I handled the business with Nadine and Trish rather badly, but I assure you I have no intention of getting involved—"

"Damn your intentions!" Bricusse swept away James's hands. "Your 'handling' people—women, I should say—is the whole problem! A relationship with a woman isn't 'business to be handled—'" Gasping as if he were unable to force air in or out of his lungs, Bricusse pressed one hand to his chest until he could regain his composure. "James," he choked out finally, giving a shake of his white head, "do you care for me?"

James gasped. "My God, what a question!"

Reaching out, Bricusse grasped James's shoulders with his two gnarled hands and pulled James's forehead toward his own, so close that James could feel his breath on his face. "I'm asking you…do you love me? Do you *love* me?"

James stepped back. "You know I do, more than anyone in the world… more than my own father! What is it you *want* from me for chrissake!"

"For Christ's sake, I want you to promise me, on your love for me, that you will not seduce Lupe Cruz. That you will not hurt her as you have, unintentionally perhaps, so many others."

Now that Bricusse had dared to name the temptation that in only three hours had overtaken him like a fever, James began to glimpse what such an unusual promise was likely to cost him. It was several seconds before he could bring himself to say, almost inaudibly, "I promise."

With a sigh, Bricusse patted James once on the cheek, apparently satisfied. James, ashamed beyond words, reached for his briefcase.

"Before you go," Bricusse added in a frail but cheerier voice, one hand extended as if to hold him there, "I brought back something for you, too, from Mexico." With effort, Bricusse stepped to his desk and hoisted a thin but sizeable rectangular package that had been leaning against the side. The box, at least four feet tall and wrapped in brown paper, had *Dieguito* scrawled on the front in Bricusse's distinctive calligraphy.

James eyed the package with unconcealed suspicion. "What's that mean?" he said, pointing at the writing.

"What, almost a PhD and you can't you even recognize your own name in Spanish?" Bricusse chortled. "*Dieguito*, dullard, is the diminutive for *Diego*, which, like 'Jacob' in Hebrew or 'Iacobus' in Latin, is the Spanish equivalent of 'James.' Iago is yet another variation. In other words, it's something like 'Jimmy.' Much as I know you hate nicknames, I couldn't resist. You'll see why when you read the literature inside."

Setting down his briefcase again, James lifted the package, obviously a picture of some sort. "A religious image, I suppose," he said with a patent lack of enthusiasm.

"I suppose," Bricusse agreed with a gentle smile. "But don't fret yourself. I believe you'll find it to your taste, like it or not."

Chapter Two:
The Tempter or the Tempted

What's this, what's this? Is this her fault or mine?
The tempter or the tempted, who sins most?
                              ...Most dangerous
Is that temptation that doth goad us on
To sin in loving virtue: Never could the strumpet,
With all her double vigour, art and nature,
Once stir my temper; but this virtuous maid
Subdues me quite. Ever till now,
When men were fond, I smiled, and wonder'd how.

Shakespeare, *Measure for Measure*

Friday dawned a sticky morning in that armpit of North America known as the Great Lakes. Lupe Cruz spent a tedious if at least air-conditioned four hours learning the rubrics of her part-time position as Research Assistant in the Heisler Institute Archives. When she finished at noon, she changed into shorts and headed down to Bradford Beach for an afternoon of studying Book I of *The Færie Qveene*.

She had just finished a first reading of Canto I when she looked up into the blinding glare of mid-afternoon sun to see James Ireton, barefoot and in a threadbare Oxford tee, his sneakers strung around his neck and his hands stuffed in the pockets of rolled-up jeans, strolling toward her along the water's edge. The Englishman wore such a pained and self-absorbed expression on his suntanned face, that Lupe hesitated before finally raising her arm to solicit his attention with a wave.

James's head began to rotate toward her, but at that moment a gaggle of rowdy teenagers ran between them, tossing a volleyball back and forth. By the time the kids had passed, James had pivoted on his bare heels and was striding swiftly away, kicking up sand behind him. After that, Lupe could no longer focus on Spenser's Elizabethan romance of Una and the Redcrosse Knight. She gathered her belongings and headed for the pedestrian bridge spanning the six lanes of traffic along Memorial Drive.

A few feet from the bridge's steps, Lupe's attention was once again diverted, this time by the sight of a man's huge pale body stretched out on the sand like a beached parmacetty, his great white nakedness covered only by a skimpy pair of tiger-striped Speedos. It was only when a flash of sunlight coruscated off the man's thick glasses as he squinted into the pages of a fat book that Lupe realized that the pale Goliath was Mitch Showalter.

A passage from Melville leapt uninvited to Lupe's mind: *It was the whiteness of the whale that above all things appalled me.*

Suppressing a growl, Lupe hurried away before the big man could catch sight of her. Why on earth, she wondered, to cap off what was unfolding as a perfectly dreadful day, had she ever agreed to go out with this guy?

Lupe had agreed to meet Mitch Showalter that evening at Beans and Barley, a small east side restaurant coupled to a sprawling natural foods store. As she approached the door, the wide skirt of her floral-print dress swaying in the scant breeze, Lupe felt a good deal like an ill-prepared freshman on her condemned way to a Calculus final.

She hadn't the slightest idea, frankly, why Mitch Showalter had asked her out. In spite of the fact that she and Mitch (and Richard Krato too, of course) had taken Fr. Bricusse's Mature Tragedies course together this summer, and had even car-pooled for the class field trip to an American Players Theatre production of *King Lear*, neither man had addressed more than a dozen words to her in almost eight weeks. For another thing, Mitch was a member of the Student Apostolate of North America, and SANA members didn't date, or so the whisper went. Either way, Mitch and Richard were so infrequently seen apart that when Mitch made the surprising dinner invitation in the Institute bookstore after the seminar the day before, Lupe had been tempted to ask whether Richard would be tagging along to serve as chaperone.

It wasn't that she had taken a dislike to Mitch, Lupe argued silently with her own reluctance as she pushed through the door of the restaurant. Mitch's obvious struggle to overcome some chronic form of shyness was even rather endearing; but in spite of his remarkably well developed physique (the product, or so said Jack Sigur, of a daily hour on his Nautilus in the basement of SANA House) and reputedly photographic memory ("the Encyclopedia Showalter" was another of Mitch's nicknames at the Institute), Mitch's personality as a whole seemed as unformed to Lupe as a blob of unbaked Wonder Bread, and about as flavorless. Indeed, it was an irresistible temptation for Lupe to compare, or rather contrast, Mitch Showalter with James Ireton, who, for better or worse, had made an immediate and forceful impression on her, even before she had met him.

According to Jack, who in matters of Institute dish was as good as a Chorus, the beautiful five hundred seat Redmond Theatre, a last minute addition to the new Institute building, had been generously funded by the local philanthropist and thrice-divorced arts *aficionada*, Leila Redmond. Mrs. Redmond, it was noised abroad, had become suddenly persuaded that performance experience was an invaluable pedagogical device for graduate literature students largely by means of James Ireton's alcohol-induced volubility one evening at an intimate cocktail party thrown two years before at

Franco Lanciano's lakeside villa. Ireton's subsequent week-long excursion to Door County with the attractive forty-something socialite hadn't hurt his case either. Such tales about the man were so common, in fact, that Lupe had found herself, and in spite of herself, very eager to get a good look him, particularly after Fr. Bricusse shared Ireton's soon-to-be published Master's thesis with her over the summer. Behind almost every one of Ireton's finely crafted sentences, Lupe had perceived an aggressive intelligence and a soul of unusual, and perhaps unusually bitter, sensibilities. Considering the man's reputation at the Institute for the number and brevity of his sexual liaisons, Lupe had also initially imagined someone unusually magnetic, perhaps even as strikingly handsome as Barry DeBrun—she had shuddered a bit at *that* thought—but from her first sight of Ireton in the seminar room on Wednesday, she had concluded, with a note of puzzlement, that the man resembled not so much an Oxford-bred Don Giovanni as a North Atlantic fisherman who had survived many a nor'easter, and one too many dockside brothels.

Whatever the case, Lupe Cruz had certainly "recognized" James Ireton Wednesday afternoon; had known who he was right off before he ever introduced himself in class. Whether he could be considered handsome probably depended on one's taste. He had blondish hair framing weather-beaten features that made him look older, or at least more worldly-wise, than a twenty-nine year-old grad student had any right to be; but handsome or no, Lupe had thought afterward that James Ireton could somehow look no other than as he did.

Lupe had also recognized in herself an immediate attraction to the man that afternoon, or at least a curiosity so intense that it had felt like a punch in the stomach; but evidenced by Ireton's skittishness about taking her on as a partner, and his obvious efforts to avoid her this afternoon, hers was an attraction that was obviously not reciprocated.

Just as well, Lupe decided with a riff of regret. The rogue male was by all accounts toxic on the personal level.

Pausing in the open doorway of the dining room, Lupe gave a brave shrug of her shoulders and scanned the restaurant.

Mitch Showalter was already seated at a corner table, frowning myopically into his latest book. When he finally spotted her, he lifted his bulk to his feet, making an annoying scraping sound with his chair, and gave a quick scratch to his fanny before finally greeting her with a "Heya!" that sounded a good deal like a burp of indigestion.

Lupe seated herself and smiled back at him with as much warmth as she could muster.

"About finished with the Lawrence?" she said, pointing at his book.

"Oh, I'm way beyond that," Mitch informed her, holding up his latest volume so that the spine faced her. It was not Lawrence's *Plumed Serpent* this time, the book he had been reading yesterday, but Harold Bloom's lit crit classic *The Anxiety of Influence*. "My third go-round with Bloom," Mitch added, his boyish face taking on a sudden earnestness of expression. "This time it's really hitting me how scholars have missed the book's prophetic significance."

"Prophetic?"

"You bet. Especially if read in conjunction with, say, Spengler's *The Decline of the West*. Or even the Lawrence. I mean, just look at it." Mitch swept his well-muscled arms in a gesture that incorporated the room, perhaps the world. "It's as if Clio's shifted the stick and history's gone into full reverse! Our present era is clear evidence of Spengler's thesis that the world-historical senescence of expansive and energetic cultures into static, enervated civilizations is the result of the inevitable loss of faith. And therefore energy. When that happens, all that's left for the artist is rebellion against previous forms, which is nothing if not a sort of backhanded copycatting. Which reminds me of Vico's cyclic theory that theocratic ages always rise again after democratic ones have collapsed. Or, to quote Spengler, *Cæsarism grows in the soil of Democracy, but its roots dig deep into the underground of blood tradition.*"

"Is that so," Lupe responded noncommittally, having no views to offer on the subject, since she didn't know what the hell Showalter was talking about. She was rather more interested this evening in the man himself; there was something different about Mitch tonight, and it took Lupe a few moments of discreet observation to realize what it was: besides having acquired a painful-looking sunburn this afternoon on Bradford Beach, Mitch wasn't wearing those bottle-thick glasses of his. An outcropping of spidery red veins around his welkin-blue corneas suggested that he had just switched to contact lenses. Too, Mitch's buttoned-down SANA livery of white shirt, navy tie, and navy slacks, the only clothing she had ever seen him (or Richard Krato, or any of the SANA members) wear, had been shucked this evening in favor of a brand new pair of khakis topped by a gold-colored tee-shirt with PRAIRIE SCHOOL scrolled in maroon letters across his impressive pectorals.

Mitch leaned forward, as if he were about to share with her some extraordinary new discovery. "I'm personally convinced that the contemporary wave of nostalgia for archetypes gleaned from the ideographic ages is a movement along the trajectory of Bloom's and Spengler's and Lawrence's prophecies. As Jung pointed out, a religion can only be replaced by another religion. The question is, Cruz, *which* religion? Or as Nietzsche put it, and ever so much more colorfully, *the weirdest of all guests stands before the door.*" Mitch opened his huge arms as if to say, *There you have it*. Then he sat back, apparently awaiting some appreciative response in kind. When all Lupe could manage was an amiable "I'm sure you have a p-p-point there," Mitch fixed his Delft-blue contacts on the doorway of the restaurant, as if expecting the arrival of some long-lost relative.

Lupe winced. From the looks of it, she had blown the first question on the Calculus test. She was relieved, therefore, when the waitress came up to take their orders. Folding her menu she said, "I'll have the avocado sandwich and a glass of rosé."

Mitch took his time, as if mentally calculating nutritional ratios, before finally ordering a rice and bean dish and a pot of herbal tea. "Avocados are loaded with fat," he cautioned *sotto voce* after the waitress had left.

"Good heavens, Mitch, surely you don't expect me to be abstemious on a night out?"

"Now, I wonder if that is a truly Christian attitude," Mitch observed with a speculative air, casting lugubrious eyes at the ceiling. "You're wearing a religious medal," he added, pointing at the silver Guadalupe medal around her neck, his eyes still heavenward as if he could see the object without looking at it. "Jack Sigur told me you were a devout Catholic."

"I am a devout Catholic. Not a devout Puritan."

Mitch tried to smile at that, but the pleasant expression wouldn't stick. "I don't understand," he said tightly, "why every time a person tries to inject some discipline into his life, other people knee-jerk label him a Puritan. We get called that at SANA all the time, you know. And 'fundamentalists,' and 'the Catholic Taliban,' and all kinds of crap."

There was another uncomfortable stretch of silence as Mitch indulged himself in a fit of watery-eyed pouting. When the waitress finally returned with their drinks, Lupe took a substantial swallow of wine before venturing on in a more appeasing tone.

"I guess what I was getting at," she said, "was that everything should be leavened with a b-bit of, well, joy. I mean, even good things, like discipline, for instance, well, don't you think, if they're taken too far, or without a sense of humor or humility, that they can flip over by sheer momentum into their opposites?"

For a moment, Mitch Showalter stared at her with thick incomprehension, as if waiting for understanding to filter into his mind like sunlight through dense foliage. When it finally did, he began to chuckle, then to laugh—a deep rumbling laugh that vibrated through the tabletop and rattled her silverware. "Oh, that's good," he said. "Yep, Mr. Krato could learn a thing or two from you! But the point is," Mitch hoisted a thick forefinger, "we at SANA are an army, and an army requires discipline. We're in a spiritual war here, you know, that's just the way things are. We've got to take the world as is. Want it *as is*, want it again, want it eternally."

Mitch's words echoed with familiarity, as did so many of his obscure and apparently borrowed phrases, but Lupe couldn't identify the source. Downing another swallow of wine, she was grateful, after another ungainly silence began to scrape on her nerves like sandpaper, to see the waitress arriving with their dinners. She took a bite of her sandwich and chewed, content to let the subject remain shelved; but when she glanced up, she realized that Mitch was looking at her, head cocked to one side, obviously waiting for a response.

"Well," she offered cautiously, "I guess I know what you mean, but I've always had a problem with the use of military metaphors when discussing the spreading of the Gospel. They usually end up communicating the willingness to k-k-kill for one's beliefs, rather than the willingness to die for them. Or live for them."

Mitch wiped his bow-shaped lips with a swipe of his napkin. "Now, don't forget that great men like Mr. Krato are almost exclusively men of action. And men of action, as Goethe pointed out, are conscienceless. More or less. Besides, Mr. Krato would say that there are no innocent bystanders in a war anyway, especially a spiritual war."

"B-b-but, Mitch—"

"Now don't jump to conclusions. I know what you're thinking, and you'd be wrong. I mean I really am trying to work this thing out. There are some thorny meta-moral problems to be worked out here, and I don't want to go tossing out the less pleasant possibilities before I've tested the limits. For instance, Mr. Krato always says that the enemies of Christ blow us out of the water because we Christians are too fastidious to fight fire with fire. Well, isn't that true?"

"But—"

"Besides, how many average Joes do you know who are willing, let alone equipped, to deal with complicated ethical decisions anyway, about war or anything else? To paraphrase Hamlet, conscience makes cowards of more than most. Perhaps the inevitably hierarchic nature of fallen human society necessitates that the responsibility for right and wrong falls ultimately on the shoulders of the superior officers…got it?"

"But Mitch," she insisted, flinging her hands in distress, "as Shakespeare said, *every g-g-good servant does not all commands.* Or Yeats: *There are things a man must not do to save a nation.* I d-don't believe you really mean what you seem to be saying. Or else you haven't stopped to think about the potential implications."

He nodded pensively, as if moved by her argument, then giggled a bit and turned his gaze to the vase of flowers at his elbow. "One thing, Cruz, you're awfully intense about things. I noticed that right off. We're just having an abstract philosophical discussion here, and there's no reason to get so intense. I mean, I'm more than willing to concede that you may be right. As I said, some things have been…well, bothering me." He waved his fork. "I'll sort it out eventually. Always a few wobbles along the road. A little spiritual vertigo. So much good has been done at SANA too. Conversions, all kinds of conversions. You've got to weigh that in the balance, too."

"Yes, of course, but which kind of—"

"And don't think I don't know what's what." Mitch emitted an athletic grunt. "Yeah, when it comes to the Church Militant, I'm a pawn. Cannon fodder. One of the dogfaces of glorious Agincourt, whose name never makes it on King Henry's battle rolls, let alone his casualty lists. Lumped with the *Lumpen*, that's me. *Mine is not to reason why, mine is but to do, and die.* Huh! The Brits didn't name Tennyson Poet Laureate for nothing. *Dulce et decorum est pro patria mori.* In wartime, you know, the gates of two-faced Janus stand wide open, and even poetry ends up as little more than just another weapon in the arsenal, another form of propaganda."

"Wow, that sounds so cynical."

"I'm tempted by cynicism sometimes, sure, aren't we all? Honestly? Truth is, I've had to swallow a lot, make a lot of sacrifices for my vocation, don't you know. Even the girl I loved. And I'd like nothing better than to throw myself into my studies, if I had the time to spare for it. But to tell you the truth, the world could probably get along fine without another Shakespeare scholar. As Melville said, *The sunken-eyed Platonist will tow you ten wakes round the world, and never make you one pint of sperm the richer.*"

Beginning to feel as if her capacity to make sense of present reality had been suspended, Lupe shrugged and said, "If that's how you feel, why are you studying literature?"

He waved. "Oh, I was caught up in it all for a while, too. Yeah, *my library was dukedom large enough.* In fact, it's a constant temptation for me. Books, that is. Reading, reading, always reading…I've got an itching mind. But I've begun to think that the postmodernists are the honest ones, and that literature is little more than a postgraduate game of Semiotics, set up to provide sedentary pedants with tenure and a regular paycheck. A Scrabble tournament on board *Titanic.*"

"Yes, but—"

"And of course the Powers-that-be support the whole charade because they'd rather have their resident intellectuals in the chattering classes cocooning themselves in their ivory towers, preoccupied with word games, instead of out on the barricades raising a *real* revolution. Literature doesn't put food on anyone's table, or change the world. If you ask me it seduces people into contemplative sloth. Besides, it's second-hand experience. *Words, words, words.* Whipping cream. Scrofula. Mr. Krato says we should want to make history, not read about it. He says literature is a sugary soporific, and most of the time, I think he's dead right. Hell, even Yeats admitted that poetry makes nothing happen."

Yearning for an interruption, Lupe glanced around the restaurant, hoping she might see someone she recognized. "Actually," she said distractedly, "that wasn't Yeats, but Auden in his *In Memory of W.B. Yeats.*" She suppressed further comment when she noticed that Mitch's sun-pink cheeks had flushed crimson; it seemed that the Encyclopedia Showalter didn't appreciate correction where his much-bruited memory was concerned.

Mitch reached for a toothpick in the dispenser beside her arm. "Personally, I'm prepared to give up literature—" He snapped the toothpick in half. "—like that." He shoved one end of the broken toothpick between his two front teeth to dig out a kernel of rice, and spoke mushily around his probing fingers. "As Mr. Krato always says, we Christians have to be willing to sacrifice anything."

"Anything but Christ," Lupe muttered.

But he must have heard her, because he smiled suddenly, tossed his toothpick on his empty plate and laughed out loud. "Not bad," he exclaimed, "not bad at all. Yep, very clever. You know more than you know."

"S-S-Sorry?"

In answer he looked up and to the side, somewhere over her left shoulder, and began to recite from memory:

> *"For that old man of pleasing words had store,*
> *And well could file his tongue as smooth as glass:*
> *He told of Saints and Popes, and evermore*
> *He strewed an Ave-Mary after and before…"*

"W-W-Wow," she said several minutes later after Mitch concluded his impressive performance by putting his hand over a burp, "you *do* have a photographic memory."

He inclined his curly brown head by way of a bow, and in the ensuing pause—he sat scratching his sunburned ear, his mind apparently a universe away—she brought her nearly empty wine glass to her lips, trying to remember the context of those familiar lines from Book I of *The Færie Qveene*. She choked on the last swallow when it finally hit her that Mitch was alluding to Mr. Peter Krato, his spiritual leader and SANA's founder, as Spenser's Archimago, the malicious sorcerer disguised as a holy monk who plotted diabolic mayhem against the Redcrosse Knight and his beloved Una.

After several seconds spent collecting her wits, Lupe decided that it might be wise, rather than risk another of Showalter's soliloquies, to fall back on the social niceties. She pointed at the maroon lettering on the big man's tee-shirt and inquired if he was an alumnus of Prairie School, the elite prep school in nearby Racine County.

"You've heard of it?" Mitch said, obviously pleased by her interest.

"Sure. Who hasn't?"

"It is a pretty swank place," he agreed. "'Course my family and me, we were just 'comfortably off' as Jimmy would say, not like some of them. My mom was an English prof at Carthage College. We had a big house right on the lake down in Kenosha County." Turning away suddenly, Mitch fixed his eyes like two blue marbles on the doorway of the restaurant, as if still waiting for the arrival of that long-lost relative. "But my family's gone now. My brother ran away from home when I was seventeen. His name was J. Edgar." Mitch chortled. "Bet you can guess who *he* was named after. Jeez, my folks were such reactionaries, my brother was bound to rebel. Poor fool probably ended up in some California commune or something. Anyway, after that my mother lost it completely. As in forever." Mitch slapped the table top with the palm of his hand. "End of family, end of story. Like Artaud said, *now I am my son, my father, my mother, and me.*"

"Wow," Lupe said with compassion.

Mitch's lips contracted in a pucker of detachment. "Well, that's life. This world's a shadow, our faith teaches us. At least I've still got my Aunt Abby up in Green Bay."

Lupe frowned, not quite able to connect all the dots. "You lost your father, too?"

Mitch waved. "Hell, yeah. A lump of fish-food to feed the ecology of accident. It was twenty years ago, I was just a kid. His sailboat sank in Lake Superior, on the anniversary of the wreck of the *Edmund Fitzgerald.* You know, the ship Lightfoot wrote the song about. My Dad's brother was one of the crewmates. In fact, Dad was on his way to a memorial for the big ship when he got rolled over by a rogue wave himself. Spooky, huh? Queer timing, for sure. But then November's a helluva bad time of the year to go out on the Big Lake in a small boat."

"W-W-Wow," Lupe repeated. A seven-hundred-foot ore freighter with a crew of twenty-nine, the *Edmund Fitzgerald* had set sail from Superior, Wisconsin on November 10, 1975, carrying twenty-six thousand tons of taconite ore for the steel mills of Cleveland. Within hours it had been lost in a freakish gale on Lake Superior — the "Big Lake," the "Graveyard of Ships," as it was called, where no body, so legend had it, ever washed ashore. The brute size of the ship and the inexplicable suddenness of the catastrophe had set minds reeling in a region where gales and boat disasters were hardly uncommon. Lupe had grown up hearing tales of the great wreck, its memory hauntingly preserved by the famous Gordon Lightfoot ballad, and Steven Dietz's play *Ten November.*

Mitch's red-rimmed eyes retreated behind a curtain of staged indifference. "I guess it was hard, sure, getting orphaned like that at so young an age. But at least I returned to the faith through Aunt Abby's good influence. Yeah, she prayed for me for years, like St. Monica did for Augustine. Can't say she's been crazy about SANA, leastways not since Bricusse withdrew his support. She thinks Bricusse is the next thing to Fulton Sheen, you know, because of his retreats and religious conferences and all." Mitch reached for his tea and took a sip. "But speaking of SANA, I need a break from all the coolie labor over there. Krato doesn't know it yet — either Krato — but I'm heading up to Green Bay next weekend to visit Abby. Yeah, I think I'll do some serious writing up there."

Lupe suppressed the smile hovering around her lips at the dizzying thought of Mitch Showalter taking pen in hand.

"I'm working on a modernization of *Lear*," Mitch added, as if anticipating some further expression of interest on Lupe's part, which she had no intention of offering. He wrapped his pudgy jaws around a forkful of rice, chewed a bit, and tongued it down his throat. "That production we saw at the APT kinda inspired me. I've been thinking of talking to Fr. Bricusse about making an independent writing project out of it. Which reminds me…" Mitch cleared his throat. "Well, I thought someone had better talk to you about, well, Jimmy."

She blinked. "Who?"

"You know, Ireton. James Ireton. Sorry, I always called him 'Jimmy' at SANA House."

"I d-d-don't follow."

"Didn't you know?"

"Didn't I know what?"

"Jimmy used to be one of us. At SANA."

Lupe's eyes grew big, like a child's at its first sight of a giraffe or a hippopotamus.

"Gotcha!" Mitch giggled at the jaw-dropping success of his ambush. "Ah, don't feel bad. It's always a shock when people first find out, Jimmy's changed so much. But yeah, he was one of us until, oh, about three years ago. He's a convert, too, can you believe it? His dad's an Anglican priest. Not that they ever got along."

Lupe shook her head again, her thoughts in a blur. The heart of every person, she had always believed, was a tremendous mystery, but the mystery of James Ireton was rapidly becoming a subject of profound interest to her.

"Yeah, we know all about Jimmy over at SANA. That's why I wanted to talk to you tonight. Or at least one reason." Mitch reached for his teacup, his sunburned face turning a deeper shade of pink. "I mean, Jimmy Ireton is a terrific guy in many ways. Honestly, he was like a brother to me. But he's not exactly what he seems. I just thought I should, you know, one Christian to another, warn you." Mitch leaned across the table to whisper. "The guy's gonads are on overdrive. Bel Gunderson, Nadine Jeffrey, Trisha Perl…the list is endless. Why, he did Jeffrey and Perl so bad, Jeffrey up and dropped out of the Institute, and Perl turned dyke!"

Lupe reached for her wine glass, then realized once more that it was empty. "Th-This is all very interesting," she stammered, "but why tell me?"

Mitch cocked back his head as if it should be obvious. "'Cause he wants *you* now. I mean, there wasn't a person in that classroom the other day who didn't see how he reacted when old Bricusse assigned you two as partners. Jeez, where was the old guy's head? But you being a Catholic and all, I thought you deserved to get the bigger picture before you let yourself get—" Mitch screwed up his tiny nose. "—intimately involved."

Lupe's brief stab of pain gave way to a burst of laughter.

Mitch pouted. "You don't believe me."

"Mitch—"

"I'm telling you, I can read Jimmy like a book! Hell, even Richie Krato saw it, and he's as thick as a Cream City brick when it comes to relations between the sexes. He said to me after class, 'That poor Cruz girl, she's next!'" Mitch gave an emphatic nod. "And don't think your religion will save you when push comes to shove, 'cause for Jimmy Ireton a closed door is as good as an open invitation! Know what they call him around here?" Mitch slapped the table. "*The General.* He's a descendent of Oliver Cromwell, you know, I kid you not. Not to mention that he's pounded more positions than Norman Schwarzkopf. Jesus, everyone knows about it at the Institute, but with all the AIDS and VD going around, you'd be wise to pay double heed. Jimmy—I know for a fact—Jimmy's ambidextrous. I mean, why do you think he's always hanging out with Jack Sigur? I promise you, when Lionel Krato was still alive—that's Mr. Krato's older brother, he started SANA—Jimmy used to follow him up and down like his evil angel—"

"Enough!" Lupe clapped her hand over her mouth and swallowed several times, as much to suppress the nasty kiss-off that was springing to her lips as the bile surging in her esophagus. "Really, Mitch," she said after a final swallow, "I do appreciate your, uh, concern, but I think we'd better change the subject. Li-Like right now."

Mitch Showalter looked more than a little shot down. "Okay," he said, opening his arms, "but don't say I didn't warn you."

Unlike its muggy predecessors, Saturday morning dawned clear and balmy, the felicitous result of a high pressure system that had moved through southeastern Wisconsin overnight. Lupe's memories of her weird encounter with Mitch Showalter evaporated into the fresh air as she set out for a morning jog.

She headed first for the Lake Michigan shoreline, and then took a path up the bluffs and through Lake Park; then onto North Wahl Avenue, an "old money" neighborhood of period mansions in a variety of styles, which realtors loved to froth over as "brimming with Old World Charm." Though Lupe had jogged this way many times this summer without particular interest, it wasn't until she turned at the intersection with Newberry Boulevard that she admitted to herself, consciously, that she had chosen this morning's route for a special reason: Newberry Boulevard was home to the Student Apostolate of North America.

To be sure, a heightened sense of curiosity was one of Lupe Cruz's predominant traits, and she had rarely refused an opportunity to explore some exotic species of foreign language and culture; but nothing outside her usual orbit had ever struck her as more exotic or foreign than the language and culture of SANA, at least as personified by Mitch Showalter and his oh-so-grim little confrère Richard Krato. After the disorienting experience of the night before, Lupe felt compelled now to take a good long look at the building, which she had once heard Richard Krato describe, in perfect earnest, as "SANA's global headquarters."

SANA House turned out to be an imposing but architecturally uninteresting red brick neo-colonial with a large aluminum SANA sign rooted in the weedy front yard. The sign displayed a cheesy line-drawing of an Aryanized boy Jesus in the Jerusalem Temple, lecturing a group of Scribes and Pharisees whose sinister, swarthy faces looked like rabid caricatures lifted straight out of a cartoon-illustrated edition of *The Protocols of the Elders of Zion*. Next to the sign stood a concrete Virgin with bovine eyes and a blue veil, above which an American flag in fluorescent colors hung limply from an aluminum pole.

Lupe clucked, wondering, as she jogged in place to keep her muscles warm, whether such a weird hybrid as the Student Apostolate of North America could sprout in any other place than her beloved home state of Wisconsin. The Badger state, after all, had produced more than its share of eccentrics, at both ends of the socio-cultural spectrum, from singing

Socialist Milwaukee mayors to Senator Joe McCarthy; from Orson Welles to Liberace; from Spencer Tracy, Frank Lloyd Wright, and Georgia O'Keeffe to Harry Houdini and Jeanne Dixon. Even Golda Meir had lived here for a time. And then, of course, there was Jeffrey Dahmer.

Well, Lupe thought, making a face at the ugly building, a joint like that was certainly the perfect setting for an acronym. For the life of her, she couldn't imagine James Ireton, whatever his vices, ever having been a part of such a place.

Whooping out loud, she resumed her jog in a homeward direction, still so preoccupied with gaping at SANA House as she passed that she almost ran headlong into a contingent of identically dressed young men, like Karmic residue from the Children's Crusade, marching double-file up the street toward the house. She didn't have to see Richard and Mitch among them to know that these were SANA members, no doubt returning from the Saturday morning Mass.

She waved at Richard and Mitch as she jogged around them. Richard gave a civil nod in response, but Mitch pretended he hadn't seen her.

No hay problema, Lupe mused silently, more than content to allow last night's farce to pass without acknowledgement.

By the time Lupe reached the more modest Stowell Avenue neighborhood in which she rented the attic apartment of her grandparents' well-worn but respectable turn-of-the-century Victorian, she had to pause to shake out an annoying cramp in her calf. Bending over to massage the muscle, she glanced behind her and caught a glimpse of a red Ferrari with tinted windows and starfish hubcaps idling in the middle of the street about ten or fifteen yards behind. At first she didn't think anything of it, but as she limped the last short stretch home, she looked over her shoulder once more and realized that the flashy vehicle was pacing her.

By the time she had reached the steps to the elevated yard in front of her house, Lupe's sense of uneasiness had exploded into an adrenaline panic. She flew up the steps and around the dense border of spruce trees that secluded the house from the street. Peering between the prickly branches, she saw the Ferrari stop directly in front of the house. The car idled there at the curb like a purring tiger for about ten seconds before pulling rapidly away with a screech of rubber.

When she had assured herself that the car was not going to return, Lupe hobbled with relief toward the outdoor staircase that led up to her third floor apartment. It was only when she had reached the top step and was unlocking her door that she realized that she had just led the Ferrari, and whoever was driving it, right to her door.

*Whoever was driving it...*but suddenly Lupe knew who was driving it. Seven years before he had been behind the wheel of an old red Mustang.

A brisk shower washed the red Ferrari out of Lupe's mind, and the Mustang, and after changing into shorts, she collected her books and went out to the little screened-in porch that was tucked into the big house's east-facing gable.

The porch overlooked her grandmother's backyard flower garden. Shielded from the alley behind by a fence of whitewashed concrete blocks, entwined with roses and honeysuckle, clematis, and morning glories, the garden's curved flowerbeds were bursting with annuals in the prime of their late-summer bloom. Up here, Lupe could study in the open air, and catch a whiff of sea breeze if the wind was right. The house was less than a mile from the beach, but even from the third floor, Lupe couldn't see the lake over the roofs of the neighboring houses. It was the one disappointment that she experienced in this second home she loved so much; that and the fact that she always sat up here alone.

After a couple of hours of study, and beginning to glimpse a possible approach to the seminar paper — if her spiny colleague Mr. Ireton approved, that is — Lupe put aside her work for a glance at the morning newspaper to see if her father, a long-time city journalist, had contributed a byline.

Matteo Cruz's most recent contribution to *The Milwaukee Journal Sentinel* turned out to be a front-page headliner about the murder, the night before, of the owner of the largest porn video store in the city. According to the article, the man had been shot in the back of the head and tossed off a high-rise ramp at the Marquette Interchange. The execution-style slaying was being viewed by police, Matteo Cruz reported, as the first fatality in an organized crime war that had been heating up for some months over the control of Milwaukee Vice. The contenders: the so-called "Rainbow Mob," led by Chicagoan Nick Calabresi, and Milwaukee's own youthful Cream City *mafiya*, captained by Vyacheslav Nesterov. The victim in this case, heretofore under the "protection" of Nesterov's gang, had, it was rumored, recently switched loyalties and accepted the patronage of Nick Calabresi. Next to the article was a photo of the rather dashing Nesterov, hip to hip with one of his employees, a stunning raven-haired "professional escort" named Candace "Candy" Duffy.

The rest of the front section of the newspaper served up more of the usual daily fare, including a bomb threat at a local synagogue, the announcement of a planned closure of the Hoan Bridge for a week in November for routine repairs, and the attempted abduction of a ten-year-old girl at a school bus stop in Waukesha. At the bottom of the page was a report on the funeral Mass of Leonard Swiatko Jr. held in St. Josaphat Basilica.

Lupe frowned. Her brother Ramon had mentioned having worked the Swiatko suicide case. Saying a silent prayer for Swiatko and his family, Lupe wondered what sorrows of daily life could move a person to suicide — something which in her remarkably happy life had never remotely occurred to her.

Lupe turned finally to the Life section and was startled to see the pea-cock-blue contact lenses of Bel Gunderson staring back at her from a full-page color spread for Stark's Dark Beer. The model was wearing—barely wearing—a tiny black lace bra and pair of bikini panties that was almost as revealing of her shapely derrière as a thong. The photo, shot in profile, showed Bel bent over at the waist, her fanny thrust up in the air like a gorilla in heat, a foaming bottle of Stark's Dark poised precariously on her rump. Bel looked challengingly into the camera lens as if daring the viewer—rath-er, *voyeur*—to come and snatch the rocket-shaped bottle away from her.

Lupe dropped the paper beside her leg and slumped against the wall behind her. If *that* was James Ireton's taste in women, she thought, then no wonder he had no use for her.

She let out a little growl.

James Ireton lay stretched out on his back with one arm draped over his face, wide awake to the early morning darkness. He had worked till midnight, bent over his dissertation like old Master Marner at his loom, accomplish-ing little more than a desultory rearrangement of papers on his desktop. The habitual consolation of work had neither settled his mind nor collected his errant thoughts, for tonight, attempts to concentrate on his studies had only served, perversely, to impress the image of Lupe Cruz even more firmly into his imagination. He had switched off the light well past midnight, all too aware that closing his eyes was futile.

He gave it another hour, as was his custom when sleep would not come, then sat up on the edge of his bed and tried to conjure up some purposeful activity to hurry the dragging hours until drowsiness, or the dawn, would bring relief. When nothing came to mind, he pulled on a pair of shorts and padded on bare feet into the living room.

James's apartment, a spacious one-bedroom flat on the top floor of the old St. Ives building, one of the many gracefully aging apartment houses strung along North Prospect Avenue on the bluffs above the lake, felt miser-ably hot and stuffy after another almost tropical downpour in the late eve-ning. The fact that a mere grad student could afford to live in such a building on Prospect Hill, Milwaukee's Gold Coast, was one of the many intriguing elements of James's personal mystery which fueled the rumor mill at the Institute. But then, because the only visitors James permitted within the walls of his hermitage were Bricusse and Jack Sigur, none of his other col-leagues could possibly know that his was the least pretentious suite in the building, decorated as it was with little more than the spectacular view of the inland sea beyond his living room windows.

James lived there like a monk. He never entertained, didn't even own a sofa or guest chairs, and when he broke his sporadic attempts at celibacy, it was never here. His furniture was second-hand and Spartan. There was a squarish old trestle table next to the sliding-glass doors that opened on to the balcony, and a whitewashed brick fireplace that he never lit. The rest of the living room was furnished only with the scarred oak desk that had once belonged to Lionel Krato, and row after row of heavily laden bookshelves that banked the walls from bare floor to white ceiling. There were no house-plants or pictures here, no signs of any life at all outside an intellectual life furnished with scores of books.

Climbing in semi-darkness atop the trestle table, James sat cross-legged, staring into the darkness beyond his lake-facing window like a shaman awaiting a vision. Outside, the soupy night was illumined only marginally by the ghostly amber of sodium vapor lamps strung along Memorial Drive. He could see nothing of the lake beyond, nor even the lights of the downtown skyline and the Hoan Bridge to the south.

The murmur of intermittent traffic rose up the side of the building in a mild crescendo and decrescendo. The foghorn of the North Point Lighthouse moaned every twenty seconds or so, providing mournful basso continuo to his mental composition of need. He thought about trying to scrounge up something to read, but he really didn't feel like reading. Indeed, he felt as if he had read every word ever written, and that there was nothing new to read, ever again. And so, James's mind, bereft of the usual distractions by the emptiness of night, settled on the image of Lupe Cruz once again.

He thought she must be in bed by now, and wondered what she looked like, sleeping. Pulling his knees up to his chin, he tried to imagine her sleep-ing; but since he did not know what her bedroom looked like, or the form of her odd possessions, he could only draw this inner portrait from images already stored in his memory. And so it was that he found himself imagining her sleeping in his room, in his bed, her legs stretched between his sheets, her black hair undone from the braid and fanned across his white pillow. These fantasies were so unlike his usual mental pictures when confronted with sex-ual need, so different from any he had ever conjured in his mind before, that their novelty briefly brushed aside the other images with which he had been wrestling since Lupe Cruz walked out of his sight Wednesday afternoon.

James was determined to forbid himself those other, more primitive mind pictures. If he allowed them easy passage in his fancy, he knew he would not be able to resist the impulse to act on them. James Ireton was out of practice when it came to the keeping of the Commandments, but in his mind at least one categorical imperative remained: he must not break a promise to Arthur Bricusse. And so, when his mind refused to let go of her image, he struggled at least to erase from it any suggestion of the erotic. Surely, he hoped, time would make easier what tonight seemed impossible.

One nail drives out another nail, he reminded himself, *one pain another pain.*

Heaving a sigh, James turned his eyes on a pile of freshly printed copies of his first published book, neatly stacked on the table beside his leg. "*The Conscience of the Prince,* by James Henry Ireton," declared the glossy dust jackets, suitably designed in Hamletesque black and white.

Ah, yes, something to celebrate, that. The publication of his first book, a more polished version of his Master's thesis on *Hamlet,* was a milestone in his life. A significant road marker on the path of his career. Or just another nail in his coffin. Lifting his hand, James let his fingertips drift along the book spines. He felt not the slightest spark of joy in this accomplishment, although he was certain that he was supposed to. Oh, he had felt a brief flush of genuine satisfaction when he presented the first copy to Arthur Bricusse; the old man had beamed with paternal pride and said, "You have a great gift, James, and a wonderful future ahead of you!" And for a moment, James had believed so, too; but now he could only sit here and wonder how in the devil he might rid himself of the five remaining copies of the half dozen that the Heisler Institute Press had so obligingly sent him upon publication.

Mentally scanning a list of his personal and professional contacts, it suddenly occurred to James that Lupe Cruz might enjoy having a copy of his book. For some reason, the thought of Cruz holding one of his books, leafing through it, perhaps thanking him in that ridiculous stammer of hers, was intensely pleasurable. So much so that he climbed off the table and went to the telephone on his desk to ring her up; then remembered the lateness of the hour; then remembered that he had made a firm decision to resist these dangerous impulses, whatever the hour.

Deciding at length that there was nothing for it, James padded to his bathroom and reached for a bottle of prescription sleeping tablets from the medicine cabinet. He tapped one into his sweating palm, hesitated, then another, and downed them both with a gulp of water from his cupped hands.

Finally, he carried a pillow and his sleeping bag out onto the balcony where he stretched out, face down. Though there was scant breeze off the lake, his breath began to come more easily. At last, and after many minutes of benumbed listening to the distant traffic below, the lowing of the foghorn, and the droning of the lapping waves, he finally fell into a dragon-ridden sleep.

The Newman Center chapel, ministering to Catholic students on the east side of Milwaukee, mostly from UWM, was little more than a converted garage attached to the back of a red brick house. Finding an empty seat near the back, Lupe was so preoccupied with the jumble of conflicting thoughts in her mind that she found herself standing with the congregation for the entrance hymn, no missalette in hand, and without the slightest idea which hymn number the lector had just announced. Before she could turn around to hunt for a booklet in the pew, the person next to her had shoved one in front of her nose, folded back to the correct page.

Lupe turned to nod her thanks to whomever it was, and was surprised to see Jack Sigur's *café-au-lait* face looming above her. She smiled up at the tall Creole and he grinned back, all the while booming out the artless, folksy tune in his resonant, almost operatic, baritone. Training her eyes on the sanctuary, before which a dozen or so SANA men were lined up laterally in the front pew like a row of plastic pigeons in a carnival shoot, Lupe's smile was instantly killed.

Except for Mitch, whose Brobdingnagian shoulders made him easy to differentiate, the SANA men all looked remarkably alike from behind, with their neatly trimmed hair and stiff, snowy collars. Finally, she saw one of the SANA men turn to whisper something into his neighbor's ear, and recognized Richard Krato's imperious profile. When the congregation sat, Lupe took the occasion to study Richard's gray-haired interlocutor, who, obviously too old to be a student member, must be, she concluded, the legendary Peter Krato himself.

In the three or four years since SANA's founding, Peter Krato had already become something of a byword in Cream City. Lupe remembered having seen one of his occasional TV specials a year or two before on one of the local cable channels, but remembered not a word of the man's message; only that it had been served up with such a treacly concoction of pious verbiage that she had been left with a bad case of spiritual indigestion. For the life of her, Lupe couldn't now remember what the man had looked like.

At this moment, only the back of Krato's head was visible, along with the pale cylinder of his ropy neck and the oversize square of his shoulders — mismatched, it appeared, to the rest of the man's smallish physiognomy. Too, Krato's hair was not the silvery gray usually associated with distinguished middle age, but a steely, almost blue-gray, like the gunmetal of an aircraft carrier. Though cut military-short like his men's, the wiry stuff sprouted down the back of his neck in bristly patches that made Lupe think of some ancient forefather of *Homo sapiens.*

Suddenly too warm, Lupe took to fanning herself with her missalette. Though from time to time a word or phrase of the prosaic liturgy penetrated the surface of her consciousness, for the most part a carnival of random pictures paraded in her mind: James Ireton's suntanned face against a blue expanse of water; Richard Krato's Roman profile over a bleached collar; Mitch's red-veined eyes behind some fat book; the woolly back of Peter Krato's neck.

When everyone stood for the Gospel, the last vestige of Lupe's peace fell suddenly and frighteningly away. The words of the reading came forward briefly in her mind, ringing like a carillon; but no sooner did the sounds strike her ear than the words faded again, to be replaced by a frigid and unquiet silence, as if a door had sprung open somewhere in her imagination, letting in dead winter.

At long last Lupe became aware of a *different* spirit within the pedestrian confines of the tiny chapel; a spirit criminal and predatory that was...and wasn't; was everywhere and nowhere at the same time. Her fingers gripping the back of the pew in front of her, Lupe gasped for air, forgetting—suddenly incapable of memory or any other human faculty—that she was in a house of God.

It seemed like a century of emptiness and terror before she heard the words, "Lord, deliver us from evil, grant us peace in our day..." Reciting the prayer in an apathetic tone, the priest called on the congregation to turn to their neighbors and offer the sign of peace. Lupe felt the comforting touch of Jack Sigur's hand, extended in friendship.

"You all right?" Jack whispered, bending down.

She reassured him with a nod and turned around to offer the sign of peace to whomever was standing behind her.

Barry DeBrun was standing behind her.

One side of DeBrun's thin mouth curved up into a sneer. He extended his hand.

Lupe focused her horrified eyes on the pastel buttons of DeBrun's designer shirt, and lifted her trembling hand. DeBrun took firm hold of it, squeezing it just a bit harder and longer than was appropriate. She pulled her hand out of the man's lingering grasp and extended it to the woman standing next to him, a tall, plump brunette wearing a pleasant face and a pink suit—DeBrun's wife, by the looks of their matching wedding bands.

Finally Lupe turned again to face the altar, her blouse soaked with sweat, the heat of Barry DeBrun's green eyes like a blowtorch on her back.

"Hey, girl," said Jack Sigur when they stepped out into the morning sunshine a few minutes later, "what happened to you in there? You weren't off having an apparition of the Blessed Virgin, now were you?"

"N-N-Not exactly." Glancing around, Lupe spotted DeBrun and his wife, DeBrun looking drowsy with boredom, climbing into a sports car parked by the corner—a red Ferrari with starfish hubcaps. Lupe shuddered. "It was more like that old saying about feeling as if someone had wa-wa-walked over your grave."

Jack emitted a concerned cluck. "Now, now, girl, this is Cheddarville, heartland of curds and whey, not voodoo dolls and hocus-pocus. However, now that you mention 'graves,' hither sallies a first-class whited sepulcher."

Following the direction of Jack's dubious glance, Lupe turned to see Richard Krato, his classic features set like an antique bust over his SANA-white shirt, approaching them with a purposeful air of disapproving inquiry that would have looked quite at home, Lupe thought, on Tomás de Torquemada.

"I wondered," Richard said to Lupe without greeting or preamble, "if I could have a word with you. In private."

Jack pivoted for a speedy exit, but Lupe caught hold of his shirtsleeve. This, she thought, had to be some sort of SANA business, and not something she wanted to suffer through alone. Besides, that cold thing that had troubled her at Mass was still haunting her imagination, like a whiff of skunk spray lingering in the air hours after the animal's carcass had been removed. She gave Jack a meaningful look before finally letting go of his arm and saying to Richard, "You c-c-couldn't possibly say anything to me that Jack shouldn't hear."

Tilting his head to starboard, Richard Krato leaned heavily on his left leg. "I just wanted to talk to you about your date with Mitch the other night."

Jack's eyebrows shot up like a rocket at liftoff.

"I'm not sure I would c-call it a date," Lupe said.

"Well, are you planning to see him again?"

Lupe was unsure of how she wanted to answer that question. God knew she had no intention of seeing Mitch Showalter socially ever again, but she hardly thought it was any of Richard's business. "If he asks me again, I guess I'll just have to cross that bridge when I come to it," she replied.

Jack chuckled at the evasion. Richard, however, attempted to mask his obvious disappointment with an uncertain survey of the overcast sky above. He rubbed his palm up and down the back of his head as if filling in the conversational gap with a bit of stage business until he could think of something to say. When he finally did, it was to Jack: "You know, I think the seminar is shaping up just great."

Lupe was taken a little off guard by this sudden turn, but Jack didn't seem the least disoriented. Responding to cue, the lanky Creole stepped off the sidewalk, eased his backside against a telephone pole, and slapped one outstretched thigh as if he were already off-book with this much-rehearsed scene. "You bet," Jack exclaimed, "Cruz here's *mighty* lucky to get Ireton as her partner, now ain't she, Rich?"

"Oh, without a doubt," Richard agreed, much too quickly. "James is one of the most talented people I've ever met. He probably knows more about Elizabethan lit than anyone in this city. Except Fr. Bricusse, of course. Too bad he doesn't know how to use all the gifts God has given him."

Uh oh, Lupe thought, crossing her arms and preparing herself for the worst: it appeared that the subject was once again to be James Ireton.

The resulting interview turned out to be even bumpier than Lupe expected. She had been able to laugh off Mitch and his tall tales of 'Jimmy' Ireton's omnivorous sexual appetites, but Richard Krato, who had heretofore impressed her as a colorless soul, so bloodless as to be unable to sustain a passion for more than ten seconds, had proven instead to be a long-winded Savanarola of righteous indignation when the subject was James Ireton; which, with these people, it always seemed to be. Richard had concluded his scripture-trinketed tirade by casting a sidelong glance at Jack while warning Lupe about "near occasions of sin." To which Lupe had instantly and heatedly responded, with a comical little stamp of her foot that only accentuated her furious stutter, that at that moment he, Richard K-K-Krato, was her nearest occasion of sin, and that she would r-r-really appreciate it if he made himself and his unsolicited opinions sc-c-carce. Richard had obliged her by turning on his heel.

"What is it with these people?" Lupe harrumphed to Jack, who, on the pretext of making sure the fuming young woman made it in one piece, had offered to walk her home.

Jack waved. "Never you mind ol' Richie Krato. He's SANA's herd dog, don't you know. It's his job to bark the strays into fenced pasture."

"But I don't understand their fixation on James Ireton."

"Ah. Well, it's like this: five years in this town have given Ireton an Orson Welles-sized reputation in the Institute. Yep, he's our very own *enfant terrible. Ergo*, everyone wants to claim him. Or damn him. I mean, he's too postmod for the medievalists, too aesthetic for the metaphysicals, and too religious, *malgré lui*, for the artsy-fartsies. Not to mention that he's got a knack for getting under your skin that a chigger could envy. Let's face it, the guy's as driven as a maniac, and it's hard to relax around a typhoon." Jack nodded vigorously. "But one thing's for positive sure, if James Henry Ireton was the sexual democrat those people make him out to be, I'd be the first to know."

On that note, Jack stopped in the middle of the sidewalk, bent over at the waist, and slapped his knees as if to keep time with his guffaws.

"Wha-What's so funny?"

"The pictures in my head, the pictures! See, when I first came to the Institute, I heard those same rumors about ol' Jim-bo. And he was friendly and charming and cute and all, so naturally, I...well, one evening when we were sitting on the beach, I..." Jack winced.

Lupe's residual anger dissolved into a giggle. "Oh my. What did he do?"

"About what you'd expect from the General at his butchiest."

"He p-p-punched you in the nose."

"In the *jaw*." Jack massaged his chin with a stoic air. "Clicks like an old typewriter ever since."

When they had reached the elevated yard of her house, Lupe was astounded to see the subject of their colloquy sitting on her outside steps, reading. James jumped to his feet when he saw them. His expression was cross.

Jack held up five spidery fingers as if to fend off fisticuffs. "Not a word, *cher*," he protested. "I was merely doing my knightly duty and escorting Milady through the forest. There were dragons abroad today."

"Dragons?" James said.

"Richard positively accosted the poor girl after Mass."

"Richard?"

"*By Heaven, he echoes me!*" Jack cried in an Othello bass.

James glared at Lupe. "What the devil did the Groom Arrogant want with you?"

"Good question, but I'm not really sure of the answer. Look, g-guys, howsabout we discuss all this over some beer and sandwiches?"

Jack glanced at his watch. "Thanks, but I've got a tennis game in an hour. But let me chat with James here a sec, d'ya mind? Then I'll send him up."

Once Lupe had climbed the stairs and shut the third floor door behind her, Jack described, in vivid detail, what had transpired with Richard Krato after Mass, and what Lupe had told him about her dinner with Mitch Showalter.

"Can you beat that about ol' Goliath," Jack concluded, "asking a girl out on a date?"

"Probably just flexing his muscles a bit after three years in a straitjacket," James said, not the least interested in Mitch Showalter's many eccentricities, now that he had been assured, by way of Jack, that Lupe Cruz wasn't interested in them either.

Jack fingered a tuft of his goatee. "I guess the real question is, after three years, why are these guys so hepped up about you again all of a sudden?"

"I neither know nor care. Except…"

"What?"

James refused to elaborate, though he was thinking of the anonymous letters. Another had arrived in yesterday's mail, this one copied from the chapter in *Revelations* about the war in heaven between Michael the Archangel and the Red Dragon.

Jack wagged his forefinger in front of his silent friend's flared nostrils. "One of these days, Jim-bo, you're going to wake up and discover that you just can't cut yourself off from your friends. Like it or not, your life has an effect on other people. Especially those who care for you."

"I've never expected anyone to care for me."

Jack looked away with a rare show of anger; then up at the door to Lupe Cruz's apartment. "Yeah, and that's why you were sitting here this morning. And don't give me that crapload about you two having a paper to write. I got eyes."

James plopped down on the stairs, his hands limp between his knees. "So, apparently, does Peter Krato and his faithful minions, else they wouldn't be setting to work on Lupe." James swore. "And me the last man in the city capable of throwing stones at their crystal cathedral."

"Why's that?"

"Because I, too, live in a glass house. The kind with prophylactic vending machines in the hallways and mirrors on the ceilings."

Of all the things that Jack had related to James about the morning's interchange with Richard Krato and Lupe's date with Mitch Showalter, everything was ultimately cast into the shade of James's troubled musings by Jack's comment-in-passing that, in response to some aggressive question on Richard's part about how well Lupe's Christian loyalties were likely to withstand James Ireton's corrupting influence, Lupe had defended herself by insisting that she firmly adhered to all the Church's more difficult moral teachings, including the ban on premarital sex.

Well, jolly good, James thought as he spiraled up the outside stairs that led to Lupe's third floor apartment. If he ever weakened in his promise to Bricusse—so went his reasoning—the pious Miss Cruz would send him packing with prissy indignation.

"Hello!" James called, pushing open the door and letting the screen door fall to behind him.

"Be right with you!" Lupe answered, apparently from the kitchen.

James entered onto a small landing that was the turning point for an interior flight of stairs coming up from the second floor. Climbing the three steps that led up to Lupe's living room, he laid a copy of *The Conscience of the Prince* on her tiny two-chair dining table and looked around, trying to read some ideographic meaning into her modest collection of possessions.

The structure of Lupe Cruz's attic apartment was reminiscent of the cabin of an old sailing ship. A low ceiling, paneled with scarred tongue-in-groove oak, followed the slope of the roof to meet low-slung dormer walls painted in cream. The floor was planked in scuffed oak as well, as were bookshelves fitted into the walls in several places. A faded sofa faced a tiny brick fireplace in the corner, over which a rough-hewn plank of wood served as a chimneypiece. A familiar American Players Theater poster hung above the fireplace: a darkly conceived photo of a papier-mâché Shakespeare dressed in a ruffled Elizabethan collar. The Bard's face was shot half in shadow, and he was holding at each shoulder, arms crossed, papier-mâché masks of Comedy and Tragedy. THE ULTIMATE SHAKESPEARIENCE read the caption in large white letters below.

James pulled his eyes away from the vaguely sinister-looking poster and turned them on the more brightly illuminated central wall separating Lupe's living room and what he presumed was her bedroom. A fifty-gallon saltwater aquarium squatted on a stand by the bedroom door, its swimming light casting a shimmering turquoise glow against the wall behind.

James was scrutinizing one of her more exotic-looking fish when Lupe emerged from the kitchen, barefoot, in shorts, and bearing a tray of sandwiches.

"Brew or soda?" she asked.

"Beer please," James said, trying not to stare at her shapely legs. "Sorry, didn't intend to invite myself to lunch."

Lupe's smile widened when she noticed *The Conscience of the Prince* on the table. She set down the tray and snatched at it with undisguised eagerness.

"It's…for you."

Lupe studied the black and white jacket, the title page, and then the foreword written by Bricusse. "Wow," she breathed, "this is…wow. How does it feel to have a book published?"

"It feels good," he admitted, smiling. Now it did. Now it finally felt good.

Replacing the book on the table, Lupe patted it once, almost possessively, James noted, and returned to the kitchen to fetch him a beer. When she returned, she led him through a low door that opened out on to her screened porch.

He crossed the porch floor in three steps and gazed out the screen. "Splendid," he said, surveying the flower garden three stories below.

"Isn't it great? I practically lived out here during the summer. In fact—"
Lupe crossed her feet and sat down like an accomplished yogini. "—I like to
pull out my sleeping bag and sleep out here."

James eased himself to the floor with a groan.

"Sorry?"

"Er, nothing."

Lupe sighed. "Now all I need is the lake."

"Beg pardon?"

"N-Nothing." Her cheeks flushed; a charming habit of hers.

Digging into their sandwiches, they chatted between bites.

"Jack put me in the picture about your little misadventure with Rich
today," James began, chewing. "I appreciate your taking up for me with these
SANA people, but I'm not sure it's necessary. Or prudent. It could ruin your
reputation among your co-religionists." He glanced up, seeming to be, but
not, lost in distracted contemplation of the flowers far below.

"Can't say I'm very worried about it, one way or the other." Lupe swallowed her giggle with a drink of beer and pointed down at the garden. "Oh,
look, *abuela*'s mums are finally beginning to bud down there. She had to
water almost every day during the summer, because of the drought—"

"I dare say you were wondering," James broke in, "but were too polite to
inquire, how the profligate son of an Anglican clergyman managed to get
himself ensnared in a rad-trad Catholic cult."

Lupe sat back, eyebrows lifted. "You're right, I was too polite to ask."

And with that, to James's enormous relief, Lupe Cruz changed the subject.

———————

Poor James, Lupe thought as she climbed into bed that night, intending to
write in her journal, he actually began to have some fun today, in spite of
himself. Ten years had dropped from his face in one hour. At least until...

Lupe reached for the journal on her night stand, her eyes darkening in a
frown. It was odd, what had happened this afternoon. They had been having a
productive, even warm exchange of ideas about their research paper—James
had become positively animated, even fervent, when the discussion turned to
Shakespeare—when, not knowing what had moved her, Lupe suddenly suggested that she put on some music. James acquiesced with pleasure, almost as
if this had been his very plan, until he heard the opening strains of the music
she had chosen, one of her favorites, a fantasy for orchestra and solo violin
by Vaughan Williams called *The Lark Ascending*.

Humming quietly to herself as the violin soared, imitating a lark in
its heavenward ascent, Lupe took no notice at first of the peculiar expression that suddenly appeared on James's face. Instead, she retreated into the
kitchen to fetch them more beer, feeling suddenly embarrassed at her own
impulse. This was, after all, music that since she was a child had resonated in
a special yearning place in her heart where something, or someone, ought to
be and was not yet. It suddenly hit her that she had chosen to play this par-

ticular music for him as a kind of barometer, because she was infatuated; was even hoping against hope, perhaps, for some response from him that might give her a clue to his deeper nature. Oh God, she thought, and in the next minute or so, when she got up the courage to walk back out there, the man to whom she was exposing this little corner of her soul—a man about whom there were enough salacious rumors floating around to fill a supermarket tabloid—would be yawning, or blowing his nose, or fidgeting with those big peasant's hands of his, as if he were bored beyond endurance. What had she been *think*ing?

Bottles in hand, Lupe turned resolutely, thinking to shut the blasted stereo off before she made a complete fool of herself. She stopped short in the porch doorway.

James was bent over, his fingers gnarled in an almost arthritic curl as they pressed hard into the hollows of his temples. At first Lupe's heart skipped a beat, because it seemed that, yes, he *was* moved by the rapture of the violin; he wasn't the cynic he worked so hard to persuade people that he was; but it took her precious few seconds to comprehend that, whatever the nature of his obvious emotion, rapture played no part in it.

Apparently hearing her approach, he looked up at her; then his dark and hollow-seeing eyes traversed the corners of the little porch, lighting listlessly and as if unseeing on the sky outside and the flowers below; then again on her face. Then his look of anguish folded into another expression entirely; an expression that she couldn't translate from her own experience into meaningful words, until it settled finally into something that looked very much like fear; or no not fear, she decided, but panic.

"My God," she whispered, "what is it?"

James rose unsteadily to his feet, like a man waking from heavy sedation. He stepped up to her, so close that she couldn't breathe without her breasts brushing against his chest. Lifting the silver Guadalupe medal that hung at her throat, he turned the thing over several times with a startled, stricken expression on his face.

"I forgot," was all he said. He dropped the medal back on her throat, stepped past her, and walked quietly out the door.

Lupe had tried calling him that evening, but James was not at home, or, more likely, not answering. She left a message on his voice mail, but he didn't return the call. She didn't really expect him to, after what had happened with the music, without knowing why, or what any of it meant...

Opening her journal, Lupe picked up a pen and began to write.

It wasn't the same, Lupe soon realized, as when James had tried to avoid her before. Now it was as if she didn't exist. When she and James arrived separately on Tuesday for the first of their weekly scheduled meetings with Fr. Bricusse to discuss the progress of their paper, James had been charming enough—lucid, professional to a fault—but his dumbshow of smiles was obviously performed for Bricusse's sake, not hers. The smiles disappeared altogether the minute they walked out the door and he vanished without so much as a see-you-later.

And of course by the end of Wednesday's seminar, during which time James didn't so much as speak to his so-called partner, even Jack got the picture. The tall man approached Lupe afterward with a warmly sympathetic air to inquire, discreetly, whether "Himself" had asked her to Lanciano's *fais do-do* on Friday the thirteenth.

"Of c-c-course not," was Lupe's bewildered reply.

"Well, then, Milady," Jack offered with a gentlemanly demi-bow, "allow Yours Truly to escort you to the *fête*. The ass-hole hasn't asked me, either."

James stepped into Bricusse's office after the Wednesday seminar, just in time to see the old man chucking a tiny pill into his mouth.

"What's that for?" James said, pulling up an armchair and motioning at the prescription bottle on Bricusse's desk.

Bricusse washed down the pill with a lemon-lime soda and coughed on the carbonation.

"My ticker," he choked out, and then laughed, as at some private joke.

James worked on a smile, but couldn't quite manage it. Instead he crossed one ankle over the other knee and began snare-drumming his fingers on the sole of his shoe. Bricusse had asked him to drive him to Mitchell Field for a commuter flight to Chicago, where Bricusse was to chaplain some sort of religious conference for laywomen, and James, frankly, was eager to get going before the late-afternoon traffic transformed his headache into a rush-hour migraine.

Bricusse wiped his eyes with the back of one age-spotted hand. "James, what's troubling you? You haven't been yourself since the term began."

James sat up. "Why, nothing's troubling me," he said, startled that Bricusse had seen so much. "I've not been sleeping well, that's all." He shrugged. "The usual."

But Arthur Bricusse was probably the one man before whom James Ireton's native talent for theater had ever come to naught. "Lupe?" Bricusse said.

James hesitated, then dropped his forehead to his propped-up fist.

"My dear boy, is it that bad?"

"It's a bloody disease," James admitted. "But you know I'll keep my promise," he added quickly. Unable to look Bricusse in the eye, James directed his attention around the room, searching for some remarkable object to inspire a change of subject. "By the way, the place is looking better. You've somehow managed to pull it—"

James's eyes had faltered on a large picture on the wall behind him. It was the astonishing color that caught his eye first, the dusty but luminescent turquoise of a floor-length mantle covering the head and body of a dark-haired young woman. Golden rays streamed outwards from behind the woman's back, as if she were blocking out the noonday sun. It was in the same instant that James realized that something in the woman's gentle face reminded him of Lupe Cruz that he also realized, by the woman's reverent posture and folded hands, that he was looking at an icon of the Virgin Mary, painted in a style such as he had never seen.

Then James felt as if he couldn't breathe, because he *had* seen something very much like this before; in a waking dream from his other life—a vision of beauty, glory, and terror, which he had spent the better part of the last three years trying to blot from his memory.

A birdlike tremolo warbled in James's mind, and his nostrils filled with the forgotten scent of roses.

Bricusse smiled lovingly at his picture. "Beautiful, isn't she? Not at all like those candy-faced Madonnas one so often sees, with their cartoonish WASP features and Hollywood makeup."

"I had no idea," James whispered.

Bricusse turned. "James," he said, clearly astonished and perhaps a little hurt, "don't tell me you haven't opened my present yet!"

James's arm shot out in pointing accusation. "You gave me *that*?" he shrieked.

When Bricusse didn't answer, James's arm fell limp to the armrest. "I'm sorry, I didn't mean that the way it sounded. I just hadn't had a chance to open it yet. Of course, she's…beautiful."

"She's Our Lady of Guadalupe," Bricusse explained, his face scrolling a pattern of deepening concern. "The Dark Virgin of the Americas. The Mexicans call her *la Guadalupana*. I'm surprised you've never seen her before. She's probably not that well known in Britain, but in America, and in SANA—"

"Lionel Krato was a devoté of Eastern icons," James observed. "Our Lady of Czestochowa and Vladimir. Peter was partial to candy-faced Madonnas with cartoonish WASP features and Hollywood makeup."

"Yes…yes, I can imagine."

James cocked his head at the picture, but didn't look at it. "Who painted it?"

"Now thereby hangs a tale. The iconographers call it *achieropoetoi*. 'Not made by human hands.'"

"Ah."

Bricusse cracked a smile at James's expression. "The image dates from 1531, ten years after the Spanish Conquest of Mexico. It appeared in the possession of an Aztec convert named Juan Diego. There's a complete account of the story enclosed with the picture I gave you. If you can bring yourself to open it, that is."

James glanced at his watch. "We'd better go. Wouldn't do to have you to miss your flight."

Bricusse reached for his briefcase. "There's something I urgently need to discuss with you en route. Something that you're going to find even less congenial than miracle tales about pictures painted by God."

"And what might that be?" James asked, thinking that there were precious few things in life that fit that description.

Bricusse glanced once more at the image, and wiped what looked like a tear from one wrinkled cheek. "You and me and SANA, and a young man named Lenny Swiatko."

Chapter Three:
The World's Report

Read not my blemishes in the world's report;
I have not kept my square, but that to come
Shall all be done by the rule.

Shakespeare, *Antony and Cleopatra*

Lupe laughed at Jack Sigur's efforts to fold his long spindleshanks into the passenger seat of her grandparents' Toyota. Once inside and they had pulled away from the curb, Jack's survey of Lupe's white halter-top party dress elicited a long, high-rising whistle.

"My oh my," he exclaimed, "ol' Jim-bo's gonna like that, I do declare."

She shot him a sideways glance. "I thought you said he wouldn't show."

"Well, now," Jack said in a mock English accent, "I couldn't have done. Ireton's not exactly overflowing with *bonhomie*, for sure, but he'd hardly be so rude to Lanciano as to pass up his gala to-do in honor of the dedication of St. Max's Cathedral, now would he?"

Lupe focused on her driving. When she had finally negotiated the turn onto Lake Drive, heading north, she glanced once again at Jack out of the corner of her eye. He was leaning one bony elbow out the window, distractedly fingering his goatee. "Jack?" she said.

"Yo."

"You can tell me to go to hell if you want…"

"What?"

"You're hung up on him, aren't you?"

Jack discharged a puff of air. "I already told you, *his affections do not that way tend*, whatever the rumors. So I'm stuck like some gay comedian in the sweet-but-pathetic Best Friend role." He looked at her. "Tell you what's the truth, James Henry Ireton can be one primo pain in the butt, but he's also, I don't know, *nonpareil*. I believe we understand one another about that, you and me."

Lupe shrugged, thinking that was true enough, though she was still unable to identify the precise nature of her own emotions toward James Ireton — she who usually, and perhaps too quickly, knew just what she felt about everything and everybody.

Neither of them said anything for a minute at least. Finally, Lupe administered an emphatic blow to the steering wheel that briefly sent the car swerving over the center line.

"Whoa, girl, what?"

"I guess I'm just having a hard time not imagining him and..."

"Madame Pythoness?"

Lupe growled.

"Tush, that's cold as any stone. In fact it was never warm, even when it was hot."

"I'm sure Bel's, um, very g-good at what she does," Lupe said, not quite able to let go of the images her mind insisted on conjuring. "There's no way for me to compete with that."

"If you tried to play her game you'd lose, that's sure. *Great mistress of her art was that false Dame*. But James is beyond that. He hit the wall last spring, and hasn't touched a woman since the one-night fiasco with Trisha."

Lupe bit her lip. "Why is Bel at the Institute anyway? She hardly seems the academic type."

Jack spun his forefinger in the air. "Our Isabel's a well-oiled literary weathervane. She twirls with the slightest breeze, fresh or stale, from de Sade to De Man. If she sees the words 'risk-taking' or 'cutting-edge' in a *New York Times* review, she's on top of the thing in a heartbeat."

Lupe giggled.

"Oh, yeah. Only Bel hasn't got James's passion, or Showalter's memory, so she really has to *work* at it." Jack whooped aloud. "Fact is, Bel Gunderson sees herself at the vortex of some incestuous circle of glitterati. Every semester or so she tries to start up a *salon*. Bloomsbury-on-Bradford Beach, or Montmartre-on-the-Menomonee...man, would she love to play de Beauvoir to Jim's Sartre! You know, each sleeping around liberally, while being perfectly *devoted* to one another. But I'm afraid our James turned out a big disappointment to her. Don't know why he dumped her — he never tells me anything — but it must have stung, honey, 'cause ol Belzebub's been trolling like a Great White on a feeding frenzy ever since. Right now I'm just waiting to see which direction she turns. My best guess is she'll go after Trish, just so she'll have something new to brag about at parties. But if not that she'll be putting out her claws for one of the SANA guys...egad!"

Lupe found a curbside parking spot about a block away from Lanciano's house in suburban Whitefish Bay (or "White-folks Bay," as Jack called it). The neighborhood was an impressive collection of upscale older homes, some of them outright mansions, in a motley of styles and designs. Lanciano's, unsurprisingly, was an Italianate villa, complete with stucco archways and red tiled roof. Across the street was a stuffy-looking neo-colonial owned by brewmeister Fred Stark of Stark's Brewery. Just a half mile to the south in Shorewood, and arguably the most lavish home in all the northern suburbs, was Max Heisler's gargantuan white neo-classical.

"Ever been in the Heisler place?" Jack said as they stepped out of the car and began making their way toward Lanciano's villa, lit up like a house on fire with luminaria lining the driveway.

"No, what's it like?"

"It was modeled after the *Vittorio Emmanuele* in Rome. I mean, have you *ever*? But it just looks to me like Godzilla stepped on a gigantic tube of Colgate. Heisler's got this humongous living room with marble floors and Cupid-pissing fountains, and trashy eight-foot replicas of famous Roman statues—" Jack heaved an imaginary spear. "You know, Zeus chucking thunderbolts, and other such-like imperial dreck." He pointed at the villa looming before them. "At least Lanciano's got taste." Jack waved at the big house, its facade emerging from behind some overgrown lilacs as they reached the flagstone walkway. "You ever been here before?"

"Years ago. My mom knows Adèle from the Catholic Women's League. You?"

"Oh, James and I get invited to dinner several times a year. Bricusse and Lanciano have high ambitions for our James, you know, albeit in slightly different directions." Jack bent over, lowering his voice as if afraid someone might overhear. "Rumor hath it that Bricusse wants to give James an Assistant Professorship as soon as he gets his diploma. Jim-bo would be Bricusse's right hand man in the new English Renaissance Program."

"What new English Renaissance Program?"

"You haven't heard?" Coming to a halt in front of the ornately carved front door, Jack rubbed his palms together, obviously delighted to have a pair of virgin ears for his latest morsel of academic dish. "Well, it's like this…Max Heisler wants to keep Fr. Bricusse happy, right?"

"I g-guess."

"So, how better to keep *il grigio* content than to make sure his favorite student stays here after he gets his sheepskin? Like, by building an English Renaissance program around him?"

"You mean they'd do all that just to keep James here?"

"Well, there's more to it than that," Jack admitted. "It would also be a prestigious innovation for the Institute. A cross-disciplinary program probably unique in the country. But mum's the word!" Jack leaned against the doorbell. "A certain Calabrian art historian and Deputy Director might not be too happy about any English Renaissance Program."

"Why not?"

"The 'English' part brackets out his own specialty in the *quattrocento*. Academic funding's a zero-sum game, and Heisler must be freaking out at how much he's already sunk into this place."

The massive front door was swept open by their hostess.

"*Bonsoir, Jacques! Bienvenue, Lupe!*" Adèle Lanciano cried in Canuck-accented French, straining her voice to be heard over the live jazz band's upbeat rendition of *Take the A Train*. An attractive blonde with a champagne tray balanced precariously on the be-ringed fingers of one hand, she escorted them into the terrazzo-tiled foyer, bearing herself with an ageless quality of cultured grace that made it difficult, without prior knowledge, to guess that she was well past fifty. "My dear Lupe, how is your mother? I haven't seen her for ages!"

Lupe endeavored to oblige her hostess with an update on Oonagh Cruz's latest doings, but her narrative was abridged by another summons from the doorbell.

Adèle gave an exasperated sigh. "You'll have to excuse me, m'dears. I think the butler we hired for the evening has closeted himself with a bottle of Perrier Jouet." She shoved her champagne tray into Jack's hands and rippled her fingers by way of an *adieu* before hurrying again toward the front door.

Making their way toward the living room, Lupe helped herself to a glass from the champagne tray, her widening eyes surveying Franco Lanciano's eclectic but well-integrated collection of tapestries, icons, and black-and-white photographs. The latter included some of Lanciano's own compositions, mostly soft-textured studies of long-limbed women in various stages of undress. A room-sized Aubusson or Aubusson-style carpet in shades of apricot and brown warmed the burnished parquet floor, and a huge terrazzo-tiled fireplace dominated the far wall. French doors led out onto a flagstone patio that stretched the length of the lake-facing side of the house. Beyond the patio the professionally landscaped yard was framed on each side by ornamental trees that ended abruptly at the bluffs overlooking the beach, twenty or thirty feet below.

"Be it ever so humble," Lupe quipped.

It had become something of a game for Institute students to speculate on how Dr. Franco Lanciano had managed to acquire such a fine art collection, in such a home, in such a neighborhood, on an academic salary. It was commonly known that he had been born in Calabria during the war, and that his impoverished parents had emigrated first to Chicago, then to Kenosha — "*Kenosha, that dirty little town!*" as Lanciano invariably related the tale, quoting Kenosha's more eminent but equally reluctant native son, Orson Welles.

A burg of some eighty thousand souls on the Illinois-Wisconsin border and comprised of large Italian, Polish, German, Irish, and Mexican subsets, Kenosha had become something of a byword in the region for blue-collar mediocrity. Lupe frankly had a hard time picturing the silky Italian, whose customary sartorial splendor no tailor could observe without emotion, growing up there. Kenosha, it was said, had more taverns per capita than any other city in the state, in a state with more taverns per capita than any other in the Union. But Lanciano had managed to overcome these obscure origins by graduating Phi Beta Kappa in art history and education from the University of Chicago. And though no one was hailing him as this generation's

Bernard Berenson, Lanciano's academic career and professional publications had been distinguished, and his present six-figure income from the Institute was better than good...but hardly *this* good.

Lupe, like many others, had also heard that Lanciano was a whiz at investments, particularly the buying and selling of art objects and antiques. Others speculated that Lanciano had turned his Canadian wife's modest Great Lakes shipping inheritance into a significant fortune by investing early in Stark Brewery stocks, which had climbed rapidly on the exchange and split several times since the company went public just a few years before. Still others insisted that Lanciano had made a killing in the skyrocketing real estate market in southeastern Wisconsin—particularly back in that "dirty little town" of Kenosha, which, bowling-alley reputation or no, had become attractive of late as a safe and inexpensive bedroom community for Cook County Yuppies fleeing their source of income.

And, of course, Lupe knew, more than a few people had rendered Lanciano's Italian surname and Calabrian origins into a Mafia connection. Unfortunately, Lanciano's mandarin attitude and affected *hauteur* did little to dispel the rumors. If questioned on this delicate point, Lanciano would invariably give a dismissing wave of one fine-boned hand as he quoted Browning's *My Last Duchess* about the ignominy of stooping to explain, well, anything.

Taking a glass of champagne for himself, Jack deposited the tray on the nearest piece of furniture, a mahogany display case containing Chinese porcelains. "Every time I come here," he said, "I think the Mafia rumors must be true. Either that, or the guy's made a pact with the devil to rival Faust. Academics just do *not* grow this kind of green."

Before Lupe could express her own limited views on the much-discussed subject, Jack's eyebrows shot up into a bow. Lupe followed his amused glance to a spot nearby where the gracile contours and swanning gesticulations of the impossible-to-overlook Bel Gunderson stood revealed in a lavender silk lounge suit. The young woman appeared to be in the process of bewitching an obese, middle-aged gentleman who emitted an odor of ill-gotten-gain that could be sniffed all the way across the room. Nor, Lupe noticed, was the perspiring little plutocrat alone in his admiration for Bel Gunderson: a few feet behind Bel stood tiny Trisha Perl, slouching dejectedly in a nearby corner, her sad eyes fixed on Bel.

Jack bent down to Lupe's ear. "Speaking of the Mafia, the rotundity yonder with She Who Must Be Obeyed is Norman Rygiel, a lawyer and art collector who also happens to be Vyacheslav Nesterov's personal attorney. As in the Cream City *mafiya*, girl. What that means for Lanciano, your guess is as good as mine, but for Bel I'd say it translates into rent money for at least six months, if she plays her cards right and practices a little *omertà*."

"You're horrid," Lupe said, her shoulders trembling with laughter.

"A girl's gotta live," Jack declared, lifting his glass. "*L'Chaim*."

Some time later, two glasses of champagne having progressed through her system and the first floor powder room having proven to be already occupied, Lupe made her way to the Lancianos' second floor in search of another bathroom. She found one beyond an open door in an alcove just off the main hallway.

The fading light of evening shone silver through a louvered window that looked out, between the toilet and sink, on to the second floor verandah. Lupe was struggling to close the louvers for privacy—the crank was rusty, no doubt from the lake air—when her attention was snagged by a black and white photograph on the wall above the toilet, the breathtaking sensuality of which seemed somehow wasted on the wall of a mere bathroom.

The photograph showed a slender but bosomy dark-haired woman, stretched out on a Lake Michigan beach with nothing but a sheer white scarf to decorate her opulent nudity. It was in the same instant that Lupe noticed the title and signature—"*Wishful Thinking*, F. Lanciano"—that Lupe also recognized, or thought she recognized, the model: Candace "Candy" Somebody—Dougherty? Dennehy? Some Irish name beginning with a D—the "professional escort" whose photo beside Vyacheslav Nesterov had graced the newspaper the weekend before.

Before Lupe could make any sense of it, there was a patter of approaching steps on the verandah outside the window, accompanied by an exchange of male voices. Realizing in a tizzy of embarrassment that the men were stopping right outside the open louvers of the bathroom window, Lupe pressed herself against the wall between the window and the sink to wait for them to move on.

But the men did not move on. Instead, they continued their conversation. The hushed urgency in their voices sent the dial on Lupe's curiosity meter spiking into the red zone.

"How did you get her for something like this?" she heard one man whispering hoarsely.

Another, apparently older, man answered: "Simple, friend. She needs the money. A girl's gotta live."

Lupe sucked air.

"What was that?"

"What was *what*? Jesus, why are you so jittery, I mean who's to know?"

"Look, I've never done business with the likes of…your people. It's making me fucking nervous."

"It's making you fucking rich. And rich, fucking. I'm telling you, son, with your equipment, you could make a career in Hollywood."

A wave of raucous laughter from the patio momentarily drowned the conversation.

"How much does she expect?" the younger man was saying when the noise finally subsided.

"Thirty thousand up front, plus ten percent after it hits the streets."

"Who the fuck does she think she fucking is, Linda Fucking Lovelace?"

"Oh, she's not some table-top stripper," the older man replied, "she's a real Ecdysiaste. An *artiste*. We'll get our bang for the buck. Yeah, what she don't wanna give, we'll take out of her. We'll make that other shoot with Candy look like a chick flick for the Romance Channel."

Frozen with inexplicable apprehension—the younger man's voice had begun to sound horribly familiar, though it was impossible to tell with all the party noise off the lawn—Lupe's eyes moved to glance again at the photograph of "Candy" Somebody above the toilet. Unable to make out several sentences of the conversation because the jazz band on the first floor had finished it's set with a raucous trumpet solo, she finally heard the older man saying, "—if we can ever shoot the fucking thing. When's the house free?"

"Next Friday's our best shot. They're heading up to Door County."

"Another *week*?"

"Look, we can't push this thing. The old boy didn't get where he is by being stupid. If he starts adding up those figures at the office—"

"Son, what you need is a little pharmaceutical support, followed by a chime-ringing blow job. Let's scrounge us up a john for the first, then see who we can lasso for the second."

As the hushed conversation veered into a debate over the comparative merits, quality vs. price, of Milwaukee vs. Chicago whores, the two men finally began to move off toward the north end of the verandah. Disgusted almost to the point of nausea, Lupe remained motionless beside the window a few seconds longer, just to be on the safe side, before finally throwing a nearby bath towel over the immovable blinds so she could use the toilet. It was only as she was washing her hands that it suddenly dawned on her that the two men might unchancily choose *this* bathroom to do their "pharmaceuticals."

Lupe hurried to the door and opened it a crack. Hearing only the murmur of party sounds from below, she stepped out and peeked around the corner of the alcove: nothing. Sliding quickly and noiselessly along the hallway wall, she descended a set of back stairs that led down to the Lanciano's designer kitchen, a-bustle with tuxedoed caterers and an assortment of loitering band members, helping themselves to the hors d'œvres during their break between sets.

Hoping that some munchies might settle her churning stomach, and some more champagne her nerves, Lupe filled a paper plate with stuffed mushrooms and crackers, grabbed a glass of bubbly off a nearby tray, and headed back toward the party.

She paused in the archway between the dining room and the living room, her searching gaze skipping over familiar and unfamiliar faces alike, none of them Jack's, blast it, until it came to a bemused rest on the gigantic figure of Mitch Showalter.

The big fellow was standing near the fireplace, trying to manage the contortionist's feat of sipping a glass of champagne with one hand while smoking with the other, all while reading a paperback propped up between his elbows. Lupe had by no means any intention of seeking out Mitch for companionship, but when he looked up from his book and spotted her, he smiled so invitingly, even pleadingly, that Lupe couldn't think of a polite way to avoid joining him.

"Heya!" Mitch greeted her, tossing his cigarette butt into the fireplace as she threaded her way toward him through the milling throng. He laid his dog-eared copy of Foucault's *histoire de la folie* on the mantel and looked hungrily at her plate of hors d'œvres. "D'ya mind? Foucault always makes me so bloody hungry. Especially in French."

"Be my guest," she said, handing him the plate. "So, um, you here with Rich?"

Mitch bit daintily into the edge of a cracker, chewed a bit, and then washed it down with some champagne. "I was," he said, "but Rich took off a few minutes ago. We're supposed to be stuffing envelopes for a fundraising mailing tonight, but I told him I was staying on a while. I need a break, big-time."

Before Lupe could comment, Bel Gunderson materialized out of no-where. Brandishing some sort of vaporous foreign cigarette in one hand, and dangling little Trisha on her other arm like a charm bracelet, she swept into the circle of firelight and proceeded to give Lupe and her dress a Joan Rivers once-over, up and down and up again, her eyebrow lifting higher and higher on her forehead. Right behind the pair was Jack Sigur, his meaningful winks in Lupe's direction suggesting that he thought she might soon be in need of rescue, whether from Bel or from Mitch, or both, Lupe couldn't tell.

"By the pricking of my thumbs," Bel quipped, "if it isn't the Weird Sisters."

"Double bubbles, balls, and baubles!" Jack chimed in.

"Don't you people know how unlucky it is to quote the Scottish Play off stage?" Mitch warned with an officious pucker of his lips.

"I was just paraphrasing," Jack insisted.

"And I'm *always* on stage," Bel purred, letting go of Trish's arm. Lupe got a heady dose of clove-scented smoke in her face as Bel exhaled. "Say, Cruz, I'm surprised to see you here with Sigur. Did someone finally decapitate the Lord Protector?"

"S-Sorry?"

"General Ireton, dearie. I heard he'd thrown his grappling hooks into you. *Boarded a land carrack, eh, General?*" Bel reached out to adjust one of the halter straps of Lupe's dress.

Lupe swatted away her hand, then did a blinking double-take: under her platinum bangs, Bel's too-observant eyes peered out this evening a cool Elizabeth Taylor violet, while in class they had sparkled a coquettish peacock blue. Contact lenses, Lupe concluded, color-coordinated.

"Honeybun," Bel protested, "I'm on your side. Or you'll soon be on mine. There's a first time for everyone, but my advice to you, when yours comes, is just close your eyes and think of England. Afterward—after Ireton's fin-ished with you—you and me and Trish here can round up all the other women he's harpooned in this town and launch an amphibious assault. Yessiree, we'll send that prick to full fathom five, where he can sleep with the fucking fishes!"

"Dammit, Bel," Trish said, shoving her little fists into the pockets of her dress slack.

As for Lupe, she did not reply to Bel's taunt, deciding it would be *infra dig*. Mitch, however, was obviously much amused. "You'll need the QE-II for that voyage," he declared, chuckling. "Too bad Nadine Jeffrey dropped out of the Institute. She'd for sure want to be on board when Jimmy walks the gangplank."

"Oh, she had it bad. Not that you can blame her." Bel gave a rolling guttural sound, like a tomcat with one paw in the fishbowl. "Ireton packs the metabolism of a hurricane in that four-square Anglo-Saxon trunk of his. And really, he can be so charming when he's on the prowl. 'Course, once he's got a woman where he wants her, on her back, he's all business, you know, and the business is war. That's why they call him 'the General,' you know. Must be his Cromwellian ancestry."

Mitch giggled. "*Once more into the breach, dear friends, once more!* Hard to imagine Jimmy being the descendant of a Puritan."

"Don't you believe it," Bel waved. "James *is* a Puritan, right down to his XY chromosomes. That's what makes these wannabe saints so irresistible. They try ever so hard to withstand temptation, but when they fall, they fall down and *dirty*." Bel reached around to goose Mitch's backside. He jumped, causing some champagne to slosh on his hand, which Bel promptly bent over to lick up, all the while looking up at Lupe from the side of her eyes as if to make sure that the frowning young woman was paying attention.

She was.

"Ah, you guys are all wet," Jack said, as usual defending his friend. "The 'General' business has got nothing to do with sex. I was the one who started calling him that during *Othello* rehearsals last year. See, I was hoping he'd take my sage, racial-blind advice and cast himself as the noble Moor opposite my own villainous Iago."

"You just wanted the part because Iago's such a scene-stealer," Mitch broke in.

"He's got some of the best lines in Shakespeare," Jack agreed. "But my main thought was what a terrific Othello Jim-bo would make—noble, angry, naïve in a cynical sort of way. And jealous as every devil in hell."

"Jealous!" Bel shrieked. "Are we talking about the same man?"

"Just 'cause he wasn't jealous about you, Belzebub, doesn't mean he ain't got it in him. With the right woman and the wrong circumstances…trust me, the man would be combustible like you wouldn't believe."

Bel snorted. "James Ireton may be burdened with an excess of testosterone, but I can promise you that the man's only real passion is Shakespeare. And perhaps large bodies of water. I mean, the jerk never gives a girl presents, never remembers a birthday, never takes you out—"

"Come on now," Jack protested, beginning to sound a little irritated at Bel's lengthening recital of James Ireton's faults. "He took you out to Mader's for your birthday."

Bel took a deep hit off her clove cigarette and exhaled into Jack's face. "Only because I told him he had to feed me before I anted up."

Jack coughed. "Jezebel, you got a mouth tonight the size of the Mississippi Delta."

"And about as p-p-polluted, too," Lupe volunteered.

"Tut, tut, that'll be two Hail Marys for pride and rash judgment, Cruz." Bel tossed the butt of her cigarette into the fireplace. "Not that I mind. The simple truth is, I'm an erotic gourmande, eager to sample every dish on the buffet table. Pity how society has become so diet-conscious these days. *Nouvelle chasteté* and all that. Puh-*leeze*. The anorexia nervosa of the libido!" Bel tapped her temple in the semaphore for lunacy and turned a sweet face to Jack. "Before I forget it, *cher*, you got any rag money I could beg, borrow or barter my body for? My step-daddy's late on his blackmail check this month."

Grumbling under his breath in Creole French, Jack pulled a couple of twenties out of his wallet and slapped them into Bel's open palm.

"You know, Isabel," Mitch said suddenly, apparently lagging a few sentences behind, "I would suggest that despite the inherently heterologous nature of human concupiscence, you might find that intellectual promiscuity is ultimately a more satisfying form of indulgence."

Pocketing Jack's cash, Bel whirled to the big man, eyebrow cocked. "Now would that be from *first-hand* knowledge?" she teased. "Really, Rosenstern, aren't you getting tired of those nightly solo concerts? But getting back to Ireton, dammitall, where *is* the man? Have you seen him, Lambchop?" As finger accompaniment to her verbal taunts, Bel was once again doing something with her hand behind Mitch's back, something that was making the big man break into a sweat, and his Adam's apple work up and down.

"He's probably with the old padre, wherever he is," Trish suggested quickly, obviously trying to get Bel's profligate attention.

"Nope," Bel said, her come-hither glance fixed on Showalter, "Bricusse was held up at some conference in Chicago."

"What conference in Chicago?" Mitch said. The big man was smiling impassively, apparently unmoved, but the liquid trembling in his glass gave evidence of the fact that Bel was still actively engaged with his backside.

"A conference for third-order Carmelites at the O'Hare Sheraton," Lupe said.

"Now, Guildencrantz, tell me truthfully," Bel cooed, slipping the glass out of Mitch's hand to finish it off for him before he spilled what was left of it, "do you sleep *alone*, or do you have a *roommate*?"

"Uh, not—" Mitch swallowed. "—anymore. We had a break-in at SANA House last month. The Blessed Sacrament was stolen, along with this really weird wooden chalice Mr. Krato picked up in the Holy Land over the summer. Anyhow, Mr. Krato put me down alone in a room on the first floor, to act as watchdog."

"Bow-*wow*. But weren't you once Jimmy's roommate?"

"No, uh, Richard was Jimmy's roommate."

"C'mon, can't we talk about something else," Trish pleaded. "Or at least someone else?"

"Hear, hear," Lupe concurred.

"Rubbish," Bel said. "You're in the army now, creampuffs, and *sauve qui peut*. I'm merely conducting, as the sociologists might say, an independent, informal, sexological survey of our colleague Ireton." She directed her violet contacts at Jack. "*Dis-moi, bonbon, as-tu couché avec lui?*"

Jack groaned, long and loud.

"I mean, besides all the rumors about oysters and snails, haven't you all ever wondered about him and St. Richard the Chickenheart? If you ask me, Ireton's entirely too *hot* about little Richie. And vice-versa. Theirs is more like a love affair gone sour than a falling out over religion, of all the medieval things. And how about old Bricusse? To borrow one of Ireton's own favorite Limeyisms, James thinks the sun shines out of Bricusse's ass. Or is it 'arse'? And everyone knows they're arresting priests right and left these days—"

Bel was unable to finish her thought because Lupe's remaining half-glass of champagne was dripping down her exquisite face onto her expensive lavender lounge suit.

Lupe handed her emptied glass to a stupefied Jack and shouldered her way through the crowd toward the French doors that led out to the Lancianos' patio. She didn't hear Bel exclaim, as she stepped outside, "Pious little bitch! She's going to wish she hadn't done that, one of these days."

It was almost dark outside, the breeze off the lake chilly and damp. Pausing on the flagstone patio to watch the half moon setting over the lake, Lupe did indeed wish that she hadn't done that. She also wished she had brought a shawl; or better yet, hadn't come here in the first place.

Her shoulders slumping, she descended the stone steps to the back yard where other guests strolled the beautifully landscaped greensward in subsets of murmuring chatter. Behind the snatches of words, Lupe heard the droning white noise of the lake beyond the bluffs, and the sibilant sound of it beckoned her to venture farther out, to get a breath of air and a shot of tranquility before going back inside to see if Jack had had enough torture for one evening.

Spotting the contours of a redwood rail sticking out from behind a yew, underlit by landscaping lights, Lupe found the set of stairs leading down to the deserted beach below. At the bottom, and in defiance of the chill, she sat down on a boulder and kicked off her slings to let the cool pebbly sand, crunching between her toes, massage away her anger and humiliation. Straining her eyes, she could just make out the vanishing horizon, a stretch of cold blackness that seemed to drain what little light remained of the dying sky.

After a few minutes of sour musings, the chill off the lake started to get the better of Lupe's impulse to wallow in melancholy. She was reaching down for her shoes, intending to go look for Jack, when a set of strong fingers gripped her shoulder.

Letting out a yelp of surprise, Lupe looked up to see Barry DeBrun's powerful figure blocking out the half moon like an eclipse.

"Fancy meeting you here," DeBrun said, squinting down at her as if sighting along a gun barrel. "The moonlight and the beach…brings back old times, eh Lu?"

Swallowing hard, Lupe struggled against a wave of fear and nausea. She tried to move off the boulder, but DeBrun only squeezed tighter. Then she opened her mouth to cry for help, but all that emerged was a dry, insubstantial cough — a gargled expression of impotence that only made DeBrun laugh.

"What the matter, Lu, an ornery cat got your limping tongue?"

When she still couldn't reply, DeBrun jerked her to her feet and pressed her hips against his, his face into her trembling neck. "I still say you were the most luscious girl in the whole damned school. Not the most eloquent, maybe, but certainly the ripest."

"DeBrun!" rang an angry male voice behind them. "You'll get your fancy dress boots all soggy down here!"

Letting go, DeBrun pivoted, affording Lupe the welcome sight of her rescuer: James Ireton stood at the bottom of the stairs, his tie undone, his dinner jacket flung over one shoulder. The expression on his face was alarming.

Lupe scrambled barefoot across the sand toward him.

DeBrun's eyes darted from James to Lupe, then back to James again. "Jesus, Lu, you're with *him?*"

"She is now," James said, draping his jacket over a nearby boulder as if thinking he might soon need two free hands.

DeBrun jerked forward, then just as quickly pulled back, shooting a skittish glance at the bluffs above.

"Looking for your wife? She's up at the house, wondering where the devil you are. So is her father. You know, they don't call him 'Mad Max' for nothing. I wonder how he'd react if he knew you were down here cornering an unwilling woman who is not his daughter. And not for the first time, I take it."

DeBrun's handsome eyebrows shot up. "Oh, now don't tell me she's suckered you with that old chestnut about how she really didn't want it, but couldn't spit out the word '*no.*' I mean, Jesus, Lu, how long you gonna milk that one for?"

That did it. Breaking free of Lupe's grasp, James hurled himself at DeBrun, his fists whirling into a blur of fury that sent the unprepared man reeling on his tailored haunches. In the next instant, James was on top of him, punching him viciously about the face. Unable to fend off the attack, DeBrun finally rolled over on his stomach and covered his face to shield his handsome cheekbones and dimpled chin from James Ireton's maddened fists.

Lupe was about to cut loose with a whoop of delight at the punishment James was inflicting, but bridled it when the sight of DeBrun's blood soaking up on James's shirtsleeve made her afraid that James might actually *kill* the man. She was about to fling herself into the fracas—or at least kick some sand at them, or rush up the stairs for help, or *some*thing—when James suddenly straightened himself, straddled DeBrun's hips, lifted the man bodily by his Gucci belt, and gave a strenuous heave that sent DeBrun's trunk splashing into the gently lapping lake water a few feet away.

"Now bugger off!" James yelled, his lungs pumping. "Get back up to the house and tell Mad Max you decided to take a moonlight swim!"

DeBrun crawled on all fours back onto the beach. Staggering to his feet, he spat out a briny mixture of blood and sand and threats, the latter of which only made James laugh. It took Lupe a moment to realize why: in his apparent eagerness to protect his pretty face, Barry DeBrun hadn't so much as landed one blow on his smaller but far more aggressive opponent.

DeBrun gave his mangled lip one last swipe with his dripping jacket sleeve before aiming his trigger finger at Lupe. "That's two you owe me," he barked, cocking his thumb as if letting fly an imaginary bullet. Then he spat some more blood on the sand by James's foot, and stepped around them, his soggy dress boots squishing in the pebbly sand as he labored toward the stairs.

James followed DeBrun's stumbling progress until his shadowy figure dissolved into the darkness at the top of the bluff. "*A most devout coward,*" he commented contemptuously. "*Indeed, religious in it.*" He turned to look down at Lupe.

A lank of black hair had fallen over her eyes, shining in the glow of landscaping lamps and the half moon that grew larger as it set over the water. The remnants of fear in her face commingled with traces of another emotion, one with which James was a good deal less familiar: gratitude.

Lupe threw her arms around him and heaved a great sigh against his chest that made his heart thump all the harder. "Th-Th-Thank you!" she sobbed into his shirt. "I was so f-f-frightened, and I couldn't get away! Feminism to the c-c-contrary notwithstanding, I don't th-think you men realize how much stronger you are than w-women."

"Feminism to the contrary notwithstanding," James said, "yes we do." Unsure at this moment as to what to do with his hands, which were damp and smarting from the blows they'd given, James finally gave in to instinct or long habit and rested them on her quivering shoulders. A moment later they were slipping down her back to her waist, then up her back again and into her hair. Finally, he pulled back her head and kissed her.

After the briefest of hesitations, Lupe leaned into his kiss. James felt more than heard the moan that vibrated in her throat as his lips moved all over her face, her eyes, down her nose to her lips again; then down her warm neck, where they brushed the cool metal of a silver chain.

James stepped back. "Oh, God."

"What's the m-m-matter?"

Glaring at the Guadalupe medal at her throat, James fully intended to tell her there, as the lake rumbled at their feet, that he hadn't intended to kiss her, and that the whole thing had been the ill-considered consequence of heated circumstance; but before he could gather the words—some lines from a BBC comedy of manners would do nicely, if he could only remember them—she had reached up again to put her fingers in his hair and was pulling his head toward her; not to kiss him again as he thought at first, but apparently so that she could study his face in the moonlight. Frowning with concentrations, she seemed to be looking for something in his face, he didn't know what. A moment later, he didn't care. He pulled her to him again for another kiss.

At length, he lifted his head. "Cruz, this is impossible. You know that."

"A few minutes ago I knew that. Right now, I only know I like this."

Oh, bloody marvelous, he thought, since he was in no state of mind to know anything either, other than that he liked this, too, very much indeed. Still, he pushed her dutifully away and, shoving his disobedient hands in his trouser pockets, began to pace a narrow circuit that extended from the base of the bluff to the edge of the water, back and forth.

Finally he stopped full in front of her. "I promised Father this wouldn't happen!"

Lupe was incredulous. "You p-promised Father you wouldn't kiss me?"

"I promised Father I wouldn't seduce you!"

"Well, you just k-k-kissed me."

James grunted a laugh. "I can't remember the last time I 'just kissed' a woman. I think I was fifteen."

At that, a twinge of doubt crinkled Lupe Cruz's heavy-lidded eyes, an expression of renewed anxiety that led him to understand, given what had happened just a few minutes before, that she was suddenly wondering whether James Ireton were the sort of man who, if he failed to have his way, might resort to force.

Like a bolt dropping at the turn of the right key, the fuller implications of DeBrun's words finally hit home. "He raped you?" James gasped. "The slimy git! DeBrun *raped* you?"

Lupe's chin trembled in humiliation. "Tri-tri-tried. Years ago, in hi-hi-high school. I only got away because I...because I..." Lupe blinked several times, then all at once broke away from him with a violent scissoring of her arms. She rushed barefoot to the dark water a few feet away and vomited violently into the lake.

James winced. "I think I get the picture."

Gagging, sobbing, hiccoughing, Lupe, still bent over, splashed lake water in her face and wrung her wet hands.

At a loss as to how one might render aid in such a peculiar situation, James finally approached and offered his assistance by pulling a handkerchief from his back pocket and waving it in her face. He even tried to take her into his arms again, but she only snatched the handkerchief from his fingers and pressed it to her mouth with gurgling noises of protest, as if too upset or too embarrassed to let him kiss her again in her patently unappetizing condition. That, then, made him laugh. Finally overcoming her resistance with the sort of soothing words and nonsense syllables one spoke to a child after a night-mare, he held her close and nuzzled her hair until her fingers were once again clutching the back of his shirt.

Chapter Four:
Dead Men from their Graves

Oft have I digged up dead men from their graves
And set them upright at their dear friends' door,
Even when their sorrows almost was forgot,
And on their skins, as on the bark of trees,
Have with my knife carved in Roman letters
'Let not your sorrow die though I am dead.'
But I have done a thousand dreadful things
As willingly as one would kill a fly,
And nothing grieves me heartily indeed
But that I cannot do ten thousand more.

Shakespeare, *Titus Andronicus*

James sat in his narrow sixth-floor Institute office the next afternoon, absorbing the drum roll of thunder that vibrated through the building. Restless from the moment he had awakened at half past three, he had gone to the marina to rent a daysailer in the clearer sky of morning, only to learn that foul weather was approaching from several directions and that a Small Crafts Advisory had been issued. After walking for several hours, nowhere in particular, as a flotilla of sullen clouds assembled over his head, he was now huddled before his computer, half listening to the storm erupting outside as he pretended to work. His mind was not on his dissertation but on Lupe's warm lips, and on the sea scent in his nostrils as his hand rode her back.

On top of it, his computer was giving him fits. Whether from the thunder-storms pulsing through the city, or from some server or hardware malfunction, he couldn't tell, but he hadn't received any e-mail all day, not even spam, and his terminal, an appendage of the Institute's fabulously expensive mainframe, kept sending him error messages in the middle of the simplest commands.

Five minutes later a streak of lightning cracked just outside his window, shutting down the electricity, and his terminal with it. When the power came back on a few seconds later, James discovered that he'd lost fifteen minutes of unsaved work. Swearing loudly, he logged off his terminal and decided that it would be more productive to head for the Meir Library at UWM to hunt down a couple of misplaced references.

Remembering that the phone had rung several times during the afternoon — as was his custom when he was writing, he didn't answer it — James was about to check his voice mail before he left, when it occurred to him that Lupe Cruz had probably been among the callers.

He paused, hand suspended over the telephone: sod all, he didn't even want to hear her voice. This had all happened way too fast.

James retracted his hand and glanced at his watch: ten minutes after three. Odd that Fr. Bricusse hadn't stopped by, or at least phoned or e-mailed. Adèle had told him the night before that Bricusse had been delayed at the conference in Chicago, but she had also said that she would be picking him up at the airport this morning. James reached for the telephone and dialed Bricusse's office.

"He got in about lunchtime," Bricusse's secretary informed him. "I know he tried to call you."

James exhaled a puff of relief, though he couldn't think of a reason to have been anxious. "I was out earlier," he said. "May I speak with him now?"

"Sorry, but Fran DeBrun's in with him right now, and she's in a real dither. Father left instructions that they not be disturbed. You know, the 'on pain of death' kind."

James chewed his lower lip. Bricusse was notorious for dropping everything when someone came to him with urgent personal needs. If he was with Fran DeBrun he might be tied up for hours, especially if Fran's 'dither' had something to do with her husband's wayward activities on Lanciano's beach the night before.

Leaving a message for Bricusse with the secretary, James rang off, and then jotted a note to himself to check with the Institute Sysop on Monday about what was happening with those error messages. He was about to walk out the door when a nagging sense of unease about the security of his dissertation, in the event of some serious computer malfunction, got the better of him. He had a CD backup of his files at home, but hadn't updated it in months. Shutting the door again, he re-booted the terminal, logged on and downloaded his entire dissertation, notes, references and text, onto a blank CD, just in case the problem with the computer turned out to be something serious.

He exited the building twenty minutes later, the first signs of a headache pressing against his temples. The thunderstorms had passed to the east, but the mid-September heat, coupled with the Midwestern humidity, was oppressive. In the end he decided he was too enervated to make any headway at the library and opted for another walk. After an hour of aimless traipsing under a sky as murky as smoke, it began to rain again in earnest. He sprinted home in a downpour.

James was a good twenty minutes late by the time he finally descended the stairs of the John Hawkes pub, tucked into the basement of the landmark 100 East Wisconsin Building downtown. Lupe was standing in the waiting room, probably had been for some time, admiring a print on the wall of Nelson's flagship, *HMS Victory*. She smiled so eagerly when she spotted him that James's prior intention of keeping this encounter brief and on a collegial footing was instantly annulled. Taking her arm, he offered a clumsy apology for having been "delayed." They followed the hostess out sliding glass doors to the restaurant's patio, fronting the Milwaukee River.

The off-and-on storms of the day had abated for the nonce, inducing the pub staff to dry off the patio furniture for one final attempt at *alfresco* serving. Taking seats at a table under a red-and-white striped umbrella, James filled his lungs with the comfortingly fishy air that rose damp and cool off the river. Normally a muddy green, the river was painted in drab shades of brown this evening from the silt-disturbing runoff of several hours' worth of pelting rain. A Mozart sonata, tinkling over the outdoor speakers, was occasionally drowned out by the roar of passing trucks crossing over the Wisconsin Avenue bridge above them.

"You're not playing the game according to the rules," he commented over the top of his menu.

Lupe looked up. "'Scuse me?"

"You're supposed to pout and treat me coolly for being unforgivably late. Letting me off so easily implies over-eagerness. I'm liable to take advantage."

She leaned her cheek against her open palm. "I guess I was just glad you showed up at all."

He slapped shut the menu. "What the devil's that supposed to mean?"

"I-I-I just thought you'd have…well, second thoughts. About everything."

He backed off. "Clever girl."

"Not really. It's just that the only thing that's been perfectly clear to me for the last two weeks is that you'd made up your mind to have as little to do with me as possible."

James was rescued from the necessity of an immediate response by the arrival of their waitress with a carafe of Pinot Gris. Watching Lupe as she ordered, he noticed that a thin layer of carefully applied makeup wasn't entirely masking a puffy redness around her normally pellucid eyes.

"Why were you crying?" he asked bluntly when the waitress left.

"I haven't c-cried since this morning!" she protested.

"Then why were you crying this morning? Was it because of DeBrun or because of me?"

"DeBrun doesn't make me cry. He terrifies me speechless and makes me throw up. As you noticed."

This, James thought, was progress, but not yet what he was groping for. He lifted the stem of his wine glass and rolled it back and forth between his thumb and forefinger, ostensibly to admire the shimmering hue of his Pinot Gris. "Jack told me that you got an earful from Bel Gunderson last night. And that she got a glassful in return."

"Half a glassful," Lupe corrected with a giggle that came a second too late. Finally her eyes met his with a level gaze. "Look, I like you, I admit it. In spite of what everyone insists on telling me about you. Can't that be enough for now?"

James set aside his wine, having suddenly realized that his hand was trembling and that she would soon be noticing it, if she hadn't already. "Well, backchat about me is something of a cottage industry at the Institute. If it's any comfort, every third word or so is a lie." He waved it away. "Sorry I barked at you. I'm on edge tonight for some reason. I had trouble with my computer this afternoon, and a headache, and I only just realized I hadn't eaten any lunch. The world's run quite out of square for me today."

"Oh, you, too?" Lupe's expression cleared. "I had a flat tire on the way home from the grocery store, right in the middle of North Downer. It's the Triumph of the Cross, you know."

"Beg pardon?"

"September 14th, the Feast of the Triumph of the Cross. I always write it off as a day of reparation, like Good Friday and Ash Wednesday and all the Fridays in Lent. The universe d-doing penance, I think."

"Ah, yes. We Anglicans called it Holy Cross Day. My father used to give the same dreary sermon from the pulpit every year, about how we all had to learn to 'bear our crosses,' which I always took as a reference to me..." Catching himself, James sat back, marveling not a little at Lupe Cruz's astonishing facility at eliciting personal information from him. "But you don't want to hear about all that."

"Actually, I'd love to hear about all that. You just don't want to talk about all that."

"Another time," he said, thinking that the time would be never and that she damned well knew it. "But speaking of bad days, we aren't the only ones. I ran into Franco Lanciano at the Institute this afternoon. He told me that someone had made off with one of his art works last night, right in the middle of his *soirée*."

"No! What was it?"

"One of his own photographic compositions. A *nuda erotica*, or so he said, hanging in an upstairs bathroom. Odd place to hang an erotic nude, wouldn't you say?"

Over coffee and dessert, James brought Lupe up to speed on Dr. Franco Lanciano's elaborate plans for this evening's program, as well as the civil brouhaha which had mushroomed this last year over the fabulous new Institute building. Lupe had been studying in Madison during the school's formative years, and hadn't realized the degree to which the Heisler Institute for the Study of Western Civilization had become a *casus belli* in her home town. Bricusse had confessed to James on more than one occasion that if he'd realized what a kerfuffle in the Culture War the project would turn out to be, he would have never attempted it, least of all with colleagues as pugilistic as Max Heisler and Franco Lanciano.

In fact, James explained to Lupe, only Fr. Bricusse's good name, much admired in all sectors for his outstanding work in establishing the excellent Oratory school, which provided free private education for low income children, had come close to working the sort of wizardry required to endear the Heisler Institute, with its unabashedly Western and Catholic bias and conservative funding sources, to the multicultural and sometimes politically polarized citizenry of Milwaukee. The success or failure of tonight's program, which Jack Sigur had mischievously subtitled, *Paradise Explained: Justifying Mad Max's Ways to Milwaukee*, would reveal whether Bricusse's lead-to-gold alchemy had succeeded.

A duet of weather systems, such as usually crossed paths only later in the season, was converging over the city. A Texas Hook of warm moist air was boiling up from the southwest and colliding with a cool, dry, high-pressure Alberta Clipper pressing in from the northwest. A gust of wind blew over a patio umbrella as James and Lupe were preparing to leave the pub, and they heard on the car radio en route to the Institute that a tornado had touched down near Janesville. Several local sports and cultural events had already been canceled this evening, but the Heisler Institute Dedication Program was apparently not one of them.

"And I can tell you why," James said to Lupe as they parked his old Jeep on the street several blocks away from the Institute because the Institute's basement parking structure was already full. "Max and Franco are hoping that the inclement weather will give them a face-saving excuse if all sorts of important people choose to stay away from tonight's festivities."

But it was, they soon discovered, far worse than that. The nauseating smell of burning rubber greeted them as they crossed the crowded street in front of the Institute, hands over faces, past an untidy curbside pile of smoking tires. After progressing a few yards further up the sidewalk James was able to make out, through the acrid smoke, a colorful assemblage of a hundred or more protesters, bandannas tied over their faces in lieu of gas masks, parading with placards near the Institute steps. They chanted, "*Hey, hey, ho, ho, Western Civ has got to go!*" as black smoke billowed toward the massive clouds overhead.

And then James saw Nadine Jeffrey in the midst of the dissident band. Tall, big-boned, and magnificent as ever in dreadlocks and tight jeans, Nadine stood at the foot of the Institute stairs, staring at him with serene hostility over the edge of her bandanna, her black eyes following the trajectory of his approach, and that of his companion.

In the next instant James saw Nadine's placard, which she lifted aloft as if challenging him to read it. His eyes swiveled obediently upwards: AND THIS ALSO, read the sign in neat block lettering, HAS BEEN ONE OF THE DARK PLACES OF THE EARTH.

James unconsciously let go of Lupe's hand. He had just about made up his mind, in fact, to flee this appalling scene, Bricusse or no, and with or without Lupe Cruz, when the silvery light of evening suddenly faded. Blinking as if coming awake, James lifted his eyes to a malicious-looking storm cloud ballooning directly overhead. A sudden silence descended on him, as if he were in an atmospheric bubble, and he felt a peculiar sizzling up his spine, a crackling of static that rustled the hair on the back of his head. He grabbed Lupe's wrist and was about to push her to the ground, himself on top of her, when a bolt of lightning ripped open the cloud above, stunning them with an apocalyptic flash and a deafening *bang* as it struck a tree on the bluffs directly across the street.

The crowd scattered in a torrent of shrieks, hail and rain.

Drenched from the sudden downpour and badly shaken, James and Lupe ran blindly into the Institute atrium, the scent of smoking rubber trailing them like the afterburn of war. They were met inside by the paradoxical vista of a sea of neatly turned-out guests, many obviously wealthy, their glittering chatter and tinkling wine glasses sounding notes in startling antithesis to the roar of human and climatic turmoil just outside the atrium doors.

James shook himself off like a river rat come ashore, wondering anxiously how, in what should have been his crowning hour, Fr. Bricusse was taking this miserable dénouement. Even the marble-white atrium looked unusually gloomy tonight, in spite of all the glitter. At first James thought that the storm had meddled with the electricity again, then he remembered that Lanciano had planned to extinguish the lights on the upper floors so that those seeing the place for the first time could get the full impact of the soaring atrium during a dramatic lighting-up in the intermission.

"W-W-Wow," Lupe stammered, flapping water out of the skirt of her dress, "my ears are ringing. How'd you know that was coming? The lightning, I mean."

James raked his fingers through his dripping hair and loosened his sticky-wet tie. "I shipped with a North Sea fishing trawler after university. Lightning struck us off the coast of Norway. One man got fried, two went overboard, and the rest of us damn near sank. It's not a sensation one soon forgets."

Lupe's eyes grew wide. Declining James's offer to fetch a drink for her from the cash bar, but demanding to hear all about his seafaring adventures when she got back, she took temporary leave of him to retreat to the Ladies Room to stand under a hot-air drier for a few minutes. James took the occasion of her absence to whip off his wet jacket and have a look around.

Moving toward the cash bar, James's drifting gaze quickly shoaled on an island of SANA members in the sea of guests, their bleached shirts rising above the wash like whitecaps on a Lake Michigan storm surge. Peter Krato stood erect as a mainmast at the center of the whorl of acolytes, who were listening in rapt silence as their Spiritual Guide addressed himself to no less a personage than Mr. Max Heisler. The Institute's patron, James noted with a chuckle, was wearing that telltale deer-in-the-headlights look common among Peter Krato's interlocutors. The expression on Krato's homely face, meanwhile, alternated in swift succession between bold sketches of urgency and overworked sincerity. He pumped his arms piston-like back and forth, too, as if he were reeling in a whopper Coho.

Krato, James concluded with a smirk, was winding up the Mother of all sales pitches.

When perhaps five minutes later Lupe was once again at his side, James, having fortified himself with a whiskey and soda from the cash bar, pulled her into the shadows under the gallery near the stairwell where he reminded her of the kiss he was owed from the night before. After assuring him that she hadn't vomited all day, Lupe let him back her up against the wall, where he licked a few remaining raindrops from her face and neck as he kissed her.

A steely pair of fingers prodding his shoulder cut short James's sport. "What the—" James's irritation yielded to mirth as he whirled around to see Jack Sigur standing over them, his tawny face flushing with pink embarrassment.

"Sorry to butt in on your, uh, conference, people," Jack said, his eyes skittering away, "but Adèle's backstage, meowing like a treed kitten. Seems no one can find Franco or the Padre, and it's almost showtime. She wondered if you could, you know, give her a hand tracking the old guy down."

"Lead on," James said, squeezing Lupe's hand.

As Jack preceded them through the shifting crowd, the atrium lights dimmed and re-lit twice, signaling that the program was about to begin. The trio ended up in a narrow hallway that led to the backstage door of the Institute's Redmond Theatre.

Spotting the trio's entrance from her vantage point in the wings, Adèle Lanciano cut loose with an cry of perturbation. "Oh thank God, James," she exclaimed, "do you have *any* idea where Franco is, or Uncle Arthur, or Max? They're not answering their office phones or their cell phones and I can't think where they could be!"

"Max is out in the atrium. Peter Krato's practicing his 'assumptive close' technique on him, poor sod. Haven't a clue about Father or Franco."

Adèle's eyes, which had rolled into the back of her head at the mention of Peter Krato, suddenly focused on some object over James's shoulder. James turned to see Max Heisler tapping swiftly toward them.

Jack leaned over and drawled in James's ear that he needed to make a pit stop, and took off before James could say anything.

"Max!" Adèle cried, this time wringing her hands, "have you seen Franco or Uncle Arthur? Franco ran upstairs twenty minutes ago to fetch his speech notes and hasn't come down yet. He's supposed to start this thing—" She glanced at her watch. "—two minutes ago! And I haven't seen Uncle Arthur since I picked him up at the airport this morning! I'm terribly worried. The security people have already apprehended protesters upstairs, trying to spray paint slogans on the windows!"

A robust widower in his mid-fifties, Maximilian Gerhard Heisler had wide-set blue eyes over a wider mouth, the unique combination of which always made James think of a talking fish. Right now, those wide-set eyes were darting around the backstage as if in several directions at once.

"All I know is that Arthur's been holed up with my daughter most of the afternoon. Damned newlyweds, think the universe revolves around their diddly squabbles…he wouldn't even see Franco and me to go over the program!"

"Why don't I run upstairs and have a look," James offered. "You know how Father is. He may have lost track of time."

"Go for it," Heisler said with a take-charge gesture that doubled as a pontifical dismissal. "And as for Franco," he added, turning to Adèle as if James were already gone, "if he doesn't get his butt down here in the next thirty seconds, I'll go on without him."

There were only a few stray guests lingering outside the theater doors when James and Lupe returned to the atrium. James seated Lupe on one of the lounge chairs, pecked her on the cheek, and jogged to the north side stairwell.

He took the stairs two at a time, the damp fabric of his slacks clinging uncomfortably to his legs. The whiskey, too, on top of the wine at dinner, was hitting him with surprising force. A low rumble of thunder shuddered under his feet as he mopped sweat from his forehead and rounded the turn past the second floor fire door.

After the thunder passed, James began to hear an odd sound coming from somewhere within the building. It was a keening sound that rose and fell and rose again, like the in-heat mewing of a cat; but James could not make any sense of it, muffled and distorted as it was by the massive masonry all around him.

Winded, James paused to catch his breath on the third floor landing and listened. The keening sound, he finally realized, was a female voice, wailing almost operatically. He was reaching for the latch of the third floor door, just to see what the hell was going on out there, when the wailing suddenly ceased. In the next instant James heard the *click*-and-*clang* of a fire door opening and closing in the stairwell directly above him. Then a patter of footsteps. Then a sort of *plop*, as if something had fallen to the floor, or been dropped. Then silence.

James leaned over the stairwell railing, craning his neck. "Hey, there!" he called out, looking up. He could see no one on the stairs above. "What's all the commotion?"

There was no reply. Instead, after the briefest of silences, no more than an intake of breath, James heard again the patter of rapid footfalls in the stairwell above him, a dozen or two at the most, followed by the sound of another stairwell door opening and closing.

Certain now that something was wrong and that he must find Bricusse, James bolted up the remaining flights of stairs.

His lungs were heaving by the time he slammed through the fire door onto the seventh floor. The darkened galleries that stretched to his left and right were lit only marginally by the reflected glow of white marble from the atrium below. There was no light under Bricusse's door, nor under any of the doors on the entire floor.

James felt more than heard a beehive drone in his ears, which he at first dismissed as a rush of blood to his head, but finally identified as the accumulated Babel of many distant voices, rising from the atrium below. He was about to go to the railing to look down when he detected movement across the way: the shadow of a hunched-over figure was moving swiftly along the seventh floor railing on the far side of the atrium near Max Heisler's office. In another second a rectangle of yellowish light burst open behind the shadow, silhouetting it in the form of a man. The south side stairwell door had opened, then closed, swallowing up the moving shadow with a distant *click*.

The buzzing below crescendoed briefly, then was silenced by the renewed eruption of the female voice James had heard before. At last James recognized the voice, and understood the words:

"For God's sake," Lupe cried from far below, "someone c-c-call the police! He fell from the top floor!"

On the top floor, James lurched to the railing and looked down: a dozen or more miniscule human figures were scurrying across the atrium like ants fleeing a fire. They were running toward a clump of people gathered on the northeast side of the atrium. Edging swiftly along the railing to get a better look, James braced himself against the rail and leaned over; then over some more. He saw Lupe at the center of the grouping directly beneath him, kneeling next to a large lozenge-shaped object in smeared colors of black and white and red. It was some seconds before the picture came into devastating focus: the black was Fr. Bricusse's cassock, the white and red the old man's shattered head.

Lt. Calvin Masefield knelt beside the County Medical Examiner, who was busy tying a toe tag to the elderly victim's badly swollen right foot.

The first thing Masefield noticed was the crushed skull, the forehead point-of-impact easily discernible; but otherwise there was little to remark. There were no apparent stab wounds, bullet punctures or ligature marks anywhere evident on the body, and any blunt force trauma to the head prior to the fall would probably prove difficult to differentiate from the impact of the fall itself. No, it looked like there was precious little to go on, save for the purplish discoloration all over the victim's head, neck, and shoulders — the so-called "coronary collar" that indicated that Fr. Arthur Bricusse, whatever else may have befallen him, had been the victim of a massive heart attack. That, and the weird fact that the corpse was wearing only one shoe.

Masefield stayed the CME's hand from bagging the victim's horribly swollen and shoeless right foot. He pointed at the black sock dangling from the grotesque appendage.

"What do you make of that?" he said.

"What, the sock?"

"And the missing shoe. B of I found it on the seventh floor, probably where he went over."

The CME grunted. "Loose, it wasn't. Any shoes the priest could've gotten over *those* feet had to have been custom made."

"You're saying the shoe couldn't have come off by accident?"

"Don't think so."

"Swell."

"Swell*ing*. Typical with congestive heart failure. Goes with the collar."

"Please tell me you're saying the old man had a heart attack and keeled over the rail."

The CME grunted. "I've got some problems with that scenario."

"Such as?"

"Such as look at this lividity." The CME tugged at the sock, revealing more of the dead priest's purple ankle. "He had to have been upright when his heart stopped. Probably sitting. The blood had time to drain to his feet. A fair amount of time."

"Dandy. Now you're telling me someone heaved him over the rail *after* he was dead from a heart attack?"

"That would be my first guess. Never seen anything like it. Any evidence of foul play upstairs?"

"Just that gigantic shoe. There are two different sets of prints on it. I mean, how many people, besides you, handle your shoes?"

The CME shrugged. "Even my wife won't touch my smelly shoes."

"And no wife here, that's sure." Masefield stood up, leaving the CME to conclude his dismal business alone. Masefield turned to the young detective now standing on his other side. "Cruz," he said sourly, "we've got to stop meeting like this."

Ramon Cruz sneezed as if in comment. A nasty cold made the otherwise handsome young detective look like he'd just stumbled out of a State Street cop bar.

"Damned Wisconsin weather," Ramon groused, reaching for a tissue.

"How's your sister?"

Ramon blew his nose. "A lot better than her dipsy-doodle date."

"What's the matter with the date?"

Ramon wiped his nose. "Two things. First, he's half mad. Every time I tried to question him, he answered in mumbled Shakespearean. I didn't understand a word of it."

"And the second thing?"

"He's a Brit. So help me, Professor, a walking definition of 'Anglo.' Gripes my soul, both halves, Mexican and Irish."

Masefield chuckled. "So where's your bunk?"

"On the seventh floor with B of I." Ramon shook his head. "We're in trouble with the primary scene. One of the Institute big-wigs was tromping all over Bricusse's office upstairs before a uniform could secure it."

Even dandier, Masefield thought, trying to avoid the sickening sight of the CME using tweezers to collect chunks of brain tissue from the greasy floor. His drifting eyes came to rest on the six tiers of gallery railings overhead. In City Hall, it had been seven. "Cruz," he said, eyes to the glass ceiling panels, "you know this ain't right. How long's it been since Lenny Swiatko?"

"Ten days. But c'mon, Professor, this wasn't a suicide. Trust me. My family's known the old guy for years."

"The CME says not," Masefield said with a disappointment he couldn't mask. But then no one ever wanted to think a friend or loved one was capable of suicide, even though it happened all the time. Lord, didn't *he* know that. "Still, I'd like to know if he had any kind of connection to Lenny. I mean, this is just too weird."

"Well, while we're at it," Ramon said in a voice bespeaking sarcasm and clogged sinuses, "why don't we compare notes with the graveyard shift? They're working that video store owner's murder, and he was tossed off the Marquette Interchange."

Masefield's return was swift: "Why don't you can the commentary and tell me what you *do* know? Which right now doesn't sound like much."

Ramon Cruz cleared his throat. "What I know is that Fr. Arthur Bricusse was seventy years old and on a clock. Bad heart. He was on daily Lanoxyn, as well as several other heart and blood pressure meds. Worse, he went to Chicago to some church conference Wednesday evening and forgot to take his pill dispenser with him. His secretary said he had to get a bunch of emergency scrips filled at the hotel. Even so, she said she wouldn't bet money he stopped long enough to take any of them."

In defiance of the CME's more ghoulish on-the-spot analysis, Masefield felt suddenly hopeful. "So maybe he did have a heart attack. Lord, I hope so, what with the politics of this mess." This time it was the potential political fallout of the unnatural death that had induced Ramon Cruz to lure his busy lieutenant away from his file-buried squad room desk. Masefield pointed up at the galleries over their heads. "What do you think? If he had a heart attack, could he have keeled over by accident…maybe tripped out of that shoe?"

Ramon looked doubtful. "The old man was tall, over six feet. But those railings up there are pretty high. Higher than code, anyway. His center of gravity would've been way too low for a trick like that. Not without help."

"What about witnesses…protesters?"

"Lupe was the only witness to the fall itself. A couple of protesters managed to get in and spray graffiti in the elevators earlier on, but they were apprehended by the Institute security people a good half-hour before all this went down. And none of them ever got past the fourth floor. Everyone else was already in the theatre by then. The Institute Deputy Director—"

Ramon glanced at his memo book and spelled out Lanciano's name. "—was supposed to start the program, but he hadn't showed up yet. Max Heisler went on stage without him."

"So where was this Lanciano?" Masefield pronounced the *c* of the man's name like a soft *s*.

"*Ch*," Cruz corrected, "Lan-*chee*-ah-no. And get it right when you talk to him, Professor, or he'll give you a half-hour Italian lesson."

"Okay, okay, so—"

"So, yeah, well, Lan-chee-ah-no says he misplaced his speech notes, and by the time he'd found them and got back to the atrium, it was all over. Oh, and by the way, Lanciano was the big-wig tromping around Bricusse's office when we arrived. Seems he thought he could Sherlock Holmes this thing for us by seeing if anything was missing."

"*Was* anything missing?"

"Not that he could tell. Or so he said."

Masefield snorted. "I like the man already. Better take him downtown."

"He's there already, along with my sis and Ireton, and another student named Jack Sigur."

"What's with Sigur?"

"He's a friend of Ireton's. He was the one who found Ireton up on the seventh floor after the old man went over."

"That's interesting."

"Oh, but it gets more interesting." Ramon reached in his breast pocket and pulled out a folded sheet of paper. "Being a Saturday, Bricusse didn't have any scheduled appointments. But he had several drop-in visitors this afternoon, and his secretary is just the type to come in on the weekend and keep a list of them." Ramon snapped open the paper. "First there was this Jack Sigur. He was in with Bricusse for almost an hour. Then there was a student named Richard Krato. He talked to Bricusse for about twenty minutes, then, according to the secretary, came slamming out of the old man's office looking like a big red balloon about to pop."

"Hm. Was Richard Krato here tonight?"

"Not when we got here to secure the scene."

"Better look him up."

"Will do. But Professor, Bricusse had another visitor this afternoon, one I think you ought to know about."

"Who's that?"

"Max Heisler's daughter, Fran. The secretary said she was in a real state, and talked with Bricusse for over two hours. The secretary suspected it was about marital troubles. See, the poor girl just got herself hitched to one Barry Anthony DeBrun—who, by the way, *was* here tonight, though he claims he was in a first-floor john when everything went down. But then I wouldn't believe a word out of that *rulacho*'s mouth if he swore on a stack of Douay-Rheims Bibles that he was the slimiest bastard in the city of Milli-wau-kay, which he most certainly is."

Masefield was definitely interested now, but not particularly happy. "Just tell me this guy isn't related to Big John," he said. 'Big John' DeBrun was one of Milwaukee's leading defense attorneys, universally known and cordially despised by the entire law enforcement community for his startling record of getting patently guilty clients off on reduced charges, plea bargains, and technicalities, usually by means of suggesting some form of police miscon-duct.

"His son," Ramon said before leaning over to a nearby potted palm and lobbing a wad of spittle into the dirt. "It was my pleasure to beat the *cagada* out of him once after he tried to mess with Lupe."

Thinking that Ramon Cruz must really hate this DeBrun —the ambi-tious young detective took refuge in Spanglish only when he was almost too riled to talk at all— Masefield glanced at his watch and sighed. He'd been on duty since four, and half his shift was already working a gang drive-by from earlier in the evening. "Let's head downtown," he said wearily.

———————

After completing a cursory review of witness statements, Masefield stepped into the fishbowl-like waiting room in the Police Administration Building where the witnesses, kept apart until then and interviewed separately, had just been gathered together. Masefield was followed by Det. Ramon Cruz, who introduced them all while Masefield studied his little assemblage.

James Ireton was seated silently against the wall, his elbows on his knees, his tousled blonde hair hanging limply over his shell-shocked eyes. Lupe Cruz, whom Masefield recognized from assorted police functions attended with her brother, sat across from Ireton. Jack Sigur, a tall, skinny mixed-race fellow with a neatly trimmed goatee and one gold earring, sat next to Lupe, one long arm draped protectively around the back of her chair, his eyes fixed anxiously on Ireton. Dr. Franco Lanciano, his white linen suit underscoring sparse black hair and a waxed mustache, stood tensely at the room's only window, next to his wife, Adèle, who, though the nearest relation to the vic-tim, seemed the only person in the room not too stunned to move.

When Cruz finished the introductions, Adèle spoke up, addressing Masefield.

"Lieutenant, I think we should see James home. He was *so* close to my uncle. This has all been too much for him. Too much."

Taking the hint, Masefield bent over James Ireton, who, Ramon Cruz had told him, had not uttered a word since being brought to the PAB.

"Mr. Ireton?" he said gently.

It was some seconds before the young man looked up, but when he did, any suspicions about James Ireton and foul play, which might have been floating in Masefield's mind, vanished on the instant. Masefield had been at his job long enough to read the faces of men who had something to hide. There was nothing in young Ireton's face but raw, bleeding pain, like a knife gash exposing a pumping heart.

Rising slowly, James almost lunged at Masefield, pulling on the lapels of the lieutenant's sports jacket.

"He didn't *jump*," James said with a groan. "There was another one up there. And another one..." Letting go, James pointed in the air above his head as at some apparition.

Lupe Cruz leapt to her feet and cried, "Please, let me take him ho-ho-home!"

"He must go home with us," Adèle advised her mute husband in matronly tones. "James shouldn't be alone tonight."

Masefield reluctantly agreed. The witness statements had spurred more questions in his mind than they had answered, and he was wanting to spend some time of his own with these people, but he realized he'd get little coherent out of James Ireton tonight. He'd have to take the chance that if the distraught witness had anything of importance to remember, it would still be there tomorrow.

Masefield motioned to Ramon, who looked inquiringly at Lupe—she said something in Spanish and gave him the thumbs-up—before helping James to his feet. Adèle Lanciano moved to his other side and together they led James out of the room.

As soon as the door shut behind them, Lupe burst into tears.

Offering her some tissues from his pocket, Masefield addressed the remaining witnesses: "I know that you've already given statements, but there are a few things I'd like to clear up. It would help move things along if you all could remain a little longer."

"We'll help you any way we c-c-can," Lupe volunteered through her sniffles, though Masefield was certain that Franco Lanciano, at least, was about to launch a heated objection.

Masefield led the three into a vacant interview room.

Accepted procedure was to question important witnesses separately, but that had already been done, it was late, Calvin Masefield was exhausted, and the rest of his shift detectives were working this or other cases. Besides, what with the Heisler Institute being something of a foreign country to him, Masefield thought it important to see how these people related to one another under the stress of police interrogation.

"Miss Cruz," Masefield began, seating himself on the edge of the interview room table after the others, except Lanciano, had pulled up chairs, "would you mind going over it again?"

"I st-tutter," Lupe reminded him, blowing her nose.

"Take your time."

Throughout her thorough and calm narrative of the evening's tragic events, Masefield glanced up from time to time to observe Franco Lanciano: the skinny Italian leaned against the wall and nibbled aggressively on a thumbnail—an annoying habit that made Masefield think of an agitated rodent; a well-groomed pet white rat perhaps, who would sink his little teeth into your hand if you messed with his food.

"Okay, I follow thus far," Masefield said, corralling his vagrant thoughts and turning back to Lupe. "So you and Mr. Ireton parted in the atrium. Are you sure he took the stairs?"

"Now wait a minute — !" Jack Sigur intervened.

"Mr. Ireton was first on the scene where Fr. Bricusse went over the rail," Masefield explained, choosing his words carefully. "I'm not implying any wrongdoing on Mr. Ireton's part, but I have to have all the relevant facts."

Sigur backed down.

"I see what you're asking," Lupe said. "Yes, I definitely saw James go through the northside stairwell doors. I guess I noticed because it surprised me that he didn't take the elevator."

Sigur spoke up again. "James never uses elevators if he can help it. He doesn't like to admit it, but he suffers from claustrophobia. Fr. Bricusse had to finagle him a staff office, because the windowless student carrels freaked him out."

"True enough," Lanciano agreed, not sparing a glance for any of them.

"Either way," Lupe said, "it all happened too fast. Father f-fell just a few seconds after James went through the stairwell door. He couldn't possibly have gotten up there quickly enough, either to see or do anything."

"Okay. Why don't you just tell me, minute by minute, what happened after you parted company with Mr. Ireton."

"James went through the northside stairwell door. It was at about that time that I first heard applause coming from inside the theatre."

This time it was Lanciano who interrupted. "We were running a tad late," he said, pushing himself away from the wall, "but see, Max —"

Masefield motioned him to shut up. "Go on, Miss Cruz."

"Well, I got up to walk around a little. My dress was wet from the rain, and I didn't really feel like sitting on it, so I decided just to roam around the atrium a bit until James returned. I hardly made it ten feet across the floor before it happened. Please don't laugh, Lieutenant, but before I saw or heard anything, I f-felt it."

Masefield leaned forward.

Lupe stretched out her hand as if she had something in it to show him. "I felt this awful…th-*thing*. Like something terrible had just walked into the building. I felt it once before, too. In church a week or so ago. Anyway, that's when I heard something, I don't know what, way up and far off. Suddenly there was a flash of lightning through the ceiling panels. I looked straight up. That's when I saw him fa-fa-fall." Lupe took a deep breath. "It happened in less time than it's taking me to tell it!"

"Did you see him actually going over the rail?"

Lupe shook her head. "Already in the air."

"What position was the body?"

"Sorry?"

"Was he falling sideways, head-first…rotating?"

"Oh!" Lupe's hand went to her throat, where she fingered what looked to Masefield like some sort of religious medal. "Head-head first," she said. "His head hit the marble first."

Masefield stood up and planted his fists on his hips, his forehead furrowed with concentration. Lenny Swiatko had gone the same way, but the boy had deliberately dived head-first after stepping up on a chair. How had Ramon put it, *just like off the high dive at the pool.* "Did you look up after he fell," he asked Lupe, "to see if anyone was up there?"

Lupe shook her head. "It never occurred to me. Not that I could have seen much, the lights were all off up there. And then there's all that grillwork on the railings."

"How much time passed before you saw Mr. Ireton up on the seventh floor?"

"A couple of minutes. I'd been screaming for help and people were beginning to come out of the theatre and gather round. All of a sudden I heard something up high again and looked up. I don't know how I knew it was James, it was so dark up there. Maybe he cried out or something, I don't really remember. But I could tell it was James and, oh God, he was leaning w-w-way over the rail. I thought he was going to fall, too, so I called out, *James, no!* Or something like that. And he pulled back." Lupe clamped her hands over her mouth as if she might be sick.

"It was at that moment," Lanciano said, once again pushing himself away from the wall, "that I came through the elevator doors into the atrium."

Masefield pivoted. "Which elevator, north or south side?"

"The north side elevator."

"Bricusse fell not far from the north side elevator."

Lanciano bristled. "I was coming up from the basement, Detective, not down from the seventh floor. I chose the north side elevator because my car was parked on the north side of the basement lot."

"Oh, yeah, you had forgotten your speech notes, you said, and were looking for them in your car." Masefield turned again to Lupe. "Did you see Mr. Lanciano?"

She shrugged. "Can't say I did. But I wasn't paying much attention at that point."

"What about a student named Richard Krato, did you see him?"

Lupe looked surprised. "No, not then, though I remember seeing Richard beforehand. He was there in the atrium with a b-bunch of the other SANA guys before the program began."

Masefield straightened. "Richard Krato's a member of SANA?"

"We have a number of SANA members studying at the Institute," Lanciano said. "They aren't very popular, to be sure, but I can't say they cause any trouble."

Ignoring Lanciano, Masefield stepped back, turning this new and somehow troubling information over in his mind and laying it alongside what he had learned in the last ten days about Lenny Swiatko. Where Masefield sat, this was just too much coincidence.

Finally Masefield swiveled to Jack Sigur. "Mr. Sigur, you said in your statement that you were in the first floor men's room at the time of the incident, and that you ran out when you heard Miss Cruz's screams. Did you happen to see Richard Krato when you came out? Or Mr. Lanciano, for that matter?"

Sigur shrugged. "No. I ran upstairs after James, first thing."

"Was there anyone else in the men's room? Anyone who might corroborate that you were there during the incident?"

"I don't think so. Everyone else had gone into the theatre." Jack adjusted his posture. "But I did see somebody on the stairs when I was on my way up. Oh, who the hell was it..." Jack whirled to Lupe. "Why, it was DeBrun, yeah, Barry DeBrun. You know, Heisler's son-in-law. I passed him on the way up." Jack Sigur settled back into his chair, obviously relieved that he now had a witness to his activities.

Masefield retrieved the folder containing witness statements. Flipping it open, he found Barry DeBrun's and scanned it.

According to the statement, Barry DeBrun claimed that he had been in the south side atrium men's bathroom at the exact time that Sigur said he *didn't* see DeBrun there, but saw him instead, a few seconds later, coming down the south side stairs. Masefield looked up again, his eyebrows meeting together in one jagged line above his nose. "You're telling me," he said slowly to Sigur, "that you saw Barry DeBrun coming down the stairs *after* Bricusse fell?"

Sigur nodded vigorously. "For sure."

"Which stairs?"

"Like I said, the south side stairs. They're right there next to the bathroom."

Masefield awarded the young man a severe frown. "Would you mind telling me why you didn't mention this when you talked to Det. Cruz?"

"Look, man, I didn't think of it, I was thinking about James, you know? I had other things on my mind."

"That's another thing." Masefield dropped the folder on the table, his every movement tracked by the anxious eyes of Jack Sigur. "Can you please tell me why your first reaction, on coming out and seeing this...this catastrophe, was to run upstairs after James Ireton?"

"My dear Detective—" Lanciano began with an air of annoyance.

"Stop interrupting!" Masefield boomed. "Your turn is coming soon enough!"

Lanciano muttered something in Italian. Masefield heard the word "*cretino*" but preferred not to understand it. "Mr. Sigur," he said, "can I assume you have a more than casual interest in James Ireton?"

"Okay, so sue me. But no, to answer your next question, the feeling isn't returned, so too bad so sad. He likes girls." Jack cocked his head at Lupe. "Her, specifically. Still, in the crunch, I thought of James first. Before the old padre, or Lupe, or anyone else." Jack shrugged.

Masefield reseated himself on the table. "So you're saying you ran up the stairs, and when you came out on the seventh floor gallery you saw…what?"

"I saw James leaning over the railing there on the north side, by Bricusse's office. It scared the holy crap out of me, too, I mean he was leaning *way* over. Then I heard Lupe yell at him from down below, and he finally pulled back. Then he just, I don't know, slumped over on the floor, like a rag doll. So I ran down the hall and around the corner and—" Jack barked out a little laugh. "—I stumbled over something. Fell flat on my kisser."

Masefield leaned forward. "What did you stumble over?"

Jack thought a moment. "It was a shoe," he said finally. "A man's shoe. A whopper."

"You *handled* it?"

Sigur nodded, eyes wide.

Damn, damn, *damn*, Masefield thought, the second set of prints!

Jack sat up as if someone had applied a cattle prod to his hind quarters. "Oh shit," he muttered, apparently just now realizing whose shoe it was he had handled.

"You didn't mention this to Det. Cruz either, did you?" Masefield almost growled.

"Hey, I just now thought of it! Brother, you're on a mission. I'm telling you, it all happened too fast. And it was dark up there!"

Masefield held up his hand. "All right, calm down, Mr. Sigur. Just finish your story."

"Well, that's almost all," Jack said, regaining a modicum of composure. "Anyhow, I went to James. He was just sitting there on the floor outside Bricusse's door, his head between his knees. I thought he was fixing to pass out or puke or something. But then he just got up and pushed me aside and said, 'I've got to see him' or 'see it this time.' It was kind of incoherent. Then he headed for the stairs. I followed him down again, just to make sure he made it in one piece."

"Just one more question, Mr. Sigur."

"Shit, shoot."

"I understand you were in Bricusse's office this afternoon for almost an hour. Mind telling me what you two talked about?"

Jack licked his lips. "It was personal."

"I can ask Miss Cruz and Mr. Lanciano to step outside."

Jack glanced at Lupe and Lanciano, and then shrugged. "Oh, what the hell. I went to confession."

Masefield was stunned. "For an *hour*?"

"Well, I don't think it took *that* long."

"Father always gave lots of counseling during confession," Lupe piped in supportively.

Thinking he'd heard everything now, Masefield turned to Lanciano, almost with relief. The scowling Deputy Director, as uncomfortable-looking as if he had an orchestra baton stuck up his tight little rectum, was still loitering by the window. "Would you mind having a seat, Mr. Lanciano?"

Lanciano made a peevish face and yanked up a chair. The whiteness of the man's suit almost blinded Masefield under the fluorescent lighting above the table. And why, Masefield wondered, was Lanciano so edgy? Shock and grief Masefield could understand, but not this fidgety electricity, like a downed power line sparking in a mud puddle after a storm.

"As I told your other officer," Lanciano began with an enervated wave, "I hadn't seen Arthur since he left for Chicago. Max and I tried to meet with him to go over the program this afternoon, but he was conferencing in his private office and refused to be interrupted."

Masefield glanced again at Ramon Cruz's scribbled notes. "He was meeting with Mrs. Fran DeBrun," he said, looking up for a reaction. "And, before her, Richard Krato and Mr. Sigur."

Lanciano shrugged with apparent indifference. "It was an annoying habit of Arthur's to drop everything, no matter how important, if some young person came running in to seek his counsel on a personal matter. I must admit that Max and I were a trifle disturbed at the sloppy state the program was in. As a priest, I suppose Arthur was used to 'winging it,' as they say, but I am not. At any rate, I was so distracted by the whole disorienting business that I took my speech notes home with me, to glance over them at dinner, then forgot that I had done so."

"What time did you leave your office?"

"Close to five. I went straight home. Adèle and I had a quick supper. Canned soup and leftover hors d'œvres from last evening's party." Lanciano shuddered. "We returned a little before seven for the cocktail hour in the atrium. You see, we had an understanding with Arthur that we would meet backstage at a quarter till eight. But then when I couldn't find my notes—"

"When did you realize you didn't have your notes?"

Lanciano leaned forward. "Yes, well, you see, I was in the atrium, deep in conversation with Isabel Gunderson, one of my students, and her companion, Mr. Fred Stark of Stark's Brewery—Fred's been *most* generous with us in the past—when I glanced at my watch and saw how late it was."

"What time was it?"

"I beg your pardon?"

It took an act of the will for Masefield to relax his jaw. "What time was it when you looked at your watch and realized it was late?"

"Oh. It was seven forty-five. I took my leave of Fred and Bel and rushed backstage, only to realize, to my horror, that I didn't have my speech notes with me. And worse, couldn't remember for the life of me where I'd left them. I was positively quaking at the thought that I might have to deliver the speech *senza aiuto*." Lanciano gave a pointed glance at his watch. "Speaking of the time, Detective—"

"Lieutenant," Masefield corrected between his teeth.

Lanciano showed some teeth of his own. "Yes, well, Lieutenant, I'm usually long in bed by now —"

"The sooner you finish your story, Mr. Lanciano, the sooner you'll be snuggled up under the covers."

"*Doctor* Lanciano."

Masefield suppressed an expletive.

"As I was saying—Lieutenant—I hurried up to my office to see if I'd left my notes there. I avoided any personal contacts, of course, as it was already frightfully late."

"Is this a roundabout way of telling me that you somehow managed to roam all over the Institute without being seen?"

Lanciano's black eyes narrowed to pinpoints. "Now, I wouldn't be able to say if anyone saw me or not, would I? I only know that *I* didn't see or speak to anyone. But as I was riding up in the elevator—excruciatingly slow, the damned thing—I suddenly remembered that the notes weren't in my office after all." Lanciano gave a decisive nod. "I suddenly had the clear and distinct memory of taking the folder from my office and placing it in the trunk of my BMW. In my mind's eye, I could see the manila folder next to my maroon gym bag against the taupe upholstery of the trunk. It made for a rather attractive color combination. In fact, it reminded me of one of the guest bedrooms on our second floor—" Finally taking note of the fact that Masefield's temper was at the boiling point, Lanciano cleared his throat. "Yes, well, so when the elevator door opened on the seventh floor, I didn't go out, I just pushed the button for basement parking."

"Was there anyone in the elevator with you?"

"No, there wasn't."

"Did you see anyone on the seventh floor when the elevator door opened?"

"No, I did not."

"You didn't step out on the seventh floor?"

"No, I'm afraid not."

"How about in the underground parking structure, was anyone down there?"

"Well, you see, Det—Lieutenant, it was already after eight o'clock by then and the parking structure was full. Anyone who would have parked there would have already gone upstairs, long since."

"You want to concoct a better non-answer, Dr. Lanciano?"

Lupe Cruz jumped to the rescue. "Pardon me, but that's true. About the basement lot being full, I mean. James and I tried to pull in there at about twenty till eight, but the g-g-gate was down and the sign said 'full,' so we had to park on the street a couple of blocks away."

Lanciano awarded his student with an ardent nod of gratitude. "I do believe I was the only person down there. Although—" He glanced up hopefully. "—now that I think of it, I did hear the stairwell door opening just as I was getting back onto the elevator." Lanciano frowned a bit. "Perhaps, perhaps not. I wasn't paying much attention. I was in a good deal of pain."

"What are you saying, 'in pain?'"

Lanciano held up his bandaged middle finger—cautiously, perhaps, but with sufficient bravado for Masefield to note that the dapper academic was in effect flipping him the bird. "I slammed the trunk hood of my car on it," Lanciano said amiably.

Masefield winced.

"Indeed," Lanciano murmured, as if grateful for the barest hint of sympathy from the belligerent policemen. "BMWs are so airtight."

"I wouldn't know. So you got back on the elevator to the first floor, is that right, Dr. Lanciano?"

"That's right. And came out on the chaos."

Masefield sat quietly on the edge of the table, one leg swinging gently. He was eager to interrogate Lanciano on the business of his snooping around in Bricusse's office after the fall, but he was also tired, irked, and desperate for a cigarette. After a ten year hiatus, he had resumed the nasty habit after Lenny died, much to his wife's annoyance. As for the conflicting testimonies, sorting it all out would take time, and much would depend on the autopsy. Really, why fuss over all the loose ends, details, half-truths, and mixed motives that surrounded every police investigation, if the autopsy ended up showing that it was all just some freakish accident, after all?

"I think we may as well call it a night," Masefield said finally, once again on his feet. "I'll have an officer drive you all home."

"That's very kind of you," Lanciano said in an officious tone, rising to smooth out the wrinkles in his trousers, "but I'll see my students home."

"Then thank you for your cooperation," Masefield countered, casting as ironic a glance as he could produce in Lanciano's direction as he pulled some business cards out of his breast pocket to hand to each of them. "But I'd appreciate it if you all kept me informed of your whereabouts for the next few days. Nothing to stress about," he added, noting Sigur's instantly crestfallen expression. "Just in case we need to clear up any details. Oh, and I'll need to talk to Mr. Ireton. Please have him give me a call in the morning after he's gotten some sleep."

"Whew!" Jack exclaimed as he and Lupe climbed into the back seat of Lanciano's sparkling white BMW. "That man's trapping pelts, and I think he's after mine."

"Or mine." Lanciano turned the ignition and the BMW's engine purred into life. "*You want to concoct a better non-answer, Mister Lanciano?*" he mimicked puckishly.

"I wish your 'alibi' were someone other than Barry DeBrun," Lupe said to Jack, then, noting Lanciano's glower in the rear-view mirror added hastily, "Sorry, Dr. Lanciano, I don't mean to speak ill of Mr. Heisler's family."

"Yes, well, *êntre nous*," Lanciano said, glancing over his shoulder as he backed out of the parking space, "I didn't get a particularly favorable impression of young DeBrun, either." Lanciano braked at the exit, but before he pulled out into the street he turned again, this time to Jack. "You don't happen to have any more of those lovely English cigarettes, do you?" he said hungrily.

Jack handed him a cigarette from a pack of Players he extracted from his breast pocket; then reached over the seat to light it for him with a Bic.

Lanciano sucked deeply. "Ah, you've saved me again," he said, exhaling. "Ghastly habit," he added. "Makes the car smell like a *trattoria*."

Storm-driven waves had tossed up dead fish, driftwood and sea-litter along Milwaukee's beaches, while ninety-miles-per-hour wind gusts had strewn amputated tree branches all over the city's muddy streets. As dawn cracked silver through sooty clouds, the storm front fled east and broke apart over the uneasy waters of Lake Michigan, giving way to a still morning of clearing skies and delicate breezes.

James awoke at nine, thick-headed from the sedative Adèle and the gruff young detective had forced down his throat the night before. Laying on his back in the strange bed, trying to figure out who all those people were last night, and what exactly had happened, it took some minutes of staring at the ornate blur of plaster moldings around the ceiling of the Lancianos' guest room, designed in a chi-chi combination of maroon and taupe, before he realized where he was, and why, exactly, he was here.

Then the brief shock of recognition gave way to the dull ache of grief.

James rolled out of bed and tottered into the guest bathroom. Adèle had set out a disposable razor and some of Franco's expensive French shaving lotion, but he didn't even have the energy to pick them up. He used the toilet, fumbled into his clothes and his shoes, and shuffled down the back stairs into the Lancianos' spacious kitchen. Adèle had left a note on the granite countertop: she and Franco had gone to eight-thirty Mass at the Oratory and would return directly. James was to make himself at home. Hot coffee was in the thermos pitcher on the table, a plate of scrambled eggs in the fridge, cereal and bread in the pantry.

James gulped down some black coffee and scribbled a note to the Lancianos: "I'm all right. I feel like walking. Ring you later. Thanks for everything. James."

He stepped out the back door, and the sight that met his bloodshot eyes all but took his breath away: the cloudless sky directly above his head was a pale powder blue, but the rising sun, shrouded by the bank of retreating storm clouds, had turned the eastern sky that met the lake on the vanishing horizon a deep midnight blue. The midnight hovered over a murmuring sea of opalescent sea-foam green, dappled here and there with peaks of snowy whitecaps scrolling restlessly to shore. In the five years James had lived on the lake he had never seen anything approaching this light-dark beauty, and for a few minutes he forgot everything and just looked.

After hours of aimless walking all over the muddy city, James found himself at last on the east side again, in his own lakefront neighborhood, every muscle in his body knotted and heavy with exertion. He ate a carryout sandwich on a bench facing the marina, and watched the boats bobbing in their slips, their white masts rocking back and forth on the water like clock pendulums ticking off the endless seconds of his morbid afternoon.

He was shoving his refuse into a garbage can when his eyes fell on a curious grayish lump sloshing in the water at his feet. Stepping to the edge of the pier, James looked down to see a large dead Coho floating on its side, its scaly carcass bumping rhythmically against the pier, its fish-eye fixed unseeingly on the hazy sky above, its ugly mouth wide in rictus as if flash-frozen in a scream. Closer observation revealed the source of the salmon's calamity: an eel-like lamprey had attached its maw to the fish's flank, sucking it dry like some antediluvian vampire.

James glanced uneasily over his shoulder: nothing…no one. He was alone on the pier. Shrugging off the creep, he turned again toward Prospect Avenue and the St. Ives.

There was a bar and grill tucked into the ground floor of the St. Ives building, and on milder days from May to October the management rolled out a sidewalk cafe. As James approached, he saw Lupe Cruz sitting at one of the tables, her face half hidden by a newspaper. There were remnants of a sandwich and beer on the table beside her arm, making it obvious to him that she had been waiting there for some time. He felt a surge of anger that on the force of their few kisses she had presumed a relationship that would permit her to intrude on his private pain on such a day as this. He stopped in front of the table.

"What the devil do you want?"

His tone was so brutal, even contemptuous, that it took Lupe a few seconds to get her mouth moving.

"They d-d-did an autopsy this morning."

"So?"

"Father d-died of a heart attack, James. Long before the fall, maybe an hour or more. But because they can't explain the fall, they're marking it down as 'pending further evidence.'" And then as if she guessed his personal hell Lupe added, "You didn't get there too late. You couldn't have saved him. However the fall happened, he was dead long before he hit the ground."

James made no sound, no move.

Lupe reached into a zippered pocket of her backpack and fumbled for a business card. "Lt. Masefield wants to talk to you," she said, holding it out to him, "when you fee-fee-feel up to it."

James extracted the card from her fingers and pocketed it.

"I g-grieve for you. He loved you, like a son."

"Well, now, I certainly disappointed him like a son."

"I'm sure he d-d-didn't—"

"What the fuck would you know about it? Christ, just…go home. I don't want anyone's sympathy today, least of all yours."

Her chin began to tremble, and a lank of hair shivered over her reddening face. Finally she flung her backpack over her shoulder and retreated quickly up Prospect Avenue toward Lake Drive and her home.

James shoved his key into the door of his apartment and stepped inside, the utter routineness of his own movements reminding him of other times when he had returned home feeling this peculiar sense of satisfaction at having caused someone else pain.

So he had roughed her up a bit, he thought as he went into his bathroom and peeled off his clothes. Better for her in the long run. No use having her getting the wrong idea.

In the glare of the overhead fixture, he stared into the bathroom mirror at his own sweaty, unshaven face. The dreary sight of it suddenly reminded him of something, or someone else: blonde hair matted and stringy, gray eyes cold and lifeless, like the dead eyes of a shark...where had he seen such a face before?

And then it hit him: he had seen a face something like this in a newspaper photograph beside an article commemorating the anniversary of the arrest of Jeffrey Dahmer.

James hurried into the shower.

Wincing at the shock of cold tiles against his feet, the blast of hot water against his back, James reminded himself that though he was no saint, he was certainly no murderer. If he had hurt people at different times in his life, well, it hadn't been intentional. It had been a normal human reaction to suffering. Everybody did it. *One nail drives out one nail*, he reassured himself, *one pain one pain.*

He thrust his face into the steaming torrent, then just as quickly stepped back, gasping and shaken at the distant but potent voice whispering in his memory: *James, do you care for me? Do you love me? Do you love me...?*

Fifteen minutes later, dried off and dressed, James stepped out the sliding glass door that opened on to his balcony. Resting his elbows on the balcony railing, he watched as the reflected gold of the setting sun stirred on the wrinkled sea at his feet. Only a brownish band of water near the mouth of the harbor, where silt and mud had been emptied into the lake by the rushing rivers, gave witness to the pelting rainstorms of the previous evening. Within a day, he thought, the lake would be all blue again, the throbbing of the waves against the shore having done their work to scrape away the shallow-clutching mud.

Finally James was able to think squarely of Arthur Bricusse, to see him in his mind's eye. The vitality of the image there did not comfort him, however, but only burdened him even more with a heavy weight of remorse. Believe it, he told himself, who believed in very little anymore, you failed the one man who loved you in the world. But before all else, before the shame and guilt and remorse, James felt the all-hollow emptiness of abandonment.

Damnation, he thought, a remnant of defiance surfacing at last, he must get used to it again. After all, this was not new. Others who had at one time been precious to him had been taken away, and he had survived. God knew there was no one now to rescue him and make it all right again; to give him life and energy and purpose, let alone hope, that cruelest of all the fantasies of the human imagination.

The cool evening breeze began to dry his damp hair and skin, chilling him to the marrow. James dropped his head against his bare forearm, feeling his body going numb and cold all over, like a slow death working outwards to his extremities from the core of a frigid heart.

And then, without warning, just when he had decided that it might be better just to let go and let the cold take him, James felt a sudden spark of warmth in his toes, as if the summer sun were rising at his feet and its heat were working its slow way up his legs to his chest, even to the sluggish muscle of his heart—a warmth that savored just a little of dreadful hope.

What else was it that Bricusse had said to him that first day of class? Oh, yes: *Put on the whole armor of God*. As many times as he had heard them, James had never really known what those tidy old words were intended to mean; but Bricusse had also said, *God is a God of the living, not of the dead*, and for all his apostasy James suddenly had a pretty damned good idea of what was behind *that* old obscurity; for along with the unheralded return of warmth and hope, James was once again hearing the old man's voice in his heart, as distinctly as if he were standing there beside him.

James scanned the emptiness of water and sky around him and gave a self-deprecating chuckle, amazed that even now his brutalized soul could resist the siren-song of wholesale skepticism—that time-out-of-mind argument for despair that consisted of one part stoicism and surely three parts laziness. But try as he might, James would never be able to persuade himself that the death of someone like Arthur Bricusse was no particular loss in the great scheme of things; that none of it, not even his own mourning, mattered. How could he ever make himself believe that Arthur Bricusse—that unrepeatable essence of living, thinking, feeling humanity—had somehow dissolved into nothingness like yesterday's storm? Could *I am* become *I am not* because of the spasm of a central muscle, or the momentary collision of bone and marble? No. Not when the words that voice had uttered still lived, still sang, still echoed back from the eternity into which they had been spoken that afternoon, when James had first set astonished eyes on Lupe Cruz, and Arthur Bricusse had given him the package with *Dieguito* scrawled across the wrapping paper.

James glanced back through the sliding doors into his living room: Bricusse's package, unopened still, was propped against the side of his desk. Like it or not, James thought, straightening, the picture would serve as the priest's final admonishment against despair and final urge to hope. His final word to James.

———————————

James hung the picture of Our Lady of Guadalupe above the fireplace he never used, where, he thought, he could look at it as he studied at his table by the window. He would read, work, glance up at it from time to time, then out at the lake; then return his thoughts to his books. Such would be the rhythm of his life from now on, and like it or not, *la Guadalupana*, the Dark Virgin of the Americas would be the bittersweet companion intruding on his former solitude.

But one nail, one fire, one pain drives out another, James reminded himself, and finally, just maybe, this was the right pain, the right fire, the right nail.

Remembering that Bricusse had said there would be literature enclosed with the picture, James rummaged in the scraps of wrapping paper on the floor until he found a pamphlet narrating the image's miraculous history. Flipping through it, James's eyes fell on an italicized section of print, relating the Virgin's words to the Aztec visionary Juan Diego, translated from the ancient Nahuatl:

> *Juanito, Juan Dieguito!*
> *Do listen to Me,*
> *My Littlest One, Juanito!*
> *Do know this,*
> *do be assured of it in your heart,*
> *My Littlest One,*
> *that I Myself, I am the Entirely and Ever Virgin*
> *Saint Mary,*
> *Mother of the True Divinity,*
> *God Himself:*
> *because of Him, Life goes on,*
> *Creation goes on;*
>
> *His are all things afar,*
> *His are all things near at hand,*
> *things above in the Heavens,*
> *things here below on the Earth.*
>
> *For truly I Myself,*
> *I am your Compassionate Mother,*
> *yours, for you yourself,*
> *for everybody here in the Land,*
> *for each and all together,*
>
> *for all others too,*
> *for all Folk of every kind.*
> *Do listen,*
> *do be assured of it in your heart,*
> *My Littlest One,*
> *that nothing at all should alarm you,*

should trouble you,
nor in any way disturb
your countenance, your heart.

For am I not here,
I, Your Mother?
Are you not in the Cool of My Shadow?
In the Breeziness of My Shade?
Is it not I that am
your Source of Contentment?

Are you not cradled in My Mantle?
Cuddled in the Crossing of My Arms?

Act Two:

Wounded Hearts

My true love hath my heart, and I have his,
By just exchange, one for the other giv'n.
I hold his dear, and mine he cannot miss:
There never was a better bargain driv'n.
His heart in me, keeps me and him in one,
My heart in him, his thoughts and senses guides:
He loves my heart, for once it was his own:
I cherish his, because in me it bides.
His heart was wounded, with his wounded heart,
For as from me, on him his hurt did light,
So still me thought in me his hurt did smart:
Both equal hurt, in this change sought our bliss:
My true love hath my heart and I have his.

Sir Philip Sidney, *Arcadia*

Chapter Five:
What I Have Been, and What I Am

Let me put in your minds, if you forget
What you have been ere now, and what you are;
Withal, what I have been, and what I am.

Shakespeare, *Richard III*

James knocked on Lupe's door. When she opened it, he held up the bouquet of long-stem red roses he'd picked up en route. She hesitated, then took them. Then burst into tears. Without a word, he led her up the three steps into her living room, laid the roses on her dining table and hugged her to his chest.

The phone rang.

Face flushed, Lupe pulled away to blow her nose and answer it, while James, grateful for an opportunity to further prepare himself to deliver the apology he'd been writing in his head for the last hour, retrieved the roses and chased up a glass from the kitchen cabinets to serve as a vase.

"That was Adèle," Lupe said when she rang off. "She asked me to remind you that Lt. Masefield wants to ta-ta-talk to you. When you feel up to it."

Promising to contact the good lieutenant first thing in the morning, James recited his apology with some stammering of his own. He concluded his speech with the announcement that he had taken the liberty of bringing some takeaway Chinese with him, seeing as how he was so rudely inviting himself to dinner.

When he had fetched the cartons of shrimp and noodles from the back seat of his Jeep, they seated themselves at her tiny dining table. They talked quietly about the wake scheduled for Tuesday night, if the County Medical Examiner saw fit to release Fr. Bricusse's body by then; then about Lanciano's coerced decision to cancel all Institute classes until after Bricusse's funeral. The police, it seemed, were insisting on keeping the building secure until they were satisfied that everything possible had been learned at the scene.

At one point a tiger-striped tomcat purled itself around Lupe's ankles, begging for some table scraps. Lupe introduced him to James as one "Prince Hal." Extracting several large shrimp from one of the cartons, James arranged them on a saucer and set it on the floor beside his foot.

"See?" he said, as the cat abandoned his mistress for her more generous guest, "a friend for life."

"More like a pest for life. That *gato* knows a sucker when he sees one." Her fork poised in mid-air.

"What's on your mind?"

"Oh, just something Ramon said."

"Ramon?"

"My brother. You know, the detective who took you to the Lancianos' last night."

"Ah, yes. I thought he looked oddly familiar, now that you mention it. Same amazing eyes, you know. Though they don't look nearly so amazing on him. But then I only noticed him at all because he insisted on shoving a fistful of sleeping pills down my throat. And none too gently."

Lupe grunted. "That's Ramon all right."

"So what was it he said?"

"That Lt. Masefield wasn't very happy about the autopsy report. See, even if Father d-d-died of a heart attack—"

"Dead men can't throw themselves over a gallery railing. Yes, I know, I've been pondering that little conundrum all afternoon." James pushed away his plate. "So what does this Masefield think?"

"Ramon says he doesn't know what to think. But I got the distinct impression last night that he suspected both Jack and Lanciano of lying about what they were up to when it all happened."

James gave a decisive shake of his head. "Masefield's barmy if he thinks Jack's a murderer. And Lanciano's Catholicism may have more to do with aesthetics than faith, but he's too civilized to be a killer. Even if he had a motive. Which he doesn't."

"He'll b-be Institute Director now."

"He was going to be anyway, when Father stepped down in January. No, the only man I know with a motive for killing Fr. Bricusse is Peter Krato." Seeing the look on Lupe's face, James added, "I promise you, his religion to the contrary, when it comes to dealing with threats to SANA, I doubt very much that Peter Krato's conscience draws six inches of water."

"But how could Father have threatened SANA?"

James propped one elbow on the table and began to massage his forehead. "The day I took him to the airport, Father showed me a letter he was intending to send to the Archbishop. A letter expressing his concerns about Peter's leadership of SANA. Coming from one of the most highly regarded priests in the country, it would have carried considerable weight. He wrote it as a sort of cover letter for a rather lengthy report I wrote myself, three years ago."

"Report...you mean of what happened to you at SANA?"

"And more. It was a narrative of my entire religious history, really. From my Anglican upbringing to my conversion to Catholicism to my last contact with SANA." James reached again for his plate and thrust his fork into a dripping chunk of shrimp, but promptly set it down again. "Father persuaded me to write it. More as therapy than anything else. He knew I was eaten up with anger."

"Why d-didn't you send it then?"

"Father counseled me against it. It wasn't the most balanced of documents, you know. I wrote it in a fever, Lupe. It finished up more as revenge play than history, though God knows it's all true. Either way, Father knew Peter would try to discredit it by trashing my reputation. Of course he's done that anyway." James pressed his fist against his teeth. "And so it remained for three years. But the day he left for Chicago, Father told me that he thought it was finally time, if not too late, to intervene. And of course I agreed."

"What made him change his mind now?"

"That young man who jumped to his death in City Hall."

Lupe's eyes widened. "Lenny Swiatko...what did he have to d-d-do with SANA?"

"Plenty, as it turns out, so Father told me. The poor kid had been in and out of psychiatric hospitals for years, diagnosed as a schizophrenic. But last September, semi-functional by then on maintenance-level Thorazine, he went back to college at UWM. He began attending Mass at the Newman Center. That's where he got himself recruited into SANA by our very own Rosencrantz and Guildenstern."

Lupe winced. "I bet SANA didn't help his schizophrenia."

"Too true. Although according to Father, Lenny actually did surprising well for a while. Religious fervor can mask a cornucopia of symptoms, don't I know it. But by the spring Lenny's symptoms had once again gotten completely out of hand. They'd find him up on the roof of SANA House, writing lengthy letters to himself and babbling passages from *Revelations*. That's Peter's favorite casual reading, by the way." James chuckled at Lupe's expression. "Honestly, I'm not sure anyone who hasn't been on the inside of that place can possibly appreciate the Orwellian degree of doublethink that goes on there. On top of the schizophrenia, it must have worked like pure brain acid."

"Still," Lupe commented with a frown, "it's a wonder Mr. Krato kept him around. Think of the potential scandal."

"Oh, Krato's no fool, that's certain. But you must appreciate the *subtext*. The man's been in fiscal hot water from the get-go. Why, he was borrowing up the wazoo to fund his grandiose schemes even before I left. Getting well-heeled backers to co-sign loans, or donate property, that sort of thing. But in Lenny Peter discovered a potential cash cow."

"I thought he was just the son of a c-c-cop."

"A cop who was killed in the line of duty," James said, finger raised. "Besides his father's sizeable life insurance policy, the police union set up a trust fund for Lenny. Lenny started to draw on it when he turned eighteen.

The bulk of it was to come to him on his twenty-first birthday. All Peter had to do, you see, was tough things out until April, when Lenny turned twenty-one."

Lupe sat back. "D-Don't tell me. He squirreled the money out of him then cut him loose."

"In June."

Lupe shook her head. "How the heck did Father find out all this?"

James sat back, the question giving him considerable pause. How much, he wondered, had Lupe heard about him and Nadine Jeffrey in her few short months at the Institute? Probably enough. "Um, Father learned about it from one of Lenny's co-workers," James said finally, "a former Institute student. She took Father out to lunch last week. Then she put him in contact with Lenny's mother."

If Lupe had heard about his relationship with the "former Institute student" she was tactful enough not to mention it. "So you're thinking," she said with a frown, "that Mr. Krato was worried that Father was about to t-t-take what he'd learned to the Archbishop? Maybe even your SANA report?"

James let out a little sigh. "Absolutely," he said. "How Krato would have known, I can't imagine. But I'm certain he found out somehow."

"Richard," Lupe said without missing a beat.

James looked up.

"I could t-t-tell he was feeling me out about something that day we got into it after Mass. He knows my mom works for the Archdiocese, I mentioned it over the summer. Maybe he thought you were going to get to the Archbishop through me. And Ramon told me that Richard had an argument with Father Saturday afternoon. Father's secretary heard raised voices, and saw Richard storming out of Father's office." Lupe reached across the table for James's arm. "But please d-d-don't repeat that, it could cost Ramon his job."

James laid his hand over hers. "Christ," was all he said.

"I know a quick way to get your report directly under the Archbishop's nose, if you still want to g-go for it."

He lifted his head.

"My mother, remember?" She gave his arm a squeeze. "She sees the Archbishop every day."

———

A while later, with mugs of tea steaming beside them, James and Lupe sat out on her screened-in porch, arms wrapped around one another as the shadows lengthened in the garden below.

"I meant to ask you," he said, nuzzling her hair, which smelled of some rose-scented shampoo, "what DeBrun meant the other night when he said, 'that's two you owe me.'"

He felt her stiffen at the question. He suspected that her obvious anger wasn't directed so much at him, however, as at the memories his question had elicited.

"I f-filed charges against him," she said finally. "But I had no witnesses. And Barry's father is a big-shot defense lawyer. After a week or so of investigation, an assistant DA t-t-told me that it wasn't looking good. He said I might even have the tables turned on me with a malicious false charge suit. So I...I withdrew the complaint."

James gave her a squeeze. "Probably the wisest thing to do under the circumstances."

Lupe's chin trembled as if she were about to cry. "I was afraid, James, after that night. I've been af-f-fraid ever since. I'd see Barry's red Mustang roaring down K-Kinnickinnic and almost faint on the street. I swear, I think they're going to write my epitaph, *And she lived c-c-carefully ever after.*"

"Now, that's quite enough, Cruz. You were, what, seventeen?"

She said nothing, and sensing that his arguments, however cogent, were making little headway against her conviction of her own cowardice, James pushed her head back to kiss her instead.

"What's so damned humorous?" he grumbled a few seconds later, feeling her chuckling under his kiss.

"The story isn't finished," she said with a sniffle. "'That's *two* you owe me,' remember?"

James listened patiently at first, then more eagerly as Lupe proceeded to narrate, in her increasingly broken speech, how Ramon and her younger brother Patrick, and even her eldest brother, Martin, who had been home on vacation from seminary, agreed amongst themselves on what Lupe described as the '*Che G-G-Guevaran' solution to the problem of Barry DeBrun.*' Wearing nylons over their heads like terrorists, the three resolute young brothers had hijacked DeBrun on the way to a Fourth of July picnic. After beating him senseless and depositing his unconscious body behind a warehouse under the Hoan Bridge, they had phoned in his location from a pay phone downtown. Then all three Cruz men had come home arm-in-arm singing *La Bamba*, each man in a different key.

"Bloody well done," was James's emphatic assessment when she had finished. He took advantage of the occasion to pull her across his lap. When she finally put a stop to his increasingly amorous moves, he took hold of her hand and pressed it against his chest, so tightly that he could feel his own heart thumping under her palm.

"Lupe," he said, struggling with a feeling of embarrassment that had nothing to do with sex and everything to do with a wholly different and less familiar form of intimacy, "I have a copy of my SANA report in the car. I want you to read it. Yes, tonight. I need you to know...who I am."

After James left, Lupe curled up on her bed with her journal by her knees and his bound manuscript in her lap. She felt a thrill of expectancy working up her spine, as if she were about to set out on a long-awaited journey to an exotic country.

She turned over the cover page and began to read.

My Experience with the Student
Apostolate of North America

by James Henry Ireton

Given that this narrative may be read by officials of the Church, I tried in the first draft to keep my personal life out of it. I realized in the editing process, however, that this would not be possible, particularly in view of some of the public accusations being leveled against me by Mr. Peter Krato and his acolytes. And so I will simply "tell all." The opinions expressed here are, of course, my own, and the reader will have to judge my credibility as a witness. I will not withhold detrimental personal information which might serve to impugn my character, as it may be relevant.

Bowing to Aristotle's dictum that tragedies are ultimately family stories, let me prologue my own with some personal history.

I am the only son of an Anglican clergyman. My father, the Reverend Dr. Cyril Ireton, now pastors a deteriorating parish in a largely working-class immigrant neighborhood of East London. His days are occupied with joyless labor to bring the Gospel to the sort of people he would not see socially if he could otherwise manage it. No longer encumbered by family responsibilities, he is now free to give this martyr's effort his undivided attention. That is a great relief to him, I don't doubt.

Tidbits of family lore: there was an Ireton listed on the battle rolls with Henry V at Agincourt, and since that time the male members of our family have gravitated towards the military vocation. In the seventeenth century one of our name, Major General Henry Ireton, broke through the ranks of the unacknowledged by embracing ascendant Puritanism and marrying the daughter of Oliver Cromwell. With his father-in-law, Ireton co-signed the death warrant of King Charles I during the English Civil War—"that late, unhappy confusion," as the old *Book of Common Prayer* so decorously describes it.

These famous (or infamous) ancestors of mine are also remembered for quelling a rebellion in Ireland with grisly ferocity. The statistics, I have read, suggest that up to a third of the population of the Emerald Isle was annihilated in "Cromwell's War." I have been told by bemused Irish seamen of my acquaintance, who gasped at the mere mention of my name, that one can lay no more fiendish malediction upon another than to cry, "the Curse of Cromwell on ye!" I thought the phrase terribly funny the first time I heard it, but have since learned to regard it with a respect approaching superstition, given that the curse of Cromwell's temperament, fusing religious fervor with military zeal, seems to have been transmitted through the blood lines of the Ireton family, and pulses in full vigour generations removed. I thought I was getting away from all this rot when I came to America; but I had forgotten, perhaps, how many Puritans emigrated to these shores well before my own arrival. But I am getting ahead of my tale.

Iretons of our little familial branch have trained at Sandhurst for generations. When I was very young (that is, still close to my uncle and grandfather,
both military men) the officers of the Duke of Edinburgh's Royal Regiment
(Wiltshire) were as second family. My grandfather Henry served in North
Africa in World War II, and my uncle James lost an arm to an Ulster sharp-
shooter in the seventies. I have cousins who served in Iraq and the Persian
Gulf.

My father, too, was originally set upon a military career until he was
sent down mid-year from Sandhurst, victim to an unexplained case of tuber-
culosis. His weakened constitution precluded a military career, of course,
and upon his complete recovery, he went up to Cambridge to read Modern
History at Christ's College, the *alma mater* of his literary hero, John Milton,
Cromwell's secretary. In spite of the fact that our immediate ancestors had
returned to mainstream Anglicanism by the early nineteenth century, Cyril
became convinced at Cambridge that something of the Cromwellian spirit
was wanting in the Established Church, and that the prelapsarian 'Paradise'
of pre-war English society had been lost due to the deterioration of discipline
and moral fiber. *Ergo*, so Cyril reasoned, the rebuilding of the Established
Church would restore civic virtue, if not regain Paradise. He experienced
this shift in intellectual orientation as a "call" to ministry. One might say he
took to religion with the same sort of pre-millennial fervor that others of his
generation took to Trotskyism or post-structuralism.

In order to better serve the Church, Cyril planned originally to remain
unmarried; but in his last term at Cambridge he made the acquaintance
of the daughter of a Milanese textile heiress and an English naval commander. My mother Gina was everything my father was not: warm, beautiful, musical, gregarious, wealthy, and, like her mother before her, Roman
Catholic—which is to say, more than a little "foreign," from my father's
point of view. I can't imagine how it came to pass, as it appears completely
out of character for them both, but like uxorious Adam under the sway of
Eve, Cyril succumbed to temptation and got Gina pregnant. Doing the done
thing, he offered to marry her on condition that she shift her religious allegiance to his own denomination.

The result: I was born by emergency Cesarean section shortly after my
father became an ordinand at the theological college at Salisbury—two
months prematurely and only four months after the marriage, to pile insult
on top of injury.

After his ordination, Cyril took a minor position under the Canons of
Salisbury Cathedral. My only sibling, Anne, was born when I was three. We
lived in a small house in the Cathedral Close until I was twelve, and I have
always remembered these years as the least troubled of my life. My father, I
was made to understand, was on the "fast track" of ecclesiastical preferment.
An eventual appointment to a canonry seemed inevitable, did he but keep
his nose clean and keep his more eccentric theological opinions to himself.

Even in the happiest times, however, religion was a battlefield in our home. Mother expressed concern, from time to time, that the tenor of our religious upbringing was too severe. After many stalemated battles she and Cyril, Solomon-like, divided up their two children: my mother was allowed to pander her "sentimental" brand of Anglo-Catholicism to the weaker vessel, my sister, while I was left to the more robust ministrations of my father.

Religion, need I say, was never a "personal" matter to me, as the Evangelicals like to describe it. Rather I absorbed, willy-nilly, the spirit of my father, for whom religion was not a love relationship with one's God and Saviour, but a meta-moral prop for a decaying class and civilisation. He viewed my mother's occasional lapses into fervent piety with open contempt, and expressed an almost aesthetic repugnance for the manifestations of "Mariolatry" in which she and other Anglo-Catholics indulged.

But Cyril's extremist tendencies are by no means the crux of my lifelong complaint against religion. No, my argument is that religion deprived me of a father, as most people understand the word. Certainly, as long as we lived at Salisbury, near my mother's friends and extended family, I felt relatively nurtured. Cyril's brother James was a generous, giving uncle, and my little sister and I played happily with our three cousins in St. Ann Street. Single-armed as he was, Uncle James played football with us, took us salmon fishing on the Wye, and taught me to shoot. When I took the blue riband, aged thirteen, at a regional marksmanship contest sponsored by the Wiltshire Regiment, my uncle James was ecstatic; my father never showed.

Cyril assumed I would eventually study at the military college at Sandhurst. Like many boys my age, I dreamed for a while of military glory, though not on land; my heart's desire was to captain a ship in the Royal Navy, like my mother's father, whom I never knew. Perhaps Cyril took this as a rejection of the Ireton tradition in favor of my mother's. I certainly never thought of it this way, I just wanted to go to sea.

In a related vein, it was also a source of considerable anxiety for Cyril that I preferred my mother's and sister's interests to his. I shared my mother's love for music, for example, and she taught me violin. My father tolerated the music-making as a sort of necessary evil in the education of a well-rounded Englishman, but whenever I tried to express my love of music to him I was coolly rebuffed. Personal warmth, beauty, joy…such luxuries found no place in the Rev. Dr. Cyril Ireton's short list of life's necessities.

I early on discovered the delights to be found in books as well, especially Shakespeare, and enjoyed nothing more than reciting speeches from *Henry V* or *Hamlet* to my mother and sister. My father, observing that I had an absorbent memory, tried to turn me to the study of Scripture and Milton. I don't hesitate to say that I resisted the suggestions because they came from my father. Occasionally, when I forgot myself, I would fall in love with a passage of *Isaiah* or a Psalm from the BCP; or even a sonnet of Milton's. But these rare enthusiasms were eclipsed by the niggling carrot-and-stick approach to this rote learning which Cyril took with me: faint praise, if I recited perfectly, isolation in my room for further memorization if I did not.

Perhaps as a consequence of his own "fall" at Cambridge, Cyril was also on the alert for the inevitable appearance of concupiscence in his rebellious son. He discovered this remnant of the old Adam in me at an early age and dealt with it severely, usually by having me study lengthy passages of *Jeremiah* and the Prophets, or Book IX of *Paradise Lost*. His intention was to sear my consciousness with the conviction that fornication was the very essence of sin, which was his own understanding of Article IX of The Thirty-nine Articles. As a result of this unusual form of punishment for sexual precocity, I can safely say that by the time my mother died I had committed most of the Prophets to memory, and the Psalms as well.

When I was eleven, the Broad Church Dean of Salisbury Cathedral was given a bishopric in the North and was replaced by an Anglo-Catholic gentleman for whom Cyril conceived an instantaneous and vehement dislike. After six months, unable to stand it any longer, Cyril requested a parochial assignment, well aware that such a move could constitute a major setback to his career. I was not quite twelve when he took the living at St. George's in Wylford, a one-church hamlet near to Salisbury on the Wylie River, a tributary of the Wiltshire Avon.

Almost instantly, our family was cut off from all the little normalcies of the outside world. I'm sure there was no need for this as Wylie, though representing the back of beyond to me at the time, was but a short drive from Salisbury; but the isolation seemed to be my father's preference. My mother, of course, quickly became miserable.

For example, Cyril, as vicar (and now "in charge" as it were, of this tiny corner of the world), began speaking from the pulpit in an openly quarrelsome vein, preaching an eccentric creed that I would now, years later, describe as a peculiar syncresis of liberal theology, muscular spirituality, political conservatism, and moral fundamentalism. Too, and in spite of frequent cautions from our Archdeacon to be "more sensitive" to his Evangelical and Anglo-Catholic parishioners, Cyril proceeded to conduct the services at St. George's with the minimum of what he termed "emotional Roman varnish" or "ritualized theatre." To me, who had always loved the glorious liturgies in Salisbury Cathedral, it seemed that all the beauty and feeling had been pressed out of our religion, to be replaced by a pastiche of outdated nationalism, militant moralisms, and an endless stream of preaching in the most turbid prose imaginable. Mordant apothegms replaced the dramatic narrative power of our faith. I felt I suddenly understood how the children of England must have felt that first bleak midwinter when the Puritans canceled Christmas. I hated the preaching and longed for the abandoned theatre.

Another problematic development: after the move to Wylford, my mother supported my desire to stay on in school at Salisbury, where I had my cousins and friends, but Cyril insisted I be packed off to Winchester, my father's school, where my name had been set down since birth. All that being the case, I couldn't help but think that Winchester's primary attraction for my father was that it was a greater distance from Wylford than Salisbury or Wyndham Hall, and I would have to board.

My mother and little sister were as heartbroken as I when I left. With the exception of one or two inspiring form masters and the odd companion, I hated every minute as a Wyckehamist. I visited home on the major holidays and long vacation, and sulked at the mere thought of returning to school. For solace, I turned more and more to books.

The move to Wylford also ratcheted up the tensions in our family life in other ways. We all lived in the same house, of course, but my father was never at home. He was in other families' homes, or in Church, or attending some conference or symposium or diocesan council, or locked in his study working impossibly long hours on his next sermon.

Worse, Cyril's understanding of his prior allegiance to the Kingdom of Heaven seemed to require of him a strict hierarchy of interests that placed his family somewhere in the rear of his affections. Cyril insisted that his ordering of priorities was in fact quite spiritual, even selfless; it would be immoral, he insisted, for him to put the needs of his own family above that of his flock. My own feeling however, which has not changed over time, was that this "higher" reasoning served as salve for Cyril's conscience, since in the end he did what he desperately wanted to do anyway: pursue his interests as if he had no wife or family.

As for my mother, she did her best to perform her duties as a parson's wife, but Cyril was never satisfied, and he left no doubt in our minds that he believed that she was holding him back in his progress up the ecclesiastical ladder. But for Gina, her occasionally notorious bouts with alcohol and pills, and the unfortunate circumstances of her death, Cyril was certain he would have eventually made Archdeacon, or even bishop.

The climax: shortly after a Cornwall holiday, as I was readying myself for the Michaelmas term at Winchester, my mother and father quarreled violently. My mother packed herself and my sister Anne in her old Rover, apparently with the intention of staying with friends on the southern coast. Instead, high on alcohol and anti-depressants, she drove her little Rover into the sea on Michaelmas, the twenty-ninth of September. I was fourteen.

An aside about my father's subsequent career.

Unable to face the murmuring villagers of Wylford, Cyril resigned his living and returned to Cambridge. Upon receiving his doctorate three years later, Cyril taught at Winchester for five years before finally requesting another parochial assignment. My suspicion is that Cyril needed to prove that he was capable of making a go of pastoral work, now that he was "unencumbered"; but that may be unfair. At any rate, Cyril is now vicar of the poor parish of St. Aidan's-in-Spital, in the heart of the East-end London neighborhood once haunted by Jack the Ripper.

Where was I while Cyril was 'pulling himself together?' I was shipped off the day after the accident to live in Toronto with Cyril's sister Jane, whom I had never met, and whom Cyril himself hadn't seen in nearly twenty years — this, even though my uncle James warmly offered to take me into his home, which would have allowed me to remain among family at Salisbury and finish at Winchester. I heard through the family grapevine that assorted maternal aunts and uncles had likewise offered to take me in, but I suspect that Cyril didn't relish seeing me reared among my mother's people or religion. I can also only conclude that Cyril wanted me, the sole (and most bitter) reminder of his mockery of a married life, as far away as possible. For this purpose Canada served as well as Timbuktu.

Aunt Jane and her husband had a lovely home on the shores of Lake Ontario, which in Iroquois means "Shining Water." It was there that I first fell in love with the North American continent, particularly those mysterious inland seas known as the Great Lakes.

Deeply attracted as well to what I read about Native American cultures, my adolescent imagination was stimulated by one story in particular, about the famous Sioux chieftain Sitting Bull. Considering what happened to me later, the story may bear relating.

Before the battle of Little Bighorn, Sitting Bull, aware that a major confrontation with the U.S. Cavalry was in the offing, climbed a mountaintop in Montana to pray for a vision. He prayed to *Wakan Tanka*, The Great Mysterious, promising to offer up a sacrifice of his own blood if he were given a vision to guide him in the coming war. The prayer was answered, and Sitting Bull received the vision. Back at camp Sitting Bull, as good as his word, proceeded to dance the Sun Dance with his warriors, a self-immolatory ritual whose courageous but grisly choreography would have made a medieval flagellant faint dead away. Whatever the outcome of the long-term war, the immediate battle was won.

I admired all this tremendously, of course, and once, when Aunt Jane and Uncle John (unhappily childless) took me for a holiday to their cabin on a remote section of Lake Ontario, I attempted Sitting Bull's spiritual exercise myself. I climbed a bluff overlooking Lake Ontario and offered up various (and woefully minor) self-inflicted wounds to the Great Mysterious in hopes of receiving some life-explaining vision. Alas, my petty sacrifices were hardly up to those of a true spiritual warrior, and I never experienced the hoped-for vision. I did nod off a few times, however, and had some shiningly vivid dreams, always of battles of one sort or another. I always died in these dreams, I might add, but I died gloriously.

It was also on Lake Ontario that my uncle taught me to sail. We made a circle tour of the five lakes that first summer I was in Canada. By the time we returned to Toronto, I had fallen in love with sailing, and felt the lakes had become my one true home.

Lest this new life in Canada sound idyllic, I must quickly add that I was only "home" on holidays and the long vacation. At my father's insistence I was sent to a Canadian military school to board, "to be made a man."

It was far worse than Winchester. In prompt succession I was thrown out of the military academy in Toronto, another in Ottawa, and barely passed out of a third in far-off Calgary. My marks were always excellent, but my behavior was rebellious in the extreme.

The truth is, I hated the military schools with a passion to which I cannot do justice on paper. Upon graduation, and breaking the long-established Ireton tradition of attendance at Sandhurst or Cambridge, I returned to England and went up to "the Other Place," Oxford, where I read English literature. There, I fell completely and definitively in love with Shakespeare.

The next stanza in this, my swan-song to religion, is puzzling to relate. It is the story of a conversion. I don't pretend to understand it, and can barely describe it.

That I retained any attraction to the divine at all is, I suppose, a miracle of grace of sorts; but I often think a purely psychological explanation for my eventual conversion is ultimately more reasonable, and certainly more honest: i.e., that I took up God as a way of having some tenuous contact with my father; or that I took up God as the ultimate rebellion against my father, as the case may be, since the form of religion I finally stumbled into, much to my astonishment and my father's chagrin, was my mother's.

To begin, I tried to put my somewhat eccentric past behind me in a setting where eccentricity was often applauded. I felt entirely free of restraint at Oxford, never attended services, and consciously rejected everything my father had taught me in terms of religious practice and belief, not to mention sexual morality. However this rejection of my religion was a decision, or rather a series of decisions, made in conflict. The conflicts were occasionally debilitating to the point of extreme lethargy and depression, and alternated with periods of intensely purposeful activity. The ups and downs were unpredictable and frightening, and it never occurred to me that there might be a clinical explanation for the emotional ping-pongs. At the time I felt it was all simply my own blameworthy and Hamlet-like inability to "get on with it." On several occasions I skipped a term and cut off all contact with family and friends altogether by drifting to some remote corner of the British Isles where I remained, idling, for months at a stretch, and felt nowhere at home. As a result I became a bit of a term-trotter; it took me over four years to get through nine terms at Oxford, instead of the usual three.

The one form of catharsis which seemed to satisfy both my own personal needs and my father's rigid code was academic success. If Cyril didn't appreciate my choice of studies, at least he seemed a little proud of my achievements; perhaps a little envious as well, as he never took better than a second, even in his beloved History. Both prospects pleased me.

In sum, I became what the Americans describe as an "overachiever." A few well-meaning dons and my senior tutor advised me that I was pushing myself too hard, but I took my philosophy from *Coriolanus*: *one fire drives out another*. Truth was, I didn't mind the dizzying whirlpool of exhaustion and dissipation nearly so much as the roaring memories that rose like Leviathan from a dead-calm sea of inactivity.

I suppose it is impossible for anyone remotely engaged with religious issues to get through a term at Oxford without the figures of John Henry Newman and the Inklings breaking into one's consciousness. These great men's words echo from wall to courtyard wall there, and vibrate in the colours of the summer snapdragons. Yet they made not the slightest impact on me, that I am aware, in the realm of belief or praxis. As Newman himself once said, "It is not at all easy (humanly speaking) to wind up an Englishman to a dogmatic level." I knew some Catholics, for instance, who gathered in the so-called Newman Rooms, and an ecumenical literary group that met weekly in The Eagle and Child, the pub that hosted the Inklings, to discuss mythopoeic literature, but I did not join them. I did not care, in fact, to be associated with, let alone evangelized by believers of any stripe, even when their arts appealed to me.

My last term, the winter Hilary term in my peculiar stop-and-start case, I suffered a particularly rancorous break-up with a girlfriend, the humiliating details of which need not be recorded here. I had thrown myself into a student production of *Hamlet* in which I played the lead. Though the experience was grueling, the production was warmly received. A producer from the RSC actually came backstage after one performance to encourage me to try out for the company. I thanked him, but demurred, unable to put into words the gut-churning feelings I had been experiencing on stage, something well beyond stage fright.

The final performance was the most blistering of all. I stumbled back to my rooms in a complete brain fag, played out from too many projects, too much all-night swotting, too many visits to the local battle cruisers, and too much sex. Alone at my desk, my Oudsian roommate having gone into town for some post-performance carousing, I remember packing away my notes and papers. A thin sheet of manuscript poetry floated to the floor. When I bent over to pick it up, the floor began to spin wildly. My entire body tingled and vibrated, as if my skin was a porcupine's coat turned inside out. I collapsed on the floor, certain that I was dying. My mate discovered me early the next morning, curled up in a fetal position.

I was rushed to hospital where, so they tell me, I repeated the words over and over, "I want to go home, let me go home…" At some point a doctor asked me, "Where's home, Mr. Ireton?" And I replied, "In my mother's womb…in my mother's womb." For the first few days my physicians thought my mind had shattered in so many pieces they'd never collect them all.

I remained in hospital for some weeks. Schizophrenia was initially suspected, but was eventually ruled out in favor of a diagnosis of bi-polar disorder when my manic psychosis swung like a pendulum into a suicidal inertia, the details of which I no longer even remember. Fortunately, I rapidly began to respond to a combination of drugs, particularly Lithium and tri-cyclic anti-depressants.

My grandfather visited me several times in hospital, but my father, an hour's drive away, not once. Easter is the busiest season of the Church year, after all.

Thus I spent my Easter in Bedlam. After my release, I continued to see a Harley Street psychiatrist once a week, who kept a keen eye on my Lithium levels and gave me to believe that my breakdown had been a case of scrambled brain chemicals, probably induced by stress and exhaustion. He was even hopeful that I could eventually be weaned off the medication—a controversial position, I have come to understand. In any case, thank God this has proven true: I've been off the Lithium for almost two years now, without incident, in spite of more than my fair share of "stress," as the reader shall see.

Upon leaving hospital I decided, I don't know why, that I must go back to visit Wiltshire, the locus of my aboriginal calamity.

My uncle James and his family were in Cornwall at the time, visiting my grandfather, and I was invited to house-sit their home in St. Ann Street, Salisbury.

I day-tripped frequently to Wilton House. Designed by Inigo Jones and home to the Earls of Pembroke, Wilton House was the beautiful Arcadia of my childhood—a magic Prospero's isle of flowers and fruit orchards, singing birds, great cedars of Lebanon, stone bridges, and vining roses. Spenser was familiar with the place, and Sidney composed his *Arcadia* there. Tradition has it that Shakespeare himself brought his company to Wilton House to perform for the Earl of Pembroke.

It was a balmy spring. I sat for hours on the banks of the Wylie with books of Shakespeare in my lap. I visited my mother's and sister's graves at Salisbury, and I walked. The Cathedral Close held largely pleasant memories. Henry Fielding had lived at Number 14, next to St. Ann's Gate, and Trollope's *Barchester Towers* was modeled after the city and its great cathedral. I frequented the Cathedral library and museum, ogled their copy of Caxton's edition of *The Golden Legend*, and re-acquainted myself with the rooms of the Regimental museum. Above all, I haunted the echoing vastness of the magnificent Gothic cathedral itself, whose image still towers over my imagination like a great and mighty fortress, at once dreadful and inviting.

I made a few excursions into the surrounding countryside, visiting famous places Mother had taken us as children. I especially loved the numerous chalk carvings that decorate the hillsides of Wiltshire and Oxfordshire, my favorite being the famous Uffington White Horse. Many believe this In huge figure, cut into a hill in Oxfordshire, to be a depiction of the pagan horse-goddess, *Epona*, but my mother insisted it was the dragon slain by St. George on nearby Dragon Hill. There's a large bald spot on Dragon Hill where no grass will grow, and Mother, who fiercely believed all such folk tales, said it was where the blood of the dragon had fallen from St. George's lance, poisoning the soil forever.

In the end, however, I couldn't bring myself to go to Wylford, my father's parish. A fissure had opened in my soul, and a visit to Wylford, I feared, would finish the bisection. I didn't know which would be the more dreadful possibility in such a pried-open state: that some essence of my self might leak out, or that some alien thing would enter through the aperture.

The evening of April 23rd, Shakespeare's traditional birthday and death-day, I was rambling near the Close. I heard the Cathedral organ opening the Evensong service, but walked steadfastly by. It began to rain. I kept walking until I found myself in front of the unimposing stone facade of a tiny Catholic Church. I was drawn inside more by a desire to get out of the rain than anything else; but upon entering, I saw that there was no vestibule, really, and that I would have to find a spot in the pews or make a scene. I shuffled into the back pew, determined to suffer through the service until I warmed up.

I remember the liturgy as rather plain — not as aesthetically pleasing, all in all, as an Anglican service, even one of my father's. The music was dull and the homily rambling, but I remember one of the readings with astonishing clarity, from *Revelations*:

> And he that sat upon the throne said, Behold! I make all things new. And he said to me, Write: For these words are true and faithful. And he said unto me, It is done. I am Alpha and Omega, the beginning and the end. I will give unto him that is athirst of the fountain of the water of life freely. He that overcometh shall inherit all things; and I will be his God, and he shall be my son...

...and he shall be my son. That evening, sitting in the creaky, saddle-worn pew of this dreary little church, a profound stillness enveloped me. It was an interior silence that seemed to emanate from within, more than without, but which was pierced from time to time by the sound of those familiar old words from *Revelations*.

All at once the congregation in front of me seemed to fade into a shining mist. A young Woman appeared before me. Dressed in a golden robe and turquoise mantle, she was barely more than a girl, but magnificent and beautiful and strange and simple, all at once. Her body vibrated with light.

I was, I suddenly realized, no longer huddled in a damp macintosh in a prosaic Wiltshire church, but lying on the white strand of a powder blue sea. I was naked, my skin bruised and broken as if from many battles, and layered with a smear of dried blood and foul-smelling filth. Notwithstanding my disgusting condition, the beautiful Woman took me by the hand and led me to the edge of the blue sea. Ashamed of my stinking self, I leaped into the water, which was surprisingly warm, eager to wash or at least hide myself. But the Woman insisted on bathing me herself and tending to my wounds as if I were her only son.

When I stepped back up on the strand I was astounded to see that my bodily wounds had been completely healed, though a good deal of ugly scarring remained. Smiling now, laughing even, the Woman dressed me with great solemnity in a white tunic that had a red cross emblazoned on the chest. Then, with a slow wave of one graceful arm, she led me away from the strand and up a nearby hillock. There, fixed on a rough and rocky base that might have been the sea-cooled vomit of some underwater volcano, rose a fantastic Tower carved of black obsidian.

Following the Woman up dark glassy steps, I entered the obsidian Tower through a low archway, so low I had to stoop. We climbed a narrow staircase that wound up and around inside, its walls carved in a confusing motley of patterns and symbols seemingly borrowed from a thousand cultures and ages of men. At the top, open to the air by means of unpaned, diamond-shaped windows, was a platform on which was mounted a fabulous altar chiseled from the trunk of an ancient cedar. A chalice, carved of myrtlewood in an elaborate knot-and-key pattern, whether Celtic or Middle-Eastern or Meso-American or Anglo-Saxon, I could not tell, sat atop the altar and was filled to the rim with what could have been blood, but which I assumed, I don't know why, was consecrated wine. Directly behind the chalice, thrust into the altar blade-first, was a star-bright sword with a luminous disc of silver gleaming at the crosspiece, like a full moon rising over the waters. It was some seconds before I realized it was a Host in a sword-shaped monstrance, shining forth in rainbow rays of divine power. A flock of perhaps a half dozen brown-winged birds with white breasts and black bands around their throats flew merrily in and out the windows and around the altar, singing with an excited, high-pitched *kee-kee-kee,* and finally gathering in a hush on one of the rafters above.

"*Emmanuel!*" the Woman cried out in an exultant voice. "*Verbum Dei, qui tollit peccata mundi!*" She bowed low before the Body and Blood, and I did the same.

Prostrate on the stone floor beside her, a great light began to radiate from the Body and Blood, a light that pierced my troubled heart with a killing heat. Gasping in pain, one hand over my burning heart, I looked up to see that the Host at the sword's crosspiece was growing brighter and brighter, until it resembled no longer the moon but a blazing sun. The resplendent light did not appear to trouble the Woman, however. Her body seemed at once to absorb and reflect it, making her grow in stature and power.

The Woman pointed at the altar and said in a resounding voice, "Take the sword. It is for you."

"And the chalice?" I said rather stupidly, pushing myself to my knees but as yet unable to stand. I pointed at the myrtlewood cup, once again fascinated by the hypnotic patterns of its peculiar knotwork.

"The Grail is for your son," the Woman replied, "and your son's sons." Without further explanation, she stretched out her hand towards the altar and with a sweep of her arm pulled the sword from its cedarwood sheath. The sound of it burst against my ears like a crack of lightning. Then she brandished the sword over my head in such a mighty pose of angelic power that for a moment I believed she was going to cleave me in two with it, as we both knew I well deserved; but instead she merely lowered the blade to touch me gently on each shoulder. Then with her free hand she slapped me hard across the cheek. The pain in my heart vanished on the instant, and the radiant light returned quietly to its Source.

Dumbfounded, I realized that I had just been dubbed a knight. Far from reveling in this unexpected honor, however, I was now more ashamed than ever, certain that some terrible mistake had been made. Surely, I thought, this magnificent being had chosen the wrong man for whatever service was presently required; but the Woman, who had by this time returned to her former diminutive proportions, ignored my protestations of unworthiness and, resting the palm of her right hand over my heart, extended the sword to me with her other hand, hilt first.

The great Sword was so heavy I could barely lift it. When I finally got it firmly in hand, the Woman raised her face to the cerulean sky beyond the diamond-shaped windows, as if making an announcement to Heaven, and cried out, "*Ex mille electus miles!* One knight chosen out of a thousand!" The flock of birds above us broke again into rapturous song.

Finally, the Woman drew me to the window and pointed arrow-straight towards the murmuring blue sea below.

Within moments, the lazy waters beyond the strand began to churn and boil, as from some sub-surface disturbance; but my attention was quickly drawn to a new and even stranger vision: at the foot of the Tower now lay three bodies, three men, bloodless and death-pale, one set apart and two aligned side by side with the boots of one even with the head of the other.

The first man was middle aged with thinning hair, but tough and sinewy, like a veteran of many campaigns. In a way, I would have said he was quite ordinary looking, except that he was wearing sandals and a blood-red Roman toga. One of the Roman's arms covered his face, whether in shame or fear or as a remedy against some fierce sunlight, long since faded, I couldn't say.

The other two men were younger than the Roman, perhaps in their late thirties. Both were, if differently, attired in solemn black. The first man was blond, blonder than myself, and dressed in an SS uniform with the familiar lightning-bolt insignia on his collar. The second man, slight of build with thinning, mousy brown hair, was wearing a priest's cassock. The Nazi's right arm was stretched out, his index finger pointing towards the boiling sea, while the priest's left arm was stretched out in the opposite direction, his index finger pointing towards a distant hillock lit by the setting sun in shades of gold and green.

A fourth man stood on the distant hillock, his figure telescoping in my sight as if I were observing him through invisible binoculars. Much younger than the other three men, he was bright-faced and sturdy, with dark, unruly hair and laughing eyes. The charming young man—I don't hesitate to say I was immediately drawn to him, and would have wished to make his acquaintance—was wearing a rather medieval-looking costume consisting of baggy brown trousers and an open-necked white shirt that laced up the front, such as some I've seen at Renaissance Faires. He was standing in front of a picturesque cottage of the familiar Cotswold variety, but with a hobbit-round door framed by wisteria.

And then I saw the volcano. It was an immense humpbacked, snow-capped peak of vast bulk, larger than any mountain I had ever seen. It smoked ominously behind the hillock, and I knew with sudden, silent certainty, I know not how, that the great hulk of molten energy was about to erupt, about to bury us—hillock, cottage, Tower, everything—in a sea of scorching ash.

"Who are these men," I said to my Lady in an anxious voice, "and what do they have to do with me?" That they had something important to do with me I knew without knowing how I knew.

"Do not trouble yourself with Past and Future," the Woman answered, and the little flock of black-striped birds *kee-keed* above us, as if in agreement. "Your task is the Present, and the Present is upon you. I say, wake up!"

Following the direction of my Lady's still-pointing arm, I saw that the boiling waters below us were turning to blood in a spreading wave, like wine blotted up by a tablecloth. An incredible stench rose from the bloody sea and began to fill the air around us, as if all the rotting graves of the earth had been emptied into the restless waters. Finally a monstrous dragon rose from the boiling, bloody sea, a great metal beast that thrashed about, cursing and screeching in a vicious, inhuman tongue. The thing had blazing green eyes and rusty iron scales that sprouted slime, like feathers, all along its misshapen body. Its scaly tail, twice the length of its huge body, coiled and uncoiled and slashed at the sea like a scythe, sending gigantic red waves scrolling ashore that threatened to swallow up the beach and the Tower altogether.

The flock of birds fell one by one from their lofty perches, as if stunned by an invisible blow. Dropping to the Tower platform, they began an almost dance-like display: they hopped around on one leg and thrust out broken-looking wings, dragging them on the floor behind them, *kee-kee*-ing furiously as they did so. Knight though I was, at least in name, I too fell quaking to my belly, dropping the sword the Woman had given me. When I finally summoned the courage to look up again, I saw that the dragon had risen high into the darkening sky beyond the window and was licking its gory chops with an asp-like tongue that, like its tail, uncoiled and uncoiled until it uncoiled a second and smaller but much more hideous dragon's head. The vicious little thing fixed its beady green eyes on the Woman.

Turning to follow its gaze, I saw my beautiful Lady gesture with a quivering hand at the great sword, now abandoned on the Tower floor. "If you love," she said in a small voice as shaky as her hand, "you must embrace the Sword. With it you must cut off the dragon's little head. If not, you will watch it consume all that you love."

There was little doubt in my mind in that moment what or rather who it was that I loved, but though I had now been told what I was to do with the sword, I still could not fathom why I, of all men, had been the one chosen to do it. Even so and terrified as I was, I became suddenly so incensed by the foul creature's design that without another thought for my own safety I found my feet at last, and my courage. Taking up the sword again with both hands, I lifted my head to the sky and gave a shout, thinking to attract the dragon's attention away from my Lady.

Startled by the noise, the hobbling birds at my Lady's feet scattered in all directions as at a gunshot. As for the great beast, it seemed startled as well. It hovered in the air, its mighty wings creaking and flapping like the arms of a windmill, its monstrous form blocking out the setting sun. Turning its vile gaze at last on me, who had thus far escaped its notice, the little dragon head, then the larger, seemed amused as well as surprised by my no doubt pitiful challenge. I could swear it—they?— sort of laughed; but a moment later it drew itself up in new preparation to strike.

I lifted the star-bright sword over my head as the foul and fearsome dragon hurled itself towards me, its rapacious jaws stretched wide, its scaly wings beating the air like a hurricane.

The vision ended precisely there, as unexpectedly as it had begun.

––––––––––

Afterwards, I don't know for how long, I sat huddled in the back pew of the little Salisbury church in a stupor of exhaustion, fear, and enchantment. Of course as long as the vision lasted, the whole episode, albeit both wonderful and terrifying, made some sort of perfect "sense" to me—but so goes madness, I'm told.

I was eventually awakened to the present by a tap on the shoulder. I looked up to see that the church was now empty, but for myself and the elderly priest, the one who had said Mass, who had come to the back of the church to see if I was all right. There might have been nothing extraordinary in any of this were it not for the brown-winged bird with the black bands around its throat that perched on the old priest's right shoulder. The priest gave no indication, then or later, that he was aware of the bird, which *kee-kee-keed* from time to time in a sweet, almost melancholy little tune; but whatever the case, the priest, who introduced himself as Fr. Lucian Delmar proceeded to ask me, as clergymen are wont to do I suppose, if he could be of any service.

Impervious in that moment to any concerns that I was about to give evidence of mental instability, I pointed feebly at the altar, then at the bird on the priest's shoulder, and blurted out my fantastic tale in half-formed words, which concluded with the announcement, "Look, here, Reverend—you're Roman, aren't you?—well, I don't give a damn about theology or who the hell was right or wrong in 1534, but I must belong to this church. On the spot."

The mystified old priest didn't toss me out on my ear as one might expect, or ring the constable. He didn't even look concerned when I informed him, as it seemed my duty to do, that he had a bird perched on his shoulder. Instead, he took me into his rectory, bird and all, and fed me hot cocoa and stale biscuits from a tin while he listened to my extraordinary story from start to finish. Then he bid me rest—I must have looked a sight—while he went into his library to look up some references to "this sort of thing," as he put it.

Returning some time later—I dozed off—the old priest, with the bird still piping on his shoulder, informed me that there were "precedents" in the lives of sundry saints and mystics for experiences such as mine, though he was in no position to judge with any assurance whether mine was a purely spiritual manifestation, a purely psychological one, or some quirky fusion of the two. His best guess, he told me frankly, was the latter—that my vision had been a true spark of the Divine alighting on my troubled soul, which, humanly limited as it was, had translated the movement of the Spirit into literary and religious imagery with which I was familiar.

Finally Fr. Delmar asked me if I remembered what day it was.

"Shakespeare's birthday," I replied distractedly. At the time it was all I remembered.

"It's also St. George's Day. The feast of the knight who slew the dragon."

I had completely forgot. "But that's a myth!" I exclaimed.

"Yes, well, so are 'visions.'"

With one last melancholy *kee*, the black-striped bird finally took flight out the kitchen window, never to return.

In the days immediately following the vision, or whatever one wishes to call it, I was burdened with an acute form of sensitivity such as I have never experienced, before or since, even in the thrall of nervous meltdown. It was as if I were suddenly unequipped, physically, mentally, or emotionally, to deal with the heavy *thing*ness of the world around me—the world of food and drink, of buying and selling, of nonsense and noise. I was extremely sensitive to lights and smells and strong colours. A sudden sound or movement, however slight, would send a thrill of pain through my nervous system.

I remember, for example, on an errand to the market for Fr. Delmar, feeling oppressed by the transitory materiality of this old, familiar world of clay and rot, as if I were seeing, like a film running double-time, the ineluctable future disintegration of every object I observed. Green trees, lush with springtime leaves, appeared to me already winter-bare and sepulchral, as if stripped by some new Ice Age. Ripe fruit piled in baskets in the marketplace smelled of next month's decay. Glittering trinkets in the shop windows—applianc-es, jewelry, silverware—turned to rust, then ashes, before my mind's eye. Human beings alone, passing to and fro on the sleepy streets of Salisbury, seemed vibrant and fresh and alive, and tremendously mysterious to me.

To boot, though my father had taught me to know shame at the earliest possible age, I experienced now an unprecedented weight of disgust at the memory of the rotting life I had led up to that time, particularly at Oxford. Discrete memories of this or that infidelity or petty meanness actually made my heart ache, as if I were struggling uphill against a Sisyphean burden.

When my uncle James and his family returned to their St. Ann Street home a week or so later, I, unable for the nonce to bear the busy sounds and activi-ties of a boisterous family, moved into a small guest room in Fr. Delmar's rectory. I helped him and his housekeeper with household chores, tended the garden, and spent hours sitting silently in the drab parish church. I rested, walked, and took instruction from Fr. Delmar. I dutifully visited my London psychiatrist once a week, on Father's insistence, but couldn't bring myself to discuss the vision with him, fearing that he would receive the whole business as new evidence of psychosis.

Finally, after a few weeks, the residual sense-related effects of my brush with the Numinous began to dissipate, but my conviction that I had experi-enced the Divine only strengthened.

For his part, Fr. Delmar also came to the conclusion that I was neither mad nor mad in craft, but he adamantly refused to attempt an interpretation of my particular visitation. It wasn't that he didn't believe my experience to be real, he told me, on the contrary; it was just that he had no expertise in mystical theology and believed himself unfit to meddle in such lofty and potentially dangerous matters. Besides, real or not, Fr. Delmar felt I'd do well to put the thing behind me, certain as he was that God and my life experi-ence would make the deeper meanings clear to me, sooner or later, and jolly well without his meddling. To tell the truth, I got the distinct impression that Father thought the whole business of little importance one way or the other, as long as the vision, or whatever it was, brought me back to God and induced me to respond to the more "daily" forms of divine grace, available to all Christians, as the vision was indeed inspiring me to do.

Fr. Delmar was a rather traditional priest and a rigorous catechist, but he was oddly, to my mind, reluctant to encourage my conversion to his faith. He frequently quoted Newman about the need to "count the cost." For my own part, I accepted without demur anything he taught me about Catholic dogma or practice, so certain was I of the reality of my experience, and that its occurrence in this particular church imparted the implicit command for me to join that communion under Fr. Delmar's tutelage. Father insisted, however, despite my "grass is greener new-convert enthusiasm," as he bluntly put it, that Catholics, even graced as they were with the fullness of the sacraments, could be just as silly and vexing a bunch as those I was leaving behind.

Oh how prophetic the dear old man soon proved to be. But once again I am getting ahead of myself.

In time, I told Father the entire story of my life. After a general confession (a bitterly difficult affair for my Protestant soul), he received me into the Catholic Church in June, on the Feast of the Sacred Heart.

Fr. Delmar also introduced me to the rudiments of a prayer life and a spirituality of personal entrustment to Christ through Mary. He believed that devotion to the Virgin, with whom, by way of my peculiar vision, I had fallen unutterably in love, would help me with my difficulties with chastity, although in the first flush of moral disgust after the vision I thought I was cured of that temptation forever. (I discovered, in due course, that I was not.) Taking inspiration from the vision, Fr. Delmar went so far as to encourage me to think of myself as a Knight in Our Lady's service, like St. Edmund of Canterbury, or St. George, or Galahad in the Arthurian romances. To my embarrassment, I soon came to understand that most of my contemporaries, Protestant and Catholic alike, tend to view this remnant of chivalry as a quaint and obsolescent form of spirituality. The occasionally caustic humor expressed at my expense over this subject cut me sharply, and I learned to hold my tongue.

———————

I was also facing the usual decisions of anyone my age about my future. I intended to study literature further, but I also felt very drawn to travel and the sea. Moreover, I was also almost superstitiously disturbed by the possible vocational implications of my vision, as if the giving of the sword implied that God intended me to enter the military, as my father had always wished.

"Yours may be a rather different sort of knighthood," Fr. Delmar said to me at last, "not to mention a different sort of dragon."

Sadly, Fr. Delmar died shortly after I left Salisbury. I can't help but wonder, as the last of his "spiritual" children, if I didn't wear the poor old man out. Especially now, as my foray into the realm of the Numinous has taken such a nightmarish turn, I have come to the inconclusive conclusion that I haven't the slightest idea what the whole thing was about.

———————

I left Salisbury in August and headed for the coast—many coasts in fact. After two years working aboard assorted fishing boats, just to be at sea, I decided it was time to do something more with my life; something to do with my great love for Shakespeare, someplace near water.

I eventually turned up in Milwaukee to pursue a doctorate in Shakespeare Studies at the newly founded Heisler Institute for the Study of Western

Civilization. I understand that many students choose the Heisler Institute for their graduate work because of its perceived "conservative" bent. A few of us, however, have chosen it in spite of that reputation, for the sole purpose of studying with Fr. Arthur Bricusse, a world-renowned Shakespeare scholar who is also an Oratorian priest graced with a deep humanity.

At the time of my arrival in Milwaukee, though I had been a practicing Catholic for over two years, I felt I still had not come to satisfactory terms with the meaning of my conversion experience, much less my problematic childhood. As I look back on those early days, I recognize now how fragile I was. I seemed to function in a sort of spiritual Limbo — no longer suffering and in pain, perhaps, but nonetheless deprived of the vision of God's face. For some reason, the beautiful Woman of my conversion experience had not completed her work in me. I wish I could be more specific, but the man blind from birth cannot describe what he has never seen. In truth, I kept waiting for something *else* to happen, something even more extraordinary, which would consummate the vision. What happened instead served to deconstruct it.

———————————

I sought spiritual counsel from Fr. Bricusse, who directed me to Mr. Lionel Krato, the inadvertent founder of a sort of fraternity for Catholic university students situated near the Milwaukee campus of the University of Wisconsin.

This is what I knew then about Lionel Krato: he was a widower in his late forties, had no children, and was a professor in the Department of Education at UWM. With a heart as wide as his girth, I have never met a finer, kinder gentleman in my life. When anyone says the word "saint" in my hearing, I think instantly of Lionel. To know Lionel and his brother Peter's family history is at once to understand everything, and nothing, but I will set it forth here, as Lionel told it to me, for what it may be worth.

Lionel and his younger brother Peter were raised on the south side of Chicago in a large family of Greek Uniate descent who, lacking a Uniate parish in their predominantly Italian neighborhood, went over to the Roman Rite. Though Mr. and Mrs. Krato had little in common, they did share a passion for the bottle, and Lionel and his siblings were the victims of alcohol-induced abuse by both parents. The abuse took both verbal and physical forms and, from an isolated comment of Lionel's about one of his sisters, perhaps sexual as well.

Interestingly, though his father's erratic but brutal discipline landed Lionel in the neighborhood Emergency Room on several occasions, Lionel always thought that his younger brother Peter had the worst of it, at least among the Krato boys. Mr. Krato, Lionel said, always viewed his middle son, Peter, as the boy-child most like himself. He therefore bestowed on Peter the sort of pressurized attention that was not to be squandered on anyone save the perceived heir to the throne. In turn, Peter was the child who accepted his father's personal fictions with the fewest reservations.

A talented entrepreneur, Mr. Krato successfully juggled a number of business ventures, both legitimate and felonious, most notably the Krato Advertising Agency. He also owned a locally notorious Mediterranean restaurant, "Krato's Palace," which catered then as now to the members of the small but deadly Calabresi mob, a crime family of originally Calabrian origin that ran their Chicago neighborhood like a banana republic. Filippo Calabresi, the patriarch of this infamous little dynasty, even became a close friend of Mr. Krato's, if one may speak of "friendship" among gangsters. Calabresi bankrolled Mr. Krato's many business ventures, with much profit to both, and Peter and his brothers have maintained the Calabresi connection to this day, especially by handling advertising for Calabresi's legitimate business operations; but Lionel, realizing that the better part of valor might be to go where he wouldn't be tempted, left Chicago after receiving his doctorate in Education from Loyola. He eventually took the teaching position in Milwaukee which he held until his death.

It would be difficult to imagine brothers more unalike than Lionel and Peter Krato. Peter was precisely the sort of man one would expect to emerge from a radically disturbed home: sour, angry to his marrow, and fluent in the language of coercion. He has, since his own self-described "conversion," become a whirling dervish of evangelical activity, deflecting his inner furies centrifugally, as it were, and dousing his darker passions with bucketfuls of holy water. He is also, paradoxically perhaps, the most colorless and prosaic individual I have ever met. How he has managed to exert such a level of influence over the young men of SANA I cannot explain, though I shall have to try.

A born teacher, Lionel took the kind of personal interest in his students that later made him the victim of his brother's most malicious slander. Essentially a Christian Humanist (or "Personalist" as he described himself), Lionel viewed education as a lifelong commitment to broadening and refining every capacity that was authentically human. He observed, however, that many university students could never get past their own painful formative experiences to open themselves to the benefits of learning. In his view, the West's *fin-de-siècle* epidemic of drug-taking, promiscuity, and the compulsive pursuit of entertainment, wealth, and power were symptomatic of a fundamental lack of affirming love. Young people, Lionel often said, did not view themselves as unrepeatable gifts of God's love, worthy of respect and dignity, because no significant adult had bothered to view them in such a manner.

Immaculata House, as Lionel named the place, was founded four years before I arrived in Milwaukee, when Lionel decided to take a new kind of personal initiative in the broken lives of two of his students: one had been abusing drugs and the other was struggling with deep, suicidal depression. Lionel encouraged these two young men to seek professional help as needed, but he also saw that there were two things which the professionals could not provide, but which he might: faith and affirming love from a stronger, more mature man—something which most of us who eventually turned up on his doorstep lacked to one degree or another.

After consultation with the Oratorians, Lionel invited these two students to take rooms in his home while they attended UWM. Other students soon asked to join them, from Marquette and MATC as well as the fledgling Heisler Institute. Lionel eventually sold his comfortable home on Prospect Hill to purchase an older three-story monstrosity in one of the run-down neighborhoods between the Oratory and UWM.

By the time I walked through the front door at Immaculata House—the name came from the title given to the Virgin by St. Maximilian Kolbe, a martyr of Auschwitz—there were already eleven men living there, two to a room. The way of life was loosely based on Newman's Oratorian principles, originally conceived as a cross between the spirituality of St. Philip Neri and the fraternal camaraderie of an Oxford college.

Lionel codified as little as possible, believing as he did that "over-organization" could only engender alienation and anonymous conformity—the prevailing diseases of our time. The need for love and respect, he believed, could only be filled through human relationship. "We're all connected, you know, in the communion of saints and sinners," was Lionel's favorite explanation for this way of life. "God is a God of human mediations."

Lionel also encouraged all of us at Immaculata House to spend time with one another, to make friends, and to share whatever talents we possessed. Consequently, I developed the first close friendship of my life with Richard Krato, Lionel's nephew, who arrived shortly after I did and was assigned to room with me. We hit it off first thing when he made an appreciative comment about the poster that hung above my bed, a reproduction of the Morris-Rossetti stained glass window of St. George and the Dragon. In turn, Richard taped a map of Middle Earth, a favorite literary haunt of my own childhood, to the wall on his side of the room. We quickly became inseparable. I look back now on these warm times as on a dream, what followed seems so inexplicable.

Whatever was to follow, I know at the time that I felt that Richard *knew* me, knew who I was in the deepest sense, as few friends or even lovers do. For one thing, Richard and I seemed to share some innate form of emotional pessimism about love relationships, though perhaps from opposite ends of the spectrum. Though I had given plenty of evidence of an intense desire for the opposite sex, I, for instance, feared I would never be any good at monogamy. Richard, however, convinced that he had only gotten involved in intimate relationships because his peers expected it of him, had become a determined celibate after discovering that he had no constitutional attraction to conjugal life. I have, in fact, heard the notion bandied about the Institute that Richard's lack of interest in women is implicit evidence of homosexual inclinations; but after living with him in the closest of quarters for almost two years, I came to think this an incredibly simplistic explanation, driven more by contemporary social myth, as if every man were equally driven by libido. There were times, frankly, that I envied Richard his detachment.

Richard and I also shared the experience of a hostile relationship with our fathers. At the time we first met, Richard and his father Peter were, to put it mildly, not on speaking terms. In a story much reminiscent of my own, Richard told me that he had only known his father as the brute choleric stranger who came home from time to time, inflicted whatever paternal discipline was deemed necessary for the occasion, and gave his only son one-minute pep talks on the Gospel of Success.

At first I thought Richard was embroidering his father's faults with predictable filial exaggeration; but when Peter Krato's marriage finally hit the skids and he began to pay his son more frequent visits at Immaculata House, I quickly saw the acuity of Richard's descriptions.

From the beginning, Peter had difficulty taking part in any activity or conversation not centered around his own affairs. He would make grand entrances through the front door of Immaculata House every month or so, flourishing monetary booty from Krato Advertising like Cortes returning to the Spanish Court with the pillaged treasures of Montezuma. It was at this point that, punning his own name, which is derived from the Greek word for "power," Richard began referring to his father's periodic visits to the House as *kratophanies*, epiphanies of power.

Peter's only other association with Immaculata House during this early period was to keep the books for his brother Lionel, who, by his own admission was impatient and inept at financial matters. According to Richard, Peter regarded Lionel's "home for wayward boys," as he called it, as a phenomenal waste of energy and time. For his own part, Peter would have preferred to devote his abundant energies to more "pro-active" political organizations, had he not believed that he could eventually turn the House and his brother Lionel to some better use.

About sixteen months into my tenure there, Peter's relationship to the House, and mine to Richard, underwent a sea change. It began one afternoon just before Christmas when Peter came calling to inform his son that his estranged wife, Richard's mother, had been granted an annulment from the Archdiocese of Chicago. Worse, Mrs. Krato was already planning to remarry. Given what I knew about the Kratos' morbid relationship—they had been living separate lives for over a decade—I was astonished by Richard's reaction. He was not only surprised, he was devastated. He suddenly felt as if his mother, whose side he had heretofore always taken in the Kratos' domestic disputes, had, in effect, and with the blessing of a corrupted Church, declared him a bastard. Almost overnight, Richard's sympathies were transferred to his father, and a strong bond of mutual grievance was forged between father and son that began to exclude everyone, even me.

In short order Peter's monthly visits became almost daily ones. Finally, Lionel felt compelled to invite Peter to live with us in Immaculata House, thinking that the fellowship there would "warm" him. After all, Lionel told me, Peter was as much a product of dysfunctional upbringing as the rest of us.

We had a weekly discussion group at the House, which Richard had dubbed "the Areopagus" after the club formed at Wilton House around Sidney and Spenser with the intention of revitalizing English literature. In our own less lofty forum we discussed House matters, current events, and any other subject that spurred the general interest. From time to time we would read works of literature together, from Flannery O'Connor to St. John of the Cross.

In the beginning, Peter, who had neither knowledge of nor appreciation for literature, sat through these gatherings in testy silence. But after several months, Peter developed a sudden interest in the Areopagus, and commented to Lionel that, for an allegedly religious house, it was too bad we weren't using the group time more "profitably." Peter went on to suggest that the meeting be divided in twain: one a House meeting with a practical agenda and the other a discussion group with a keener focus on what he termed "spiritual formation." Delighted that his brother was finally taking some interest in communal affairs, Lionel agreed to give it a go, and even asked Peter to "provide a little direction" in the discussions.

What Peter did was direct the Areopagus into a discussion of what came to be called "the book of the month." Residents were initially invited to take turns in choosing the book to be read, but Peter, I soon learned, had a way of influencing the choices of a majority of the residents towards his own tastes. Peter' tastes, by the way, were far from literary—he regarded literature as fanciful and impractical—but of the genre which most people call "self-help" or "pop-psychology." But whichever book was read in the Areopagus, Peter, taking the helm, approached it with a distinctive, eccentric, and rapidly all-encompassing vision.

Peter is a firm believer in that uniquely American form of popular business religion known as "the power of positive thinking." I don't suppose any native-born citizen of the United States can comprehend how peculiar this little footnote of American culture appears to a foreigner; only a comic genius like Chaplin could do justice to this Babbitt spirituality; but to Peter this was what America was all about. *"You become what you think you are!"* Peter repeated incessantly in the Areopagus. *"Nothing succeeds like success! The best defense is a good offense! You become what you think you are!"*

Peter's mind is neither rich nor deep. The color of his personality tends to a muddy gray, and his voice resembles a southside Chicago police siren. Peter is, however, forceful. He is more than capable of wearing down an opponent in an argument by sheer vehemence of temperament. When he gets hold of an idea, and the more simplistic the idea the better, he's like a dog with a bone; there's no yanking the conversation out of his teeth until the subject is safely chewed and interred. Even in the most casual exchange Peter takes an interlocutor's comments, not as meat for consideration, but as prey to be wrestled out of an opponent's grasp.

Given his temperament, it was not surprising that a few of the residents who attended the Areopagus began to complain to Lionel of Peter's influence, even hegemony. Mitch Showalter actually went to Lionel in private to warn him that he believed Peter had it in mind "to take over the whole damned place." But Lionel, one of those great innocents who can't imagine subterfuge in another person, thought Mitch's fears were overwrought. I'm struck now by Mitch's perceptiveness, as well as puzzled that he was unable to hang on to his own indignation when the event came to pass precisely as he prophesied.

I was too absorbed in my studies to notice what was happening, but from a number of the younger members there was a surprisingly positive response to the new order: Peter, they enthused, was inspiring them to "make something of themselves." Too late did the rest of us discover how critical these meetings of the Areopagus were in the development of ideas that later transformed our casual little fraternity into a secret society.

Testimony had by this time spread in the Church about Lionel Krato's work with college students, and he was being called upon with increasing frequency to speak to campus groups around the country. Lionel was also a respected educator and author in the secular world, and drawing on both these capacities, he was asked to participate in a major international conference in Rome on the subject of the spiritual care of Catholic youth in secular universities.

Before Lionel left, Peter and Richard took advantage of Lionel's absorption in travel and conference preparations to concoct a revolution based on a research paper Richard had written on the Knights Templar.

The Order of the Poor Knights of Christ, later known as the Knights Templar after their headquarters in Solomon's Temple in Jerusalem, was founded in 1119 by Hugh de Payens after the First Crusade. A military order, the Knights wore a white mantle with a large red cross emblazoned on the back, and took religious vows. It was the springtime of chivalry, and the Templars' purpose, at least in the beginning, seemed a noble one in a troubled time: to protect Christian pilgrims making their way to the holy city of Jerusalem. Quickly becoming more successful than they ever dreamed, the Templars eventually moved back into Europe and amassed such wealth and influence that kings and popes felt threatened by their power. Indeed, it would not be going too far afield to say that the Poor Knights of Christ became the bankers of Christendom. Many also contend that they devolved into a sort of *contre-église*, a diabolic secret society whose influence reaches into the present in a spectacular diversity of forms, from the Freemasons and the Priory of Sion to the Ku Klux Klan. Whatever the case, the masters of the order were convicted of Satanism in 1307, and the order was suppressed in 1312.

Together, Peter and Richard Krato pored over every available document, reliable or otherwise, relating to the Templars. The fruit of their devoted research was a self-styled *Program for an American Crusade*, which they presented before the assembled members of the House in the last meeting of the Areopagus before Lionel's departure for Rome. As might be expected, however, in adapting the Templars' spirituality to the situation at Immaculata

House, Peter and Richard rigorously applied the aspects of the Templar Order that suited them, and vigorously ignored any cautionary elements to be drawn from the order's controversial history. I enclose a copy of the information Peter and Richard passed out that evening, but I paraphrase their Program here in brief:

> 1. A two-week guided "formation retreat" (or "boot camp," as it came to be called) for all new recruits or "aspirants" at Immaculata House.

> 2. An elaborate business plan for organizational expansion by means of modern methods of management and fundraising. (What Peter described as "taking the best of American culture to serve the Church.") The goal was a "franchise" network of identically operated and centrally-controlled subsets spreading across the college and university campuses of the nation, hybridizing the unity of purpose of a military battalion with the financial sophistication and "product familiarity" of a fast-food chain.

> 3. Charismatic leadership supported by the absolute loyalty of a small but disciplined "Gideon's Army" formed in military-style obedience.

> 4. The development of Spiritual Power through the *Four Pillars of Spiritual Power Program*, which included the practice of Prayer, Poverty, Persistence, and the counsels of Perfection.

Without prior consultation with Lionel, Richard and Peter unveiled their Program before the assembled Areopagus, their pale faces shining as if they had just descended from Sinai with the stone tablets of the Law. Peter was whipping out his flow charts when Lionel arrived, several minutes late and obviously distracted.

Talking without pause like a fringe-party orator in Hyde Park, Peter proceeded to announce to the assembly that God was calling Lionel Krato and the young men of Immaculata House to be the founding members of a well-organized and disciplined army of young apostles that would be to the third millennium what the Knights Templar had been to the Crusades. Moreover, because of America's unique position of leadership in the world (so went Peter's reasoning) the conversion of America's youth would inevitably lead to the conversion of America itself; then the world at large. This in turn would bring about the eventual downfall of all godless regimes, finally ushering in the Reign of the Immaculate Heart. A domino theory of the spirit, if you will.

Though he said nothing at first, Lionel's expression throughout the presentation resembled that of a man who has just seen a thousand souls die in a televised terrorist attack. Noting his distress—the poor man couldn't speak—I was the first to take the floor when Peter and Richard finished.

I began by declaring with some energy that as the descendent of a general in Cromwell's New Model Army, I had long since been persuaded that when Our Lord told his followers that the Kingdom would be taken by violence, he wasn't calling for the faithful to storm the walls of Jerusalem in the First Crusade. History proved nothing, I argued, if not that the Kingdom would ever suffer violence in this world, and the Christian would always be doing battle with sin, his own first. But what happened to the Templars, not to mention St. Peter in the Garden centuries before them, should provide warning enough about what was in store for power-hungry men who viewed the Sword of the Spirit as a weapon of mass destruction.

My friendship with Richard had been strained for several months, but this was the first time I ever crossed him publicly. His face went white as I spoke. Peter, however, having apparently anticipated some such resistance, delivered an obviously pre-packaged reply, in the most vehement if formulaic terms imaginable, to the effect that prophets were never welcomed in their own countries. Anyone, he said, who stood in the way of his holy work was unquestionably a fifth columnist in league with the Enemy of all souls.

Eager to lower the temperature of the heated interchange, Lionel finally pointed out, very quietly at first, that there were many vocations in the Church just as there were many styles and temperaments in the structure of the human personality. Nevertheless, the vocation of Immaculata House, Lionel maintained, was not at all consistent with Peter's crusading vision. "No matter how noble the cause," he said, "when you mix fallen human nature with ideology and a militant organizational structure, alchemy will operate in reverse: gold will be transformed into lead. Genuine renewal occurs heart to heart, one person at a time."

Undaunted, Peter challenged his older brother to put the matter to a vote. Lionel, his broad face purpling, refused outright. Instead, rising to his feet, Lionel declared in a resonant voice supported by the full weight of his frame, "You're all free to stay or go as your conscience dictates. If you go, then God be with you, you can try out your scheme someplace else. But I swear as I stand here that I will personally close Immaculata House before I see it turned into the headquarters of a militia!" With that, Lionel exited the room.

I followed Lionel into his office. There, broken-hearted and remorseful, Lionel laid all blame for what had just transpired on himself. He must have failed miserably, he told me, in his mission of teaching and healing, otherwise the young men of Immaculata House wouldn't be grasping at the straws of spiritual megalomania that Peter was holding out to them.

I argued with Lionel, but to no avail. He returned to the library a few minutes later, where, though he reiterated his rejection of Peter's proposal, he apologized publicly for losing his temper.

Peter, visibly shaken by the strength of his older brother's rebuke, suddenly burst into the smiles of a Wall Street trader whose junk bonds had inexplicably trebled in value overnight.

Lionel left Milwaukee in early March. Expecting to be away for at least six weeks, he stated publicly at a House meeting that Peter would handle "financial matters alone" in his absence, while I, as one who 'knew the drill,' was to act as a surrogate House leader. Lionel was worried, I knew, about the turn of events in the Areopagus, but was never able, in his own immense benevolence, to suspect his brother of anything more than misguided enthusiasm.

To paraphrase Suetonius, so much for the Emperor. I must now tell the story of the Monster.

No sooner did Lionel set foot on the airplane, than Peter began to annex Immaculata House. In the smallness of daily events, the ambiance of mutual trust that Lionel inspired gave way, step by inexorable step, to an atmosphere of anxiety, resentment, and surreptitious backchat. I frankly did not know how to meet the challenge that Peter posed to Lionel's ideals. It was like boxing with a shadow. I did write e-mails to Lionel in Rome, as did Fr. Bricusse and a few of the older residents. No doubt sensing that some game was afoot, Lionel even made plans for an early return to Milwaukee before the conference was to have concluded. Tragically, he died of a sudden and massive stroke in the taxi on the way to the Vatican. It is easy for me to remember the date: April 22, the eve of the fourth anniversary of my vision, Shakespeare's birth- and death-day, and the feast of St. George.

Lionel's death was a blow to me, but a rout for Immaculata House. For Peter, who had, before the advent of the Program, been singled out in Lionel's sloppy will as the one to manage House affairs in the event of his death, it was a sign of providential election. Carrying a majority in the Areopagus by one vote, Peter swiftly declared himself "Spiritual Guide" of Immaculata House and put his Program into action.

His first act was to rename the place SANA, the Student Apostolate of North America. Then, like some petty self-crowned Napoleon, he proceeded to parcel out his subjugated territories to his assorted minions: Richard became his "Ex O," while Mitch Showalter, at that time still mourning and wavering, accepted the lowly duties of an organizational gofer.

For the public view, Peter put his sweetest face forward as he made sure that no one nearby could prove an obstacle to his rule. His statements to visiting prelates and Catholic journalists remained moderate and submissive. He spoke in glowing terms of continuing his brother's "important work." He saved the meat of his new doctrine for the "inner circle." Thus to outsiders and visitors Krato spoke in treacly tones of community, of faith, of charity.

To the inner circle he spoke the language of combat and discipline, of leverage and pressure. He spoke the language of Power.

The changes came swift and hard. The Areopagus was renamed "the Cenacle" after the traditional name of the Apostles' meeting place in Jerusalem. This Cenacle was no longer a common room for group discussion, of course, but a thrust stage for Peter's increasingly doctrinaire soliloquies.

Peter also launched a wide-ranging fund-raising scheme. We students (or rather, "foot soldiers of the Student Apostolate") were called upon to sacrifice our academic goals, which Lionel had seen as appropriate ambitions for laymen seeking to "restore all things in Christ," for the sake of eighteen hour days engaged in recruitment and fundraising activities for SANA. To my profound surprise, the money started coming in. The first thing Krato did with it, since there proved to be some trouble over the disposition of the House in the terms of Lionel's handwritten will, was to make a hefty down payment on an impressive neo-colonial mansion on Newberry Boulevard.

At the time that the move was being discussed—"announced," I should say—I was the only remaining "Royalist" still living in the House. All the others faithful to Lionel's vision had left within a few weeks of his death; but oddly I was not the only one to object to this spendy move. Mitch Showalter, again, was scandalized that we young apostles would suddenly be living in a finer home and in a more prestigious neighborhood than ninety-five percent of those who were contributing their widows' mites to the Cause. He even summoned the nerve to point out to Peter that several less ostentatious homes, nearer Marquette perhaps or west of UWM, could have been purchased at the price Krato was paying for the mansion.

Peter received this argument with patient condescension. While he appreciated Mitch's "idealism," he said, Mitch's outlook was nonetheless "shortsighted." Mitch, after all, had no firsthand business experience and "didn't understand consumer psychology." To be perceived as substantial, Peter explained—something worth contributing to—SANA needed to look substantial. And the Newberry Boulevard house was nothing if not substantial.

Peter then took Mitch into his office for a private conference that lasted over three hours. I don't know what transpired there, but Peter, who had three parts of Mitch already, emerged from the meeting with the man entire. From then on Mitch Showalter, like all the rest, was wholly imbued with his leader's "vision" for SANA. *Propter hoc*, Mitch's attitude towards me, the last holdout of the old regime, was leavened with Peter's malice.

In preparation for the move to the new House, Peter drew up guidelines for communal order and cleanliness that would make an allergist ecstatic. All "secular" art works and decorations were to come down off our walls, to be replaced by a choose-your-poison motley of pious prints that had to be pre-approved by Peter, whose taste runs to the Velvet Elvis end of the artistic spectrum.

I refused to remove my Rossetti-Morris St.George, with its depiction of a semi-nude captive virgin, but Middle Earth disappeared from Richard's wall—fiction, according to Mr. Krato, was by definition a form of lying, and fantasy fiction, with its wizards and elves and references to magic, was "patently demonic." Even Mitch, though in tears, discarded a long-cherished photograph of his high school sweetheart when Mr. Krato, stopping once by his room, declared that the memories it evoked might prove a temptation to Mitch's vocation.

A dreary and conformist dress code was announced at a meeting of the Cenacle, consisting of the now-familiar white shirts, navy slacks and tie, and black shoes. Richard, who at that time still retained a vestigial sense of humor, was the first to comment that we would all look ridiculous to our academic colleagues, like a horde of door-to-door Jehovah's Witnesses or the Blues Brothers. "I always thought Catholics had taste at least," he concluded. I burst out laughing, but quickly stifled it when Peter proceeded to rebuke his only son in a manner so vicious, that it stunned even me, who after two years on North Atlantic fishing boats thought myself inured to every form of verbal crudity. The normally stoic Richard fled the room in tears.

This form of potty-mouthed discipline was meted out on a regular basis, by the way, primarily to poor Richard, but sooner or later to everyone. It was almost entertaining, for instance, to witness Peter, a strong but smallish man with the physiognomy of an ape, verbally abusing a giant like Mitch Showalter, while the big fellow just stood there, all six-foot-four of him, shaking with fury but nonetheless taking it like an adolescent caught batting a baseball through a parlor window. Mitch's transgression in one particular case: he had dared request a day off and the use of a car to drive to Green Bay to visit his beloved Aunt Abby, who was recovering from hip replacement surgery.

Unquestioning obedience quickly became the sole criterion for preferment at SANA. From the beginning Peter kept tabs on everyone by a stooge system worthy of a federal penitentiary or the Nixon White House. Having spent many years in English public schools and Canadian military academies, I am an old sweat at that particular game, and more than familiar with the techniques. For example, Peter sent everyone out "two by two," whether to the grocery store, to class, or to the loo. Parents and guardians, such as they were, were surprised to find their sons coming home, on their increasingly infrequent visits, with at least one fellow SANA member invariably in tow. This measure was implemented primarily to prevent "imprudent disclosures" about the newly-reformed way of life at SANA House. The idea was that there would always be someone standing over your shoulder to hush you up if you spoke out of turn, or rat on you if you sneaked a smoke.

The final element of the makeover of Immaculata House into SANA was the codification of Peter's eccentric private theories of angelology and sexology. Krato liked to refer to the angels as "sources of immense power that can be tapped like electric lines." He "tapped" this angelic power by demanding our daily attendance at his early-morning chapel services, during which we mouthed repetitive prayers enlisting the aid of dozens of angels, archangels, and saints, each one patrons of this, that, or the other thing, for the success of the apostolate. The daily incantation, in the hushed stillness of early morning, had the exotic flavor of a séance.

Krato likewise managed — the intellectual process eludes me — to link this whole angelic business to his personal theories, derived from I know not what source, on the degraded and bestial nature of human sexuality. Where Lionel had promoted chastity and sexual maturity, Peter believed that the love of men and women had become so polluted that the only sure way to heaven was to bypass conjugality altogether and become "like the angels." Warning us against "distractions to the apostolate," he encouraged us to "avert our eyes" whenever confronted with the sight of a comely female, much as he encouraged us to avert our eyes from heady glances of Lake Michigan, thus "offering up" a (to me at least) daily source of inspiring beauty on the apostolic altar.

By the time I left, some members were making private "promises" of celibacy for increasingly extended periods of time, with a view to a possibly permanent "covenant." Krato didn't use the word "vow," of course, because vows are governed by the Code of Canon Law, and Archdiocesen oversight would interfere with his grace as Founder. Notwithstanding its non-canonical status, however, Peter managed to impose the concept of these promises with a feat of verbal gymnastics that I am unable to replicate, except to say that it communicated Krato's belief that, if anything, such a promise would be "spiritually" if not "formally" even *more* binding on our souls than the vow of a cloistered religious.

Needless to say, I made no such promise, though I understand that some of the members have since made life-long commitments, both to celibacy and to SANA — Mitch and Richard, to name two. These commitments are wholly one-sided, however. SANA's by-laws make it clear that the community's "Spiritual Guide" (read: Peter Krato) can dismiss anyone, anytime, as he sees fit, no explanation given. In this as in the rest I kept waiting for Krato's petty kingdom to perish of its own diseased imagination, or for a prince of the Church to ride in on a white horse to rescue us all from the lunacy. Neither prospect materialized.

One day Peter, having learned of my unsavory pre-conversion sexual history by way of Richard — it could have come from no other source — took me aside and said, "Okay, Jim, I know you're doing okay right now, but you're the kind of guy that's never going to get your act together with women. You're like an alcoholic who can't sip the booze without draining the bottle. The only way for a guy like you to handle it is to swear off the stuff — I mean females — once and for all."

Before I could produce a suitable reply — as ever, Peter had the capacity to throw me off balance by sheer ballsiness — Peter launched into some pseudo-scientific drivel about the debilitating effects of sex, even between marriage partners.

To this analysis I believe I replied, after I sufficiently recovered my wits, "No wonder your wife divorced you," and turned on my heel.

Whenever I waste my time trying to come to grips with the question of whether Peter's motivations are sincere or hypocritical, I always remember one incident which lives in my mind as the apotheosis of Peter's method.

The week after the spring term ended, finally acknowledging that the situation was hopeless, I had just about made up my mind to leave Immaculata House—SANA, rather—but felt that I needed to get away from the place for a while to clear my mind and spirit before I made the final decision. Having decided to launch my summer vacation with a sailing holiday on Lake Superior, I was surprised when Mitch Showalter graciously offered to let me use his Aunt Abby's vacant cabin near Grand Marais in the Michigan Upper Peninsula.

In several of his chapel tirades before I left, Peter used my planned vacation as the perfect illustration of *fiddling while Rome burned*. I ignored Peter's thinly veiled allusions, of course, as I ignored almost everything he said; but then, as I was about to walk out the door, luggage in hand, Peter suddenly pulled me into Lionel's office and proceeded to exhort me, in the warmest, friendliest tones I had ever heard him use towards me, to "relax, Jim, have a good time, take a much needed rest. You're still getting over Lionel's death, after all."

I suppose I was still naïve enough to suspect nothing untoward by this sudden turn, only a measure of surprise and relief. I even wondered if the man had perhaps come to his senses finally, like Scrooge on Christmas morning. I drove to Grand Marais feeling that if I no longer fit in at Immaculata House under Peter Krato, at least there would be no hard feelings if I decided to leave.

When I returned several weeks later, however, it was as if to a different...*institution*. Indeed, I don't hesitate to say that our little brotherhood had now been fully transformed into a sophronistery, like one of those model polyopticon prisons so beloved of New Historicists like Foucault, in which every criminal inmate is at every moment under the watchful gaze of a jailer. My every move was scrutinized, and the shunning which I had previously experienced as a sort of morose wariness had hardened into the wholesale denial of my very existence.

Mitch was the only one of the men with the decency to blurt out, after a little prodding, what had occurred in my absence. Although he naturally tried to put the best possible face on it, he confessed that the evening I left, and not two hours after Peter's uncharacteristically warm send-off, Krato, having determined that there was no hope of getting his hands on my trust fund, had assembled a "war council" in his office consisting of Mitch, Richard, and one other enthusiast who has since left, like me, under a cloud of innuendo. The main purpose of the conclave, which went on for the better part of three days, was, of course, to figure out how to make James Ireton's life so miserable at Immaculata House that he would be forced to flee.

According to Mitch, who seemed surprised (a little flattered, too, I think) to have been included in this elite confab, Richard initially resisted the idea, arguing with his father that I might prove more dangerous to SANA outside the fold than within. Agreeing that this could indeed prove problematic, Peter countered that there were surely ways to persuade me to keep my mouth shut, and proceeded to extract every drop of personal confidence I had ever shared with Richard about my private life, going so far as to put Richard "under obedience," as the monastic phrase goes, to disclose all my personal secrets — for my own spiritual welfare, of course, as well as the good of the apostolate!

How he felt about it I suppose I shall never know, but thus it was that Richard coined me into the gold of his father's approval. Thank God I have a reticent nature, and had not given my friend the key to *all* my counsel. I had never revealed to him some of the more painful details of my family life, nor of my conversion experience, but what Richard knew was enough to do me considerable damage.

The sleazier details of my sexual history were quickly broadcast Housewide, unlacing my reputation with the more timorous members. Mitch, as he confessed to me, was frankly appalled — not by Peter's violation of my privacy or Richard's betrayal, but at my history of carnal failings, the likes of which he had never imagined. It seemed that the god of Mitch's idolatry had turned out more Dionysus than Apollo, and his respect for me was shattered.

Furthermore, according to Mitch, Krato ordered Richard, while I was away up north, to rifle my computer files and e-mail, and sift through my personal belongings with the intention of unkenneling any attempts on my part to document the events of the past months. Letters that Lionel wrote me from Rome disappeared. I suspect, too, that it wouldn't have been intrinsically repugnant for Richard to have uncovered some particularly unsavory personal item to expose my occulted guilt to the other men, such as a copy of *Playboy*. A copy of *Playgirl* would have been better yet. On that score, at least, I disappointed them all.

When I returned from Lake Superior, my room was in a shambles, my laptop a buggy mess of deleted files and programs, and Richard, my erstwhile roommate and best friend, had moved in with Mitch Showalter. I felt absolutely *persona non grata* in what was as much my home as anyone else's. Even my St. George and the Dragon picture had disappeared from the wall above my bed. I found it in a garbage can outside, covered in hamburger grease from the previous night's dinner.

In my own defense, I *did* try to argue against each of Peter's innovations as they were introduced, but I made about as much headway with the man's chop-logic as Prince Hamlet did against the Gravedigger's. Instead,

I learned on my own flesh that words do not hold the same meaning to every person. As a literature student coming head to head with Semioticians, Deconstructionists, New Historicists, Feminists, and Queer Theorists on a regular basis, I suppose I should have already known this, but it took several months of "dialoguing" with Peter Krato for the concept to become enfleshed. To me, words represented the communication of my soul to other sentient beings, and theirs to me — imperfect certainly, as is everything this side of the Beatific Vision, but nonetheless meaningful. To Peter, however, words were tools, instruments; weapons to be sharpened on the nearest interlocutor who, by definition, was put on this earth to get in his way. Discussion between us was schizophrenic, and any hope for mutual understanding, remote.

As for my peers in SANA House, whenever I attempted to draw upon fraternal feeling and communal experience in order to challenge Peter's new ideology, I discovered that the well had long since been poisoned. Fr. Bricusse, not wanting to betray confidences by speaking to me directly of the things he was hearing from some of my House "brothers," was able to persuade Mitch Showalter (again) to reveal to me what Peter was saying behind my back in his father/son conferences, and through his primary mouthpiece, Richard: that before his death, Lionel and I had been engaged in a torrid homosexual affair, and I was now supporting Lionel's prior "mismanagement" of Immaculata House out of homoerotic loyalty.

For some reason, perhaps because of my unconcealed devotion for Lionel Krato, the lie took deep root among the members of SANA. Mitch, for instance, after explaining the situation to me, frankly told me that he was inclined to believe it all, in spite of my dumbfounded denials. He couldn't imagine, he said, that a Christian man like Peter would lay such a charge at my door, let alone that of his own brother, unless it were true.

The Big Lie, SANA-style.

It goes without saying that Peter has never made his accusations public, but then he has hardly needed to. When it comes to rumor-mongering, Peter could put the murderous Machiavel to school. Especially in the suffocating atmosphere of SANA, where everyone studies everyone else for signs of Election or Declension, such a scandal would, and did, completely undermine my credibility. Who is James Ireton to call Peter Krato a crook and a charlatan and a petty tyrant? He's a sex addict who swings like a double-hinged door in both directions at once. Could such a demi-devil possess any grace of discernment, any grace at all? How convenient that Lionel is no longer around to defend himself, while I, a self-confessed sinner, am left in the unenviable position of proving a negative.

For the record, let me state that Lionel had no prurient interest in young men; it is Peter who is the true fetishist, using his boys at SANA like rubber inflatables for his midnight purposes. And Krato not only gets by with it, he is interviewed in reverential tones by religious talk show hosts; oblivious journalists from the Catholic press seek him out to write of the important work he is doing "for the youth of America"; he is lauded as a man of vision and noble purpose, "a man of faith," while Lionel's name is clean forgotten after a mere eight months.

A word about the state of my conscience during this period:

Until I met Lionel and Fr. Bricusse, most of what I understood about conscience I learned from Newman, who affirmed in his *Apologia* that "obedience even to an erring conscience was the way to gain light." Fortunately for me, the subject of personal conscience proved to be one of Lionel's preoccupations as an educator. He feared, in fact, that our contemporary culture was spawning an army of conscienceless drones at an alarming rate.

My own interest in the subject came to a head when I was writing my Master's thesis on *Hamlet*, entitled *The Conscience of the Prince*. The problem of Hamlet's conscience is an old one in Shakespeare criticism, but had fallen on hard times in the wake of the triumph of Theory in the postmodern academy, enamored as its proponents are of textual analyses removed from "contextual" philosophies and ideas—save, of course, those ideas, usually left unidentified, which happen to preoccupy the minds of the Theorists themselves. It was a risk, I suppose, professionally speaking, that I was disinterring the notion of conscience for my Master's thesis, but I suppose I was fascinated because, in a sense, the shaping, unshaping, and reshaping of my personal conscience has been the summary theme of my life story. As a boy, my conscience had been press-ganged into the service of my father's private little war with modernity. Unchaining myself from his dyspeptic perspective, and learning of my own free will to commit to something outside myself has been the uphill battle of my adult life.

When I took the issue to Lionel for one of our late-night chats, we were soon engaged in a passionate and heated exchange which forged, in truth, a far more intimate bond than any of Peter's lurid imaginings of sodomy or fellatio. For me personally, as well as for my Master's thesis, the discussion was formative.

Lionel called the conscience one's "original face." To be true to one's conscience, he said, was to be true to that image of God, molded in the shape of Christ, which paradoxically made every human person unique and irreplaceable. "It's recognizing who we are," Lionel said. "God's name is I AM WHO AM." Thus understood, the conscience was like a work of art, and like a work of art it had to be formed and crafted. When I asked Lionel how one went about forming one's conscience, he replied that it was done by "revelation, thought, suffering, experience, and beauty."

I was surprised. What on earth, I asked, did *beauty* have to do with it?

"Spoken like a Puritan," Lionel cried, laughing out loud, "and you a lit scholar, too!" It was the aesthetic element, he went on to explain, which had been neglected in these last utilitarian centuries, but was understood by the ancient philosophers and the Fathers of the Church. To them and to Lionel, Truth, Goodness, and Beauty were one, a seamless garment, and where there was no appreciation for beauty there was liable to be little for truth or goodness either. Lionel then quoted Newman to the effect that Truth had two attributes: Power and Beauty. *Real* power, he added; power to attract, not to pressure or force. Force, he said, quoting Simone Weil, turned persons into things, and was one of the sure signs of the diabolic. Or, to use the language of the police, Lionel said, *forced entry is the sure sign of crime.*

And then Lionel looked at me with a pained expression on his face that did more to shame me than a month of my father's jeremiads. "That includes, James," he added, "the form of psychological forced entry we so delicately term 'seduction.' We have to look for beauty in the Shadow of the Cross, of course," he added, quickly letting me off the hook. "It isn't the same as prettiness." Nor was it to be found, he said, among the glamour merchants of Madison Avenue or Sunset and Vine, let alone Times Square or Wall Street. It was even difficult, he concluded, to find it on Church or Main Street.

Suddenly reminded of Emerson's wonderful line, *What you are shouts so loudly I can't hear what you're saying,* I made the comment that there were some people whose personalities were so crass, so ugly, that they shouldn't take up the preaching of the Gospel, however much they proclaimed a desire to serve it.

At that, Lionel heaved a great sigh: he loved his brother, but he was no fool.

———————————

This conversation haunted me as I sat amidst my boxes in July as the rest of the men were preparing to make the move to Newberry Boulevard and the new SANA House. I had just had an up-and-downer with Richard on the subject of my intended "desertion," as a matter of fact, which included childish displays of temper on both sides, and concluded with my snatching up the King James Bible I had given him the year before as a birthday present, and throwing it in his face.

As I sat there on the porch steps I looked around the haunted timbers of our monstrous old House. Lionel Krato's Immaculata House was creaky and dusty and in a lousy neighborhood, as such things are judged in Milwaukee, with a crack house a block to the west and a Gangster Disciples meeting-house in an abandoned building two blocks to the north; but the place was beautiful to me, the way Lionel was beautiful, and Shakespeare.

The new SANA House, on the other hand, to which the rest of the members were moving, was expensive, sanitary, and in a leafy upscale neighborhood. It was, in Peter's phrase, *substantial.* It was also conveniently distant from the "meddling Oratorians" and the immigrant poor who, Krato claimed, brought down real estate values. But the new House was as ugly as sin to me, and I suddenly understood the truth of that old adage, which had never before struck me as particularly descriptive. So when Mitch Showalter, hoping I might still be persuaded to change my mind, volunteered to help me load my boxes onto the Ryder truck bound for Newberry Boulevard, I shook my head and said, no, my conscience wouldn't permit it. "I'm leaving this New Model Army for good."

There is, by the way, one important page in this storybook of horrors that I cannot bear to turn, though I shall allude to it. My spiritual life is, if anything, darker now than it was before the Woman made me her knight in that little church in Salisbury. I can only remember with great effort what she sounded like, and looked like, and it's a less-than-zero emptiness that makes me wonder if the whole business weren't a manic delusion, after all.

Krato silenced my Lady, too, as forcefully as he has silenced the consciences of his drones. He took Lionel's concept of a chivalrous knighthood of the Immaculata and twisted it into a spiritual blackjack with which to thump us. What he did to the Immaculata is the one part of his creed that I can't bear to discuss in any detail, although it became in many ways the cornerstone of his ideology. I will have to leave it to the reader's imagination, and refer anyone interested to SANA literature, which drips with references to the Virgin, the Pope, the angels, and all sorts of celestial higher-ups, like a schmoozing name-dropper crashing a Hollywood premiere. The Immaculata was the most beautiful thing I had, perhaps the only good thing in me; but even she was defiled in those last months.

In spite of my obduracy, Mr. Krato gave me one last chance to "get with the Program." The week after the move, the first such overture in many months, Richard suddenly took it upon himself to ring me up and invite me to dinner, on his "nickel," as he put it. While I suspected at once that it might be some sort of fishing expedition, and that every word I uttered would be repeated, verbatim, to Peter, I accepted the invitation anyway in the feeble hope that Richard might have retained some vestigial sense of genuine friendship towards me.

Richard's first mistake was to set the venue for our dinner meeting at Karl Ratzsch's, one of the finest and most expensive German restaurants in Milwaukee. Richard, I knew, had far too few "nickels" to afford such a splurge, and therefore I felt safe in assuming that this fine meal was to be financed by Peter's corporate MasterCard. Since I knew full well that Peter was not in the habit, keen businessman that he was, of making such "substantial" investments without expecting some sort of "substantial" return, I couldn't help but be curious as to what sort of return Richard could hope to extract from me.

It took over an hour to find out that Richard wasn't coming cap in hand for a donation, which had been my first guess. The conversation limped along trivial and mostly academic lines through the salad and main course, and it was only when the *Linzertorten* and cappuccino were set before us that Richard finally got down to business. Laying aside his fork, Richard suddenly inquired, without preamble, what I intended to do with my life, now that I had abandoned the apostolate. Since Richard knew perfectly well that I was working towards a doctorate in Shakespeare Studies, I knew that he must, in fact, be trying to find out what, if anything, I might be intending to do re: SANA.

Disappointed at the transparency of this maneuver, I replied, in an ironic tone, that I was thinking of doing a bit of "creative writing" now that I was on my own and didn't have to worry about people mucking about in my manuscripts and private correspondence. After all, I said, I had had some fascinating experiences of late that would make for terrific Theater of the Absurd. This was mere banter, of course; I had no intention of writing about SANA at all, at least not before Fr. Bricusse suggested it. I was merely trailing my coat to see if Richard might trip over it.

He did.

"You know," Richard responded after a telling minute of jaw-clenching silence, "a man with a your reputation should be careful about what he says. Or writes."

Threats were very much what I had come to expect from the Kratos, *père et fils*, but I hardly thought it possible for them to tarnish my reputation any more than they had already. "Surely you can do better than that," I said.

But then Richard said something that *did* surprise me. "You could still come back, you know," he said. "We could be roommates again. Start over."

In truth, there was such a sincere, even humble look of appeal on Richard's face as he spoke that for a second, possibly two, I actually entertained the idea. "On what terms?" I asked finally, certain that there would be terms, probably steep ones.

"We'd like to pray over you," Richard replied. "In the chapel."

I was puzzled. "Pray over me about what? For what?"

"We think you're being...well, oppressed by a spirit of rebellion. You wouldn't be the first, you know," he added quickly. "We did it with Mitch last week. He's doing much better now."

I was thunderstruck. "Sweet Christ," I shrieked, startling several diners at neighboring tables, "you want to perform an *exorcism*? On *me*?"

"Well, you don't have to call it *that*," Richard said, looking around with obvious embarrassment.

For a moment my innately sardonic sense of humor got the better of me and I opened my mouth to produce some smart-assed remark about the best possible uses, in SANA's proposed rite, for crucifixes and split-pea soup. But all at once the sheer obscenity of Richard's suggestion struck me like a thunderclap.

I was suddenly reminded of the famous Recorder scene in Act III of *Hamlet*. As often as I had studied it, I believe I comprehended fully only that night the nature of the violation that Shakespeare was attempting to portray in that extraordinary scene, where Guildenstern, at Claudius' behest, attempts to "feel out" his erstwhile friend. Recognizing the maneuver, Hamlet responds by grabbing a Recorder from a passing musician, thrusting it in Guildenstern's face, and comparing himself to it as an "instrument" to be played upon and made to "sing." Sitting there with a cup of cappuccino in my hands, surrounded by fine food and wine, by bone china and crystal and silver and every artifact of a world of culture and civility, I was struck so violently by the analogy that I was momentarily lost in thought, my mind turning over Shakespeare's astonishing words:

Hamlet
Will you play upon this pipe?

Guildenstern
My lord, I cannot.

Hamlet
I pray you.

Guildenstern
Believe me, I cannot.

Hamlet
I do beseech you.

Guildenstern
I know no touch of it, my lord.

Hamlet
It is as easy as lying. Govern these
ventages with your fingers and thumb,
give it breath with your mouth, and it
will discourse most eloquent music.
Look you, these are the stops.

Guildenstern
But these cannot I command to any
utterance of harmony; I have not
the skill.

Hamlet
Why, look you now, how unworthy a
thing you make of me! You would play
upon me; you would seem to know my
stops; you would pluck out the heart
of my mystery; you would sound me
from my lowest note to the top of
my compass: and there is much music,
excellent voice, in this little organ; yet
cannot you make it speak. 'S'blood,
do you think I am easier to be played
on than a pipe? Call me what instrument

you will, though you can fret me, yet you
cannot play upon me.

Too late, I understood Lionel's insistence on the role of art and beauty in
the sculpting of conscience, for by means of this passage I suddenly understood what might have otherwise remained a fearful mystery to me: that I
was no longer a man to Richard; no longer a person made, like him, in the
image of God, with a dignity and worth wholly separate from my potential
utility to SANA and Peter Krato. I was but an instrument, a thing; a pipe to
be played upon and made to sing a madman's tune. Moreover, the man who
had for almost two years been like a brother to me had somehow become
willing to *erase* me; to make me, or at least anything unique about me, disappear, like a blotted-out reference in a Stalinist history text.

Setting aside my cappuccino lest I spill it, I grasped hold of the edge of
the table with both trembling hands, within an inch of turning it over — dessert plates, candles, cappuccino, and all — into Richard's tidy lap.

"You'll agree to it?" Richard said eagerly, apparently misinterpreting my
extended silence.

My head swam. Finally, I let go of the table, scooted back my chair,
reached for my wallet, and pulled out a hundred-dollar bill. I dropped the
money on the table.

"When pigs fly," I said, and walked out.

The most ironic part about this entire mess, given the Krato-inspired rumors
floating around about my sexual appetites, was that I "fell," morally speaking,
for the first time in years that very night. Exiting the restaurant, I made my
furious way to a nearby Water Street bar, intending to drink myself into oblivion. Unhappily, I ran into an acquaintance there, a fellow student and fashion
model who, as it happened, was under contract with Krato Advertising to
pose for Stark's Dark Beer ads. Since she had been pursuing me for some
weeks, and since SANA-gossip had me in bed with her already, I suppose I
thought I might as well be hung for a goat as for a sheep.

I don't precisely know what my own motivations were, because I did get
stumbling drunk, and the next thing I remember clearly was waking up in
the woman's bed at three in the morning. I left as quickly as I could manage,
thoroughly disgusted with myself, and came back the next night. And the
night after that.

Thus it may be argued that Peter Krato has been proven right about me
after all. The Old Adam has been resurrected, and I have not received the
Sacraments since that dinner with Richard. Father Bricusse keeps assuring
me that Christianity is not truly reflected in the carnival mirrors constructed
by my father and Peter Krato. Nor will I deny that I still retain some sort of
obscured faith; but even so, I cannot bear it. That is all I can say: I cannot sort
it out, and I cannot bear it.

Now that I've gone, one would think Peter Krato would be delighted to see the back of me; but no, he will not leave me in peace even now. I suppose I should take his paranoia as a sort of backhanded compliment, but his attentions to me are loathsome. I get weekly missives, unsigned, containing Bible passages cut out and pasted neatly on a sheet of paper. To boot, I often feel as if I am being spied upon by sundry members of SANA, at the same time that I know that I am still being shunned by them. This last term, when two SANA members discovered that they had signed up for a class that I was also taking, they dropped out by the second lecture—much to my relief, I might add. For the hell of it, I have taken to sending copies of my intended schedule to Peter in advance, thus sparing his boys the trouble of inadvertently registering for a course he won't permit them to complete.

As for Richard, he hasn't spoken a word to me since that night at the restaurant, unless social protocol requires an exchange of meaningless pleasantries.

I have but one final comment. Around the time I left SANA, Fr. Bricusse said to me, "The spiritual formation in that place leaves a vacuum in the soul where conscience ought to be, and human nature abhors a vacuum. Christ warned in his parable that we should fear a house which has been swept clean of one devil; if it is not soon indwelt by the Spirit of God who is love, seven devils will return to fill the emptiness where the one was cast out."

I hope Father was not referring to me.

Chapter Six:
I Am Not What I Am

I follow him to serve my turn upon him...
In following him, I follow but myself;
Heaven is my judge, not I for love and duty,
But seeming so, for my peculiar end:
For when my outward action doth demonstrate
The native act and figure of my heart
In compliment extern, 'tis not long after
But I will wear my heart upon my sleeve
For daws to peck at: I am not what I am.

Shakespeare, *Othello*

The Oratorians had decided, in anticipation of a sizeable crowd, to hold Fr. Bricusse's wake in the Oratory School gymnasium. The body lay concealed in a closed casket of polished cedar, on top of which Adèle Lanciano had placed a photograph of her uncle with his Oratorian brothers. Arriving early to help ready the gym, James choked every time he looked at it, and even tried for a while to avoid sight of it altogether, only to decide in the end that it induced a less painful form of mourning than its dolorous alternative: the memory of Bricusse's brains spilling onto the white marble of the Institute atrium.

After helping arrange the folding chairs and set up trays of drinks and snacks on a banquet table, James sat down opposite Franco Lanciano, his attention drifting in and out as the new Heisler Institute Director nattered on and on about nothing in particular, returning at length to the troubling subject of the autopsy report.

"I think it's preposterous to suspect someone of wanting to kill Arthur." Lanciano picked a speck of lint from his trousers. "Except...what about your cult-friends on Newberry?"

James peeled open his drooping eyelids. "You've heard about the SANA report?"

"I didn't read the damned thing, if that's what you mean," Lanciano replied irritably. "*Il vecchio padre* was unusually protective about your role in the whole affair. But he told me about it in broad terms, in case it went public. In case the Institute got dragged into it. Which no doubt it would have been. As the other evening proved, there's a vocal little faction of troublemakers in our fair city who would love to get hold of something like your SANA report and use it to prove that the Institute is a breeding ground of right-wing mullahs. God knows I try to distance myself from crackpots like Krato, but what, reasonably, can I do? Refuse to let his people study here?"

"Then I'd better warn you," James said. "My SANA report was put on the Archbishop's desk yesterday afternoon. I expect to be contacted about it any day now."

Lanciano put his thumbnail to his teeth. Crossing his tailored legs with a snap, he conferred a severe frown on James before conceding, most reluctantly, that such a development was probably unavoidable. "But on a more pleasant note, before I forget," he added, "I have a copy of Arthur's will for you back at the office. It'll take a while to get the legal formalities taken care of, but Arthur's intention of leaving you his Shakespeare library and unpublished papers is quite clear. As executor, Adèle wants you to feel free to start going through his office at your leisure."

A steady current of mourners filed in and out the gymnasium doors to pay their respects to the body of Fr. Arthur Bricusse, to light candles, and to offer condolences to Adèle, James, and the Oratorians. Max Heisler attended the wake with his daughter Fran, but Barry DeBrun, James heard Fran telling Adèle, was not feeling well and couldn't make it. Thank God.

Clinging to her father's arm with an almost childish dependency, Fran DeBrun stepped up to James.

"I'm so very, very sorry," she said in a shaky voice, reaching for his hand. "Father spoke of you so warmly every time he came to the house."

"You saw him, I believe," James said gently, "that last day."

"I went to him often for couns—" Fran's lips quivered. "For a chat." Sniffling loudly, she let go of James's hand to snatch a handkerchief from her purse. "I knew he wasn't well," she almost wailed into her linen, "but I had no idea, I'm so sorry!" Her hankie to her face, she whirled away, apparently making for a ladies' room. She was almost to the door before James suddenly remembered having seen something odd as he shook Fran's hand: purplish crease marks, like a tattooed bracelet, encircling the woman's fleshy wrists under the cuff ruffle of her blouse.

James grimaced. Ligature marks.

Stepping forward to take James's arm in a firm grip, Max Heisler frowned over his shoulder at his retreating daughter. "You'll have to excuse Fran," he said. "I think she feels guilty."

James recollected himself. "But, why?"

"She was with him for hours the day he died. She thinks she should have noticed that he was sick. Or that she overtaxed him. You know how the man was. He would have never said a word."

"Yes...yes I know."

Heisler gave James a resounding thump on the shoulder. "Well, I know you came to the Institute because of Arthur. But I hope you won't go rushing back to England now that he's gone. He thought the world of you, and as a scholar, too. He wanted to build the English Renaissance Program around you."

"I didn't realize. He never really said much about it."

Heisler grunted. "Typical. The man had no head for administration. But he was the heart and soul of this place. I wouldn't have been lunatic enough to bankroll it for anyone else, let me tell you." His fish-eyes growing moist with tears, Heisler seemed to yank himself up by an act of the will. "Now, you think about what I said. We'll get together with Franco one of these days, you and me, and see what's what. Right?"

"Yes, Sir. I'll think about it. Thank you."

James had just about made up his mind to search out a seat in some inconspicuous corner when he spotted Lupe's arrival. A middle-aged woman was at Lupe's shoulder, no doubt her mother, Oonagh O'Donnell Cruz.

Lupe resembled her pink-cheeked Irish mother very little in the face, but the two women shared the same lush figure and ready smile. After the requisite introductions and expressions of condolence, Oonagh Cruz put James quite at ease by planting a warm kiss on his cheek before moving on to embrace her old friend Adèle Lanciano. James made the most of his opportunity by grabbing Lupe's wrist and pulling her into a deserted hallway of the old school, where he took her in his arms in a needful embrace.

Coming up for air after a minute or more, Lupe whispered into his neck, "I seem to have d-discovered, these last couple of days, that I love you. Including all the things that w-w-worry you so much."

James stepped back. Whatever he had expected, he hadn't expected *that*.

James had, in fact, always prided himself on possessing a special instinct, a sixth sense that warned him, Sibyl-like, when those terrible words were about to be spoken in a relationship. This was a useful faculty when one's standard operating procedure included a protocol for severing ties as soon as the partner to hand began exhibiting symptoms of excessive attachment. But James's instincts had utterly failed him tonight, and he was too taken by surprise to formulate a glib response.

His first thought was to joke away Lupe's statement with something like, *Far too early for all that, surely*, or *You don't really know what you're saying*. But then the whole thing seemed suddenly right somehow, or at least inevitable. So instead of mouthing a dismissal he wasn't yet prepared for himself, he gave a nervous little laugh and took her face in his hands to kiss her again, this time in such a way as to express his, well, *gratitude*. At least in a general sort of way—providing emotional support in a trying time, and so forth. In the process, his body began to respond in a fashion that communicated his sentiments more eloquently than a soliloquy.

It was Lupe's turn to step back.

"If you love me," he protested, trying to subdue himself by thinking of less inspiring activities, such as dinner with his father, or cleaning fish, "why does it offend you that I'm attracted to you?"

"It doesn't offend me. I'm attracted to you, too, I d-d-don't mind saying it. It's just…" Her face grew redder still. "It's hard to explain."

"Try."

After chewing her lip a moment longer she said, "It's like this story I read, about St. Margaret Mary. She had visions, you know, like you. Visions of the Sacred Heart of Jesus. I was born on her feast day, you know, and I would have been named after her, too, but my oldest sister had already been named Margaret Mary, so they named me Guadalupe Oonagh after my—" She broke off. "D-D-Dammit, James Ireton, you're laughing at me!"

"I am not. Well, all right, I suppose I am. But Guadalupe Oonagh—" He kissed her nose. "—you're the only woman I know who would think to introduce the subject of the Sacred Heart of Jesus into a conversation one step away from becoming an argument about sex."

"We were one step away from an argument about sex?"

"We weren't one step away from an argument about sex?"

Lupe prodded his chest with her forefinger. "Well, ok-kay, maybe we were. But then maybe if you didn't try to keep sex and religion in separate little boxes all the time you wouldn't have so much trouble with either of them. Everything's connected, you know, especially the really important things, like sex and religion—"

"Uncle!" he cried, hands aloft in a posture of surrender. "I believe you were about to tell me all about St. Margaret Mary and the Sacred Heart. You have my undivided attention."

By now looking more defiant than embarrassed, Lupe took James's hand in her much smaller one, as if by way of illustration, and interlaced their fingers. "They exchanged hearts," she said, "like lovers. Jesus and St. Margaret Mary. That's what religion's all about, isn't it? And sex? It's just that most of us learn how to exchange hearts with G-G-God by doing it first with another person. Like what you wrote in your SANA report. What Lionel Krato used to say. *God is a God*—"

"—*of human mediations.*" James was no longer laughing. He pulled away his hand.

"I knew it. You're peeved."

He was also incredulous. "You want to exchange hearts…with *me*?" James ran the back of his hand across his damp forehead. "Well, now, that would be a rotten trade for you. This heart of mine is as cold as any stone."

Lupe's turquoise eyes fastened on his. "No one who hurts as much as you do could have a heart of stone," she said, sounding as if she'd already given the matter a good deal of thought and had quite made up her mind.

In lieu of a reply, James gripped her shoulders, a little more roughly than he intended, and shoved her against the wall. "I think," he said in a throaty voice, "we'd better have that argument. And bloody soon."

"I think we'd b-b-better go back into the gym," she parried, slipping out from underneath his arm. "I think they're about ready to say the Rosary."

"I don't remember how to say the bloody Rosary."

"Yeah, well, it'll come back to you."

He caught her at the door. "Lupe, about the SANA report..." He took a deep breath. "I've never shown the thing to anyone but Fr. Bricusse. Even Richard doesn't know most of it. I don't give a rat's ass what those priests at the Archdiocese know about me, or even the police, but people at the Institute, not to mention your family..."

"'Tis in my memory locked," she assured him, *"and you yourself shall keep the key of it."*

James unlocked the door of his office the next morning, already doubting the wisdom of trying to concentrate on any work before the one-o'clock funeral. He had hardly slept the night before, his head was thick, and his dark gray suit, though woven of lightweight linen, seemed to be absorbing the heat and humidity of the hazy Midwestern day like a solar panel. He shrugged off his jacket and yanked loose his tie, then cranked open the narrow window overlooking the North Point Lighthouse before seating himself at his desk to scan his week-long accumulation of mail.

The first envelope contained a note from Jack with a return address in Chicago:

> Yo, Buddy,
>
> I've *carpe diem*'d during this unexpected hiatus from class and took the train down here to look up someone I haven't seen in a long time. You can reach me here, if you (or Lt. Masefield, yee-hah!) need to get hold of me. Otherwise, I'll be back in time for next week's seminar.
>
> Yours ever,
>
> Jack

When James tore open the next envelope, he was startled by the unwelcome sight of another photocopied Bible page. This time the selected passage was from the sixteenth chapter of *The Book of Ezekiel*:

> **37** Behold, therefore I will gather all thy lovers, with whom thou hast taken pleasure, and all them that thou hast loved, with all them that thou hast hated; I will even gather them round about against thee, and will discover thy nakedness unto them, that they may see all thy nakedness. **38** And I will judge thee, as women that break wedlock and shed

blood are judged; and I will give thee blood in fury
and jealousy.

Swearing violently, James crumpled the paper into a ball and tossed it
into the trash can. It was a good minute or more before he was calm enough
to finish reviewing his mail, then turn his attention to his phone messages.
He dialed the number of his voice mailbox and keyed in his security code.

"*First message sent Saturday, 11:13 a.m.*" the programmed voice announced. Then came the shocking but unmistakable prosody of Fr. Bricusse's
wheezing voice saying, "James, I need to talk to you as soon as you're free."
A loud cough. "I'd appreciate it if you'd stop up as soon as you get a chance.
It could be important."

"*End of first message,*" announced the programmed voice.

There was a second message from Bricusse as well, recorded an hour or
so after the first, but in a breathier voice, and spoken in a timbre of urgency
that was audible through the telephone static: "James, I really must see you
as soon as possible. Something very disturbing has come up. I'm afraid it
involves you. I really shouldn't say more on the phone, but it's something
that requires our immediate attention." Several deep, wheezing breaths. "As
honest Iago said, *I am not what I am*, eh?"

"*End of second message.*"

James's heart thumped against his chest. Soon the familiar anxiety symptoms progressed to sweating to nausea to a roaring in his head that almost
made him swoon. Swallowing some bottled water from the shelf above his
desk, he had to listen to Bricusse's message several times over before he could
persuade himself that he wasn't hallucinating. Finally, he rummaged through
the inside pockets of his briefcase until he found Lt. Calvin Masefield's business card. He punched out the telephone number with trembling fingers.

His call was answered by a female voice in a particularly catarrhal version of the Milwaukee twang. Masefield was out of the office, the woman
said, and asked if James wanted to leave a message.

"Yes, tell him I need to speak with him as soon as possible. About the
murder of Fr. Arthur Bricusse."

No sooner had James rung off than Franco Lanciano called, wanting to
know if James needed a ride to the funeral.

James rubbed his forehead in a daze, "Um, I thought I might walk to the
Oratory."

"Walk!" Lanciano exclaimed. "Don't tell me that miserable little office of
yours hasn't any windows."

James glanced at the narrow rectangle of glass that was his vantage point
on the outside world: a cloudburst had liquefied the outside world into a
slate-gray smear. "In that case," he said dully. "I gratefully accept. No, wait…"
James glanced at his watch. "Bloody hell, I'm supposed to collect Lupe in an
hour."

"Then we'll save a spot for you in the front row. By the way, I hate to be critical under the circumstances, but don't you think you got a little, er, carried away in Arthur's office?"

James reached again for the water bottle. "I'm sorry, Franco, I'm not tracking. What was that?"

"I simply noticed," Lanciano said slowly, as if enunciating for a slow-witted child, "that you got a little carried away going through Arthur's things. In his office. James, are you still there?"

"Look, I'm sorry, but I don't know what the hell you're talking about. I haven't been in Father's office since before he died."

After a brief silence of his own, Lanciano said, "James, if you're not too busy, I'd appreciate it if you'd come up here. At once."

Out of breath from the sprint up the stairs, James stopped short in the open doorway of Fr. Bricusse's office.

Books and papers were strewn all over the desk, floor, and shelves, and Bricusse's remaining half dozen or so moving boxes had been sliced open and emptied like garbage. In the center of the debris stood Dr. Franco Lanciano, immaculate as ever in a charcoal-colored silk suit and black wingtips.

"I take it," Lanciano said with a sweeping gesture at the room, "that you aren't responsible for this…shambles?"

"I haven't even got a key!" James exclaimed. "Father hadn't got round to giving me one yet, not to his new office."

Pursing his thin lips, Lanciano fumbled in his trouser pocket and pulled out a key, which he held out to James then just as quickly retracted. "Never mind," he said, dropping it in the nearest wastebasket. He leaned over Bricusse's desk to punch a button on the intercom. "Christine," he growled into the speaker, "would you kindly get a locksmith up here, at once. I want all the locks changed, at least the ones for which Arthur had keys."

"There was no sign of forced entry?" James asked when Lanciano had signed off.

Lanciano shook his head, his eyebrows gathered, his face shrouded with preoccupation. "What did he want for God's sake," he mumbled.

"What do you mean, 'he'? What did who want?"

Lanciano looked up. "I mean…well, whoever the hell did this!" Lanciano yanked a silk handkerchief from his breast pocket to daub at his beading forehead. "Dear God, do you think you could, I don't know, take inventory? See if anything's missing, I mean. You know Arthur's collection better than anyone."

Feeling faint again all of a sudden, James lowered himself to the floor. He sat in a huddle, his head between his knees.

For his part, Lanciano slumped into Bricusse's chair and thrust his thumbnail between his teeth. "The police didn't find Arthur's keys on the body, you know," he said finally, his mouth working around his thumb. "He always carried his keys in his cassock pocket. I suppose I'll have to question the security people and the janitorial staff."

James lifted his head. "Don't you think we should inform the police about this before we go stumbling around up here?"

Lanciano bolted from the chair. "Absolutely not. As if this Institute hasn't had enough bad publicity for one decade. Haven't you seen the papers these last few days? They've been printing wild speculations from every two-bit conspiracy theorist in the city!"

"Some very strange things have been happening here," James insisted. "Perhaps a thorough investigation would be for the best."

Lanciano perched his fists on his narrow hips. "Easy for you to say, my friend. A 'thorough investigation' will involve looking at the Institute finances. You haven't seen the spreadsheets as I have these last few days. I'm telling you, there are a couple of accounts in such disarray that I can't make heads or tails of them. I mean, you and I know that Arthur was a saint, there's no question of deliberate malfeasance. But the man was a complete retard when it came to fiscal management!"

Finally noticing the darkening expression on James's face, Lanciano braked himself, and resorted once more to his hankie. "*Perdona me*," he said, daubing at himself. "This whole business has rattled me. Arthur's papers and books and so forth are legally yours...yes, I'm not thinking clearly. There could be insurance money coming to you from the Institute's policy if anything valuable should prove missing. I believe there are riders for just this sort of eventuality—"

"Father owned nothing of value," James interrupted. "Not of monetary value anyway. Only his papers and manuscripts and a few old books."

Lanciano suddenly looked more hopeful. "Wait a minute, what about Max's private detective, the one at the bank? We could ask her to look into this business." Lanciano gestured at the pile of emptied boxes. "Then if the person who did this proved to be someone connected to the Institute—" Lanciano winced. "Well, we might be able to settle the matter without resorting to a public exposé. Not to mention the goddamned police."

James lifted his weary eyes to *La Guadalupana* hanging on the wall behind Lanciano's head, the sight of which he'd been avoiding since he walked through the door. "It's no good, Franco. We have to involve the police. This mess could be somehow connected to Father's death."

Lanciano's handkerchief went back into his breast pocket and his thumbnail back in his mouth.

The Requiem Mass, celebrated by the entire congregation of Oratorians, was held in the old Romanesque inner-city church which now served as the Oratory of St. Philip Neri. James, Lanciano, and Heisler were among the pall bearers who carried the casket up the aisle. By the time James returned to the front pew, the steamy raininess of the afternoon complementing his mental fog like a Pathetic Fallacy, he felt as if a soundproof wall of transparent Plexiglas had slammed down between himself and the altar. He only knew when to stand or kneel or sit, as the familiar rubrics demanded, by keeping one eye on Lupe's serene figure beside him.

She nudged him gently at Communion time so that she could step over him into the main aisle, where two slowly-progressing queues moved past him towards the altar rail. It was the sudden swelling of the organ, accompanying the boys' choir's rendition of Father's favorite hymn, Newman's *Lead, Kindly Light,* that finally breached the dam. He wept openly as the mourners approached the altar to receive the host which united them, not him, with the dead priest in the Body of Christ. Among them Peter Krato and all the young men of SANA.

James started to rise, too, aching to do the thing that Bricusse had so longed to see—to take the Sacrament again. To *put on the whole armor of God.* But a second later he collapsed against the pew, unable to summon the will for so hypocritical a gesture. He hadn't been to Confession, let alone Mass, in over three years. And James Ireton needed to be purged of a great deal more than sins of apostasy and fornication.

Anger's my meat, James thought, *I feed upon myself, and so shall starve with feeding.*

It had ceased raining by the time James and Lupe drove in the funeral procession to Holy Cross Cemetery. The moisture hanging heavy in the air felt like a pillow pressed against James's face. After the casket had been lowered into the turf and the final prayers intoned, James persuaded Lupe to get a lift home from the Lancianos so that he could spend some time alone at the gravesite.

The marble stone that was to mark the priest's grave had been set aside near the casket under a blue striped awning. Looking down at it, James noted the Latin inscription, drawn from the twin mottoes of Cardinal John Henry Newman: *Ex umbris et imaginibus in veritatem, cor ad cor loquitur.* "From shadows and images to the Real, heart speaks to heart."

"Look, let me spell it out," Lt. Calvin Masefield began the next afternoon. He had just seated himself at James's dining table, fully aware that the scowling young Englishman was more than disappointed that Masefield had so little to report about MPD's progress, or lack of it, in the Bricusse case. "The autopsy report left us with a lot of questions, you bet. But it also showed that Bricusse died of natural causes. A myocardial infarction to be specific. Chances are the fall was some freak accident, the nature of which we haven't yet been able to determine. I mean, the worst we could be looking at—grant you, it's not pretty—but the worst we could be looking at is malicious tampering with the body some time *after* he died of natural causes."

It seemed to take a moment for Masefield's statement to sink in. When it did, James looked Masefield straight in the eyes and said, "You're telling me that the American justice system is so relaxed in matters of life and death that it permits a layman, perhaps some malicious bystander, to determine whether or not a sick man is beyond the reach of medical help and dispose of his body over a seventh story railing just for…what, the theatrical experience of it?"

Masefield leaned back against his chair, finally cracking a smile; he couldn't have put the case better himself. "Point taken," he said, picking up the SANA report lying on the table in front of him. "Okay, let's see what you've got here."

As Masefield scanned the pages, James fixed them both some coffee, then recounted the chronology of his and Bricusse's intended involvement in the Archdiocesan investigation of SANA; then his belated discovery of Bricusse's unusual phone messages, and Lanciano's of the vandalization of Bricusse's office. After a thorough search through the debris in Bricusse's office, James informed the lieutenant, the only thing that had proved missing was any trace that Fr. Arthur Bricusse had any knowledge or opinions on the subject of Peter Krato and the Student Apostolate of North America.

Franco Lanciano's reluctance to involve the police frankly bothered Masefield more than the rest, especially in light of the fact that Lanciano was still the most likely candidate, from Masefield's point of view at least, for the person James had heard in the stairwell the night of Bricusse's death. Besides, for Masefield's money, any effete sonuvabitch who invited men like Norman Rygiel to his home for cocktail parties was also the type of man who might have something to hide.

When James finished speaking, Masefield followed the young man's frowning gaze towards the picture of the Virgin Mary hanging above the fireplace. Similar to ones Masefield had seen in Hispanic homes throughout the city, it looked somehow out of place in this stark, masculine, and very Anglo domain, stripped clean of everything but a few sticks of cheap furniture and heaps of books. But then this Ireton, Masefield mused, looking once more around the room, was obviously a man who lived inside his own head; who judged the affairs of the real world by the words and ideas inside his own mind. In Masefield's experience, such people were eccentric observers of outside events. Their perceptions might be brilliant and incisive, or super-subtle and way off base. Right now, Masefield couldn't tell which was the case.

"Do you mind if I ask a personal question?" he said, lifting his coffee cup.

"I doubt you can ask me anything more personal than what you're going to read in there." James gestured at the SANA report.

Masefield swallowed some coffee and set down his cup. "I realize that paranoia is selling right now at fire sale prices, but is it a habit of yours to suspect homicidal conspiracies behind otherwise explainable events? Or do you just plain hate Peter Krato's living guts?"

James seemed neither surprised nor offended by the question, but he still had to think about it for a half minute before answering, "I suppose I have enough Christian sensibility left in me to say I struggle against the impulse towards hatred. Not always with success."

Masefield pulled a notepad and a ballpoint out of his breast pocket and jotted a note: KRATO—SANA—LENNY—BRICUSSE. "Well, I'll tell you," he said, flipping shut the notepad before James Ireton could get a look at it, "the two Kratos and Mitch Showalter all gave each other sterling alibis for the time of Bricusse's death."

"Of course they did."

Masefield looked up. "Most of it's corroborated by outside witnesses. The three of them ate supper at Ma Fischer's Diner, then arrived at the Institute at half past seven for some schmoozing in the atrium. Then all the SANA guys, except the Kratos and Showalter, left for home at about seven-forty-five. The three strays hung around fifteen minutes longer so they could hit up Max Heisler for a donation. When Heisler wisely sat on his wallet, the three finally left, just before eight o'clock. They told Heisler that they couldn't stay for the program because they were scheduled back at SANA house for a nine o'clock online chat-room discussion with some internet visionary on the topic of 'Megacharged Lay Evangelization.'" Masefield snorted. "Several men at their house concur that they all three arrived home at around eight-forty."

"It hardly takes that long to drive from the Institute to SANA House," James observed tartly.

"They didn't drive, they walked. And there was the storm, remember? They took shelter on a porch for almost fifteen minutes during the worst of it. The homeowners weren't at home, unfortunately, so that part can't be substantiated."

Ireton leaned forward. "Then why did they walk? I assure you, Peter Krato loathes physical exercise of any sort. And he owns two cars at least, not to mention other vehicles belonging to SANA members."

Masefield gave a brusque shake of his head. "Sorry, but they've sold all their cars except two: Krato's Lincoln Towncar and a SANA-owned Chevy van. Seems they're strapped for cash. The first contingent of men went home in the van, while Krato's Towncar was in the shop getting a new muffler."

Ireton glanced over his shoulder again at the Madonna, lines of disappointment and something like desperation cutting several paths across his face.

"Let's talk a minute more about Bricusse's missing SANA stuff," Masefield said, hoping to nudge Ireton away from his obvious personal animus towards Peter Krato. "What should Bricusse have had?"

Ireton took a deep breath, apparently re-focusing. "Computer and CD files of my SANA report, certainly, as well as the draft of his letter to the Archbishop. These would have been on the Institute's main computer system. It was also Father's practice to keep a hard copy of important documents. For example, I've found CDs, zip disks, or old floppies containing his entire correspondence dating back almost fifteen years, but none for the last three and a half years. In other words, for the time period since Peter Krato took over Immaculata House and turned it into SANA."

Masefield was surprised. "You had access to Bricusse's personal files?"

"I've been Father's official and unofficial research assistant for years. He always had me edit his published papers, and gave me access to all but his most sensitive files. We certainly shared all our SANA information. And I believe I was the only person, besides his secretary, who knew his computer user password. But I examined every directory, every disk, and every file in that office, and there was no trace of anything related to SANA." James leaned forward on his elbows. "Bricusse was a careful man, Lieutenant. Everything that should have been there relating to SANA has gone missing."

Masefield scratched his chin, his thoughts veering back towards the circumstances of Bricusse's death. In his experience, homicides were often clumsily disguised as attempted burglaries gone sour; but in this case, the burglary had occurred several days *after* the suspicious death. Masefield stabbed his finger at Ireton's cell phone, which lay on the table between them. "Okay, then, about these phone messages. Any idea, even a wild guess, what Bricusse meant when he said that something 'disturbing' had come to his attention?"

James's frustration was evident. "Not a clue."

"What about that last bit, '*as honest Iago said, I am not what I am*?'"

James absent-mindedly fingered his coffee cup. "It's a reference to Shakespeare's *Othello*. '*I am not what I am*' is a line spoken by the villain, Iago. His most famous line, actually. Father had just published an article about Iago in *The Shakespeare Quarterly*. A comparison study with Edmund, the villain in *King Lear*." James pushed aside the cup. "But bloody hell, I even sifted through Father's manuscript files, in case he'd made any suggestive notes, but I found nothing. And yet he clearly meant something by it, something by way of a warning, I just can't think what."

Masefield drained his coffee to the bottom. "You're going to have to refresh my memory," he said, setting down his cup. "All I remember about *Othello* is that it's about a black man who kills his white wife."

James shrugged. "The central theme of the play is Othello's jealousy, I suppose, but it's Iago who gets the ball rolling. Iago uses a simple trick to make the credulous Othello believe that his wife, Desdemona, has been unfaithful to him. Iago plants one of Desdemona's handkerchiefs in another man's apartment, then makes sure that Othello sees it. The upshot is, Othello kills his wife in a jealous rage."

He knew it was the cop in him, but Masefield just had to ask, "What was Iago's motive?"

James Ireton actually smiled, albeit crookedly. "That's the sixty-four thousand dollar question of all *Othello* criticism. Some racism, to be sure, and class resentment. Othello had passed him over for a lieutenancy, you see, in favor of a handsome upper-class bloke. Then there's lust. Lust for Desdemona, or even Othello himself perhaps, if you're into Queer Theory.

Believe me, Lieutenant, oceans of ink have been spilled over the knotty question of Iago's motive, but there are still no definitive answers. Never will be, I dare say."

Masefield chuckled.

"A dead cert, though, Iago's a fabulous liar. An actor really. Or better yet, a sort of playwright, like Shakespeare himself. Chesterton once said that Shakespeare's plots are usually about plots. Well, Iago has an absolutely splendid time concocting his little plots, all the while pretending to be Othello's most trusted officer and loyal friend. I suppose it's because Shakespeare was a theatre man, that was his world. Any actor will tell you there's something inherently schizophrenic about it."

Masefield sat silently for some seconds, digesting this peculiar information — not the sort of thing he usually had to consider in homicide investigations. James, meanwhile, equally pensive, finished his coffee with enervated slurps. Finally, Masefield glanced at his watch. "Mercy," he said, collecting the SANA report, "I've got to run." He gestured at Ireton's cell phone. "Don't erase those messages. I'll want to make a copy."

James was preceding Masefield to the door when Masefield paused again to ask, "You didn't by any chance know Lenny Swiatko, did you?"

James shook his head. "He joined SANA long after I left. But it was his suicide that persuaded Father to intervene in the Archdiocesan investigation." James face folded in a frown. "Odd, isn't it, that they both should have died as they did?"

"There was that video store owner, too…"

"Beg pardon?"

"You didn't read about it? Part of the Milwaukee Vice war."

"I don't read the papers much."

"The guy owned an adult video shop," Masefield explained. "He backed the wrong side and got himself dropped off the Marquette Interchange for his trouble. I mean, whether falls or drops or dives, this is the kind of thing that happens maybe once in a decade, not three times in a couple of weeks, know what I mean?"

Noting the confusion on James Ireton's face, Masefield snapped out of his momentary brain funk. "Probably just a weird coincidence," he added quickly, quoting Ramon Cruz, who had only yesterday complained that Masefield was paying too much attention to the "drops" angle. The unstated but obvious inference, of course, was that it was due to his feelings of guilt over Lenny's suicide. Not that Masefield was about to tell a civilian, least of all one as suspicious as James Ireton, that he had answered Ramon with the remark, "Maybe so, but if it's a coincidence, it's a whopper. In my experience they don't come in that size."

"Say," Masefield said instead, producing a reassuring smile intended to lull Ireton's uneasy mind as he moved once again towards the front door, "you got a copy of *Othello* I could borrow? Maybe a movie of it or something? And that article Bricusse wrote, while you're at it. I think it's time I brushed up my Shakespeare."

It appeared that the local meteorologists had cooperated admirably with James's romantic plans for the afternoon, sending him what was very likely to be the last summery day before a major Canadian-born cool front descended on the state over the weekend. The southwest wind sent the thermometer hiking well above the sweating mark, even on Bradford Beach, while faint brush strokes of cirrus-white decorated a clear sky over powder blue waters—a palette, James thought, unique to Lake Michigan in summer. A dozen or more sailboats spirited along the horizon, their canvasses alternately drooping or swelling in the finicky breeze.

James thrust the handle of a beach umbrella deep into the sand while Lupe unpacked the picnic lunch he had brought, complete with an expensive bottle of Merlot recommended by Jack. The latter elicited a whistle from Lupe when she saw the label. They chatted for a while about nothing in particular, taking their time as they ate and drank, and soaked up the heat of the sun, and the growing warmth of their intimacy. Finally, James set aside his almost empty plate.

"Well, now, I believe we were due for a little argument. About sex."

Lupe chased her last bite of bread with a swallow of wine before securing the stem of the plastic glass in the sand next to her leg.

"Shall I g-go first?"

"By all means. Though I dare say I know your opinions on the subject, at least in theory."

"You think so?" Tucking her legs underneath her, Lupe waved the thought away and ventured on in a let's-not-beat-about-the-bush tone. "First, an analogy. My brother Martin—he's the Carmelite priest I told you about—he once told me that penitents in the confessional fall roughly into two categories: sacks of potatoes, or sacks of flour."

James chortled. "There you go again with that lofty mystical theology. Too deep for me, by half."

"Now really, it's perfectly simple. Your sack of potatoes is just someone who spills his or her guts in one heave. You know—" Lupe made dumping motion with her arms. "—you turn the sack upside down, and all the spuds t-t-tumble out in a heap. Nothing left in the sack. See?"

"Perfectly."

"But now your sack of flour…well, think about it. If you turn a flour sack upside down, the flour all comes out in a cloud of dust, and there's always a layer of flour still sticking to the inside of the bag. To clean it out, you have to reach up inside the sack and scrape and scrape, and you get flour dust all over you, and-and-and—"

James raised his hand. "I catch your drift. You want things straight, no tacking and jibing. Well jolly well so do I. I may be a sack of flour about everything else in my life, *Señorita* Cruz, but when it comes to sex, I'm pure Idaho."

Lupe grunted. "You just want to know whether it's 'yes,' 'no,' or 'm-m-maybe.'"

James's mouth slipped open, then he fell on his back, shaking with laughter. After his shoulders finally ceased quivering, he reached out and pulled her over on top of him. That she kissed him back was encouraging, to be sure, but then her Guadalupe medal struck him in the face and he swore.

She sat up. "We were discussing whether I was g-g-going to sleep with you," she said, reaching for the wine bottle.

He snatched it away. "Is the prospect of sleeping with me so frightful that you need to get ripped even to consider it?" Noting signs of irritation emerging in her swift-moving face he added, "Look, this whole thing's a little frightening for me, too, all right? I'll even go so far as to say…well, I don't know exactly what. But in any case, let me remind you, as a student of literature, that Shakespeare wrote an entire series of sonnets protesting the stinginess of those who refuse to share their gift of beauty with the opposite sex."

"Shakespeare wrote that sonnet series to protest the stinginess of those who refuse to marry and pass on the gift of beauty by procreating," Lupe corrected. "I'll have you to know I'm fully prepared to do my, uh, duty in that regard. I'm not a prude, d-dammit, I'm a Christian!"

"Who went out once too often with Barry DeBrun."

She looked away. "I wouldn't read too much into that. It's not like it made me afraid of being loved. From wanting a man's face to show me G-G-God's face." Looking up, she fixed her turquoise eyes on him with a surprising fierceness. "For me, in the language of the body, sex means that I give myself to you and I take you in return. All of me and all of you. A very great thing which is also a sign of something even greater. A sacrament. A holy communion. Or not at all."

"Ah, yes," he said tightly. "*With my body, I thee worship.*"

"Yep. The whole sack of potatoes."

Frowning out at the melting blue of water, James felt his skin tightening across his cheekbones. It was happening again, he thought; he didn't know why she always had this effect on him, but once again Lupe Cruz was peeling off the scabs of his inner wounds and exposing the sores beneath to air and sun, exposing them to pain.

Finally, James gave a bitter sounding laugh and said, "The language of the body…what an imagination you have. Unfortunately, one better suited to the twelfth century than to the twenty-first. You do realize, don't you, that there's no word in modern English for the sort of sexual love you're describing? As far as I know there never has been. Too bad, too, when we have so many picturesque and to-the-point coinages for all the less sublime variations on the theme of coitus. In any case, 'worship' is a language I do not speak."

She just looked at him, her dark eyebrows gathered.

"Well, now," he continued when it became clear she had nothing further to say on the subject, "considering how I'm feeling myself right now, I can well imagine the reactions you've had, hitting a man with your sublime version of 'Hell, no' when all in the world he was wanting was to empty himself between your beautiful legs."

She colored. "It's been the end of the relationship, every time. Like Gregor Samsa, I woke up one morning from uneasy dreams to find myself transformed into an Anachronism…something a little lower on today's evolutionary scale than K-Kafka's cockroach."

He felt a stab in his gut at the thought of those other men, her other possibilities. He couldn't help but wonder what they did together, how far those men had got with her…not far, from the sounds of it, though he didn't know whether to feel relieved or more worried still. Was this, he wondered anxiously, what people called 'jealousy'?

Then, tumbling after that, James also recognized a now-familiar sense of shame in Lupe Cruz's presence; in her certain knowledge of all the things he had done before with other women, so many other women. For three long years he had felt no compunction about the whole business other than an occasional flutter of abstract, once-removed guilt—the dust and debris of exploded Christian morality settling into the cracks of his interior life. But in this moment, her turquoise eyes frowning darkly in the shadow of the umbrella as she struggled to understand him and his wayward desires, the sting of self-reproach felt like a poker thrust in his belly. God, what did all this *mean*? Why couldn't he sort out these feelings like a normal man?

"Tell me," he said, resisting the temptation to hold his breath, "have you ever been in love before?"

"Oh, no." She squinted up at the sky, one hand circling the air as if she were groping for the words. "No. I didn't know it, but I was looking for something. Something that's p-p-pretty rare."

"What? Specifically."

"P-P-Passion," she said matter-of-factly.

He cocked back his head. "I don't believe for a moment that no man's ever been passionate about you."

"That's not what I meant. I meant 'passion' as in an intensity towards things in general. A religious intensity."

He turned his face towards the glare of water. "Then you've come to the wrong shop. Religion is dead to me. It means nothing." When she didn't respond, he added, "Bloody hell, Cruz, I can see the gears turning. You may as well say what you're thinking."

"You're not going to like it."

"Have I liked anything you've said since the hour we met?"

She fidgeted with her Guadalupe medal. "Here's what I think. I think you're a good actor. You put on a good show, but it's all show. You say 'nothing' with the passion of St. John of the Cross—*nada!* Oh, no. Truth is, I think you're the most religious man I've ever known."

Feeling the sweat on his chest soaking through his Oxford tee, James yanked it over his head and flung it down on the sand beside his leg. "*Religious,*" he almost spat, "that's enough to make a cat laugh." He scooped a handful of hot sand and let it sift through his splayed fingers. "I'll tell you about my religion. It's like a chronic case of TB. My ability to function may improve over time, but my immune system is impaired, my temperament's been skewed by an awareness of my own contagion, and I'll never lose the goddamned bug." He leveled his eyes on hers as the last particle of sand dropped from between his fingers. "Sorry, *but I am rough, and woo not like a babe.* I don't suppose your love and my religiosity are sufficient argument to persuade you to come home with me tonight."

"N-N-No, they're not."

He sucked in his breath. God, she had said it, flat out. He felt sick.

"But look," she added quickly, reaching for him, "we could still be friends, you know. I said w-way too much the other night, I know I did, but we could make a pact never to speak of love again. I mean, maybe if we didn't k-k-kiss anymore—"

"Stop kissing you? Jesus, why not suggest I stop breathing!" He yanked away his hand. "Oh, I'm getting the picture. You're thinking that you're the one who loves, while for me...well, boys must get their greens, and this thing of mine is just one of those irritating physical reactions randy young men are prone to." Scooping up another handful of sand, he closed his fist until the particles oozed out between his fingers. "You may have an uncanny knack for spiriting confessions out of me, but this time you haven't quite got it right. Bloody Christ, you want *all* of me? That means my past, too, you know, including the several score women I've banged in the last fifteen years. Better have your multiplication tables up to speed, 'cause if I gave you the complete roster we'd be here for days. But just for starters—"

"I don't need to know all that to-to-to know it."

"Oh, but I think you do. Honesty's one of my few remaining virtues, and I'd hate to have you taking me on without the complete picture. Probably need a wide-angle lens." He raised his hands like a film director framing her face for his next shot. "Fact is, dearest girl, I've seen better faces in my time than yours. You're hardly as pretty as Bel Gunderson, if 'pretty' is the word. But then Isabel could turn a Fra Angelico into a leering whore with that *haute couture* smirk of hers. But if we were to set intelligence and character wholly aside, it's not in the face but in the measurements where *you* really begin to excel. Oh yes, as exquisite as Bel is, you're streets ahead of her there, at least for a man of my tastes."

"James, this is cruel."

"So it is, but it's also the truth, so I suggest you listen up." Dropping his hands, he turned away as if searching out some pleasant fragment in his memory. "Of all the women I've known, until you, I think Maggie Claymore had the finest cleavage. You wouldn't know Maggie, she's an actress with the Milwaukee Rep. True, she could freeze the god Priapus with that Kate Smith voice of hers—Jack and I used to call her *Magnum Clamor,* because she could shatter glass at a thousand yards. But, mercy, what miraculous breasts. Praise the Lord for two big hands!" Lowering his two big hands, James turned his attentions to another part of Lupe's anatomy. "Let's see... hips, thighs, and...ah me, the holy trinity. Or let's say, the Bermuda Triangle, where so many unwary ships are lost without a trace. Sad but true, I don't supposed I've ever done so well before there, you've got quite a package. But then one's memory does begin to play tricks. I've had so many women their images have begun to commingle in my mind like mushy vegetables in an overcooked stew."

"James—"

"Then there's your exotic color combination of turquoise eyes and black hair. I would have never guessed I had such a thing for dark women. Want to hear who it reminds me of?" He didn't wait for a response. "It reminds me of Nadine Jeffrey. You've not met her either, I think, but she's Bo Jeffrey's little sister. If the truth be told, I was sailing too close to the wind with Nadine." He waved his arm in a haphazard arc. "All right, I guess I was just a little in love with her. Now I recognize the emotion, I didn't then. Not that I would have ever said I loved her even if I did, just as I'll never say it with you. But no question I was floundering. The night I took her to Lanciano's party last spring, I could tell she was about to give me the old heave-ho, like the intelligent woman she was, and I was actually trying, in my hamfisted way, to keep her. We were up in one Lanciano's second floor bathrooms when Nadine said to me, in the midst of things—I was paying some masculine lip-service to the feminist notion of the valorization of the clitoris—that she needed time to think about our relationship. She needed to think about our relationship because she didn't know *who I was*." He barked a laugh. "Didn't know who I was, and me the most obvious bastard this side of the Atlantic? Well, it irritated the hell out of me, I can tell you. I made up my mind, on my knees right then and there, to lose her once and for all. I wrote a speech in my head on the spot. Wholesale garbage about our not suiting one another, about our cultural differences and all that pious rot. There may be fifty ways to leave a lover, but I've perfected only one: the Gilbert and Sullivan *short sharp shock*, too blunt to be anything but farce. But wouldn't you know, right out of the blue, I was rescued from the hoisted guillotine by a knock on the door. We were obliged to pull ourselves together. We went back downstairs where little Trish Perl, afloat on Lanciano's expensive champagne, made a drunken pass at me. I went home with her without so much as a word of explanation to Nadine. And now Nadine hates my guts, and jolly well should."

He wiped sweat from his forehead with the back of his hand, his eyes to the sand. "Now, about Trisha. God knows she can't compare to you in looks, but she's a brainy, feisty girl, and has a sort of innocence and intensity, like yours, which I found utterly irresistible. For about twenty minutes. Poor girl just shook while I worked her over, damned if I know why. And tell you what, no matter what I did I couldn't get her fuse lit. So finally I just told her, like the gentleman I am, to lay there so I could finish myself off. And damned if she didn't do it, too. There have been so many bodies, I've known so many bodies...*For several virtues have I liked several women; never any with so full soul but some defect in her did quarrel with the noblest grace she owed, and put it to the foil.* Megan Phillips' cheekbones, Kim Prohaska's pianist's fingers, Leila Redmond's woman-of-the-world finesse..." He laughed. "Of course with Leila I was whoring myself selflessly for Western Civ. She's our most generous patroness, you know. She had a wonderful scent about her, some sort of terrifically expensive perfume that I imagine I shall for the rest of my life associate with silk sheets and five-star hotels. She wrote out the check for the Redmond Theatre the day we got back from Door County, and hasn't troubled me since. I tell you, that week must surely reign in my imagination as the perfect assignation."

He finally got up the nerve to look at her: Lupe was hunched over, hugging her knees.

Smiling slightly, James continued in a brutally flippant tone, "So you see, with all the bodies I've known, I can almost come up with one whole woman, stitched together like the Bride of Frankenstein. But speaking of body parts, your legs remind me of the last girl I knew, biblically, at Oxford. I stuffed her for a couple of months. That must have been a record for me, until Bel. In fact, everyone in the *Hamlet* production that term thought I was hooked, and said so. But then I panicked one night when we got a little too athletic and the Durex broke. I called it off after the next day's rehearsal. The director threatened to ax me for fucking up the morale of the cast. In this case quite literally, since the girl was my Ophelia. But whether it lasts a month or a week or just one night, something puzzling happens to me, sooner or later, in every affair." He tilted his head to one side, the question mark in his eyes reflected in hers in an expression of horror. "I think the word is 'revulsion.' Yes, stomach-emptying, never-touch-a-woman-again revulsion. Do you imagine that could happen with us?" He waved it away. "About two months later, long after we'd broken up, I ran into my Ophelia in front of Blackwell's. She slapped me full on the face. Damned near knocked me flat, too. And when I demanded, like the injured party, to know what the hell it was for—you're going to love this—she said, she said, *that's for your baby I just got shot of*—"

James's voice broke, the sound of glass under a jackboot. When he dared look up again a half minute or more later, the suffering etched in Lupe's face positively frightened him. He had gone way too far, he knew it, and the only decent thing would be to offer some form of explanation or apology. But when he began to speak again he heard himself saying entirely different words from those he intended, and in an even more savage tone:

"Why, I haven't told you the half of it, and you're blubbering already! Have you any idea what all that serene bullshit about 'love' and 'communion' and 'exchanging hearts' makes me feel? Christ, I haven't been a virgin since I was fifteen years old. I'm sure I've only managed to escape all the nasty diseases of the last few decades because I seem to have this inveterate penchant for *nice* girls. Except Bel, of course—*a palomino that any man can ride if he comes with sugar in his hand*. But she does take all the proper precautions, our Bel. Or so I thought. But then I haven't really told you about *that* relationship yet, have I? Not that you could call it a 'relationship' exactly. Precisely the case where a bit of four-letter nomenclature comes most in handy, and anything but the L-word. But just for a moment, climb down from that mountaintop of yours and try to imagine what it was like for me three years ago, coming out of that religious lunatic asylum where nothing was just what it seemed. Well, Bel Gunderson at least was exactly what she seemed." He thrust out his open hand. "In-your-face eroticism, nothing more, nothing less. She was like a strong hit of morphine after a botched surgery. I would go to her to make the pain stop for a few minutes. I would, as it were, make an *appointment* with her two or three times a week, when the sexual tension would strong-arm my puritanical self-loathing."

"Stop—"

"Nasty thing about lust, though, it won't stay gone when it's satisfied. *The expense of spirit in a waste of shame is lust in action*—Sonnet 129 and all that crap. In fact I don't know why I haven't gone the solo route, since most sex is little more than mutual masturbation anyway. Fewer hassles, less fuss, no human complications, no diseases. It's just that I can't seem to get past that need for some sort of, some sort of..." He gasped. "...human contact... however truncated..." His voice trailed off. He hadn't realized it himself until he had said it.

A moment later he shook away the thought, like shooing away an annoying bumblebee. "Have I made myself understood? Dammit, look at me! Does this look like the face of God to you?"

"I kn-kn-know what I see," she whispered, her bleached cheeks damp with tears.

"Then let's soldier on. Now as for Bel...trouble with Bel Gunderson, she has this rather kinky sense of humor, have you noticed? She came back one evening after a week down in Chicago and told me, as casually as if she were describing a Thirteen-Hour-Sale at Marshall Fields, that she, too, had just had herself hoovered out."

Lupe doubled over, clutching her belly.

"Well, now," he said, feeling very pleased with himself, "I thought that would get a reaction."

Lupe's eyes flew up to his face—startled, angry eyes. She gave a shake of her fists beside her knees. "You w-w-wanted that reaction? Well, try this on for size: *I* would have kept your child. Or is that the last thing on earth you want to hear? Sweet Savior, what's the matter with you, didn't your father ever tell you where b-b-babies come from?"

"Oh, that's rich! Sad to say, the Rev. Dr. Cyril Ireton was never very fluent in the language of the body. In fact I could never quite imagine how he got it up long enough to beget two children. Cyril was adept, however, at brutalizing his wife. Must have picked up all my latent hostility from him. You see? Bad gene pool, Cruz. When it comes to the domestic arena, I've only been trained for to-the-death battles. *Morituri te salute!*"

He leaned into her face, his voice rising in pitch and volume like the sound of a scream through a slowly-opening door. "They explained it all to me in hospital. What a stew of *words, words, words* those trick-cyclist quacks served up for their daily purgatives: dysfunctional, codependent, addictive personality, sexual compulsive, and bi-polar in the manic phase...Lord, the labels! Of course it all depended on whether the shrink in question was Freudian, Adlerian, Rogerian, or Jungian. One fellow there, a *devoté* of Laing and Szasz—or was it Foucault?—thought I was the only sane man in the whole place." He aimed his forefinger at her. "You'd better have all hands on deck sailing me, Cruz, because you know what they say about us bi-polars: *the higher the peak, the deeper the valley.* I'm the sort of nightmare that finishes up as a rapist, or a serial killer. Or just a garden-variety wife-beater. You don't want communion with that kind of mess. You don't want to wake up with that every morning. You don't want *my* children!"

With the last word she flung herself face-down on the hot sand. When after a minute or so he couldn't stand her crying any longer, he grabbed a beach towel to wipe her face.

She yanked away the towel. "Ok-k-kay," she sobbed, daubing her face, her lower lip quivering, "I may be slow, but I'm getting the picture. You want me to take it all b-b-back, don't you, everything I said before? Isn't that what all this is about? Hurting me as badly as you can so I'll take it all back and you won't have to deal with it? Well, too bad, because I won't. I know what I've seen. And if you're so damned honest, then tell me why it makes you feel better to hur-hur-hurt me. God, if you can't deal with how I feel, then why don't you just tell me to go to hell and we can just—"

"Lupe—"

"—call it quits and I can drop the class, take it next year. Now that Father's gone, I don't give a damn. But I won't take it back. Not any of it. That's not the way it works. When I said I loved you, I didn't just mean when I felt like it, or when you turned over a new leaf, or when you made it *easy* for me, d-d-damn you—"

He lunged forward, pushing her on her back and flinging his arms around her waist as if grasping for a life preserver in a gale-dark sea. "I didn't know you were coming," he cried, his face in her belly.

Catching her breath, she lifted one arm to shield her eyes from the sun, while the fingers of her other hand inched along the sand to his shoulder. Then up to his neck and damp hair. "Funny," she whispered, "I always knew you were coming."

He rested his chin on her belly to look up at her. "Everything I said is true. Everything. How could you love that?"

She looked surprised by the question, not as if she didn't know the answer to it, but as if she couldn't imagine that he didn't. "You're glorious," she said. "Dark and light and shocking as a midnight by Caravaggio."

"You got the midnight right at least. And you're as bright and clear and clean as a morning by Vermeer. A greater mismatch can hardly be conceived. I suppose that's what I've been trying to tell you this afternoon, no doubt brutally."

"Silly, silly man."

"Come home with me tonight. *If ever any beauty I did see which I desired and got, 'twas but a dream of thee.*"

"No."

"Because of your goddamned religion."

"Yours, too."

"I don't speak that language anymore. I don't speak theology!"

Sitting up, she cradled his damp head in her lap. "Then let's speak poetry. You understand that language well enough. Think of me as a p-p-poet, working in sonnets. To craft a sonnet, you have to keep to the form: fourteen lines in iambic pentameter, three quatrains and a couplet. Otherwise it's not a sonnet, it's...free verse."

"Great poets know when to break the form," he countered. "And free verse has its own beauty."

"But I'm not a great poet. And as for free verse..." She smiled crookedly. "Be honest. Whether it's a matter of taste or something a little more, you wouldn't find me worth reading twice in free verse."

James lay grinding his teeth for several seconds, the sweat dripping from his forehead onto her thigh. Finally he jumped to his feet. "This is impossible," he announced.

James drove Lupe home in brittle silence before returning empty-handed, against all his hopes, to his steamy apartment, where he changed into a pair of running shorts. Forty minutes later, after a furious sprint up and down Prospect Avenue failed to sand down his sexual edge, he showered, threw on a bathrobe, drank a quart of water, cursed a great deal, then paced his living room for several minutes before finally giving in to humiliating need and padding back into his stuffy bedroom for five furious minutes of Vaseline-greased masturbating that left him feeling sick. Then, perhaps fifteen minutes later when his sexual tension inexplicably returned, sicker. He lay there afterwards for twenty minutes or so, sweating and panting and raw, before finally dozing off.

Waking up an hour later to the dreadful dragon-dream, he rolled out of bed, took another shower—so cold it hurt—then changed into khakis and a rugby shirt, having decided that he was long overdue for an evening of pulling birds downtown. Bloody hell, he hadn't felt like this in years. Three years, to be exact.

He stood before the image of *la Guadalupana* some minutes later, his attitude defiant, his mind a littering of impulses and images, like a year's accumulation of party refuse. He needed to organize this mess in his head, he thought; sort it out and collate it into a neat, paginated little bundle; then maybe the text would make some kind of sense.

Somewhere in the sorting process an image of Barry DeBrun emerged, trigger finger aimed; then the sound of DeBrun's taunting words that night on the beach, which James, thus far, had been unable to square against Lupe Cruz's version of events—that five-hankie tale of violated innocence that had wrung from him first compassion, then a kiss; then a torrent of feeling that was threatening to sweep him into the sea. Now, a week later, DeBrun's challenging words rang in his mind with hollow brilliance: *C'mon, Lu, how long are you gonna milk that one for…?*

James paced some more beneath *la Guadalupana*, whose sightless eyes seemed to observe his every impulse like a paranoid Superego. Really, he wondered, could Mr. Soap Opera have pulled those unnerving words so quickly and casually out of his pocket that night if they weren't true? Could a man like DeBrun—any man—be that good of an actor? Or was *she*, perhaps, the one that had been indulging in a bit of histrionics—about DeBrun, about herself and her oh-too-sublime convictions?

James paused, fists in pockets.

The most reasonable explanation, he began to think, had been right in front of him from the beginning: DeBrun had seduced Lupe once in high school, had even got a little rough perhaps—undoubtedly unpleasant for a sensitive girl's first time—and she had panicked. Maybe she had even been afraid she was pregnant. As the product of immigrant parents and a strict Roman Catholic upbringing her instinctive reaction had been—of course!—to fabricate a martyr's tale.

At long last a new and strange, but nonetheless compelling image formed in James's mind, like a negative soaking in film emulsion: the features and figure were those of Lupe Cruz, but there was an older, more knowing expression on this woman's face; a look of cunning and calculation which subtly transformed those familiar open features into a mosaic of dark complexity. James couldn't remember ever having seen such an expression on Lupe Cruz's face before—the muscles of her lips, for example, slanted at just that provocative angle; but he could well imagine it, yes clearly, as if he had seen it many times, and its credibility began to take shape in his mind as a kind of fact.

Lord, James thought with a snap of his head, what a case he'd been these last few weeks! First lust, then grief, now lust again…he'd been upended. Under such trying circumstances, it was not to be wondered at if he had resorted to a bit of emotional day-tripping. Or worse, a psychosexual version of two weeks on Fantasy Island. Almost too late he was realizing that Miss Guadalupe Cruz had been playing, and expertly too, a very old game with him. The marriage game. Oh, she hadn't said so in so many words, but that was unquestionably the subtext, printed in boldface type.

To give the girl the benefit of the doubt, perhaps a feminine need for that mediocre form of emotional security had been planted in her as deeply as revulsion for the institution had been in him. Well, James could imagine that. Women were like that, so they said. And then there were the tales floating around the Institute about his private income, which, though hardly luxurious, might prove sufficient stimulus for the ambitions of your average middle-class girl. If that were the case, then an expensive present alone might turn the trick, or the merest hint of a wedding after he got his degree.

James stepped to his desk and reached for his keys and wallet. *Bait the hook well*, he concluded, heading for the door, *and this fish will bite*.

After a half hour's worth of agitated meandering along Milwaukee's near east side, James's sexual tension finally gave way to the itch of mere restlessness. Looking for something reasonably intelligent to do to waste the rest of an already ghastly evening, he brightened a bit when he spotted the Oriental Theatre up ahead, an historic east side film palace that served up the usual art house fare. James's face sagged, however, when he got close enough to make out the lettering on the marquee: the cinema, it appeared, was hosting a week-long Kubrick retrospective. Tonight's feature was *Eyes Wide Shut.*

Bloody hell, James thought, that wouldn't help.

After opting instead for a cup of coffee at nearby Ma Fischer's Diner, he stepped out onto the sidewalk twenty minutes later, dismayed to hear a too-familiar voice hailing him from a distance. Turning, he saw Bel Gunderson sashaying out of the Oriental, tarted up tonight in a black fedora, tube top, and leather leggings. On her arm was Trisha Perl, mismatching her partner in her usual frayed overalls. The unlikely pair was followed, *seriatim*, by Jack Sigur and Bo Jeffrey. James was most surprised of all to see Mitch Showalter making up the caboose of this weird train, dressed this evening in khakis and a polo shirt — the first time James had seem him in civvies in over three years.

"Ireton," Bel scolded as James approached, bending down so that Trisha could light her clove cigarette for her, "I've been leaving messages for you all day. You were playing hooky, I knew it."

"Maybe Jim-bo wasn't in the mood tonight for Grand Guignol," Jack commented, reaching inside his shirt pocket for a lighter and a pack of Lucky Strikes.

Bel seemed inclined to argue the point, but finding no interest in James's closed face, directed her fashion magazine pout on Mitch Showalter. Disengaging herself from Trisha's clinging arm, she sidled up to Mitch, pulled the big man towards her by the collar of his polo shirt, and whispered something in his ear, their faces hidden by the brim of her fedora. By the time Mitch straightened, a flush of pink was mounting from his thick neck to his cheeks.

"I ca-an't, Isabel," Mitch said, his voice cracking comically. "I, uh…well, the Cenacle's meeting tonight and I'm already late. Maybe another time?"

"Now that's progress!" Bel announced. Whipping off her hat, she slapped it down on Mitch's oversized and clammy head; but before Mitch could bring forth his impending expression of befuddled gratitude, a look of sudden recognition erupted on Bel's face. Tossing her clove cigarette into the gutter, she waved her slender arms in a dramatic arc at some object over James's left shoulder.

James turned to see an ivory-colored roadster, a classic-styled convertible with tinted windows and the top up, pulling up to the curb on the opposite side of North Farwell.

"My next appointment, children," Bel trilled, adjusting her tube top with a quick yank. "I'm off to a bona fide little orgy of my very own, performed in campiest Roman style. It's gonna be filmed, too, can you believe it? In Cream City? Decadence has made its way to Brewtown even before civilization!"

"Bel," Trisha said as the invisible driver of the car tooted impatiently, "what the hell are you doing?"

Bel chucked Trish under the chin with affectionate condescension. "Now, child, don't get clingy on me. Life's a crap shoot, you know, and it's my turn to roll." With that, Bel whirled away, her final gesture a diva-like benediction from across the street as she climbed into the passenger side of the two-seater. The ivory roadster burst away with a squeal of rubber down Farwell.

"Well, I like that," Jack commented sourly.

"What's to like or dislike about the Whore of Babylon getting into a flashy car?" Bo Jeffrey smirked. "Same old same old."

"That flashy car's a *Baci*," Jack explained, blowing out smoke. "Only one of fourteen made by hand on the south side. Probably worth upwards of a hundred grand."

Trisha's lower lip quivered. "You know who it belongs to?"

Jack shuddered. "Norman Rygiel, he of the Cream City mob. Hope to hell ol' Belzebub knows what she's doing."

Mitch's comment on the situation consisted of a cracking of his thumb knuckle with a sickening punch. James had to restrain himself from an outburst of laughter: in Bel's ill-fitting fedora, the big man resembled a round-rumped circus bear, peregrinating the high-wire in a top hat. "I gotta skedaddle," Mitch said, yanking off the fedora and raking his pudgy fingers through his curly hair, which looked both longer and more golden than heretofore in the wash of marquee lights. "Rich thinks I'm at the library, but if *Der Führer* finds out I've gone AWOL, I'll be peeling potatoes till the Last Trump."

Bo Jeffrey snickered with appreciation, but seeing no similar response from the rest of the group, Mitch gave an ironic salute and turned on his size thirteen heels. Bo turned as well, as if he were about to follow the big man.

Jack called after him, "You going to the Cenacle meeting, too?"

Bo paused to face his friend. "I'm due at my sister's, and I'd lay odds on her temper over Peter Krato's any day." He laughed out loud. "Care to join me? We're having a party. All the old gang."

"I'm getting too old for your parties, man."

Bo rolled his eyes. "Honestly, Sigur, you've got the wrong temperament to be gay. I think it's time you settled down on the south side with a fat wife and a passel of rug rats."

"I don't recall needing a Bo Jeffrey seal of approval on my coming-out papers," Jack retorted.

"Maybe it's just the scummy company you're keeping, you know?" With that, Bo Jeffrey thrust his middle finger in the air in front of James's face and wheeled around, exiting the circle of marquee light in long, athletic strides.

James didn't react. He'd been expecting it, or something very much like it. But Jack flung his cigarette on the pavement and cut loose with a string of bawdry that sounded filthy even in French.

"Let it go," James said. "You can't blame the man."

Still gazing forlornly at the corner where the Baci had disappeared, Trisha suddenly burst into tears. Jack wrapped his arm around her shoulders, sympathy for her humiliating situation apparently superseding his irritation at his old friend Bo Jeffrey. "I fall for the lousiest people!" Trish wailed into his armpit. When she realized what she had said her eyes flew up to James's face. "That's not what I meant," she cried, stamping one boy-sized Reebok.

James cleared his throat. "I'm afraid I never got round to apologizing for that night. I was bloody, to you and Nadine both."

Trish dug into her dungarees for some tissues. "Worry about Nadine, not me. If you knew the whole story—" She cut off her own sentence with a wave of her tissue. "Tell you what, guys, I'm sick and tired of these lipstick lesbians. I'm tired of lesbians. Hell, I'm tired of sex. Honest to God, I think I hate sex. I mean, I just don't know what everyone sees in it. Maybe I'll turn nouveau celibate or Second Virgin or whatever the hell they call common sense these days." She honked into her tissue. "You know, we're all three of us Purple Heart casualties of the Sexual Revolution. *N'est-çe pas?*"

Jack had to laugh. "Yeah, well, me, I love sex. Problem is, sex just hasn't taken a liking to me yet."

They both turned to James.

"Don't look at me," he said. "I'm beginning to think I don't even know what it is, let alone whether I like it or not."

Jack reached for another cigarette, his eyes on the sidewalk.

"Jack," Trisha's voice was taut with sudden urgency, "I don't suppose I could talk you into walking me home, could I? Sounds like there may be a rapist roaming the east side." Trisha's pale little face sagged in the light of the marquee. "Bel told me Kim Prohaska was attacked last week. The guy broke into her apartment on Farwell, just up the street from you, Jack."

James gasped.

"Jesus," Jack murmured.

"Bel said the cops haven't got a clue. The bastard crushed her fingers with steel-heeled boots or something. They don't know if she'll ever be able to play the piano again. I mean, she never even *saw* the guy. The attack was from behind, know what I mean?"

"Jesus," Jack repeated. "Well, by all means—" He cocked his bent elbow towards her. She hooked her arm through his. "And where are you off to, my lad?" he said to James, who was still stunned by the news about Kim.

"Um, I've got to stop in at the chemist's to fill a prescription."

"Not sleeping well again?"

James shrugged. "The usual."

"Yeah, well, you were never one to take advice, but if you'll take mine, I think you'll find that the best remedy you got for insomnia lives in a big three-story house about a half a mile over yonder." Jack waved his fresh Lucky in the direction of Stowell Avenue, then lit up. Not waiting for a response, he signaled his intention to depart to Trish. "*Adieu, good Monsieur Melancholy.*"

James watched in silence as the lopsided pair headed up the street arm in arm, looking for all the world like a cartoon of a Dream Team basketball player escorting a Russian gymnast to an Olympic *fête*. When they had finally turned the corner, James, feeling suddenly sick to his stomach, closed his eyes, a memory surfacing of Kim Prohaska's beautiful fingers playing his instrument under a Lake Park yew.

A puff of cool air found its way under his shirt, causing gooseflesh on his chest and arms. Slipping the barbiturate prescription out of his wallet, James made his way to the corner drugstore.

After showering and changing into a nightshirt, Lupe lit a vigil candle beneath the poster of *La Guadalupana* in her bedroom and offered up a silent prayer for…God knew. Then she set her mind to scrounging up something to do; something that might displace the memories of this afternoon's beach debacle in her tumbling thoughts.

In spite of his chronic fury at All Things Religious, Lupe had nonetheless expected James to be a little more, well, sympathetic to her moral predicament. After all, unlike most of their contemporaries, for whom religion served little purpose other than to bless life's sundry passages with hoary ritual, James, at least, had once been on her side of the divide that separated the believer from the skeptic, the committed from the lukewarm. But sympathetic James was obviously not, and the usually decisive Lupe Cruz suddenly didn't know what to think about it all, let alone what to do about it.

Settling finally on the performance of some long-neglected chores to salve her bewilderment, Lupe set about washing dishes, clearing and wiping down the kitchen counter, putting away the clothes she'd brought up earlier from the basement laundry, and organizing her desk. Those little triumphs of hope over despair accomplished, she concluded her exercise in tidying up by carrying a plastic trash bag from room to room to empty the wastebaskets.

Having stuffed the bag into the big plastic garbage can on the landing of her outside stairs, Lupe was replacing the lid when she felt a droplet of rain on her nose and looked up: a bank of clouds, heavy with rain, was moving across the full moon.

Suddenly she heard footsteps. Whirling around, she saw a figure emerging from the darkness below. She reached in panic for the screen door latch, then saw in amazement and relief that it wasn't Barry DeBrun as she had feared, but James, spiraling up the stairs two at a time. Before she could calm her galloping heartbeats, he had reached the top step and was lifting her off her feet in a fierce embrace.

She was at first too surprised to respond, but within moments she was flinging her arms around his neck and returning his kiss with every ounce of strength she possessed. A radiant energy passed from her lips to his, then back again, from his body to hers, in a shudder that reverberated through her belly and thighs. It was some time before he put her down, and a while later after that before she realized that it was raining in earnest, and that they were half-sitting, half-lying on her puddling wooden steps, their wet clothes clinging to their bodies, his heart thumping against her cheek.

She lifted her head. "I thought you were home, furious at me and nose-deep in some book."

"The only book I seem to be able to read this term is you." He framed her wet face in his hands. "I love you, you know. I suppose it's the only word for it. And just so you believe me—just so you know I've never said those words to anyone before tonight—I promise not to ask to come in. God knows I don't know what's to be done about all this, about us, but I can't bear to think—" James's voice broke. He wiped a hand over his dripping face. "This has not been one of my better days. I'm so ashamed, Lupe. I've got to sort myself out before I...before we..." With a shake of his head James moved to rise.

"Don't go yet!" she exclaimed, clutching at his shirt.

Laughing at her transparent eagerness, James fell back and stretched himself clumsily on the landing, pulling her half on top of him. She felt his hands on her hips, the tickle of rain on the back of her knees, the salty taste of his stubbly cheeks on her tongue. It was only then that she realized, some seconds too late and her breath coming fast and shallow, that she was naked but for panties and the nightshirt, and that he had slipped his hand underneath it to feel his way all around her warm wet skin as he kissed her.

Hardly able to get her breath and unaware that she had begun to cry, Lupe reached down to echo his gestures. She scanned the length of his side with her hand and pulled his shirt out of the waistband of his jeans so that she could stroke the fine, curly hair of his chest, damp with rain. Finally, her fingers closed around the zipper of his jeans.

Having grown up with three unruly brothers, Lupe was hardly a stranger to male anatomy; but until James, her only direct experience of masculine arousal had been a vicious one of Barry DeBrun seven years before. The memory of it stopped her cold.

James clasped her hand in his and hugged it to his chest. "I said not tonight. When the time's right, you won't be crying. And I won't be shaking like a goddamned teenager."

Relieved, disappointed, embarrassed, all at once, Lupe clutched at his shirt and sobbed. He let her cry for a bit, then kissed her on the nose before standing up, pulling her up with him. She grabbed his hands, still not quite willing to let him go.

"C-C-Come with me to Bay View tomorrow," she pleaded. "My family's having a party."

"What's the occasion?"

"My father's birthday."

He moved a lank of wet hair away from her eyes. "Well, why not. I'll ring you early tomorrow then."

With that, James turned without another word. A flash of lightning illuminated his retreating figure as he made his way down the stairs. By the time the inevitable crash of thunder followed, the night had swallowed him.

Shivering at the top of the stairs, cold and soaked and not caring, Lupe realized as she stood there, her senses wholly absorbed in watching him, that somewhere in the course of the last few minutes all grace to resist him had abandoned her. If he turned back now she wouldn't be able, or wouldn't want, to say no.

———————

But James did not turn back. He walked home in a quiet, steady rain that washed away the city's noise and dirt, transforming the gritty urban horizon into a penumbra of shimmering night. He strolled as if it were a warm, dry night in June, his steps measured, his hands hanging loosely at his side, his thoughts on her lips and breasts and between her thighs, and in her wet, black hair. Soaked through to his skin, he felt no part of him that wasn't bathed in a baptism of rain and night and desire. The thought crossed his mind that perhaps the theologians were right, after all, about this much at least: that of the two great forces that strove, time out of mind, to rule the hearts of men, perhaps love *was* the stronger.

A long-forgotten word rose quietly from James's bruised memory and pulsed in his inner ear: grace, grace, *grace.*

Chapter Seven:
The Green-Eyed Monster

O, beware, my lord, of jealousy!
It is the green-eyed monster, which doth mock
The meat it feeds on. That cuckold lives in bliss
Who, certain of his fate, loves not his wronger;
But O, what damnèd minutes tells he o'er
Who dotes, yet doubts — suspects, yet fondly loves!

Shakespeare, *Othello*

L upe directed James, at the wheel of his Jeep, across the Hoan Bridge into the southern suburb of Bay View; then down a narrow side street to a Craftsman-style home overlooking South Shore park. There were already people sitting inside the screened-in porch at the top of the steps, and upon entering, James recognized Ramon Cruz sprawled on the porch swing. The young detective's keen turquoise eyes, the exact color of his sister's, were veiled this afternoon behind reflecting aviator glasses. Ramon's arm was draped around a petite Hispanic woman with a chubby infant in her lap, presumably his wife Gloria. Though out of uniform in jeans and a sweatshirt, the scowl fixed on Ramon's face as Lupe introduced them all was identical to the one James had seen the night Bricusse died.

"Are things settling down at the Institute?" Ramon said, his tepid politeness sounding rehearsed as the two men shook hands.

"As much as can be expected, I suppose," James replied, realizing, as he pulled away his hand, that his palms were sweating and that Ramon couldn't have failed to notice. He raked his fingers through his Anglo-blonde hair. "I, uh, don't imagine there's anything new. I mean with the police investigation."

Ramon peeled off his shades and squinted at him. "We aren't really in the habit of keeping civilians posted about investigations."

"Ah," said James, shoving his hands into his pockets. He was more than a little relieved when Lupe, remarking the awkward silence that ensued, hastily encouraged him to follow her to the park across the street, ostensibly to seek out her brother Patrick, the youngest of the Cruz children, who was taking a run on the beach.

Patrick Cruz met them just on the other side of the street. An athletic college Senior, he was known as "the Bay View Bomber" of the UWM Panthers soccer team, or so Lupe introduced him. His dark red hair, much darker than his mother's, stood out in shocking contrast to his navy sweats. Lupe was obviously fond of him, and somehow more at ease with him, James noted, than with their older brother Ramon. After the two men shook hands, Patrick stepped back to look James over with the air of an NFL recruiter about to make his bid.

"Lu here says you're a rugger," were Patrick's first words. "And Ramon says you're a descendent of the Devil Cromwell," were his second. Cackling at James's expression, Patrick went on to express his relief that their oldest brother, Martin-the-Carmelite, would soon be there to see to it that a certain young detective minded his blue-crew mouth and manners.

"M-M-Marty's coming?"

"He's got a wedding to perform at Holy Hill first, but he told dad he'd be able to get away for dinner and an overnight. Even Carmelites get vacation time these days, you know."

James was puzzled. "A monk performing weddings?"

"*Friar*, if you please," Lupe corrected. "Don't ask me the difference, but the Carmelites are fierce about it. And Holy Hill is a parish as well as a shrine and a monastery."

Patrick slammed his fist into the palm of his other hand. "Yeah, nice of Martin and Maggie to get the religious vocations out of the way for the rest of us, eh Lu?"

"Phooey," Lupe declared. "Paddy here, aged seventeen, announced to the entire family that he was going into the Oratorians after he graduated from college. That was about—" She squinted up at the cloudless sky. "—five girlfriends ago."

"Four!"

"Interesting," James commented. "What made you change your mind?"

"Simple. Sex."

Lupe sighed. "I think I'll leave you b-boys to discuss this, er, guy stuff while I go help *Mami* with supper or something." Giving a half-completed wave, she turned towards the street before James could volunteer to accompany her.

Patrick, looking a little shot down, flicked a covert glance at James. "I don't suppose you and she…?"

"No," James said succinctly, studying a knot of crabgrass at his feet.

Patrick was obviously impressed. "Jeez, don't you find it kinda hard? I mean you strike me as a been-there, done-that kind of guy."

In lieu of words, James tucked his hands under his armpits and offered Patrick a flinty arrangement of facial muscles that was designed to forestall further inquiry.

"Sorry., didn't mean to get nosy. It's just…well, Lu deserves a little fun. I keep thinking if it hadn't been for that goddamned bastard DeBrun…" Patrick shook his head and fell silent.

James looked up. "Speaking of the devil, it falls out that Mr. DeBrun has married the daughter of Max Heisler. Lupe has already had the unsettling misfortune to run into him on several occasions. In fact, he and I had a bit of a punch-up at a party the night before Fr. Bricusse died."

"*Dios mio*, what happened?"

"He cornered her down on the beach. I clocked him a couple, then heaved his sorry ass into Lake Michigan."

"Yes!" Patrick cried, hammering the air with upraised fist as if applying an undercut to the dimple on DeBrun's chin.

When the two men returned inside a few minutes later, Lupe, emerging from the kitchen, took James's arm to lead him on a tour of the Cruz home.

There weren't that many rooms in the house, only three bedrooms on the second floor, and the converted attic over the garage, which had served as a dormitory for the Cruz boys; but all the rooms were spacious, cheerful, and furnished with comfort rather than style in mind. It was, James thought, his chronic emotional diet of bitterness spiked this afternoon with a pinch of envy, what Cyril Ireton would describe as "shabby-genteel."

Only the dining room proved exceptional. Oonagh Cruz, Lupe explained, had long since given up any thoughts of fine decorating with such a large and rambunctious family, but after the last of her six children had matured beyond the destructive stage, Oonagh had insisted on renovating the dining room, the heart of the house, in grand style. The walls were papered in a floral motif in shades of peach and green, and a brass chandelier was suspended over a massive oak dining table. Irish lace hung at the south-facing bay windows, where potted and hanging plants gathered the sunlight filtering through beveled glass. One wall of the dining room was decorated almost from floor to ceiling with family photographs, some of them going back more than fifty years.

"This is our Wall of Memory," Lupe explained, cataloging the pictures for him. Here were black and white and sepia, as well as color photos of four sets of Irish and Mexican great-grandparents, a number of weddings, Martin's ordination, as well as Maggie's Profession of Solemn Vows; graduations, baptisms, and First Communions.

James' eyes settled finally on a small picture of a chubby black-haired toddler dressed only in nappies, muddy red tennis shoes, and a shabby straw hat perched crookedly atop her head as she stood on the beach with her little fists on her diapered hips as if inviting the world to a boxing match.

"What a wonderful picture," James exclaimed. "The diaper manufacturers would pay megabucks for that. One of Kate's children?"

"That's me," Lupe said. "Mercy, what a hellcat! *Mami* still accounts me responsible for three-quarters of her gray hair."

Looking at her, then at the picture, James found himself thinking a completely new thought, one such as had never before presented itself to his mind in his almost-thirty years: what, he wondered, might their children look like, hers and his?

In the center of the pictorial arrangement was a large color photograph of the entire extended family gathered for Ramon's wedding in front of a twin-spired, neo-Gothic brick church. "Let me guess," James said pointing, "Holy Hill."

"B-B-Bingo."

He fell silent, his eyes roaming the photographs with an almost sensual relish. "You have absolutely no idea how lucky you are," he said finally. "*Her faithfull knight faire Una brings to house of Holinesse.*"

The tour continuing, Lupe guided James through the large square kitchen, then into the family room where Ramon's five-year-old daughter Margareta was sprawled in a yellow bean bag near the fireplace, mesmerized before the large-screen image of a Bugs Bunny cartoon. Two fluffy and corpulent caramel-colored Persians, Winkin' and Blinkin', had assumed Sphinx-like poses along adjoining windowsills of the west-facing wall, their ugly pug faces to the sun. Nod, Lupe told him, the gouty third of the ancient feline triumvirate, had recently passed on to kitty heaven.

There was another, but smaller, fireplace in what Lupe described as the "parlor"—a sort of sitting room at the front of the house, facing the screened porch. A beat-up upright piano with yellowed keys squatted in the corner. "We usually have a bit of music and *craic* after supper," she said, pointing at the upright. "It's Mom's, she's the parish organist. *Mi abuelo*, my grandpa, he plays the fiddle when his arthritis isn't too bad. The rest of us just sing. Ramon's got a nice voice."

"Yours is better!" Patrick called out, foraging in a bowl of Chex mix as he approached from the adjacent dining room. "And she doesn't stutter when she sings!"

Lupe looked at her watch. "Are you sure Marty's coming?" she asked her brother.

"Yeah, what's the rush?"

She copped a glance at James. "Well I need to go to c-c-confession. If Marty wasn't coming, I thought I'd run down to church before supper. It wouldn't hurt you to go, either, you heathen."

"Yeah, I know," Patrick readily agreed, "but it's always the 'firm purpose of amendment' part that gives me fits. You know, 'O, God, make me chaste... but not yet!'" He giggled wildly. "You guys wanna beer?"

"Sounds good," James said, trying to remember the last time, if ever, he had subjected himself to the excruciating dating ritual known as "meeting the family." It was thirsty work.

Patrick scooped up another fistful of Chex mix. "So what'll it be, MGD, Guinness, Tecate, Corona? Oh, and Ramon brought some Stark's Dark, too, but I'm too PC to drink the swill. Lu here gets madder than hell when she sees those kinky ads."

"I'll take a Guinness, thanks," James said, his social anxieties suddenly displaced by an image from last Sunday's newspaper, which Patrick's comment had called to mind: Bel Gunderson in a stop-sign-red teddy, straddling a bottle of Stark's Dark pointed up at her crotch.

"Oh, g-give me a Stark's just this once," Lupe grumbled. "Ramon's been bugging me to try it for months. Seems the entire MPD swears by the stuff."

Patrick muttered an obscene remark and trotted off. James let a few seconds pass, to assure himself that they were quite alone, then took hold of Lupe's arm. "Was what we did last night so sinful," he whispered hoarsely, "that you need to go to confession?"

"It was more what I almost did," she replied, coloring. "I d-don't know where to draw the line all of a sudden. I went too far last night. I was out of control."

After a telling pause, James let her go. "Well, now, General Cruz," he said, "dicey move, that. You've just slipped strategic information to the enemy. Last night was a truce, you know, not an armistice."

Suddenly Ramon's wife Gloria stuck her head around the pantry door.

"Your dad just called," she said to Lupe. "He'll be here in about twenty minutes. Could you guys maybe set the table?"

"Uh, sure...sure thing!"

Lupe made a hasty move towards the pantry, but James once again caught her arm. "Please don't go to confession to your brother," he pleaded. "Anyone but your brother."

She reached up to touch his cheek. "Ok-kay."

Pushing through the swinging pantry doors, Lupe began rummaging through cabinets for plates and silverware. James, right behind, glanced around the windowless, closet-sized room and stopped dead.

Little more than a short, narrow galley of cabinets fitted from floor to ceiling, and exiting at the opposite end with another set of swinging doors that led into the kitchen, the Cruz pantry was the sort of room that his mother had always called a "larder."

Tapping herself on the head as if remembering something, Lupe swept through the swinging doors into the kitchen, calling out her mother's name. On the other side of the wide-swinging doors James caught a fleeting glimpse of Oonagh Cruz, an apron tied around her waist, leaning casually against the kitchen sink as she chatted with her daughter-in-law. The doors swung back and forth, back and forth a couple of times, then shuddered to a close.

James was alone in the windowless room. The oak cabinets on each side of him seemed to press against his face. There was a roaring in his ears and he felt certain that something dreadful was about to happen, something to do with those doors. Unable to get his chest wall to expand to take in enough air, he leaned against the cabinets, tingling, trembling, his heart pattering wildly.

After what seemed like an hour of agony the kitchen doors flew open again. "Say, James—" Seeing him slumped against the cabinets, Lupe moved quickly to support him. "My God, what's the matter?"

He made a weak, waving gesture. "Feeling a bit queer. Just get me out of here, please."

Pulling his arm around her shoulders, she helped him out of the pantry and into the front parlor. Sweat dribbled down his whitened forehead as she eased him onto the sofa.

"James, what happened?"

"A cross-sea of memories," he whispered. "Silly, really. Be all right in a jiffy."

"Well, stay put for a bit, alright? I'll get the dishes."

Giving a nod, he collapsed against the back of the sofa, his head lolling to one side as he followed her movements with unfocused eyes. When, after a couple of minutes, his trembling began to subside and his head to clear, he took a few more deep, relaxing breaths, as his sundry doctors had always advised him to do when suffering a panic attack, and finally turned towards the window behind him, hoping for a glimpse of the inland sea.

His eyes fell on a puzzling sight, something which even in his foggy, fuzzy-headed state he knew was somehow all wrong: an ivory-colored roadster with the top up was idling on the far side of the street, directly in front of the Cruz home.

Stumbling to his feet, James burst out the front door to the porch. But by the time he had navigated the front steps on wobbly legs the car was pulling away in a shriek of burning rubber.

Exhaling expletives, James watched in helpless, inexplicable fury as the car careened around the corner towards the Hoan bridge.

The dining room table had been lengthened by three leaves, and the place of honor festooned with drawings and a homemade birthday card sent by Kate's children. Standing a little below medium height, Matteo Cruz beamed at the childish artwork, then at the crowded, crazy houseful. He was stocky like his son Ramon, James observed, and both Ramon and Lupe had inherited his black hair and turquoise eyes.

James was frankly relieved when Matteo didn't seem in the least wary or surprised by the unlooked-for presence of the British newcomer, or even overly curious. He simply shook hands with "Lu's new friend," squeezed his shoulder once as he said a few kind words about Fr. Bricusse, then went about the more urgent business of catching up with his grandchildren. Within five minutes of the introduction James felt as if he had been incorporated into the family, and frankly, didn't know how he should receive this unprecedented welcome. He even indulged himself for a half-minute with the gloomy suspicion that Lupe might somehow have gotten ahead of herself; might have said something to her family that was suggestive of a formal commitment on his part, which he was wholly unprepared to make.

By way of testing this theory, James approached Matteo once more before supper and said, as a sort of backhanded prompt, "I'm very grateful to be included in your family gathering on such short notice, Mr. Cruz."

To which Matteo Cruz replied, as if it should be obvious, "Any friend of Lu's is always welcome in this house. And my name is Matt."

And that was that.

Fr. Martin Cruz arrived in his brown Carmelite habit just as everyone was assembling in the dining room. He was taller than his father and brothers, with chestnut hair and beard, and though he shared the air of good-humored ease that seemed to be the Cruz family's predominant trait, he didn't participate as readily in the banter of his younger siblings. James wondered if this quieter demeanor were due to temperament or the product of monastic training.

After the compulsory polite exchanges, everyone stood behind their chairs as Fr. Martin led them in saying grace. Then the briefest of silences gave way to cacophony. Chairs were scooted in, plates and condiments passed on this side and that, and several separate conversations, in English and in Spanish, broke out or were resumed with the final "Amen."

"Hey, Dad," Patrick called from his seat on the other side of Lupe, "what's this big story you're working on? Ramon says you've been hanging around the strip joints doing—*ahem*—research."

Matt lifted a slab of soda bread as if threatening to toss it at his youngest son's head.

"Don't even think about it," Ramon warned, tapping the rock-hard crust of Lupe's soda bread with the blade of his knife. "I'd have to arrest you for assault with a deadly."

"At least I tried to contribute something to this meal," Lupe grumbled. "These Cruz men think their beards will stop growing if they step into a k-k-kitchen."

"More than that will happen if Ramon Roberto Cruz steps into *my* kitchen," Lupe's grandmother declared in a thick Guanajuatan accent behind a perfectly straight face.

"Whoa, granny, screen and roll!" Patrick exclaimed, scooting back his chair to head into the kitchen for another beer.

Gloria grunted. "No point in trying to initiate these brain-deads into the higher mysteries, eh? Hey, Paddy, grab another for me, too!" At that, an infant's cry was heard from the parlor, where Gloria had put her baby's bassinet. "Infallible timing," the young mother commented, now likewise scooting back from the table.

"That's what you get for yelling," Ramon chided.

"That's what I get for sleeping with you," Gloria countered.

With a foreigner's slack-mouthed fascination, James watched as Gloria padded into the parlor and retrieved her fussing infant. She took him to the sofa where she nonchalantly lifted her tee-shirt to give him her breast. The child's ululations were instantly transformed into sucks of greedy contentment.

"What was that about strip joints?" old Nemencio said to his son in a tone of placid innocence.

"I'm working on a series on the Milwaukee vice war," Matt said. "It's the first of a six-part series for the annual Fall circulation drive. Can't imagine where the Metro Desk editor got the idea that sex and violence sell newspapers." He punctuated his commentary with a shrug—a tell-tale gesture that suggested to James that Matt wasn't entirely squared on the whole seedy business.

Oonagh Cruz lowered her pint. "Don't tell me you actually go *in* those places."

"Just doing my job, honey." Matt leaned over to whisper something in his wife's ear. Whatever it was brought a wash of red to Oonagh's pink cheeks.

"Watch your back, *Papi*," Ramon cautioned as James sent the butter down to the head of the table at Matt's request. "These guys may not like all the publicity you're giving them. And it's gonna get way uglier before it's over."

When Patrick asked his brother who he thought was going to come out on top of the so-called "war," Nesterov or Calabresi, Ramon, after giving the matter some deliberation as he sucked on his bottle of Stark's Dark, finally voiced the opinion that, though Vyacheslav Nesterov was known to be a "crazy mean bastard, that's sure," he'd have to put his pesos on Nick Calabresi. Not only, he explained, had the Calabresi family been in the business longer, but "Nicky C" was determined to prove that the demise of the Italian Mafia had been announced prematurely.

"Oh, but the Calabresis aren't just Italians anymore," Matt observed, knifing up a pat of butter on his corn-on-the-cob. "On the contrary, the Rainbow Mob is a model of multicultural hiring in the corporate criminal sphere. I heard Calabresi's even recruiting Native American kids from up north. He wants the Wisconsin trade real bad, I think."

"Well he sure as hell didn't sit still for Nesterov's whacking his video store owner," Ramon concurred.

Matt looked up. "You heard about the prostitute, I suppose."

"What prostitute?" Oonagh asked.

According to Matt, whose narrative was interlaced with factoids of a more colorful nature from Ramon, a prostitute named Candace "Candy" Duffy, an employee of Nesterov-controlled Bonsoir Escorts, had been stabbed to death two nights before in nearby Racine. Racine PD had not yet identified any credible suspects, but was operating on the assumption that it was Calabresi retaliation for Nesterov's recent murder of the video store owner. The theory was supported, RPD believed, by the fact that Duffy's mutilated body had been dropped from her twelfth story apartment balcony.

James looked up from his plate. "She was dropped?"

"Racine thinks it's tit-for-tat for the Marquette Interchange," Ramon explained, masticating his second ear of corn.

"I was down there this afternoon," Matt said, wiping his mouth with his napkin, "that's how come I was late. Hope to God I didn't put the Calabresis on to her with that picture of her and Nesterov…" Frowning suddenly, Matt blew out a puff of air and turned his gaze on his older son. "But what, I'd like to know, did you hear about it that RPD neglected to tell me?"

Ramon stabbed his forefinger in his father's direction. "You can inform your readers that 'unnamed sources close to the investigation,' or whatever you guys call it, believe that if Duffy was killed by the Calabresi mob, then the bodies are gonna start dropping from the skies like ducks in November, seeing as how she was Nesterov's hooker of choice. Our one consolation is that all these slimeballs might end up killing each other."

Ramon's mother did not seem to derive much comfort from this prospect. "Innocent people always get hurt in these things," Oonagh said, turning to her husband. "Matteo…"

"Don't worry, *bonita*, I'll be careful."

"Hey, g-g-guys," Lupe piped up, "do you think we could change the subject? I'm about to hurl this wonderful supper." She glanced at James, then her mother. "Anything new at the Archdiocese, Mom?"

"Some good news about the SANA investigation at least," Oonagh reported with a smile at James. "The Archbishop has read your documents, James. In fact, His Excellency told me he was 'horrified' by them. SANA's a private organization, so there's not a lot he can do directly, but he's withdrawn the privilege he'd given them of letting them keep the Blessed Sacrament in their chapel. And he's conferring with canon lawyers about what other measures can be taken, if he can't persuade Mr. Krato to change his ways, that is."

James wiped his mouth. "You'll see Nesterov and Calabresi kneeling side by side in the Cathedral first," he prophesied.

Sour thoughts were sweetened by cake, coffee, and Bailey's, and a riotously inharmonious rendition of Happy Birthday, after which Matt opened his birthday presents and after-dinner jobs were divvied up. At little Margareta's insistence Lupe and James were assigned the (to James) dauntingly unfamiliar task of getting the child to bed while her father drove his grandparents home and her mother nursed her baby brother to sleep.

The bedroom where Margareta and her aunt Lupe were to be enthroned for the night was a haphazard collection of angular corners, sloping ceilings, and fitted cupboards, designed with extravagant overkill by the professional carpenter who had remodeled the house before the Cruz family had bought it almost twenty years before.

Lupe fumbled Margareta into her jammies, then presented her with a book she had bought for her, an illustrated version of *St. George and the Dragon*. When the child begged her aunt to read it to her, Lupe promptly passed the buck to James, whom she praised as "a g-great Shakespearean actor who really knows how to read a story!" Margareta proceeded to hang on James's legs until he agreed to perform.

He settled her on the floor at his side, his back against a twin bed, while Lupe lay on her stomach across the bed to read over his shoulder as he paged through the book.

"This is my favorite fairy tale," James began, his initial reluctance overcome by the wide expectancy in the child's eyes, "the story I wish Shakespeare had got to first, before Spenser." Lupe swatted him from behind. "But while you look at the pictures, I'll tell you *my* version of it."

"What's it about?" Margareta asked warily.

"It's about a valiant but foolish young knight, known only as Redcrosse, who gets himself tricked by an evil sorcerer into believing that his beloved Princess Una has been playing him false."

"What's that got to do with dragons?" Margareta insisted.

"Yes, well, when Redcrosse realizes that he's been tricked, he regains his honor by doing battle with a vicious dragon who's been making off with all the fair maidens of Una's kingdom. That's how Redcrosse earns his name, you see, 'St. George of Merrie England.'"

Margareta still looked dubious. "I'm kinda scared of dragons."

"Not to worry. The story has a happy ending, more or less. And you know what?" James leaned into the child and whispered, "Princess Una reminds me a lot of *you*."

"Shameless f-flatterer," Lupe commented. Margareta, however, squirmed happily on her skinny knees.

James cleared his throat. "Once upon a time…"

Matt Cruz, dressed in a faded navy robe over his pajamas, stepped into the attic dormitory where Martin and James were climbing into one of the two sets of bunk beds.

"I know it's late," Matt said in a low voice so as not to wake his youngest son, who was already sawing logs in the other bunk, "but could Oonagh and I talk to you boys a minute before you go to bed?"

Martin and James followed Matt back down into the kitchen, where Oonagh was already pouring hot cocoa from a pan. The four gathered around the kitchen table with steaming mugs.

Oonagh lifted her cup. "Where's Lu?"

James informed her that Lupe had already gone to bed.

Matt glanced at his wife, then at Martin and James. "Well, I don't like to talk behind her back, but Lu looked all done in this evening. Look, guys, Oonagh and I need your help. Martin, your spiritual sense about things, and James…well, you're seeing more of Lu than the rest of us."

"It's about Barry DeBrun, isn't it?" James said.

Matt sighed. "Patrick told me what happened at that party."

Martin suggested that they begin with a prayer. James was surprised to see Lupe entering the kitchen as Martin was praying. Whispering to James that she couldn't get to sleep, she pulled up the chair next to him.

"I don't understand that man," she said when Martin was finished. "He just got married. I've never met Fran Heisler, b-b-but I'm sure she's very nice."

"I'm sure she's very rich," James dissented, taking up his mug.

"There may be an element of revenge in this thing, too," Oonagh offered quietly.

"Are we talking about what I think we're talking about?" Detective Ramon Cruz shuffled through the door with a Stark's Dark in one fist.

Lupe threw up her hands. "Stupendous. The war party is assembled. Now all we need is Patrick to come cheer-lead."

"Now, Lupe—"

"I appreciate everyone's concern, but Barry's probably...I mean, I don't think he'd *really*—"

"Hold the phone," Ramon broke in. "I was the one who picked you up that night, remember?" For some reason Ramon glared at James as he vented his heated words. "Her dress was ripped to shreds and she was shaking like a paint-mixer. You could see his goddamn fingerprints on her neck! I say we remind the bastard that he's not immortal."

Martin raised his hand to speak. "*Revenge is Mine, says the Lord.* As unpalatable as it might have been, I don't think Lu would still be having this problem if we had let it alone seven years ago. As it is—" Martin nodded at his brother Ramon. "—you, me, and Patrick pounded her into his memory."

"It's not revenge I want." Matt Cruz looked near tears. "I admit that Barry DeBrun is the only man I've ever wanted to kill...and don't think it didn't cross my mind again tonight! I mean, don't we have any legal recourse? There are laws against stalking...Ramon, how about the Sexual Predator law?"

Ramon gave a snort. "It only applies to convicted felons. Barry's never been convicted of jaywalking, thanks to his daddy. But, now listen." Ramon set down his beer and leaned forward. "I've been doing some snooping of my own. Before Barry married Heisler's daughter, he was picked up in Forest County for a whole slew of stuff. DUI, possession of narcotics, solicitation of a minor, and sexual assault, just for starters."

Lupe gagged.

"Yep, trolling for little girls is Barry's favorite recreational sport. And that was just in Wisconsin. C'mon, Lu, a guy like that isn't going to change his habits just because he hooks himself some upscale in-laws."

"Forest County?" Matt's forehead was troughed with worry. "What was he doing up there, gambling on the reservations?"

"Yeah, and don't think the local tribal leaders weren't sitting around a table then, just like we are now, trying to figure what the hell to do about him. The victim was a little fifteen-year-old Potowatomi girl. He picked her up off the street in Carter, loaded her with cocaine in every orifice, then dumped her in the middle of the Nicolet National Forest."

The color drained from Matt's face. "I can't believe we never heard about this at the paper."

"Big John takes care of his baby boy," was Ramon's interpretation of events. "And I can even tell you how. I called this guy I know who works security at the Potowatomi Hall on West Canal. He's an ex-tribal cop from Carter. He knew all about DeBrun. He said the local men would've gladly strung him up, if they could've got hold of him. But Big John dug up some unsavory stuff about the victim's older brother. He threatened to have the brother arrested on outstanding warrants if the girl prosecuted."

"Don't tell me." Matt waved. "She dropped all charges. What was the unsavory stuff about the brother?"

"He took off for Chicago and became a two-bit *pachuco*. Then got himself recruited by Nick Calabresi, of all people. The family claims they haven't seen him in years."

Matt's hands fell to his lap. "So what the hell do we do?"

"Not to sound monkish," offered Fr. Martin, "but there's always God."

James cleared his throat. "There's also Max Heisler."

All eyes turned on him.

"Heisler's not a man I would want to cross," James elaborated. "If he were ever to be apprised of his new son-in-law's extra-curricular activities, I wouldn't change places with Barry DeBrun for the Powerball jackpot."

There was a moment of collective silence. Then Ramon whistled.

It was, James thought with a peculiar feeling of satisfaction, the closest thing to a "welcome to the family" he would probably ever hear from Ramon Roberto Cruz.

Patrick was still out like an unplugged appliance when James and Martin stretched themselves out in their bunks, James in the upper bunk with a book of Irish religious verse from a nearby shelf opened in his lap. He had just scanned C. Day Lewis's *Offertorium* when drowsiness finally overtook him. He turned off the wall lamp behind him with the soothing sound of Patrick's heavy breathing lulling him to sleep.

He awoke hours later, sweating and gasping for breath. A telephone was chirping loudly on the table beside the lower bunk. Patrick didn't stir, but Martin finally groaned, stretched out one arm and pulled the receiver off the hook.

"Hello…?"

Pale grayish light shone through a crack in the curtains. James jumped down from the bunk and reached for his robe, thinking to head for the bathroom to wipe his face and get a drink of water.

"Oh, you got it, *Papi*?" James heard Martin saying into the phone. "Right…*buenos noches*." Martin fumbled the phone back in its cradle before turning his sleepy eyes on James. "Sorry about that. It was for Dad. Sounded like someone from the newspaper. Say, are you all right? You look sick."

"Nightmare," James croaked, mopping his face with the sleeve of his robe.

Martin propped himself on his elbow. "How about a glass of juice?"

James accepted gratefully.

"Do you suffer from nightmares often?" Martin asked in the kitchen a few minutes later, pulling a plastic pitcher of orange juice from the refrigerator.

"I'm so used to them, I hardly pay attention anymore. The details change from time to time, but the plot remains roughly the same. And I always wake up just before I'm about to be lunched upon by a dragon."

"A dragon! Ouch." Martin handed James a glass. "Wonder what it means."

Nodding his thanks, James took the glass and stifled a yawn. "Nothing, I dare say, other than that I was very fond of fairy tales as a child. To tell you the truth, I've always had the superstitious feeling that if the dragon ceased haunting my dreams, he might take up residence in my waking hours. Besides, why does it have to 'mean' anything?"

"Oh, I was just thinking of a passage from the Talmud. Something like, 'a dream that isn't understood is like a letter unopened.'"

"Some letters, I assure you, are better left unopened."

Martin cocked his head to the side, a gesture connoting reflection, James thought, not necessarily agreement. "Well, nice thing about being raised in a big family, there was always someone in the next bed when you woke up with a monster after you."

Swallowing some juice, James gestured at the modest kitchen. "I envy what you've all had here."

"Happy families have to struggle with the big Whys and Wherefores, too, just like everyone else. Bad things can come in from the outside."

"Things like Barry DeBrun."

"Yeah, well, we're a tight bunch, we Cruzes." Martin chuckled. "Kick one and we all limp. I mean, you read about things happening to people in the paper, other people, but to have it happen to one of your own, especially someone like Lu…" Martin fingered his glass. "Seminarians aren't supposed to like beating the daylights out of people, but I did. I could have killed the man that night, and not turned a hair."

"I know the feeling."

Martin smiled slightly. "I bet you do. I understand you had a lousy experience with Peter Krato at SANA."

The quick turn of subject caught James off guard. He felt Martin's eyes on him, and didn't much care for the sensation. "It was a different kind of rape attempt," he said finally, "only it succeeded. I've been wondering ever since how many casualties will have to pile up in our little side-aisle of the universal Church before someone wearing purple or red finally stumbles over a body and says, 'Oh how dreadful, we have a problem here.'"

"Do you mind if I ask why you didn't try to do something about it your-self, when you first left?"

James cut his eyes away from Martin's level gaze. "Let's just say the wounded aren't fit to fight."

Martin said nothing to that, but took advantage of the caesura in con-versation to get up and pop two slices of bread in the toaster. "Have you ever noticed," he said finally, one elbow propped on the kitchen counter as he waited for the toast to brown, "how people with a great gift for something are often tempted by its opposite?"

One corner of James's mouth curled up. "An interesting theory, but I have to wonder if it's of much use in everyday life. There are an awful lot of us with nary a 'great gift' to call our own."

"Oh, I disagree. We've all got at least one. Though it may be a great gift for a small thing. Unfortunately, many of us never bother to track it down."

"And how might one do that?"

"If it's not obvious to you, you might try working in reverse. Try asking yourself what your greatest temptation is."

The toast popped up. While Martin took plates from the cabinet and spread the butter, James's thoughts turned at once to his own shabby his-tory of womanizing. As overwhelming as that temptation seemed to be for him — in Martin's scheme of things perhaps suggesting a capacity for love or fidelity which James had never had reason to suspect he possessed — it wasn't, after all, the worst thing James had to struggle against.

Taking a slice of toast with a nod of thanks, James bit into it, chewed a moment, and chased it with a swallow of juice. "I usually have a lot of energy," he said at last, "and yet sometimes I feel completely becalmed. Like a racing yacht stalled in the summer doldrums. That's when I'm tempted to give up."

"Give up what?"

"Fighting. 'Soldiering on,' as my father would say."

"Then fighting for what, or against what?"

James chuckled. "As it happens, I'm rather good at fighting against things. I just can't seem to get up enough steam to fight *for* anything. A little too much like Hamlet that way, I guess."

Martin smiled. "We call that 'acedia' in the theology trade."

"Good God, there's a name for it?"

"Psychology wasn't invented by Freud, you know. Acedia is just a fancy word for laziness, especially spiritual laziness. It often takes the form of a sort of disgust."

James downed the rest of his juice in several gulps, the disturbing thought crossing his drowsy mind that Fr. Martin Cruz was hitting a little too close to home. He wondered, with a flush of sudden suspicion, if Lupe had gone to her brother for confession after all; but then the moment the thought was formed, James realized, with a whopping measure of relief coupled with a sting of self-reproach, that there had been no possible opportunity for her to seek out her brother for such a conference, so busy had they all been this evening with group activities of one sort or another.

"Acedia," James said finally. "That's lovely, that is."

Martin's smile grew wider. "Everybody suffers from it to one degree or another, especially nowadays. Maybe even especially men. It's not like we're animals, you know. We don't have automatic instincts to tell us when and how to act, and force us to be brave." Martin laughed suddenly.

"What?"

"I was just thinking of a newspaper article Dad wrote last spring about a bunch of construction workers on I-94. They dug up a nest of killdeer under an on-ramp. Amazing birds, killdeer. They build their nests in the weirdest places. The male has this incredible tactic for protecting the nest when a predator approaches." Martin circled his hand in the air, a gesture so reminiscent of Lupe, groping for the right word. "He sort of, you know, lifts his wing and flops around. Seriously! The bird keels over on one side and jerks around, as if he's got a broken wing. It attracts the predator's attention away from the mother and the eggs. With possibly fatal consequences to himself, I might add...what's the matter?"

James had frozen, his slice of toast suspended halfway to his mouth. "What did you call this bird?"

"A killdeer. It's from the *kill-dee* sound they make."

Swallowing, James put his toast back on the plate. "I don't suppose you know what these birds look like."

Martin looked surprised by James's sudden ornithological interest. "Yeah, I've seen them. They're white with brown wings. And they've got a couple of black bands around their throats. Pretty common in this part of the world."

Matt appeared in the kitchen doorway, bleary-eyed and clumsily dressed in a rumpled suit and mismatched socks. The clock ticking silently over the sink, James noticed, read a little after four.

"*Madre de Díos,*" Matt said, rubbing his eyes, "didn't one of you boys have the sense to put on some coffee?"

"Actually, I don't think we were planning to stay up." Martin frowned at his frowning father. "What was the call about?"

Matt ran some tap water in a mug, shoved it in the microwave, and punched some buttons. "Another mob hit. This time the owner of The Harem Club, a Calabresi-controlled business. Probably Nesterov retaliating for the murder of Candace Duffy." Matt paused, frowning out the large kitchen window into the inky curve of blind night. "The poor louse was emasculated, then thrown off one of the high-rise ramps at the Marquette Interchange."

James awoke in his own bed Monday morning, feeling as if he had just disembarked from a month-long Caribbean cruise. Grinning for no reason, he shaved, dressed, and put on some coffee while he called Lupe, just to hear her voice; then Franco Lanciano, to discuss how Max Heisler might best be approached about the Barry DeBrun situation.

Regarding the latter, Lanciano was not a bit happy with James's less-than-subtle hint that he, Franco, would be the best person to deliver the news to Mad Max Heisler about his son-in-law's unwholesome proclivities. After all, Lanciano quipped, James's favorite playwright had often commented on the reception a bearer of ill tidings could expect to receive from testy monarchs. When James pointed out, however, that Heisler's private intervention might prove less troublesome for the Institute's reputation than a public police investigation, should Barry's harassment of Lupe be allowed to reach the point where her only recourse was to press charges, Lanciano did a one-eighty, as James anticipated, and agreed with alacrity that it would be *far* better if he were the one to broach the delicate subject with the Institute's patron-founder.

Satisfied that more could not be done, at least for now, James fixed himself another cup of coffee and sat down at Lionel Krato's old oak desk, thinking to make some headway on the final edits of his dissertation. He booted up the terminal, logged on to the Institute's server, and keyed in his user name and password; but when he double-clicked on the folder containing the dozen-odd research and document files that comprised the substance of his almost completed doctorate, an empty screen box came up.

James swore aloud. When a slow and careful retracing of his steps still yielded nothing more than an empty screen box, he broke into a sweat. Finally, James resorted to the system's "Find" program; but each time the program completed its search circle, the screen box remained empty and the message at the bottom read, "0 file(s) found."

Staggering to his feet, James rifled through an assortment of plastic boxes on a nearby shelf, where he kept his CDs and floppy disks. One of the boxes should have contained a hand-labeled CD in a plastic case—a backup of his dissertation, notes and text, made before he had left for his Caribbean sailing vacation.

It wasn't there.

"*Du calme,* James, *du calme,*" Lanciano soothed, laying aside the issue of *La Cucina Italiana* he had been reading when James thundered into the room.

"Don't try to tell me that this is some weak-hinged fancy," James said, one fist slamming into his other palm as he paced like a caged animal in front of Lanciano's desk. "There was a key to my flat on Fr. Bricusse's missing set. Whoever has it almost succeeded in deleting three years of my life. Franco," James concluded, still shaking with the might-have-beens, "the twenty minutes it took me to get over here and assure myself that I still had a backup of my dissertation in my office were the longest twenty minutes of my life."

Lanciano shoved a thumbnail into his mouth, then just as quickly yanked it out again. Finally uttering some Italian oath that was well beyond James's limited tourist vocabulary, he reached inside the drawer of his desk for a silver cigarette case and matching lighter.

Wound up as he was, James couldn't help but laugh: Lanciano had given up smoking some years before at Adèle's behest, and it was quite against the building's rules; but for a man whose self-discipline was exceeded only by his vanity, the butchery Franco had committed on his once-immaculate fingernails these last stress-filled weeks was more than sufficient incentive to fall back on a foresworn vice or two.

Lanciano exhaled, his thin shoulders rippling with satisfied need. "Worst case scenario," he said with a sigh, "you could have pieced most of it together from the chapters farmed out to your dissertation committee. Besides, if it were deliberate vandalism and theft using Arthur's missing set of keys, why didn't the resourceful thief steal your office copy as well?" He waved his cigarette as if to say, *Get a grip!*

James, who had already considered all the angles, proceeded to explain, consuming his every remaining ounce of patience in the process, that while Fr. Bricusse had long since had a key to his apartment, James hadn't got round to giving his mentor a key to his office after the move to the new Institute building over the summer.

Lanciano tapped his ashes into an empty coffee mug and headed for the great window overlooking the lake. "There must be an alternative explanation," he declared. "Did you speak to the Sysop? If the vandal somehow hacked into our server, then surely other students or faculty have complained of similar problems."

"The Sysop said I was the only one who had complained of anything. That led him to believe that it wasn't a hacker at all. He said he thought someone must have got hold of my password, logged on as me, and then just…deleted my files."

Lanciano clasped his hands behind his back, the cigarette dangling between his fingers. "Then I suppose the next question is, how did someone discover your password? Have you ever revealed it to anyone? Lupe, perhaps, or a previous, er, girlfriend?"

"No one but Fr. Bricusse," James snapped, moving to join Lanciano at the window.

"Yes, well, I only ask because Arthur told me his password in case I needed to get into his files when he was away. Of course, I told the dear old fool he should pick some other password than 'Othello.' Or at least add some numbers to it. Any half-wit who knew his literary predilections could have guessed it."

Looking for an instant as if he'd been slapped, James dropped his forehead against the sun-warmed window glass.

"Now what's the matter?"

"If someone could have guessed Father's password, then sussing out mine would've been simplicity itself."

"You don't mean…dear God, you actually used 'Hamlet' for your password?"

James nodded against the glass. "I'm dyslexic with numbers. And 'Hamlet' was so easy to remember."

"So it was," Lanciano said dryly, retreating to his desk to flick off his ashes in the coffee mug.

James turned. "Sorry I barked at you. Still, easy to guess or no, there's one thing for sure about all this."

"And what's that? No, don't tell me." Lanciano held up his hand. "Barry DeBrun's behind it. Or no, not Barry, Peter Krato."

James crossed his arms, no longer even trying to hide his irritation. "As a matter of record, I'd be willing to bet next term's tuition that Krato is indeed mixed up in it, right up to his eyeballs. Remember, Father's SANA files have conveniently gone missing, too."

The Institute Director paused to stare at James, his expression that of a man confronted on the street by an escapee from Bedlam. "Now, really, don't you think you're carrying this thing with Krato, this...this..."

"Vendetta?"

Lanciano clucked. "It's all been too much for you. Arthur's death, the vandalism of his office, this computer tampering—"

"Don't patronize me!" James exploded. "Even the Archdiocese is finally taking Krato seriously. You may well think I have a tile loose, but you don't know the man as I do!"

Now Lanciano looked a little hurt. "I'm sorry, James, really I am. But when all is said and done, I find individuals like Peter Krato generally as harmless as they are obnoxious. A charlatan, to be sure, but *dangerous*...?" Lanciano snorted. "You speak of him as if he were a Mafia Don from the Capone era."

"You said it," James muttered. "Must have been all his rubbing shoulders with the Calabresis when he was a boy."

"*What?*" Lanciano shrieked.

James was startled by Lanciano's reaction. "Don't tell me you didn't know," he said. "Krato's family owns a restaurant in Chicago, frequented by gangsters. It's the only place in the neighborhood, I understand, which isn't required to pay street tax to Nick Calabresi."

Lanciano mashed out his cigarette. "Krato's Palace," he said, *sotto voce*. "I should have guessed. It's an unusual name." Clasping his hands behind his back, Lanciano began to perambulate the room in unhurried steps, like a monk in a Florentine monastery courtyard, saying his beads. When he spoke again, a good half-minute later, his face bore the marks of a man who had made up his mind, God knew about what.

"No wonder Arthur didn't get anywhere with Krato," he announced. "He and I both made the mistake of dealing with the man as if he were a sentient being, at worst an over-the-top fundie with an inexplicable interest in higher education." Lanciano leaned across his desk, his fingers splayed on the polished wood in the pose of a jungle cat ready to spring. "Permit me to give you a piece of advice about dealing henceforth with a creature like Mr. Peter Krato. First, don't waste your time trying to reason with him. In fact, the less you say to him the better. A man who's used to dealing with Calabresi street soldiers on a daily basis doesn't play by the rules of an Oxford debating society. He'll only use what you say as ammunition to shoot back at you." Lanciano aimed his forefinger at James. "Second, walk close to the wall. And last of all and above all, if you ever sit down to negotiate with a man like that, you make sure you lay your biggest weapon on the table." Lanciano slapped the desktop. "Your biggest weapon. *Capisce?*"

James sat glumly at the seminar table Wednesday afternoon, waiting, like everyone else, for the substitute lecturer to arrive. He time-killed the remaining minutes by listening, his attention only minimally engaged, to the energetic debate Lupe was having with Mitch Showalter over the meaning and merits of Artaud's *The Theater and its Double*, Mitch's tome-*du-jour*. James had been forced to muck through the dizzying essay last spring in a colloquium on poststructuralism, and the mere memory of it gave him a headache. Jack loped in just then and took the seat on the other side of James. Interrupting Showalter in the middle of a quotation-laden sentence concerning the metaphysics of speech, Jack challenged the class at large to guess what had happened to Bel Gunderson, whose usual seat next to Mitch was vacant this afternoon.

Richard Krato looked up over the top of his Catholic weekly. "Where the heck is she?" he said. "We were supposed to meet Saturday for a research session at the library, but she never showed."

"She's laid up in St. Mary's hospital," Jack reported, "lookin' like she got a baby grand dropped on her."

Trisha sat forward. "Good God, what happened?"

Jack shrugged. "She wouldn't tell me. But it looked kinda serious. I was thinking we could all take up a collection for flowers or something. Better yet, considering how much pain she's in, a bongful of Colombia's finest."

Richard, who had briefly appeared sympathetic to Bel's plight, puckered his lips and returned his disapproving attention to his newspaper. The rest of the class reached into their respective briefcases and purses and backpacks for loose cash to send Jack's way.

All at once Lupe cocked her head sideways to peer at the headlines on the front of Richard's *Rambler*. Nudging James, she pointed at the headline at the bottom of the front page: **MYSTERIOUS FALL KILLS FR. ARTHUR BRICUSSE.** Next to it was a small sidebar titled, "Archdiocesan investigation of SANA continues in shadow of famous priest's death."

Finally noting James's progressively hostile scrutiny, Richard shifted in his seat. "There's a, uh, nice obituary," he said, folding the tabloid and passing it down the table towards James by way of Mitch. "You're welcome to keep it, if you want."

"Uh oh," Mitch said, glancing at the article before handing it on. He gave a shake of his newly golden curls—recently tinted, or so Jack had told

James, at Erik's of Norway. "I know someone who is not going to like seeing that in the papers."

"Don't worry," Richard said placidly, "Dad doesn't read newspapers, not even Catholic ones."

It was miserably hot the following day, and the Institute's brand new air conditioning system was on the fritz again. The swelter of sweat and stale air trapped in the windowless A-V room, where the seminar students had assembled to watch a DVD of Branagh's *Henry V*, was doing nothing to ameliorate James's claustrophobia, let alone cool his temper.

"We already re-scheduled this once to suit Rich's schedule," James snapped at Mitch after the big man informed him that Richard wouldn't be making it to the screening this afternoon. "What is it this time, Peter have him out on the knocker pushing tracts?"

"Lay off the poor guy, Jimmy," Mitch whined, his defense of his SANA-mate accompanied by a juicy belch. "It was really my fault. See, Rich and I were supposed to finish the typesetting for our updated Policy and Procedures Manual last night, but I ended up blowing chow from some twenty-four-hour stomach bug. Rich was up all night finishing it by himself. He just had to get some snooze."

Before James could bring forth the comment springing to his lips concerning the best possible uses for an updated SANA Policy and Procedures Manual, the A-V room door opened. James looked up with a surprise rivaling Mitch's to see the object of their colloquy standing in the doorway. Dark circles of sleeplessness haunted Richard's handsome brown eyes, underscoring his pallor.

"I need to talk to you," Richard said, addressing Mitch as if he were the only person in the room.

The oath James uttered was drowned out by the *clang* and *bang* of a folding chair, kicked by Mitch, going end over end and smashing against the audio-visual stand. "Jesus fucking Christ!" Mitch cried, "can't you people leave me in peace five fucking minutes?"

The assembled students gasped as one at Mitch's unprecedented and most un-SANA-like outburst. Richard Krato couldn't have looked more thunderstruck if Mitch Showalter had just announced his conversion to Islam. He stood mute in the doorway, his bloodless mouth forming a large round O. Mitch pushed past him into the hallway, still muttering obscenities under his breath.

It was three or four minutes later when a very subdued Mitch returned to the A-V room, his Prairie School tee-shirt drenched in sweat. Richard trailed in glumly behind him. "Jimmy," Mitch said, wiping his damp face with his forearm, "I gotta go."

James sat fingering the DVD remote like a set of rosary beads. He was close to kicking something himself.

"It's not that, Jimmy, it's not the manual." Mitch trained his moist eyes on the empty doorway. "I gotta drive to Green Bay. My Aunt Abby passed away."

James sat forward.

"Oh, Mitch," Lupe exclaimed, "is there anything we can d-d-do?"

Mitch gave a slow shake of his blonde curls. "Nothing I can think of," he said softly, looking up and away as if sniffing for a trace of smoke. Finally he turned to Richard. "Drive with me up to Green Bay...?" His voice trailed off into a little-boy whine.

"You know I can't," Richard said, not unkindly. "Dad needs me to get the manual to the printer."

"For chrissake," Mitch cried, his doughy face scarlet, "couldn't your god-damned manual wait one goddamned day? I'm all alone now!"

"You know as well as I, that in our vocation true charity lies in obedience and abandonment—"

"I'll go with you," James said.

Mitch looked at first as if he didn't realize who had spoken. Then he whirled to James, his expression rapidly morphing from one of sorrow for the woman who had practically raised him, into one that James could only identify as something resembling terror. Backing away, as at the approach of an assail-ant, he threw his arms in front of his face. The two men stood staring at one another for a moment, eyes locked, the entire class watching them in silence, until the weird spell of it was broken by a piercing whistle of incredulity from Jack. Finally, Mitch dropped his arms to his sides and blinked like a man com-ing awake from a long sleep. He took a deep, calming breath, as if practicing a yoga posture. Then another. Then his shocky face relaxed into a kind of forced lassitude, pale with self-control. "It's real nice of you, Jimmy," he said, "but I think it would be better if I went alone, after all. Thanks all the same."

With that, Mitch snatched up his briefcase and exited the room.

"For God's sake," Lupe exclaimed to Richard, "go with him. He's in trouble!"

"She's right," agreed James. "I know a man on the verge of a breakdown when I see one."

Richard shifted his weight back and forth from one leg to the other. "God will give him a special grace to get through this difficult time," he said.

Lupe was appalled. "God *is* giving him a special grace to get through it. He's giving him you—a friend, almost family. Someone to be with him. Someone to—"

Before Lupe could finish her thought or Richard reply, James had stepped forward, grabbed Richard by his starched white collar and dragged him to the doorway. "Get out of my face!" he yelled, giving his former friend a violent shove.

Richard fell out into the gallery, tripping and stunned. James turned his back on him. "We'll reschedule when Mitch gets back," he announced to the class.

"Well, *I* won't be back!" Richard cried, grabbing hold of the gallery railing to pull himself to his feet.

James wheeled around in the doorway. "Oh, yes you will. You'll be back because Peter will tell you to come back. Someone's got to keep an eye on Mitch and me and Lupe and God knows who all. Christ, Rich, if Peter told you to jump off the seventh floor of the atrium—" He waved at the galleries gyring above their heads. "—I do believe you'd ask him if he preferred a swan dive or a half-gainer. Although perhaps suicide isn't the crime he'd be demanding of you. He'd be losing his most useful appendage. No, I can see a much more likely scene in my mind's eye: Peter Krato, his mighty shoulders sustaining the weight of the sinful world, beset on all sides by rebellious Judases and the meddling clergy, turns one evening to his loyal lieutenant and says, *Is there no friend who will rid me of this living fear...?* How did you answer him, Rich, hm? What did you say to him when he asked you to take care of 'the Arthur Bricusse problem' for him?"

Richard just stood there a moment, his mouth opening and closing, while James, leaning one arm against the doorjamb, looked him up and down as if trying to identify the source of a rancid smell.

"How could I—" Richard began finally, "—how could you possibly think that I—" He mopped his dripping forehead with his white shirtsleeve. "It was an obscene accident...the old man had a heart attack!"

James waved it away. "Just a rhetorical question, Rich. Just a hypothetical scenario, that's all, because I simply can't figure out where you people draw the line. If murder's too foul for you, how about vandalism or theft? Suppose Daddy told you I needed running out of town, or my career ruined. Would you see to it my computer files got erased and my dissertation shredded? Or suppose he needed something that didn't belong to him. Would you steal it for him, like the SANA report I wrote?"

"—Oh, for heaven's sake!" But the protest of innocence had come a second too late for James not to see the hesitation, the quick glance to the floor. "You've got to believe me, James, all I ever wanted—all my father ever wanted—was what was best for you."

James snorted contemptuously. "Put a sock in it. You don't even take care of your own. But then, I knew that, didn't I?"

"James..." Lupe said, coming up behind him and laying a hand on his shoulder.

Looking around, James saw that the rest of the class had congregated near the doorway and was observing them in fascinated silence. Turning, he waved at Richard, as if shooing away a late-summer mosquito, and said, "Go home, Rich. Go finish your Policy and Procedures Manual."

———

The day was clear and crisp, awash in sunlight, and the lush trees sailing past the windscreen of James's rusty Jeep were just beginning to turn the colors of autumn. The simplicity of the rolling south-central Wisconsin countryside, along with the farm smells and slower traffic, briefly afforded James, who'd been feeling increasingly stressed for weeks, a sense of expansiveness and peace such as he usually only experienced when surrounded by an ocean of sky and a thousand square miles of water. He and Lupe were en route to the rural community of Spring Green for one of the last American Players Theater performances of *Othello* before the company closed for the winter.

Upon arrival, James and Lupe parked the Jeep in one of the grassy lots at the bottom of the hill and climbed the sandstone gravel path to the theater. The open-air auditorium, with its rustic, multi-level stage, built entirely of graying wood, was lit by high-powered lamps atop plank towers that rose in back of the stage. Settling into their weathered seats, they scanned the horizon for approaching weather—several performances, James had heard, had already been rained out this month. But the stars continued to shine clearly against a backdrop of sky darkening from blue to ebony, and finally the houselights dimmed. A shaft of spotlight slanted down, transforming the rural Wisconsin stage into the midnight streets of Renaissance Venice.

The production, James thought with an appreciation born from considerable personal experience, was clean and energetic, and the leads were impressive. The Iago in particular was both brilliant and unsettling, giving the enthralled audience an unnerving portrayal of the famous villain's fetching combination of cunning and needfulness, of ribald *joie-de-vivre* and truth-telling, truth-twisting voyeurism—so much so that by the time the stage lamps faded on the inevitable fifth-act scene of carnage, and the audience was making its murmuring way down to the parking lot in the haloed glimmer of pathway lights, the only thing James could remember clearly about the production was the actor's chillingly light-hearted reading of Iago's most famous line: *I am not what I am.*

"I c-c-can't imagine Jack playing Othello," Lupe commented on the late-night drive back to Milwaukee. If James had had his way they would have stayed over night at the Springs Resort, but Lupe for some reason had not regarded the plan with favor.

Behind the wheel, James concentrated on willing his racing heart to beat at a more moderate tempo. He'd begun to feel jittery again in the middle of that last act. As the veteran of several extremely unpleasant manic episodes, he didn't want to think about what the familiar sensations, after years of freedom from the disease, might betoken. "Why not?" he said distractedly, thinking that this couldn't be happening at a worse time, and that he'd better make a doctor's appointment, "Jack's a natural ham. He was wonderful."

"But he's so—" Lupe shrugged. "—good-natured. Othello's got a beastly temper. D-Darned if I can see Jack getting that excited about anything."

James shifted in the driver's seat to get a little more blood flowing to his tingling right leg. He wondered if he should turn over the wheel to Lupe. "Oh, I don't know. Our Desdemona said she thought he was going to throttle her during the final performance, he got so caught up in it all."

Lupe turned her face to the passenger side window where the darkness beyond was broken only occasionally by yellow or white farmyard lights, or the approaching headlamps of a lone long-distance truck.

He glanced at her. "What's the matter?"

"I was just thinking about the scene where Othello k-k-kills Desdemona. I've never seen it done that way before."

The play of shadows on her face brought the chiaroscuro image rushing into James's mind: spotlights slashing the stage like lightning as Othello, facing the audience with inflexible determination, smothered his tiny wife's face against his own broad chest. Most productions had Othello smothering Desdemona with a pillow, as the text suggested, but this terrific little innovation had provoked a collective gasp from the audience. James had thought Lupe was going to jump up and leave. His spine jerked with a start at the mere memory of it. "Uh, it's a splendidly effective way," he argued, clearing his throat, "dramatically speaking, for a man to murder the woman he loves and hates at the same time. I wish I'd thought of it last year myself."

Lupe's shoulders rippled with a shudder.

"Want something to drink before you g-g-go?" Lupe hinted as she unlocked her apartment door and switched on the landing light. It was almost three in the morning and James could tell that she was wanting him to say his goodbyes and let her get to bed.

"I wouldn't say no to a nice warm cuppa," James replied, calculating, as he trailed her inside, snapping a kink in his neck with a twist of his shoulders, that tea would take longer to prepare than instant coffee. Just too damned edgy to face his big white empty bed alone. It was as if all the ordinary lubricants that greased the gears and pulleys of his body had been suddenly and maliciously drained, and everything inside was grinding. In the effort to persuade himself that it couldn't be the mania returning, not after all this time, James had settled instead on the thought that it was probably just the scent of fall in the air. He loved the season, it was especially beautiful in Wisconsin, but in the five years he had lived here he had learned to dread autumn's bitter promise of winter. For James, a Wisconsin winter meant the cold and the dark, and above all, confinement.

"You've got to let me get some sleep," Lupe complained, tugging him into the kitchen. "Blast it, *you* may be an insomniac, but I'm not. Besides you've only got one lousy class and an almost letter-perfect dissertation to edit. I'm carrying twelve hours and a part-time job!"

"I'll go home like a good boy," he promised, hand raised and speaking with unusual rapidity, "if you just let me stand here and make love to you—

antiquated usage—whilst the tea is steeping. A brief interlude of snogging, I feel certain, would be just the thing. I'm all at loose ends tonight."

She put the kettle on the burner and turned on the stove. "I suppose three minutes won't hurt."

"It takes five minutes to brew a decent cup of tea," he declared, backing her up against the kitchen wall.

When she pushed him away well over five minutes later, James, mumbling to himself, turned to fetch the milk from the refrigerator. In the process, his elbow knocked the tea tin from the counter. It clattered to the floor, depositing several dozen tea bags at their feet.

Lupe reached for sugar in the cupboard. "Sheesh, Diego, you *are* at loose ends. You on speed, or what?"

Not answering—not hearing really—he knelt to collect the tea bags and put the tin away. When he had finished, he retreated to the dining table, a smile pasted to his face. He thrust his fists into his lap so that she wouldn't notice that his hands were shaking, but the smile disappeared when he glanced up and saw that the wall above her mantel was no longer decorated with THE ULTIMATE SHAKESPEARIENCE poster, but with an original pen-and-ink seascape which he distinctly remembered having seen in Jack Sigur's apartment only a week before. What the hell did Jack think he was doing, giving Lupe expensive presents?

Joining him at the table, Lupe handed him an envelope. "This came for you yesterday, by the way. Can't think why it was sent here."

James pulled his eyes away from Jack's seascape—what rubbish, he told himself. What competition could he have from Jack?—and studied the envelope: first-class stamp, no return address…he ripped it open. Inside, instead of the familiar Bible photocopy, which he had been expecting, was a sheet of plain white paper containing a limerick in boldface type:

'TIS A PITY SHE'S A WHORE

There was a sly maiden from Brewtown
Who said to her Englishman, "Get down,
 Yes, down on your knees,
 And marry me—please!
Or you'll never get me to lie down."

Now what a bad deal that would be,
When DeBrun has enjoyed her for free;
 She's baiting you, dunce,
 It's your money she wants,
Plus a ticket to Anglicity.

Unaware that he was mumbling again, James stared at the thing, then up at the seascape, then at her. He dropped the paper on the table.

"James, I don't understand a w-w-word you're saying," he finally heard Lupe complaining, though the sound of it was as from a great distance, not three feet away on the other side of a table. "What on earth is the matter?" When he didn't answer, she reached for the paper. He snatched it away. The paper crinkled in his fist as he rose to his feet, so quickly that he knocked over the chair behind him. Crunching the paper in his fist, he hurled it as if it were a baseball. But instead of striking the seascape, which he'd been aiming at, the clump of paper struck Lupe's cat, heretofore asleep on the mantelpiece. Hal leaped to the floor with a howl of protest.

"James, for God's sake what's the matter with you!"

Still not answering, refusing even to look at her, James kicked the upended chair on which he'd been sitting, strode across the room, and slammed his way out the door.

The brisk night wind is ebbing, sighing into stillness. Though the doors and windows are open, not a breath of air stirs against your face. You are perched atop your table, cross-legged and rudderless, your mental sails drooping in the dead calm, your blank eyes staring out the window into middle-of-the-night nothingness. Your body struggles against opposing urges: half of you is numb, groggy, while the other half races like an engine with the idle set too high.

The abyss cracks wide.

And when I shall put thee out, I will cover the heaven, and the moon shall not give her light... you're talking to yourself, screaming really, mouthing syllables pressed into your memory like wrinkles under a hot iron: *Put out the light, and then put out the light, and put out the light...*

You hear a whisper and sit up, spine burning.

Something is after you. An unseen hand strikes wide, nail-ripping a gobbet of flesh. You cry out, scramble off the table, your eyes swiveling against the dark for the shadow you cannot see. Whirling, whirling again, you find yourself eye to eye with the Woman. The amber glow from the streetlamps transforms her turquoise mantle into a sanitarium green. But she's not looking at you anyway, and you think, *good thing, jolly good she ain't looking,* because you wouldn't want her babbling again. No, not a pleasant thought, that, her babbling again...the game's afoot!

(*Thunder and lightning. Enter three witches.*)

Fingers slide through damp hair. The shadow of wild music curls up the side of the building, pouncing through the open glass into your room. You recognize it, and don't: raging, ripping, runaway bass, faint, roaring, faint, roaring. Motion, motion—she can turn and turn and turn again. Knives in the air, unseen, unseeable, whistling past the ear. *Is this a dagger I see before me...?* Shut up, you fool, wrong play. Wrong, *wrong* play.

Scramble to the door, chest pounding. Hesitate. Grab the knob with both hands, jiggle it. Locked. No one could have come in. Did someone come in? Isn't there someone—something—in the room? Look around, look around.

Hiding, it is. Under the desk. At the bottom of the closet. Something ugly. Whining, whispering, wheedling...not quite word somethings. Not quite true. Not quite not true. Somethings. Press your back into the door, your wide eyes scraping the empty dark to follow the waves of Nothing.

Shut the eyes, breathe deep, press a foot against the door, run the gauntlet—run for your life!—beat the air with scissoring arms—to the desk, to the desk—to the chair, the lion's lair—seize the phone—hold the phone!—punch the button, punch another—numbers, numbers, never good at numbers—slam it down. What's her number? Have it out—why can't the idiot remember her bloody number? Address book. No, mail file, yes, computer. Push the button, disk drive, screen thing, thing ring, wring the hands—a monkey with a boom box. Chances of a monkey sitting at a typewriter and typing out *Hamlet*: Minuscule. Modest. Modern. Postmodern. Modem. Disk drive. Driven. *Rrrriiinngggg*. Sound piercing air. Bullet through the throbbing, bang, bang, head. Lunge at it. Knock it off the cradle. *Knock it off, dickery-dock*. Look at it, stare at it, glare at it, twice—a voice—a voice calling a name, from far away, from underwater, *Under the Sea*—

"James...James...!"

That's your name, by the Mass, someone's calling your name. The phone, hold the phone—*hold the phone, Molly Malone*—tap at it, yap at it, might be hot, electrified, alive, a shape-shifter—not what it seems, not what it seems!—might morph at your ear—oh, bless me it's quite dead, can't bite, swallow terror and hold it to your ear.

"Hall*ooo*...?"

"Oh thank God...James? James, please say something!"

Amazing, that. You're breathing again. You're closing your eyes. You're hearing the sound of your own voice saying her name, unbearable, wonderful, glorious—you haven't run aground yet, you can remember her bloody name, because yes that's you closing your eyes and breathing and her talking, and you've forgotten now what it was all about, what you wanted to have out with her, why you wanted to strangle her.

"James, that thing...you-you-you don't really...look, blast it, I'm frightened!"

"I'm frightening."

"Oh, God...have you taken something? Have you hurt yourself?"

"Hurt myself? I? My, oh my. Bit off my stride, girl. Shaky hand on the tiller. *Save me, O God, for the waters are come in, even unto my soul, and the sea is the sea, and drowning men do drown.* Bad quarter of an hour, this. Earnestly unglued. Quite Uncle Dick. Pack me off to the Tall Chimney. Twist and twirl, somebody's fucking with my *head*—!" He's screaming. Then sudden silence. Booming silence like the pounding of the sea.

"Are you still there?"

"Still where? Here, there, and everywhere. Yes, quite. I'm quite here. I'm not quite here."

"What c-c-can I do? Tell me what I can do!"

"You can…you can tell me what…what day?" He's forgotten something. Remembered something. Remembered he's forgotten something.

"Are you asking what day it is? It's Sunday, early Sunday morning!"

"No. I mean yes. I mean what month the number is the day?"

"What, Oh God it's, uh, September 29. It's September 29, what the hell—"

"Oh hell yes it's hell. September twenty-twenty—"

Shatter. Break. Crash and burn. Crave and yearn. Starve and learn.

"What's happening…are you still there?"

"Am I here? Why am I here? Why aren't I there? I'm stuck, I tell you. *Stuuuck.* Stuck at home with the pope of Rome."

"Jesus help me…look, I'll come there, okay? What's your apartment number?"

"Six. No, seven. At sixes and sevens. At twos and eights. An inch short of a two-foot rule—"

"James, *think*. Your apartment number. Quiet down and think!"

"He's thinking, he's thinking! It *is* six. *Bzzt.* Something six. Six, seven, eight, nine, ten, eleven, eleven, eleven…*twelve*! Oh yes it's twelve and… twelve and…twelve and six, yes, twelve naught six!"

"Twelve-oh-six. Are you sure?"

"More or less. Give or take. To have and to hold, from this day forward—"

"I'll be there as fast as I can. Oh, wait, James! James…?!"

"James is here."

"Is there some sort of building security?"

"Ring—" Swallow. Need to swallow but can't. "Ring the lobby. No, ring the button by the…by the…oh God by the shiny brass thing with letters."

"I understand, by the mailboxes in the lobby. I'll be there as soon as I can."

"*He shall stay until you come.*"

"Oh, wait! First tell me what you're going to do when it rings in your room!"

"Rings in the room? I haven't any rings in the room. I've got a ring in my closet somewhere…oh don't you see I'm so very tired and I want to sleep?"

"James *please*. C-C-Concentrate."

"C-C-Concentrate. Think. Speak. Do. Be. *Do-be-do-be-do.*"

"James—"

"He's thinking, he's thinking! He's thinking it will ring. It will ring and he shall walk. To the door. Then he'll…oh dear."

"Try to—"

"He'll push the goddamned button by the goddamned door!"

"Okay, okay, now just hold on. Can you hold on?"

"He shall jolly well hold on. Hold up. Hold out. Hold down. Down a hole—"

"Look, I think I'd better bring some help—"

"No, no, please, no helpers! I've already had so many mother's little help-ers and I still can't sleep!"

"Okay, okay, I'll be right there. Now I'm going to hang up the phone, okay?"

———————————

Lupe wondered if she were just picking up on James's chaotic state of mind, or if the stresses of the last month had finally undermined her sanity as well, because she felt eyes on her from the instant she stepped outside her apart-ment door. Like a cold hand down her bare back, the sensation of approach-ing horror was almost as tangible as it had been that strange morning at the Newman Center Mass, and the night Father died.

She paused at the foot of the stairs, listening…for what? The early morn-ing was so quiet, so perfectly still, she could hear the slightest movement of every cat, every squirrel in the neighborhood.

Telling herself to get a grip, Lupe made it to the garage on shaky legs and started up her grandparents' Toyota. She was backing slowly into the alley when she was startled by the gleam of metal in her rearview mirror: a car, its headlights off, was turning into the alley behind her. Lupe became even more alarmed a few moments later when she realized that the car wasn't pulling into a garage anywhere along the alley, but was following her back out into the street. A click of a button beside her elbow locked the car doors.

She breathed a sigh of relief when the car behind her passed under a street light: it wasn't the red Ferrari, thank God, but some sort of old-fash-ioned looking roadster, whitish.

By the time she turned east on Kenwood towards the lake, the pale-colored roadster had moved up right behind her, it's headlights now on and glaring in her mirror like owl's eyes. Lupe was so distracted by their shine that she missed her turn and continued through a yellow light towards the lake. The car didn't stop on the red behind her, but took advantage of the empty night streets to stay right on her tail.

After making a last-second decision to turn south on Lake Drive, just to see if the fellow behind her meant business, Lupe swung abruptly left onto North Wahl. The car turned with her.

Lupe was beginning to feel sick; but pulling over to throw up was not an option, it would make her too vulnerable, so she coughed back the bile and made another sudden left, she didn't know exactly where. It turned out to be a narrow wooded street that curved down the Lake Park bluffs. It was also a perfect place for a lone female to get herself hijacked.

Near panic, she pressed the accelerator, momentarily pulling away from the roadster. She sailed down the hill, then out onto Memorial Drive with-out so much as a pause at the stop sign at the intersection. But it was no use. By the time she passed under the pedestrian bridge at Bradford Beach, the owlish headlights were shining again in the rearview mirror.

Lupe's eyes flew from side to side, finally spotting—*Madre de Díos!*—an idling police car to her left, no doubt lying in wait for his next speed violator or drunken driver. Or taking a nap.

Lupe floored the gas pedal, leaned hard on the horn and prayed, *oh, God, let him make his quota tonight!*

The roadster revved its engine and was on her bumper within seconds.

Then finally, *finally*, Lupe saw the red and blue strobes swirling in her rear-view mirror, and heard the wail of the police siren, more beautiful to her in that moment than a choir of the heavenly hosts. The cop—bless his blue-crew soul!—was pulling over the roadster.

Lupe managed to get James's hefty frame into his bed, which was nothing more than a box springs and mattress set on the hardwood floor of his bedroom. When she tried to get up, he cried like a little boy and wouldn't let go of her, so she laid down beside him and let him fall into a twitchy sleep with his head on her breast, his hand clutching at her sweatshirt.

James awoke some three or four hours later with a head that felt like it had been stuffed with asbestos. He rubbed his puffy eyes with his fist and looked up. Lupe was standing at the foot of his bed, her cheeks flushed as she tugged at her disheveled clothes. It took him a moment to remember why on earth she was here and what exactly had happened. When he did, he opened his mouth, but couldn't think of a thing to say.

Suggesting that they talk later, after he'd had something to eat and some coffee, Lupe coaxed him up, then into his kitchen, where she managed to get him seated, more or less upright, at the small butcher-block island in the center of the room.

"Oh my God…"

The alarm in her voice sent a spike up James's spine and into his throbbing head. He looked up to see her staring with horror at three prescription bottles and a half glass of some clear liquid sitting atop the kitchen counter, none of which he had any memory of putting there.

She took a sniff of the liquid and made a face. "Whiskey," she said incredulously, "with these goddamned pills?"

He'd never heard her swear like that before, and the mild shock of it cleared his brain a little.

"No wonder I feel so bloody awful," he said. "I could tell something was coming. I suppose I tried to…" He glanced at the pills. "Well, I guess it was too late."

"How many were in there?" she demanded. "How m-m-many did you *take*? Oh, Jesus, this is a terrible mix. I should have—"

"For chrissake calm down, can't you see I'm all right?" He wiped his forearm across his clammy forehead, groping inside his foggy brain for something pacifying to say. "Look, there couldn't have been much left. I haven't taken that stuff in years. Except the sleeping tablets."

"But, even the-the sleeping tablets, mixed with the—"

"I tell you, I don't remember! I don't remember *any*thing after I got home!"

The plastic bottles rattled like castanets as Lupe replaced them on the counter with trembling hands. "Are you seeing a d-d-doctor?"

"If you mean a shrink, the answer is no. Just a GP for sleeplessness."

"But from everything I've heard, bi-polar disorder isn't something you have once and just g-g-get over, like the measles. At the very least, you ought to be checking in with a specialist!"

He turned away, unable to look her in the face as he lied. "I didn't have that serious a case, you know. And last night was a fluke. I feel perfectly steady this morning, just a little tired. Really." James knew he could be a pretty decent actor when he needed to be, but Lupe Cruz was obviously not buying it. "Look," he said with a sigh of exasperation, "it's all so damned complicated, and I'm too fagged right now to sort it out. Let's just...please, let me just sit here a bit, all right?"

Lupe glanced anxiously at James from time to time while she foraged through his cabinets and fridge for their breakfast fixings, and put on a twelve-cup pot of coffee, hoping to caffeinate him into a semblance of lucidity. He got up once to go to the bathroom, or so she presumed, until she heard the sound of the shower turned on full throttle. That would surely help.

She was stirring the scrambled eggs when he stepped into the hall-way again, naked but for a towel around his waist. He stood there for a few moments, one suntanned arm propped against the doorjamb, while she focused her eyes on the frying pan so that he couldn't see her blushing. Finally he turned and padded away into the bedroom, returning a few minutes later wearing jeans and a tee-shirt with a Great Lakes shipwreck map on the back.

"I feel better," he told her, and for once this morning she believed him. He bent over to pull a tray from the cabinet beneath the stovetop. "Let's eat out in the living room. There's a nice view."

Diffuse sunlight filtered through his huge east window, and a touch of fog lingered over the lake, dimming the horizon line between sky and water. "W-Wow," she said, pulling up a chair and silently concurring with the rumors she'd heard about James Ireton having one of the best views in the city.

James took the chair opposite; but when he just sat there for several seconds, as if he didn't know what he was supposed to do next, Lupe loaded his plate, fixed him a cup of coffee, and set them in front of his sagging face with a command to eat. He did apologize for scaring her the night before, but other than that, said nothing. Instead, she saw him looking around his room from time to time, between bites of food and sips of coffee: at *la Guadalupana* hanging above his fireplace, then at her, then out the window at the shimmering water, then back at her.

All of a sudden, and wasted as he was, James raised his arm and brought his fist down on the table. "How dare Rich send that bloody-minded thing to you!" he exploded like a popped balloon. "I have half a mind to march over to SANA House and rip out his spine, if he's even got one, the miserable little lizard."

The eruption was so sudden and violent that Lupe, almost jumping out of her chair from the surprise of it, instantly forgot the questions forming in her mind about the nasty limerick, and why he was so certain it had come from Richard Krato, and when he was going to make a doctor's appointment. Instead she burst out laughing.

"What's so damned humorous?"

"You, Hotspur! Or at least the thought of you, in your present condition, getting past Mitch Showalter!"

James screwed up his face in an expression of imagined pain. "I'd be loathe to tackle Mitch Showalter on a good day," he admitted, "let alone now. Not that I'm so sure that I'd have anything to worry about from him anymore, even if I arrived on the doorstep of SANA House with a bazooka on my shoulder. If you ask me, Mitch is finally waking up to the fact that Peter Krato may not be the Second Coming of Christ after all."

Lupe's residual chuckles evaporated. "If you ask me, Mitch's Catholic faith is going down the tubes right along with his faith in Peter Krato."

"Well, now," James drawled, "there are precedents."

"But all that Theory g-g-garbage he reads. I can't believe Rich doesn't snitch on him to Peter Krato. I almost wish he would. He's beginning to sound in class like he's channeling Michel Foucault."

"You're awfully interested in Mitch Showalter all of a sudden."

Lupe could hear the sharp edge of jealousy in his voice, but couldn't quite believe it. James, jealous of *Mitch*? It was absurd. In fact, it was downright— she shuddered at the word that had formed in her mind: *insane.* "I'm a lot more worried about you right now than Mitch Showalter," she said quietly.

James looked away, his jealousy quickly transforming into irritation, or so it appeared to her, that she was not allowing him to steer their breakfast conversation away from what should obviously be the topic at hand. "I am sorry about last night," he said again at last, in a tone suggesting he thought she might need some convincing on the subject, because so few of his statements this morning were proving trustworthy. "It was the prospect of the day, I suppose, as much as the pills. Michaelmas is always a bad day for me. You can always tell a clergyman's son. We mark everything by the liturgical calendar."

"M-Michaelmas?" She frowned, wondering what the feast of St. Michael and the Archangels had to do with anything. Then, suddenly remembering the significance of September 29th for him, her hand shot out to grasp his. "Oh my God…your mother and sister."

Taking her hand in his, he squeezed it hard, then let go so he could run his forefinger around the lip of his coffee cup several times before picking it up and draining it to the bottom. "I didn't tell it all in the SANA report," he said finally, shoving aside the cup with the back of his hand. "What happened that day."

Lupe said nothing, just waited.

He glanced over his shoulder at *la Guadalupana*, as if gathering strength for some herculean effort. "I don't suppose it came across in the report, but I adored my Mum. She had few reasons to smile, God knows, but when she did, it was like the sunrise over the cathedral steeple. But I couldn't count on her, Lupe. She'd retire to her bedroom with a bottle of Glenfiddich to get pissed-up on the worst possible occasions. Leaving me to look after Anne and handle my father, alone. That's how it started, that day."

Turning his gaze on the lake, silky under a sheer veil of sun-dappled fog, James's gray eyes grew smoky under the shadow of his eyebrows.

"I don't even remember what their argument was about that day. What was it ever about? Well, about me, often enough. But all I remember that day is that Mum had been drinking since breakfast. She passed out in her bedroom with her stereo going full blast. It was that violin fantasy you played that day, the one by Vaughan Williams. It was her favorite piece. My father hated it, of course. He thought it sentimental and romantic. That was probably why she was playing it that morning, to annoy him."

James jerked his head, as if pulling away from a snag of cobwebs. "After a while, the stereo went silent and Mum stumbled downstairs. Almost fell down the stairs, actually. Probably looking for more booze. That's when she and Colin got into it. Christ, I could hear them all the way up in my bedroom. Little Anne came running into my room, terrified at the commotion. To quiet her, I promised to sneak downstairs and fetch her something to eat. Mum hadn't fixed her any breakfast.

"So we tiptoed downstairs and into the dining room. Then the larder. What you call a 'pantry' here in the States. Very much like the pantry in your parents' house, with a swinging door that opened into the kitchen. I was in there reaching for a biscuit tin when I heard Mother say, scream really, *I'm divorcing you, you bastard. Even if it means exposing the ugliness of our marriage all over the parish, the entire Church!'* Lord, she couldn't have chosen anything worse to say than that. My father's career meant the world to him, and she knew it."

"What did he d-d-do?" Lupe whispered.

James gave a vacant wave. "I couldn't hear the words, he spoke so quietly. But the tone of it…it was as cold and smooth as glass. I was trying to peek into the kitchen through the crack in the swing door, but all I could see was Mother's shadow on the kitchen wall." James held up his right hand. "Suddenly she — the shadow — pulled her wedding band from her finger and tossed it —" He flicked his wrist. "— into the dustbin. Then she slammed out the kitchen door into the back garden. Annie must have thought she was leaving without her or something, because all at once she pushed past me into the kitchen, screaming, *Mummy, Mummy, don't leave me!*"

James's hand dropped to the table. He cocked his head to one side as if he were regarding a piece of artwork hung crookedly on the wall. "She left, all right. Took Anne with her. She didn't take me. Perhaps she didn't know I was in there. Or probably she just…forgot. All I know is, the next thing I remember clearly, it was a day or two later. I was being shoved onto an airplane at Heathrow, bound for Canada. Mum and Anne were dead, and I was to live with my Aunt in Toronto."

Covering her mouth with her hand, Lupe watched James peering at the empty horizon with emptier eyes. When he finally began to speak again, his voice sounded distant and hollow, as if he had fallen down a well.

"It was as if Mum and Annie just…sailed away. The whole business is sort of smudgy now, like a stain on my imagination where a memory ought to be. But I do remember my father's last words as he shoved me into the plane at Heathrow. He said to me, *Boy, these fourteen years of misery have all been because of you. We'd have all been better off if I could have talked her into the abortion.*" James gave a slow nod. "It's the darkness, Lupe. The darkness behind…"

Lupe grabbed his hands. "I love you. You know I love you. D-D-Darkness and all. All of you."

He leaned forward slightly. He looked almost puzzled. "Do you? Do you really?"

"So much it frightens me. Everything about you is…m-m-more. I'm afraid there's not enough of me to hold it all."

He enfolded her hands in his much larger ones. "Your heart is as wide as the sea. More than enough. Problem is, Lupe, you say you love me, but you're not willing to love me as I am. If you loved me, *me*, you'd love me here, where I am. Not someplace I may never be." Letting go, he reached up to nudge her cheek, to make her look at him. "If you could just give me a month of your life. Two. Just give me six months of your life. Six months of your love, your great love. Here, with me. It would be an act of charity, you know. More than you know. I'd get better, I know I would."

"But how-how-how could that help anything? I don't see—"

"You're the channel of grace for me, that's all I see!"

Lupe's fingers reached instinctively for the medal at her throat. Fingering it, her mind a whorl of thoughts, impressions, emotions, as she struggled to stretch her little self around his huge need, she couldn't remember all of a sudden the convictions that had made her put it on in the first place. All she could see was the man in front of her. "I n-n-need some t-t-time," she stammered.

He gripped her hand again. "At least give me a date, for pity's sake. A date I can circle on my calendar. A date you'll come here to be with me, stay with me. It'll help me hold on. Then, if you change your mind…"

Unable to come up with anything better in the press of the moment, Lupe picked the first date that came to her mind. "My b-b-birthday," she said. "No, no wait! My birthday's a Wednesday, I couldn't possibly come on a Wednesday. I have to work the next morning and—"

"Then when?"

"The wee-weekend after my b-b-birthday." She clapped her hand over her mouth, appalled at the wretched sounds coming out of it.

"Friday, the 18th," he whispered, his eyes shining again with a remnant of delirium. "We'll make a celebration of it. We'll exchange hearts."

She started to say, "What if…?" but couldn't bring herself to mouth the words. Not now, not when he was so fragile, so needy, so close to the edge. Instead she turned her eyes towards the indifferent sea beyond the glass, praying that her silent God would make an exception, just this once; would unseal the heavens and give her a sign, show her what to do…

The morning sun disappeared behind a puff of cloud.

Chapter Eight:
Once More Into the Breach

How yet resolves the governor of the town?
This is the latest parle we will admit.
Therefore to our best mercy give yourselves
Or like to men proud of destruction
Defy us to our worst: for, as I am a soldier,
A name that in my thoughts becomes me best,
If I begin the battery once again,
I will not leave the half-achieved Harfleur
Till in her ashes she lie buried.
The gates of mercy shall be all shut up,
And the flesh'd soldier, rough and hard of heart,
In liberty of bloody hand shall range
With conscience wide as hell, mowing like grass
Your fresh-fair virgins and your flowering infants...
What say you? Will you yield, and this avoid,
Or, guilty in defence, be thus destroy'd?

Shakespeare, *Henry V*

After a cursory perusal of the limerick, and wishing for the fourth or fifth time that afternoon that he hadn't forgotten his cigarettes back at the office, Lt. Calvin Masefield re-folded the sheet of paper, replaced it in its envelope, then dropped the envelope inside a plastic specimen bag. Yanking off his disposable gloves, he leaned back in the chair and took a sip of the coffee James had fixed for him.

"Have there been any others?" he said addressing his host, who looked, Masefield thought, as if he hadn't slept in a month.

"Three," James said, rubbing his red-veined eyes. "Or I should say, three recently. Two before and one right after Fr. Bricusse died. I used to get them all the time, after I left SANA, but not in almost three years."

"This is the only one you kept?"

James gave a frustrated-sounding sigh. "Richard Krato's a little shit, Lieutenant, but I guess I always thought he was an essentially harmless little shit. Until this." He waved at the letter in Masefield's specimen bag. "This took time and effort. And he directed it at Lupe, for pity's sake. Not that he'll admit it."

"You confronted him?"

"This morning, as a matter of fact. At the Institute. He denied it, of course. But I could see the guilt behind his eyes. It was everything I could do not to throttle him right there in the atrium."

"A gift for reading faces is not an infallible source of information," Masefield cautioned, thinking that throttling people might be the sort of thing this obviously angry young man contemplated doing on a regular basis, "even with a guy's who's as lousy an actor as Richard Krato."

James leaned forward. "Look, Lieutenant, the letters with Bible passages were all photocopied from a Bible I gave Richard. I mentioned it in my SANA report. I recognized the edition and the translation. I've got one just like it, I can show it to you. Even the pagination matches up perfectly. So there's no question in my mind who's behind it. My concern is, could these letters of Richard's be somehow connected to some of the other things that have been happening around the Institute?"

Masefield scratched his chin. "Could be. As far as your computer vandalism is concerned, I'd say most likely. I mean, other than Richard Krato, how many Bible-thumping enemies do you think you have around here?"

"No one over there at SANA likes me," James admitted, collapsing against the back of his chair. "Peter's seen to that. But Richard and his father are the only ones who've made giving me grief part of SANA's evangelical mission statement."

His bushy eyebrows arched high over his nose in a bemused expression, Masefield placed the plastic specimen bag in an evidence envelope, sealed it, then extracted a pen from his breast pocket to fill out the identification label. "Well, I'll do what I can with this," he said as he scribbled, "but I'm not holding out much hope that we'll find any fingerprints on it, except yours. The thing that's worrying me, and I think should worry you, is that, generally speaking, people who get their jollies out of this sort of harassment are usually on their way to bigger and badder things."

"What the devil do you mean?"

Writing his signature with a hasty flourish, Masefield tucked away his pen. "I mean that criminals aren't born overnight, James. They acquire their confidence and skills, and shed their morals, by degrees. Like the guy, whoever he was, who tossed your dead priest over that seventh floor railing. Five'll get you ten that wasn't his first act of public mischief."

Ashen to begin with in the dull light of the overcast afternoon spilling through the window, James seemed to pale even further. "You think that Richard—I mean the person who sent these letters—is the same man?"

"Now I didn't say that," Masefield pointed out hastily, thinking that the last thing he needed was James Ireton going Dirty Harry on him over on Newberry Boulevard. "I'm only suggesting that if making you squirm is a major priority for this guy—" Masefield patted the envelope. "—then petty stuff like this, or even the computer tampering, won't satisfy him for long. If I were you, I'd prepare myself for some escalation."

"That's lovely, that is."

Cracking a smile, Masefield tucked the evidence envelope under his arm and pushed himself to his feet. "By the way," he said in a suddenly cheerier tone—he had just remembered he had a pack of Marlboro Ultra Lights in the glove compartment of his car—"do you happen to remember any of the Bible passages from those other letters?"

As if coming awake, James rose and trailed the lieutenant to his front door. "Um, one was from *Revelations,*" he said, "the famous bit about the red dragon. Another was from *Ezekiel,* about punishing Israel for her sundry whoredoms. And the first one…" James thought a moment, then made a disgusted face. "Oh yeah. It was from *Isaiah.* About the fall of Lucifer."

Masefield's hand paused on the door knob. He turned. "*How art thou fallen, O Lucifer, son of the morning?*"

"Spot on, Lieutenant. Don't tell me you're a preacher's son, too."

"Grandson," Masefield said, his voice beginning to tighten up on him. "What version was it?"

"Beg pardon?"

"You said you recognized the translation, that these passages were from the same version as the Bible you gave Richard. Which one was that?"

"Oh. Well, it was the King James, of course."

The lieutenant was momentarily speechless. Finally noticing the expression of alarm flowering on James's face, Masefield backed off to give the guy some breathing room. "Why did you give Richard a King James Bible?" he asked finally. "Why not a Catholic version?"

James was obviously puzzled, perhaps troubled by Masefield's peculiar line of questioning. "I gave it to him as a bit of a joke, really. It used to vex Richard when I claimed that, whatever its Protestant shortcomings, the King James was the only English version of sufficient literary worth to merit the title 'the word of God.' Good Lord, what does it matter?"

Even if he had known the reason—he only knew that it mattered, not why—this was one question that Lt. Calvin Masefield was not prepared to answer. Yet.

Lupe hung up the phone with a sigh that commingled weariness and relief. Going into the bedroom to fetch the three-ring notebook that served as her journal, she jotted a quick entry regarding the private retreat she and Martin had just scheduled for Holy Hill in December, around the feast of Our Lady of Guadalupe. By then the term would be over, of course, and all the difficult decisions she was facing already made, for better or worse; but even the simple act of planning some time alone to think and pray had given her a moment's reassurance.

But only a moment's. Replacing the notebook on her bedside table, she shuffled to her kitchen to fix herself a sandwich while she mentally sorted out the day's events, if for no other reason than to avoid having to think about those upcoming.

First had come Jack's surprise announcement in class that Bel Gunderson had dropped out of the Institute, citing poor health and a deteriorating financial condition. Word was that Bel's once lucrative modeling career was in the toilet after her recent hospitalization, which she still refused to explain even to her closest friends.

Then Lupe and James had walked to the Golda Meir Library to track down some secondary sources for their seminar paper, only to run into one of James's old flames, the busty Milwaukee Rep actress with the Kate Smith voice named Maggie Claymore who James had mentioned so cruelly on Bradford Beach. Lupe had overheard *Magnum Clamor*'s graphic *what-it-was-like-to-get-laid-by-James Ireton* remarks, spoken to a companion at the Reference Desk in what the woman no doubt believed, wrongly, to be a whisper, from nearly ten yards away. Worse, James's subsequent attempt at reassurance—"It only lasted a week, luv"—had depressed rather than consoled Lupe. He had tried to coax her out of her testy mood with the offer of dinner and a movie. Claiming exhaustion, Lupe had demurred, which only made James pouty in turn. When Lupe proposed the alternative of a quiet evening watching a movie at his place, James grumbled that *no*, they couldn't go to his place, his place was a bloody mess. At which point, Lupe, now the one pouting, complained that she couldn't fathom his reluctance to share his private space with her, given his recent demand that she move in with him.

In short, they had quarreled.

Lupe paused, milk glass in hand, to stare at the calendar tacked to the kitchen wall. The red circle drawn around Friday, October 18th prompted images to resurface in her mind, images that had tormented her off and on for weeks: James and Bel, James and Nadine Jeffrey, James and Trisha Perl, James and Leila Redmond, James and Maggie Claymore, James and…God.

Setting aside the milk, Lupe pulled a bottle of Guinness out of the refrigerator, wavered, then exchanged it for a much larger bottle of Irish whiskey from the cupboard—a souvenir from her parents' recent trip to Oonagh Cruz's native Donegal. Filling a tumbler half full, Lupe added some ice cubes and a splash of water as she'd seen her father do on similar occasions, and calmly decided to get plastered.

She gagged a little on the first sip, then chugged down the rest; then refilled the glass. Halfway through the second round her spine began to tingle with the welcome beginnings of inebriation. Burping, her lolling eyes drifted once more to the red circle on the calendar: what James had taken to calling her "belated coming-of-age party" was less than ten days away.

Curious, Lupe thought, pouring round three, this time without the water, James actually seemed to be enjoying the wait—James Henry Ireton, who wasn't accustomed to waiting for, well, *anything*. Indeed, he seemed to be looking forward to next Friday with the same heady anticipation that she would have expected to feel before her wedding night. The fixed date, the planned festivities, the postponement of amorous satisfaction, all lent a patina of ritual and sacramentality to this scheduled overture to their coupling.

At least for him.

Lupe's stomach heaved. She bolted for the bathroom.

A short while later, her stomach emptied and her mouth tasting like brine, Lupe sat wrapped in a blanket on her screened-in porch. Far below, framed by October-scarlet trees, her grandmother's snapdragons swayed lazily in the evening breeze, their petals full and plump as if oblivious to the bite of frost in the air. The subdued vesperal light on the summer colors evoked in Lupe a stab of emotion that felt perilously close to nostalgia, as if this particular autumn evening heralded the coming of a winter that would never again wheel to spring.

Lupe was reaching for her journal again when a flash of metal-reflected light from the setting sun shone into her eyes. She looked up to see a car idling in the alley behind the house.

It was that roadster again.

Lupe looked so very young, James thought, her face framed by a nimbus of black hair and her winter white jacket zipped up to her throat. There had been something reticent and inward-looking about her all day, like a flower closing its petals against darkness and cold, and he had begun to worry. Still, here she was beside him, climbing the eleven flights of stairs to his twelfth-floor apartment, a duffel bag slung over one shoulder and hauling a large package wrapped in brown paper—obviously a picture of some sort. In her other hand she clutched a bouquet of flowers rescued from her grandmother's garden before tonight's anticipated hard freeze. The petals were nipped black around the edges, but the summer colors against her white jacket made her look like a schoolgirl going up to her First Communion. James felt he could fly up the stairs.

"God, what a barbarian I am, let me carry those," he said, suddenly remembering his manners. He took the flowers and the picture and gestured at her duffel bag. "You can't have much in there."

"It's just enough for to-to-tonight," she stammered. "I'm worried about Hal. You know, my cat."

"What's the matter with him?"

"He didn't come home when I called him this afternoon. It's supposed to get down in the twenties tonight."

"I thought you were going to ask your grandmother to look after him when you moved out."

"I was, b-b-but…"

James paused on the twelfth floor landing, out of breath. "You haven't told her yet, have you. Any of them. Dammit, Lupe, you've got to tell them."

"Tomorrow," she said, leaning against the stairwell door. "I'll tell them tomorrow. I wasn't supposed to know, but Mom and Dad are throwing a surprise b-b-birthday picnic for me at Holy Hill."

James's eyebrows gathered. "Odd they didn't invite me," he said feeling surprisingly hurt by the apparent snub.

"But that's how I found out," she said hastily. "They were g-g-going to call you, but when they realized you had an unlisted number, they had to ask me. And of course, I wanted to know what was going on and, well, *Papi* was never good at keeping secrets from me."

"They still didn't call me."

She hesitated. "I told them I th-th-thought you had other plans for the day."

Now he was definitely hurt. "*You* didn't want me there?"

She flapped her hands. "You know it wasn't that. I just thought it might be better if I told them about us alone. They're going to need a little time to get used to it. They're going to be…d-d-disappointed."

James was not about to accept this. "Come on," he argued, "what about when your sister converted to Judaism when she got married? I dare say your family was disappointed then, too, but it's hardly made them love her less. Or her husband and children."

"Yes, that was hard. But it was different, too."

"Now, really, how?"

She thought a moment. "That was like a poet putting aside sonnets in favor of villanelles or sestinas, because the man she loves lives for them. This is like…" She shrugged and reached for the door latch.

He held the door shut. "Like what, Lupe?"

She looked up at him. "Like a poet who lives for sonnets, but who can only get published if she writes limericks. *There was a sly maiden from Brew-town…*" She pushed aside his arm to open the door.

James followed her down the dimly lit hall to his apartment, where several seconds' worth of digging for his keys gave him some much-needed time to conjure his next move—something to erase that disturbing collation of guilt sifted with accusation in her face. Finally getting the door unlocked, James set the picture and the flowers inside, then scooped her off her feet like a bridegroom. He kicked the door shut with his heel and headed for the bedroom.

"Aren't you even g-g-going to feed me before I ante up?"

Setting her down, he kissed her deeply, admonishing himself to slow down, to remember how new and, given her traumatic experience with Barry DeBrun, even frightening this first time might be for her. After slipping off her jacket to hang in the hall closet, he pulled her towards the living room. "I have a surprise for you," he said, guiding her before him through the archway. "The real reason I've been keeping you out of the flat the last two weeks." His hands resting on her shoulders, James surveyed his own handiwork with a tactile sense of satisfaction:

The east-side glass of his picture window was now framed with hanging and standing plants. The old trestle table had given place to new dining room furniture carved of ebony, set this evening with an eclectic mix of sterling, crockery and chiseled crystal. Lionel's desk and the bookshelves on the west side of the room remained as before, now even more heavily laden with the addition of some of Bricusse's books, but an expensive entertainment system had replaced his old portable television and DVD player. A hand-woven rug in shades of brown, gold and turquoise carpeted the center of the hardwood floor, while another, smaller rug of similar design was laid out in front of the fireplace, setting off an ebony-and-glass coffee table and a sofa upholstered in ochre corduroy. A lavish bouquet of salmon-colored roses sat atop the mantel under *la Guadalupana*, still the only art work in the room.

"This is beautiful…" Lupe breathed.

He embraced her from behind. "I've been bivouacking too long," he said into her neck. "I wanted us to have a home."

She looked up at *la Guadalupana*, her eyes damp with tears. "It's g-g-going to be all right," she said. "*All's well that ends well.*"

Releasing her, he stuffed his hands in his pockets. "Ah yes," he said, a sharp bite of vexation in his voice, "*God's in His heaven, all's right with the world.* In my experience, Lupe, things don't 'end well.' They just end."

She began to turn away, but his hands shot out for her. "Dammit, don't you see, having you here with me is more than I ever expected from life. And certainly from God."

It took her a moment, but she smiled again after that. Yes, she wanted to be here, he told himself. Most of her wanted to be here, anyway. He would content himself with that much.

She took a seat on the sofa while he poured her a glass of sherry, then started up a fire with a couple of prefab logs — the first fire, he told her, in the three years he had lived here. Glancing once at his watch — the caterers would be here any moment — he sat down beside her, pulling her head on his shoulder while his fingers stroked her face, and her hand caressed his knee. Within a minute, she was asleep.

When the doorbell buzzed, she awoke with a start.

"The caterers," he said, rising.

He returned a minute later balancing two trays on his rigid fingers, having assured the caterers with a generous tip that he could manage from there. He couldn't bear anyone else in the room.

Watching him lay out his feast with clumsy ebullience, waving away her help, she shook her head at his extravagance; but he could tell she was charmed, nevertheless. Finally seating her by the window, James scanned his mental list of all the little "extras" he had planned to make this dinner perfect: smoked salmon fettuccine, her favorite, and the Oregon wine Jack had recommended to go with it; roses, music…damn, the music! He went to his new entertainment system and fumbled with the unfamiliar buttons and knobs until he got the CD going, a Yitzhak Perlman recording of the Bach double-violin concerto he had purchased the previous afternoon.

They said little as they ate. Instead they listened to the music, achingly beautiful, and watched the silver waves outside the window crumble into gold in the setting sun. She made an enthusiastic remark about the entrée at one point, and then giggled until she was nearly sick when he told her that he had ordered seafood out of respect for her traditional habit of abstaining from meat on Friday. The incongruity of it all seemed obvious to her, but it took an explanation for him to see the irony:

"Wh-Wh-What's the point of keeping the little rules," she said, "when we're breaking such a big one?" Then she, too, ceased laughing altogether.

"What's the matter?" He held his breath.

"After tonight," she said, as if it had occurred to her for the first time, "I won't be able to receive c-c-c-communion."

James winced. He was about to say, *Oh, but many Catholics these days…* or words to that effect, but thought better of it. The everyone's-doing-it argument wouldn't wash, not with her. "Thank you for what you're giving up for me," he said instead. "I…wait here a moment."

Putting down the butter knife he'd been gripping in his fist, James hurried into the bedroom, thinking bloody hell, that was a close one. He returned a moment later with a festively wrapped box. "Your birthday present," he announced.

Lupe's face lit up as she tore it open. There was a garment inside the box, a turquoise dress spun entirely of cashmere.

"Go put it on."

Shutting his bedroom door behind her, Lupe set the box on his bed and took off her sweater; then her slacks. She folded her clothes on his dresser, thinking that the next time she undressed it would be here, tonight, with him.

She held up the dress in the half-light. It was designed as a simple wrap-around with a bodice-length collar that folded back to form lapels in front. Secured only by a tie belt of the same cashmere, the dress, she thought, would be easy enough to get out of in the clinch…not that James was that calculating. No, that was the sort of thing she'd expect from Barry DeBrun. Besides, James had a right to think what he was thinking, to expect what he was expecting. She had given him that right.

Spotting her own reflection in his mirrored closet doors, Lupe pressed her palms against the cashmere at her thighs. No question, it was a beautiful dress. And it had to have cost an awful lot of money.

Her eyes drifted to the package leaning against his dresser. In it was a sonnet she had written about their encounter on her stairs in the rain, and a poster of the Rossetti-Morris St. George, identical to the one he had lost at SANA house, or so at least she hoped. The sonnet was no masterpiece, to be sure, and the prospect of a Shakespeare scholar reading it made her want to weep; but the picture at least was really quite striking, and not easy to come by, and she was sure he would be glad to have it again, even in its thrift-store frame; but laid side to side in her mind against the refurbished apartment, the fine dinner, and the fabulous dress…

She sighed. All she had to give him, really, was herself. All of a sudden it didn't seem nearly enough.

James rapped on the door, but entered without waiting for an invitation. He caught his breath when he saw her in the turquoise dress. Never in his life, he thought, stepping into his own familiar room with the reverence of a pilgrim on the threshold of a shrine, had he seen anything more beautiful. Except once. He stopped dead.

"I d-d-don't think I can accept this," she said, gesturing at the dress.

James was startled out of his troubled reverie. "What's wrong with it?"

"Nothing, it's p-p-perfect. But cashmere…I can't imagine what it must have c-c-cost."

"Nonsense," he said, thrusting his hands in his trouser pockets. "I knew it was made for you the instant I clapped eyes on it. If you must, think of it as a present I bought myself, just to see you in it. Besides, I'm sure you've heard—" He caught himself mid-sentence, about to say, *I'm sure you've heard all the backchat about how well-lined I am.*

Their eyes circled one another's in a wary dance, each hoping for some word or gesture from the other that would set them in a common rhythm again. James even thought to make his move, right there and then, in the bedroom, but his nerves were screeching like a violin stroked by a razor, and the expression on her face warned him that it would be very poor timing indeed.

Instead, he gently took her arm and led her back into the more neutral territory of the living room. "I've got something to show you," he said, seating her on the sofa before going to his desk. He returned a moment later with an envelope. "Jack gave me an early birthday present. Two tickets to Stephen Dietz's *Ten November* at the Milwaukee Rep. It opens next week."

"What a sweetheart," Lupe said, smiling as at the mention of a favorite uncle. "You know, he gave me another one of his seascapes for my birthday. I don't know why he's being so generous. Except maybe because he's got so much stuff, and his apartment's so tiny, he has no place to put any of it." She laughed. "I think he's been using me as his U-store-it garage."

"Jack does love giving expensive presents," James said after a moment's pause. "But he hasn't the cash for it he used when he had a steady job." A sliver of wood popped in the fireplace, sending sparks up the chimney. Seating himself, his elbows on his knees, James reached for his sherry. He twirled the stem of the glass back and forth between his fingers, back and forth. "You go to Jack's place often, do you?"

"Couple times a week," she said, apparently not hearing the peculiar tension in his voice. "He's got a fabulous CD collection. He's been trying to educate me about opera." She chuckled. "Hopeless."

Rising, James snatched the decanter off the chimneypiece to pour himself another glass. He bolted it down in one swallow. Seeing Lupe yawn, he chided himself silently for being an idiot—what nonsense to be jealous of Jack of all people!—and seated himself again beside her. He was leaning over to kiss her when he realized that she was still wearing that goddamned Guadalupe medal. Pushing aside the chain, she groaned with pleasure as he buried his lips in her neck.

Finally, finally, he felt a kick of electricity between them. Rather than risk any more problematic words, he rose, took her hands, and pulled her after him into the bedroom.

The room was all but dark. Only a slant of yellowish light washed into the room through the open doorway, casting contrasting shadows on the polished floor, the low bed, her face. Letting go of her so he could unbutton his shirt, James was suddenly aware that he was a little flushed with the wine, but that it was probably just as well: the liquor might slow him down, preventing what he dreaded might otherwise be a famine-induced, trigger-happy misfire.

Never taking his eyes from her half-shadowed face, he removed his shirt and tossed it on the floor, then his shoes and his socks; but when he unbuckled his belt and began to unzip his trousers, her eyes slipped away, reminding him that there was still one shallow channel to clear before he made safe harbor. She would have to be worked gently, until he got her to the place where her senses took hold of the moral tiller, like the night on the stairs in the rain; where she would be too absorbed in feeling to notice his powering through the tacks and jibes. Then, then…downwind sailling in the tropics of desire.

Reaching for her, he kissed her and stroked her back, drawing her towards him and against him until he felt her heat as well as his own, and heard the low moans syncopating her breath. Then he pulled, ever so gently, on the belt of her dress until it came undone.

He knew the responses of women. He could tell she was totally absorbed in feeling now, in the sensation of hot skin against hot skin. Pressing his mouth into hers, his hand rode down her shoulders and across her breasts, then gripped her hips before she could take conscious note of the fact that her dress had slipped to the floor, that they were half-naked, and that he was pulling her down on his bed.

His hands were behind her back, his fingers working on the hooks of her bra, when his lips made contact with the cold silver of her Guadalupe medal. Chuckling uneasily, he reached up to unclasp the chain. Finally getting it undone, he set it on his bedside table, then pulled open the top drawer to rummage inside for a condom.

Lupe looked at the medal, then the limp, flesh-colored condom. She sat up. He tried to pull her down again, but she pushed him away. "I-I-I can't d-d-do this," she said shrilly, flapping her hands. "I thought I could but I can't. Dammit, James, I want *you* inside me, flesh and blood, not some fucking piece of Latex! I can't believe I forgot about all this!"

He gasped at the word he'd never heard her use. But his surprise was instantly translated into a flare of anger. "Jesus, forgot about all *what?*"

"I-I-I…" She reached instinctively for the medal that was no longer around her neck, and when she realized it wasn't there, flapped her hands again. "You're being very patient with me, I know you are, it's just—oh God, everything's c-c-connected, and we're trying to cut it up, and I don't know how or where to cut. There's bone everywhere beneath!"

"I don't understand a word you're saying," he broke in. He was lying, of course. He knew what she was getting at, though he couldn't have phrased it a word better. It was the thing that was all wrong this evening: the sensation of cutting something up, of grinding something down; of grating against raw bone and exposed nerve everywhere he pressed.

"James, for God's sake, there are some things we've got to talk about. I can't believe we haven't talked about them before now!"

"I'm miraculously free of venereal disease, if that's your concern," he snapped. "I even had myself checked for HIV last week, just to be on the safe side."

She heaved a great sigh. "That wasn't really what I meant."

"Then what, dammit?"

She threw a skittish glance at the condom, still in is hand, and folded her arms over her breasts. "What if," she said slowly, "no matter what we do, or don't do...what if I g-g-get pregnant?"

Finally meeting her gaze, he saw her turquoise eyes glittering black and surprisingly fierce in the half-light; the expression in them shining in marked contrast with the caution he was hearing in her voice. James looked down at the condom in his hand. "You tell me," he said thickly. "I don't recall ever being asked my opinion about it."

She didn't speak for a half minute at least. When she did, she said, "Well, I'd be a mother then, wouldn't I? And you'd be a father. You're going to have to decide if you can live with that."

Something snapped inside. He threw the condom on the bed and stood up. "You'd just love that, wouldn't you, getting up the spout by me, so I'd have to do the done thing and marry you!"

Lupe licked her lips. She was silent for some seconds, then finally swallowed and said, "If that's what you think of me...how could you want me?"

When James couldn't answer, Lupe bit her lip and said, "James, *do* you want me? I mean, do you want *me*?"

James stepped back. The words rang in his mind like a carillon of bells: *Do you care for me, James? Do you love me? Do you love me?* "I love you!" he cried. "I love you! This isn't a seduction, it isn't!"

She held out her hand, palm up. "Then try to understand. My religion isn't like a necklace I can take off at night and put back on in the morning. It's who I am. Without it, I don't know what I'll be. I don't know what else to say."

"We *could* marry, I suppose," he said hastily, desperation now mixing with the old familiar anger bubbling up in him like a pot on an accelerating boil. "I wouldn't mind a civil ceremony so much, as long as there was no fucking priestly hocus-pocus. That way, if things didn't work out, there'd be no—"

"For God's sake," she cried, "stop negotiating with me! I'm trying to give you my *self*, not sell you a goddamned sports car!"

He squinted down at her. "You know, I always begin to sweat when you lose your stutter. That tongue of yours becomes as sharp as hedge clippers."

Lupe sighed, her breath evaporating in another and longer silence that seemed to deepen the darkness in the room, thickening it until it almost seemed to have a weight and measure of its own, like a woolen blanket thrown over their heads. "Look," she said finally, "we're both…off. We'll have cooler heads in a d-day or two. Why don't we just—"

"Why don't you just get out of here, you bitch."

It was an unspeakably long moment before he realized that he had been the one who had spoken the terrible words, and that it was far too late to rope them in again. His own breath catching in his throat, he fastened his eyes on a shadow falling like a scarf around her neck.

She blinked a few times, then nodded. Glancing stiffly around the room, apparently looking for her clothes, she stood up and stepped around the cashmere dress lying on the floor at the foot of the bed.

He didn't move, hardly breathed. When she had finished dressing, she nodded once at the Guadalupe medal on his bedside table—a peculiar gesture of leave-taking—and walked past him into the freezing night.

The fireplace had long since burnt out when James finally noticed that the corduroy upholstery of the new sofa on which he was sitting still reeked of chemical fabric protector, and that the fumes had given him a headache.

He felt himself teetering on the familiar edge—numb, exhausted, enervated, and exhilarated near to wildness, all at once. Oh, he hadn't taken any pills this time, or drunk too much, but there it was again all the same: the edges in the air, the nerves jangling out of tune…the dragon rising from the foam.

Taking silent survey of the evening in his mind, he shivered with belated apprehension at the catastrophe unfolding in his memory. He remembered especially her quiet retreat from his apartment. He had sat there in his bedroom for God knew how long before he realized that she wasn't coming back, and that he might as well get up; then his stiff, clumsy motions to retrieve the Guadalupe medal she had left on his bedside table; then the picture. He had brought them both into the lamplight of the living room to look at them, and here he was still, untold hours later, shirtless to the drafty air and trying to swallow down the dragon.

Once more, he picked up the medal from the coffee table. Possibilities took shape, then disintegrated in his mind as he fingered it. He had decisions to make—decisions that would determine the course of his life and hers as well. The really awful thing about it, it seemed to him, was that the choices were all his to make.

He knew Lupe Cruz well enough to know that she had not changed, and would not change, her mind. He imagined her as she must be now, sleepless no doubt as he was, perhaps bundled up on her attic porch—confused, angry, hurting as if from a knife wound, oh yes; but whatever her feelings, she would remain as single-minded as Una, and as loyal as Desdemona, unable to talk herself into the one decision that might bring her material relief: to cut him off.

He couldn't fathom why she wouldn't do it, why she wouldn't cut him off. Hers was a quixotic form of constancy, as reckless as it was fierce. It was also the thing above all other things that made him love her. Made her, oh God, need her. And so, like it or not, he was the one who now had to make up his mind.

It took little thought for him to dismiss out of hand the first possibility. To go on as they had, or as they had almost done tonight, was unthinkable. Tilting his head this way and that as he studied her medal, then *la Guadalupana* above the fireplace, James knew that he had blown his one chance, hardly real in the first place now that he considered it, of persuading Guadalupe Oonagh Cruz to act against her own deepest convictions.

He could, however, imagine another scene, one more appropriate to his performance tonight, which he had been rehearsing on an almost daily basis for some years now: the scene of himself, standing on a chair and lifting the Dark Virgin off the wall; of tossing it in the trash, or burning it in the fireplace. Then ringing Lupe up—no, going to see her would be the only decent thing, if he could manage it—and explaining to her in rational but not indifferent tones, his voice resonant with concern, that they were simply *wrong* for each other, that "*it would never work.*" Wasn't that the stock phrase he always used in these tawdry episodes? That, at least, was the speech he'd prepared for Nadine Jeffrey that last miserable night, and he still had it down cold, word for bloody word. Then, of course, Lupe would drop out of his life and probably out of the Institute, as Nadine had done before her, and he would somehow marshal the energy to finish his degree and…what? Do what? Feel what? What the hell for?

Shoving the medal in his trouser pocket, James pushed himself to his feet and went to Lionel Krato's ancient desk. He stood there for a while looking down at it, trying to imagine himself sitting there as he had always done, pounding away at his computer keyboard as if he were still the same man who had sat there before the term began with nothing to trouble his imagination beyond the next chapter or paragraph or sentence of his dissertation.

James laughed out loud at the very thought of it. Truth was, the possibility of that alternative universe had disappeared almost from that first day he had met Lupe Cruz. To be in the world was to love her, to be loved by her. That was just…life. The only life he had left.

Closing his eyes in a shudder of anxiety, James could not resist toying a bit with that last-but-one possibility: the possibility of slipping into the bathroom and opening a vein; or stepping out onto the balcony to take his final bow. *To be or not to be* and all that sophomoric bullshit. One thing for sure, James thought with a nod, if he did it, this time he'd bloody well do it *right*—

—*and fry in hell for it.*

James's eyes popped open. The suddenly clear and distinct imagination of that cheery little theological construct sent him retreating once more to the sofa. Even three years of determined apostasy, it appeared, had not obliterated the holy fear that centuries of choirs and cathedrals and candlelit liturgies had bred into him. Indeed, James Ireton's unshakable belief in hell was a kind of quirky, backwards faith; faith in the negative, when he couldn't even imagine the positive. Oh yes, James Ireton still believed in the Dragon, because he'd seen his lowering shadow through the larder door, and his face in the bathroom mirror. Wish as he might, death for him could never be the nothingness that all suicides yearn for, but a no-exit timeless repetition of the same-old same-old; an eternity of having to hear himself say to her, over and over and over, *Why don't you just get out of here, you bitch?*

The limits of his imagination exhausted, James glanced once more at *la Guadalupana*, the image of the enchanting Woman who had once, somewhere in his soul, made of him more than he was. Or at least made him want to be more than he was. He suddenly remembered that there was a picture just like it, only a little smaller, in the Cruz family parlor, and the thought of it turned James's mind to the old frame house in Bay View, with its shabby furnishings and picture-wall of treasured memories. There, for the space of a weekend, James had almost become a different man. Yet wasn't that man… himself? Wasn't that James Ireton, holding her hand on the lakeshore, and sitting beside her at the dinner table, surrounded by her family, and reading little Margareta a bedtime story—?

James wiped his arm across his damp face. That was it, wasn't it, the stopper? The thing that terrified him before all else, as some men shrank before snakes or spiders or fire? To Lupe Cruz love meant marriage and having a family. That's what it seemed to mean to, well, most people. Normal people, at least. To James, however, marriage and family had always meant, not love and security, but a claustrophobe's vision of hell.

Noticing that an envelope had fallen to the floor where he had unwrapped the St. George poster, James reached down to pick it up. Inside was a single sheet of paper containing a sonnet, handwritten in Lupe's neat, upward-sloping script:

Strange Pearls

On slick wooden steps, a premarital bed,
Rain played our senses like a stop-sounding pipe;
Your heart told its mystery, rare and unread—
Wordless moans held unharbored archetypes.
The heart of my mystery you grasped, having sought—
Braille-scanning fingers my soul's flesh perceived;
Your hands wrapped my pulse in charged, soundless awe—
Nothing remained to shield my temple, now cleaved.
Surprised, suspended, my body decided—

To surrender was gain, no scruples now;
Will-less, yielding all till now we had hid—
But you held back, wondering, with reverence bowed.
    In silence, the painful fleshed truth of our worlds,
    We 'changed mysteries, hence-sealed: luminous strange pearls.

The paper slipped from his fingers.

Some time later, he didn't know how much later, James got to his feet and padded barefoot to his bedroom closet, where he rummaged in the shelving until he found a shoebox with three years' worth of dust on the cardboard lid. At the bottom of the box was the thing he was looking for.

The morning dawned bright and cold in a cloudless sky. Spectacular fall colors, dappled with sunlight, quivered playfully in the countryside as James drove his Jeep through Washington County. According to the directions given him by the gas station attendant in Germantown, he was still a mile or more from Holy Hill when he first glanced to the left and spotted the dark profile of twin spires rising like a dream above the treetops.

James made a left turn at Station Way, which the attendant had identified as the most likely venue at Holy Hill for the Cruz family picnic, but wasn't sure he'd found the right spot until he saw a phosphorescent yellow Frisbee come flying out between the trees about fifty yards ahead, and Patrick Cruz's athletic figure chasing after it.

James pulled off on the shoulder and honked.

Patrick jogged to the driver's side, his cheeks flushed, his damp hair a tangled red mess.

"Hey, man, am I glad to see you!" Patrick leaned breathlessly into the open window. "Criminitly, some birthday party, Lu looks like last week's dog food! I mean listen, I like you a lot, liked you from the first, but I've never seen Lu like this, and if we find out you're playing with her, man, Ramon and I will *personally*—"

James flung open the car door, knocking Patrick aside. Momentarily silenced, Patrick dropped the Frisbee and began jogging in place, like a boxer preparing to feint or strike. The rest of the Cruz family, James noted, was congregated around picnic tables on the far side of the clearing.

"Where is she?"

Finally dropping his guard, Patrick pointed up in the direction of the shrine where a footpath wound up the hill. "She went up there," he said, "about a half hour ago. Outdoor Stations of the Cross."

The outdoor Stations of the Cross at Holy Hill consisted of fourteen field-stone grottoes strung along a steep footpath. The grottoes housed life-sized limestone sculptures depicting the Passion of Christ. Trudging up the path, the denim of his jeans pressing against his straining thighs, the quiet cadence of James's steps was embellished by the piping tremolo of little birds perched high above him in the shivering leaves.

As he passed the first station, *Jesus is condemned to death*, James found himself making the sign of the cross and saying an Our Father as he used to do, before Peter Krato, when these little rituals had brought him solace instead of vexation. Reining in the vexation this exquisite morning, James finished the prayer, then recited another at the next station, deciding that he could jolly well use a little ritual propping up right now, whether he liked any of it or not.

Rounding a turn in the path approaching the Sixth Station, *Veronica wipes the Face of Jesus*, James saw that the Seventh Station up ahead was positioned between a fork in the path. Lupe was sitting on a boulder beside the grotto, her head hanging between her knees. Approaching silently, he knelt beside her.

"Lupe..."

Her eyes flew up. The look of ripe suffering on her face almost knocked James on his backside.

He gripped her shoulders. "Oh, Jesus—"

"I thought I'd ne-ne-never—"

He put his fingers to her lips. "We'll talk later. First—" He pulled her to her feet. "—will you take me up to the Church? There's something I need to say, and I need to say it in a church. Before the Blessed Sacrament."

Neither said a word as Lupe led James up the path, then underneath a large concrete portico at the top of the hill, which served as porch for the main church above. Climbing the stairs on the other side, they emerged onto the porch itself, which was bordered by a chest-high wall that resembled the ramparts of a medieval castle.

It was hardly as imposing as his beloved Salisbury Cathedral, James thought, but the Carmelite Shrine of Holy Hill, dedicated to Our Lady, Help of Christians, nevertheless reminded him a good deal of a grand European abbey, sitting like a queen atop the highest hill in the Kettle Moraine. Forest colors of opal, emerald, ruby, and garnet, set against a sky of lucent blue, cascaded downward on all sides of the Shrine like precious jewels sown into the trailing silks of her majesty's robe.

"Come on," he said, pulling her through the main doors into the Shrine.

Taking holy water from the stoops in the vestibule, they entered the nave hand in hand, their steps up the main aisle echoing gently in the nearly empty church. They knelt in the front pew, the dark old wood creaking noisily under their weight. James looked towards the sanctuary where a red candle, burning atop an iron pedestal beside the high altar, heralded the presence of the Blessed Sacrament. The tabernacle itself, wrought of gold, was curtained by an Ordinary Time veil of dusty turquoise—the color of the mantle of *la Guadalupana*, he thought, the color of Lupe's eyes.

"Promise me," he began in a whisper, "that you won't interrupt me until I'm finished."

Pulling a tissue out of her jeans pocket to blow her nose, she nodded.

"First, I have a confession to make. I broke my promise to Fr. Bricusse. I tried to seduce you, after all."

She squirmed.

"Now don't argue with me, you promised. There's a fragment of truth in what you're thinking. I really did believe your living with me would some-how…well, make things better. But all in all, I was using my problems as a form of psychological warfare." James shuddered away a remnant of despair. "God, how can I explain it. For all my 'privileges,' I feel as if I've been a scav-enger all my life, surviving off the scraps of other people's dinners. Then all of a sudden, you come along and invite me inside a palace for a great feast, and I'm absolutely petrified." He squeezed her hand. "But I seem to have discovered, these last few hours, that terrified or not, not loving you is not an option for me anymore. Loving you is knit in my bones, something I was made to do. Other things, too, I think. Things I can't see yet. But whatever those things are, I don't think I'll ever be able to do them, or even know what they are, if I don't…love you first. That much is clear now. *You're the fountain from the which my current runs, or else dries up.*"

Hearing her noise of surprise, James turned to see Lupe staring at the Guadalupe medal dangling from a chain around his throat.

"You can't have it back," he said, reaching up to finger it. "But I have something for you in return." Thrusting his hand into his jacket pocket, James drew out a white-gold wedding band. He held it up in the dim light. "It was my mother's," he whispered. "I fished it out of the trash that awful day. Probably not the best legacy…"

Lupe reached out to stroke his damp face with her fingers. He took the opportunity to clasp her hand and slip on the ring. When he found his voice again he said, "I asked you last night—well, no, I was bargaining with you last night, but I'm asking you now—will you marry me? Really and truly. I mean here, in church. Before God Almighty, your family, a priest, and the whole damned world. Lupe, you must know I can't promise to have every-thing…well, perfectly under control. If ever there was a work in progress, it's me. But if you say yes, we'll do it right. All according to form, priest and all."

Chuckling at the expression on her face, James leaned over and brushed his lips against her cheek. *"How yet resolves the governor of the town? To our best mercy give yourselves, or like men proud of destruction defy us to our worst."*

A crackle of laughter escaped her throat. She looked around guiltily.

"Come, your answer in broken music," he prompted, *"for thy voice is music and thy English…broken.* And don't you dare reply, like Harry's Kate, *I cannot tell."*

Wiping her face on her jacket sleeve, Lupe struggled for the words in broken music: "*Therefore, g-g-great k-king…*oh, b-b-blast, James, I can't remember the lines the w-w-way you can!"

"My dear, if ever there was a time for a simple 'yes,' 'no,' or 'maybe,' it is surely now."

"Then…y-y-yes. With all my heart."

He lifted her fingers to his lips and his eyes to the tabernacle. "*Take it, God*," he said with a perplexed expression, "*for it is none but Thine.*"

After lighting a vigil candle in a side chapel dedicated to the Sacred Heart of Jesus, James and Lupe made their way again outside where Lupe, taking James by the hand and promising him a "t-t-treat," led him down the porch stairs to the driveway in front of the Shrine. A set of double doors stood open at the base of the right hand tower.

"What is this," he asked, craning his neck to look up, "the bell tower?"

"The bell tower's the one on the left. This one's called the Scenic Tower. There's a spectacular view up there, if you're not afraid of heights."

"Oh, I love heights," he assured her. "It's itty-bitty closed-in spaces I'm not overly fond of."

After dropping a couple of dollars in the donation box inside the door, they began the nearly three hundred foot climb up the Scenic Tower, taking the ever-narrowing stairs single file. The dark stairwell—an itty-bitty closed-in space if ever there was one—made James feel as if he were climbing to the bottom of the sea. He was grateful when he finally felt some fresh air against his face.

They stepped out into a small platform near the top. It was perhaps ten feet square and constructed of sandblasted brick walls and a floor of cement tiles. Pairs of tall, narrow lancet windows beneath large rose windows, all crisscrossed with iron grillwork and open to the air, afforded an unobstructed view of the spectacular countryside at all four points of the compass. Raising the collar of his leather bomber jacket against the fierce wind, James surveyed his perimeter: the Shrine's bell tower was to the north, the main body of the church to the east, and the rolling Wisconsin countryside to the south and west everywhere resplendent.

Stepping to the lancet window on the west side, James peered between the iron grillwork to look down at the blacktop driveway directly beneath them. The distance didn't seem so terribly great until he spotted a pair of pilgrims approaching the door far below. In the warping perspective of nearly three hundred feet, the two women looked like little more than colorful leaves blown to the ground by a hilltop gust of wind.

Turning around, James wrapped his arms around Lupe's shoulders. "We'd better join your family," he whispered into her neck. "Your oh-so-clever brothers have seen through me completely. I don't doubt they're at this very moment readying a rope and tree."

"Oh, but this is so nice…" Lupe burrowed deeper into his arms. "Besides, are you sure you want to, you know, announce it right away? I know how these things work. The Archdiocese has its rules and regs, and they'll make us wait a couple of months while we attend pre-Cana classes and stuff."

"A couple of months," James exclaimed, letting go. "That's inhuman!"

She giggled. "Don't forget, we have a good six weeks left in the term. We're not likely to get that paper written in your bed."

"Our bed," he corrected.

"But really, James, this is a huge thing for you. Wouldn't you, you know, rather wait a bit?"

He stiffened. "You're afraid I'll change my mind."

"I just don't want you to feel p-p-pressured."

"Absolutely not." James gave her a firm squeeze. "We're going to do everything according to form. Shakespearean sonnet form, that is: fourteen lines in iambic pentameter, three quatrains and a couplet. And I'm especially looking forward to the couplet."

After a boisterous picnic lunch with the assembled Cruz family, sauced with much astonished back-slapping, hand-shaking, and toasting of beer bottles all round in celebration of James's touching announcement of their engagement, the couple met with Fr. Martin Cruz, who was of course to witness their vows.

The friars of Holy Hill, Martin explained, had been forced some years before to restrict the Shrine's acceptance of non-parochial wedding dates, so many non-parishioners wanted to marry in the spectacular church; but when Lupe suggested their home parish in Bay View as an alternative wedding site, her brother wouldn't hear of it. The date was duly set for Saturday, January 4, the Eve of the Epiphany.

It seemed to James an unconscionably long time to wait, but Martin assured him that the January date was only available because of a recent cancellation. Besides, Martin added, wearing an owlish expression peculiar, James thought, to clerics, the delay would give the prospective couple plenty of time to fulfill the Archdiocesan prerequisites of four pre-Cana classes and a course in natural family planning.

"Lupe already knows all about that stuff," James objected.

"I bet you don't," Martin returned.

"Good Lord," James grumbled, "getting hitched in the sight of God has become more arduous than a medieval pilgrimage to Santiago de Compostela. Romeo and Juliet got married by good Friar Lawrence the day after they met!"

"Yeah," Martin snickered, "and look what happened to them."

It was nearing suppertime when James and Lupe climbed the spiraling stairs that led up to her apartment, pausing every few steps to kiss. Reaching the landing at last, Lupe pointed at what looked like a large shoebox, wrapped in brown paper, set atop her garbage can.

"You didn't get me another birthday present, did you?" she asked, digging in her backpack for her keys.

"Not I," James assured her, lifting the box to examine it as she unlocked her door. It was heavier than he would have expected, and there were no stamps or labels or writing of any kind on it. He was about to suggest that it might be another present from Jack—Lupe was now leaning over the stair railing, whistling once more for Prince Hal, who still hadn't come home, or so she informed him—when he felt something sticky on his hands and looked down: a brownish-red stain had soaked through the wrapping paper on the underside of the box.

"Lupe…"

Turning, she looked from James's frowning face to the box. "What's the m-m-matter?"

"Get me some scissors."

When she returned a minute later with the scissors, he ordered her back inside and shut the door behind her.

He came in a few minutes later, his face drawn, his hands empty.

"James, what is it?"

James stared down at his bloodstained hands. *"All the dead cats of civilization,"* he murmured.

"Wh-What?"

He swallowed and looked up. "It's escalation."

Act Three:
St. George and the Dragon

Vpon a great aduenture he was bond,
That greatest Gloriana to him gaue,
That greatest Glorious Qveene of Faerie lond,
To winne him worship, and her grace to haue,
Which of all earthly things he most did craue;
And euer as he rode, his hart did earne
To proue his puissance in battell braue
Vpon his foe, and his new force to learne;
Vpon his foe, a Dragon horrible and sterne.

Edmund Spenser, *The Faerie Qveene*

Chapter Nine:
A Roaring Hideous Sound

With that they heard a roaring hideous sound,
That all the ayre with terrour filled wide,
And seemd vneath to shake the stedfast ground.
Eftsoones that dreadfull Dragon they espide,
Where stretcht he lay vpon the sunny side,
Of a great hill, himselfe like a great hill.
But all so soone, as he from far descride
Those glistring armes, that heauen with light did fill,
He rousd himselfe full blith, and hastned them vntill.

Edmund Spenser, *The Faerie Qveene*

Lupe was at James's flat several evenings later when the doorbell rang. "We've got to talk," Max Heisler growled, stepping inside before an astonished James could think to proffer the invitation. Looking a decade older than the last time James had seen him, at Bricusse's funeral, Heisler shouldered his way out of his overcoat, which he unceremoniously tossed over James's sofa, gave Lupe a preoccupied greeting, then pressed something into James's hand.

James looked down to see a handful of thousand dollar bills.

"What the—"

"Consider it compensation for the crap you and Lupe have had to put up with from my cocksucking son-in-law."

James had five years of experience with Max Heisler's no-holds-barred mode of expression, but Lupe almost lost hold of her glass of wine.

"I want you two to go do some skylarking," Heisler insisted, evidently misinterpreting the nature of Lupe's discomposure. "And I won't take no for an answer, so don't even start."

Casting a bewildered glance at his fiancée, James pocketed the money with a flourish of embarrassment. "What's happened?" he said, knowing full well that Maximilian Gerhard Heisler wouldn't darken a student's door, let alone toss him several thousand quid, without some extraordinary provocation. He gestured at the sofa.

Heisler paced a bit, then took a seat, obviously reluctant to begin. "Franco told me what you found out about Barry," he said finally, leaning forward as if to project his words more forcefully into their bewildered ears. "I've had my private investigator trailing him ever since. He's been tooling around with Norm Rygiel in Rygiel's fancy-shmancy roadster."

"Roadster?" Lupe and James exclaimed in unison.

"Yeah, they've been patronizing just about every unsavory establishment between here and Chicago, with women ranging from teenage streetwalkers to the spendier ladies of the Bonsoir Escort Service." Heisler prodded James's coffee table with a steely forefinger. "I wasn't born yesterday, I know why he married my girl. Hell, I can't prove it yet, but I'm pretty sure he's been garnishing money from a couple of my Institute endowment funds, too." Heisler waved, as if it were the least of his worries. "No question, he and Big John DeBrun will do their damnedest to take Fran and me to the cleaners at the divorce. But I'm telling you right here and now, if Barry tries to play hard ball with me, I'll throw him one right in the bollocks."

"What's this got to do with us?" James said.

His fierce gaze suddenly faltering, Heisler shook out his shoulders, a tic-like gesture that spoke to James of an uncharacteristic fear. "We all know he's a sleazeball, but I guess I'm just starting to wonder how deep the corruption goes. Not only with my Fran, but..." Heisler regarded Lupe. "According to my investigator, Barry's been spending a lot of time lately watching your house."

James and Lupe glanced at one another. Lupe swallowed.

Heisler's fish-like eyes flitted wildly about the room as if he were looking for something to throw. "The man's a sadist. I don't suppose you young people have heard about this new porn video making the rounds in town, *The Rape of Lucrece*?"

James shook his head, but Lupe said, "My father mentioned it. He's looking into it for his series in the newspaper on the vice war."

"Barry and Rygiel produced it. They're probably the 'stars' of the thing, too, as if anyone could tell one prick from another, the men are all masked. The first part's just your usual kinko stuff, but it ends with a torture and gang rape. Believe you me, even if the rest of it's Amateur Night, that part looks real." Heisler produced a sound in the back of his throat that made James think of a sick wolf. "The filthy thing was filmed in my house, in my living room, on my furniture! But tell you what, if Barry's got a brain cell sparking in that pretty numbskull of his, he'll worry a lot more about Nick Calabresi than the cops. He and Rygiel cut a distribution deal with the Nesterov mob. Which transaction, given the current state of mob relations, put the pair of them on Nick Calabresi's shit list. I mean, Barry even took it upon himself, without Rygiel's okay, to drive a truckload down to Chicago. That was like thumbing his nose at Calabresi and Nesterov both!"

"Do the police know about this?" James asked.

"No," Heisler said emphatically, "and we're keeping it that way. The less police involvement, the less publicity my daughter will have to endure. Besides, I can take care of this quicker and cleaner than the cops."

"But—"

"Look, I only told you this at all because I didn't want it on my con-science if Barry goes and tries something with Lupe here, and you had no warning. Understand?"

Lupe stood up, then promptly sat down again.

"What?" James said.

"That p-p-prostitute who was murdered in Racine. Candace Duffy. She worked for Bonsoir Escorts. I think she was in that v-v-video."

James was astonished. "How would you know something like that?"

Taking a deep breath, Lupe explained to James and Heisler both what she had seen and overheard in Lanciano's second-floor bathroom the night of the party, the full meaning of which she had only this moment under-stood.

"But even if she was in Barry's video," Heisler argued with a dismissive wave when Lupe had finished, "her murder was a Calabresi hit. Everybody knows that."

James was beginning to catch Lupe's drift. "With all due respect, Sir, nobody knows that, not even the police. Barry's been stalking Lupe, you've said as much yourself. Well, what if he's a murderer as well as a stalker and a sadist and a pornographer? What if he dropped Duffy from her balcony just to make it look like a Calabresi hit? And it's not only this prostitute. I've been driving myself mad with the thought that Richard Krato had some-thing to do with Fr. Bricusse's death. But Barry was up there on the seventh floor that night, too."

"What the hell are you talking about?"

"I saw someone moving along the gallery near your office. He exited by way of the southside stairs. I couldn't identify him, but Jack Sigur said later that he saw DeBrun coming down the southside stairs after Father fell. What if Father found out about Barry's activities and Barry killed him for it? Or at least brutalized him till he had a heart attack, then dumped him over that railing to make sure he was dead?" James threw up his hands. "The police have got to know about this!"

Heisler rose. "My Fran's in a living hell right now."

"But so is Lupe! DeBrun's wanted her for years, and sooner or later he's sure to go after her. He killed her cat last weekend, you know. Chopped it in a dozen pieces."

James hadn't intended that Lupe ever learn the graphic details of her beloved pet's killing, but now that it had slipped out, her reaction was pre-dictable. She jumped to her feet and made straight for the bathroom.

Heisler observed her retreat, then fastened his wide-set eyes again on James. "I understand your feelings, believe me I do. But at least give me a couple more days. That's all I ask, just a couple more days. Let me see what my investigator can dig up about Barry and this prostitute. Then, if it…well, if I can't take care of it, I'll call Masefield myself. I swear."

"All right," James relented. "A couple more days."

The business with Heisler having thus concluded on a nerve-wracking wait-and-see basis, James was surprised the next afternoon, and more than a little alarmed, to see Lt. Calvin Masefield, his hands stuffed in the pockets of his shabby all-weather coat, waiting for them in the Institute gallery after the seminar. The policeman's expression was so grim in fact that for a split second James nurtured the misgiving that some horrible mistake had been made, and that Calvin Masefield was about to chuck *him* in the nick for God knew what enormity.

"Sorry to muscle in on your schedule," Masefield said soberly, "but we need to chat."

"What about?" James said.

"Norman Rygiel's been murdered. He was tossed off a bluff in Atwater Park, up near Lanciano's house. The man had enough coke and speed in his system to make Dumbo fly, but it was clearly no accident. Seeing as how you people are friends with Rygiel's buddy Lanciano, I just thought maybe you might have some light to shed on the subject."

James caught Lupe's eye. "Was it the Calabresi mob," he said to Masefield, "or Barry DeBrun?"

Masefield lifted a bushy eyebrow. "Now what, I just have to ask, made you think Barry DeBrun might be involved? Or should I say, how'd you hear about *The Rape of Lucrece*, and why the hell didn't you tell me about it?"

Lupe let out a little groan, but James experienced no such impulse towards regret. Now that another murder was involved, all keep-it-mum agreements with Max Heisler were off. "Max Heisler told us about it last night," James explained. "He wanted to keep it mum because of his daughter. He only told us about it as a warning, in case DeBrun tried to go after Lupe."

"Too late for keeping it mum," Masefield said crisply. "Not only is Barry DeBrun a murder suspect, he's also gone missing, and I intend for every man, woman, and canine in the state of Wisconsin to know about it."

Accepting the lieutenant's offer of a lift home so they could talk some more, James and Lupe followed Masefield down to the basement parking lot, Lupe hanging on to James's arm as if it were a life preserver in a choppy sea.

"Howsabout this for coincidence," Masefield said as they all three climbed into his brown Chevy, Lupe and James in the back seat. "DeBrun not only hired Candace Duffy as his 'personal escort' on several occasions, we also got a positive ID from Duffy's parents on her role in the opening scenes of *The Rape of Lucrece*. So far, nobody knows the identity of 'Lucrece' herself. Not that the poor woman's likely to come forward, even if she could." Masefield glanced over his shoulder at Lupe. "Your brother thinks they snuffed her."

James opened his mouth to speak, and then just as quickly closed it. The 'Lucrece' in question was quite alive, as he well knew; but Bel Gunderson, he quickly decided, was having a difficult enough time as it was right now without his dragging her into a murder investigation by speaking out of turn.

Lupe clung tightly to James's hand. "So Barry's a suspect in Candace Duffy's murder, too?"

"And Bricusse's. Personally, I think Racine's all wet with their mob war theory on Duffy, and I told them so. They're not letting out the gory details to the media, but from what they showed us, Duffy's murder was sheer overkill. It had all the markings of a crime of passion."

"I don't understand," James said.

"Professional hit men don't take the time or trouble to do what was done to her. Dozens of stab wounds. Even piquerism. You know, knife wounds in sexual areas as a substitute for rape. In other words, overkill. That's a giveaway of tunnel-deep anger. The sort of thing crazy, jealous lovers do. Or headcases." Masefield glanced once more over his shoulder at Lupe. "Which means I concur with Heisler about that much at least. That it wouldn't hurt for you to be extra careful right now, given your history with DeBrun."

"It must have been B-B-Barry who stole that picture of Candace Duffy in Lanciano's bathroom," Lupe said, almost to herself.

The car swerved as Masefield tossed her another, rather more probing look. "What picture of Candace Duffy in Lanciano's bathroom?"

Lupe winced. "He's going to k-k-kill me."

The Rygiel murder made the front page of the *Journal Sentinel* several days running, and Barry DeBrun's picture appeared in a prominently displayed "Wisconsin's Most Wanted" ad, complete with an 800-number tips hotline for the FBI's violent fugitive task force. Masefield hadn't included James's and Lupe's names in his press-releases about the case, but Lupe had explained all to Jack, the Institute's unofficial loudspeaker, and within a day's time James and Lupe had become minor east-side celebrities, barraged with probing questions from their fellow-students about their role in *l'affaire* DeBrun. They fielded all queries with the obscure reply that they had been asked to say nothing until the police were able to "bring charges."

Even the constitutionally anal Franco Lanciano, not at all troubled, it appeared, that the latest developments were shedding the harsh light of notoriety on Heisler's family, succumbed to a fit of laughter and back-slapping when James filled him in during their weekly racquetball game, so delighted was he that culprits had been identified, if not yet apprehended, and that all the mysteries and conundrums of the last two months were, well, *almost* solved. James refrained from comment when Franco failed to mention, in this context, his still unaccounted-for photograph of Candace Duffy. Or even if it *was* Candace Duffy. Either way, James had every confidence that Calvin Masefield would not let the matter rest for long.

Max Heisler, meanwhile, secluded himself with his distraught daughter in their Door County hideaway, and could not be reached for comment.

James stood on his balcony, watching the darkening sky dissolve into the slate-gray lake. A slant of light cut through the clouds, lighting the arches of the distant Hoan Bridge like a fluorescent McDonald's. Turning his eyes to the north, he could just make out the midnight-dark bluffs along the northern suburbs above the lake, near Atwater Park, where tubby little Norman Rygiel had met his inglorious end.

God, James thought, what an awful way to die.

Bending over, James pressed his forehead against the cold iron rail and tried to imagine the moment of his own death. What, he couldn't help but wonder, would come to his mind when faced at last with his own obscure eternity? Nadine Jeffrey's glowing face came instantly into his mind's eye, followed by Bel Gunderson's. And others.

He had made his peace with Trisha, he thought, but he owed the rest. Bel and Nadine above all. Before he could move on—before he could make straight the crooked paths of his wandering life—he needed to try and set things right with Bel and Nadine. Somehow.

Matteo and Oonagh Cruz hosted a shindig at their Bay View home the following weekend—part engagement party, part going-away party for Lupe's grandparents, who were departing for Oregon to visit one of Matt's siblings, and part Halloween party. Lupe's grandfather Nemencio, full of sail from the spiked cider, toasted James's and Lupe's engagement with some well-oiled Guanajuatan hyperbole that made Ramon scowl. The young detective did manage to shake James's hand at least.

But there were less convivial topics of discussion that evening as well. To begin with, between soccer matches and the usual social life of a college senior, Patrick and his teammates, who occupied the entire second floor of the senior Cruz's Stowell Avenue house, would be away a good deal of the time while Lupe's grandparents were in Oregon, leaving Lupe too frequently alone in the big house. With Barry DeBrun still at large, Lupe's safety was in the forefront of everybody's mind. Lupe's grandparents even offered to postpone their trip, but Lupe, with typical stubbornness, would hear none of it; which attitude finally induced James to promise them all that he would doss down on Lupe's couch whenever Patrick was away. This announcement had gone a long way to assuage the anxieties of parents and grandparents, but it had raised brother Ramon's hackles.

"You'd think Ramon had been raised in a Los Angeles *barrio*," Matt observed with a wry smile when Ramon stepped out of the room. He hoisted his steaming cider in a not altogether convincing pantomime of cheerfulness. "Well, as the Irish say, *the Lord between us and all harm.*"

"Come hell or Cromwell!" Patrick added, raising his pint and winking at James.

A moment later, James noticed, Matt's weary eyes were fixed on a spread of photographs on the front page of the newspaper lying open on the kitchen table, beneath one of his own bylined articles on the hunt for murder suspect Barry DeBrun—photos of Norman Rygiel, Candace Duffy, and Arthur Bricusse.

In spite of the general merrymaking, in fact, Matteo Cruz remained subdued throughout the evening. Remarking Matt's quiet exit from the parlor in the middle of some hilarious old Mexican drinking song that Nemencio had dug up from the cellar of his memory, James finally found his future father-in-law seated at the kitchen table, sipping hot cocoa and once again staring at the newspaper photographs. Though doubting the wisdom of an intrusion, before James had had a chance to turn and head back into the parlor, Matt looked up and motioned for him to join him.

"There's some hot cocoa in the pan," Matt said, casting a nod at the stove.

James helped himself and sat down. The two men sipped their cocoa in silence for several seconds, until James, who certainly hadn't intended to broach the subject, heard himself saying, "You know, Lt. Masefield feels certain that Candace Duffy was killed by a disgruntled boyfriend, not the Calabresis. Or even DeBrun. Unless DeBrun was the disgruntled boyfriend."

Matt gave him a wary look. "What makes him think so?"

"The excessive number of stab wounds to the face and body. 'Overkill,' he called it."

Matt fingered his cocoa mug. "Well, you may be right—and I appreciate the effort to cheer me up. But the whole thing's got me thinking."

"What?"

"Sex and violence sell newspapers, James, just like they sell movie tickets and dish soap. *I* was the one who greenlighted that picture of Duffy with Nesterov back in September. Even if it wasn't the reason she was targeted, and even if it wasn't the Calabresis who killed her…well, just maybe I'm not doing the public a service by telling them every ugly goddamn thing I find out that's going on out there."

"People can't change what they don't know about," James argued.

Matt sighed. "Okay, let me put it this way: maybe I haven't got the stomach for it. The Medical Examiner does a service to the community when he performs his autopsies, but few of us are cut out for the job, if you'll pardon the expression."

"Well, if you'll pardon an outsider's observation," James said, "your family is altogether too innocent for this sad old world. I don't think any of you are quite as desensitized as the rest of us. Except perhaps Ramon." Smiling slightly, James looked around the old kitchen. "Yours is a fairy kingdom, Matt. Beautiful, good, and true-hearted. Lupe could have come from no other place, I think."

Matt scratched his head, his blue-green eyes finally twinkling with a trace of merriment. "You're wrong about one thing."

"What's that?"

"You're not an outsider. You're a member of our family. Still, I see so much garbage in my job—things I never could have imagined as a boy back on that sleepy sheep farm outside Guanajuato. God, what a shock when we moved up here."

Still recovering from Matt's first sentence James managed to say, "How old were you?"

"Eleven. I was sixteen when I met Oonagh, at a parish dance." Matt smiled, a sweet, fond smile that curled behind a wisp of steam that rose from his mug. "She had just got off the boat herself. We got married when we were nineteen. She was the first, James, and only. Everything I know I learned from her." He laughed out loud. "*Mami* always used to say that when it came to growing big juicy red tomatoes, it was sunshine and good soil that gave the plant strength, but hot nights that made the fruit ripen. Stupid me, I was married before I caught on to what she was saying."

James coughed into his mug. In the ensuing silence, Matt sat sipping his cocoa while James just stared at his. But at length James could stand it no longer. He licked his lips and said, "Matt?"

Matt looked up, apparently startled by James's sudden tone of intensity.

"I wish I could say to Lupe what you just said to me. But I suppose you know I can't."

Matt put down his mug and nodded, then cocked his head to one side and studied James intently, as if looking for something in the younger man's face. "You really love her, don't you? You're not marrying her just to sleep with her."

James fell back against his chair: the straight-up honesty of these people was simply unnerving. In spite of himself he broke out laughing. "I love her," he said.

Apparently satisfied, Matt reached across the table and thumped James on the shoulder. "*Bueno*. But before we get back to the others, I'd like to leave you with a final word. An overused, and maybe even trite word. But one that has served me well over the years."

"What's that?"

Matt gave a decisive nod, as if agreeing with himself. "Romance."

James caught his breath, suddenly reminded of the last time he'd heard someone use the word.

Matt slapped the palm of his hand on the table top. "People make the same damned mistake with love that they do with religion. And with life. They forget that it's either a great and terrible and wonderful adventure, or it's brutish slavery to the god of our stomachs. Don't ever stop wooing your wife, James. When you build your house, along with your kitchen garden and cash crop, make sure you surround it with beds of fragrant flowers. That's the blessing I'd like to give you two: *romance*."

The first weekend in November, an unseasonable heat shimmered above Lake Michigan in the Indian Summer sun. After Sunday Mass, and basking in their brief respite from the onslaught of rapidly approaching winter, James and Lupe dined *alfresco* on the Lancianos' patio, sipping Piedmontese wine as if it were an early spring, and taking their time over the soup and salad courses in the Italian manner. At one point a flock of Canada geese honked brassily overhead, flying in a southwards arc.

"How's that depressing line from *Lear* go?" Lupe said, eyes to the sky and nudging James under the table.

James daubed at his mouth with a linen napkin. "*Winter's not gone yet, if the wild geese fly that way.* But winter, like death, is inevitable," he added philosophically, reaching for his wine glass. "You Wisconsinites should know that better than the rest of us. By the way, did anyone get a photo of Franco sporting an apron in the kitchen? I could hustle some serious blackmail out of that back at the Institute." Returning Lupe's under-the-table nudge he added, "Er, why don't we take a little stroll on the beach after lunch?"

"Oh, I wouldn't if I were you," Adèle cautioned. "A crop of dead alewives floated ashore this morning. The stink down there is incredible. I assure you, if the wind weren't from the west today, we'd be eating inside, balmy temperature or no."

At that moment, Dr. Franco Lanciano, his white linen suit resplendent under a blood red chef's apron, emerged through the patio doors bearing a silver tray. He swept off the lid.

"*Aragosta fra Diavolo,*" he announced. "Braised lobsters in a wine and tomato sauce."

"Splendid," James said, smacking his lips.

"Sure as heck beats the parish fish fry," Lupe agreed as Franco served her first.

Finally seating himself, Lanciano adjusted the napkin on his lap so that the four corners squared neatly with the table. "Allow me to propose a toast," he said, lifting his glass. "To the best damned week we've had since this miserable term began, to James and Lupe on their engagement, to the Institute, free of mysteries at last...and to the Fr. Arthur Bricusse Program in the English Renaissance!"

"Hear, hear!" they agreed in unison, clinking glasses all around.

Having fortified himself with a lusty swallow, Franco set aside his wine. "By the way, I ran into Jack Sigur yesterday afternoon. He told me the most frightful news."

"What now?" James said anxiously.

Lanciano gave a *harumph* of disapproval. "Why, that you weren't going to be acting in our student production of *Hamlet* next term."

James's face relaxed into a smile. "I won't be a student any longer next term, remember? I'm to get the doctorate in January, or so the members of my dissertation committee keep assuring me."

"Yes, of course," Franco said with an impatient wave, "but I thought Arthur had persuaded you to take the role, notwithstanding."

"Father persuaded me to direct the play, not act in it," James said in a tone of finality. "*If* I stay on at the Institute in some sort of teaching position, that is." James pulled a face. "But act again, and as the bloody Prince of Denmark...? I'd sooner walk barefoot to Jerusalem."

"Of course you're staying on in a teaching position," Adèle said, aiming a meaningful glance in her husband's direction. "Who else better to get Uncle

Arthur's program going? But why don't you like acting, my dear? You're so very good at it."

James finished off his wine. "It's rather too much like masturbating in public."

The women giggled at the reply, Lupe almost losing a mouthful of the expensive wine, but Lanciano, picking a grape from the clump on his plate, was apparently unmoved. "I still say it's a shame," he declared. "Adèle's right, James, you're gifted. Why, your Iago last year was delightful…if one can use such a term in connection with one of the most fiendish villains in theatrical history."

Before James could respond, Adèle turned to Lupe. "Speaking of news, your mother told me you're going down to Chicago to lend a hand with your niece and nephew while Kate has a C-section."

"Leaving in the morning," Lupe said. "James has p-p-promised to sit in on my classes and take notes. That would be another picture worth taking. Him with all the first-years."

"Sod all," James said, flinging down his napkin, not thinking so much of his temporary academic demotion as of his prospective six-day separation from his fiancée. "What about tonight?"

"Wh-What about tonight?"

"Will Patrick be in the house, or any of his soccer mates?"

Lupe sighed. "You always ask me that."

"And I'll keep asking it, until Barry DeBrun's tailored arse is sitting in the nick, where it belongs."

When the Lancianos hastened to express their own concerns about Lupe's safety until that longed-for time, Lupe finally admitted that her brother Patrick and his soccer roommates had gone to Minnesota for an important series of games, and wouldn't be home until the Sunday evening after she returned. James received this news with patent disapproval, knowing that Lupe wouldn't have told him if she hadn't been asked. "Then you may expect me on your doorstep this evening," he announced, "just in time for dinner. Fear me not," he added with a wink to Franco and Adèle, "my intentions are wholly chivalrous."

"To be sure," Lanciano concurred with a gentle smile.

In lieu of sexual intimacy, James had knit himself into the weave of Lupe's life in other, less direct ways. He went with her to Patrick's soccer games, to the grocery store, and even to Mass, as if wanting to see her in every possible setting and attending to the most quotidian details of her life. He had long since had a key to her apartment, and she would often come home from class or an errand to find a bouquet of flowers on the table, or a book he had picked up for her, or a scarf. He left personal items in her apartment as well, ready for his almost daily visits: the brand of French roast coffee he liked, and bottles of Spanish sherry; the crackers and Munster cheese he munched on when he studied. He handled her odds and ends of thrift-store dishes and flatware as if they were china and sterling, almost caressing them as he set them out on her table, or put them away in a drawer.

There was something sensual in this new-found domesticity, as if he were making love to her through her things; getting to know her body through the objects which made up the stuff of her day-to-day life; but there was one barrier she had raised that he had learned to respect: she kept her bedroom door shut when he visited, and he didn't feel free to open it even when she wasn't there.

Lupe stretched out on her living room sofa that night, surrounded by books and papers, intending to finish drafting her allotted portion of their research paper. James, meanwhile, had commandeered her desk to work on his. At one point, and for no ostensible reason, he pushed away from the desk and went to her, pulling aside her hair so that he could nibble on the back of her neck.

"*Dieguito*," she complained, putting her hand over a yawn, "you know I c-c-can't concentrate when you do that. I thought you were supposed to be the monomaniac, always studying."

"I am the monomaniac, always studying. I've simply changed the subject, that's all."

"Easy for you to say," she grumbled. "You're two months away from your PhD." Lupe jabbed at her collarbone with her forefinger. "*I'm* the one on overload. Before the term's over, they're g-g-going to be scraping me off the walls! Hey—" Her head flopped against the back of the sofa so she could look up at him. "Why don't we finish up that chess game we started weeks ago."

"Easy for you to say," he countered. "As I recall, you were within two moves of mating me."

"That's what you get for putting your queen at risk to go after my lousy bishop."

He kissed her nose. "All right, Cruz, half a minute. Let me just tidy up that last paragraph."

"Done. Now then, where'd you put the chess set...?" Looking around, James saw that Lupe had fallen asleep on the sofa. One of her arms lay limp in her lap, while the other hung over the side, almost touching the floor.

Rising, he turned off the lamp beside her head, then looked around for something to drape over her. The air was chill, and the furnace in the old house wasn't the most efficient. Finding nothing to hand, James stepped noiselessly to her bedroom door, hesitated, then turned the knob.

Inside, he fumbled for a light switch. A lamp came on atop her bedside table. There was an afghan crocheted in an Irish knotwork design folded at the foot of her bed, which he took back to cover her. He returned to the desk with the intention of doing a bit of reading, but couldn't concentrate on the book: his thoughts were drawn again to her bedroom. Finally glancing over his shoulder at the open door, he got up, turned off the desk lamp, and walked silently into the inviting field of light.

Lupe's bedroom was fitted with the same tongue-in-groove oak ceiling panels as the rest of the apartment. The low walls were painted in a pale peach, and a dormer window was tucked into the outside wall. A small closet was carved out of another wall, under the eaves. Her dresser, he decided, had to be either second-hand or the battered survivor of several Cruz generations. It had an equally ancient jewelry box on top, and two photographs; the smaller was a copy of the family picture from Holy Hill that he had seen in her parents' home, and the larger a picture of the two of them, taken by Patrick the day James had asked her to marry him. On the mirror above the dresser she had taped a prayer card, yellowed with age and in Spanish, addressed, as far as he could tell, to *La Guadalupana*.

He turned towards her bed, over which hung a poster of Caravaggio's *Deposition of Christ*. A cheap Victorian-style lamp on the bedside table cast an antique glow of flesh tones on the picture, as well as the bed and the walls surrounding it. Next to the lamp was a small collection of books, including a three-ring notebook—no doubt the journal she'd spoken of several times. He smiled when he saw his SANA report stuffed inside it, and had to fight a powerful urge to open it.

On the wall opposite the Caravaggio, as if hung strategically for the best view from her bed, was a print of *La Guadalupana*. Looking at it, James's smile of contentment dissolved into a yawn. A sultry fatigue settled rapidly on his mind and body and drooping eyes, and for the life of him he couldn't imagine walking out of this room and descending the stairs to fetch his sleeping bag from his Jeep.

Kicking off his shoes, James pulled down her white counterpane and fell into the bed. Rolling over on his back, he sank into her sheets as if he were lying naked on the deck of a sailboat, his face to the sun, the warm sea below rocking him into a peaceful dreamless sleep.

After seeing her off the next morning—Lupe had blushed all through breakfast—James struggled against a relentless impulse to glance at his watch and calculate the remaining hours until her return from Chicago five days later.

He kept himself occupied, the several days after, with work on his dissertation and their research paper, and was surprised Wednesday afternoon, after the seminar, to discover Bel Gunderson waiting for him outside the door of his office. He hadn't seen her since the night in front of the Oriental Theatre, when she had gotten into Norman Rygiel's *Baci*.

Bel was dressed in a heavy black overcoat, scarf-hood and dark glasses—a get-up, James thought, befitting a Russian spook in a Bullwinkle cartoon. She kept glancing over her shoulder, too, as he unlocked the door, as if afraid someone might recognize her. It took James a moment to realize that, considering her own role in *The Rape of Lucrece*, Bel's obvious anxiety might have something to do with what had happened to Norman Rygiel two weeks before. Still, in spite of his pity for her, and his prior intention of speaking to her sometime soon—to square away the past and all that—James wasn't prepared at this moment to deal with the difficult woman. It took some considerable effort on his part even to bring forth an invitation to step inside.

He tossed his keys and his briefcase on the desk and motioned for her to sit. Bel shut the door behind her but remained standing.

"I've been calling you for days," she complained, the dark glasses concealing her expression. "Is what I've heard true?"

"Is what true?"

"That you're going to marry her."

James pulled his lecture notes out of his briefcase and turned to file them in a nearby cabinet. "It's true."

"*Why?*"

He slammed the drawer. "For the oldest, tritest reason you can possibly imagine."

"Because she won't fuck you otherwise."

He rounded on her. "Because I'm in love with her. Because I want to spend my life with her. Because—" He scraped his fingers through his hair. "That's all I'm going to say about it."

"But this is very reckless of you. Have you signed a pre-nup? What if you find out after the wedding that you're not sexually compatible?"

Unable to detect the smallest hint of irony in Bel's earnest tone, James had to check a cruel impulse to laugh, and was more than a little grateful when a rapid series of knocks on the door postponed the necessity of a reply. Jumping at the sound, Bel quickly cornered herself behind the door, her frantic sign language making it abundantly clear that she wanted her presence in his office undiscovered.

James opened the door a crack, shielding the view of the room with his body. It was Jack. "What can I do for you?" James said, rolling his eyes to let his friend know that he was in something of a predicament.

"Uh, yeah, sure, buddy, sorry to bother you, but I, uh, forgot to ask during class…could I borrow your copy of Greenblatt? The Encyclopedia Showalter's got the only library copy, and you know what that means."

"Sure, just a sec." James retrieved the book from a stack on his filing cabinet and handed it over. Jack promptly saluted his thanks and took off. When the door was safely shut and James turned, Bel was leaning against the wall, wringing her gloved hands.

"Bel, for God's sake what's the matter?"

"Long story…well?"

"Well, what?"

"How do you know you're compatible without trying it out first? You're so damned impulsive. A Saturn-ruled Scorpio, astrologically pure Dorian Gray. And she's a Libra, or so I'm told. Lovers in neighboring signs can be a tricky business. At least let me do a Tarot reading for you."

James gave way to exasperation. "Look, I'm supposed to be in a meeting with Lanciano in five minutes. We're planning the new English Renai—"

"Goddammit, Ireton, whether you like it or not, we're connected!" Stepping up to him, almost in his face, Bel pressed a gloved fingernail against his chest. "The least you can do is make a fucking appointment with me!"

Tethering himself, James stepped back. "Okay, fine…look, when's good for you?"

"I can't tonight," Bel said matter-of-factly, "I've got a client. And tomorrow I'm going out of town till Saturday evening. But I think I can get rid of my Saturday client by eight-thirty. How about nine?"

James was stunned. "*Clients*? Bel, what in God's name are you doing?"

"Oh, don't pretend to be scandalized, you of all people. Can you make it or not?"

James lifted his hands, then promptly dropped them again. "I can make it. But I won't be able to stay long." Lupe would be getting home about then, though he certainly had no intentions of informing Bel about it.

Later, in the darkening purple of evening, the collar of his leather bomber jacket raised against the cold as he stood outside Lupe's door, James rifled through his briefcase, then his jacket and jeans pockets, hunting for his keys. Coming up with nothing but some breath mints and a little loose change, he punched Lupe's door with his bare fist.

Sometime during the day he had lost his keys. Again.

James reached for a beer in the fridge, popped off the cap, and glanced at his kitchen clock: six minutes after four. Barring a worse-than-usual traffic jam through Chicago, Lupe should be home in less than five hours.

The phone rang.

"Buddy, we've got to parlay, and pronto,' Jack said on the other end. "I've got something to show you that will *blow* your little mind."

James shrugged off a kink in his shoulders. He was getting that razor's edge feeling again. "Come on over," he said, grateful at the thought of a little company to kill the time. "I was about to throw a frozen lasagna in the oven. We can have ourselves a real matey meal."

A little over sixty minutes later, the two men were seated at James's dining table with steaming plates of lasagna and Jack's bottle of cheap but surprisingly good Chianti.

"I'm waiting with bated breath," James prompted, digging in.

Jack grunted. "You were never much into porn, were you, Jim-bo?"

James looked up in surprise. "Um, can't say I ever was. You know me, Jack, I've always been a simple boy-meets-girl, boy-beds-girl, boy-leaves-girl kind of guy. Though now that you mention it, Bel was kind of into it."

Jack's face burst into a triumphant *I told you so* expression over the top of his wine glass.

"And your point is?"

Jack reached behind him for his jacket and pulled a DVD out of an inside pocket. He held it out to James.

"Where in God's name did you get this?" James exclaimed, staring at the copy of *The Rape of Lucrece* in his hands.

Jack seemed a little disappointed that he hadn't taken his friend wholly by surprise. "I got it from Bo Jeffrey," he said, as if it should be obvious. "Hey, everyone's who's into this sort of thing is talking about it, love it or hate it."

"Since when were *you* into 'this sort of thing?'"

"Oh, not I," Jack protested, hand over heart. "I just brought it to your attention 'cause word's getting around the 'hood that 'Lucrece' is our very own Jezebel Gunderson. Given the, uh, present morbid interest of the regional Mafia in All Things Pornographic, it occurred to me that this kind of notoriety might not be a particularly salubrious thing to have bandied about." Jack scooped up a heaping forkful. "*N'est-ce pas?*"

"You're certain it's Bel?"

Jack nodded. "And tell you what's the truth," he added after swallowing down his gigantic mouthful, "either there was some Oscar-level acting and special effects going down, belied by the dimestore quality of the rest of the production, or those boys really did a number on her."

James stared at his own dim reflection shimmering in the blood red bottle of Chianti. "DeBrun and Rygiel were behind it," he said. "They filmed it in Max Heisler's house, the night Bel got into Rygiel's *Baci*. I have no doubt it was the reason she landed in hospital."

Jack whistled, long and loud. "Heisler's house? I thought I recognized that kitschy statue of Zeus." He took a moment to finish off his most recent bite of lasagna then said, "Maybe someone ought to encourage her to lay low for a while. I mean, she was wearing a wig and loads of makeup, but if Bo recognized her, so will half the population of the near east side."

James speared at his food, in and out, not really eating. "I'm running over to her place tonight, I'll mention it." Double-taking at his friend's saucer-eyed expression, James added, "It was Bel in my office Wednesday when you came to pick up that book. She acted terrified, didn't want anyone to know she was there. She said she needed to talk to me about something. Something important."

Setting aside his rapidly emptying plate, Jack took to fingering his goatee. "You got any idea what ol' Belzebub wants?"

"Not a clue. But I figure I owe her one. She, uh, she's taking 'clients' now."

Jack made some distressed noises, but in spite of his obvious agitation, retrieved his plate. A moment later his fork paused halfway to his mouth.

"What?"

"I was just thinking about your *tête-à-tête* with She Who Must Be Obeyed. My friend, *I smell a device*. I mean, maybe she'll just hit you up for money or something. If she's doing clients she must be hurting. But I'm tellin' you, Jim-bo, don't you ever let yourself feel so sorry for Isabel Gunderson that you forget she's got a tyger's heart wrapped in that woman's hide o' hers. And worse. She knows the exact latitude and longitude of each and every one of your hot buttons."

"I'll be careful." James smiled. "Um, you're a good friend, Jack."

"I know it," Jack said, reaching again for his fork.

After Jack left, James inserted *The Rape of Lucrece* into his DVD player and sat down to watch. The "story," such as it was, was absurd, even by the degraded standards of pornography. The production values were as cheap as they were outlandish. But like Masefield before him, Jack had not exaggerated the bizarre nature of the film's climactic set piece, nor it's brutality.

Nor was there any question in James's mind that the awful thing had been filmed in Max Heisler's living room, kitschy statue of Zeus and all. Rygiel was easy to identify by virtue of his ponderous belly, and James thought he recognized Barry DeBrun by his arrogant carriage, but it was hard to be sure since the otherwise naked actors were all masked—all except Bel, of course, the slender and frangible female focus of sadistic masculine desire, left at the end dangling unconsciously from some ghoulish trapeze.

James hadn't intended to watch the whole thing; in fact, only enough to assure himself that it was indeed Bel; but there was a momentum to the erotic savagery that he found difficult to resist. When he finally pressed the STOP button some eighty minutes later, exhausted and sick to his stomach, he was loathe to admit that he was also more than a little aroused. In spite of his efforts to bend his mind in more wholesome directions, the prurient images lingered, summoning visceral, half-forgotten sensations, urges, impulses...for a moment he even considered turning the thing back on and—

James bolted from the sofa. Lupe would be home soon. Goddamn, he needed to see her. He was desperate to see her, to talk to her, to hold her, to feel her vibrant warmth burning away these ghastly images. Why, he could pick up some fresh flowers and champagne on the way to her place—things bright and beautiful to summon his better angel.

Grabbing the keys he had just had made to replace the set he'd lost, and his jacket, he headed for the door.

It was only when he had climbed into his Jeep in the basement parking lot and saw the clock on his dashboard reading five minutes before nine that he remembered his prior appointment with Bel Gunderson.

Bel's apartment complex, Jackbourn Towers in the Yankee Hill neighborhood, was a bleak heap of tall rectangles in white concrete, brown brick, and glass, with narrow, cantilevered balconies clinging to the sides. This particular architectural mess, designed in what someone had dubbed the "Brutalistic" style, had for many years placed either first or runner-up on *Milwaukee Magazine*'s annual list of "Ugliest Buildings in Milwaukee." The appellation had made the place irresistible to Bel, however, who was fond of declaring that the Towers' exorbitant rent and gruesome aesthetics were a fair exchange for its California-style amenities, including a heated underground garage and indoor swimming pool.

Climbing out of his Jeep, James raised the collar of his bomber jacket against the wind howling off the lake. By the time he jogged across the street and pushed through the revolving door on the ground floor, already fifteen minutes late for their appointment, his mind had emptied and his mouth had gone sour from ill-digested lasagna. Unable to remember Bel's apartment number, he ran his finger across the upper-floor mailboxes, finally finding "Gunderson" by number 1531. He pressed the button.

"It's James," he said in response to Bel's shrill query. "Sorry I'm late."

A familiar-sounding *bzzt* signaled the unlocking of the security door. James pushed it open.

Climbing the familiar stairs, one foot after another, the palm of his hand sliding up the railing, James's body began to slip into some primitive form of muscle-memory laid down three years before. His thoughts, too, revolved back to mind-pictures from those months when he had climbed these stairs several times a week, often wearing this same leather jacket, and usually in the throes of that old familiar sexual tension; up and up, then into the fifteenth floor corridor; then Bel's living room—a breezy Art Deco pastiche of checkerboard tile, neon lamps, pistachio walls, and a huge *trompe d'œil* mural Bel had painted herself on the wall in vertiginous perspective. James would usually find Bel elegantly recumbent on her black-and-yellow tiger-striped sofa, dressed—undressed, really—in one of those lacy things she wore in the Stark Ads. Flinging aside his own clothes almost as soon as he closed the door, he would only half-listen as Bel described, in grisly detail, some new technique she was determined to try, distilled from her exhaustive supply of *how-to* sex videos and manuals, when all in the world he wanted was just a few minutes of release from the tension.

Pushing open the fire door on the fifteenth floor, James paused to catch his breath. A man was coming out of the door next to Bel's, a familiar-looking little fellow in a business suit, with thinning hair and wire-rimmed glasses. It was the glasses that finally placed him in James's memory as Somebody Philpot, a CPA and busybody who obligingly supplied Bel with high quality dope from what he liked to describe, as if it lent the transaction an aura of glamour and danger, "a Russian source."

Philpot burst into a whiplash of smiles.

"Ah! So glad to see you, again, er..."

"James."

"Of course, James Ireton, the one who always walked up fifteen flights of stairs! Still leery of those elevators, eh?"

"Afraid so."

"Well, so glad to see you coming around again, however you get here. Bel was happier when she was with you. I've been getting a little worried lately, you know, she's been seeing so many, er..." Philpot put his fingers to his lips, apparently catching himself in an indiscretion. "Well, running late! Do tell Bel that I'll be back with her stuff around ten-thirty, okay?"

"Sure."

Philpot scurried toward the elevator with *Have a good one!* on his thin lips.

James rapped on Bel's door. When there was no answer, he tried the knob and was surprised, after Bel's flagrant exhibition of paranoia a few days before, to find the door unlocked. He pushed it open a few inches and called into the room. Bel answered, apparently from the bedroom, saying she'd be right with him.

Stepping inside, James blinked.

Bel had completely redecorated. Her previous Art Deco motif, though affected and rather childish, had at least been cheerful; but the room James faced now was dark and oppressive — a jumble of untended houseplants and massive, noisily upholstered furniture in a Joseph's coat of rabid color: black and emerald, magenta and puce, Mars orange, sulfur yellow, and bishop's purple. Unable at first to discern any order in the chaos, it finally occurred to James that Bel had been aiming at a British Colonial motif, but had overshot the mark by a furlong. The tiger-striped sofa, the one piece of furniture he recognized from before, crouched amidst the foliage of two huge potted palms like a carnivore in the jungle, ready to pounce. A steel drum band pinged and ponged from her stereo, reminding him of rain patter on a tin roof. There was a haze of acrid smoke hovering near the ceiling that mingled her signature *Narcisse* with marijuana smoke and the pungent scent of those clove cigarettes she fancied. Dog-eared magazines, books, and dusty bric-a-brac littered every grimy surface, alongside smudged glasses, crumpled napkins, greasy plates.

James felt a film of closed-room sweat beading on his scalp. Taking a deep breath, he crossed the floor to the least cluttered section of the room, a whitewashed wall adorned only with one large picture and an antique buffet. A decanter of sherry sat atop the dusty buffet, along with an arrangement of long stem red roses in a crystal bowl. The roses had gone off and the slimy water was beginning to stink from jungle rot.

James studied the huge picture above the buffet. It was a reproduction in a primitive style, Central or South American he guessed, depicting a busy marketplace from some ancient civilization. It was only when James spotted the blood-dappled pyramid in the upper background that he guessed that the civilization in question must be pre-Columbian Mexico at the apogee of the Aztec empire. Absorbed in this exotic alchemy of beauty and horror, James didn't hear the sound of the bedroom door opening and closing behind him.

"Diego Rivera," Bel said. "A gift from an admirer, along with the roses. You never gave me roses, you conceited, self-absorbed motherfucker."

James turned, startled at first only by the utter dullness with which Bel had spoken the violent words. Then his mouth slipped open.

An emaciated Bel Gunderson stood before him wearing only a flimsy scarlet teddy that hung from her bony shoulders by two spaghetti straps. The woman's once elegant line, so lovely it could take a man's breath away, had wasted to little more than a brittle collection of ribs, nipples, and joints—a stick figure more appropriate to an Auschwitz *Lager* than a Paris cat-walk.

"Oh, don't mind this," Bel said, gesturing at the teddy and misreading his expression of shock. "I'm not out to get fucked. God knows I've had enough fucking for one night." She pushed a strand of oily hair away from her face—so thin, so translucent, that James could see the vein throbbing at her temple. "My last client likes this Frederick's of Hollywood trash. Well, most men do." Bel stepped to her coffee table and reached out a spectral arm for a pack of Djarums. The coarse tobacco crackled as she lit it, and the harsh scent of clove-drenched tobacco wafted to his nostrils. "Of course you were an exception to the rule," she added, exhaling. "You never cared what I wore. Or didn't. As far as you were concerned I was merely the nearest available spillway. And here you had all kinds of money and I never asked for a shilling." She laughed. "But, I'm learning, friend. You bet I'm learning."

James put his hand over a cough. "Christ, Bel, it wasn't that bad, was it?"

Dropping onto the sofa, Bel shook her head at his obtuse, masculine incomprehension. "Never mind, darling, that was another life." She aimed a chipped red fingernail at the rattan armchair on the other side of the coffee table. "Sit. *Sit.*"

James didn't sit. He took a few steps towards her, intending to speak, to get this gruesome interview over with, but his words were stopped by the sight of her knocking her cigarette ashes into an obscene-looking ashtray on the coffee table. Shaped like a human skull with the cranium scooped out, the ashtray was so overflowing with butts—Djarums, Players, joints—that it looked as if it were sprouting grizzled hair. Next to the hideous artifact was a small silver tray dusted with coke, and a pack of oversized playing cards spread out for what James presumed was Patience, until he looked closer and realized that they were Tarot cards arranged in some sort of cross figuration.

"I'm in the middle of your reading," Bel explained, answering the dumbfounded question in his face. "Must say, yours is the most ambiguous situation I've seen in some time. Look here." Sitting forward, Bel laid a fingernail on each card as she spoke. "The Queen of Hearts covers you, while the reversed Knight of Cups is your obstacle. Now, the reversed Three of Wands crowns you, the Devil is beneath you, the Four of Swords is behind you, and before you—" Bel waved her skeletal hand over the card that formed the left wing of the cross. "—the Tower. Tricky business, the Tower. It suggests adversity, even deception...or an opportunity. We'll see which one." She laughed. "Or both."

Reaching for the cards that were still face down in the deck, Bel picked out the next one, turned it over, and laid it to the right of the cross. "This represents your disposition to the situation at hand...ah, yes, the reversed Three of Swords!" She snorted. "Typical." The next card went face up above the last one. "This is your house, representing the influence of others...the Moon! But of course. Son, you're ensnared by hidden enemies!" She nodded with stagey solemnity, as if to say, *how true*. "Next, your hopes and fears—they're always the same you know, hopes and fears. Hm, the Eight card. That signifies strength, power, courage..." Bel's mouth worked up in a frown. "Don't quite know what to make of that..."

"Bel—"

"But finally—" She held another card over the others, face down. "—what will come. This is what everyone wants, and dreads, to know. Shall we turn it over?"

James sighed. "You know this is all meaningless to me."

"I know!" Bel slapped the card down above the other three, as if in defiance of his indifference. "Well, well, well," she exclaimed with what appeared to be genuine astonishment, "the Hanged Man, the most ambiguous card of all! But then, that's you all over, isn't it, Ireton?" She laughed as at some private joke that James could not possibly share, and retrieved her cigarette.

"I've seen the video," James blurted out.

"Have you now," she said without missing a beat. "Give yourself a good lube and oil job while you watched, or was Little Miss Curds and Cream there to service you?"

"For chrissake," he said, coughing again on the smoke she was aiming in his face, "it's getting around town that you're the star of the thing. Doesn't that worry you?"

Bel hooted. "Li'l ol' me, the *star*? Puh-*leeze*. DeBrun's prick was the star of the thing, I was just a random collection of orifices. A stage prop. My trademark role."

"But don't you think it might be wise to go home for a while?"

Intentionally or not, James had finally found a vulnerable spot in Bel Gunderson's thorny armor. "*Home?*" she nearly shrieked. "You mean to *Daddy*?" She snorted. "At least my clients pay me."

James hesitated. "What about the police? I'm sure Lt. Masefield—"

"What good would some cop do me, besides getting me dumped over my balcony like pigeon shit. Though why a bunch of Chicago goons should give a damn about me, I can't imagine. I haven't seen a dime from the fucking thing since Rygiel took a dive. Only blood and bruises and nightmares and doctors' bills." She sniffed. "But thanks ever so much for the warning."

He swallowed, and nodded.

"Well, if you're not going to sit down, you might as well make yourself useful and get us a drink." Bel motioned at the decanter on the buffet.

Feeling a drizzle of sweat coursing down his back, James peeled off his jacket and dropped it on the floor beside the rattan chair, then went to the buffet.

"A habit I picked up from you," Bel commented a few moments later, taking the proffered glass of sherry from his trembling hand. "You English are so bloody civilized."

Seating himself at last, James took down half his glass in one swallow. "By the way," he said, fingering the stem of the glass and making a ridiculous stab at a conversational tone, "I ran into Philpot outside. He said he'd be back around ten-thirty with your stuff."

Bel gave a distracted nod.

"Well, now, you said there was something you wanted to discuss with me?"

James wondered for a moment if Bel had heard him, because she didn't answer right away; instead she laid her cigarette in the skull's head ashtray and frowned down at her legs stretched out in front of her. It must have been a good minute at least before she finally whispered, almost inaudibly, "*Whose legs are those...?*"

James looked at her looking down at her own legs.

Finally, Bel pushed a strand of greasy hair from her face and reached again for her cigarette. "I lied to you," she said, the words sighing out of her like air from a leaky balloon. "I didn't have an abortion. I was never pregnant. I can't get pregnant."

James sat up, a drop of spilled sherry spreading on his jeans. "Then for God's sake why did you—"

"I wanted to get some kind of human reaction from you! Even a slap or a *fuck you* would have been better than your goddamned civil indifference!"

Their eyes locked. James knew it was his turn to say something, but he couldn't think of a word. Instead he bent over and shook his head from side to side, he didn't know for how long, and when he looked up again, he knew his brief opportunity to make some genuine connection with Isabel Gunderson had already been lost. A door had shut in her mind; he could see the slamming finality of it in her face.

"So much for that," Bel said, rearranging her stickly legs. "So what's this I hear about your writing a soppy letter of apology to Nadine Jeffrey? Jesus, Ireton, what is this shit, some lower rung on a twelve-step ladder for sexoholics?"

James's initial surprise at Bel's knowledge of his recent correspondence quickly gave way to a sigh of weariness and exasperation. "Nadine wouldn't speak to me over the phone," he said, "so, I wrote her a letter. I was glad to be able to speak to you in person."

"Speak to me?" She lifted one arched eyebrow. "About what?"

"Well, to tell you how sorry I am. About everything. How I handled everything. How I mishandled everything. With us."

Bel clapped her hands. "And by Christ," she exclaimed, "performed with all the last-act penitence of Shakespeare's Angelo!" She jumped to her feet, some color finally blotching on her pale cheeks. "Tell you what, Ireton, the lit-crits don't call *Measure for Measure* a 'Problem Play' for nothing!"

"But I *am* sorry."

She wheeled on him. "And...? What, that makes everything okay now, is that how you think it works? You chant *mea culpa* a few times and I'm obliged to stand here and give you absolution, so you can trot off and shag Lupe Cruz between your freshly laundered sheets?"

James held up a warning finger. "Nothing of her, that's my one condition. You can say anything to me you like, and I'll sit here and take it. I know I deserve worse. But I won't hear anything about her." He threw up his hands. "For pity's sake, if I have a chance at happiness for the first time in my life, why should you resent it?"

Bel bent over to grind out her cigarette with a fierce twist of her bony wrist, then turned toward the bedroom. For a moment James thought she was going to leave the room entirely, but she pivoted before she reached the door, her face as scarlet as her lingerie. "*Resent*?!" she cried. "The word hasn't been invented that expresses how I feel about you! But I'll tell you one thing. You have no *right* to be happy, no goddamned right. I've been fucked by men like you since I was twelve years old...twelve years old! You owe me, goddamn, you! You, Ireton, especially you! You owe me!"

James rose to his feet, and just as quickly sat down again. "Christ, Bel, do you need some money?"

"*Money?*" she cried shrilly. "Gawd, isn't that you in Technicolor! Look at me, you motherfucker, *look at me!*" Bel jabbed her bony forefinger into her almost concave chest. "Money couldn't begin to pay for it! You owe me, damn you! You owe me, pain for pain!"

James opened his arms. "Bel, I didn't mean...honest to God, I just wanted to help you. Please, let me help you, in whatever way I can. Even if it's only money. Just because...because we're connected."

It took Bel Gunderson a few seconds to compose herself. When she did, her words came a split-second too late and a degree too warm to be anything but imposture.

"Well, that's really good of you. And of course I'll take your money. Send me a goddamned check, the bigger the better. It would be a help right now."

James nodded, marginally relieved, and bent over to retrieve his jacket.

"But before you go, permit me to give you something in return. Just because we're connected!"

James hesitated—the gnawing in his stomach was becoming acute, and her voice had taken on a peculiarly triumphant tone, which he knew he should distrust. "What?" he said cautiously, dropping his jacket.

"Think of it as a birthday present, a mere trifle. You turn thirty tomorrow, right? November tenth? I always remember because it's Dorian Gray's birthday, and Richard Burton's. Two great actors, like yourself."

James shrugged. He'd been so preoccupied with Lupe's absence he'd forgot about his own birthday.

"Well, my gift to you on your thirtieth birthday is an amusing little morsel of Freshman doggerel someone recently brought to my attention. Want to hear it?"

James opened his arms. "You obviously want me to hear it."

Bel unveiled her teeth in something like a smile and reached for another cigarette. Sashaying to her entertainment center as she lit it, she leaned one wasted arm on top of it, like a chanteuse poised beside a grand piano. "Speaking of actors, Gielgud I'm not," she declared with a flourish as she blew out the match and dropped it on the carpet, "but then this poetry ain't Shakespeare, either." She sucked on the clove cigarette, blew it out in a plume, then cleared her throat: *"On slick wooden steps, a premarital bed, rain played our senses like a stop-sounding pipe; your heart told its mystery, rare and unread—wordless moans held unharbored archetypes—"*

"Jesus Christ," James cried, unaware that Bel's recital had lifted him to his feet, "where did you hear that!"

If Bel was shocked by the explosiveness of his reaction, she recovered quickly. A chunk of ashes fell unnoticed onto her bare foot as she took another long self-satisfied pull. "Where I heard it," she said, exhaling, "is no business of yours. What is your business, or at least should be, is that the love of your life has been pandering it all over the Institute. Gawd, James, surely you knew."

James gripped his stomach, his mind spinning. "She wouldn't have showed that to anyone, I know she wouldn't. She must have left a paper lying around class...something..." He shook his head, trying to think, unable to think, hardly able to breathe as the clove smoke swirled in his face like a foul dream. He looked around him, his eyes wide open and staring, trying to get his bearings in the oppressive surroundings as Bel just stood there laughing at him in open derision. "I don't believe this!" he cried finally. "She wrote that for me. For *me*. She wouldn't have shared that with anybody!"

Bel whooped at his desperate determination to avoid the obvious. "Oh, Ireton," she exclaimed, "this is classic...*classic!* I have to admit, I didn't think the simple little bitch had it in her, but she's gulled you like a pro. Don't you get it? She didn't write that thing for you, she wrote it years ago for some high school jock who knocked her up. *Zounds*, man, look at you! You're like some stupid Elizabethan cuckold, his hobbyhorse topped by the general camp and he the last to know! Tell you what son, you're paying a good deal too dearly for what's been handed out to others free of charge!"

James inched his way over to the buffet on the other side of the room, thinking that he had to put some distance between himself and Isabel Gunderson, he had to, or else he would curl his fingers around her scrawny throat and *squeeze*.

"At a loss for words?" Bel taunted. "The mellifluous and honey-tongued James Ireton? Now that's a first. But the girl's lying is just the half of it. In fact, for a man who cherishes his privacy as much as you do, I'd say it's her truth-telling that ought to come as the biggest outrage."

"What are you saying?"

"I'm saying that your pious she-love is the most gifted actress since steamy little Jennifer Jones got the Oscar for *The Song of Bernadette*. I'm saying that while she's promised you her undying discretion and devotion, she's been telling everyone at the Institute about her precious little birthday celebration, and how you redecorated your apartment for her, and begged her like a dying man to move in with you. Unkindest cut of all, you selfish egotistical bastard, I wasn't good enough to invite up for a lousy soda, but you'll call your fair savior in the middle of the night when you're having an-other nervous breakdown! *Thy vile lady has robbed thee of thy sword*, General! Fool, she's told people all about your nervous breakdown at Oxford—"

"No—"

"—and how she's come to interpret your legendary nocturnal exploits as emotional over-compensation for your guilt over your mother's suicide."

"Oh, God, this is a—"

"A nightmare? Well, welcome to the Twilight Zone, goats and monkeys! Idiot, *she's* the one who stole your precious dissertation, because it was the only thing you cared about more than her. Gawd, she's been parading your lousy CD like a hunting trophy. Don't you know that's the reason she won't let you into her bedroom? She's afraid you'll find the disk on a shelf in her closet! Jesus, but the absolute kicker for me was that hysterical vision of yours…dubbed a knight by the Blessed Virgin Mary, now, were you? Fight-ing dragons…puh-*leeze*!"

One moment hyperventilating, a moment later hardly able to breathe at all, James bent over against the biting pains in his stomach. The floor seemed to heave beneath his feet like the deck of a trawler on a heavy sea. "Who did…who did she talk to?" he gasped out finally. "Was it Jack? It was Jack, wasn't it? She talked to Jack! She told Jack everything and then he told you!"

Bel slipped the cigarette between her teeth and took one last hit before mashing it out in the skull's head ashtray. "Does it really matter?" she said, seeming suddenly to have grown weary of her spectacular triumph. "The point is, she talked. And talked and talked and talked. For you, that should be more than enough to know."

And it was.

James lurched towards the door.

The clock on his dashboard read nine-fifty-four. Screeching to a halt at a parking space near the intersection with Downer, James flung open the Jeep door and ran jacketless like a man on amphetamines against the red light to the other side of the street; then into the nearly deserted drugstore. The pharmacist seemed a little peeved when he noted the time—the pharmacy closed at ten—and that James hadn't called in the prescription first, but swallowed his complaint when James paid with a hundred dollar bill and didn't wait for his change.

By the time James had pulled out into the Saturday night traffic again, there were no thoughts at all in his mind, only the echo of Bel's words in his overheated brain, the raw sensation of betrayal, and a rage cold as January.

A maddening picture developed in his imagination, a picture as real to him as if he had actually seen it: Guadalupe Cruz in that flower-print dress of hers, sitting in Jack apartment with her hand upon his friend's warm knee, unburdening herself to Jack, in her childish stammer, about her "difficult relationship" with James Ireton. To Jack—Jackson Beauregard Sigur, who in his immense and awful innocence couldn't keep a secret about anybody or anything!

James slammed on the brakes in front of her house and ran up the steps to her yard, taking the prescription sack with him but leaving the flowers and champagne he had bought earlier in the back seat. His rage mounted with each step up her spiraling stairs. Unlocking her door, he almost laughed out loud when he discovered that she had left the chain off the hook, no doubt for his expected arrival. If necessary, he had been prepared to break down the door. Her brother and grandparents were out of town, no one would hear what was about to happen.

He shot the bolt behind him and hooked the chain. Her living room was dark, but for the ultramarine glow of the salt-water aquarium. A light came on under the bedroom door just as he was dropping the sack on her table.

Her door opened an inch and she put her head around it, then opened it wider when she saw who it was. She was dressed like very sanctity in a white nightgown that absorbed the sea-light of the aquarium. The gold of her bedroom lamp shone like an aureole behind her back.

"James," she said with relief, "you gave me such a scare! I meant to wait up, but I was so tired I...well, for a moment I th-th-thought..." Her voice trailed off when she got a good look at his twisted face; then at the white paper prescription sack on the table. The planes of her face began to droop, and she lifted one hand to her breast, obviously about to retreat.

He was on her in an instant, shoving her through the bedroom door. She fell sprawling on the floor inside, the back of her head striking a bedpost with a thud. Putting her hand to the back of her head, her eyes blinking in disbelief, she scooted away from him until she was huddled in the corner beneath *la Guadalupana*.

He took two steps to her closet door and flung it open, then yanked clothes off their hangers and tossed them on the floor until he remembered that Bel had mentioned it being on a shelf. Reaching up, he swept everything off the shelf above the clothes rail—shoe boxes, blankets, purses—until he spotted what he was looking for: a corner of a CD jewel case peeping out from the open lips of a purse that had fallen at his feet.

He bent down to retrieve it, but still didn't quite believe it. He had to open the jewel case and turn the CD over several times, reading and re-reading his own scribbled labeling in black marker before he could finally accept the fact that he was holding the stolen backup of his dissertation. Finally closing the jewel case with a snap, he fastened his gaze on her, his gray eyes icy as a northern lake.

She cowered in the corner, her arms wrapped tight around her trembling knees as if she could will herself to disappear into the wall behind her. Her eyes flickered from the CD to his face, then to the CD again, as if—God, what an actress!—she didn't *understand*. And still didn't understand, not even when he tossed the CD on her bed and began to unbutton his shirt.

It was only when he dropped the shirt beside the disk and began working on his belt buckle that she finally began to absorb the meaning of his actions. The sight of her quivers, the exhilarating feel of old-house drafty air against his naked, sweaty chest, sent a thrill of exhilaration up James's spine so potent he thought he would detonate. He unhooked his belt, and pulled it slowly out of the loops of his jeans. When it came free from the last loop she threw her hands in front of her face as if she thought he was going to strike her with it. But he didn't hit her with it; no, of course not, he had no intention of hitting her with it; what he was going to do to her he wanted to do with his two bare hands.

He dropped the belt on the floor. The leather and metal slithered and banged against the wood planks at his feet.

Letting out a great sigh, she opened her lips as if to speak.

He took two steps and grabbed her before she could utter a word, yanking her to her feet and shoving her against the wall. One of her shoulders knocked hard against *la Guadalupana*. She cried out, a muffled whelp, and he responded by clapping his hand over her mouth—not because he needed to, the house was empty, but because he wanted to feel his own strength forcing her silence. She managed to get one of his fingers between her teeth and bit down hard. He jerked away his hand with a yelp of pain.

"Barry, stop—!" Her hands flew up to her mouth when she realized what she had said. But James only stepped back to wipe his bleeding finger across her white counterpane.

"Ja-Ja-Ja—"

"Shut up!" He rounded on her, his arm flexed high above her head; but in the last second before he struck her, the rest of his body pivoted and his fist whirled past her face and into the image of *la Guadalupana*. The glass shattered in a starburst. The picture fell to the floor at their feet.

His knuckles dripping blood from cuts he didn't feel, he reached for her throat and shoved her head against the wall. "You believe in a language of the body? Well tonight you're going to hear most eloquent speech from me!"

He threw her on the bed. She tried to scramble to the other side, but he yanked her back by her ankles and pinned her with his own weight. He wrenched her over underneath him until he could brace her arms against her sides and stretch himself on top of her. He crushed his mouth into hers as if he would jump down her throat. When she finally gagged, he shoved his knee between her legs, feeling the punishment he was inflicting on her only as thumps against his chest as she struggled uselessly, a gurgle against his tongue as she groaned, and a rush of dark pleasure up his spine.

And then he suddenly realized, with a shudder of disappointment, that he wouldn't be able to finish it until he learned the one detail that Bel had refused him.

He lifted his head. "Who?" he yelled in her face. "Who did you talk to! It was Jack, wasn't it!"

She said nothing, perhaps could say nothing, and her choking silence, the wildness in her eyes, and her body's vain struggles beneath him began to undermine his violent resolve. He stiffened his purpose by administering a slap across her face that produced a trickle of blood at the corner of her mouth. Her eyes swiveled up to the ceiling, her black pupils large and glazing over.

"Who was it?!" he yelled again.

"God," she whispered. "God…"

"God! You talked to God? I'll tell you about God, I've got him memorized. *Oh, ye who kindle fires and set firebrands alight, this is your fate at my hands: you shall lie down in torment.* Oh, I am keen tonight, and *it will cost you a groaning to take off my edge!* Let's get your term in Purgatory out of the way right now, shall we, isn't that the pious theory? Pay now, so you don't have to pay twice as much later? Well, I think I can help you with that!"

He tore open her nightgown at the neckline and pried her legs apart with his knees, just now realizing himself, in vivid, violent detail, his body burning, exactly what it was that was going to do. The decision was made in an instant. Done.

But he couldn't look her in those damned eyes of hers and do it, so he pushed her face to the bed with one hand while he reached down with the other to finesse the zipper of his jeans. He had just got himself unzipped, and had buried his face in her naked shoulder again, when he suddenly felt something cold and metallic against his lips.

He lifted his head. A bit of silver sparkled against the black of her hair, a bit of silver that dangled from a chain around his own neck. A word rang in his mind: *Bricusse.*

A noise escaped James's lips that swelled into a roar. He ripped the chain from his neck and flung it against the wall. The medal struck her dresser mirror with a *ping*, then fell clattering to the floor. He folded over almost double and rolled on his side, sharp pains stabbing at his belly.

He laid there for some time, gripping his belly, before he finally heard himself saying, "How could you do it? How could you…"

She had curled up and was clutching at her bruised throat. "Do wh-wh-*what*?" she almost screamed.

He straightened against the pain. "Bel told me everything…everything! Things only you and I knew. My breakdown at Oxford, and the vision in the church. How I redecorated the apartment for you, and tried to get you to move in with me. She even had your miserable little sonnet memorized. Told me you had written it first for DeBrun. God, Barry DeBrun! Why couldn't you just *tell* me you were lovers, that you'd had to get an abortion? Do you think I'd have held it against you, I, who've done as much myself?" He snatched the CD case beside her leg and shook it in her face. "But this… this! What could it have meant to you? What kind of trophy-hunting sicko *are* you!"

She just looked at him, as at a lunatic, then at the CD. She gestured feebly at the closet. "I d-didn't put it up there. And all th-th-those things about you, ab-b-bout us, I never told them to anyone!" She shook her head. "And the sonnet…d-d-don't you remember that night? In the-the-the rain, on the steps…how could I have written that for *him*?"

James sucked in his breath, the words drumming in his mind. *On slick wooden steps, a premarital bed—purging rain played our senses like a stop-sounding pipe...*

The CD case slipped from his fingers.

There was a perfectly sane explanation for all this, he thought, working with trembling hands to do up the zipper of his jeans as his mind stirred in one direction then another, like a whirligig in a finicky wind. Why, he must have stumbled in on himself in the middle of another nervous breakdown. Yes, that was it. He was barking. Barmy. Raving mad. None of this was really happening. It was a psychotic episode. Brain chemicals gone lollapalooza. If he just gave it a little time, and sat here a while to catch his breath and get his balance again, this mad scene he'd stumbled into might suddenly dissolve again into something resembling solid reality.

But seconds passed, and more seconds passed, and the scene refused to morph into something he could deal with, let alone understand. Instead, he saw bruises sprouting on Lupe's face and neck as she sat up and checked herself, or so it would seem, for breakages. A triangle of torn, blood-dappled cloth had folded down over her breast, exposing a white shoulder marbled with purple. Beads of blood from her battered lip decorated her throat like a necklace of rubies.

Feeling he would burst from the pressure if he didn't move, James jumped up and began pacing around the bed, from wall to door to window and back again, his arm slicing the air. "Then how is it, how is it—" Coming to a frantic halt in front of her, he grabbed her shoulders and shook her. "Oh my God, I know what happened, you talked to a priest! Of course that's what you did, you went to confession to that goddamned brother of yours, and he—"

She wrenched herself out of his grasp. "I haven't confessed to Martin since before we met!" she cried, a ring of anger beginning to supersede the fear in her voice. "Except..." Suddenly her eyes grew wide, as at some other horror in the room beside himself that he could not see. Then she turned her head slowly, very slowly, towards the bedside table.

"What is it?" he whispered. The look on her face was somehow more terrifying than anything that had gone before.

Her eyes, hollow with exhaustion and confusion and a kind of deathly sadness, swiveled slowly towards him again, then back towards the bedside table. Then they clamped shut, as if she could not bear to see what she was seeing. She lifted one hand, her fingers curled as if she would strangle the air, and gestured crookedly at the bedside table. "My j-j-journal," she stammered, "it's go-go-gone."

He followed her gesture to its source: there was a gap in the collection of books on her bedstand where the three-ring notebook ought to be. He rushed around the bed to bat through the remaining books, knowing before he did so that the notebook he'd seen there a few nights before was gone, and with it his SANA report.

He whirled around. "Couldn't you have taken it to Chicago?" he almost pleaded.

She shook her head, but still didn't open her eyes.

He stepped back, then back some more until he bumped his head on the sloping ceiling under the eaves. Then he looked down at his blood-smeared hands. "I lost a set of keys the other day," he said finally, still looking at his hands. "The key to your apartment was on it."

She nodded, but still didn't open her eyes.

James took a shuffling step to leave the room before she could open her eyes again; to put himself out of her sight, to spare her the sight of him; but he couldn't get his feet to move properly, and his sudden lethargy must have given her the time she needed to gather her wits, because all at once her eyes popped open. Only she wasn't looking at him any longer, nor at the bed-stand, but at something beyond the bedroom door. In the next instant she had leapt off the bed and was running past him into the living room, her torn gown billowing behind her like a spinnaker in a freshening breeze.

He thought at first that she was running for the bathroom to be sick, but her footfalls stopped too soon, and he looked up to see her standing by her little dining table, her hands shaking violently as she clutched his prescription sack and tried to read, in the wash of light from the bedroom, the receipt stapled to the bag. It was only when she ran with the sack into the bathroom, slamming and locking the door behind her, that he realized what she was doing, and that she had somehow anticipated his next move before he had even had a chance to formulate it himself.

He lurched after her, yelling at her, begging her to let him have the pills. When she didn't answer, he put his ear to the bathroom door. He heard the sound of coughing and gagging, and the rattle of capsules inside the plastic bottle. Stepping back in the narrow passageway, he threw his full weight against the door. It crashed open against her, sending her reeling into the shower with windmilling arms. He fell over the toilet, and in the harsh light of the overhead fixture, saw his sleeping pills whirlpooling down the pan amidst a greenish swirl of vomit.

"Oh, God," he moaned, pushing himself to his feet and unaware that he had begun to cry. He stumbled back for the bedroom—for his shirt, for his belt, for he didn't know what; but she was quickly on her feet again and right behind him, calling his name, begging him to stop, begging him to talk to her.

"Listen to me!" she cried finally, yanking his shirt out of his hands and whipping it across his face to get his attention. When it didn't do the trick— he was still moaning, babbling really, still shaking his head, still waving her away—she pulled back and slapped him hard across the face with the flat of one hand, then the other, almost knocking him off his feet. "Damn you, listen to me!" she screamed. "You wouldn't give me a chance before, you miserable bastard, but you're going to listen to me now!"

He collapsed on the edge of her bed, his head nodding stupidly up and down, his hands folded meekly between his legs, willing to take anything she might do or say to him, willing to give himself up to whatever punishment she might wish to inflict. The problem was, no punishment she could possibly invent would be sufficient, and as he heard her furious and remarkably fluent words — *You're not alone anymore. You have no right to throw away your life as if you'd never met me!* — he knew at once that he had to get out of here. He had to get out of this room, this house, this body, this waking nightmare of a soul and go *any*where, because anywhere was better than sitting here and having to listen to Lupe Cruz trying to forgive him.

Finally he could stand it no more and stood up. "You don't understand," he said. "You don't understand what I was going to do. What DeBrun tried to do. And more. Oh much more…"

"What I understand," she replied, calmer now but still defiant, "the only thing I understand right now, is that you didn't go through with it. Believe me, Barry would have." She wiped her face on her nightgown sleeve. "He wouldn't have thought of the pills, either."

He opened his mouth to argue with this preposterous bit of naïveté, but she stood firm. "Shut up and listen to me for once!" she demanded. "I tell you, you're not like him, whatever you may think. You're a good man, I kn-kn-kn-ow it." Faltering suddenly, she swallowed a sob. "*They say b-b-best men are molded out of f-f-faults…*"

James recognized the quote, too well. "They don't call *Measure for Measure* a 'Problem Play' for nothing," he whispered. Taking a single step, he swayed, then folded in a heap at the foot of her bed. "Oh my God," he moaned, his forehead thumping hard against the floor, "what a wedding night I almost gave you here…"

At that, Lupe's vestigial strength abandoned her at last. She clutched at the torn nightgown, trying to hold it together across her breasts, and wailed.

———————

Too strung out to clean up either herself or the shambles of her apartment, Lupe lay shivering in her bed several hours later, her nightgown safety-pinned together, listening to the intermittent groans of James's troubled sleeplessness as he lay sprawled on her living room sofa under the influence of more Tylenol PM than could possibly be good for him, but not enough. So far, a similar dose had done nothing for Lupe, either, except to make her feel sluggish and sick to her already emptied stomach.

She had spoken words of hope to him a few hours before, to rescue him from his self-destructive befuddlement, and in the moment she had believed some of them herself; but now, in the early morning stillness, the moonlit blood stains on her bedspread dancing to the rhythm of her shivering body, she faced a long night of sleeplessness and uncertainty, a sunrise that would bring no easy answers, and a swelling of ambivalence which she feared was the prelude to a failure of nerve.

First Barry, now James…was there something about *her*, she wondered; some habitual and unthinking signal she gave out to the world at large that drew masculine violence like a whistle summoning a pack of dogs? It was horrible enough coming from Barry, but from *James*, the man she loved and thought she knew...

She had known almost from the beginning, she reasoned with herself, that James Ireton was one of the walking wounded; was bringing a burden of emotional baggage to their relationship that she, at times, might be forced to help carry; but she had had no idea, none at all, how crushing the burden might prove to be. Right now it seemed insupportable. Certainly, to go on as they had before—the warmth, the trust, the intimacy—was impossible after so radical a breach. Surely caution was in order now, extreme caution. Not to mention a postponement of the wedding and some time apart to...

To do what?

Lupe let out a little growl: *and she lived carefully ever after.*

Eventually lost in a drugged sleep, Lupe was awakened by furious pounding on her outside door. After glancing at the alarm clock—it was a little past four— she stumbled groggily into the living room where a peek through the spy hole revealed that her middle-of-the-night visitor was none other than—what the hell?—her brother Ramon.

"Ramon, for heaven's sake, what's the matter?" she said, unlocking the door but leaving the chain on the hook.

"Where is he!" Ramon demanded. He pushed against the door, but the chain held.

"What are you talking about?"

"Ireton's Jeep's outside! Where is he?"

"He-he-he's sacked out on the sofa."

"Dammit Lu, let me in! The sonuvabitch killed a woman tonight!"

"Wh-Wh-Who?" she said, hearing James stirring on the sofa behind her.

"An old girlfriend named Isabel Gunderson. He raped her, sliced her into ribbons, and dumped her off her fifteenth-story balcony. They found his jacket in her apartment, soaked in her blood."

Chapter Ten:
'Tween Sleep and Wake

Thou, Nature, art my goddess; to thy law
My services are bound. Wherefore should I
Stand in the plague of custom and permit
The curiosity of nations to deprive me,
For that I am some twelve or fourteen moonshines
Lag of a brother? Why bastard? wherefore base?
When my dimensions are as well compact,
My mind as generous, and my shape as true,
As honest madam's issue? Why brand they us
With base? with baseness? bastardy? base, base?
Who, in the lusty stealth of nature, take
More composition and fierce quality
Than doth, within a dull, stale, tired bed,
Go to the creating a whole tribe of fops
Got 'tween asleep and wake? Well then,
Legitimate Edgar, I must have your land.

Shakespeare, *King Lear*

Lt. Calvin Masefield stepped up to the one-way glass that separated him from the interview room where James Ireton, dressed in an orange jail jumpsuit, this one made of paper because he had been put on a suicide watch after what Lupe Cruz had told them, had been brought from the city lock-up. Masefield rubbed his stubbly chin. Sure enough, he thought, the ragged young man, as wilted as an unwatered flower, looked like he would gladly walk to the nearest electric chair. But then this morning James Ireton was both surprising and disturbing Masefield on any number of scores.

At least Ireton's story about stopping by the drugstore after leaving Gunderson's place had checked out. The pharmacist had had no difficulty remembering his five-minutes-to-closing customer who paid with a hundred dollar bill and left without his change. Too, though the autopsy report hadn't come in yet, so they didn't know the estimated time of death, the victim's high body temp, coupled with a lack of rigor mortis, indicated that Isabel Gunderson hadn't been dead long when her mutilated body was found at one-thirty-five a.m. Nor did it seem likely that this was a hurry-up job. Whoever had inflicted all those ghoulish marks of sexual torture on the victim had clearly been savoring every moment. Masefield doubted very much that it could have been accomplished in the thirty or forty minutes between

Owen Philpot's spotting of Ireton outside Gunderson's door, and Ireton's subsequent appearance at the drugstore.

Ramon Cruz, however, who until last night had been certain that Barry DeBrun was behind all the recent mayhem, was now equally convinced that James Ireton had not only killed Isabel Gunderson, but had also dropped Bricusse and murdered the prostitute Candace Duffy as well; worse, that his "naïve" sister was providing a false alibi out of a misplaced sense of loyalty. Indeed, Ramon was so persuaded of Ireton's guilt, particularly after he saw what Ireton had done to his sister, that he had administered some significant pre-emptive punishment on the unresisting Englishman before putting him under arrest and reading him his rights in Lupe's apartment. If the news people got hold of that, Masefield thought with a groan, things could get real dicey on his shift, real fast.

Blood samples had been taken, along with Ireton's clothes. Masefield suspected that the isolated blood drops on Ireton's jeans would turn out to be his own and Lupe Cruz's. Ditto with the bite on Ireton's finger. God knows, he couldn't imagine that Gunderson's killer had gotten off so clean. Also in Ireton's favor was the fact that he had been unusually cooperative thus far, identifying his own blood-soaked jacket (after throwing up at the sight of it) and volunteering to sign every search request they had shoved in front of his nose. Not to mention, passively withstanding a grueling interrogation earlier this morning. No, from Masefield's vantage point, Ireton was far too preoccupied with his self-confessed violence against Lupe Cruz to comprehend the gravity of the charges being leveled at him in regard to the murder of Isabel Gunderson. He had even signed a waiver of attorney, though if he were held much longer one would be assigned to him, whether he wanted legal representation or not.

With a pre-arranged signal, Ramon emerged from the squad room to observe Masefield's upcoming interview of James Ireton through the one-way glass.

"Don't let him smooth you," was Ramon's sole comment.

Masefield turned the knob and stepped inside.

"Did you get any sleep, Mr. Ireton?" he said, shutting the door behind him.

James sat up and seemed to do a weary double take when he realized that he and Lt. Calvin Masefield were no longer on a first-name basis.

"Not really," James said, a shudder percolating up his trunk as he glanced around the windowless interview room. "Is there any chance we could talk somewhere else? There's not enough room to swing a cat in here, and I've got a touch of claustropho—"

"This won't take long," Masefield said, thinking that a little more discomfort might persuade Ireton to get this over with sooner.

Swallowing hard, James closed his eyes and broke into a sweat.

"First of all, I want to apologize on behalf of the police department for the, er, damage." Masefield gestured at James's black eye, broken lip, and swollen jaw. "I think you should have let us have a doctor look you over. I'm afraid it's not going to leave the representative from the British Consulate with a very favorable impression of American justice."

James scraped his fingers through his rumpled hair. "I deserved worse. I hope Ramon isn't going to be in any trouble."

"Even though you've chosen not to press charges, Det. Cruz may still have to face an inquiry by the Internal Affairs Division."

"Then tell them—you can write it down—" James pointed vehemently at Masefield's notebook, his first sign of life all morning. "—I resisted arrest. Ramon was using whatever the hell the term is for proper use of force."

Masefield held up his hand. "I'll talk to Internal Affairs myself. That's the best I can do." The lieutenant pulled up a chair. "Son, you've got one whopper of a temper. If it had been *my* sister—"

"I should be put down like a rabid dog."

Masefield started to chuckle, then realized that the young man had spoken in perfect earnest. "Look," he said, "I know you're not feeling too good about yourself, but I'm afraid I don't have the luxury of giving you the time to get over it. Now, I've read your statement, but there are some things I need clarified."

James stared at the wall in front of him.

"First, you said you told Miss Gunderson last night that she might be in danger because of *The Rape of Lucrece*. What made you think that?"

"You told me yourself that the mob war between Calabresi and Nesterov was a possible motive for the murders of Norman Rygiel and that prostitute in Racine."

"Rygiel's murder, maybe," Masefield agreed, "but as for Candace Duffy and your friend Gunderson..." Masefield studied James closely. "If those were mob hits, I'll eat my badge, they've gone and hired themselves a first class sicko."

James looked up at him with bloodshot eyes; he didn't seem to be understanding a word Masefield was saying.

Masefield rose to his feet. "Look, Mr.—hell, James, I'm facing a very disturbing situation here. I'd like to think you weren't Gunderson's killer, but at this moment I'm the only one in this building who has any doubts about it. To my way of thinking, you were too busy brutalizing your own girlfriend to have any thought, let alone time, for Isabel Gunderson. But you may still be connected somehow, or know something that can help us."

Frowning suddenly at the lieutenant's words, James gripped the edge of the table. "Oh my God, Barry DeBrun...is someone watching Lupe? She mustn't stay in that house alone!"

"She's fine," Masefield insisted. "She's in Bay View with her family. Besides, we don't have any evidence right now that DeBrun's killed anybody."

"But I thought—"

"It's a good working theory," was the furthest Masefield was prepared to commit himself. "Our problem is—" Masefield pointed at James. "—or should I say *your* problem is, a lot of bad stuff's been happening around the Institute lately, and most of it, one way or the other, involves you. I keep thinking that the answer to all our still-unsolved riddles may be locked up somewhere inside that smart little brain of yours."

A drop of sweat fell from James's chin to the collar of his paper jumpsuit. "Smart? God, Lieutenant, you've come to the wrong shop. I'm the stupidest man alive."

Masefield played with the keys in his trouser pockets, weighing his options. Ramon Cruz wasn't going to like what he was about to say to James Ireton, and probably not their Commander, either, if he ever found out, but to hell with that. Ireton would never be able to help them if he didn't wake up to what was at stake here.

"Okay, let me spell it out," Masefield said. "I can't go into detail, but there's no question in my mind that Isabel Gunderson was murdered by the same person who killed Candace Duffy. Of course, both Duffy and Gunderson were engaging in some high-risk sexual activities. Even if they weren't mob hits, there's a chance their killer's a mutual client. Maybe some drifter blown in from Boise, for all we know. But I don't think so. I think we have a sex killer on our hands, James, a local one. And what's really scaring me is that it could take another killing or two, or three, before we begin to see a definite delusional scheme emerge. I mean before we begin to suspect what the killer is *really* after. What the killer himself may not know he's after."

James looked dazed. "You mean like a symbolic structure?"

Masefield's eyebrows perched high on his forehead.

"Oh, you know," James waved, "hidden patterns connecting otherwise random-looking events. Chesterton once wrote that symbols weren't disguises really, but displays. The best expression of something that couldn't otherwise be expressed. But then, we lit scholars are very fond of telling authors what they didn't know they meant."

Masefield chuckled. You could take the man out of Academe, he thought, but not Academe out of the man. "Yeah, something like that," he said. "Say, want some coffee before we move on?"

Waiting impassively while Masefield stepped outside to fetch them some coffee, James looked at the large mirror on one wall of the interview room, wondering if it really were one of those two-way things he had seen in films, and if so, whether someone was watching him now. Surely, he thought, they weren't having *him* up for Bel's murder, what with the pharmacist having corroborated his and Lupe's version of events; but then, Calvin Masefield hadn't told him yet exactly when Bel was murdered, or even if they knew. Nor had anyone mentioned letting him go.

A spasm of pain gripped his left kidney, where Ramon had punched him with particular relish the night before. James gripped his side, sucking air. None of it mattered, he lectured himself, willing himself to sit still and just take the pain without complaint. Neither the pain mattered, nor the charges being raised against him, nor even the shredding sense of guilt, worse than ten beatings. They could all do with him what they liked. His miserable young life, only thirty years old this very day, was being rolled up like a scroll.

Masefield returned a few minutes later with a thermos pitcher, three Styrofoam cups, and stone-faced Ramon Cruz. James groaned inwardly at the sight of Lupe's brother, whose presence not only shamed him, but also implied another less than civilized grilling. He took a sip of coffee and grimaced; he could taste the aluminum of the pot it had been brewed in.

Without preamble, Masefield began by asking James if he knew of anyone who Gunderson was seeing on a regular basis.

"You mean, romantically?" James said. The word sounded odd in reference to Bel.

"In any kind of relationship."

James shrugged. "She told me she had someone in her apartment before I arrived, but she called him a 'client.' In fact, when I came in she was still wearing a bit of lacy red lingerie. You know, a teddy. For a moment I even thought she was trying to get something going with me again, but then she said something like, 'don't worry, I've had enough fucking for one night.'"

Ramon set down his coffee. "We found no red teddy last night. Gunderson was nude. Did you take it for a souvenir?"

James just looked at him.

"C'mon now, any recent lovers of Gunderson's you can identify for us?" Masefield persisted.

James shrugged again. "She had many. In fact her neighbor Philpot said last night—"

"Hold the phone!" Ramon had jumped to his feet and was yelling in James's face. "You admit Philpot saw you last night?"

James cocked back his head, as much to distance himself from Ramon's coffee breath as his fuming anger. "Why shouldn't I?" he said. "I ran into him outside Bel's door."

"You *talked* to him?" Masefield said eagerly.

"For a minute or two, yes."

Straightening, Ramon turned to glare at his boss, whose till then grave expression had finally begun to relax into a hint of a smile. "What did you talk about?" Masefield said.

James recounted the brief conversation, concluding with Philpot's promise to return with Bel's 'stuff' around ten-thirty.

"What 'stuff?'"

"He didn't say, specifically, but he's been her supplier for years."

"Supplier...as in *drugs*?" Ramon's morning-long fury was rapidly dissolving into stupefaction. "Owen *Philpot*?"

"Yes, Detective, Owen Philpot. As in pot, coke, speed, pain-killers... name your poison. Bel used to call him—" James's voice cracked. "She used to call him 'dear old goofy Pill-pot...'"

Masefield handed James some tissues from his back pocket so James could wipe his nose. Ramon emitted an indecipherable grunt. It was only when James was looking around for a garbage can in which to toss the used tissue that he noticed the "I told you so" look on Masefield's face, directed at Ramon, and finally realized why this particular bit of information seemed so important to the two policemen: James *was* their prime suspect, due in large part to Owen Philpot's identification; but Little Mister Pill-pot had apparently not made it clear that he had actually *spoken* to James Ireton the night before, probably because it would have revealed the substance of their conversation and Philpot's on-the-side drug trafficking. Perhaps it had also just occurred to Det. Ramon Cruz that it was unlikely that the ruthless murderer of Bel Gunderson would have allowed himself to 'chat' with a neighbor in front of her door right before he slaughtered her.

Finding no trash can to hand, James dropped the clump of tissue on the table top. "Look," he said to Ramon, sniffling, "I'm guilty of more crimes than even you can guess, but I'm not guilty of murdering Bel Gunderson. If I murdered anything it was her soul, three years ago. But as I well know from my own experience at SANA, no one gets thrown into jail these materialistic days for killing souls. And as for quaint little Mr. Owen Philpot, I should think a natural-born busybody like him would have a rather exact memory of our brief conversation. In fact, I imagine that if you had pressed him half as hard as you've been pressing me this morning, you might have even discovered whether Philpot saw Bel, alive and well, when he delivered her 'stuff' long after I left."

"Let's follow up on that," Masefield agreed.

Ramon glared at his boss. "Ireton's still got plenty to explain," he grumbled before fixing his flinty turquoise eyes again on James. "At least let's cut the shit about your not knowing Candace Duffy. Which prick was yours in that video?"

Declining even to attempt an answer to such a question, James rubbed the back of his aching neck, which Ramon had come close to breaking the night before, and shook his head.

Ramon drew a four-by-six photograph of Candace Duffy out of his breast pocket and held it up within inches of James's face. "How did you meet her? Through Lanciano or through Bonsoir Escorts?"

James gripped the arms of his chair. "Look," he said tightly, "after what I did last night to Lupe, I'm not prepared to launch defenses of myself about much of anything. All I can say is, I was not and never have been in a pornographic movie, certainly not in *The Rape of Lucrece*, and did not know Candace Duffy. Let alone have sex with her, either personally or professionally, in public or in private. I've never even been to Racine!"

"Look at the picture, dammit! You know this woman, I know you do!"

James shoved aside Ramon's hand. "I tell you I've never met her, even if—" James hesitated, his jaw working.

"What?" Masefield said, leaning forward.

James released a sigh. "Okay, I admit I feel I ought to know her, or that I've seen her somewhere. But my God, I haven't slept with so many women that I can't remember their names or what they look like! I tell you, I didn't know her! If she looks familiar, it must be because I've been seeing her picture in the paper! Or in Lanciano's bathroom!"

Before Ramon could approach the subject from another angle, there was a series of raps on the door, followed by the entrance of a smallish woman in a cheap polyester suit. The woman requested that Masefield, whom she addressed as "Professor," follow her outside. Masefield disappeared behind the door, leaving James and Ramon to catch their breaths, drink their awful coffee, and eye one another in an intensely uncomfortable silence.

Masefield returned a few moments later, and not a moment too soon, carrying a manila folder, which he promptly flipped open and shoved under Ramon's nose.

Ramon followed the direction of Masefield's pointing finger. A few seconds later his mouth slipped open. "I don't believe it!" he cried.

"What is it?" James said to Masefield, who had stepped over to give him a hearty clap on the shoulder.

"I'm sorry, son, I know this has been hell on wheels, but we've had to do our job." Masefield nodded at the folder, which Ramon was still reading with the frowning concentration of a pre-schooler sounding out his first vowels. "It's the autopsy report. For one thing, Miss Gunderson's blood type does not match any of the stains on your clothes. Except the jacket of course."

James closed his eyes, breathing as if for the first time in many hours.

"For another thing, Miss Gunderson died between midnight and one-thirty a.m. That is, midnight at the earliest. You had already been at Lupe's for almost two hours by then. Last and best of all, at least for you, we finally located the resident of the ground floor apartment outside of which Gunderson's body was found after it was dropped from her balcony." Masefield clucked. "It seems that residents of Jackbourn Towers are not supposed to keep pets. Which is why Mr. Schwinn took his Yorkie for a walk on the sly a little after one a.m. The dog peed right there by the bushes where the body was found, and Schwinn swears up and down that the body wasn't there then, nor when he came back from the walk fifteen minutes later. In other words, the body had to have been dropped shortly before it was found at one-thirty-five by another resident. You were already at Lupe's three-and-a-half hours by then. It puts you clean out of the ball park."

James's hands were shaking so badly by this time that he had to set his half-empty coffee cup, which he had just picked up, back on the table.

"Tell you what," Masefield added, awarding Ramon a similar back-slap, though this one looked more like one of sympathy than congratulation, "obviously James is a free man now, but I'd like him to come with us to take a look at Gunderson's apartment." He turned to James. "Besides the killer and maybe Philpot, you were the last person to see Isabel Gunderson alive. I need you to take a look at the scene and tell us if anything's changed since last night. Oh, and I believe your friend Sigur brought you a change of clothes."

It couldn't have been later than three in the afternoon, James thought, steeling himself to face the crime scene as he trailed Masefield and Ramon past the threshold of Bel's apartment, but the shades, pulled down tight over the windows, lent the place an impression of deepest midnight. A fetid smell lingered in the room, mingling with the more familiar scents of clove smoke, marijuana, and Narcisse. Masefield flicked a switch on the wall. Several lamps came on.

"Looks like a Caribbean knocking-shop," Ramon commented with a smirk.

James, his insides grinding and too tired for any more verbal sparring, swallowed a wave of nausea and looked around. He noticed the tiger-striped sofa first: the cushions were gone. There were splotches of dried blood all over the back and sides, and on the carpet beneath, portions of which appeared to have been scissored out. A trail of blood smeared the remaining carpet from the sofa to the balcony doors. His hand over his mouth, James pointed, speechless.

"We took the cushions and some of the rug for lab analysis," Masefield explained. "He killed her on the sofa, then dragged her body to the balcony."

"Did you sit on the sofa last night?" Ramon asked. "We'll need to know so we can separate any physical evidence from you."

His hand still over his mouth, James shook his head and pointed at the rattan chair. "Only there," he gasped out.

"Did you walk around—use the john or anything?"

James cleared his throat and wiped his hand over his beading forehead. "Um, well, I walked in the door of course, but Bel was still in her bedroom. So I went over there to the buffet." James turned toward the spot where he had stood the night before, and blinked: the picture that had been above the buffet was gone, leaving a gaping white hole in the room's chaos of color. James waved at the blank wall. "Why on earth did you take the picture?"

"We didn't take any pictures," Ramon said, looking at his boss. "We found an empty frame in the bedroom."

"What was up there?" Masefield asked James.

"A reproduction of a Diego Rivera mural. Bel told me an 'admirer' had given it to her."

"What did it look like?"

"Uh, well, it was an Aztec scene, or so I presumed. You know, pre-Columbian Mexico. It was colorful, in a primitive folk-style…I would have called it beautiful, even. Except for the pyramid in one corner, dripping with blood from human sacrifices."

"Say, *what*?" Masefield exclaimed. Ramon, who had been scribbling furiously in his notepad, looked up as well.

James was surprised by Masefield's reaction, but could make nothing of it. "The Aztecs had a very advanced, orderly civilization," he said with a shrug. "But they fed their gods human hearts, occasionally by the thousands.

I read an article about it recently, in a pamphlet Fr. Bricusse gave me before he died. Not that uncommon a practice in ancient civilizations, I understand, but the Aztecs seem to have taken it to an unusual degree."

"Professor!" Ramon barked at Masefield, who had unconsciously laid one hand over his heart and opened his mouth as if he were about to speak.

Masefield looked at Ramon, and closed his mouth. James, who didn't want to think he was correctly filling in the blanks of Masefield's silence, was more than content to abandon the subject as well.

"What else do you see that's different?" Ramon said with a take-charge demeanor.

"Um, it was very hot last night, and smoky. Bel was chain-smoking those Indonesian clove cigarettes. Djarums, I believe they're called." He pointed at the coffee table, now almost bare. "There was a hideous ashtray there, a plastic skull's head. At least I assumed it was plastic. It was overflowing with cigarette butts."

"All Djarums?"

"Mostly. But there were also a few joints, I think. And some Players."

"Gunderson smoked Players, too?"

"No, just Djarums."

"Do you smoke Players?"

"Used to. Haven't done since college. God, I could use a cigarette right now."

"Players are an English brand, aren't they? Masefield said, reaching into the pocket of his overcoat to offer James a Marlboro Light, which James took gratefully. Masefield lit James's cigarette, then one for himself. "Do you know anyone who smokes them?"

James thought a minute. "No," he said finally, rubbing his watering eyes and suppressing a cough. "All the smokers I know buy American brands."

"Anything else missing or different?" Ramon asked.

James shuddered a bit from the swift kick of nicotine, and gestured again at the coffee table. "There were books and magazines there, and Tarot cards spread out. Also a small silver tray with some coke in it. And no, I didn't do any, Ramon, to answer your next question. I've long since decided my brain chemistry's scrambled enough as it is, thank you very much."

Masefield seemed to be thinking out loud. "So he took the teddy, the picture, the ashtray…maybe even the Tarot cards and the coke." He gave a perplexed shake of his head. "The guy must have been hauling a steamer trunk when he left here." Masefield turned again to James. "Anything else different or missing? Anything at all."

"It's certainly a lot cleaner," James said. Except for the…all the blood."

"What do you mean, 'cleaner?'" Ramon asked.

"The place was a shambles last night. Dusty, grimy, stuff piled everywhere, plates of leftovers on every surface…" James gestured at the buffet. "There were dead roses in that bowl last night. It's been emptied and washed." He bent over and ran his fingers across the top of the coffee table. "The place is still dusty, I guess, but a lot more tidy."

"That's fingerprint powder," Ramon said. "It was spotless when we came in last night. Except for all the blood."

"Would it be like Gunderson to suddenly go on a cleaning spree right after you left?" Masefield asked incredulously.

"She wouldn't have had the time!" Ramon exclaimed.

James took another drag on the cigarette and noticed that his hand was shaking again. "Are you saying your people didn't tidy up?"

"We don't get paid to be Merry Maids," Ramon snapped, then turned to Masefield. "The couple living in the apartment beneath this one heard a vacuum cleaner running up here a little before one a.m. It woke them up."

"Gunderson was dead by then," Masefield announced. "The killer was cleaning up after himself. Did you get the vacuum bag?"

"The canister was empty. It wasn't in the garbage chute, either."

Masefield looked as if he were about to curse, but refrained. "James," he said, after pondering the situation a moment longer, "you said in your statement that you thought Bel Gunderson lifted your keys the afternoon she came to your office."

"She must have done," James said, "to get into Lupe's flat. To plant the CD and steal her journal. It's the only way she could have known some of the things she said last night. Lupe's journal, and the SANA report inside it."

"Only problem with that theory," Ramon offered, "is that we didn't find either your keys or Lupe's journal in here."

Frowning deeply, Masefield stepped over to the buffet to stub out his cigarette in the empty flower bowl. "You didn't happen to run into Peter Krato that afternoon, did you, or anyone from SANA?"

James joined Masefield at the buffet to extinguish his cigarette as well. "No, not that I recall."

"How about Jack Sigur or Franco Lanciano?"

James shrugged. "I saw them both, at the Institute. In fact, Jack stopped by my office when I was talking to Bel. That was probably when Bel swiped the keys off my desk, while my back was turned."

"Is that so," Masefield said, rubbing his chin.

The next morning, no more rested than he was the day before even though he had slept, or tried to sleep, in his own bed, James climbed the stairs of the *Journal Sentinel* building downtown, his body aching cruelly from Ramon's professionally-applied beating, his senses brutalized by a humiliating strip-search and hours of grueling interrogation in a smelly, windowless room the size of a broom closet; and last but not least, by the grisly visit to Bel's apartment. Never in his darkest moments had James ever thought anyone could survive a nightmare like this; could so much as find the will to roll out of bed in the morning. Or resist the temptation to end it all as swiftly as possible. The only thing that prevented him from taking the latter course himself was the certain knowledge that he would be buying his own relief at Lupe's expense, and he had already hurt her more than he could bear to think.

His sluggish thoughts moving at a glacial pace, James circumscribed his dread of the upcoming and unavoidable interview with Matt Cruz, at least as well as his ragged condition and faltering courage would permit, by reminding himself that he deserved everything he had gotten thus far and was about to get. And a good deal more.

The newsroom was a large open space on the fourth floor of the *Journal Sentinel* building, a chaos of workstations and computer terminals pushed together back-to-back. James was about to ask someone for directions to Matt Cruz's desk when he felt eyes on him and turned. Matt Cruz stood at one corner of the hallway, glaring at him with a hefty measure of rage and more than a little disbelief.

Matt cocked his head in a gesture that James understood to mean, "Follow me, you sonuvabitch."

James shadowed Matt's brisk steps around the corner into a small, one-window lounge. Matt shut the door behind them and motioned James to sit. His side throbbing, James lowered himself gingerly into an ugly Naugahyde chair, his elbows on his quivering knees. Unable to look Lupe's father in the face, he fixed his red-veined eyes on Matt's black wingtips, pacing the utility carpeting in front of him. Matt got straight to the point.

"I want you to give me one good reason why I shouldn't break your goddamned neck right here and now."

James licked his swollen lips. "Other than the fact that you'd probably be sent to prison for it, however undeservedly, I haven't any reasons to offer."

The wingtips paused. "I heard two different versions of what happened. One from Lupe and one from Ramon."

"Ramon's version would be closer to the truth. Lupe dips all my faults in her affections."

"James, we've welcomed you into our family—"

"You've been more than gracious—"

"Shut up, you—!"

James didn't understand the rest of Matt's harangue because it was in a blazing jumble of rapid-fire Spanish; but without warning, James felt himself being yanked up by the lapels of his overcoat and slammed against the nearest wall. He turned over a lamp on the way down to the floor.

A few seconds later, the door flew open and a young woman in gold-rimmed bifocals rushed into the room.

"Oh, for goodness…Matt, I heard such a racket!"

"I fell," James offered, brushing bits of broken glass from his corduroy slacks as he levered himself to his feet, wincing against the pain in his side. "Of course, I'll be happy to pay for any of the damages—"

"I said, shut up!" Matt yelled. "Dammit, Harriet, I need some privacy here!"

The befuddled woman fled in a flurry of embarrassment, leaving Matt Cruz to mumble a gritty apology before resuming his tense circuit on the carpeting.

James once again eased himself into the chair.

"Look, I can't tell my daughter what to do anymore," Matt said. "She swears up and down that you've never touched her before, and that there were extraordinary circumstances that night, and that it was a freak occurrence that couldn't possibly happen again." Matt's shoes came to rest again in James's peripheral vision. "But I want to hear it from you. I want to know that nothing like this will ever happen again! Ever!"

Bracing himself on the arms of the chair, James looked up. "I know this will sound hollow to you, but I do...I do...love Lupe. At least, well, as best I can. Which I realize isn't very well...but that's not the reason I've come. The reason I've come, Sir, is to assure you, in person, that I won't be troubling Lupe much longer. That I intend to break it off as soon as I can. I mean our engagement. If she doesn't break it off first, of course."

"She won't break it off," Matt almost growled.

"Yes...yes, I guess I knew that." James brought his hand down over his face as if to draw a veil over his pain. "Actually, I was hoping you might speak to her about that. It occurred to me that she might face the facts about me more clearly if they came from you. You see, I can't seem to make her understand that we can't just...start over. That I can't permit myself even to hope for that. I know what I must do, it's just...well, I can't see my way to doing it just yet. Not as long as Barry DeBrun's still at large."

Matt grunted. "What the hell's he got to do with this, other than that my daughter seems to have an unnatural talent for attracting abusive men?"

James bit the inside of his cheek until he tasted his own coppery blood.

"Look, that was out of line. I've got things of my own to deal with here."

James opened his hands. "On the contrary, that's precisely my point, you've got right to it. Lupe won't be told how much alike we are. But I'm afraid she'd be alone too much if I broke it off now, and I guess I won't be easy about that, leaving her alone I mean, until DeBrun's been put away. After that, after they catch him...well, I give you my word, I'll vanish without a trace. As quickly and quietly as I can manage it."

Matt's mouth puckered into a curl of doubt.

"Of course I'll gladly pay for any expenses incurred in the wedding arrangements, just to keep up appearances. If Lupe won't be persuaded to call it off, that is. That might at least get her through the term."

When Matt Cruz still didn't have anything to say in response to this unusual offer, James pushed himself to his feet and stepped to the door. Leaning against it, his right foot pawed the carpet as if he were a wounded bull, preparing to charge or flop to its knees. "I won't insult you with an attempt at an apology," he added, before pulling open the door and stepping out.

"*Madre de Díos*," Matt whispered to the empty air.

James's next stop was the Police Administration Building on State Street. As perversely cheerful this cold and overcast November morning as James himself was morose and a little crazy, Calvin Masefield shepherded James into his office with a slap on the back that jarred James's sensitive insides and motioned for him to sit.

"A bit early for you, isn't it?" James said, unable to produce the requisite smile of greeting as he took the chair in front of Masefield's desk.

Masefield blew out a puff of air. "Until we put this one down, the whole squad's on overtime. The higher-ups are even discussing the possibility of a task force. Coffee?"

"Please. By the way, I wanted to thank you for the referral to Dr. Simon. He seems like a good man. Not as eager as some to push the pills."

"You've seen him already?" Masefield fixed their cups from a hotpot in the corner, under a shelf where volumes of the *Law Enforcement Bulletin* and *Crime Control Digest* were arranged with military precision.

James shrugged. "Talked to him on the phone. My first appointment's next week." Nudging the thought from his mind that he had little reason to believe he would live long enough to keep the appointment, James cleared his throat. "So, um, what did you want to see me about?"

Masefield stirred some creamer into James's cup and handed it to him, a faint smile playing around the corners of his mouth. "After a little, uh, persuasion from Detective Cruz, Mr. Owen Philpot knuckled under and corroborated your story from A to Zed. According to his amended statement, he returned to Gunderson's apartment at ten-twenty with a large bottle of Vicoden. She paid him in cash. Scared the daylights out of him, too, because she insisted they conduct the transaction in the hall."

"Peculiar," James agreed.

"Philpot was pretty sure she had a visitor inside, someone she didn't want him to see. In fact, he thought it was you and said so. To which Gunderson replied—" Masefield pantomimed quotation marks. "'—Ireton left a while back. And after the number I did on him, I'll wager you a pound of Pure that they'll find his little Mick-Spic floating in the harbor before the week's out.' End quote, as nearly as Philpot could remember it. The 'Mick-Spic' part was a new one on me, but Philpot was emphatic about it."

James considered his coffee.

"Fortunately for Philpot, he brought three other people home with him for a little marijuana party of his own, or he'd have been under suspicion himself."

"Odd," James said at last. "Jack Sigur always insisted Bel was in love with me. Funny kind of love."

"Funny kind of love you showed your woman the other night, too," Masefield observed. "But that's just the beginning." The lieutenant reached for a manila folder on his desk, flipped it open and pulled out a sheet of paper. "Take a gander at this."

The paper was a photocopy of a Bible page from *The Book of Isaiah*. There was a passage circled in red—*How art thou fallen O Lucifer* it began—and a handwritten note in the margin: "*Introibo ad altare Dei,*" which James recognized as the opening line of James Joyce's *Ulysses*. The Latin phrase was followed by a signature in the same handwriting: *Lenny Swiatko, Jr.*

"Except for the marginal note and the signature," James said, a note of wonder in his voice, "it looks exactly like the first letter I got back in September. The exact same passage…even the precise way it's circled in red." He handed it back to Masefield. "Why is Lenny Swiatko's name on it?"

"It's his handwriting. This was his suicide note."

James sat back. "I don't understand."

"Neither do I, but I'm beginning to have a few guesses. For instance, neither Lenny nor his mother owned a King James Bible. They're Catholics, after all. But his Mom found two more pages similar to this one in Lenny's room after he died. Since we don't have your original letters to compare them with, we can't be sure, but I think that whoever's been sending these to you, was also sending them to Lenny. And maybe for the same reason."

"But what reason could that be?"

"Both of you had griefs against Peter Krato and SANA, and both of you knew enough to do some major damage if you wanted to. I think the sender wanted to scare you off." Masefield's eyebrows gathered. "In Lenny's case, the letters may have worked better than anyone planned. Besides the bit about Lucifer falling, one of the other pages was that passage from the apostle Paul about *meeting the Lord in the air.*"

James winced. "Lupe told me about your connection to Lenny Swiatko. I'm sorry."

Masefield looked away. "I completely forgot about the kid," he said, letting the sentence hang there between them for a moment before rapping his knuckles on his desktop and adding, "But that's not your concern. What is your concern is that we got into Miss Gunderson's home computer. Seems she'd been writing some risky e-mails the last while." The lieutenant swept another sheet of paper from the folder and held it out to James.

It looked to be the printout of an e-mail, headers and all, dated October 31. By the time James was in the middle of the second paragraph, his hand was shaking so badly that he had to lay the paper on Masefield's desk to finish it:

> Happy Halloween, Pietro! I've been following the articles in the paper about the Archdiocesan investigation…*Double, double toil and trouble, fire burn and cauldron bubble!* So sad to hear about your troubles, but to paraphrase another historical conflict with religious overtones, *your danger is my opportunity.* On this Rock, I will hatch my nest egg.
>
> To be brief, I need more money. Let's make it five grand. Not only has Stark dumped me, but I've had a lot of medical bills of late, and I have nothing to lose now by letting the world know—and James, and the Archdiocese—that you put me up to seducing him, three years ago in exchange for the Stark contract. Hey, it took me months of hard work and all my finely honed skills to finally get him prone! With

any luck, I might even manage it again, if I could only separate him from his Virgin Queen. You'd like that, wouldn't
you? I know about her connections to the Archdiocese, and
so far, your boys have gotten nowhere trying to scare her off.
Well, she'll find out her mistake, soon enough, if I know
General Ireton.

Pietro, I gave you plenty of ammo to help you keep Ireton's
reputation in the mud, and his sweet lips zipped. I need
some motivation now to keep mine similarly sealed.

Your creature in the Lord,
(Oofdah!) Jezebel

"It never occurred to me," James whispered, lifting his head at last.

"Krato's alibi the night of Gunderson's murder is reliant on the testimony of his son Richard," Masefield said, "and you can guess about how much
I think that's worth. We also know that Gunderson made a cash deposit of
five thousand dollars into her checking account on November 4th, which is
about what you'd expect with a blackmail payoff. It'll take a little time, but
we'll soon find out if there was a similar withdrawal of funds from any of
Krato's or SANA's accounts at the same time."

Suddenly too hot, James unbuttoned his flannel shirtsleeves and rolled
them up above his elbows. "Are you going to arrest him?" he asked, getting
up to orbit Masefield's desk in an enervated half-circle, back and forth.

Masefield grunted. "Arrest him for what, hypocrisy? Look, we've got
a motive for murder, sure, but not necessarily *this* kind of murder. C'mon,
settle down, have a seat there. You won't help either of us by stroking out, or
going ballistic on Peter Krato. And in case you were thinking of dropping by
SANA house for a little nose-to-nose with the man, he took off this morning."

James ceased pacing long enough to say, "Krato left town?"

"Yup. Seems the Archbishop of Milwaukee has been a little disapproving of late, and almost half of SANA's members have taken the hint and
moved out. Richard says his dad's trying to fix things by shmoozing with
higher-ups in Rome." Masefield chuckled. "Lord knows I don't know much
about the Catholic Church, but my guess is we'll be hearing those Vatican
doors slamming all the way across the Atlantic."

Finally seating himself again, James found a minimal outlet for his frustration by rat-a-tat-tatting his fingers on the sole of his boot.

Masefield pointed a pen at James's scowling face. "There's still DeBrun
and his video," he reminded him. "And we can't forget Lanciano's missing
photograph of Candace Duffy, either. 'Course, Lanciano swears up and
down that he never knew Duffy by name, and didn't remember her as one of
three Bonsoir models he hired a couple of years ago to pose for shots on the
beach." Giving a quick shake of his head, Masefield grunted and fell silent.

"What is it?" James said. "I can see the wheels turning."

Masefield leaned forward on his elbows. "If I end up telling you way more than I should, it's because I think you can help me. But you've got to promise me that what we talk about in here you'll keep to yourself. That includes Lupe Cruz and her clever but ornery big brother, understand?"

James shrugged. "I guess you know what you're doing."

Masefield folded his hands. "First some brute facts. Both Duffy and Gunderson were savagely sodomized. And both women had a crude mark carved on their foreheads and hands. Sound familiar to a preacher's son?"

"The mark of the Beast in *Revelations*...can't remember the chapter all of a sudden."

"Chapter thirteen. Believe it or not, this kind of screwy religious ideation is not uncommon in brutal sex crimes. In this case, the 'mark' was a letter. Care to take a guess what it was?"

"Haven't a clue."

"The letter J."

"J?"

"Yep. J as in...?"

"Jezebel?" James suggested, thinking of the e-mail. "The biblical Jezebel was thrown from her window. And dogs licked her blood."

"Why do you suppose Gunderson called herself 'Jezebel' in that e-mail to Krato? Was it a nickname?"

James hesitated. "I've heard a few people use it."

"People such as...?"

"Okay, Jack Sigur. But he always meant it in jest. He also called her 'Madame Pythoness' and 'Belzebub' and 'She Who Must Be Obeyed.' Look, Jack and Bel were chums."

"Tell me about Jack Sigur. What are his sexual preferences?"

"Men," James said emphatically.

"Exactly. So howsabout 'J' as in 'James?'"

James was incredulous. "Then why would he rape and kill Bel?"

Masefield leaned forward. "We're dealing with pathology here. If it's a pathology about you, for instance, then it could be the killer's way of getting at you, or getting a piece of you, by taking something that was once yours. Without killing you outright, that is, which would end all his fun. That might even explain, in a twisted way, the killer's handling of Fr. Bricusse."

"Your theory has a flaw," James said, feeling panic tightening his chest, "and her name is Candace Duffy. She was never 'mine,' as you call it."

"But you admitted she looked familiar. There may be a connection you're not remembering."

"Then let me put it this way." James slapped his palm on Masefield's tabletop. "Jack Sigur couldn't kill anyone if he tried."

"Take it from me, James, there's no such critter. There's also nothing much recognizable about murderers until you actually know they're murderers. Then you look back and say, good God, why didn't I notice this, or notice that?"

"I am not what I am…"

"Huh? Oh, yeah, good ol' Iago." Masefield snapped his fingers. "Fascinating play, by the way. Thanks for letting me borrow it. My wife and I watched the video last week—" Masefield faltered, then rose slowly to his feet.

The look on Masefield's face almost pulled James to his feet as well. "What is it, Cal?"

Masefield began snapping his fingers as if to keep time with his thoughts. "Iago got his wife to steal Desdemona's handkerchief, then planted it in another man's apartment to make Othello believe that Desdemona was unfaithful to him. Then Iago killed his own wife to shut her up. In our case, someone— *our* Iago—got Bel Gunderson to steal your keys, then used them to plant your CD in Lupe Cruz's apartment. Then he killed Bel Gunderson, in part to keep her quiet, in part to turn the screws on you. Maybe even set you up for the murder." Masefield fixed his eyes on James and whistled. "Son, somebody's done *Othello* on you, but good. I'd bet my paycheck on it."

James sank into the armchair, overwhelmed by the scenario Masefield had just laid out for him. "In Shakespeare's play," he said finally, his thoughts once again as sluggish as he words, "Iago was Othello's most trusted officer. Someone he believed to be a friend."

"Which leads me to wonder, which one of your nearest and dearest is also a sexual psychopath, out for your skin for good measure?" Masefield winced. "Or should I say, out for your heart."

James's gray eyes glittered with fear. "Lupe's my heart."

Chapter Eleven:
Human Mediations

Our indiscretion sometime serves us well
When our deep plots do pall; and that should learn us
There's a divinity that shapes our ends,
Rough-hew them how we will...

Shakespeare, *Hamlet*

The news media were feeding like piranhas on the juicier leavings of the Bel Gunderson murder case. Reporters and editorialists commented volubly on its similarities to the Duffy and Bricusse cases, the possible connections to the Chicago-Milwaukee mob war, and, after the connection to *l'affaire* DeBrun was brought to light, the possible involvement of James Ireton and the Heisler Institute. Since he hadn't been charged, James was never mentioned by name, only described as "a Heisler Institute student and citizen of Great Britain." Unfortunately, since James was the only man in Milwaukee who fit that description, no one at the Institute was in any doubt as to the identity of the much-discussed suspect. Masefield neglected to mention to the press that though James was on record as a "person of interest" in the case, he had a firm alibi and was no longer a suspect. This tactic even surprised the otherwise unforgiving Ramon Cruz, who queried his boss as to his reason for allowing the finger of common opinion to be pointed at the innocent Englishman.

"Because if I'm right," Masefield replied, "and everything that's happened these last three months is connected, then our killer already has James Ireton in the cross-hairs. Right now we need to keep him there."

Rumors floated freely, as if carried on a lake breeze. James's entry through the main doors of the Heisler Institute the Wednesday after Bel's murder elicited an unmistakable and unsettling response: he was being watched, discussed, shunned. It was a visceral, almost tangible sensation, as if the fabulous Heisler Institute building, which had felt so hollow to James in the weeks after Bricusse's death, had in the two months since become infested with some obscure but distinctly malevolent spirit. It was everything James could do not to look over his shoulder as he crossed the atrium en route to the stairwell and the fifth floor Shakespeare seminar.

A medley of student chatter was killed the instant James stepped through the door, and many pairs of eyes trained on him like rifle barrels. But at least everyone was there, James thought, more than a little surprised. He took his usual seat next to Lupe, just in time to hear Jack ask her, "Say, what happened to your face, girl?"

"Oh, uh, I ra-ra-ran into a wall," Lupe lied, her cheeks aflame with the blush of an unpracticed liar.

Jack looked unconvinced in any case, and when he spotted James's equally battered condition, he did a pie-eyed double take. "And who hung the mouse on you, bub?" he asked. "Or did you run into a wall, too?"

"More or less," James said.

In the two excruciating academic hours that ensued, the discombobulated substitute lecturer spent the better part of the class time with one wary eye on James, as if she thought the notorious Englishman were going to whip out a dagger and assault her in the middle of their half-hearted discussion of Spenserian allegory as a narrative strategy. Nor did she know what to say when Richard Krato came right out and declared that he didn't think it was proper to be holding class four days after the brutal murder of a classmate. "Former classmate," Mitch reminded his confrère, setting aside his copy of Georges Bataille's *Theory of Religion* long enough to brush a golden lock of curly hair away from his doughy face, "whom you otherwise regarded about as highly as a wagonload of chickenshit." Jack had seemed the only one of the group not too stunned to speak, and had practically taken over the class.

As they were all leaving at ten to three, and having deflected Lupe's quiet invitation to go for a beer, James was surprised to see Dr. Franco Lanciano standing in the gallery just outside the door, observing the students' exits with silent solemnity. It suddenly occurred to James that he hadn't seen or heard anything from the Heisler Institute Director in the four days since Bel's murder; not even to wish him, albeit ironically, a happy birthday. It was an uncharacteristic silence from someone, however annoying at times, whom James had come to regard as a friend.

James waited until everyone had left—Lupe took off with Jack—then motioned Lanciano into the seminar room. "What's on your mind, Franco?" he said, shutting the door behind them. He yanked up a chair and straddled it. "Might as well out with it. It can't get much worse for me at this point."

Seating himself, Lanciano folded one slender leg over the other, apparently in no mood to sympathize.

"James," he said in a businesslike tone, "I have always supported you, you know that. Even when some members of our faculty labeled you ambitious, arrogant, and insubordinate."

"So you have. But...?"

"But as I sat down to the breakfast table this morning with yet another newspaper editorial about our 'troubled Institute' staring me in the face, I was suddenly reminded of something you said the day of Arthur's funeral. You said, 'Very strange things have been happening around here of late.' And how true it was. Thing is, it finally dawned on me that, one way or the other, you've been at the heart of every strange and awful thing that's happened here since the term began. To be honest, I've been asking myself all day if I really know you."

James turned his brooding attention to the window overlooking the frosty lake. The fact that Lanciano's words were almost identical to ones spoken recently by Calvin Masefield was doing nothing to console him.

"Oh, Adèle thinks I'm over-reacting," Lanciano continued. "She always takes up for you. But do you know I ran into Bo Jeffrey yesterday, and when I asked him where his charming sister had gone off to — I had expected to see her in my *quattrocento* course this term — Bo said to me, 'She's transferred to Marquette. And if you want to know why, go ask that prick, Ireton.'"

James scraped his fingers through his hair and stood up, his supply of combative energy long since spent. "Don't fret yourself," he said with quiet resignation. "I'll be out of here faster than you can imagine." With that, James shoved his hands in his pockets, veered on his heel, and exited the room.

It had been over ten days since James's brutal assault and Bel Gunderson's murder, but Lupe was growing more, rather than less, troubled. First, James was making excuses every time she tried to see him. The one time she had managed to get her melancholy fiancé alone for a total of five minutes, he had spent at least four of them trying to talk her into a postponement of the wedding. She had refused to consider the idea...unless, she added hastily, it was *his* desire. He had assured her with even more haste that it was not, not at all, that he loved her more than life itself — yadda yadda yadda. It was just, he had declared with an uncharacteristic lack of fluency, that he didn't think that it was "um, well, a good time to, um, well, make long-range plans, what with, you know, all that's going on...right now." Even in that moment of fumbling semi-honesty, it was as if James was only half there; where the rest of him was Lupe couldn't begin to guess.

To be sure, something had broken in James that awful night; but Lupe was also convinced that it was something that had wanted breaking — an old fracture of the soul which had never healed, or healed crookedly, and which had needed to be re-broken before it could be set properly. Unfortunately, all James could see right now was that he was broken, not that he might finally have a real chance at healing.

Of course, the other possible explanation, Lupe reminded herself, was that she was utterly mistaken, and what was appearing to her, these last ten days, as a losing battle against debilitating guilt, was in reality nothing more than a predictable lapse in James's notoriously short erotic attention-span.

On this particular Thursday evening the week before Thanksgiving, James and Lupe were walking home from the last of their scheduled classes in Natural Family Planning, their desultory conversation intersected by the sort of uncomfortable silences that only served to reinforce Lupe's anxieties about the nature of her fiancé's true feelings.

"You know," she said suddenly after one such silence, gripping his hand all the tighter as they approached the steps to her yard, "I have a b-b-beef with these classes."

"And what is that, love," he said, so quietly that she almost couldn't hear him.

"Well, they spent so much time on the family planning stuff—you know, female reproductive cycles and all that—that I never felt I learned much about men and how their bodies work. I'd really like to learn more about men."

In what was obviously a spontaneous reaction, his first in almost two weeks, James grabbed her around her waist and lifted her off the ground, as if about to twirl her around in an overabundance of happiness; but then a second later he set her down again and stepped back. "Well, now," he said, the cheerful tenor of his voice at variance with the gray pain in his face, "I almost taught you more about that than you ever wanted to know, didn't I?"

Lupe stamped her foot. "Blast it, this has got to stop. I won't break you know, I'm not a piece of glass. If you're having second thoughts about everything, I can take the truth!"

Lupe's pleas were interrupted by a rushing sound, like leaves scattering in a gust of wind. A shadow seemed to step between James and the light. Then there was a *thud* just before James collapsed on the sidewalk, almost knocking Lupe over on his way down. Lupe let out a cry of confusion as a pair of strong hands clapped around her waist, lifting her off the ground. Her arms vised against her body, she kicked back with her hard-soled shoes, eliciting a grunt from her attacker.

"Goddammit," the voice growled in her ear, "quit fighting me or I'll blow Ireton's head off!" To illustrate his words, Barry DeBrun pointed a gun barrel down at a spot between James's shuttered eyes. Lupe's imminent scream was squelched to a gurgle.

Leaving James's inert body folded on the sidewalk, Barry dragged Lupe roughly up the steps to the yard, then around the house and through the wooden gate that led to Rosarita Cruz's garden. They crashed like a pair of drunks through the beds of winter-dead flowers, then through the back gate into the alley where Barry's old red Mustang was idling next to the garage. The rusty passenger's side door squealed open as he shoved her inside. Waving the gun in her face, he commanded her to take the wheel, and climbed in after.

She turned to look at him: one strand of dark hair fell limply over Barry DeBrun's pale green eyes, which hued a little to yellow in the alley lamplights, making him look even more perfectly nightmarish to her than her nightmarish memories from seven years ago. She clapped her hand over her mouth, instantly nauseated.

He thrust the gun barrel between her breasts. "Throw up on me this time, and that's all she wrote. Understand?"

She swallowed several times, and nodded.

"Well, then, let's go!" Barry said, as if they were off for a ride in the country on a Sunday afternoon.

She hadn't driven a stick in years and the transmission groaned loudly as she put the car into first. When she asked where they were going Barry informed her, keeping the gun leveled at her, that he wanted her to drive to Lake Park. "Take the Newberry entrance," he added. "I'm looking for a nice quiet spot where no one will disturb a couple of old flames, necking in the moonlight. Just like old times, eh Lu?"

She drove slowly but her mind raced. Neither of them spoke until she crossed the Lake Drive intersection and entered the park.

"So has Ireton taken that cast-iron cherry of yours yet?" When she refused to answer, Barry put his left hand on her thigh and stroked it, moving upwards.

"You k-k-killed Bel Gunderson, didn't you?" Lupe blurted out. "And Candace Duffy!"

Barry snatched away his hand. "What the hell do you think I am, some kind of monster?"

The reaction had seemed so spontaneous, so genuinely indignant, that Lupe let out a humiliating sigh of relief; but she also had no time to sort it out, because the narrow asphalt road was coming to a dead-end. All she could remember at this moment was that there was a footpath near here that led to the bluffs, and beyond that, a steep vertical drop to Memorial Drive.

He waved the gun. "Pull over."

The gearshift creaked into neutral. He reached over and turned off the ignition, pocketed the keys, and took her arm to pull her out of the passenger side. He led her stumbling across the cold greensward, above which towering evergreens bent with the whipping wind.

They finally stopped at a park bench in a grove of trees that overlooked one of the park's many deep ravines. He sat down and pulled her on his lap, one powerful arm wrapping around her waist to secure her. "I've been waiting for this for seven years," he said, his lips brushing her hair.

"You k-killed Rygiel, didn't you?" she sputtered, yanking away her face.

"Jeez, you really need to think the worst of me!"

"Well, didn't you kill him?"

Barry waved, gun in hand. "The porky little asswipe pulled a gun on me. This one, as a matter of fact. He found out I was selling some videos on my own down in Chicago. I mean, it's not like I wanted to kill him, but it was him or me. And I promise you, he never felt a thing. I shot him a speedball. He was fucking flying when I heaved him over the cliff. He laughed all the way down to the beach."

Lupe shuddered at the vision of tubby little Norman Rygiel being rolled off a Lake Michigan bluff like an empty beer barrel. And yet suddenly she didn't feel quite so afraid. If Barry admitted to having killed Rygiel, she reasoned silently, then perhaps he wasn't lying when he denied killing Bel and Candace Duffy. "What about Fr. Bricusse?" she said cautiously.

The words weren't out a second before she felt his indignation in his stiffening thighs. "Jesus," Barry exclaimed, "I wouldn't kill a priest, I'm a Catholic!"

"What you did to Bel in that video, you didn't learn in parochial school!"

"Hey, what happened in that video wasn't my fault. I had the thing choreographed like a pansy ballet…everybody had rehearsed! But then Norm dragged in all these extras at the last minute—goons from the Nesterov mob who could barely speak English, guys I didn't know, masked, naked men all over the fucking room…it got out of hand! It was Norm and his beasty boys who started all the real violence. Don't you see, it was all supposed to be acting. But then I couldn't slow it down, and the camera was rolling…it got out of hand!" Barry's thin lips curved downwards in a childish pout. "What should you care about a common whore like Bel Gunderson anyway? Everybody knows she fucked your lover, her and a couple dozen other females I could name. That's what's been eating me alive for three months, Lu, the thought of you and that Limey prick. Why, he's no better than me, not one goddamned bit, but you were too all-fired superior to go with me!"

"You don't know him."

"Have you slept with him?"

"You almost k-k-killed me!"

"I was just trying to shut you up, calm you down! You were fucking hysterical!'

"You were trying to rape me!"

"Hey, you made me mad! Egging me on, then shutting me off!"

"I listen to your sob story for two lousy hours—how you've been misjudged and misunderstood, how you're really such a sweet, sensitive guy, and I'm obliged to go to b-b-bed with you?"

"I never had to rape anyone. That's bullshit."

She glared at him. "Oh yeah? How about that fifteen-year-old Potowatomi girl up in Carter?"

Barry cut away his eyes. "So I was a little high that night. And she reminded me of you. Things got out of hand."

"God, Barry, they'll be putting that on your gravestone: *Things got out of hand.*"

His rapid breaths turned to fog in the cold air. "How'd you hear about the Indian kid?"

"You hear things."

"Yeah, and I bet I know from where. So, Ramon Roberto Cruz is a fucking cop now. And Martin's a goddamned priest. Jesus. Your saintly brothers cost me two plastic surgeries, Lu, *two*. Don't try deny it was them, I'm not stupid. And you know what, I was even thinking of apologizing to you before they jumped me." He sniffed angrily. "I didn't forget about that night any too soon, let me tell you."

"So now I owe you, is that how it goes? So now you have the right to beat my fiancé over the head, k-k-kidnap me and rape me…is that how it works with you?"

"Is that what you think this is about?"

"What am I supposed to think!"

"Let me clue you in, babe, I've got my sources of information, too. There's a Calabresi contract out on me now, a contract with one whopping helluva difference."

"What 'd-d-difference?'"

"No innocent bystanders are to be touched. Can you fucking beat that? Never knew a Calabresi to be squeamish about collateral damage. But either way, you're my 'innocent bystander.' You know, my insurance policy. You're staying right beside me until I can figure a way to get out of this fucking town."

Lupe hugged herself for warmth. She wondered again what time it was, and whether a patrol car might be cruising the park soon. "Okay, so you killed Rygiel, but didn't kill Bel or Candace Duffy. Or Fr. Bricusse. But you were up there the night he died, weren't you?"

Barry swatted at the air with his gun hand. "Oh, sure. But I was on the other side of the atrium, by Max's office. Believe you me, when I saw the old man getting dropped, I got all my shit together and skedaddled as fast as I could load my briefcase."

Lupe gasped. "You mean you saw…my God, why didn't you tell the police?"

"Because I wasn't supposed to be up there in the first place!" Barry gave a shake of his head. "Jesus, you're supposed to be so smart, can't you figure anything out? I was messing around with Max's computer, skimming money from Institute funds. Besides, it was dark and the guy was behind the railing, I couldn't see who it was, so what the hell would it matter if I told the police?" Barry glanced around and shivered, apparently reviewing his options as he spoke. "Man, it's cold. And maybe it's not such a good idea to be out in the open like this."

"T-Take me home, Barry. I'll try to help you."

"And how do you propose to do that?"

"I believe you when you say you didn't kill those women. And Father. I'll testify for you. Running away won't help. Sooner or later, they'll catch you. At least in jail, the Calabresis can't get to you. You can start over."

Barry laughed out loud. "Get a grip. Nick Calabresi's probably got a dozen goons doing time up in Portage. I'd be in mothballs within the week."

It didn't take Lupe long to realize that Barry was probably telling the truth on that point as well. When she sighed, and commented that he was probably right, he seemed a little surprised. Perhaps a little encouraged, too, because she suddenly felt his hands on her breasts and his cold lips on her neck. Lupe pulled away, exclaiming, "God, will you never understand?"

He stood, yanking her up by the elbow. "I understand pretty damned well," he said, dragging her once again towards his old red Mustang.

"We're going to Lake Geneva," he announced as he pushed her in the driver's seat and settled into the passenger side. The gun still gleamed in his right hand, resting in his lap, but at least it wasn't pointed at her. "Norm had a cottage there no one knows about. But first we gotta stop and get some cash. Then it's the Hoan Bridge to the south side, where I've got some of my things stashed."

"The Hoan Bridge is closed for repairs. It's been in the papers for days."

"So much the better, we won't be bothered by traffic. Besides, it's just routine maintenance. It's not like they're ripping up pavement." Barry clucked. "We are *not* using the Marquette Interchange. Not only is it the preferred dropping point for the Calabresis, the cops have been perched on it like hens on a nest."

Barry directed Lupe to Lake Drive, then Farwell where they headed south. He kept glancing over his shoulder, then at his side-mirror. Downtown, they got on Astor and pulled into the drive-up automatic teller at the Cudahy Building. Barry handed her an ATM card, told her his pin number, and ordered her to get him five hundred dollars. Her hands were shaking so badly that she fumbled the buttons, twice, and he felt moved to press the gun barrel against her ribs to stimulate her concentration. She exhaled with relief when she finally heard the *pht-pht-pht-pht-pht* of the bills dropping out of the slot.

He took the card and money from her, then reached over her to roll up her window. As she drove south again at his direction, past the Quadracci Pavilion towards the Hoan Bridge, he rested his arm over the back of her seat to fondle her hair. "You, uh, seen our little art film yet?" he said.

Lupe shook her head, her stomach burbling.

"We'll watch it together. Yeah, it ain't up to Academy standards, cinematically, but God knows it passes muster on realism." Barry slipped his fingers under the collar of her blouse. When she complained that she couldn't drive if he did that, he went back to playing with her hair. "We shot a few of the earlier scenes with Candy Duffy, you know. But she wasn't half the performer that other gal was."

"B-B-Bel."

"R-R-Right. But believe me, love-of-my-life—" Barry put his arm around her shoulder and squeezed. "—I thought of you every single minute. Except, you know Lu, if I had my way, I'd never share you with anybody, let alone a whole roomful of randy men."

"Was it you who killed my cat?" she said with a sudden frown.

"Kill your—" He cocked back his head. "Darlin', I don't know what you're talking about. But you're talkin' way too much. Time to relax a little." Slipping his gun in his pocket, Barry reached over and caught hold of her jacket zipper. He was so engrossed in the process of unzipping her jacket, and copping a feel of her breasts as he did so, that he didn't notice her glancing once again at the rear view mirror: a shiny black SUV had been following them since they pulled out of the Cudahy lot.

They were curving around towards the ramp that led up to the Hoan Bridge when a flash of mirror-reflected headlights from the SUV shone in Barry's eyes. He looked up at the mirror, then over his shoulder. He sat up, the pleasures to be found beneath her jacket instantly forgotten.

"C-C-Could it be the police?" she asked as she steered carefully around the barricades at the bottom of the bridge, hoping against hope that there might be a squad car somewhere nearby to stop them for ignoring the barricades and construction signs.

"Police don't drive Range Rovers," Barry said in a shaken voice. "How long have they been following us?"

"Since we pulled out of the ATM. Oh, God, I feel sick, g-g-got to—"

"Don't toss your cookies now," he said, gripping her shoulder. "If they're who I think they are, it's going to take the both of us for either of us to get out alive. You got that?"

Lupe swallowed hard and nodded, calculating that, all in all, her chances of survival were even less promising against a carful of Chicago guns-for-hire than they were with Barry DeBrun.

The lights of the Range Rover glared in the driver's-side mirror. Lupe pressed the accelerator to the floor. The red Mustang sailed up the bridge, the concrete rising before them like a ramp into night and nothingness.

"Jesus, this is the worst place on earth!" Barry cried, twisting back and forth to glare at the arched steel spans of the bridge above them and the Range Rover approaching rapidly from behind. He reached over and unlocked her door. "If we can't outrun them, we can fishtail the car, jump the median and run like hell back downtown. There's no way they can drive over that median. Can you do that?"

"I th-think so."

"Speed up, Lu, speed up!"

She floored the accelerator, pulled the stick into third, and then pushed it into fourth. But in her side-view mirror the Range Rover seemed to be growing larger. Then she saw one of its back seat windows rolling down, and a steel cylinder emerging. "They've got a rifle!" she cried.

"It's no good. Do it now. Now!"

With no time to consider whether Barry's plan held any hope for success, she slammed on the brake and yanked the wheel sharply to the right. The back end of the Mustang swung towards the rail, and for a bad moment Lupe thought they were going to crash into the rail and over the side into the harbor; but the wheels finally gripped fast. They came to a grinding halt perpendicular to the bridge.

A cacophony of tire screeches, door bangs, and shouts sounded in Lupe's ears as she flung open her door; but before she could extricate her legs from under the steering wheel of the compact sports car, a pair of strong hands grabbed her under the armpits and yanked hard. One foot got tangled under the clutch, and for a second she felt as if her arms would tear clean out of their sockets. Finally her legs came free and she tumbled out into the whipping wind atop the Hoan Bridge.

She cried out in pain as the man behind her wrenched her elbows together behind her back. Then a dark thing flashed before her face as another man, wearing a black ski mask, leapt in front of her. He hunkered down in the open doorway of the red Mustang, pointing a semi-automatic in Barry DeBrun's terrified face.

"Get your ass out of the car!" the gunman yelled into the wind.

Barry crawled out of the front seat, all spastic arms and legs, his pale face dripping with sweat in spite of the frigid temperature. A third man, also in a ski mask, handcuffed Barry's wrists behind his back while the man with the semi-automatic—the leader, by the sounds of it—extended his arm and pressed the gun cylinder against Barry's temple.

But instead of blowing Barry's brains out, as Lupe was certain he was about to do, the leader suddenly fixed his black eyes on her. "Who the hell are you?" he demanded.

"She's not a part of this. I picked her up —"

Barry was silenced with a pistol whip across the face. "Shut the fuck up!" the leader cried, positioning himself almost cheek to cheek with DeBrun. "You've got a thing for snatching girls off the street, don't you? Well, I want you to know that I personally volunteered for this job, you know why?"

Barry shook his head wildly.

"'Cause I wanted the last sound you ever hear on this earth to be the sound of my sister's name in your ear as I blow your balls out your ass!"

Collapsing with terror, Barry had to be propped up by the gunman behind him. The leader took aim again, but this time at Barry's groin. But he hadn't forgotten about Lupe. "Let her go!" he ordered the man holding her.

"Are you nuts!"

"The man's rules are different this time, or we're all fishbait!"

A pair of headlights flashed in the distance. All heads but Barry's turned long enough to see the lone squad car approaching the bottom of the bridge from the south side.

"Let's hustle, people, we're about to get some company up here. You!" The leader pointed with his free hand at Lupe, then back towards downtown. "You run like hell, and you don't stop until you get to the Firstar Building, understand?"

She didn't even have time to answer because the gunman behind her gave her an iron-fisted shove that sent her stumbling several feet. But the shove also gave her the momentum she needed, once she regained her balance, to turn her face to the north and pump her shaky legs as fast as they would carry her.

She ran ferociously down the bridge, her legs cycling, her lungs burning with November air. She didn't pause or look back or even think about what to do next, not even when she tripped out of one of her shoes, not even when she heard the *thump-thump-thump* of the semiautomatic behind her, followed instantly by Barry's hideous screams. She kept running.

Finally, amidst the syncopated rhythms of shots and screams and screeching tires, Lupe heard a sound that made her slow up a bit—a sound wholly out of sync with the deadly modernity of Range Rovers and semiautomatics and steel arches over restless waters. It was a brilliant, almost exultant war cry released into the wintry air in a string of unfamiliar syllables that caught on the wind and sang, and then faded with a word that Lupe *did* understand:

"*Bode-wade-mi!*"

The long anticipated splash came a few seconds later; but Lupe was running full out again by then, her legs churning towards the city.

Suddenly the bridge inclined sharply downwards, propelling her into uncontrollable free-fall on the unforgiving concrete. Picking herself up, her hands and knees torn and bleeding, Lupe ran some more, and didn't stop running until she came to the barricades at the foot of the bridge. It was there that she first heard the sirens, and saw the blue and red swirls of another prowler, this time approaching from the north. The white lights of the Firstar building shone in the near distance like the Emerald City of Oz on the other side of a poppy field.

Finally, Lupe bent over, her hands on her torn knees, and vomited against a lamp post.

After giving a nearly incoherent account of what had occurred atop the bridge—the patrolman who had picked Lupe up told Masefield that it could have been a UFO abduction for all the sense he could make of it—the same ER doctor who only a few minutes before had failed to persuade James Ireton to similar measures, prevailed upon Lupe Cruz to admit herself to the hospital for overnight observation.

Hours later, with morning sunlight striping through the blinds at the hospital room window, James sat hunched in an armchair at the foot of Lupe's bed, his throbbing head wrapped in gauze. Matt and Oonagh Cruz huddled together in similar armchairs nearby, hardly speaking to each other, let alone James Ireton. At one point, a middle-aged nurse in wrinkled polyester marched into the room carrying a breakfast tray. She set the tray down on Lupe's portable table, pulled a penlight out of her pants' pocket and flashed it in James's scowling face.

"Let me see your pupils, young man," the nurse commanded, shining the flashlight first into one eye, then the other. "You're the one ought to be in that bed," she added, motioning at Lupe's inert figure. "She's just sleeping off a few contusions and a bad scare. You've got a whopping concussion."

"I'll rest later," James promised with a wave of one hand in lieu of a nod, because moving his head made him want to puke.

"Really, James, she's right." There was a tone of warmth in Oonagh Cruz's voice that was incomprehensible to James, unless the Cruz men had chosen not to inform her about what he had done to her daughter a few weeks before. "Couldn't he just lie down over there?" Oonagh pointed at the adjoining, unoccupied bed.

"I won't tell if you won't," the nurse said wryly.

Lupe finally turned her head and moaned; then sat straight up in bed, letting out a piercing wail of post-traumatic terror that drove a spike of agony into James's banging head, and drew Matt and Oonagh rushing to the bedside.

But James got there first. Taking her in his arms—Matt took it upon himself to shoo away the nurses that came bounding into the room—James cradled Lupe tightly, rocking her from side to side until her cries subsided. Finally calm as well as awake, she lifted her fingers to James's bandaged head.

"You o-k-k-kay?"

"Peachy," he lied, sniffling back tears of joy as well as pain. "Here I've got the hardest skull on the planet, and I still managed to get myself knocked down like a Milwaukee ten pin. But you…" James had to laugh, even if it was excruciating. "The captive virgin defeated the dragon single-handedly. Redcrosse himself couldn't have managed it better."

Lupe brushed the back of one hand across her forehead. "That's not how it was," she said. "I stammered and shook and barfed and ran like an Olympic athlete as they…as they k-k-killed him. Oh God, just once in my life I'd like to be brave."

He gave her a little shake, forgetting for a moment that her parents were only a few feet away. "You couldn't be more wrong," he assured her, wiping tears from her cheeks with his thumbs. "You're brave in ways they don't give people medals for. The other kind of brave, the easier kind, would have only got you killed. Take it from one who knows, trying to save a monster like Barry DeBrun wouldn't have been worth the risk, by half."

At that, Lupe's frown deepened. "But what if he wasn't the monster?" she said.

After a quick visit from the doctor on call, Lupe was declared fit to be released, whereupon Calvin Masefield promptly reappeared with the stated intention, long since grown familiar to James, of "clearing up some details."

"Whoever did the number on DeBrun deserves a medal where I sit," Masefield added grumpily, "but it still goes down in the city's statistics as an unsolved homicide. Those boys up on that bridge got clean away, and damned near killed two of ours while they were at it. Or at least could have if they wanted to. I mean, do you know how hard it is to clear an organized crime murder from your open cases file? And now that DeBrun's fish food, I'm not sure we'll ever clear up some of the other cases, either."

James could manage only the weakest of sympathetic nods; the painkiller that the ER doctor had prescribed hours earlier was rapidly wearing off.

"Barry admitted to killing Rygiel," Lupe said, pushing away her largely untouched breakfast tray, "but he didn't kill any of the others."

James sat forward at the announcement, but just as quickly collapsed again into his chair, felled by pain.

Now that she was calm and a bit rested, Lupe was able to render a much more thorough account than she had the night before. Still, she could give Masefield little in the way of useful information about the perpetrators themselves. "Can't you tell me anything about the gunmen?" Masefield pleaded. "Anything at all?"

"They wore ski-masks. I couldn't see their faces. Two of them were tall, over six feet. The leader was shorter, but stocky."

"What about their voices? Did they have accents?"

"The two tall men sounded like they were from Chicago."

Masefield leaned forward. "What about the leader?"

Lupe hesitated. The man, she thought, had wanted to do for his own fifteen-year-old sister what her brothers had done for her. And he had spared Lupe's life, to boot, when the others would have blithely tossed her into the harbor right along with Barry DeBrun. But then he was also a gun for hire who, next time, when the orders were different, might not scruple over 'collateral damage.' It was for that reason, then, though she didn't feel very good about it, that Lupe knew she would have to share with Masefield the one detail she'd kept from him thus far.

She took a deep breath. "I'm pretty sure the leader was Potowatomi."

After Masefield left, delighted with the huge break Lupe Cruz had just handed him, James stepped out of the room so that Lupe could ready herself for home. Shutting the door behind him, he noticed Matt sitting next to his wife in the waiting area on the other side of the nurse's station.

Matt leaned over to whisper something in Oonagh's ear, then got up and approached James.

"Mind if we talk?" Matt said, the skin around his turquoise eyes cobwebbed with fatigue.

"Of course."

Matt took James by the elbow and led him away from the busy nurse's station. He stopped just outside an unoccupied patient's room. As was his custom, Matt got straight to the point. "Lu said you weren't coming to Thanksgiving."

James shoved his hands in his pockets and focused on the laces of his boots. "I told her I had some research to do down at the Newberry Library in Chicago. You understand."

"Yeah, I do. Problem is, Lu does too. In fact, I'd say she understands you pretty damned well." Hands on hips, Matt blew out a lungful of air. "Look, my daughter is twenty-four years old. I think it's a little late in the game for either of us to be trying to cushion her from every bump in her road. I couldn't help her last night, any more than you could, and she came out all right. Sometimes these things are…out of our hands."

"But Mr. Cruz—"

"Matt, dammit!"

James winced, then nodded, then winced again.

"Now look here—" Matt was growing insistent. "—I pressed Lu the other night about what the hell had been going on, and she finally filled me in on a few things. Things you've been dealing with the last while, and the circumstances that night."

"You mustn't listen to her," James exclaimed. He'd been over this all in his mind a thousand times. "It drives me mad to think she's willing to forgive all my sins. Even finish up paying for them."

Matteo Cruz blinked several times, then laughed out loud, as if James had just told a joke worthy of a late-night TV monologue. "But that's life," he said, opening his arms. "Man, you're thirty years old, haven't you figured that out yet? We all end up paying for other people's sins, and they for ours. That's just how it works. Or it doesn't work at all. Especially when you love." Matt's hands went back on his hips. "And I'm not the only one who thinks so. In fact, Oonagh said to me, just this morning—"

"She knows?" James exclaimed, his head swiveling, in spite of the pain, to stare at Oonagh Cruz, who was still sitting in the waiting area, flipping through an old *Newsweek*.

Matt snorted. "You think I wouldn't tell my wife and Lu's mother about something like this?"

James swallowed hard. Oonagh Cruz, he had long since figured out, was one of those people who didn't say much, but when she did, the entire Cruz family stood at attention. Knowing somehow that his future happiness, and perhaps even his survival, might depend on how Matt Cruz answered his next question, James asked in a wavering voice, "What did Oonagh say?"

"She said there would be something missing in the family if you weren't sitting there next to Lu come Thanksgiving. Okay, so I kinda argued with her, I admit it. You gotta look at all the angles in a situation like this. But then Oonagh said—and this is what really got to me—she said, 'You know, I've often thought that when Jesus took up that cross, he was probably doing the first really original human act since Cain slew Abel. Oh, Cain probably had his reasons to kill his brother, don't we all. But after thousands of years, it's not exactly an original or effective way to respond to injustice anymore, is it? But forgiveness and a second chance…they're as rare as a heat wave in a Wisconsin winter." Matt raised his hand as if taking an oath. "I swear before the holy Virgin, that's what my wife said."

James lifted his eyes, which were filling with tears. "And I swear before the holy Virgin," he said to his future father-in-law, "that I would die before I ever hurt Lupe again. I would lay down my life for her."

Matt's face twitched. It looked to James like surprise. "How can you know a thing like that?"

"Because for a miserable fortnight I've had to face the prospect of a life without her. It didn't look much like a life worth living."

After a moment's hesitation Matt shrugged, as if that were the only sensible attitude a sane man could hold about his beloved daughter. "James, you're a member of our family now," he said, "and you just can't up and resign from a family when things get rocky. So we'll do our level best to put it behind us, okay? How does Scripture put it, *as far as the East is from the West...?*" Matt reached around James's trembling shoulders and squeezed.

The Solemnity of Christ the King, the last Sunday before Advent, fell this year on the weekend before Thanksgiving. The Oratory of St. Philip Neri was decked with resplendent bouquets of white gladioli. Kneeling in the pew while Lupe went up to Communion, his concussion headache once again plaguing him, James couldn't help but notice that there was someone else not receiving the Body and Blood of Christ on this last Sunday of the Church year: Dr. Franco Lanciano, perfect as ever in a taupe flannel overcoat and fedora, remained uncharacteristically kneeling in one of the front pews while his wife approached the altar rail in a brand new mink.

James, therefore, though he could not have explained why, was not entirely surprised when Lanciano approached him and Lupe after Mass and invited them to their home for an impromptu Sunday brunch. After Lanciano's lubricious no-confidence vote following Bel's murder, James, frankly, wasn't keen on having to fabricate a pretense of sociability; but there was such a subtle tension in Lanciano's exquisitely controlled face as he proffered the invitation that James, squeezing Lupe's hand as a signal, felt suddenly inclined to accept.

Franco, it would appear, had something on his mind.

A Vivaldi concerto provided aural counterpoint to the silvery light playing on the November lake outside the Lancianos' dining room. What Franco had characterized as an 'impromptu brunch' turned out to be a carefully orchestrated symphony of quiche and croissants, fresh fruit, Asti Spumante, and postprandial cappuccino. It was while the quiche was being served that Adèle let the cat out of the bag: Franco's restored confidence in James was due not only to Adèle's own unwavering belief in the young man's innocence, but also to a lengthy phone conversation the day before with Oonagh Cruz.

Thereafter the four of them chatted pleasantly, if a little uncomfortably in a few spots, until the brunch dishes were finally cleared; then Franco gave his wife what looked for all the world like a pre-arranged signal, prompting Adèle to sweep Lupe into the kitchen for the ostensible purpose of helping her with the washing up "while the men talk."

Franco picked up his coffee and motioned for James to adjourn with him to the library, where the fireplace was already burning in cheerful welcome.

"That's a nice jacket you're wearing," Franco commented, shutting the doors behind them before flopping into a calfskin chair with all the grace of a rhino downed by a tranquilizer dart. "That northwoodsy-preppy style suits you, as it does most Anglo-Saxons. My daughter bought me a Shetland tweed jacket for Christmas last year, and Adèle didn't stop laughing for a week. L.L. Bean, I presume?"

"Land's End. 'Buy Wisconsin,' and all that."

The opening pleasantries thus concluded, Franco pulled a silver cigarette case from his breast pocket, flicked it open with his thumb, and held it out to James.

"Not now, thanks. What's on your mind?"

Franco lit his own cigarette with a matching silver lighter. "Lately, a great deal," he said, exhaling a plume of blue-gray smoke, "but first I want to apologize for last week."

"You needn't. Things looked bad, I realize that."

"Quite right, *looked*. I'm afraid that my anxiety for the deteriorating reputation of the Institute induced me to, well, jump the gun a bit. But I want you to understand that I never suspected you of the murder itself. Or should I say—" Franco's shoulders rippled. "—murders."

"As you said, I have been in the midst of things these days." Suddenly wanting something to do with his hands, James leaned forward. "Maybe I will take one of those, after all," he said, helping himself to one of the cigarettes from the silver case on the coffee table.

Wondering what expensive and no doubt exotic brand of nicotine Franco had chosen for his exercise in self-indulgence, James lit up, took a drag, then studied the gold lettering on the white filter.

It was a Player. The cigarette fell to his lap, then to the floor.

"Been a while, eh?" Lanciano chuckled as James scrambled for the cigarette before it burned a hole in Franco's exquisite Turkish carpet.

"I thought you'd given up smoking," James countered clumsily, cigarette once again in hand and brushing ash off his corduroys.

"I only smoke when I'm a wreck. Which unfortunately has been for the better part of the term." Franco emitted a rueful chuckle. "I succumbed again the night of my *soirée* here, you know, the night all the other disasters began, thanks to those two petty gangsters, DeBrun and Rygiel. The swine." Lanciano exhaled a bolt of smoky laughter.

"What's so funny?"

"Just thinking what a picture I must have made that night. You see, I had just discovered that my little *nuda erotica* had disappeared, and I was frantic at the thought of what else might have gone missing. But what, you may well ask, was the first thing I did? Call the police? Seal the house? Oh no,

I rushed downstairs and said to the first person I saw, 'I need a goddamned cigarette.' He obliged me with a Player, and I haven't managed to shake the disgusting habit yet."

Chuckling indeed at the picture Franco's words drew in his mind, James felt a delicious wave of relaxation wash over him, part nicotine-induced, part relief at the realization that, even if Players were English cigarettes, it didn't necessarily follow that Franco was the only man in Milwaukee with a taste for them. "So when did you finally realize that your stolen *nuda erotica* was a picture of a woman who was soon to be murdered?"

Franco's cigarette paused halfway to his lips. "How did you know it was a picture of Candace Duffy?" he said crossly.

"One hears things."

"Yes, well so does Calvin Masefield, and it cost me two very unpleasant hours in his shabby little office last week."

"I suspect he wanted to know why you didn't report the theft," James said amiably. "Among other things."

Franco harrumphed. "Good God, I didn't report it because the thing was practically worthless. Certainly not worth the insurance deductible. Why, it only lacked Fabio to give it all the artistic merit of the cover of a dimestore romance! Which is why I hung it in the bathroom in the first place. It was intended as a crude attempt at humor. Adèle thought it was hysterical. She was right there, you know, during the shoot. In fact, Adèle was the one who hired Duffy for me in the first place. She got her name from a local modeling agency. Adèle's always been so supportive of my little hobbies." Franco picked a piece of lint from his trousers. "Can't imagine, frankly, with all the truly valuable art work hanging on my walls, why anyone should have wanted it enough to steal it."

"That, I suspect, was Masefield's question as well," James agreed. "Not much fun finding oneself a murder suspect, is it?"

Franco threw him a look. "Yes, well, perhaps now that DeBrun and Rygiel are out of the way, we can all go back to behaving like civilized people again."

"Hear, hear. Thing is, if you think about it, not much has really changed since their deaths."

Franco glared at him. "What the hell do you mean?"

"I mean that everyone seems to believe that DeBrun was guilty of Bel's and Duffy's murders, as well as Rygiel's. Perhaps even Father's. But Lupe doesn't read it that way. And neither, alas, does Calvin Masefield."

Franco sat forward. "What does Masefield think?"

"I'm not sure he knows what to think. DeBrun readily admitted to killing Rygiel, but he vehemently denied involvement in the other murders. In fact, he told Lupe that he saw someone else drop Fr. Bricusse that night, but couldn't see who it was." James hesitated. "I have my own reasons for suspecting someone else, but when I try to put my mind to it, I just can't believe it."

"Who?" Franco whispered.

"It's so improbable, so out of character, that I'd really better not say. And Masefield's asked me not to talk about any of it until they've got more evidence."

"Shit," Lanciano declared, pressing himself into the cushioned calfskin at his back. "I don't know if I can take much more of this. I dare say that sounds a bit querulous to you, seeing as how you've been caught square in the eye of the hurricane, as it were, but I must say these last few months have been hopelessly muddled. Between you and me, it's going to take a miracle for the Heisler Institute to recover its reputation. Why, I've already noticed a substantial dip in pre-enrollment for next term, especially among women. For God's sake, Duffy wasn't even connected to the Institute, and Gunderson wasn't a student here when she died!"

James fixed his eyes on the crystal ashtray on the coffee table: the thing was to the brim with the butts of Players.

Franco shifted his weight on his slender hips. "James," he said with a sudden earnestness that made James look up, "the reason I asked you here is…I have a confession to make."

"I'm in no position to offer absolution, you know."

"Yes, well, the priest who hears the confession I'm about to make to you is liable to have a cardiac arrest. When I get up the nerve to confess to a priest, that is. In the meantime…well, let's just say I need to be understood by someone whose opinion I value, and whose friendship I don't want to lose because of misunderstandings and rumors."

James inclined his head. "I'll take that as a compliment, very much needed right now. This is about your rumored Mafia connections, isn't it?"

Franco's sigh was more eloquent than any 'yes.' "No one knows what you're about to hear, except Adèle," Franco said. "Oh, Arthur knew some of it, of course, and Max Heisler knows a lot more than he ever needed to know, though how he found out I can't imagine. I swear, sometimes I think that man can see around corners with those piscine eyes of his."

"Money can buy a lot of information."

"So it can. Of course, I've always known there were rumors flitting around about my dealings with men such as Rygiel, even though our relationship was wholly professional."

"How so?"

"My little part-time private art dealership. Rygiel was one of my most spendthrift customers. Believe me, along with some real estate investments, I've made a lot more money from art dealing than I ever have in academia. Unfortunately for my reputation, Norman Rygiel was something of a social climber as well as an art collector, and had a nasty habit of showing up at my private parties, quite uninvited. Which is what happened the night before Arthur died. That, James, is the simple truth."

James pursed his lips. "Except the truth is rarely simple, is it?"

Franco stamped out his cigarette and immediately reached for another. "You said it. In my case, the not-so-simple truth is…well, I'm not entirely what I seem. Of course, it's the American way. Start over, break from the past—Jay Gatsby and all that. Oh, I never tried to hide the fact that I was born penniless in Calabria. But what most people don't know, in Milwaukee at least, is that Nick Calabresi's father, old Filippo Calabresi, hailed from Calabria, too. Hence the name, of course."

"Fascinating." James stubbed out his own cigarette, wishing Franco would get to the bloody point.

"When Filippo Calabresi made it big in the Chicago mob back in the thirties, Calabresis began arriving in Chicago in droves. As it happens..." Franco's cigarette trembled at the end of his fingers. "Calabresi was also my father's surname. My surname."

James's mouth fell open.

Franco averted his own eyes to the fireplace. "My father was one of Filippo's cousins. And in the end, one of his soldiers. In his defense, let me add that we were practically starving at the end of the war. My parents would have taken any opportunity to leave Calabria and have a chance at a better life. Filippo paid for our transportation money. The deal was, my father would repay it by working for Filippo in Chicago."

Abandoning his cigarette, Franco resorted to his fingernails, then when he realized what he was doing, to the nicotine again. "It was a dirty business, James. *La malavita*, my mother called it. I'm certain that my father murdered people rather casually in his line of work, like those thugs did the other night on the bridge. But just as they will, sooner or later, my father finally got what he deserved. He was killed when I was seven, gunned down by a policeman while attempting to hijack an armored car."

"God, Franco."

Franco shrugged. "My friend, I admit to no great love for *poliziotti* ever since. Just an instinctive reaction I can't seem to shake, even after all these years. Every time I come face to face with Calvin Masefield, or even Lupe's gung-ho brother, I can't help it, I just want to spit in their eyes."

"I can imagine."

Franco sat up. "Yes, well, as you may also imagine, when my mother was widowed, she took back her maiden name, Lanciano, to avoid the Calabresis as much as the police. She packed us quietly off to Kenosha, where she had relatives. She said it would take a miracle for our family to break clean from the Calabresi influence. She made endless novenas, begging Our Lady of Mt. Carmel to keep us out of harm's way."

"Her prayers seem to have been answered." James motioned around the room.

"Perhaps not as well as she had hoped." Franco leaned forward to offer James another cigarette, then lit it for him. "As you know, I got my doctorate at the University of Chicago. That's where I met Adèle. The irony was, Filippo's son, Nick Calabresi, whom I hadn't seen since we were both children, was getting his MBA at the U of C at the same time."

James looked up. "You met him?"

"At a student tavern. It was hours before I found out his last name, and realized who the hell he was. We became great chums. Of course, I never told him who I was, or that we were cousins. The perhaps silly, perhaps ugly, truth is…I admired the guy." Franco opened his arms. "Can you imagine? Quite the Renaissance man, Nick is. I can almost see him ordering his little assassinations over plates of caviar and magnum bottles of Veuve Cliquot. Things got so friendly between us that the day I received the doctorate, Nick took me aside and tried to give me a gift. It was a beautiful little Florentine Madonna, eighteenth century. I don't know how—the piece was exquisite—but I somehow managed to refuse it. Very, very politely, of course. It wasn't that I didn't want the thing, God knows. I had no money yet for original art then. But you see, I knew that if I accepted the gift, Nick would feel free to ask me for a favor sometime. By then, it would be very difficult, and perhaps unwise, for me to refuse him. That was when I realized that things had gotten out of hand—something I never allowed to happen with Rygiel, by the way. Or so I thought. At any rate, when I took the job at Marquette and moved up here, I neglected to tell Nick where I was headed. I haven't seen him now in over twenty-five years."

"It must have been unpleasant for you when you learned he was beginning to operate in Milwaukee."

"Indeed, that's where it gets complicated," Franco admitted, reaching this time for his cappuccino and speaking between sips. "I happened to make a casual comment to Max—I think it was the day after that strip club owner was killed—that, what with Rygiel's habit of showing up on my doorstep uninvited, I hoped Nick Calabresi wasn't supervising his operations in Milwaukee personally, as I didn't care to cross paths with him again, or have it thought that I was somehow in league with Nesterov. Max asked me what the hell I meant by 'crossing paths *again*,'" and I, well, I felt I had to tell him."

"Uh oh."

Franco shrugged. "Max never forgets anything, damn his fishy eyes. And when he finally found out what sort of man his daughter had married, and that Nick Calabresi was after him because of that horrific video —" Franco shook his head. "James, I could read Max's mind. He'd do anything for Fran. That's Max's categorical imperative: protect Fran. I don't know for sure, but I suspect that when Max gave the police all the information he had gathered about Barry's activities, he also, mentally, gave them a certain, shall we say, limited amount of time to take care of him."

"Or else he would take matters into his own hands. Yes, I gathered as much. What are you trying to tell me?"

Franco put down his coffee cup and stared into the fire. "Max and Fran were up in their Door County retreat the weekend Bel Gunderson was murdered. They came back the Wednesday afterwards. The day I was so beastly to you after your seminar. In fact, I went up to Max's office directly afterwards to tell him…well, to air my concerns."

"About me."

Franco chuckled. "You'll be edified to learn that Max laughed in my face, called me a goddamned fool, and said that if I couldn't read 'Barry DeBrun' all over everything that had happened the last few months, I needed spectacles. Gunderson's murder shut a door in Max's mind. He was through worrying about what the police did or didn't do in regard to his son-in-law. Especially since he believed Barry capable of something downright crazy, like taking Fran hostage. As a matter of fact, precisely, in the end, the sort of thing he tried with Lupe. But Max also told me that his private detective had uncovered something that would give Nick Calabresi the jump on the police in finding Barry, if Calabresi ever found out about it. Something to do with a secret bank account in a phony name." Franco shifted in his seat. "It was just then that Max reminded me that I had once mentioned knowing Nick Calabresi. The long and short of it is, Max asked me to arrange a private meeting."

James coughed out a lungful of smoke. "He did *what*?"

Franco recoiled. "I have a daughter of my own," he said defensively, "and a granddaughter. I understood Max's feelings. But I assure you, I did try to talk him out of it. I said to him, 'Max, *think*, these people will mow down anyone who gets in their way. Innocent people could get caught in the middle of it!'"

"My God, how did Heisler answer that?"

Franco's voice faded to a whisper. "He said, 'Calabresi will have to play it my way. I'll give him Barry's head on a buffet plate, if he sees to it that no one else gets hurt. And I'll make sure he knows that if he screws me on this, I'll spend every last penny of my fortune, and even see myself convicted of conspiracy, just to see him strung up by his bollocks.'"

"Wow."

Franco nodded, then shrugged, though it looked to James more like a shudder. "I made a few phone calls, right there in the office. Nick was on the line within ten minutes. He and Max met that very evening, at Ray Radigan's restaurant down in Kenosha."

James shook his head, too amazed to speak.

"Well, at least Max kept his word about innocent bystanders," Franco added with an unconvincing wave. "Nick, too, for that matter."

Marshaling his own depleted resources of resilience, James mashed out his cigarette. "Perhaps you'd feel better if I got indignant and told you I thought you had caved in on your principles," he said. "But so help me God, all I can think of at this moment is that those hoodlums, as you called them, may have saved Lupe's life, whether they intended to or not. And certainly saved her from a brutal rape."

"It could have turned out very differently," Franco pointed out. He had obviously been thinking of the might-have-beens as well. "And DeBrun died like a dog. I'm not sure even he deserved that."

James jumped up and began to pace the perimeter of Franco's Turkish carpet, his hands stuffed in his pockets. "Look, I'm clean out of crocodile tears this month for the likes of Barry DeBrun. I understand men like him too damned well. So if you wanted absolution, you came to the right place. If what you need is a penance, then I suggest you go to the Oratory or

Holy Hill." James stopped in front of the fireplace and massaged his temples, which were suddenly banging again. "But thanks for telling me. It took some guts. It won't go out of this room."

Franco managed a nod, then reached for another cigarette.

"Just for the sake of curiosity," James said suddenly, following Lanciano's hungry movements with his troubled eyes. He gestured at the cigarette case. "Who was it that gave you the Player that night at the party?"

Franco looked startled by James's question, and had to think a moment. "Why, it was Jack Sigur," he said finally. "Why?"

Chapter Twelve:
The Dragon's Tail

This is the excellent foppery of the world, that when
we are sick in fortune — often the surfeit of our own
behaviour — we make guilty of our disasters the sun,
the moon and the stars: as if we were villains by
necessity, fools by heavenly compulsion; knaves,
thieves and treachers, by spherical predominance;
drunkards, liars and adulterers, by an enforced
obedience of planetary influence; and all that we
are evil in, by a divine thrusting on: an admirable
evasion of whoremaster man, to lay his goatish dis-
position to the charge of a star! My father com-
pounded with my mother under the dragon's tail,
and my nativity was under Ursa Major; so that it
follows I am rough and lecherous. Tut, I should
have been that I am, had the maidenliest star in the
firmament twinkled on my bastardizing.

Shakespeare, *King Lear*

Jack propped his feet on James's coffee table, sucked on his Lucky Strike and produced a perfectly round smoke ring. "I'm heading down to Chicago for Thanksgiving, wanna join me? There are some people I want you to meet."

"Good of you," James said, "but we can't. I'm running over to Nadine's tomorrow night. And Lu and I promised to spend Thanksgiving weekend with her folks."

Jack pulled his feet off the table. "Nadine's!"

James reached for his pack of Marlboro Lights, Masefield's brand, to which he'd taken a fancy. "I won't claim she was thrilled at the prospect," he admitted, lighting up, "but she's letting me come over."

Jack gave him a sideways look. "Now what do you want to go and do that for? Isn't your life complicated enough as it is?"

James fiddled with his cigarette. "I need to apologize to her. To her face. Pray God I do a better job of it than I did with Bel." He took a deep breath and produced an asymmetrical smile. "But if you give me some directions, Lu and I could possibly pop down in the evening, after Thanksgiving dinner. I believe Oonagh's planned the meal for around two."

"That'll work," Jack said, though he was still shaking his head over the bit about Nadine. He laid aside his Lucky in the ashtray and began scribbling an address and directions on the back of a paper napkin.

"Jack?"

"Yo, buddy."

"You were smoking Players there for a while, weren't you?"

Jack looked up. "Now why in tarnation is everybody so all-fired interested in my nicotine habits all of a sudden? Even Calvin Masefield was grilling me over the coals about it, just yesterday."

"What did you tell him?"

"I told him I ran out of Luckies the night of Lanciano's party, and bummed some smokes off Mitch Showalter. The guy gave me a whole pack of Players. Said he had an extra on him."

James coughed on his smoke. "Mitch Showalter! SANA members aren't allowed to smoke."

"Yeah, and they ain't allowed to drink and wear civvies, and talk pottymouth, and tint their hair, and read doorstoppers by every nihilist from Nietzsche to Nechayev, neither, but the Encyclopedia Showalter sure as shoot does. Don't know what's gotten into little Richie. He used to be a better watchdog."

James spoke very slowly. "You're telling me that Mitch Showalter smokes Players."

"Used to." Jack held up a limp wrist. "It's so *English* you know. But I think he's switched to Marlboros now that he's seen you smoking 'em." Jack gestured at James's pack of Marlboro Lights on the coffee table and laughed out loud. "Damned if I know why those nutniks over there at SANA House don't toss him out on his tuchus."

James and Lupe strolled hand-in-hand through South Shore Park, trying to walk off some of their Thanksgiving dinner before making the drive to Chicago. After his conversation with Jack, James had also been trying to walk off his sudden anxieties about Mitch Showalter, who was in almost every way, even after almost five years of acquaintance, something of a blank slate for him. To add to his worries, Lupe had gone to bed the night before with a mild headache and awakened the entire Cruz household around midnight with nearly hysterical screams. A nightmare, she had said. "Something aw-aw-awful in the room."

They paused where a breakwater of boulders propped up the grassy embankment at the edge of the beach. A trick of light created a strip of white along the watery horizon, as if it had just snowed on an ice floe. James put his arm around Lupe's shoulder.

"The doctor said there might be repercussions from your ordeal on the bridge," he suggested supportively.

Lupe's eyes darkened in the skittish light. "It wasn't Barry."

James stopped. "Beg pardon?"

She took a step back, then just as quickly rushed into his arms, burrowing herself under his armpit. "The th-th-thing in the room last night, it wasn't Barry!"

"My darling, what are you talking about?"

"The thing I first felt that day at Mass, when Barry was sitting behind me." She shook her head against his chest. "Then the night Father died. All this time I thought I was picking up on something with Barry. But that whole evening with Barry on the bridge, as horrible as it was, it wasn't the same. It wasn't...*that*." Looking up into James's frowning eyes, Lupe's voice took on a note of panic. "James, Barry is dead, but *it*'s not. It's still here. And it wants..."

He brushed a lock of hair away from her face. "What, love?"

"Me. D-D-Dead."

They had intended to say their good-byes and head down to Chicago for their visit with Jack and his mysterious friends, whoever they might be, but when James and Lupe returned to the Cruz home from their walk in the park, they were startled to find the entire family gathered in front of the television set in the family room, listening to some sort of news break.

"To recap what we know," announced the Channel 4 anchorman, "the missing woman is a Marquette University graduate student, last seen entering her apartment building yesterday evening. She was reported missing by her family this morning. Her car was found abandoned this afternoon in Atwater Park, overlooking the lake, not far from where the body of reputed organized crime lawyer Norman Rygiel was found last month. The Milwaukee Police Department has not released any further details of the disappearance, but has said that they fear foul play. We'll have more on this breaking story in our five o'clock report."

In the end, James and Lupe didn't make it to Chicago at all that night, because a grim-looking Calvin Masefield came knocking on the Cruz's door a few minutes later.

"I can't believe this...why me this time?" James asked when the three of them were seated in the parlor.

One bushy eyebrow cocked high on his forehead, Masefield regarded James with an expression that mingled doubt with something like wonder. "A member of the missing woman's family named you right off as a likely suspect."

"B-B-But James was here all night!" Lupe exclaimed.

"I can't tell you how delighted I am to hear that." Masefield did indeed seem genuinely relieved. He pulled a pen and notebook out of his breast pocket. "Since what time?"

Lupe flapped her hands. "Uh, well, James was supposed to visit a friend last night, but she c-c-canceled, so he picked me up early, about five. We came straight here."

"*Please* tell me you have plenty of witnesses to that effect."

"The whole family saw him here at dinner and all evening…even when I woke screaming from a nightmare at midnight!"

"Oh my God," James whispered, pieces of this latest puzzle finally falling into place, and in an alarmingly familiar pattern. He thrust his knuckles against his teeth. "It's Nadine, isn't it? It's Nadine that's gone missing."

Masefield sighed. "So would you please tell me why one of her family members would name you as first on his list of possible kidnappers? I mean, the guy was nearly apoplectic."

"Bo," James said with a nod. He couldn't bear to meet Calvin Masefield's probing gaze. "Nadine and I took a class together last spring. We…we were together for about two months. I ended it very cruelly. Bo's hated me ever since. That was why I wanted to see her yesterday evening. To try to explain things. Or at least ask for forgiveness."

James's confession seemed to hit Masefield unusually hard. He sat clicking his ballpoint pen in an out for a minute at least before finally saying, "You're telling me you had an affair with Nadine Jeffrey."

His face paling rapidly, James nodded.

"And the woman who was raped, Kim Prohaska?"

James nodded again, barely.

Masefield clicked the ballpoint open, started to jot a note, then gave up and tossed both pen and notepad on the coffee table. "Besides the two porn dealers and Norm Rygiel, not to mention Lenny, we have Bricusse, Prohaska, Duffy, Gunderson, and now Nadine Jeffrey. That's eight victims dying in falls from great heights, and one rape that would have probably ended the same way, if Prohaska's boyfriend hadn't showed up unexpectedly. Even if we take away the obvious mob-related hits and Lenny's suicide, what do you think are the odds that four of our five remaining victims would be people you've loved?"

"Please God it's not five. Not yet. What makes you think—"

"James, we're not going to find her alive. I think you know that."

Lupe squeezed James's hand. "Iago," she whispered.

Masefield looked at her, then at James. "I talked to Richard Krato the other day. He swears up and down that he got rid of that King James Bible of yours three years ago. Threw it right out in the trash, he said, after you guys had an argument at the John Ernst Café."

When James and Lupe finally arrived the next afternoon at the near north side Chicago address that Jack had given James, the familial scene that greeted them, comprised of three generations of Jack's father's second family, was chaotic but oddly healing.

"I talked to Bo on the phone," Jack said in a subdued voice, answering James's question of whether there was anything he could do to help the Jeffrey family. "He said they needed to be left alone a while. At least until they get some news." Almost as pale as James, Jack grimaced. "They didn't report it on the news, but Bo said there were buckets of blood in Nadine's car. Her blood type. Masefield's told them to be prepared for the worst."

On top of the pallor, James noted Jack's red-rimmed and swollen eyes.

"You look like shit," James commented.

"Yeah, well, you wouldn't win any beauty contests neither. When was the last time you got a decent night's sleep?"

"That would be September 3rd, the day before the term began."

Lupe, whose extended silences in the last twenty-four hours was an eloquent indication that she was taking things harder than she wanted to admit, latched on to James's arm. "So, wh-wh-when did all this happen?" she asked with forced cheerfulness, gesturing at the house, the kids playing in the front yard outside the living room window, and Jack's father, snoring softly in an easy chair in front of the low drone of CNN.

Jack extracted a large drumstick from the plate of cold turkey on the coffee table and searched out the meatiest portion. "I hadn't seen Dad in years. I heard through the family grapevine that he was playing in a Zydeco band here in Chicago." Jack bit down, chewed a bit, and swallowed. "Then when Father B. died, I don't know, it shook me up. I just made up my mind to let bygones be bygones, and see what I could salvage of my family life. In the process I picked up a step-mom, a half-sister, and her three ornery moppet-heads." Jack wrapped his jaws around another chunk of dripping meat and motioned them to help themselves.

"No, th-thanks," Lupe said, cradling her tummy.

James, nursing a beer, declined as well.

"See, Jim-bo," Jack enthused, wiping a splotch of gravy from his goatee, "I've got family again! God, it's great. Especially at a time like this, when the whole world's going to hell in a handbasket." Jack dropped the half-eaten drumstick back on the plate and broke down. "Oh, God," he sobbed into a paper napkin, "First the old padre and Bel and now Nadine…this is godawful, godawful!"

Nadine Jeffrey's disappearance was not only driving James to rely even more heavily than before on the short-lived and less-than-salubrious consolations to be had in nicotine and alcohol, but Masefield's words that day in the Cruz parlor had also planted a seed of new anxiety in his mind, anxiety about Lupe's safety. He longed for the days, so short and yet so long a time ago, when all he had to lose sleep over was nasty letters in the mail, or having his dissertation pinched, or whether he could get Lupe Cruz to go to bed with him. Finally swallowing his pride, or what little remained of it after the bludgeoning it had endured the last couple of months, James paid a late-night visit to the suburban tract home of Det. Ramon Cruz, whose aid he had decided to seek in procuring a weapon.

After warning James that a conviction on carrying a concealed weapon would probably cost James a prison term and/or deportation — the least of James's worries at this point, as James hastened to make clear — Ramon, obviously scared to death for his sister, agreed with surprising alacrity to contact a retired cop and gun collector of his acquaintance, who, in Ramon's words, "owes me one." Fortunately for James, this discreet gentleman had recently installed a shooting range on his rural property, where James's rusty marksmanship might be brought up to speed.

Sunday, December 8th, after escorting Lupe to Mass for the Feast of the Immaculate Conception, James made sure Lupe was safely stowed at her parents' home before holing up in his Institute office to drink Irish whiskey from a Styrofoam cup and read Mitch Showalter's research paper, which was the scheduled topic of discussion for Wednesday's class, the last of the term. Tingling from head to toe in eerie premonition of a reoccurrence of his Oxford breakdown, in spite of Dr. Simon's most recent assurances that he was doing rather well, all things considered, James set aside Mitch's obscurantist, nearly incomprehensible paper after only ten minutes and palmed his ugly little Grendel P-12 automatic, which Ramon's retired cop-friend had chosen for him. "Small, reliable, and easy to conceal" the thing might be, as the gentleman claimed, but it still felt odd to James's big hand, even after a week of almost daily target practice under Ramon's keen-eyed tutelage.

James shoved the Grendel back in its belt holster and covered it with the black ski parka he had bought to replace his ruined leather bomber jacket. My God, he thought, pouring some more whiskey as he glanced around at the four close walls and one narrow window of his tiny office, his life had turned so hellish of late that his claustrophobia, heretofore the chronic minor terror of his everyday life, had almost entirely disappeared. *One nail drives out another*, he reminded himself grimly, wishing to hell he still had the old nails to deal with rather than the new ones.

There was a knock.

After checking to make sure that the Grendel was safely concealed beneath his parka James called out, "Come in!"

Calvin Masefield opened the door, his brown eyes weary, his hands stuffed in the pockets of the same shabby all-weather coat that James had seen him wearing for two interminable months.

"Lupe said you might be here. D'you mind?"

"Just the man I want to see," James said, flourishing his cup.

Masefield closed the door behind him and grabbed a metal folding chair that was propped against the wall. Straddling it facing James, he eyed the whiskey bottle with sympathetic disapproval. "So how are you holding up, or should I ask?"

"Other than incipient dipsomania, a re-habituation to nicotine, and the imminent advent of another cataclysmic nervous breakdown," James assured Masefield with a burp, "thing's are just tickety-boo." He pulled a pack of Marlboro Lights from the top drawer of his desk, took one for himself, and handed one to Masefield; then somehow got both cigarettes alight with a quavering Bic. "Thank God the term is nearly over," he added, blowing out a cloud of smoke. "One more class and *consummatum est.* The end of the most hellacious three months in academic history." James giggled. "God, I wish you could come to class this Wednesday. We're discussing Mitch Showalter's research paper."

"That bad?"

"So godawful bad, that after reading a fifty-page rough draft a month ago, Mitch's assigned partner managed to talk our substitute instructor into letting them each go it alone." James lifted the hefty sheaf of papers which comprised Showalter's manuscript. "Barmy. I'm shoaled on page fifteen of seventy-two. Mitch calls it *Hamlet Deconstructed,* though what it has to do with *Hamlet,* or anything else we've been studying this term, I can't begin to tell you. Translated into plain English, as best as I can decipher it, Mitch appears to be announcing to the academic world the Death of Drama, much the way Nietzsche announced the Death of God." James grunted. "At least Nietzsche could write."

"Couldn't prove it by me. How's your dissertation coming?"

"Topping." James gave a sodden nod. "I defend it in January, should I live so long."

"Good heavens, boy, when do you find the time?"

"Mostly at night, when I can't sleep, and I don't feel like drinking or medicating myself into analgesic oblivion. Sad to say—" James hoisted his cup. "—these last few bloody weeks, *I'll watch the horologe a double set, if drink rock not my cradle.*"

"What, you got a well-upholstered woman like Lupe Cruz to cuddle up to, and you can't sleep?"

"She's a bona fide Catholic virgin, a remarkable and uncommonly steadfast breed. I'll sleep on the wedding night." James burst out in a peel of nearly hysterical laughter.

"Friend, no one sleeps on their wedding night!" Smiling finally if not energetically, Masefield extracted a Styrofoam cup from the stack hard by on James's desk and waved it in front of his host's nose. "Here, gimme some of that hooch."

"*We'll teach you to drink deep, ere you depart,*" James declared, filling the lieutenant's cup as he mocked his own British speech with a pronounced slur. "And here I thought peelers weren't supposed to imbibe whilst on duty."

"Yeah, well I thought students weren't supposed to drink or smoke in this building, either."

"Damned right." James pointed at a smoke detector above the door. "I ripped out the frickin' wires."

Masefield took a bracing mouthful. "Probably against the law, but I'll let you off with a warning, this time."

"Ever so good of you."

"Say, did you hear about the game this afternoon?"

"What game?"

"What game! How long you been in Wisconsin, boy? The Pack beat Da Bears, 40 to 3!"

"I say," James exclaimed, leaning back. The sudden movement almost undid him; his head swam, then his stomach.

"The C of P and me had a twenty-dollar bet on that one, and I whooped his ass. Cheers!"

"*Salud,*" James returned, knocking his cup into Masefield's. When his revolving head finally achieved some equilibrium, James set down his cup and focused again on the suddenly silent lieutenant. "Let's out with it," he said bravely. "Nothing personal, Cal, but you're like a big, brown, ever-bearing bush of the baddest news imaginable. You didn't come up here on a weekend just to check up on my class work and gloat over the Packers' game."

A wrinkle of what looked to James like sadness creased the corners of Calvin Masefield's half-smile. "I've been talking on the phone to a profiler with the FBI. A specialist in homicidal psychology. We sent him copies of our crime scene reports. He agrees with me that everything's connected. To you."

Bloody hell, James thought, he couldn't feel his feet.

Masefield scooted his chair closer and pulled a pair of reading glasses from his breast pocket, along with several sheets of e-mail printout. "There's a lot of stuff here, so I'll just hit the high points."

"Christ," James said, more prayer than curse.

Masefield consulted his papers. "Our Iago's either a student at the Institute, or a former student, age range mid-twenties to early thirties. He's sexually ambivalent, with a cleverly masked hatred of women. The sodomy committed on Duffy and Gunderson—probably Prohaska, too, the Feebie agrees with me that that was his work—either indicates contempt or severely repressed shame. You know, that he can't bear to look the women in the face while he's assaulting them."

James took a drink.

"He's smart, and a highly organized killer. His care in removing or destroying physical evidence implies that he's a cunning sociopath who knows how to play the games of society, without really believing in any of the rules. In other words, he's got the brains to make a success on his own, but not the emotional equipment. He suffers from feelings of social inferiority and erotomania, probably stemming from a disadvantaged background."

James tapped his fingers on his knees.

"Now about the drops. It's possible that the killer underwent some traumatic experience in a high place, in which case these postmortem drops may be a way for him to feel in control after the fact. Or it could be he's just a copycat who saw the reports about the mob drops off the high-rise ramps, then Lenny Swiatko's suicide, and thought it would be a cool thing to try himself. In general terms, though, drops like this signify a need for power and self-display, because they're easily the riskiest part of the killer's MO. He's also read up on ancient human sacrifice rituals, probably from the Aztecs, and may have even dabbled in the occult. And last but not least, he is, or was, a Catholic."

James felt a drop of sweat rolling down his calf underneath his jeans. "What on earth could this grisly business have to do with the Church?"

Masefield leaned forward. "Who does it sound like? Who among the men you know?"

"You're asking me?"

"You above all."

James ran a finger across his sweaty eyebrows. "No one. Least of all about the disadvantaged part. The Institute's not a cheap education, you know."

"Except for that, then. How about Richard Krato?"

James grunted. "Every time I try to imagine it I almost laugh."

"You think he hasn't got it in him?"

"He doesn't have that much energy in him period. Let alone sexual energy. Sodomy?" James made a face. "If Richard's had sex in his life, of any variety, I'd be amazed to hear of it. I've more than once envied his dispassion."

"You may have just answered my question. See, where I sit, Richard Krato's not only 'sexually ambivalent,' I'd say he's also a very angry young man. He was angry at Bricusse the day the old priest died, we know that, and he's been angry at you for three years. Hell, angry at the whole damned world, all the time, for failing to appreciate the sacrifices he's made for his beliefs. And angry at his father most of all, I think, because somewhere deep inside, little Richie Krato is just honest enough to know that his pop's a religious illusionist. Huh! I'd describe Richard Krato as a disaster waiting to happen."

When no further comment was forthcoming from James, Masefield set aside his notes and pocketed his reading glasses. "I know you don't like to consider it, but what about Sigur?"

James bristled. "You've had a stick up your ass about Jack from the first time you interviewed him. Where I sit, it's called homophobia."

Masefield sighed.

"Cal, he's the best friend I've ever had."

"And he's in love with you. Take it from one who knows, jealousy is one of the most potent motives for murder ever invented by the wicked heart of man. Maybe the perfect motive for Iago." Masefield leaned forward, his elbows resting over the back of the folding chair. "We've got to consider the possibility that it wasn't the Kratos sending you these letters, at least the last ones, but someone who wanted you to think it was them. Did Sigur know about your getting them when you first left SANA?"

James thought a moment, and was distressed by the answer forming in his memory. "He was in my apartment once when I opened one up," he admitted. "I had just moved out of SANA house. I kicked a garbage can across the room."

Masefield slapped his knee. "Then consider this. Jack Sigur's got no alibis for any of the incidents. And you told me yourself that he knew you were intending to go to Nadine Jeffrey's that night. Don't you see? Iago was trying to set you up that night, just like he tried to set you up for Gunderson's murder. Only this time you lucked out. This time Nadine Jeffrey got cold feet and canceled on you, and you had an entire houseful of people on hand in Bay View to vouch for your whereabouts."

"If Jack knew about the letters or my planned meeting with Nadine," James said between his teeth, "then so did every man, woman, beast, and weed at the Institute. Jack's one of the most unmalicious people I've ever met, but he's also got the most wagging tongue on the near east side." His face closing, James retrieved his drink.

"Okay, scratch Sigur for the moment. How about Lanciano?"

"But you just got through saying—"

"I know he's older than the profile indicates, but these things are never a hundred percent. He certainly grew up disadvantaged, he knew Candace Duffy, and he hasn't any good alibis for the nights in question either. Other than his wife, and wives often cover for their husbands, even in cases like this." His frustration obviously mounting, Masefield slapped his palm hard on the desktop. "Then let's try Mitch Showalter. He's big enough, physically, to do just about any kind of damage he wants. And we know he was smoking Players there for a while. Maybe he picked up your Bible from the trash where Richard Krato claims he dropped it. C'mon, any 'J' as in 'James' motives you could ascribe to Showalter?"

James pressed his fingers to his aching temples. "No personal motive that I'm aware of, other than SANA. He used to be one of Krato's True Believers, and so tight with Richard that we all called them 'Rosencrantz and Guildenstern.' But he was never rabid about me like the Kratos. And lately he acts as if he can't stand the sight of them."

Masefield looked surprised. "Then why do you think he stays on there?"

"Damned if I know. The more interesting question might be why they allow him to stay on there. Peter doesn't tolerate insubordination, believe me, and Mitch has been breaking their rules four ways from Sunday."

"Well, our primary problem, right now, is that we have no reason to believe that Showalter, or anyone else around here with the exception of Lanciano, had any prior relationship with Candace Duffy. See, Duffy's our key, I'm convinced of it. She was the only one of the women who wasn't targeted because of you."

James looked away. Masefield hadn't intended to wound, perhaps, but the needle had stuck home all the same.

Masefield poured himself another inch of whiskey from the rapidly emptying bottle. "We're doing background checks on everyone. I've even got a man down in Racine right now, interviewing some of Duffy's classmates from Prairie School, but so far we've got nothing."

Feeling suddenly more than sober, James pulled his feet off his desk. "Prairie School? You must have sussed out by now that Mitch Showalter attended Prairie School."

Masefield regarded James with an amused expression. "Who told you that fairy tale?"

"Mitch!"

Masefield chuckled. "He told us he went to Bradford High in Kenosha. Which is what he did, 'cause we checked. Believe me, Clan Showalter did not have Prairie School money. His Auntie's been paying his Institute bills."

"But his family—"

"His dad was a janitor, for cryin' out loud. Worse, he died of a heart attack when Mitch was, like, seven or eight. The widowed mother only made ends meet by working food service at Carthage College. When she wasn't on unemployment, that is. She was a chronic alcoholic."

James pressed the heel of his hand against his forehead, wondering whether the liquor was affecting his thinking, or if the November concussion had done some sort of permanent damage to his brain. "I don't know where you're getting your information," he said finally, "but Mitch's mother was an English professor at Carthage College. And his father didn't die of a heart attack, he died in a boating accident en route to a memorial service for the crew of the *Edmund Fitzgerald*. Mitch's uncle was one of the twenty-nine that went down with the ship. I forget the year, but it was November 10th. I always remember it because November 10th is my birthday, as well as the anniversary of the wreck." James reached again for the whiskey, but Masefield yanked it away.

"Son, it's time to lay off the sauce."

"But—"

"Trust me, Mitch's mother worked in the cafeteria at Carthage College. And yes, Showalter's dad died on a boat, and in November—maybe even November 10th, I don't remember—but it was a heart attack, and it was on Lake Michigan, just outside Kenosha Harbor. Absolutely nothing to do with the sinking of the *Fitzgerald*."

Anxiety rising in him like a hot-air balloon, James found himself standing. "*I am not what I am*, remember? Mitch talks about his stint at Prairie School all the time. He wears Prairie School tee-shirts and—"

"So the guy's been telling stories." On his feet as well, if only to lay a steadying hand on James's agitated shoulders, Masefield added, "It's not a crime. Lots of people make up stories to make their lives seem more glamorous and exciting, especially if they've come from—"

"Disadvantaged backgrounds?" James snatched up the bottle of whiskey to pour himself one last round, but his hand was so unsteady that Masefield ended up having to do it for him. Then a little more for himself.

Masefield took his down in one swallow, then set down his cup. He took a deep breath. "James..."

James looked up, startled by the gentleness in the policeman's voice.

"Nadine's body's been found."

An arctic air mass moved across Lake Superior and down into southeastern Wisconsin overnight, icing everything in its path. Though the sun rose sharp and bright in a cloudless sky, the wind-chill was a bone-cracking and record-breaking minus-forty. Icebergs were already forming along the Lake

Michigan shoreline, an incredible sight for an early December that hadn't even seen its first snowfall.

Nadine Jeffrey's body had washed ashore in little Whitefish Bay, just north of Milwaukee. The Medical Examiner's autopsy concluded that an accurate determination of time-of-death had been rendered impossible by several days' worth of exposure to the frigid water, but the grisly specifics of the victim's ante-mortem wounds, coupled with the evidence of a postmortem drop from a great height into the Lake, left little doubt that Nadine Jeffrey had been slaughtered by the killer who was beginning to be known on the Milwaukee streets, with a ghoulish dose of compensatory trench humor, as "Dropped Dead Fred."

Lupe said little when James broke the news to her that evening. Though he refrained from filling her in on the substance of his conversation with Calvin Masefield, at Masefield's insistence, James could tell by her pallid expression that she was beginning to see the pattern, too. Nor did she comment when she learned that Masefield was placing her under guard, twenty-four-by-seven; nor even when she put her arm around James's waist and felt, for the first time, the automatic pistol holstered in the small of his back.

For James's part, he wished to God it were an Uzi.

———

Two interminable days later, James's phone rang.

"Buddy," came Jack's baritone drawl from the other end of the line, "I'm downtown here at ye olde Grand Aveenoo Mall. Howsabout you and me headin' over to the John Hawks and havin' us a gaudy night, jus' like ol' times, huh?"

"Sounds as if you've already got a hefty breeze blowing in your sails."

"I'm as pickled as a Claussen Kosher Dill," Jack admitted with a sniffle.

James leapt inwardly at an opportunity for indulging himself in a much needed dose of Jack Sigur's rollicking good-humor, until he realized that his friend was actually crying. "Jack, old friend, what's the matter?"

"Tellin' you what's the truth," Jack sobbed, "those boys down in that damned poh-leece building wanna pin all this nasty shit on me, and I haven't been with a girl since I can remember!" The pathos of Jack's weeping was counterpointed by the distant sound of a brass band, tooting out a medley of Christmas carols in the mall somewhere nearby.

"Hang on," James said into the phone, reaching for his keys, "I'll meet you in fifteen minutes at the Plankinton Arcade."

———

After a brief detour to the pissoir, James and Jack navigated the wide-planked oak floor of the John Hawks Pub, James providing starboard ballast to Jack's port-side list. James piloted Jack to one of the corner booths in the smoking section, where Jack's inebriated condition wouldn't be so noticeable. When the waiter bounced over, James ordered coffee and a Reuben sandwich for Jack, too drunk to make up his own mind, and his staple grilled tuna and

Black and Tan for himself.

"Damn, Jim-bo," Jack said, his baritone finally giving evidence of a modest return of lucidity, "you ought to be home, cozying up to the O'Cruz."

"She wasn't feeling too chipper anyway. Probably just as well for me to leave her alone a bit."

Jack was alarmed. "You left that girl alone!"

"Not to worry. Patrick and her grandparents are home, and Masefield's got a cop watching the house like an obsessed groupie."

Jack exhaled his relief, then did a pie-eyed double-take at the Christmas lights wrapped around a swathe of garland on the wainscoting above their booth. "Wowza," he declared, "it's Advent!"

"So they tell me. Feels like the last Lent before the Apocalypse."

Jack had nothing to say to this gloomy analysis. Instead he closed his eyes and promptly dozed off. As soon as the waiter returned with their drinks, James filled the downtime by sipping his brew and taking survey of the pictures hung on the wall of their booth. The frame above Jack's nodding head contained the frontispiece to some nineteenth-century edition of *Measure for Measure*, while the print above his own contained a black-and-white sketch of the stormy shipwreck of a lake freighter: *The Wreck of the Edmund Fitzgerald, November 10, 1975* read the spidery handwriting at the bottom of the print.

"Christ."

"Say, what?" Jack lifted his head, put one hand over a cavernous yawn, and with the other, reached inside his jacket for a pack of Lucky Strikes.

"I'll have one of those," James announced, realizing he'd left his own smokes at home.

Handing over the pack, Jack winked. "We'll quit when all this shit's over, right?"

"Right-o."

They fired up.

"What were you drinking before?" James asked.

"Stark's Dark, by the bucket. Remember what Housman said, *Malt does more than Milton can to justify God's ways to man.*"

"Stark's Dark! I thought you had more selective taste buds than that."

"Hey, it was Ramon's doing. He kept ordering the swill and I kept tanking it."

"You mean to tell me you went out drinking with Ramon Cruz?"

"Well, yeah. Well no." Jack frowned with drunken confusion, his brown eyes fixed on their two columns of smoke mingling in a curl towards the ceiling. "See, Masefield called me in for another interview this morning, hang him, and whadya know, them little boys blue went and shoved me in an eight-by-ten with some pit bull from the FBI. The guy gnawed my leg for *two hours* trying to get me to 'fess up to these murders, all because I smoked that pack of Players at Lanciano's party back in September. Well, hell, after a while I realized it was all just a lousy fishing expedition, and that they didn't really think I'd done it, so I sez to the guy, 'hey, bub, or have I missed something? I've never been much into girls, ya know.' 'Yeah,' sez the as-swipe, 'we were trolling for barracuda, and netted ourselves a bottom-feeder instead.'"

James winced.

"This cheesed me off, let me tell you. I won't repeat what I said. But it was at this point in the colloquy that Professor Masefield came stomping in. Apparently he'd been watching us through that two-way glass thingy and didn't like what he was seeing. So he gives the Feebie this really nasty look—you know how he does, *de haut en bas*—and ordered little Dudley Do-Right O'Cruz to 'escort' me home." Jack took one last drag on his cigarette and reached for his coffee, then, thinking better of it, James's Black and Tan. "Tell you what's the truth, Jim-bo," he said, smacking his lips and clunking the pint on the table, sloshing some beer on his hand, "I was such a quivering glob of gelatin by that time that I told Ramon to drop me off at the nearest liquor establishment. So what does Ramon Roberto Cruz up and do?" Jack snickered ferociously. "He goes and hauls me wide-eyed and innocent into some State Street cop bar. Wowza, I never seen so much leather and chains since Bo Jeffrey's last Halloween party. Well, no matter. I was happy to drink on Ramon's invite, and happy to tell him, in return, everything I knew about everybody."

"That must have taken awhile." James reached for his beer.

Jack grabbed the pint from the other side. "Whadya doin', bunk?"

"I'd like to drink my beer, if you don't mind. What the hell is 'bunk?'"

"Cop slang for 'partner.'" Jack suddenly sounded remarkably sober. "Sorry about the beer, but I don't think you should drink after me. Though I suppose the alcohol would kill anything..." Jack rubbed his knitted forehead. "I know I ain't exactly thinking clearly at the precise moment, but they've done some research into sharing toothbrushes—"

"Now, Jack, don't tell me you've got strep throat again, it's only December. This is Wisconsin. You've got five more months of winter to survive."

Jack's creamy face flushed brick red; but before he could say anything more, the waiter had returned with their baskets of sandwiches. James ordered two more pints while Jack said a silent prayer over his food—just like Lupe, James thought—then zoomed in greedily on his Reuben. "Wunnerful, wunnerful," Jack said with a full mouth behind a silly grin. "How'd you know I wanted a Reuben?"

"You always order Reubens when we come here."

"*Thou art a gentleman and a scholar*—"

"*—let us therefore eat and drink!*"

"Hey, man, it's been too long!"

James squeezed lemon juice onto his grilled tuna. "My fault. These have been a profoundly weird few months. I've barely kept my head screwed on straight."

"You're not just whistlin' Dixie. I, for one, am ready to go *en vacances*, big time. Whadya say, howsabout you and me and Trish and Lu rent a cabin up in Copper Harbor for some serious skiing during the Christmas break, huh? Surely they got some snow up there by now."

"Splendid idea." James wrapped his jaws around his tuna sandwich. "Which reminds me," he said chewing, "do you realize we've never gone sailing together? I must take you sailing as soon as the weather turns. Maybe April, if we're good and lucky."

"By golly, boy, it's about time you asked!"

James suddenly stopped chewing. "Jack," he said, after finally getting the last swallow past his constricting throat. Their eyes locked across the table. "Jack…it's not strep throat, is it. Oh God, tell me it's not…that."

Jack said nothing for a moment. Finally he shrugged. "'Fraid so, bunk."

James closed his eyes. When he opened them again, Jack was looking at him strangely: James had put his hand over Jack's and was gripping it tightly. James pulled back. "How long have you known?"

Jack shrugged. "August. I've probably had it for a couple of years. But since I hadn't been going with anyone for, well, longer than I care to admit, I never bothered to get tested." Jack picked up a French fry to eye the corrugated pattern of its crinkles. "When I got a lesion this summer, it wasn't hard to figure out what was what."

"Why didn't you tell me?"

"Friend, I may not understand much of what's been going on these last few months, but it didn't take X-ray vision to see that you're plate was fully loaded. Jeez, bud, I thought we were going to lose you to the rubber room more than once. Besides, I've been feeling great. It could be quite a while before anything else shows up. Maybe never, who knows? The meds are getting better all the time."

"Does Trisha know? I mean, you two…"

A portrait in indignation, Jack dropped his sandwich to wag a long brown finger in James's face. "Now lookee here, my romping days are over. I'm not prepared to go risking people's necks for the sublime privilege of sleeping with me."

"Can't you work around that?"

Jack glared at him. "You telling me you've never had one of them flimsy things break on you? Shit, I've had more than my share of trouble with the sixth commandment, but I'm not about to go flirting around with the fifth just for a few lousy minutes of splendor in the grass, now you hear what I'm saying?"

James tipped back his beer and drank half of it in one take, trying, with limited success, to steady his quivering hand through raw will power. "You and Lupe have a lot in common," was all he could think to say when he finally put the thing down rather than spill the rest of it all over the tabletop. "How are you doing on money…insurance?"

"Not too bad. Don't worry, I'll ask if I need help." Jack reached over the table to thump James on the shoulder. "Hey, don't worry so much. I'll be around a while, promise."

James slammed his fist on the table. "It's not fair! I'd lay odds I've been with dozens more women."

"So it goes. Probably got it from Bo, and he's been with more even than you, trust me. Not his fault, he didn't know either."

"Bo! I didn't know you two were ever together."

"Yeah, well," Jack drawled with good-humored sarcasm, "it wasn't exactly the most memorable experience of my life, know what I mean? But I was on the rebound, and maybe just a little too hungry to be careful."

James frowned. "A couple of years ago? On the rebound from whom? I didn't know you were seeing anyone since…well, since I've known you."

Jack shrugged it off. "C'mon, man, let's drop it."

"You don't mean…you mean on the rebound from that afternoon with me on the beach?"

Jack shrugged again, then sniffled, looked away, and finally wiped his nose on the sleeve of his sweatshirt as the waiter brought them two more pints.

"Tell you what," James said when the waiter was safely gone, "it would have been better all the way around if I'd slept with you instead of Bel and all the others. I lost a piece of myself with every goddamned affair, but Kim and Bel and Nadine…"

Jack frowned sharply. "Now ain't you got sins enough of your own? You talk as if some tutti frutti's out there attacking these women just because they slept with you." He shook his head as if he'd heard everything now.

"I guess that does sound a bit paranoid," James agreed, thinking that the FBI wasn't infallible, after all, nor even Calvin bloody Masefield.

"You're damned right. Dropped Dead Fred, he's just the *fin de siècle* version of a rabid dog or a runaway train. A freak of human nature, that's what Fred is. Kim and Bel and Nadine, they just ran out of luck. Wrong place at the wrong time, that's all."

"You don't understand."

"What I understand is that these things are complicated. Life's a problem play, bud. You can't always make the ending turn out just like you want."

"At least I haven't been with anyone since…" James glanced furtively out the windows overlooking the frozen Milwaukee River. The winter-cold sun had long since dropped behind the downtown buildings. Christmas lights twinkled on the potted evergreens on the patio like a constellation of midnight stars.

"Oh, don't worry too much about Trisha," Jack said with a wave. "She's one tough little critter. And to hear her tell it, you were stone drunk that night, while her own motives weren't exactly of the purest. She told me she was so desperate to prove her mom wrong, she would've laid fatso Rygiel that night, if you hadn't crossed her path first."

James was not following this line of thought at all. "What's Trisha's mother got to do with it?" Far from ever having heard her speak of any sort of family, James had almost formed an image of Trisha Perl having sprung out of the earth like a wood fairy.

Jack grunted. "She had the unqualified nerve to tell Trish she was turning sapphic because she knew she was lousy in bed. Leila's always ragging on her to make herself more attractive to men, or so says Trish."

"*Leila?*"

"Yeah, Leila Redmond. Didn't you know? She's Trisha's mom by her first husband."

James sat back, his mouth hanging open.

"Yeah," Jack said, apparently misinterpreting James's obvious shock, "strange how some women think."

"You're not just whistling Dixie," James whispered. He cleared his throat. "You and Trish have been, um, spending a lot of time together lately."

"Yepper. Been afraid to leave her alone, to tell you the truth." Then, when he finally caught James's drift Jack added, "C'mon, haven't you ever heard the word 'friendship?'"

"It's been something of a problematic concept for me." James admitted. "But speaking of which…" James cleared his throat again.

"Yeah, bunk?"

"I just wanted to tell you—" Covering the sudden crack in his voice with a cough, James fidgeted a bit, rapped his knuckles a couple of times on the tabletop, then drained his Black and Tan to the bottom. "Damn," he exclaimed, clunking the empty pint on the tabletop.

Jack Sigur's eyebrows shot up.

"What I mean to say is…I wonder where that waiter went off to? I told him we wanted more beer."

"What's on your mind, Jim-bo?"

James craned his head towards the salad bar, then back at Jack. "Oh, hell." He almost lunged across the table to clasp Jack's hand. "*Since my dear soul was mistress of her choice and could of men distinguish her election, she hath sealed thee for herself.*"

It was Jack's turn to be surprised.

"You're the best friend I've ever had. I'm not sure but that you're the only real friend I've ever had. You always want to think the best of me, and you've never tried to make me into something I'm not, just to please you."

Jack's tawny face flushed hotly.

"I know I haven't always been the best friend in return. Hell, I've even pushed you away sometimes, I know it. I suppose it unnerved me that you hoped for a different sort of relationship from what I could possibly give. But whatever the case, you stuck by me. After Bel was killed, I think you were the only person besides Lupe who somehow knew I wasn't a murderer, just because…well, just because you knew me. I love you, Jack."

They were silent for a few seconds, and Jack finally pulled away his hand. He patted James once on the arm before wiping his moist eyes with his sweatshirt sleeve. James took the opportunity to catch the passing attention of their waiter and motion for two more pints. "You know, I haven't got much of a family left," James continued a moment later, "and I'll be surprised if anyone from my side even makes it to the wedding. But I was wondering if you'd be my best man. Maybe godfather, too, if we have children."

"I'd be honored," Jack said with uncharacteristic gravity. "You know, facing this thing I have, this thing that's probably going to kill me someday sooner than I'd like, well, it got me thinking."

"What about?"

"Well, it seems to me that there's only two things in this life, maybe three, that end up mattering much."

"What's that?"

"Faith in something bigger than your little self, for one. Your family and friends for another."

"And the third thing?"

"Feeling like it made a difference to somebody I was here."

"It's made a difference. A huge difference."

Jack nodded, a kind of silent 'thank you.' When the waiter brought their Black and Tans, they clinked their pints.

"You know what," Jack said suddenly, "I think I'm going to try out for the Florentine Opera Chorus this Spring."

"No!"

"Yeah, I think I will. Hell, we're none of us going to live forever. We've got to make the most of our time, you know?"

"Absolutely." They drank deeply.

"Say, did I ever tell you about that last time I talked to Father B?"

James shook his head.

"I went to confession the day he died. Yessir, first time in…we're talkin' *years*. Don't know what got into me all of a sudden. Oh, I'd gotten the bad news a couple of weeks before, then Lupe and I went to the party at Lanciano's, and suddenly I just *knew*—don't tell me how—I just knew you and she were meant to be. Well, it hit me like a goddamned brick. 'Jackson Beauregard Sigur,' sez I to myself, 'chances are slim to none for your ever having anything like that. Especially now.' I mean, it was a little hard to accept at first, you know?"

James knew, all right: his own relationship with Lupe had fallen on him like a healing rain in a desert, unlooked-for and wholly undeserved.

"Anyhow, I felt like I had to talk to somebody. I happened to be walking by the old padre's office the next morning, so I rapped on his door, and oh Lord the poor old man looked sick as a dog. But he hustled me right into his office like I was just the person he'd been longing to talk to." Jack took a deep breath. "I told that priest everything. Sunrise to sunset."

"The whole sack of potatoes."

"Yo. And you know what the man said? Well, here I was expecting a no doubt well-deserved but wholly unwelcome lecture on chastity, and all the man sez to me is, *Jackson…*" Jack stiffened, pressed his hand against his chest and wheezed—an imitation of the old priest so perfect that James thought he would choke. "*—you're a good man, and I know you wouldn't risk anyone's* *life by acting irresponsibly, so we won't even discuss that."* Jack shook his head. "Buddy, it blew me clean out of the ballpark. Before I knew it I was telling him all about my dad, and how he'd tried to get in touch with me over the years, and how I had refused to see him because I was still so pissed at him for taking off all those years ago. Well finally the padre sez to me—" Jack sat up again and resumed his uncanny imitation. "—*Jackson Sigur, your first order of business is to forgive your father his human failings and for the love of Christ*—" He wheezed noisily. "—*go see the man!*" Jack collapsed against his booth as if he'd just managed a narrow escape. "And so I did. That's how I ended up down in Chicago for Thanksgiving. Man, did we have a lot to catch up on."

"Wow."

There was a lengthy silence, during which time the two friends finished their food. Suddenly—it was obviously unpremeditated—Jack's hand shot across the table to clutch James's shirtsleeve. "Bunk," he exclaimed, "you've got to do the same."

"Do what?"

"Forgive your father for being an ass-hole. And the Kratos. Feels like shit, I know, but it's the only way."

Over cheesecake and coffee, the conversation turned once again to the more immediate situation at hand.

"Just exactly what were they questioning you about this afternoon?" James asked, who hadn't heard anything from Masefield since Nadine's body had been found.

Jack snorted. "It was mostly about Rosenstern, if you can believe it. Ramon wanted to know if I had I ever heard one of 'em mention the name of Candace Duffy. Now, have you *ever?*"

"Well, had you ever?"

"As if! I mean, can you imagine either one of those bass-ackward bozos with a hooker?" Jack slapped the tabletop, howling in derision. "I mean, c'mon, man, they wouldn't know what to put where! Oh, but that ain't the half of it. You'll love this. Then Ramon up and asks me if I knew of any guy at the Institute who could be obsessed with someone whose name began with the letter 'J.' Now, how's that for weird?"

"It's weird right enough. What did you say?"

"Well, what do you think I said?"

James frowned. The expression on Jack's face suggested that he thought the answer to this strange question should somehow be obvious. Not really wanting to know but unable to resist asking, he said, barely above a whisper, "I know I'm slow about these things, but you're going to have to explain it to me."

Jack didn't answer right away. Instead he shook his head several times and slapped his spidery fingers some more on the tabletop, as if he'd heard everything now. "Now if that isn't you all over. Godomighty, how a man as smart as you are can be so completely clueless sometimes is just way beyond my imagination. I mean, *think* about it a sec."

"I've been thinking about little else for weeks."

"Well, who of all the guys you know would switch his brand of cigarette just because he saw you smoking Marlboros? He's such a freakin' copycat."

James opened his mouth, then just as quickly closed it.

"You know that colloquium you took last spring on all those *gauchiste* Froggy Theorists?"

James pulled a face.

"So, who is it's been trying to catch up with your reading list ever since? Foucault, Derrida, Artaud…even that wonky Aztec priest wannabe, Bataille. *Gésu*, what a sick bastard."

"You don't mean—"

"I mean the boy's been making a spectacle of his big ugly self trying to keep up with you. *Yond gull Malvolio is turned heathen, a very renegado!* Golding up his hair to match yours…man, haven't you noticed the clothes he's been wearing these last coupla months? Khakis and jeans and corduroys and polo shirts—" Jack gestured at James's flannel shirt. "I saw him flipping through a Land's End catalog last week. Just you wait, he'll be in flannel before the week's out, and him with the chassis of a Peterbilt. Don't know which he'll resemble more, Paul Bunyon or Babe the Blue Ox. Oh, and let's not forget all those hoity-toity Prairie School stuff he wears every chance he gets, just so he's got something to rack up against your ratty old Oxford paraphernalia. Buddy, I'm tellin' you what's the truth, the soul of that manchild is his clothes! Or should I say, *your* clothes."

James gripped the edge of the table.

"Hey, now, don't you be takin' it so personally. I mean, why should you be paying attention to Mitchell Showalter's little peccadilloes all of a sudden? You sure as hell never did before."

James pressed the heel of his hand against the side of his pounding head, a remnant of the late-November concussion that resurfaced whenever he felt the pressure of tears behind his eyes—an almost daily trial of late. He reached for one of Jack's cigarette's. "I had to give Masefield a list, you know," he said quietly, lighting up. "A list of every woman I've had sex with in the last three years. It was longer than I remembered. God, how humiliating. At least he hasn't bothered Trish. She's so tiny, and he's so big, it terrifies me to think—" James tripped into silence over the expression on Jack's face. .

"Yeah, he's bothered her," Jack said dully. "Masefield didn't want it getting out—something about denying the perpetrator the satisfaction of free publicity—but someone vandalized her apartment night before last. Spraypainted swastikas and Nazi slogans, in German no less, up one wall and down the other. Thank God she wasn't there. Masefield told Leila Redmond to leave town for a while, and Trish is staying with me."

James took a hit on his fag, and groaned out the smoke.

Jack licked his lips. "Are you telling me…"

James nodded.

Jack began to look queasy. "Sweet Jesus. Mr. Anxiety-of-Influence himself. God help us all."

After dropping Jack off at his apartment, James headed to the Meir Library where was to be found, or so a call to the reference desk librarian had informed him earlier that afternoon, a complete collection, on microfiche, of yearbooks from Bradford High School in Kenosha. With some assistance from this same librarian, James was soon seated in a carrel before a microfiche reader, looking for "Showalter" entries in the yearbooks for the period of time during which Mitch would have been a high school student. James didn't really have any idea what he was looking for, only that he hoped he would recognize it if he saw it.

As it turned out, there was disappointingly little to be learned in the appropriate editions about Mitch Showalter, high school student. For example, in spite of his Superglue memory, Mitch never made the Bradford High honor roll—a fact which, upon mature consideration, was not all that surprising to James, given the big man's spotty academic performance at the Institute. Gifted he might be, oh yes, but something in Mitch Showalter's mind or personality lacked a clear, individual imprint. His labors rarely brought forth anything intelligible, let alone remarkable. Equally unsurprising, given Mitch's less than stellar social skills, he had participated in few if any extracurricular activities.

What was surprising, however, was the plethora of pictures in the old yearbooks of Mitch's older brother, J. Edgar—named, if James remembered correctly (and if Mitch had been telling the truth for a change) after their father's hero, J. Edgar Hoover. Athletic, good looking, and blonde, James Edgar Showalter had not only appeared on the Bradford High honor roll three years running, he was also captain of the tennis team and the school's most acclaimed student thespian. He had played the lead in *The Sound of Music* his junior year and *Kiss Me Kate* his senior—the same year he was elected Prom King. He had even successfully auditioned for the theater program at Yale. And he went by the nickname of "Jimmy."

His mouth going dry, James scanned the prom pictures from Jimmy Showalter's senior year at Bradford High, shortly before he had run away from home, according to James's recollection of Mitch's oft-repeated tale. He paused at length before a photograph in a spread covering the Senior Prom.

"Hey, what's up?" a timid voice sounded behind him.

James whirled around. "Rich," he said, getting hold of himself with some effort, his heart thumping, "what a surprise. I believe this is the first time you've initiated a conversation with me in over three years." James stood up, mainly to deprive Richard Krato of the opportunity of looking down his aquiline nose at him.

But this evening at least, James's former roommate seemed to have lost the attitude of righteous self-assurance he normally carried around with him like a security blanket. "I was just over there, trying to read Mitch's paper," he said. "I saw you and I thought, you know, maybe I should…" Richard shifted his weight to his right foot.

"Good God, Rich, do you and Peter have any clue as to what's going on over there at SANA house," James said with exasperation, "any clue at all?"

Richard shifted to the other foot. "Lt. Masefield stopped by this morning," was all he would say.

James had a pretty good idea as to the nature of the visit. "Are you finally going to help him?"

Richard just stood there, shifting back and forth from foot to foot, his jaw working as if he had a sore tooth, his handsome eyes wavering. In spite of himself, James felt his long-standing indignation towards Richard Krato dissolving into sadness and a belated sense of mourning for the friend he had lost three years before. After all, he scolded himself, why should Richard have proved any more skilled at human relationships than he? Richard Krato, like himself, was to be counted among the walking wounded, and people were not always wounded in the same place or the same way.

"Maybe this will help you sort it out," James said, not unkindly. He aimed his index finger at the picture on the screen. "This is a senior prom picture from Bradford High School in Kenosha. It's Mitch's brother and his date. Mitch went to Bradford High, you know, not Prairie School. Did Masefield tell you how Mitch has lied about his background?"

"A little," Richard admitted, his face curling in consternation. He had been copping glances at the microfiche reader from the moment he appeared, but now permitted himself to lean forward and study it openly. "Jimmy…" he said. "That's what Mitch always calls you. He even looks like you." Richard straightened himself. "Okay, so it's kinda weird. But what's the big deal?"

"Dammit, Rich, look at the picture!"

"I'm looking at it!"

James was still pointing at the screen. "Look at the *girl*."

Leaning forward again, Richard Krato squinted at the picture of Jimmy Showalter's prom night date, then moved in closer. "It's Mitch's old girlfriend," he said with a note of wonder, "the one he used to have a picture of back at the old House. What was she doing, going to the prom with Mitch's brother?

"Rich," James said, the last remnant of his three years of anger melting into a sickening wash of pity, "it's Candace Duffy."

Chapter Thirteen:
The Dreadful Beast

By this, the dreadfull Beast drew nigh to hand,
Halfe flying and halfe footing in his hast,
That with his largenesse measured much land,
And made wide shadow vnder his huge wast;
As mountaine doth the valley ouercast.
Approaching nigh, he reared high afore
His body monstrous, horrible, and vaste;
Which to increase his wondrous greatnesse more,
Was swolne with wrath, & poyson, & with bloudy gore.

Edmund Spenser, *The Faerie Qveene*

James peeled off his parka and helped himself to one of Masefield's cigarettes. "Graduated to full strength I see."

"Friend, we're a pair." Taking a deep drag on his Marlboro, Masefield heaved his feet up on his desk like a satisfied man. "But it'll be over soon."

James' cigarette paused in mid-air.

"You were right. *I am not what I am.* Showalter's been lying about a whole heckuva lot of stuff. It'll take some time to sort it out, but it's a ray of light splitting the storm clouds."

James sat down. "What do you have?"

"Mitch's father's name was Jim Showalter. Whether it was egotism or lack of imagination I don't know, but he named both his sons after himself. The eldest, James Edgar, went by the name of 'Jimmy.' The younger, James Mitchell, went by the name of Mitch. When anyone bothered to remember his name at all. They had a two-bedroom frame house on Sheridan Road north of Kenosha. His entire neighborhood's a row of little frame houses from the fifties and sixties, some of them overlooking the Pike River flood plain and old raspberry bogs. The lakeside villa he claimed as his own is down the road a ways, and sure enough, belongs to a retired Carthage College English professor who's lived there for thirty-odd years. Unfortunately, the absent-minded old gent has only the vaguest of recollections about his neighbor who worked the cafeteria at Carthage, and even less about the woman's strapping son who mowed his lawn for pin money."

"Peculiar," James agreed, "but it's slim evidence upon which to base an assumption of multiple homicides."

"Oh you bet. But there was one other thing we've found out that may prove more significant."

"What?"

"The Outagamie County Sheriff faxed me some stuff this morning from Green Bay. One of their veteran officers heard about our troubles down here—Dropped Dead Fred and all. He remembered a series of unsolved rapes he'd worked almost a decade ago. Three UW-Green Bay girls who were abducted and brutally sodomized, all three with long dark hair. The pictures indicated a strong resemblance to Candace Duffy. Showalter was an undergrad there at the time. Took the guy six years to get his BA. But as it happens—get this—Showalter was one of about fifty different guys on campus that they pulled in for questioning, because his physique matched one of the victim's general description of her attacker's size. And he'd been seen in a student bar the same night the last girl was abducted."

"She couldn't identify him?"

"Positive IDs were out of the question because he used a condom and wore gloves and a ski mask. And Showalter's aunt gave him an alibi for the entire weekend the last girl was attacked...say, you all right?"

"It's a lot to absorb. But you look different today. You think it's him, don't you?"

"Yep."

"What about Peter Krato?"

Masefield smiled slightly. "Let it go, James. He's a charlatan and a coward, not a murderer. Sure, for a while there I thought Krato might be a textbook religious fanatic gone bonkers, but his claim to be in Rome at the time of Nadine Jeffrey's murder checked out. We talked to several Vatican officials verifying his visits. Attempted visits, rather. They refused to meet with him, said it was a local matter between him and the Archdiocese. And all our digging turned up zip on Sigur and Lanciano and Richard Krato."

"That leaves Mitch."

"That leaves Mitch. Supposedly—and conveniently—always holed up in his little room on the first floor of SANA House at the time of the murders. A sort of alibi, in that his SANA buddies were always seeing him going to bed, then coming out of the room the next morning. By the way, I asked Sigur what he thought Showalter's attitude was towards you, and he answered, without batting an eyelash, 'If Mitch were gay I'd say he was in love with the guy. But since he isn't, I'd say he wishes he *were* James.'"

James mashed out his cigarette.

"Here, have another. I'd offer you a shot of booze to chase it, but I don't keep any in the office."

James reached for the proffered cigarette, feeling he had become impervious to shock. "When are you going to arrest him?" he said dully.

Masefield lit another for himself as well. "I wish it were that simple. We could hold him on suspicion for 24 hours, but without some substantial hard evidence—prints, an eyewitness, a DNA sample—the laziest judge in town would throw us out of court for lack of habeas corpus. Then Showalter might bolt. Of course, we haven't known where to look till now. God, I wish I'd taken Sigur into my confidence earlier. He knew everything without knowing he knew anything."

James now began to feel dizzy, the last remnant of his mid-November concussion. He gripped the arms of the chair; it was either that or reach for the nearest trash can to be sick.

"One thing's for sure," Masefield continued blithely, apparently unaware of his guest's rocky state, "Showalter's a hell of an actor. You should have seen him with the Feebies yesterday. He was sunbathing in the sunshine of their attention. By the way, I'm taking the surveillance off Lupe and putting it on him, twenty-four-by-seven."

That, at last, brought some spark to James's mind. "Well, for God's sake, let me be the first to know if he loses you!" he exclaimed.

"Will do. And James, I wasn't born yesterday, I know you've got a gun. I've got a pretty damned good idea who you got it from, too." Masefield held up his hand to forestall James's imminent objection. "I'm not going to lecture you. I'm just telling you, keep your nose clean. If you go after him, you might not only do yourself more harm than him, you could mess up our chances for a conviction."

"Jack is taking Trisha Perl out of town," James said, his nausea passing but his thoughts once again engulfed in gloom. "And I'm going to ask Franco to cancel tomorrow's class. 'Out of town' sounds bloody good right now."

Masefield stood up and leaned over the desk. "I've already talked to Lanciano about that class. It needs to go on as scheduled. In fact, I'm going to be there."

James looked up, aghast. "But…why?"

"Listen to me. We've got a crapload of circumstantial evidence, but we can't arrest him because we've got no probable cause. Our only option right now is to crank up the pressure. That's how they got Gacy you know, by keeping the pressure on him till he finally slipped up. If you call off that class tomorrow he's going to smell it, and he might take a permanent vacation himself without our being able to stop him. Right now, all he knows is that we've been pushing him, just like we've been pushing you and Sigur and Lanciano and the Kratos and just about everybody else. He doesn't know we've weeded out everyone but him."

"You can't expect me to take Lupe into that classroom tomorrow!"

"James—"

James jumped to his feet, cigarette ashes dropping unnoticed on his slacks and the carpeting. "Why do I get this feeling that you're taking the guards off Lupe because you're hoping he *will* go for her? Well, fuck you, Calvin Masefield, if that's what you're doing!"

Masefield pointed his cigarette at him. "Listen, Ireton, we've got a manpower problem. We can't have the entire Milwaukee Police Department standing guard over every woman you've screwed in the last three years."

They glared at each other. James was the first to deflate. "Quite," he said softly, turning his back and moving towards the door.

Masefield was right behind him. "Damn...I'm sorry, James, that was a low blow. What's happening here isn't your fault. It *isn't your fault*. But that doesn't mean you can't help me."

James let go of the knob. "How?" he whispered.

"He's put you and me and everyone around here in the category of 'brain dead.' All these guys like him, they all want to think the rest of the world — and especially the homicide squad — are a bunch of local yokels who don't know jack. Help me throw him off, surprise him."

James turned finally, his shoulders sagging. "What do you have in mind?"

"Let's call it a play within a play. He's played *Othello* on you, now it's our turn to play *Hamlet* on him." Masefield smiled grimly. "The class is the thing, wherein we'll catch the conscience of our demon-king!"

James glanced with affected nonchalance at Calvin Masefield, who was chatting like an old chum, head to head, with Franco Lanciano at one end of the seminar table. The substitute lecturer had been asked to stay home, James had been informed, because Lanciano, at Masefield's suggestion, had decided to conduct the last class of the term himself.

James shivered. The first significant snow of the season was being predicted for the next twenty-four hours, and the mere anticipation of it was making him stiff with cold. Pulling a sweater over his flannel shirt, he reached for Lupe's clammy hand under the table, wondering how she would take what was about to happen, whatever the hell that was.

Unusual as it was, Masefield's unannounced appearance this afternoon, though a subject of some whispering, didn't seem to be taking anyone wholly by surprise. The speculation was rife, after all, that Dropped Dead Fred was a student among them. James knew that Masefield was planning, if anyone asked, to explain his presence by saying that he wanted to "get better acquainted" with the Institute and its students. Nobody asked.

Frankly, Masefield's hopes of kicking something loose in Mitch — the idea had come to him, so Masefield had told him, after reading Mitch's loopy research paper, which the lieutenant for some reason found unusually revealing — seemed altogether mad to James; a fantasy plucked from a Perry Mason episode in which the killer tearfully confesses under brilliant cross-examination, and all loose ends are tidied up before the last commercial. What James had wanted to do more than anything, and had frankly considered, was to bring the Grendel to class and shoot Mitch square between the eyes as soon as he entered the room. After all, the small-caliber pistol probably wouldn't do the job against a man Mitch's size at anything but close range, and probably with a considerable element of surprise.

But then, James reminded himself morosely, they weren't absolutely sure, were they?

Mitch Showalter loped in at five to. He was sporting a brand new flannel shirt, almost identical to James's, and his appearance in it elicited a guffaw from Jack Sigur. Apparently not realizing that he was the object of Jack's scorn, let alone why, Mitch ignored him, but eyed Masefield and Lanciano with a sideways squint, his bow-shaped lips parted in a faintly derisive smile as he pulled a copy of his manuscript, then a paperback, out of his briefcase, set them on the table, and seated himself next to Richard, who turned instantly white.

James resisted a temptation to close his eyes. God help him, he thought, he could feel Bel and Nadine in this room, standing over them all like spectral sentinels, pointing their skeletal fingers of blame in his guilty face.

The syllabus called for a discussion of Mitch's paper during the first hour, while the second hour was to be given to a summing-up lecture which James was to read from notes he had gleaned from Fr. Bricusse's scholarly leavings. Otherwise, Masefield had asked Lanciano to keep a loose rein on the class and give Mitch plenty of rope; but as the prescribed conversation loped along predictable scholarly lines for the first thirty minutes, Mitch condescended to say little about his own work, and even succumbed to an attack of narcolepsy during one of Jack's longer and intentionally goofy perorations on Mitch's jungle of jargonated weirdery, most of it lifted wholesale from Mitch's favorite Deconstructionists and New Historicists. This, for some reason, seemed to fascinate Masefield no end. The lieutenant studied the dozing Showalter with flagrant curiosity before finally speaking up, his first comment since the bell rang:

"Would someone mind explaining to a civilian, in plain English, just what this 'deconstruction' and 'new history' stuff is all about?"

The Encyclopedia Showalter was suddenly alert. "Deconstruction and New Historicism," he replied, sitting up, "are two of the leading schools of contemporary literary criticism which Professor Harold Bloom of Yale has termed 'The School of Resentment.' Specifically, Deconstruction is the method, borrowing liberally from Hegelian dialectic by way of Nietzsche, used to explicate a given text without reference to authors or authorial intentions, so that in the end the text is made to mean the very opposite of what the uninitiated reader thinks the author intended it to mean. New Historicism, on the other hand, is the critical school which, borrowing liberally from Hegelian dialectic by way of Marx, explicates a given text without reference to authors or authorial intentions, so that in the end the text is made to further the class struggle." Mitch directed his pasty sneer directly at Masefield's placid half-smile.

"Are we gonna have to sit through another ninety minutes of Showalter's glossolalia?" James heard Trish grumbling.

Donning his reading glasses, Jack raised a slender forefinger. "As for me, I prefer Jimmy's more squirrely definitions, from his recently published book." Jack lifted his copy of *The Conscience of the Prince* and waved it at Mitch like a matador taunting a bull. "Quoth he, 'A Deconstructor is the Shaman-in-the-Wilderness of postmodern literary culture who practices the sado-masochistic, surgico-linguistic art of cannibalizing the corpses, or *corpuses*, of his tribal enemy, the Dead White European Male, for the purpose of incorporating said enemy's Juju into himself.' On the other hand, Jimmy describes the New Historicist as 'the Boy Scout-in-the-Wilderness of postmodern literary culture, who practices the sado-masochistic, surgico-linguistic art of performing autopsies on the corpses, or *corpuses*, of his class enemy, the Dead White European Male, for the purpose of feeding the rotting meat to the illiterate masses…who, all in all, would just as soon have a Big Mac and a Supersize fries, thanks all the same.'"

Mitch rolled his cherub-blue eyes. "*We're all killers on land and on sea,*" he intoned, "*Bonapartes and sharks included.*"

"That's clever," a student in the back said approvingly.

"That's Melville," James corrected. "*How well he's read to reason against reading.*"

"That's Shax!" Jack exclaimed. "But didn't Harbage claim you could prove anything by quoting Shakespeare?"

"No," James said, "he claimed you could prove anything by quoting *Hamlet*. I was quoting *Love's Labours Lost.*"

"This linguistic stuff is fascinating, people," Masefield interjected, "but if you'll humor me, as a cop, I'm more interested in Mr. Showalter's opinions on Shakespeare's portrayals of evil. From what I'm hearing, Mr. Showalter here thinks Hamlet is the real bad guy of the play." He tossed his copy of Mitch's paper face down and turned to James. "I believe you edited an article by Fr. Bricusse on the nature of evil in Shakespeare. What did the good old priest have to say on the subject?"

James leaned against the back of his chair for emotional support. "Father was especially fond of Othello," he said in his academic voice, "an essentially noble character flawed by jealousy and a dragon-like wrath. As a priest and confessor, Bricusse told me he had seen such men any number of times."

"*Othello wasn't jealous*, Jimmy," Mitch interrupted, his eyes popping open after another thirty-second nap, "*he was trusting.*"

"Dostoevsky!" Jack cried, stabbing his finger in the air, "*Crime and Punishment.*"

"It's Dostoevsky quoting Pushkin in *The Brothers K*," Trisha said.

Mitch stared dreamily at the door of the classroom, as if expecting the imminent re-appearance of a long-lost relative. "I never got around to reading the old man's article. What did he say about Iago?"

Ignoring Mitch, James addressed Masefield. "The subtitle of Father's article was 'The Ecology of Evil in Shakespeare.' Father's thesis was that the crimes of villains like Iago are the very stuff of everyday sin: murder, envy, slander…lying, above all. Iago, like similar villains in Shakespeare—say, Richard III or Edmund in *King Lear*—simply take these sins to a rare and self-aware extreme. But Bricusse also points out that every one of us, in some way, contributes to the ecology of evil in which these villains thrive. Shakespeare's villains, like his protagonists, are always sinned against as well as sinning."

"Yeah, well we'd probably all turn out like Iago," Mitch agreed, "if we knew we could get by with it."

James finally looked across the table at Mitch. "That was Father's opinion, too. The Iagos of the world simply do what many more of us would do if there were no law to restrain us. Bricusse felt that somehow—" He leaned forward. "—before the beginning of the play, Iago had experienced an interior removal of restraint, of what nature the playwright doesn't give a clear answer."

"*To escape from the Castle of Conscience, we must first enter the Castle of Murders,*" Mitch quoted.

"Bataille!" Jack guessed with a slap of the tabletop. "No, Derrida!"

"*Bzzzt,* guess again!"

"Foucault," James said, "inspired, I believe, by De Sade."

"That's the whole problem with your paper," Trish said, screwing up her tiny nose. "It's not just bull, it's seventy pages of other people's bull."

"The god Dionysus was born from a bull," Mitch returned.

"And what god, Mr. Showalter," Masefield asked suddenly, "is born from a mutilated cat?"

It seemed to take Mitch a moment to absorb Masefield's statement. When he did, he shrugged his massive shoulders, a gesture of studied indifference that belied the rigid square of his jaw. "It doesn't take much study of literary history to see that villains and criminals are to us now what the gods were in classical times—agents of change. Wild cards who save civilization from the sheer boredom of goodness. *I have not time to tell you how I came to be a killer, but you should know, as time will show, that I'm society's pillar.*"

"Who the hell was that?" Jack wondered aloud.

"Jack the Ripper," James said.

"Good cannot exist without Evil," Mitch reminded them. "In fact, Good creates Evil."

"Evil is *p-p-privatio,*" Lupe spoke up suddenly, her first contribution of the afternoon. "The peculiar existence of no-no-nothing."

"*Sine d-d-diabolo, nullus red-d-demptor,*" Mitch mocked. "The archetypal *aporia.* As Derrida has shown, every structure can be shaken precisely because it's built on that which it attempts to exclude. In other words, Christianity, like every other religion, is a cult of human sacrifice, no different than the Aztecs or the Druids or the Canaanites. Even Aquinas recognized the Eucharist as cannibalism."

Lupe began to look quite shaken herself now that Mitch's pious mask had dropped from his pudgy face. "In our re-re-religion," she stammered, "God gives himself for us to eat...so we'll stop eating each other!"

"*Another one of Marlowe's inconclusive experiences.*"

Jack snapped his fingers. "Conrad's *Heart of Darkness.* The guy might have been a racist, but he could sure put pen to paper."

"Now that one I've read," Masefield said. "For sure, Conrad was a European with all the prejudices of his time and place. But like all great writers, he couldn't help but tell the truth now and then, maybe in spite of himself.

Remember that one telling line…?" The lieutenant held out an expectant hand towards Mitch, one bushy eyebrow lifted.

"*Kurtz had kicked himself loose of the earth…a soul that knew no restraint!*"

"Close, Mr. Showalter, but no cigar."

"*All Europe contributed to the making of Kurtz!*"

"That's even better, but still not what I was thinking of."

"*And this also,*" James said suddenly, looking with shocky eyes around the clean spaces, bright windows, and plush furnishings of the Institute seminar room, "*has been one of the dark places of the earth.*"

Masefield slapped the table. "Give Mr. Ireton a Kewpie doll! I do believe he's several points ahead of you in round one, Mr. Showalter."

Mitch shrugged, a pantomime of indifference. "The point is, Kurtz is attached to civilization by definition, just as much as Homer or Shakespeare. *Whatever Kurtz was, he was not common.*"

Richard, pale as his shirt, finally got up the gumption to look his fellow SANA member in the face. "I can't believe you really believe the things you're saying today."

"But he's been saying them for months!" Lupe exclaimed. "We just ha-haven't been listening."

James felt the skin on his back creeping along his spine as Mitch squinted at her, as if puzzling out a challenging crossword. Finally the big man's face lit up. "*The Heisler Institute is a place of advanced study, dedicated to the principle that Art and Idea shape the structure of the world.* You know, the old 'ideas have consequences' theory. But the truth is, we're just having an abstract philosophical and literary discussion here. Ideas are just word-games, and sooner or later every honest person wakes up one morning and realizes that, all in all, every word ever spoken by anyone is at least half a lie. In which case, the only really honest thing to do is to shut the hell up."

Masefield nodded. "*From this time forth I never will speak word,* as honest Iago says. But I can think of another response, Mr. Showalter. And that's to go more than halfway and lie to the teeth."

Mitch opened his arms. "Could it possibly matter? The lying indeterminacy of speech is an inescapable psychological condition of postmodern man. If there's one thing I learned from Peter Krato, it's that language is not about expressing meaning and truth, it's about moving people from point A to point B to serve your purposes. It reminds me of the theologian who wrote that no modern man who uses light bulbs could possibly believe in the Resurrection."

"Bricusse," James countered, "was certainly a modern man who used, and even understood, light bulbs. And he still believed in the Resurrection."

Mitch laid his palms flat on the table, his fingers splayed. "Do you, Jimmy? Do you believe in the Resurrection?"

James wavered, but not for long. "It's either true," he said, "or nothing is true."

"God knows that's true!" Mitch turned to Masefield. "How about you, Lieutenant? Do you still believe in the Resurrection, or have you tossed that out as a colonialist myth imposed on your ancestors by their white oppressors?"

Masefield smiled patiently. "Oh, I think hope in a resurrection is reasonable enough. And I've seen a lot of dead bodies in my time, Mr. Showalter. A few more even than you, I think."

Mitch sucked air, not the only one in the class. A thrum of whispers broke through the room that shattered against James's eardrums like the sound of breaking glass. He gripped Lupe's moist hand under the table.

Mitch laughed out loud. "Resurrection is just the teleological version of the Love Conquers All bromide. Bullshit. You're all reducing metahistorical narrative to the Christian tradition. As the emperor Julian learned, to his dismay, the tide of history was against him. Pan had already fallen asleep." Mitch turned suddenly and pointed a carrot-sized forefinger at Lupe. "But now the tide of history's against *you*. History's undergoing yet another inevitable metaphysical reversal, and it's the Jew-god's turn to sleep the long sleep." He laughed aloud, opening his arms. "Besides, what did Christianity ever do for anyone? *'Peace upon earth!' was said. We sing it, And pay a million priests to bring it. After two thousand years of mass, We've got as far as poison-gas.*"

"Mitch!" Richard cried, as if he could bear no more.

"Hey, it's Hardy's line, not mine," Mitch said innocently.

"I have seen the future," Lupe said, "and it is Dropped Dead Fred?"

"I told you months ago, Cruz, we're not just reverting back to classical paganism with its Golden Mean and anthropomorphic gods. That, at least, was civilization. No, we're jumping butt-first into the pre-historic worship of Force. Hail, the zero-degree of culture! The end-of-history belongs to prehistory and its pre-literary gods: Tezcatlipoca, Kali, Hecate, and the Two-Faced One of the Druids. They're all—all of them!—rousing from their slumbers. Neurotic and narcotic and necrotic flowers suddenly blooming again on the rotting graves of the old monotono-theistic mythologies." He sighed happily. "Jesus was a fag."

"*Tut, tut,*" said Jack, "*you are too shallow, much too shallow to sound the bottom of the after-times.*"

"Like it or not, Master Fool, we are not only post-Christian, we are post-humanist. God is dead, and so is Man, and western civ's gone a-whoring with the oldest mythologies, where the Dragon never dies, and may even be worshipped as a god. As Lawrence also wrote, *the dragon he is not so dead as the Spanish churches, this all-enwreathing dragon of the horror of Mexico!*" Mitch sniffed. "And, if I'm wrong, well, then *maybe I was born too late. Maybe I was an Aztec in a past life.*"

It was Masefield's turn to gasp.

"Jesus," Jack said, "Who's he quoting now?"

"Jeffrey Dahmer." Masefield pulled his fist out of his trouser pocket. "Do you have any original ideas, Mr. Showalter, or do you just regurgitate other people's words like a literary bulimic?"

Mitch's jaw twisted to the side but he did not answer.

"You know," Masefield said, "me and my colleagues in the homicide squad, we've had this same running debate in the squadroom about whether there's any value, in our line of work, in reading literature. But would you believe, Charles Manson may have gotten some ideas for his cult from Heinlein's *Stranger in a Strange Land*? There was also a sex murderer up in Toronto who slept with a copy of Brett Easton Ellis' *American Psycho* by his bedside. I've even read of two or three killers who liked to identify themselves with Holden Caulfield from *Catcher in the Rye*. First there was that guy who shot John Lennon, what was his name...?" Masefield snapped his fingers, as if unable to remember.

"Mark David Chapman," Mitch volunteered.

Masefield tapped himself on the temple. "Oh, yeah. These guys are pretty much all alike as far as I'm concerned. Yeah, as I recall, Chapman was actually carrying a copy of Salinger on him when he shot Lennon. Now let me see, the other Caulfield wannabe was that obsessed fan who stalked and killed that actress—"

"Robert John Bardo." Mitch tapped himself on the temple, blatantly mimicking Masefield. "The name of the actress escapes me..."

"Rebecca Schaeffer," Masefield said tightly. He seemed to be having trouble unclenching his jaw. "But speaking of literary inspirations for criminal activities, I'm very grateful to James here for re-introducing me to Shakespeare, under present circumstances. Yup, ever since Fr. Bricusse fell over the gallery railing out there, I've been studying Shakespeare with the keenest interest."

"Why?" Mitch said, by the looks of it genuinely curious.

"Because the day he died, Fr. Bricusse left an intriguing telephone message to James here. He seemed to think there was an Iago amongst you."

A moment's hushed silence was followed by the murmurs of a dozen confused graduate students.

"As a result," Masefield continued, raising his voice over the noise, "I've read *Othello* several times now since September, along with several other Shakespeare plays. James here tells me that many critics view Iago as Shakespeare's incarnation of evil. But as a man on the streets everyday—" Masefield screwed up his nose. "—the guy strikes me as very small potatoes. An envious little scuzzball. I see two-bit versions of him every day. But you know who I think is the worst villain in Shakespeare, at least of the plays I've read?"

Mitch snickered. "Tell us, Professor Masefield."

Masefield gave an emphatic nod. "Hamlet's uncle, Claudius. Can you guess why?"

"Because he killed his own brother."

"Somehow, I just knew you were going to say that, Mr. Showalter."

The big man's eyes fluttered. Now *that* had surprised Mitch, James thought, though he couldn't fathom why.

"Nope, fratricide's another garden-variety crime. Men have been killing their brothers since Cain slew his baby brother Abel. No, Claudius is the worst because he's so moral."

"*Moral?*" croaked Richard.

"Yes, Mr. Krato, moral. The man's no nihilist, he's a believer. Why, after the play-within-a-play, he gets right down on his knees and admits to everything he's done. Problem is, in terms of law enforcement, guys like him look so much like Mr. Churchgoing Upstanding Citizen that we cops have a helluva time catching them. Yessir, Claudius is sort of a 'white-collar criminal.' Do you recognize the type?"

Richard hunched deeper into his starched white collar.

Masefield turned again to Mitch. "The Iagos of the world are failures, that's why they kill. They know destruction is their only claim to fame. But since they're cowards and little men, their damage is limited. But now, men like Claudius are powerful. They're executives and politicians, movie producers and doctors and generals. And religious leaders. And they're smart enough never to get their hands dirty." Masefield once again directed himself to Richard Krato. "The Claudiuses of the world get their underlings to do their dirty work, guys like Rosencruntz and Guildenstern. What patsies! I keep thinking that if only those boys had said 'no' to Claudius early on, all the rest of the tragedy wouldn't have happened. But because of dupes like them, men like Claudius can get away with thinking that they aren't liars, because they get their stooges to do the fibbing for them. They can think they aren't murderers, because their soldiers pull the triggers. They can think they aren't thieves, because someone else's prints are on the goods. Yeah, and we cops have a helluva time collaring guys like this—Lordy, half the time, I think these bastards are running the country!"

"What's your point?" Mitch demanded.

"My point is...so what Iago took out Othello and Desdemona, Roderigo and Emilia? Big deal. The State went on pretty much as before, with no basic assumptions questioned. But now Denmark after Claudius was another story. Claudius's plots brought about a rather sudden change of government, didn't they? The Danish court at the end of Act Five looked like the morning after Gettysburg, and the only one left standing was the blunt solder Fortinbras. *Bid the soldiers shoot!*"

Mitch, who didn't seem to like the direction the discussion was taking, cleared his throat but couldn't seem to find anything to say.

"Now take our very own Dropped Dead Fred," Masefield went on. "The guy's an evacuated personality, a soul gutted by envy and resentment. A vacuum. Or maybe I should say a vacuum cleaner. I suspect he's never had an original idea in his entire life. 'Second Hand Rose' is what I call him in the squad room. I bet he wears clothes he sees other men wearing, men he admires and wishes he could be like, and quotes famous books right and left, pretending he's a man of culture and artistic temperament, when he's nothing but a cipher. A parrot. A ventriloquist's dummy mouthing other people's lines. Even Fred's victims are second-hand, they belong to someone else. And since he can't create beauty or attract it to himself, he trashes it. Last but not least—" Masefield looked Mitch dead in the eye. "—I bet he can't function with a woman under normal circumstances. I bet he can only get it up when he sees them tied up and hurting, and knows they can't get away."

Mitch's mouth went crooked. James saw fury for an instant, then the big man's blue contacts seemed to fog over, like a steamy windshield on a rainy summer afternoon. Without warning, Mitch exploded, "We've all been debating the question of these literary straws for five fucking years in this fucking Institute, and you're all still missing the fucking point! These 'pathetic' men you're talking about, they're our cultural heroes! They're celebrities, luminaries! Not their victims, and not the detectives who catch them. *If* they catch them. And no, they don't always get caught. There are some, like the Green River killer, who elude capture for decades. And the Zodiac killer and Gary serial rapist were never caught!"

Masefield's lips puckered. "Interesting you should bring up the Gary rapist," he said after a moment, as if mentally scanning his options. "He was a door that swung both ways. He sodomized men as well as women. And the Green River killer was a true serial killer. He picked random strangers, mainly prostitutes and street women. Our friend Fred isn't even a true serial killer."

"How do you figure that?"

"Fred knows his victims. Rather well, as a matter of fact. There's a pattern to his crimes that almost puts him in the category of a domestic murderer. He just wants us to think he's a serial killer. He's no Ted Bundy."

"Yeah, and I'll tell you what the pattern is," Richard broke in, his eyes wide and wild, his index finger pointed at James. "I realize you've slept with most of the women in the Institute, but it doesn't take a genius to figure that the odds of this guy's victims being your ex-lays are astronomical. Admit it, James, you're not just an actor in this tragedy, you're half the playwright!"

Lupe fumbled for James's hand, but James couldn't help himself: he closed his eyes and groaned.

"What?" Mitch gloated, *"frighted with false fire? We that have free souls, it touches us not!"*

"What about you, Mr. Krato," Masefield said quickly and not a little angrily, "think you might have contributed a scene or two to this script?"

His head snapping back as if he'd been slapped, Richard sat frozen for a second, then leapt to his feet and crashed out the door, abandoning his briefcase and papers, everything, in his haste to flee the room. The door banged open against the wall behind him; then there was a dead silence for about three seconds, the only sound that of Richard's shoes pattering rapidly away down the gallery towards the elevator.

The class erupted in a cacophony of consternation.

With a prompting glance from Masefield, Lanciano rapped on the table for order.

"Mr. Krato—" Lanciano began, then even more loudly, "—Mr. Krato has raised an interesting point, but I think his indignation is a little misplaced!" The class began to settle down, and Lanciano motioned for the student nearest the door to get up and close it. "James is not responsible for what has happened here," he continued in an emphatic tone. "As Lt. Masefield has said, these kinds of killers are becoming distressingly common these days. And I do mean *common*. Let us not feed into this debased killer's bloated ego by granting him celebrity status!"

James's voice crackled like static. "We make celebrities out of killers because we live in a time without the vision to make celebrities out of heroes. Let alone heroes out of ourselves. Behold, the culture of the Dragon, where the monster reigns supreme in our imaginations. They say miracles are past...yet the fabric of a murderer's and a hero's life are woven out of the same cloth, the same *textum*. But where are our Arthurs, our Galahads... even our tormented Hamlets? We're as imaginative as Homer at creating monsters, historic and literary, and surely in a world grown as devil-ridden as ours, a thirst for beauty is the most revolutionary and countercultural of passions. But in the bright sun of Nietzsche's noon, do knights in glistering armor, with poetry on their lips, roam the forests of our fancy anymore?" James shook his head. "No. St. George has been banished. Worse, transmogrified into a hit man or a terrorist. A technocrat with a smart bomb. We've jettisoned all visions of heroism that average men can aspire to, and dragons have taken up residence in the void of our imagination, like the biblical seven devils indwelling the house emptied of one."

"Well, lookee here," Mitch cried, "Jimmy's cynical mask has finally come unglued! You're about eight centuries too late, brother, this is the age of Iago! We have Shakespeare to thank for that, you know. From Iago to Milton's Lucifer, from Darth Vader to Kaiser Soze, the most attractive and articulate characters in art and literature have been the villains. God knows it wasn't his blackface Othello that made Anthony Hopkins a household word, an Oscar winner, a millionaire...and a Sir Knight!" Mitch threw back his curly golden head and roared. "Let's get *real*. No one remembers the names of Jeff Dahmer's fourteen victims, but everyone in this country knows the name of Jeff Dahmer!"

Masefield leaped to his feet. "*I* remember their names! I remember every face, every name, every brother and sister and mother and father sitting in that courtroom! Steven Hicks. Steven Tuomi. Jamie Doxtator. Richard Guerrero. Anthony Sears. Ricky Beeks. Eddie Smith. Ernest Miller. David Thomas. Curtis Straughter. Errol Lindsey. Anthony Hughes. Konerak Sinthasomphone. Matt Turner. Jeremiah Weinberger. Oliver Lacy. Joseph Bradehoft. And Jeff...Jeff, with his spooky yellow contact lenses to make him feel like the Emperor from *Star Wars*, too bad Jeff didn't live long enough for the rest of us to watch him *rot*. Jeff, who if he had lived wouldn't have smelled the clean air of freedom again for nine hundred years, do you think his infamy did him any good as he sat up there in Portage, getting fat in his eight-by-ten while his brain was studied like a cancerous liver by a bunch of shrinks trying to figure out what in the hell went wrong? Do you think his infamy did him any good that day he was scrubbing the prison toilets, and some loony-toon as crazy as he was splattered his bloody skull fragments all over the latrine walls?"

The echoes of Masefield's voice reverberated against the silence in the room, stretched tight like the skin on a drum. When Masefield was able to compose himself and sit down again, his burly shoulders were tremoring with emotion. Mitch's were tremoring with laughter.

Looking up suddenly, Lupe addressed Mitch. "Your 'precursor' never was Iago, w-w-was it? Not really. It was the bastard son Edmund, plotting against his brother Edgar...J. Edgar...Jimmy Edgar. You told me months ago you wanted to write an update of *Lear*, I just didn't get it."

"Ah, well," Mitch replied, obviously basking in his position at center stage, "there's no denying my very rapid process of self-sculpting has been a ravishing experience of transgressive transcendence. *Thus play I in one person many people.* As Derrida said, 'America *is* deconstruction.' And every person in this room is living evidence." With a self-satisfied nod, Mitch proceeded to address each person in turn. "Take Dr. Lanciano, for instance, who's forgotten more than I'll ever learn about pretending to be something you're not. It's the American way—*Jay Gatsby and all that!* Or howsabout Trisha Perl, who loves to wax indignant on the topic of women as sex objects, but who tried to prove her own suspect femininity by getting herself good and fucked one night by arguably the easiest lay in the Institute. Or *Monsieur* Sigur, who pretends he's white, and wishes he were Cruz. Or Cruz, who pretends to pray to a God who's abandoned her, because the only thing she wants anymore is Jimmy between her legs. Ditto Richard, whose missing backbone was on exhibit just now. Or how about Professor Masefield here, who earns his respectable place in white society by shooting down his own neighborhood kids?" Mitch took a deep breath. "And as for you, Jimmy...Jimmy, what can I say...?"

Jimmy could say nothing. But Lupe once again found her voice and with surprising fluency. "You think you've got him all figured out," she said, "but you don't know him. You don't know who he is, or what he feels, and you certainly don't know how good and brave he is, and sooner or later it's going to ruin it all for you. But let me tell you what *I* know. What I know about this Iago stalking Western Civ. He's the ideal Performance Artist for our Culture of Death. So why don't we be *really* honest, Mitch? Why don't we erect pyramids across the street from City Hall. Turn the County Jail into Abu Ghraib and the Bradley Center into a Coliseum. Hire professional priest-slayers and temple prostitutes to fill the spiritual needs of the populace. Put Dropped Dead Fred on the city payroll to perform the ritual sacrifices that keep the sun rising and the rain falling. That at least would be *honest*!"

Volcanic laughter rumbled up from Mitch's taut belly and vibrated the tabletop. "Hey, Jimmy, no wonder you're hanging on to this one, she's smarter than you are! '*Zounds, I was never so bethumped with words since I first call'd my brother's father dad!* Cruz, you and me are gonna have to do some work together one of these days. On my play I mean. Alas, my busy schedule this term hasn't allowed me to spend much time on the manuscript, but perhaps in the future, through the alchemy of pen-and-ink, I'll have the leisure to transform my chaotic Dionysian shape-shifting back into structured Apollonian discourse." He showed his perfect white teeth to Lupe. "And you know what, *poquita?* I'll immortalize you on the printed page, too, as the smartest little cunt I ever met."

Instantly, James was halfway across the table top, going for Mitch's throat. It took Masefield, Jack, Lanciano, and several other students besides to pull James off, kicking and yelling and swearing that he would kill Showalter if it was the last thing he did on this earth.

Mitch was ecstatic. "Jimmy, you've made my day!" he cried, jumping up and backing off from James's clawing fingers, knocking over his chair in the process. "You've made my week! My fucking year!" Getting his balance and laughing, laughing, laughing, Mitch grabbed his manuscript and his paperback copy of Bataille's *Le coupable,* stuffed them in his brand new alligator-skinned briefcase, and prepared to take his leave on a ringing note of triumph.

"Showalter!" Assured that the other men had James under control, Masefield turned his glare on his suspect. "I have some officers waiting outside. It's time you and I had another talk, downtown."

Mitch had paused at the sound of the lieutenant's booming voice, one big hand on the doorknob, eyebrow lifted. Finally swiveling, he drawled, "I realize you routinely count on your brain-dead suspects to be ignorant of the fact that they are not even required to say *boo* to you, let alone go downtown with you, unless you can show probable cause. Which you can't, or you wouldn't have been sitting here for the last hour. But I am aware of it, Lt. Ass-hole, so if you want to talk to someone, talk to my lawyer, Big John DeBrun. He's an expert defender of free speech, and right now that's all the case you've got against me, isn't it? You don't like my new religion?" Mitch raked his fingers through his shaggy golden curls. "I promise you, just put me on the talk-show circuit and give me a dot com, and within a week's time I'll have a following to rival the seers of Medjugorje!" Throwing one last wink at Lupe, Mitch fastened his cornflower-blue gaze on James, who was still struggling to free himself from Jack's and Lanciano's grasp. "You know, Jimmy, you're not as good an actor as you think you are."

With that, Mitch waltzed out the door with a swish of his fanny.

Hours later, Calvin Masefield parked in front of Lupe's house. He climbed the front steps to the elevated yard just in time to see James carrying a large carpetbag down her outside stairs, his young face a portrait in misery.

"You two going somewhere far away I hope?"

Setting down the luggage, James let out a sigh that caught in his throat like a sob. "Holy Hill for a few days. After that, as far away as I can persuade her to go."

Masefield frowned. "Who knows about this?"

"Only her family. And they all know to keep it mum. I haven't even told Jack."

"Holy Hill's a bit remote," Masefield observed, scratching his stubbly chin, "but I guess it's as good a place as any. As long as *he* doesn't know you're there."

"Sweet Christ, I don't understand why you can't just arrest him! He was practically boasting about it all this afternoon!"

"Was he? That's not what I heard. I heard a man exercising his First Amendment right to free speech. Or at least that's what Big John will argue right out of the gate." Seeing the exhaustion competing with equal measures of terror and fury in James's face, Masefield dropped his two hands on James's shoulders. "Chin up, son. He was within an inch of making a mistake today, he's bound to make one soon. Or Richard will finally prove man enough to blow chow on his tidy little alibis. I swear, if Showalter so much as jaywalks, we'll be down his throat in a heartbeat. Just don't give him the satisfaction of seeing you crumble."

"It's leave or crumble," James admitted. "But surely after today he wouldn't dare go after her…would he?"

Masefield shot him a look that suggested the comment didn't deserve a response. "He's constructed himself a parallel universe in his head, one that doesn't operate by the same rules as yours and mine. Whatever his motive, his perverted masterpiece won't be complete until he has her. Until he has her, he doesn't really have you. Then he'll either kill you himself, or have a barrel of laughs watching you crumble, I'm not sure which. That's the one thing after that class that's absolutely clear to me. Why, he couldn't keep his eyes off her this afternoon. When he wasn't looking at you, that is. In fact, I think the only reason he hasn't gone after her before now is because he wants to drag out your torture as long as he can. And he's gotten bit by the acting bug."

James' breath came out in a puff of steam. "I think Lupe's close to collapse. God knows, I know the symptoms — can't sleep, has dreadful waking nightmares…she's been crying ever since we came home."

"So what's holding you together? Besides cigarettes and Irish whiskey."

"Watching out for her," James replied without hesitation. "Otherwise, *he would himself his quietus make, with a bare bodkin…*" He shook his head.

The words summoned a disturbing picture-memory to Masefield's mind: Lenny's broken head on the City Hall floor. "You're taking your medication with you I hope, along with that gun," he said.

"The meds are in my kit," James said. "The Grendel's under the parka, in a holster around my waist."

"You a good shot?"

"Used to be. And I've been practicing every day. But it's small caliber. I've heard bullets don't work on vampires unless they're made of silver."

Masefield chuckled.

James obviously didn't see the humor of it. "He's a monster, Cal. If he had evaporated from that classroom in a puff of smoke, it wouldn't have surprised me in the slightest. I can't believe these things happen to people. Where is God in all this?"

Masefield had no answer to that question. "Hate to break it to you, but you'd better be prepared for the worst from here on. Even when we've got him, you'll be crucified a second time in the public trial. When his motives come out, I mean. Yup, the whole damned country is going to find out that Mitchell Showalter was doing all this to get at James Ireton." Nodding in somber punctuation, Masefield stuffed his hands in his pockets for warmth. The wind, picking up from the north, was sharp now that an approaching bank of cottony snow clouds shrouded the setting sun.

James seemed not to have heard any of it. "What did you really hope to gain from the classroom play today?" he said. "Did you actually think he might crack?"

"Mostly I wanted to see how his mind works. I mean, please tell me they don't teach that lofty-sounding homicidal bullshit in graduate school as a matter of course."

James shrugged. "I guess we're exposed to all kinds of rancid things, even in as conservative a place as the Heisler Institute. But Mitch was always a bit of an autodidact. I should have listened to Lupe. She told me weeks ago there was something wrong with him, just by the things he was saying in class, and the stuff he was reading."

"Look, the guy didn't learn how to take out a girl by reading Nietzsche, let alone all that half-baked lit crit. A man like that has his mind made up already. He's just been absorbing teaspoonfuls of nihilism from here, there and yon to give his conscience an injection of narcotics. If he's got a conscience. No, I'd be willing to bet Showalter's secret reading pleasures are of another genre entirely, though how he'd hide it in that prison environment at SANA, I don't know. Mr. Krato keeps his boys on a short leash."

James stepped forward with sudden urgency. "On the contrary, that's what's so odd. Krato's been giving Mitch free rein all semester. Mitch *must* have something on him. If only Richard—"

"Richard's got a misplaced sense of loyalty. 'Even the saints had faults,' he said to me when we showed him that blackmail letter Bel Gunderson sent his pop. But you know him better than anyone, what do you think? If I could get him alone, would a visit from me nudge him down the path of righteousness or drive him away?"

James thought a moment. "Approach him in terms of his Christian conscience, and he might talk. I keep telling myself that it isn't all his fault. That his father's more to blame. Some people just aren't strong enough to withstand that kind of parental pressure. And when I think what Mitch must have suffered to become what he is—"

"Don't make excuses for him," Masefield broke in, almost sternly. "In my experience, finding other places to lay blame only complicates the mystery, it doesn't solve it. I mean, I read your SANA report. Your life was no crystal stair, either. I doubt either of those boys suffered any more at the hands of life — or Peter Krato — than you did. Not as much in fact."

"You forget, I was never a true believer. Both Richard and Mitch were. That's a steep drop."

"You were never a true believer in Peter Krato and SANA. But you were a believing Catholic."

James shrugged. "I suppose so," he said a little sadly. "For me, the Church has been a beautiful but erratic mother. She wasn't there when the wolf came to the door. In fact, as far as I could tell, she was tossing him scraps of raw meat through the window."

Masefield peered intently at James. "Did your sense of betrayal ever tempt you to blasphemy?"

"Beg pardon?"

"Blasphemy," Masefield repeated. "You know, what Job's wife said to her husband, *Curse God and die.*"

James licked his lips. "I've noticed, from time to time, the impulse to take pleasure in hurting people as a kind of revenge on God, on life. But by some amazing grace I've managed to fend it off…with a few frightening lapses."

Stepping closer, so close he could feel James' icy breath in his face, Masefield said, "Why? Why didn't you give in to it?"

"Because it's ugly," James replied without hesitation, though he looked as much surprised by his own answer as he did Masefield's peculiar question. "I need beauty, Cal. I need it the way most men need air and water and bread. Dostoevsky once said beauty could save the world. I have no prophecies to offer on that large a scale, but it may yet save me."

Masefield smiled and stepped back. He had learned to like this intense and sometimes forbidding young man over the troubled course of the last three months, but never more than at this moment. The kid, he thought, was going to be all right. "A different question," he said, "this time about the *King Lear* stuff Lupe was talking about today. Refresh my memory, what's this Edgar and Edmund got to do with dotty old Lear and his three daughters?"

James began to look dazed again; he had obviously been trying to absorb the implications as well. "The thing with the daughters is the main plot," he said, "but there's a subplot, a sort of mirror-reverse of the main story. It concerns the Duke of Gloucester and his two sons, Edgar and Edmund. Edgar was the legitimate older son, while Edmund was the nihilistic younger son, a bastard."

"Let me guess," Masefield broke in. "Edmund was envious of Edgar."

"Homicidally. And just like Iago with Othello, Edmund puts on a false face of fraternal loyalty while he's ruining his brother to get his inheritance. God, how Mitch must have hated his brother." James shook his head. "I wonder how it started."

"It started early, that's for darn sure," Masefield affirmed. "I was just talking to the Coast Guard before I came here. According to their records, Mitch was eight years old when his father had a heart attack aboard their little fishing boat. It was out on Lake Michigan, November 10. Bad time of the year to be out in on the lake. I mean downright stupid, especially with a couple of kids. Mitch and Jimmy were only in grade school. Sure enough a storm came up, and the dad started having chest pains. When he collapsed, he capsized the boat. Each boy later claimed that the other drowned their father by climbing on top of him to get back in the boat again."

"God."

"Whatever happened out there, because of the date, Showalter's somehow connected the whole tragedy to the legendary shipwreck of the *Edmund Fitzgerald*. Who knows? After all this time, he may even believe it himself. Then the coincidence that November 10th turned out to be your birthday somehow got tangled up in Showalter's sticky cobweb of homicidal symbolism. It was the date he killed Bel Gunderson, you know."

James looked as if he was about to make a vigorous objection, but Masefield held up his hand. "That's not the end of the numerology, James. Next there's J. Edgar's disappearance. Everyone assumed that Jimmy Showalter had simply run away from home, like thousands of other teenagers every year. All except his ma. She doted on him apparently. She insisted he hadn't run off, that there was foul play involved. She said he had too much going for him. A full scholarship to Yale, for cryin' out loud. But the kicker for me is the date Jimmy Showalter went missing. Want to guess?"

"November 10th?"

"Nope, September 19th. The day he left for Yale. Only he never made his flight. It was the date, years later, Mitch killed Candace Duffy. The girl he wanted, but who Jimmy got to first."

James closed his eyes.

"But that's still not the end of it. So far, I don't see a link to the date Bricusse got dropped, but that may have been a simple crime of opportunity, unrelated to this other stuff. But how about this: after Jimmy Showalter's disappearance, and in spite of two months of grief counseling, Mitch's distraught mother swallowed a bottle full of sleeping pills and drowned herself in her bath tub. Open and shut suicide. And the date was…?"

James thought a moment. "Two months after September nineteenth would be around Thanksgiving." James swallowed. "Nadine."

"Yup. See, James? Your 'symbolic structure.' Bet the freakazoid doesn't take a dump without consulting his horoscope."

James shook his head vigorously. "You can't possibly expect me to believe that Mitch is doing all this because my birthday falls on November 10th."

"That's not what I'm saying. I'm just saying that's how he's picking some of his more important dates. Probably to give it some artistic or ritual embellishments. No, the real source of Mitch's mania was staring you in the face in that yearbook from Bradford High. 'J' as in 'Jimmy,' remember? *Jimmy*, his older brother. *Jimmy*, the golden boy. *Jimmy*, his mother's reason for being.

Jimmy, the popular, smart, good-looker, who always succeeded where Mitch failed, from athletics to the honor roll to theater to Candace Duffy. Hell, Jimmy Showalter even looked like you." Masefield lifted his eyes to the sky, pregnant with the season's first snow. "I'd lay odds Jimmy Showalter was Mitch's first bona fide murder victim. Then, having once got a taste for violence, he raped those girls when he was in college. Somewhere along the line he got religion, too, probably from his aunt, and tried to...I don't know, repent I guess. That happened to Dahmer, too, you know, only with his granny. What it was after all these years that started the homicide ball rolling again, we may never know. But the violence has been escalating for three months. Somehow, Mitch is finishing now what he started back on that day so many years ago when he somehow made his brother Jimmy...disappear."

"He always called me Jimmy," James said faintly. "The only person who ever did. I always thought it was odd. And he used to say—this was even odder, because we were never close—he'd say, 'Jimmy, you're like a brother to me." James shook his head. "Christ save me, I hardly knew he existed." Brushing a snowflake off his nose, James reached in the pocket of his parka for his pack of cigarettes and offered one to Masefield. "Want to come in?"

Masefield took the smoke. "Thanks, but I promised my wife I'd have dinner at home for a change. Oh, by the way, I've encouraged the Outagamie County Sheriff to re-open the books on the conveniently-timed death of Abigail Showalter. It wasn't a natural death, you know, she fell down her basement stairs. It was ruled accidental because of her bad hip."

Having just lit up, James promptly took the cigarette out of his mouth. "Mitch was sick the night she died, I remember distinctly. We were about to watch a film the next day and—"

"He used his alleged tummy-ache as an excuse to lock himself in his room at SANA house. He had plenty of time to slip out that night and drive up to Green Bay and back before breakfast the following morning."

"But why would he kill her? He adored that woman. You should have seen him that day, I could swear that wasn't an act. Nobody's that good an actor."

Masefield exhaled. "Maybe it wasn't an act. Maybe he loved her. But maybe he didn't love her enough. Especially if he thought she might be a danger to him. And remember, Mitch was Abigail Showalter's sole beneficiary. She left him property and money and an insurance settlement worth over half a million dollars. His bank statements indicate he's spending it, too, in large and frequent cash withdrawals. But what's he spending it on? He sure as hell hasn't given any to Peter Krato. And we've gone through his room at SANA, it hardly looks as if anyone lives there. I'm telling you, the guy's leading a double life somewhere."

"I still can't believe Mitch would kill Abby for money."

"Oh, it was more than money. Hold on to your shorts, James: Abigail Showalter attended that religious conference in Chicago, she and three other women from her parish. The other ladies reported that Abigail had a lengthy last-minute private conference with Fr. Bricusse. They didn't know what it was about, but they did know Abigail Showalter was sweating bullets over her nephew. She had begun to think he was unhinged. Considering the messages you got from Bricusse the next day, she must have told him plenty, too." Masefield took a puff off his cigarette and blew out forcefully. "No wonder the poor old man had a heart attack. But look, there's one last question I needed to ask you. That chapel over there at SANA. They have Mass there, right?"

Obviously surprised by the question, James's eyebrows shot up. "They used to, whenever a priest happened to visit. They used to keep the exposed Blessed Sacrament, too. The Archbishop's forbidden it all now."

"And to a Catholic, those communion wafers don't mean anything until a priest says certain words over them at Mass, right?"

"After consecration, the bread is the Body of Christ. Before that, it's just…flour and water. What on earth has it got to do with this awful business?"

Masefield felt several drops of wetness on his face, and looked up: it was beginning to snow in earnest. "There's a couple details of the murders I have to keep a secret, even from you," he replied, wiping snow from his eyes. "It's standard procedure. To protect the integrity of possible confessions." He snorted. "Not that we're likely to get one in this case. Besides, no Catholic church or chapel in the archdiocese has reported a sanctuary break-in in several years."

James turned up the collar of his parka. "Well they missed one. Mitch told Lupe months ago that SANA had a sanctuary break-in over the summer. A chalice was stolen containing the Blessed Sacrament. You may be sure Krato didn't notify the Archdiocese about it. It would have made him appear irresponsible with the sacraments, just when they had begun to investigate him."

A surge of excitement warmed Masefield's extremities. He almost hopped at the news. "Can you describe this chalice?" he said eagerly.

"Afraid not, other than that it was carved of wood. Mitch told Lupe that Peter picked it up last summer on a pilgrimage to the Holy Land."

Masefield tossed down his cigarette and stepped on it. "It's all coming together," he said, "like the spokes of a wheel, meeting at the hub." He clapped James on the shoulder. "And you, my poor young friend, are the hub. Or rather, one Jimmy Edgar Showalter, who, as far as his brother Mitch is concerned, just won't stay dead."

Chapter Fourteen:
Ex Mille Electus Miles

Now are we come vnto my natiue soyle,
And to the place, where all our perils dwell;
Here haunts that feend, and does his dayly spoyle,
Therefore henceforth be at your keeping well,
And euer ready for your foeman fell.
The spark of noble courage now awake,
And striue your excellent selfe to excell;
That shall ye euermore renowmed make,
Aboue all knights on earth, that batteill vndertake.

Edmund Spenser, *The Faerie Qveene*

James and Lupe set out for Holy Hill in the gathering darkness of a Great Lakes snowstorm. Whether it was the fierce wind and rapidly accumulating snow, near to whiteout, or the fact that they were driving steadily west, away from the lake, James endured a panic attack en route so oppressive that he had to pull over on the shoulder of the highway to fling wide the Jeep door and inhale a bracing lungful of air.

The brightly lit spires of the Shrine, normally visible from miles away, never gleamed a candle's worth in the shifting drapery of snow. They drove almost blindly. By the time they finally pulled into the parking lot at the base of the Shrine, James was so shaken by the treacherous, grinding climb up the winding, snow-blanketed hill that he pulled Lupe in his lap for a lengthy session of needful kissing.

"Lupe," he pleaded into her frosty hair, "let's go away. Get out of Milwaukee until everything's over. Go someplace warm and bright and surrounded by water."

Wiping sweat from his forehead with her mitten, she nodded out the window at the brick spires looming above in the whorl of snow. "We're safe here," she assured him, "here of all places."

The Carmelite monastery was located atop Holy Hill behind the Shrine. The visitors center, of which the guesthouse comprised the second floor, was built lower down, into the hill itself. The entire compound was secluded and terribly quiet after dark, a circumstance usually considered an asset in a retreat house, but in their present situation, one which only augmented James's feverish sense of dread. On the plus side, the friars, so Fr. Martin Cruz informed them as he escorted them to their adjacent rooms, had long since hired a security guard for the visitors' peace of mind. No one could get into the building without a key.

Their dorm-like rooms, like all the others in the retreat house, were furnished only with twin beds with a bedstand in-between, a desk, a reading chair, and a small tiled bathroom with a shower. Pulling aside the tatty, flowery drape at the large window in Lupe's room, its corners filigreed with snow, James peered out into the whited night: the guest house was separated from a steep embankment by a concrete well that was both wide and deep—so deep, James couldn't see the bottom.

"The well's mainly for drainage," Martin explained, his normally serene-to-complacent face etched tonight with worry. "The runoff from the hill is incredible. But as it happens, it will also keep anybody, who doesn't fly at least, from getting in through the window."

Dragons fly, James thought, yanking shut the curtain.

Martin handed them each room keys, which, he explained, unlocked the main outside doors as well as the individual room doors. James didn't for a moment believe that Lupe's brother, priest or no, was naïve enough to think that he would actually sleep in that other room next door, and didn't give a damn either way; God knows, sex was about the last thing on James's mind right now.

"I talked to the security guard about our problem," Martin said as James pocketed the key with a grunt of thanks. "I don't know if you noticed, but the corridor light has a movement sensor. It comes on automatically whenever someone steps into the hall."

"Besides," Lupe piped up with a cheerfulness James knew to be imposture, doubtless for his benefit, "it's over, really. He's under c-c-constant observation."

A while later, alone in his assigned room next door while Lupe got ready for bed, James snapped the mixed-load magazine back into the Grendel. He slid the weapon into the leather holster and adjusted the belt so that the weapon was tucked into the small of his back. He practiced his draw and his aim for several minutes, feeling for all the world like a kid playing cowboy, and bloody well not caring; for when he measured himself against James Mitchell Showalter, who at six-three packed at least a fifty pound advantage on him in pure, over-developed muscle, James knew that his chances of protecting Lupe in any genuine confrontation were...problematic. Unless he could get off a clean shot in the first few seconds. In the heart, or right between the eyes.

"This is an important feast day," Lupe announced next morning. They were seated in the Old Monastery Inn, their trays loaded with coffee and eggs.

"Which one now?" James said with a morning's shot of hope.

"Silly man, December 12, Our Lady of Guadalupe!" But Lupe's smile suddenly dimmed, then disappeared altogether.

James turned to follow her glance over his shoulder: Fr. Martin Cruz was rapidly approaching their table, his brown habit swishing with his steps, his face a study in anxiety.

"What's the m-m-matter?"

Martin pulled up a chair. "Lt. Masefield just called." Martin turned to James. "He said you weren't answering your cell phone."

"I left the battery charger at the flat. I've been trying to save juice by leaving it off. What the—"

"They served a search warrant at SANA house this morning. Showalter wasn't there."

James lost his breath.

"He p-promised us they-they-they were watching him every minute!"

Fr. Martin Cruz clasped his sister's hand. "It looks like he gave them the slip. Either way, Masefield said that you two mustn't under any circumstances go back to Milwaukee until they find him. Not that you could anyway, what with all the snow. The roads are closed between here and the interstate. But that's not all. I filled in Fr. Abbot on what was going on here and…" Martin took a deep breath. "He remembered Mitch Showalter."

"What the devil do you mean?" James demanded.

"I mean that Showalter was *here*, six years ago, supposedly trying his vocation." Martin was looking a little panicky. "I was away at seminary, I never met him or even heard of him. They sent him home after only a few weeks."

"Wha-wha-what has this got to do with anything?"

Martin's grip on his sister's hand tightened. "The reason they sent him home, Lu. Besides blowing all the psychological tests, Showalter would go missing every other day or so. They'd always find him up in the Scenic Tower." Martin cocked his head in the direction of the Shrine. "Showalter told Fr. Abbot that when he was a kid, his brother got him to climb the grillwork up there with him on a dare, then tried to push him out of one of the open rose windows."

"We're on the next plane out of here," James announced, "going anywhere."

"B-B-But he c-c-couldn't possibly know we're here!"

James's finger stabbed the air in the direction of the Shrine. "Don't you see, that goddamned Tower—"

"James," Martin said firmly, "the Tower is boarded up and locked for the winter. More to the point, we're in the middle of a blizzard. Mitchell Field is closed and they're predicting another eight to ten inches this afternoon. If it's any comfort to you, even when they get 167 cleared, no one's going to be getting up or down this hill for a while. Not without chains and a four-wheel drive."

"Martin's right," Lupe said, reaching out with her other hand to grasp James's. "Neither of SANA's cars would m-make it up the hill, even with chains."

James just kept shaking his head.

"One last thing. Lt. Masefield told me to tell you that, before they lost him, one of your Institute friends tried to kill Showalter last night."

Calvin Masefield had *not* had a good night. He had stayed in the office until dawn, poring over all the case files in case he had overlooked something that might give them an excuse to arrest Showalter; either that, or a clue as to where Showalter could be living his double life and stashing his murder trophies. Meanwhile, two of Masefield's detectives had chased the suspect up and down Water Street from one watering hole to another. All well and good until Bo Jeffrey, who had found out what was what from the Mouth-of-the-South, Jack Sigur, jumped Showalter outside the London Bridge Pub and Grill with a knife that looked like something out of *Crocodile Dundee*. A brown belt in Tae Kwon Do, Jeffrey had kick boxed the much larger Show-alter to the ground. He would have slit his throat, too, or some other part of the big man's anatomy, if Masefield's detectives hadn't come quickly and somewhat bass-ackwardly to the rescue.

"Swell," Masefield had grumbled to his men afterwards. "Why didn't you let Jeffrey have a go at him, and saved us all a lot of trouble and expense? Wisconsin's a no-death-penalty state, remember?" The lieutenant was left contemplating the perverse ironies of the world: Showalter had been taken to the ER, where he was treated and released with nothing more than a superficial thigh wound, while Bo Jeffrey, brother to a murdered sister, was tossed in the city lockup for assault with a deadly. Then Masefield's sleepy-sloppy detectives had somehow, God roast them both, lost Showalter at SANA house.

Last but not least of all, after phoning SANA House to get a detailed description of SANA's stolen chalice from Richard Krato (and to summon him downtown for another interview), Richard had gone missing as well.

Masefield returned to his own home for two hours of stolen, fitful sleep, and was now sitting in a daze at his kitchen table, chowing down a turkey sandwich while his wife tried to crank up his sagging spirits with a pot of coffee and a dose of family dish before he headed back downtown.

The phone rang.

"It's Ramon," said the familiar voice on the other end.

"Any sign of Richard Krato?"

"*Nada.*"

"Then, let's get another fu…another search warrant for SANA house."

"To look for *what* ? The joint's as clean as a nun's undies."

"This time we look for leads to where Showalter is living his double life. Whip up the warrant, Ramon, and call me when we're ready to roll."

"Wait a sec! Ireton just phoned from Holy Hill. He said Showalter was there six years ago, trying to become a monk."

Masefield choked on a swallow of coffee, but quickly recovered. "Weird enough for sure," he said. "But six year's ago? That's ancient history."

"Yeah, but with this guy," Ramon argued, "as the old song says, *everything old is new again*. I mean, Ireton's got a bad feeling about it, and so do I. Showalter not only knows Holy Hill, from the inside, he and his brother Jimmy had a fight up in the Scenic Tower. Ireton thinks that's the reason for Showalter's drops. He also thinks that's why Showalter hasn't gone after Lu before now, because he's waiting for a chance to get her up there in the Tower. Lu planned this retreat months ago, and James is afraid he's somehow found out about it."

Masefield had to concede that with a guy as keen on symbolism as Showalter, there were plenty of reasons for concern. The very thought of it made the turkey in his belly do a loop-de-loop. "Okay," he said finally, "it would be Showalter's kind of thing, no question. And no question James and Lupe ought to get the hell out of there—get the hell out of the state—as soon as the weather clears. But how could Showalter know they're there if no one in your family's talked about it? James told me not even Sigur knows about it."

That had ended the discussion for the time being, but no sooner had the unpersuaded Ramon Cruz hung up, and Masefield gone back to the kitchen table to finish his lunch—and debate with himself about whether or not he should phone the triggerable James Ireton himself, or even chopper them out of there—than the phone rang again.

"Lt. Masefield…?"

Masefield swallowed down the last bite of turkey sandwich. "Richard," he said, wiping his mouth with a napkin, "I am very relieved to hear from you. Where the hell are you, boy?"

"I'm in danger now, too, aren't I?" Richard said.

"You are if you know something that can incriminate him. Do you?"

"Yes, Sir. At least I think so."

"Where are you?"

"The Meir Library. I've been walking all night, thinking…" Richard's voice faded, replaced by the sound of muffled sobs, the sound of a young man coming apart at the seams.

"Richard, I want to pick you up and take you downtown, where you'll be safe. And if you tell me everything, start to finish, I'll do my level best to keep you out of jail for obstruction of justice. Son, Showalter's assorted fairy tales are all one woven fabric of lies. All it takes to unravel it is for someone to find the courage to start pulling the loose threads. Please, Richard, before someone else dies."

Silence.

"He's after Lupe Cruz next, you know that. And finally James himself, that's my guess. Do you want that on your conscience?"

Still no answer, only weeping.

It was a risk, but Masefield decided there was nothing for it: "You and your Dad gave Showalter a false alibi the night Bricusse died, didn't you?"

Masefield heard a sharp intake of breath.

"For God's sake, Richard, *why?*"

Richard issued a miserable-sounding laugh. "For God's sake," he said at last. "For God's sake!"

Masefield shook his head in silent pity. "Tell me what happened."

"That night, when Dad and Mitch and I were at Ma Fischer's…"

"Yes?"

"Dad was desperate to get a look at James's SANA Report. Mitch promised he'd get hold of a copy during the program."

Masefield snatched the memobook from the breast pocket of his shirt.

"When we went back to the Institute, we milled around in the atrium for a while, waiting for Fr. Bricusse to show up. The plan was, when we saw him, Mitch was to sneak up to his office to look for the file. And anything else he could find up there about SANA. But Father never showed. So finally Mitch just…went upstairs anyway."

"What time was that?"

"Maybe ten minutes to eight. Dad was still talking to Mr. Heisler. Neither of them noticed when Mitch took off. But as soon as Mr. Heisler left, I told Dad that Mitch had gone upstairs. Dad had second thoughts and insisted that we leave. He said that if Mitch got caught up there, trying to steal the file, our story would be that we didn't know anything about it, that Mitch was acting on his own. We waited for him across the street, but Mitch didn't come out until about a quarter after eight. And it was strange, too, because Mitch didn't come out the front door, like you'd expect, he came out from the basement parking lot. I swear to God, Lieutenant, I never suspected…I mean, he looked like he'd seen a ghost! He said Bricusse's office was unlocked, and that he found the SANA file right there on his desk, but that as he was heading for the stairwell, he heard a noise and…oh God, saw the old man going over the rail. We believed him. We needed to believe him."

Masefield looked up to give his attentive wife, who was doing dishes at the sink, a triumphant thumbs-up. "Richard," he said, checking his enthusiasm, "I want you to go to the Circulation Desk and wait for me. Showalter got away from us last night and we don't know where he is. It's real important that you stay in a public place, you hear? I mean, don't even go to the bathroom. I'll pick you up in fifteen minutes and we'll go downtown. Understand?"

"Yes, Sir…no, wait, Lieutenant!"

"What?"

"I need to go to the Oratory first. I need to see a priest."

James's boots penetrated the virgin snow in a steady, heavy rhythm, down the steep path alongside the outdoor Stations of the Cross. Every few minutes he would lift his eyes towards the great church, rising over the sea of snow like a lighthouse. From time to time a solitary bird — once a bright red-bellied robin, spitting grouchily, another time a huge blackbird, majestic in its ugliness — would perch above his head in the bare, ruined choirs, pendant with snow, and the thought would cross his mind that it all meant something, if he could only catch hold of it.

Rounding a bend in the path near the bottom of the hill, James pulled up his parka sleeve to glance at his watch: five after three. Lupe would be making a holy hour in the main church now, surrounded, thank God, by a dozen or more Third Order Carmelites from Oshkosh. He had promised to meet her in the lower church, the chapel of St. Thérèse, at four, where Martin was scheduled to say Mass at half past. He had a volume of poetry stuffed inside his jacket to read while he was waiting.

His ears stinging with cold, James pulled his seaman's cap out of his pocket and over his ears, and turned around to begin the steep climb back up the hill. Pushing slowly but steadily, retracing his own steps, he recited a litany of familiar prayers at each station, feeling a tug of emotion that savored a little of nostalgia, and a deep need.

He needed something, he knew that much. He needed something he didn't have, and had once had. Or had almost had. And he needed it now.

———————

A quarter of an hour later, James sat reading in a pew near the back of the Thérèse chapel, a puddle of water collecting at his feet from the snowmelt off his boots. He was scanning George Herbert's *Love* when he felt a movement of silky air around him — a draft perhaps, as if a door had opened nearby.

Glancing around, James saw that a light had come on above the confessional box in the side aisle to his left. Choosing to ignore his clerical company, James gave a grunt and returned his attention to his book. As he savored the words of the poem, a melancholy melody rose gently to his mind. It was a half minute or more before he remembered that Vaughan Williams had set this poem to music, in a song cycle that his mother used to play on her stereo. Closing his eyes, James let the remembered song play in his mind...

Put on the whole armour of God.

James's eyes fluttered open. It had sounded for all the world as if someone had just whispered in his ear, *Put on the whole armour of God.*

James whirled around: the chapel was still empty, but for himself and the priest in the confessional.

Telling himself to get a grip, James addressed himself once again to the poem; but the other words, St. Paul's words — Bricusse's words — continued to intrude upon his consciousness like an uninvited guest: *Put on the whole armour of God.*

All at once James found himself on his feet, navigating on unsteady legs towards the confessional. It was only when he saw his own hand reaching for the latch to the penitent's side of the box that he began to ask himself why he couldn't remember having actually decided to do this.

The door shut behind him. James knelt. The grille door slid open, and the priest on the other side intoned a benediction.

"Uh," James began after an awkward moment of silence, "I can't say I really know why I'm in here."

"Would you like me to read a passage of Scripture?" The priest's tone was polite, not in the least discomposed.

"If you wish," James replied, thinking he would have to humor the fellow until he could figure out how to get himself out of this dreadful little box without making a scene.

The priest said, "This is from the *Letter to the Ephesians*, chapter six.

> 'Finally, my brethren, be strong in the Lord, and in the power of his might. Put on the whole armour of God, that ye may be able to stand against the wiles of the devil. For we wrestle not against flesh and blood, but against principalities, against powers, against spiritual wickedness in high places. Wherefore take unto you the whole armour of God, that ye may be able to withstand in the evil day, and having done all, to stand. Stand therefore, having your loins girt about with truth, and having on the breastplate of righteousness; And your feet shod with the preparation of the gospel of peace; Above all, taking the shield of faith, wherewith ye shall be able to quench all the fiery darts of the wicked. And take the helmet of salvation, and the sword of the Spirit, which is the word of God.'"

James fumbled for the door latch.

"Please don't go," the priest said.

Shutting the door again, James wiped his sweaty face with his flannel shirtsleeve. "I just needed a little air," he said stupidly. "Feels like a bloody coffin in here."

The priest said nothing.

"Since when did Catholic priests start quoting the King James Bible?" James demanded sourly.

"My sister gave me a copy," the priest said. "She's fond of the language."

James sighed. "Martin."

"Good afternoon, James," Fr. Martin Cruz said amiably. "You chose a great day for confession, the Feast of Our Lady of Guadalupe. I understand she's a favorite of yours, too."

"I haven't been to confession in over three years, you know."

"Well, as we say every morning in the Divine Office, *if today you hear His voice, harden not your heart.*"

James threw up his hands. "What good can this possibly do? For chrissake, I keep doing all the wicked things I don't want to do, and the good things I do want to do I can't seem to find the strength to do." It was only when he heard Fr. Martin Cruz suppressing laughter on the other side of the grille that James realized he had just paraphrased another one of St. Paul's more famous *dicta*.

"Welcome to the fallen human race," was Martin's sole comment.

Like a man about to plunge into Lake Superior on a January morning, James braced himself on his already stiffening knees and said, "Well, now, if you insist, Fr. Cruz, in the three years since my last confession I've slept with a dozen or more women, hurt all of them, one of them's been vandalized and another viciously raped, and two of them have been murdered. I hardly have a clue why it's happening, but I'm told it has something to do with *me*. And as for me, God, what can I say? I almost raped your sister myself!"

"Are you sorry for what you did?" Martin demanded. It sounded like a challenge to combat.

"Of course I'm sorry! I wouldn't be kneeling here like a bloody idiot if I weren't!"

"Have you apologized where it was appropriate, asked forgiveness of the people you hurt, sought to make restitution?"

"Yes, I've begun to, but—"

"Do you intend to pull this kind of crap again?"

"Of course not!"

"Then dammit, Ireton, get on with it. Why won't you just accept forgiveness when it's offered, and start over?"

"It can't be that easy!"

"Easy?" Now Martin sounded surprised. "Look, man, it took three years to get you on your knees in here—" *You miserable sonuvabitch.* The good friar hadn't actually said it, of course, but James could hear the words distinctly. "Three years of shame and suffering, and acts of both cowardice and courage, or you wouldn't be here. No, it's not easy. But you want grace, and by God you need it, too!" James heard Martin's sharp intake of breath, as if the man were struggling to master himself. "Okay. God can take care of all that. That's why we have priests and confessionals. Right now, as far as you're concerned, I'm not Martin Cruz, Lupe's brother—who'd just as soon come around the other side of this creaky little box and give you another concussion. I'm Fr. Anonymous, *alter Christus*. For better or worse, I stand in the place of Christ. As your Lionel Krato used to say, *God is a God of human mediations*. Okay, then. I'm the mediator at hand. End of story. So get over it and get on with it."

James rubbed his forehead. "You want the real reason I haven't willingly stepped inside a church in three years? It's because I've had the devil's own time imagining myself back in the same Body of Christ with Mr. Peter Krato. The last time I went to communion it tasted like ashes on my tongue."

Martin snorted. "Well, my friend, I'm here to tell you that you're in no position to split hairs with God because He declines to toss thunderbolts at public hypocrites every time they troop up to the altar rail. Besides, amazing but true, hypocrites like Peter Krato may make it into the confessional too, sooner or later, just like fornicators like you."

James wanted to scream.

"Look," Martin said, by this time obviously as exasperated as James, "you and Ramon haven't always seen eye to eye, no?"

"True enough."

"Well, use your imagination a little. Extrapolate on that. Suppose Peter Krato was Lupe's, I don't know, uncle. Would you refuse to marry her, refuse to become part of her family, just because Peter Krato also happened to be a member of it?"

"I guess not," James had to admit.

"And when you married her, would you be thinking about Peter Krato on your wedding night?"

"God, no."

"Well, what do you think 'communion' means? Seriously now, are you going to let a sorry excuse for a human being like Peter Krato come between you and the beating heart of the world?"

James head ached. "I suppose it's not just Krato. I've done a piss-poor job of forgiving my own father, too. He's a real piece of work, Martin. Coming from a family like yours, you can simply have no idea."

Martin didn't reply right away. "Okay," he said at last, and with a good deal more caution in his voice. "I know we've been lucky that way. But just for the exercise, why don't you try to imagine how your life would have turned out if your father had been different. You know, if he had been the father you wanted and needed. Would you even be here? In the States, I mean."

James pressed the bridge of his nose between his thumb and forefinger. "I suppose not."

"You'd be back in England, wouldn't you? Probably getting your doctorate at Oxford."

"Or in the Royal Navy..." James gripped the ledge of the grille window.

"Then what are the chances you'd ever have met Lupe?"

James bit his lip. "Nil."

"So, if you could wave a magic wand to undo it all, make it all right with your father, knowing that you'd have been a happier man, perhaps, but would have never met Lupe...would you wave that magic wand?"

"God help me, no."

Martin clucked. "The defense rests."

James shifted on his aching knees. "All right, I'll lay my heart on the altar, one more time." Swallowing his shame, and a hefty measure of inbred Protestant reticence, James enumerated every serious sin he could remember having committed in the last three years. The whole sack of potatoes. It took a while. When he had finished, Martin waited a moment then said, "For your penance, say one heartfelt Hail Mary to the Virgin of Guadalupe for Peter Krato and your father. And Showalter, while you're at it. Then I want you to put all of them out of your mind and hear Mass with us this afternoon. And when you receive the Body of Christ, whether it tastes like ashes or ambrosia, I want you to remind yourself that by receiving Christ, you bind yourself more intimately to Lupe, and strengthen yourself for whatever lies ahead. All right?"

"That's all?"

Martin snorted. "You want to drag your suit of armor up Holy Hill like Robert De Niro in *The Mission*? By the way, who's your patron saint?"

"Beg pardon?"

"Didn't you take a patron saint when you were received into the Church?"

"Oh. Oh yes. It was St. George."

James thought he heard Martin chuckle. "You mean the one who slew the dragon?"

"Damned right."

Martin made an indecipherable noise. "Well, then, while you're saying your penance, ask St. George to help you fight your, er, 'dragons.' All right?"

"Right-O."

When, after receiving absolution, James didn't rise to leave the confessional, Martin remained silent for a moment and then said, "Anything else?"

"I had a vision," James blurted out.

There was a moment's silence. "Want to run that by me again?"

"I said I had a vision. Or at least the priest who received me into the Church called it a vision. It was almost eight years ago now."

"Well, some people have visions, so they tell me. So?"

"Dammit, Martin, I've never understood it. The vision I mean. And I've got to understand it. Now."

"Why now?"

"Because it…Christ save me, the thing's coming true in some horrible, unimaginable way!"

"I think you'd better start at the beginning."

James related the story of his vision, his conversion, his apostasy, and his subsequent nightmares. "I know it sounds crazy, Martin," he said when Martin's lengthy silence afterwards made him suspect that Lupe's brother might now be questioning her fiancé's sanity as well as his character, "but I'm telling you, the woman I saw was the Virgin of Guadalupe. She made me a knight, and gave me a fabulous sword. There was a chalice, too. You know, like the Holy Grail. Carved of myrtlewood like they have in the Holy Land. Only she said it wasn't for me, it was for my son, while the sword *was* for me. I was to kill the dragon with it, the dragon that rose from the sea. But the vision ended as the dragon was flying towards us, and I've never understood any of it. Especially about the sword. Dear God, what is it? I know the dragon well enough."

"Who's the dragon? Mitch Showalter?"

"I suppose. But I've seen his ugly face in my mirror more than once, too. Still, I don't understand about the sword. Obviously, it's the weapon I'm to use to kill the dragon, but what *is* it? I mean in real life? I've got a gun, but it surely can't be as simple as that."

"You're asking me?"

"Yes!"

Martin seemed to be thinking a moment, perhaps praying. Finally, he said, "It was in that passage I read when you first came in."

"Beg pardon?"

"*Ephesians.* The part about the Sword of the Spirit being the Word of God."

James dropped his forehead on the window frame. "For the love of Christ, speak to me in English. I don't know what that stuff means, I never have."

"Okay, then let's back up. You're telling me that the woman in your vision was the Virgin of Guadalupe, and that when you first met Lupe, she reminded you of her."

"Exactly."

"And how did that make you feel?"

James squirmed on his knees. "Uncomfortable. No, terrified. In fact, when I saw the picture in Bricusse's office...well, I didn't want to admit that I was falling in love with her. I mean, Lupe. Oh, this doesn't make any sense."

"No, it does, sort of. But love is an act of the will as well as an emotion, you know. It's a decision to give yourself. At some point, whatever your feelings, you had to make that decision, right? And given your history, it probably wasn't easy?"

"True enough."

"When was that?"

"Uh, well, it didn't happen all at once. But the day after Father was killed, I opened a package he'd given me, a present he'd brought for me from Mexico. I knew it was *la Guadalupana*, but I didn't want to open it. I didn't want to let her into my life. But after Father died, well, I felt I had to." James took a deep breath. "Then there was another time, one night after Lupe and I had an argument, a whopper. Over sex, of course. That's when I realized, finally, that I had to love Lupe, or give it all up."

"Give what up?"

"Everything. Anything that was any good in me. Even my work. So I chose to love." James sighed. "And, of course, I've done my usual balls-up job of it."

"No, listen, the important part is that you chose to love. Which, as I'm sure you're quickly discovering, involves a bit more than flowers and champagne and planning the honeymoon cruise. See, when push comes to shove—and it always does you know, sooner or later—loving and giving oneself completely means being willing to suffer, sometimes even die, for the beloved. Like the killdeer we talked about that night. That's the sword that kills every dragon, James, and it's a helluva weapon. It's God Himself. As the old book says, the Sword of the Spirit is the Word of God. The Word *is* God—"

"And God is Love," James whispered, amazed.

———

When James finally opened the door of the confessional, Lupe was sitting in a nearby pew, apparently waiting her turn.

She looked up at him, then at the confessional, then back at him, her turquoise eyes wide in astonishment.

He knelt beside her. "Well, now," he said, caressing her cheek and checking a modest laugh, the first in many days, "It seems that I am not what I was, but finally what I am."

The fast-approaching twilight made the unshoveled snow on the steps of SANA House look sooty as smoke. Tossing a "here we go" glance over his shoulder at Ramon Cruz, Lt. Calvin Masefield pounded on the door.

After a few seconds the knob turned. An anemic-looking individual of indeterminate age—he could have been fourteen or forty—peered out at them with bulging, thyroid-sick eyes. Masefield held up his shield and warrant before the sorry-looking fellow could launch into his no doubt well-coached refusal to allow another search.

"Is Richard Krato here?" Masefield demanded, pushing past the kid into the hallway. Richard hadn't been at the Meir Library where they had agreed to meet, nor had he shown up at the Oratory, where he had told Masefield he had wanted to go. To say that Masefield was worried as hell would have been an understatement. "What's your name again?"

"Uh, Theodore, Sir. Theodore Krieger. Richard hasn't been here since yesterday."

"Swell. Where's Peter?"

"Mr. Krato left for Rome, Sir."

Masefield pivoted. "Say, *what*?"

Krieger stepped back. "Yes, Sir, sorry, Sir. An hour ago, he left."

"What in the…doesn't he realize his son is missing!" When no intelligible comment was forthcoming from Theodore Krieger, Masefield barked at Ramon Cruz: "Radio the dispatcher to send someone after him. And call Mitchell Field security. He can't have taken off yet."

While Ramon turned away to make the calls, Masefield crossed the entry hall to the door at the bottom of the stairs, Krieger shadowing his steps. It was Showalter's door and it was locked. "You got a key, Theodore?"

"No, Sir, sorry, Sir."

Masefield stepped back and ran into the door with his shoulder; it gave way easily.

If anything, Showalter's room looked even tinier and emptier than when they'd searched it before. It contained only a twin bed, a desk, a chest of drawers, and a narrow closet. The shelves above the bed held a few textbooks and a SANA booklet, written in the *rah-rah* mode by Peter Krato and entitled *Become What You Think You Are*. Without comment, Masefield took the books down one by one and flipped through them, looking for a notation or a slip of paper—anything that might give them a clue as to Showalter's plans or whereabouts. Krieger stood in the doorway the while, his chalky hands hanging limply at his sides.

Masefield replaced the last book and stepped to Showalter's chest of drawers. "Mitch doesn't have much stuff, does he?" he commented over his shoulder.

"Oh, Mitch is very spiritual," Theodore replied admiringly. "He wants to live an unencumbered life. He took most of his things to St. Vincent de Paul last month. Even his Nautilus."

Ramon, who had just joined them, snorted loudly. "Even his Nautilus? I don't think so." He yanked open the door to Mitch's closet.

Finding nothing but a smattering of gigantic socks and underwear in the chest of drawers, Masefield stepped next to the student desk, wondering how in the dickens a guy as big as Showalter could even get his legs under the ratty little thing, which looked as if it had been made for a child and neglected in an attic for decades. The flimsy drawers—a knob came off in Masefield's fingers—contained only a few pens, a stapler, and the bulky Milwaukee Yellow Pages. The only object on the desktop itself was a dusty ceramic Madonna with a chipped nose and broken-off hands.

Masefield leaned across the desktop and pushed aside the faded green curtains at the room's only window. The window overlooked the back of an overgrown yew. The window screen, Masefield noted, had been removed and the storm window pushed up in the outside track. The wooden mullion, greasy to the touch from what smelled like WD-40, slid up silently.

Masefield stuck his head out the window. It was almost dark, but he could still see that the snow directly beneath the window had been disturbed. Directing his flashlight along the foundation of the house, he discovered a sloppy succession of gigantic footprints leading around the back of the house towards the neighboring yard.

Masefield swore. "This is where he got out this morning," he commented to Ramon, pulling back inside.

Ramon slammed the closet door. "There's nothing in there except two sets of SANA uniforms and the second biggest pair of shoes I ever saw."

Masefield noticed that Theodore Krieger was still standing in the doorway like a straw-stuffed scarecrow, guarding an abandoned cornfield. "If you were Mitch," he said to the kid, "and you were looking for Richard, where would you go?"

"Oh, that's easy," Theodore replied, as if gratified to have something to contribute to these otherwise mysterious police proceedings. "Richard can't study well in the house. His dad's always needing him for something, you know. So he goes to the Meir Library a lot. That's where Mr. Krato always sends Mitch to look for Richard when he needs him. The Meir Library."

Looking at his boss, Ramon gave a whistle that was more eloquent than an orchestral rendition of *The Death March*.

"Phone the Oratory again," Masefield ordered brusquely. "And if Richard still hasn't shown up, radio the dispatcher. I want a unit to search for him over at the library—bathrooms, broom closets, stacks. Every street and alley and dumpster between there and the Oratory."

Ramon motioned at the kid. "Show me a phone, Theodore."

Speaking of phones, Masefield thought suddenly, directing his attention once again to Showalter's desk as Theodore led Ramon out of the room. He pulled open the middle drawer and frowned down at the Yellow Pages, trying to figure out why a guy like Showalter would keep it in his desk when he didn't even have his own phone.

The lieutenant had almost given up on the annoying little riddle when the answer lit up in his mind like a light bulb in a cartoon: Showalter had been apartment hunting.

Snatching at the book, Masefield thumbed his way to the "Apartments" heading. He finger-scanned the alphabetical listing in the dim hope that his suspect, in spite of his much-ballyhooed photographic memory, might have had some reason to make a notation in the margins. Nothing...nothing...

At length, Masefield's finger fell on what looked to be a coffee stain next to the listing for Jackbourn Towers.

Masefield found Ramon seated in front of an elaborate phone system set up on one of several banquet-length folding tables in the middle of the SANA House living room.

"Any bright ideas for an alias?" Ramon said as soon as Masefield came running in, Yellow Pages in hand, to share his discovery.

"Try 'James' something," Masefield suggested after a moment's thought. "Or 'Jimmy.'"

Ramon dialed the number. As soon as he began to explain the situation to the soon-to-be-alarmed Jackbourn Towers manager, Masefield took the opportunity to pull up a chair and survey the erstwhile living room, which Peter Krato had transformed into some sort of operational center and mailing room. The banquet table was piled high with boxes of envelopes, mailing labels, and an assortment of cover letters, pamphlets, and brochures. Canvas mailbags were bundled in one corner for sorting bulk mail by zip codes. Theodore Krieger sat opposite Masefield, busying himself with stuffing newsletters into pre-stamped bulk-rate envelopes. Masefield reached for one of the newsletters.

The December issue of SANA's *New Millennium Newsletter* was printed on expensive glossy paper and illustrated throughout with four-color pictures: Peter and Richard Krato at a crowded audience with the Pope two years before, shoving a SANA publication under the Holy Father's patient nose; Peter Krato interviewing a Curia Cardinal; Peter Krato giving a talk at some Catholic college out east. On the back page was a recruitment section entitled *Workers for the Harvest*, which included a photograph from happier times: a dozen young SANA men, kneeling before the exposed Blessed Sacrament in the chapel, Mitch Showalter's white-shirted back rising above the others like a humpbacked whale.

Masefield scanned the text: *persecutions of the Enemy…Gideon's Army… we're in the business of saving souls…industrial-strength evangelization…VISA or MasterCard accepted…*

Hearing Ramon hang up the phone, Masefield dropped the newsletter back in its pile.

"'James Powers,'" Ramon said with a smirk. "He pays his rent in cash and claims to be a buyer for a Canadian import/export firm. He also drives a brand new black Jeep that sounds like a newer version of Ireton's."

Masefield was already heading for the door.

"Wait, Professor!"

Masefield wheeled around.

"You'll never believe this. Remember the guy with the Yorkie who had the ground floor apartment, where Gunderson's body was dropped?"

"Yeah?"

"He had to vacate, because of the pooch. Showalter took the place the very next day. Didn't even want the place cleaned. Said he would clean it himself."

Masefield made a face. "And I bet he did, too. Let's hustle, Cruz, we got a warrant to whip up, and I mean on the double."

Ramon trotted past him while Masefield hesitated in the open doorway, his troubled eyes trained once again on Theodore Krieger. The forlorn-looking young man, having absorbed the entire conversation in apparently uncomprehending silence, was still stuffing envelopes in the living room. "Theodore," Masefield said, stepping back inside, "the Archbishop told all you boys to go home weeks ago. Believe me, this is no place for you or anyone else right now."

His fingers curled around a newsletter, Theodore's bulging eyes turned up to Masefield's with a lost-little-kid look that instantly made Masefield think of Lenny Swiatko. "I haven't really got any place to go, Sir," he said.

Masefield sighed. "Where you from, Theodore?"

"Prairie du Chien, Sir."

"Don't you have anybody back in Prairie du Chien?"

Theodore carefully replaced the newsletter in its proper box. "Nobody who wants me, Sir."

Masefield reached into his breast pocket for his wallet and notebook. He pulled out a couple of twenties from the one and scribbled his Sherman Avenue address on a piece of paper from the other. "Listen up, Theodore," he said in the most James Earl Jones voice he could muster, "I want you to drop what you're doing and call a cab. I mean right this very moment. Don't even bother to pack, now you hear? I want you to go to my house. I'll call my wife, she'll be expecting you. You can stay with us till we can get you settled somewhere. Understand?"

Taking the money and the note with limp fingers, Theodore Krieger's protruding eyes made a slow circuit around the room. "It's finished," he said, "isn't it, Lt. Masefield?"

"Yes, Theodore, it's finished."

Chapter Fifteen:
Now Gods, Stand up for Bastards

> *....Well then,*
> *Legitimate Edgar, I must have your land.*
> *Our father's love is to the bastard Edmund*
> *As to th'legitimate. Fine word, 'legitimate.'*
> *Well, my legitimate, if this letter speed*
> *And my invention thrive, Edmund the base*
> *Shall to th'legitimate. I grow, I prosper.*
> *Now gods, stand up for bastards!*

Shakespeare, *King Lear*

Keeping one ear tuned to his portable radio for weather reports and up-dates on road conditions, James spent ten minutes next door, while Lupe got ready for bed, making a series of desperate phone calls to every public transportation facility in southeastern Wisconsin and northern Illinois. Mitchell Field had only one runway cleared, and all available flights were booked. Amtrak had at first looked promising, until James remembered that they would have to make it back to Milwaukee first, and Highway 167, the county road that connected the shrine to the state highway, had just been closed for the second time in as many days. Then James's cell phone battery died. If he wanted to recharge it, he'd have to trudge down the hill and through the eighteen inches of snow piled up on the parking lot, start up his Jeep, and hook up the portable charger (if it was still in the glove compartment where he'd last seen it, that is) to the cigarette lighter. Bloody bleeding hell.

James unlocked Lupe's door to tell her what was up, only to have it catch on the chain, hooked from inside. Hearing the *whoosh* of her shower running full throttle in the bathroom beyond, he figured that she wouldn't be ready for a few more minutes and locked the door again. He turned and trotted downstairs to the deserted lobby in front of the Shrine gift shop, thinking to finish his calls on the pay phone.

After being put on hold for several minutes, he learned that Greyhound was snowed in, just like everyone else. Worse, a call to the State Highway Patrol gleaned the distressing information that the road crews wouldn't get around to county highways like 167 until the following morning. If it didn't snow anymore, that is. He slammed down the phone.

James retreated to the men's room for a quick pee as he weighed the pros and cons of whether to brave the elements and re-charge the cell phone, or wait till morning when the Shrine's snow plow would have had a chance to clear the parking lot. Deciding that all his efforts were proving useless anyway, and that he didn't dare leave Lupe alone that long, he opted for the latter, plus a quick step outside to get a breath of fresh air and perhaps a smoke. Judging by his racing heartbeats, sleep would probably elude him once again tonight.

Lupe turned off the hairdryer and ran the brush through her hair, then gave in to desperation and reached for the bottle of prescribed sedatives on the bathroom sink. She downed two with water from her cupped hands before going back into the bedroom and slipping into the bed nearest the window, feeling for all the world like a budding hypochondriac, but determined to be asleep before James returned to take his place in the other bed. He hadn't slept a wink the night before — she knew because she hadn't, either — and she was hoping that a quiet room and a sleeping partner might prove a better soporific for him than those blasted sleeping pills, which he refused to take anyway because they made him feel so dopey, especially when combined with the other non-optional medications recently prescribed by Dr. Simon.

Lupe turned off the bedstand light, plopped her head on the inadequate dorm room pillow and closed her eyes, praying that "it," as she had come to name her almost hourly visitation by unnameable terror, would leave her alone, just for tonight. She was doing her best to put on a brave front for James's sake, who was already blaming himself beyond reason for everything that was happening; but the truth was that she was exhausted and sick with fear, and the cafeteria bratwurst she had scarfed down at supper was churning in her volatile stomach in a mélange of meat grease and digestive acids. She was also more than a little dispirited that the retreat thus far was giving her little of the spiritual consolation she was accustomed to, had been desperately praying for, and was very much in need of right now.

For a few hours, at least, her brooding sense of desolation had been ameliorated by James's unflagging devotion and Martin's sturdy serenity; but in the twenty or so minutes since James had left her at her door, kissing her nose with the promise to return within the half-hour, the abyss had once again yawned wide. Lupe gripped tight to a ragged little corner of her faith, reminding herself that the grace she had spent the entire day pleading for was surely being stored up, well, *some*where, like a savings account accruing interest, ready to be drawn upon in some unforeseen emergency.

Thirty seconds later she growled, turned on the light, threw aside the covers, and rolled out of bed. She was heading to the closet for that huge plastic bottle of antacids she had tucked in her backpack, when she saw the envelope on the floor, just inside the door. A bolt of electricity ripped up her sluggish body.

Nothing to get worked up about, she told herself, swallowing a mouthful of brine as she drew nearer the door. The door, after all, was still locked and chained—oops, she'd forgotten about that. She unhooked the chain so James could get in with his room key, reminding herself that the security guard was stalking the premises, and James was either next door or just outside having a smoke, about to return any second. She bent down for the envelope.

The note inside was in Martin's handwriting, apparently scribbled in haste:

> *Lu,*
>
> *James fell on the icy steps outside the retreat house. Fortunately, the security guard heard him yelling. The infirmarian thinks it's a broken leg. We're going to load him up in a four-wheel drive in the driveway in front of the St. Thérèse chapel, if you want to come along for the ride to the hospital in Germantown. But don't worry, he's in good hands. I'll be back to check on you in just a few minutes.*
>
> *Love, Marty*

Poor James, Lupe thought, flapping her hands; he'd been through so much, and now *this.* She burst into tears, partly because of James, partly because she could feel those potent sleeping pills already kicking in, just as she was suddenly needing to remain alert after all. Dropping the letter on the bed, Lupe reached quickly for some tissues, and her clothes.

Glocks at the ready, Masefield and Ramon stood one on each side of the door of James Powers' apartment on the first floor of Jackbourn Towers. This section of the building had been silently evacuated, and members of a SWAT team were stationed at all the entrances, elevators, and stairwells. Masefield thought the precautions would probably prove unnecessary, since James Powers' Jeep wasn't in the lot. Afraid that Showalter could be bolting for Canada, Masefield had alerted the FBI, the neighboring county sheriffs' departments, and even the Waukegan-based Suburban Municipal Assistance Response Team. An alert would be going out to the media any minute, and a couple of SMART's jet helicopters were already airborne, in defiance of the weather, to scan the arterial highways for a glimpse of the Jeep.

Masefield glanced at his watch: one minute after ten. At least the foul weather would surely slow Showalter, wherever the hell he was going.

At a nod from Masefield, Ramon slipped the key into the lock, twisted the knob silently, and kicked open the door. It banged hard against the wall.

But then there was nothing. Nothing but the sound of their own breathing. Masefield could feel it, Showalter wasn't there.

They went through the same procedures at the bedroom and bathroom doors. When they were satisfied that the apartment was indeed vacant, Ramon alerted their colleagues via radio, and they began to look around in earnest.

James Powers' apartment appeared to be the standard Jackbourn one-bedroom unit, very much like Bel Gunderson's on the fifteenth floor. The only significant difference was that the sliding doors opened out onto a small fenced patio instead of a balcony. The place didn't have much furniture yet, either, Masefield mused, but what was here was new, expensive, and remarkably similar to what Masefield had seen in James's newly redecorated digs.

There was one piece of furniture, however, not molded to Ireton's tastes: the tiger-striped sofa wasn't an exact copy of the one that had inspired it, but it came close enough to make Masefield's skin crawl.

Getting Masefield's attention with a whistle, Ramon stabbed his index finger in the direction of Showalter's Nautilus, poised in a corner of the living room like a gigantic black spider. Above it hung a large picture in a massive frame: Bel Gunderson's Diego Rivera. Gunderson's red teddy was hung over one corner of the frame like a scarf, while a bra and pair of bikini panties, probably Nadine Jeffrey's, draped the opposite corner. A pair of stiletto heels that had no doubt been on Candace Duffy's feet the night she had been cut to ribbons was propped on the upper edge of the picture frame. Gunderson's skull's head ashtray, containing the butts of a half-dozen Marlboro Lights and a couple of Djarums sat on the coffee table next to her pack of Tarot cards.

"He's got some *cojones*," Ramon commented, "putting it all out in plain view."

"Yeah, well, my guess is he doesn't get much company." Masefield took a deep breath. "It's all here. Everything we need to put him away till Doomsday…everything except that wooden chalice and the communion wafers." Frowning—given the rest of Showalter's display, he would have expected the chalice to be set out as the centerpiece of his grisly collection—Masefield headed for the bedroom.

Flipping the light switch, the lieutenant almost jumped out of his skin. Garish flashes of light attacked his eyes from a dozen different directions at once, momentarily blinding him. It took a few blinking seconds for the spots to fade and for Masefield to realize that there was only one light source, the overhead, but that it was being reflected, along with a dozen startled images of himself, from mirrors fastened on every available surface over drywall painted midnight. Showalter's bed, a king-sized mattress and box springs sprawling on the floor without a frame, was covered with scarlet silk sheets that bled like an open wound against the mirrored darkness surrounding it. Directly above the bed was a Shakespeare poster captioned THE ULTIMATE SHAKESPEARIENCE.

Hearing a noise behind him, Masefield turned to see Ramon Cruz gaping at something above his head. Following the younger detective's gaze, Masefield spotted the digicams mounted in all four corners of the room, their owlish lenses focused on the scarlet bed.

After a moment's dumbfounded pause, Masefield rushed to the entertainment center hooked up opposite the bed and batted through Showalter's video collection. *The Rape of Lucrece* was there of course, but along with a predictable assortment of retail pornography in almost every format and tending to the S & M end of the rotter scale, there was a DVD with a handwritten label on the plastic case: *Thanksgiving — NJ.*

Masefield lifted it out with the tips of his Latex-gloved fingers. Glancing up once more at the cameras on the ceiling, he felt suddenly and violently dizzy, something that hadn't happened to him since he was a rookie. He tossed the DVD on the bed and staggered to the bathroom. When he reemerged a minute or two later, Ramon was standing by the bed, the DVD in his hand, his tawny face gone pasty.

"How did he get her in and out of here without anyone seeing?" Ramon asked thickly.

Masefield wiped his lips with a piece of toilet paper. "The patio. The fence door opens out on the parking lot." He waved vaguely at the bathroom. "Lanciano's photograph of Duffy is hanging above the toilet."

When Ramon still hadn't moved a few seconds later, Masefield added, "Pull yourself together, Ramon. Radio the ID Unit and tell them to come wrap up the whole fucking place."

Ramon took a deep breath and dropped the video on the bed. "Still haven't found the chalice," he said, "and…you know. Guess I'd better check the freezer." Pulling out his radio, Ramon headed back to the kitchen with visible reluctance.

Relieved that young Cruz was volunteering for that potentially grisly task, Masefield wiped his clammy forehead on his overcoat sleeve and stepped to Showalter's computer desk. There was a bulletin board hung above the computer and covered like a mosaic with snapshots: James, Mitch and Richard in front of a large old frame house, presumably the original Immaculata House; James and Mitch, saws and hammers in hand, absorbed in what looked like some sort of backstage set-building project for one of the Institute's yearly Shakespeare productions; James on stage and in costume, probably as Iago; James lying on his back, napping on Bradford Beach.

Only one photo in the grouping did not include James: a yellowed snapshot of a teenaged Candace Duffy. Showalter had fixed the picture to the corkboard with a red thumbtack through the heart.

Pulling the chain of a green-shelled desk lamp, identical to one Masefield had seen in James Ireton's apartment, Masefield turned his attentions to the desk. The lamp threw a rectangle of yellow light on a stack of books piled next to Showalter's computer tower: a history of memory-enhancement techniques "from Giordano Bruno to Harry Lorraine," or so the back cover claimed; a copy of James's *The Conscience of the Prince*, littered throughout with Showalter's angry red marginal notations; a King James Bible with "to Richard with much love" inscribed on the flyleaf and signed by James Ireton; a copy of James's SANA Report; the Summer edition of *The Shakespeare Quarterly*, containing Fr. Bricusse's article, "Motiveless Malignity: Another Look at Iago and Edmond," also heavily annotated in Showalter's red ink; a composition book with "Lear" handwritten on the front cover label; a three-ring notebook.

Masefield picked up what he knew must be Lupe Cruz's journal. Opening it, he saw, as anticipated, Lupe's name and address taped on the inside cover, followed by sheet after sheet of dated entries containing neat handwriting that slanted slightly upward on the page. Masefield was quickly scanning the pages from the last few months when a handful of loose papers and envelopes fell out onto the table. Setting aside the notebook, Masefield lifted the top sheet of paper. It was apparently a letter written on Holy Hill stationery by Fr. Martin Cruz. Odd, though, Masefield thought as he glanced through the rest of the pile, his eyebrows gathering, there were several sheets of plain notepaper as well, all containing crossed-out and rewritten sentences, over and over, as if Lupe—no, it wasn't her handwriting—had been practicing penmanship. On closer inspection, Masefield realized that all of the letters were variations on the theme of James having broken his leg—*what the hell?*—and were all signed "Love, Marty."

It took Masefield a few seconds to sort it out. When he did, he let out a cry that brought Ramon bounding in from the living room, weapon at the ready. "Jesus, Cal, what's the matter!"

Masefield was madly scanning the rest of Lupe's journal entries. His finger lingered over a two-month-old entry dated Wednesday, October 9th:

> *Talked to Marty. Private retreat at H.H., Dec. 11–14. The decision will have been made by then, but I figure I'd better schedule the prayer time anyway...*

"He knows she's at Holy Hill!" Masefield cried, almost knocking Ramon over in his race for the door. "Get your brother Martin on the phone! And get us a helicopter, now!"

A cigarette in one hand and his briefcase in the other, James paced outside the front entrance of the Visitor's Center. The temperature was dropping, and a brisk wind had finally succeeded in blowing the remaining snow clouds off to the east, revealing a setting half moon in the clearing sky. Glancing at his watch—it was one minute past ten—it suddenly occurred to James that he hadn't seen the security guard since before dinner. Trash-canning his fag, James took to the snowy walkway that led up to the back door of the retreat house, thinking it to be the most likely spot for the guard to have positioned himself.

The wet snow clung to his boots like mud. When the unshoveled pathway proved more treacherous than James would have predicted, he paused for a breather where the walkway intersected the path leading up to the Shrine. Looking around in the play of shadows and reflected snowlight for a sign of the security guard, his eyes stumbled over a darker shadow among the shadows. The path up to the Shrine had been barricaded to prevent falls, and visitors were directed to use the elevator from the guest house. The last time James had come this way, after supper, the untrodden path had just been blanketed by another six inches of fresh snow. But now the steep and slippery way was marred by the imprints of gigantic feet, with slashes and grooves off to the side as if someone, much smaller, had been dragged up the hill.

His briefcase falling from his fingers and his legs all but giving way beneath him, James scrambled for the path up the hill. Less than ten yards ahead he tripped over the shadow he had seen from below: a man's legs, sprawled across the path.

Just off the path, in a bramble of leafless bushes, the dead security guard lay on his belly, his head twisted around almost one hundred and eighty degrees, his sightless eyes fixed on the night-dark silhouette of the Shrine above them. Swallowing terror, James, too, turned his eyes toward the Shrine, and ran.

The wind whipped down the hillside, sending a stinging spray of snow across James's face as he made his difficult way up the path through the sometimes deep drifts, slipping, clambering to his feet again, his bare hands gloved with snow, through the velvet darkness, vaulting over locked gates, up the winding, icy steps toward the Shrine, praying that he was wrong. He prayed that the thick layer of new snow on the driveway below the Tower would still lie plump and untouched in its virgin, Christmasy whiteness; that the door to the Scenic Tower would be safely locked, as it should be for the winter, and all quiet and dark and empty inside.

But as soon as he reached the driveway, shining with an arctic brilliance under the cold glare of security lights, James saw again the huge imprints, and the smaller ones alongside, leading to the door at the base of the Tower.

The door was unlocked. But then, James thought, horrified belief finally taking hold of him as he pulled it open, Mitch would be expecting him to follow, wouldn't he? Would be waiting for him, up there, in the cold and the dark. His belly churning, his knowledge of his own impotence shrouding him in a rough blanket of despair, James reached under his parka for the Grendel holstered at his back. He shut the door quietly behind him.

Brushing snow from his boots and off his face as his eyes adjusted to the interior darkness, James made his silent, careful way up the winding steps of the wind-wracked Tower, gun in hand, ascending into darkness, up and around and up again the gyring corridor of steps. He slowed as he finally

approached the narrow landing, which opened out to the right on the obser-
vatory gallery, where he knew they would be.

An unnatural bluish light clung like ice to the frosty air. Pistol at the
ready, James paused on the top step before the landing. He had begun to
think he might be hallucinating in his terror, because over the whistling of
the wind up and down the narrow stairwell, he was hearing the jolly strains
of a bit of Gilbert and Sullivan, sung in Mitch's raspy tenor.

"...*Behold the Lord High Executioner! A personage of noble rank and title.
A dignified and potent officer, whose functions are particularly vital!*" Showalter
obviously had little concern about being heard. The retreat house was hun-
dreds of yards down the hill, while the monastery cloister was on the other
side of the great church, on the other side of the hill...on the other side of
the world, for all it mattered up here in this wasteland of old brick, new
snow, and wind.

Taking one last slow step up to the landing, moving a centimeter at a
time, James peered carefully around the corner, hoping against hope that
Mitch's back might be to him. The gallery was only about ten feet square, he
knew, and he was confident he could get off a clean shot at such close range
without hitting Lupe, if only he could take aim without the big man seeing
him.

But Showalter was facing the stairs, his great beast of a figure side-lit
by battery-powered lanterns set like stage footlights on the gallery floor, his
huge body poured into black leather boots, leggings, and jacket. His back to
a pair of lancet windows, boarded up with plywood for the winter, Mitch's
trunk-thick legs were set wide apart on the snow-dappled platform. A brown
friar's robe lay crumpled at his feet. Snow had blown in through the one
unboarded window nearest James and had collected on the floor, reflecting the bluish lamplight in harsh blacks and whites, and ghostly blue-grays.
Mitch had obviously pried off that section of plywood, and James could not
help but see that no intact body could fit through the openings between the
window's iron grillwork, only body parts. Mitch's naked skull, newly shorn
of its curly locks, gleamed a spectral pearl in the lamplight. He was leaning
almost casually against the plywood over the lancet window behind him,
his massive body enfolding Lupe's like a child grappling with a disobedient
teddy bear. Blood was dribbling from a bump on Lupe's temple, and though
she was conscious, she was obviously woozy, struggling hopelessly, exhausted
already, her face death-pale in the lamplight behind limp strands of blood-
damp hair. Mitch had thrown aside her jacket and was in the process of
unsnapping her jeans.

James backed off in the dark, to get hold of his shaken nerves and await
an opportunity; but it was too late; Mitch had heard or seen something and
looked up.

"Well, now," the big man cried in mocking imitation of James's half-
English, half-American speech. "*Childe Roland to the dark tower came!*" His
fingers closed around Lupe's throat. "I was beginning to think you'd missed
your cue, Jimmy. The curtain's gone up!"

Slipping the gun back in its holster behind his back, James swallowed despair and turned the corner, stepping out onto the tiny gallery in front of the open window.

"Which of the Elizabethan tragedies are we enacting tonight?" James asked with a calculated swagger he certainly didn't feel.

"What, almost a PhD and you don't even know what fucking play we're in? Well, Jimmy, in life and lit, we're always telling the same old stories over and over again, aren't we? Tonight I play Iago, making Othello egregiously an ass. Or the bastard Edmond, getting his brother Edgar's lands. Or Cain and Abel, Jacob and Esau, Quetzalcoatl and Tezcatlipoca…" Mitch grinned, his perfect teeth glistening in the lamplight. "*Our name is Legion.*"

James inched forward. "Too true. Hell is empty, and all the devils are here."

"Now stay back, Jimmy, or I snap her neck in two, and you know I can do it."

James paused. "You've become rather accomplished at that sort of thing, haven't you?"

"Oh you bet. I've become a professional thanatic. A gynocidal auteur, deconstructing the bloody subtext of the entire Western Canon. You know, all the unmentionable stuff between the lines. But then, as you well know, I've had only the finest teachers."

"Who?" James asked, raising his voice against the crescendo and decrescendo of the cycling wind coming in at his back. "Who taught you—" He gestured at the Tower. "—this?"

"Oh, not just the Kratos, if that's who you mean. I could always count on you to blame them first. Though no question it was Peter who gave me the Master Class in the fine art of the bold-faced sanctimonious lie. Better than an acting degree from Julliard, let me tell you! But then I'm a natural polymorph anyway. A shape-shifter. Why, I've fixed myself up with a Canadian persona that's going to see me clean out of the picture when my work is done in this Castle of Murders." Mitch nodded at the Tower. "Then, arising from the ashes like a postmodern Phoenix, will be the Last Man." Mitch twirled his yellow-gloved fingers at his bald pate. "Like it? I just did it this afternoon."

"Terrific. Now you look like a thousand other skinheads in Milwaukee."

Mitch pouted. "Actually, It's an *hommage* to Foucault, along with all the leather." He gestured at his outfit. "But let's talk about more interesting subjects, Jimmy. Let's talk about what I learned from *you.*"

"All right, I'll bite. What did you learn from me?"

Mitch laughed. "You mean, besides providing me, with that kooky vision of yours, with the perfect *mise-en-scène* for my dramatic climax?"

James swallowed. "Yes, besides that."

"Why, you taught me how to eat women, Jimmy. How to eat 'em alive, then toss the leavings into the nearest gutter. And now the bloody instructions have returned to plague their inventor!"

Licking his cold lips, James felt the brutal confrontation with truth sapping his resolve. "Oh, but you've never trod the boards," he countered after a moment's hesitation, and not quite able to bring forth the requisite degree of lying bravado, "or you'd know how dangerous it is to quote the Scottish Play off stage."

"Pul-*leeze*," Mitch returned with a brassy grin, "as ol' Belzebub used to say, *I'm always on stage*. But there was one other thing you taught me, Jimmy, perhaps the most critical."

"And that is?"

"Irony, brother. The Universal Solvent. The first and final principle, which the medieval alchemists slaved to discover, and never realized they'd already found. Yeah, you were my prophet, Jimmy, my Zarathustra. I've often wondered how things might have turned out if you'd somehow managed to keep a grip on your faith. But there's no point in worrying about might-have-beens, now is there?"

"Mitch," James cried, "for God's sake what happened? When did the bottom drop out?"

Mitch clucked. "C'mon now, this delaying routine is one of the oldest plot devices in Western literature. Not that I really mind, mind you. Masefield's pacing the floor back in Milwaukee, and I've already taken care of the security guard. I've got all night, really and truly."

James opened his arms. "As you say. So here's your one chance, before you finish us, to share your triumphs with the only man on the planet who could possibly appreciate them." James straightened himself, his right hand primed for the quick reach behind his back. "So tell me, when did your conscience die?"

Mitch shifted his weight like an old-timer settling in for a twice-told tale before a roaring campfire. "It didn't happen all at once, it was murder by degrees. But I suppose the point of no return was the afternoon my Aunt Abby came down to talk to Peter. That was the first day of class. See, she'd found a notebook of mine, a first draft of my *Lear* adaptation. It upset the hell out of her, poor dear. She was hoping to convince Peter what a sick little boy I was, and how I needed help. Thing was, Peter was facing a cash-flow crunch. All he could think about was how he could weasel the old girl into mortgaging her house to keep SANA out of bankruptcy court." Mitch giggled. "I was hiding behind the door, listening to the two of them go round and round and round."

"That's...all? That's all it took to turn you inside out?"

Mitch lifted his eyes and addressed himself not so much to James as to the air a few inches above James's head, as if standing in attendance at an apparition. "Jimmy, Jimmy, Jimmy," he said, "you hopeless innocent! You think you've seen the heart of darkness in the mirror? *The horror! The horror!*" Mitch whooped. "You've seen nothing. *I met Death along the way. He wore a mask like Peter Kra...*well, you get the idea. It was a revelation, Jimmy. A fucking kratophany. Tell you what, brother, it led me to a deeper understanding of the commandment against taking the Lord's name in vain. I mean, what's a few spur-of-the-moment *goddamns* compared to a snake like Peter Krato, in the name of the Thrice-Holy-One, hissing at a long-suffering saint like my dear old Aunt Abigail with ad copy like, *You're an unwitting agent of the Adversary! If you deny this work, you'll be denying God!*" Mitch shook his bald pate. "Poor old bird fled the room in tears. That's when I said to myself, holy shit, Mitchell, you've spied into the deep secrets of Satan! In this world or in any other, it's eat or be eaten. That simple. So, I killed God right then and there. I drank up the sea. It was a decision made in a twinkling. Meaning came into focus later."

"But, Mitch —"

Mitch yelled, "If there was a God, he would have acted that afternoon! He wouldn't have been able to resist it! But what did I see, hear, taste, smell, touch…? Hm? Nothing. No thing! Zip. *Nada.* Nul." Mitch lifted his head and whistled into a gust of wind. "Power is the god of this world, Jimmy. Yeah, and I knew that once before, eleven years ago, when I dumped my drunken brother into the eighth sea with a tackle box strapped to his ankles…oh, now, I see that look on your face. Don't try to tell me you don't understand what I'm saying. You've looked in that smoking mirror."

"I've looked in that mirror." James risked a glance at Lupe: except for her violent trembling and an occasional sluggish blink, she had remained motionless throughout Showalter's outrageous narrative, as if she were struggling against some overwhelming urge to sleep.

And then James remembered: besides the bitter cold and the nasty bump on her head, she'd probably taken sleeping pills.

James planted his feet slightly apart, thinking he would have to make his move soon, probably with little help from Lupe, and before his own bare hands went completely numb from the cold. "So your religion wasn't all show," he asked finally, "at least before?"

"Let's just say I'd had one too many doses of Abby's spiritual Prozac. And I was young. Oh, but you'll be edified to learn that poor Richie finally stumbled over his conscience where he mislaid it last September 14."

"I don't understand."

"He was about to blow my alibi. And for his pains —" Mitch gestured in the cold air, as if tossing a soiled napkin in the litter basket. "— *Stout Sansjoy doth sleep in deadly shade.*"

Lupe let out a moan.

Mitch looked down. It appeared he had almost forgotten her. Stretching out both Latex-gloved hands, he cupped her breasts and squeezed. "*She speaks! Oh, speak again bright angel!* Man-oh-man would Jimmy have loved to get his pickers and stealers on these fine tits!"

"Mitch!" James broke in, "your brother Jimmy seems to be the pattern thread in the weave of your little text. But I'm not your brother Jimmy!"

Mitch looked a little offended. One huge hand moved back to Lupe's throat. "I know it. I'm not bloody crazy. *Full fathom five my brother lies. Worms are e'en at him* — going a-progress through the guts of some beggar at a Kenosha fish-fry. But it's the aesthetics of the thing that counts. The allegorical parallelism, the circularity. See, two Jimmies have fucked me over from the get-go. Annexing me, marginalizing me, getting there first…taking what was mine by rights. But not any more, oh no. As Artaud said, life is always someone's death, and in this case mine is yours. You must decrease, so that I may increase—" Mitch broke off and looked down.

After squirming for several seconds under Mitch's unconsciously tightening grip around her throat, Lupe had passed out. Irritated, Mitch put the fingers of his other hand under her cheekbones and began shaking her head. Suddenly Lupe closed her teeth around Mitch's forefinger and bit down ferociously. Mitch yanked away with a howl.

James went for the pistol in the small of his back; but his benumbed fingers got tangled in his bulky parka, and the second before James could take aim, Mitch's huge hands were once again wrapped around Lupe's head and neck, ready to twist.

"Drop it, Jimmy, or she's headless!"

James growled in fury. The gun clattered to the floor.

Mitch's eyes darted from the gun on the floor to James's face. Then back to the gun. "On second thought," he said breathlessly, steadying himself on his two pillar-like legs, "I don't think I want that thing lying around. So you're going to bend down, Jimmy, I mean *real slow*, and pick up that gun between your thumb and forefinger. Got that?"

James obeyed, never taking his eyes off Mitch in case he got that impossible second chance.

But he didn't. His muscles flexed, Mitch stood poised to break Lupe's neck at the slightest provocation. Straightening, James had no choice but to extend his arm to the side, the Grendel dangling between his thumb and forefinger.

"Step back to the window behind you."

When James didn't respond fast enough, Mitch gave a tug on Lupe's neck. She cried out, the sound of it muffled by the pressure of his carrot-sized fingers against her throat.

"All right!" James cried. His boots crunching in the miniature snowdrift that had collected near the wall, he took two steps back to the open lancet window. Reaching through the bars, dusted with snow like tinsel in the moonlight, he tossed out his one decent chance. The pistol disappeared into the snowy void without a sound.

Trembling violently, probably as much from cold now as from fear, Lupe closed her eyes and began to weep.

"I guess we knew something like that was coming, so it was good to get it out of the way." Pulling Lupe down with him as he squatted, Mitch seated himself spread-eagled on the concrete floor, his back to the wall and Lupe tucked securely in his lap. He grinned as he reached inside his jacket pocket and pulled out a small but deadly-looking knife, its blade razor-sharp and carved from smooth black obsidian. "Let's both sit down for a minute," Mitch added, waving it at James. "That way no one can move too fast. Sit *down*, Jimmy!"

James collapsed on the cold, snowy concrete.

"You know, I think I'm going to work without the gloves tonight. Tonight of all nights."

James watched helplessly as Mitch proceeded to remove the Latex gloves one at a time, using his teeth so that he could keep the knife in his free hand, ready at every moment. When he dropped the second glove on the floor, Mitch wrapped his legs around Lupe's to spread them wide apart. He lifted his arm, the knife blade aimed at her crotch.

"You dropped Father, didn't you!" James nearly screamed.

Mitch laughed, then shrugged, but lowered his hand a fraction. "Hey, no need to get so excited. I was just mentally rehearsing my options. But yeah, as for old Bricusse, dropping him was a mere flourish. The old geezer was already dead when I got up there."

James spoke rapidly. "But it was you who sent the anonymous letters, wasn't it, not Rich and not Peter."

"Sure. I sent them to you and Lenny Swiatko both."

"Why to Lenny?"

"Oh well that part *was* Peter's idea, though he didn't know about my sending them to you. He thought that if we could keep the poor loony tight-rope-walking on the razor blade with some spooksville tactics, he'd forget all about the money Peter had filched from him. Mind you, I don't think Peter thought it would go as far as it did, but you got to hand it to the kid, he went out with style. Gave me some great ideas, he did."

"And Candace Duffy? Was that you or the mob?"

Mitch's eyes narrowed. "I saw her picture in the paper with Nesterov. First I'd seen of her in years. I made an appointment with her under an assumed name." Then he exploded: "The filthy cunt didn't even recognize me!"

"What about your Aunt Abby?" James asked quickly before Mitch could translate his remembered fury into savagery in the here and now.

Mitch took several deep breaths, apparently to calm himself. "I loved her," he said, "don't think I didn't. She was the only person who was ever decent to me in my life. But she'd told me she was going to that religious conference, and when I found out at Lanciano's party that Bricusse was there, too, I knew she'd talk to him. About me. Oh, that might have been the end of it—she thought Bricusse could practically raise the dead—but when his obituary appeared in *The Rambler*, I had to act. That rag was the only newspaper Abby ever read. I knew that when she saw the article about how he fell, she'd know I'd done it. So I had to get to her before she made up her mind to call the police. Which she would have, sooner or later. Old Abby's mind worked a little slow, maybe, but her conscience was as sharp as this blade."

James groped for another question, any at all. "What were you looking for in Fr. Bricusse's office?"

"I was afraid Bricusse had taken notes of his meeting with Abby. He hadn't, I guess, but I was also looking for anything on SANA. Anything that might persuade the Archbishop to close SANA before I was ready. SANA was such a great cover, especially with the Kratos wrapped around my little finger." Mitch's eyes darted around the dark-light platform, as if contemplating the next scene in the tragedy he was so brutally scripting. "Anyway, here we are, in the Tower. Where it began, it ends, for me as well as for you." He squinted at James. "My hour's come round at last, Jimmy-me-boy. The wheel's come full circle. Trust me, a year from now my name will be an eponym. Like *shrapnel*, like *sadism*, like *America*. All the earlier scenes were dumbshows. This is the main stage. The ultimate Shakespearience, Act Five, with you and me and the aphasic Dark Lady in the middle." Mitch squirmed on his fanny, as if with an overabundance of energy. "Now, I tell you what, I think it's time for word to become flesh." He raised the knife.

"Wait! This isn't about her, it's about you and me! So, how about this—" James swallowed cold air, riding his panic like a bucking bronco. "Let her go, and you can do with me what you like!"

It seemed an eternity before James realized that his proposition had actually taken Mitch by surprise; was perhaps even tempting him. The knife glimmered uncertainly in the air several seconds before Mitch finally lowered it and said, his reedy voice sounding a little unstable, "Well, now, just what, I have to ask, besides watching me rape and gut the thing you love most in this wide world, could you really do for me…?"

"Let you…let you…do what you will with me. Anything. Everything. I give you my word, I'll offer no resistance. Completely at your mercy." As if to bait his terrible offer, James lifted his hand to the zipper of his parka and pulled down, very slowly. Lupe began to moan. He slipped off the jacket and dropped it beside his hips; then went to work with cold-clumsy fingers on the buttons of his flannel shirt. A moment later it, too, was on the floor beside his parka.

Mitch gazed at James's shivering, sweaty chest, naked to the waist but for the Guadalupe medal around his neck. Lupe's head began to roll from side to side in time with her moans, and Mitch, obviously irritated that she was distracting him from full concentration on James and his tantalizing proposition, put the knife to her throat. "Shut up, bitch," he barked, recovering his self-possession with a smirk; but he didn't take his eyes off James. "You're not going to quit there are you, Jimmy?"

His knees knocking together, James unlaced his boots and pulled them off; then his socks. His bare feet stung on contact with the icy cement. James's fingers had moved to the snap of his jeans when Mitch suddenly raised his knife hand to put a stop to James's wintry strip-tease.

"You know, I think that's about enough," Mitch said, his blue eyes blinking rapidly. "Nice try, though, I'll give you that. But I'm not exactly inclined that way, you know what I'm saying, whatever Calvin fucking Masefield might think. And I certainly don't think I should go screwing around with my MO at this critical juncture. Besides," he added, more cheerfully, as if the thought had just occurred to him, "right now I've got the both of you anyway, so why do with just one?"

Riding a cross-sea of humiliating relief and abject misery such as he had never known in his miserable life, James flattened his palms on the concrete beside his hips. "But you don't have both of us," he argued, nodding at the stairwell only three feet away from him, but almost ten feet away from Mitch. "I'm nearer the door and you're encumbered with your hostage. I can clear off any time. Run to the monastery for help."

Mitch's eyes flitted to the stairwell then back again, his huge body tensing in anticipation of some move. But then he visibly relaxed the huge muscles of his thighs and said, "I don't think so. No, you won't leave. You won't leave for the same reason you didn't run for help before you came up here. Because you know I'd still be able to give her fifteen or twenty minutes of the most nauseating savagery a human being has ever had to endure on this side of hell. Believe me, Jimmy, the pleasure would be worth the risk to me, you know it would!" Mitch laughed out loud, as if gaining confidence with every passing second in the accuracy of his assessment of his own—and James Ireton's—character. "Worst case scenario, even if I ended up in jail, I'd still have the priceless satisfaction of watching you drag out the rest of your pitiful days, knowing you'd abandoned the only thing you ever loved to my knife's point. Either way," he concluded, "it's going to be real interesting to me, these next few minutes, to find out what you're made of."

"To me, too," James agreed, drawing upon every technique he had ever learned on the college stage to mask the desolation behind his words; to keep his hands flat on the icy concrete beside his hips; to keep himself from abandoning Lupe in earnest and scrambling for the stairs only three feet away.

There was no hope. They were going to die, Lupe more vilely than James in his worst moments of rage could ever have imagined. All her love and goodness and beauty had come to naught and worse than naught; because it was her very love and goodness and beauty that had delivered her into the clutches of the Dragon. Even James's own repentance and remorse, his renewed faith in a God who had died to kill death, had proved, as he should have known it would, as he had always known it would, no more efficacious in the communion of saints and sinners than a letter sealed in a bottle and tossed out to sea. Love was dying tonight in a pit of ugliness, and the most he could hope for was to provoke the fiend, to bring things to such a pass that Mitch would kill her outright and forego his grislier choreography.

His muscles tensing, James prepared himself to lunge and have done.

Kee-kee-kee!

Mitch seemed as startled by the sound as James. Both men jumped, then turned as if one towards the source of the noise.

A bird had flown in the open window behind James. Its brown wings fluttering, it came to rest near the floor in one corner of the Tower amidst a collection of objects arranged on a beach towel next to the wall, which James hadn't noticed before in his preoccupied terror. Besides scissors, duct tape, and wash cloths, Mitch's toolkit included a hacksaw, a barbecue lighter, several razors that looked like operating room instruments, a package of condoms, and an empty quart-size plastic food container.

His mouth going dry, James realized that the *kee-kee*ing little creature, its white breast ringed with black bands, had perched on the lip of a wooden chalice, perhaps six inches in height and carved in a strange but oddly familiar knot-and-key pattern. Even in the chiaroscuro lamplight James could see the brown and gold graining, which indicated that the cup, containing a pair of large hosts, round and white as the moonlight, was made of myrtlewood.

James stifled a gasp.

Lupe's eyes had swiveled as well. On seeing the objects of torture, she went limp. Mitch didn't seem to notice. Apparently anxious that the bird might be after the communion wafers in the chalice, he flung one arm in the killdeer's direction and cried, "Shoo, goddammit, shoo!"

The killdeer hopped off the cup onto the towel, then flopped over on its side as if Mitch had somehow managed to break one of its wings by means of a blow to the air from several feet away. It limped around like that for a couple of seconds before righting itself and taking to the air again, flying out the window behind James with a final *kee-kee*.

Turning slowly back to Lupe, his concentration suddenly as focused as a laser, and all thoughts of provoking Mitch just to get it over with having flown with the killdeer, James saw the spasms in Lupe's throat, and her frantic swallowing. Half frozen and brutalized, woozy from the blow to her head, she was not thinking clearly, but yet clearly terrified that if she gave in to nausea Mitch would slit her throat with one flick of his wrist.

But James had known Mitch longer than Lupe. A shot of energy sizzled up his spine: there was still one strange chance.

Lifting his head and trying not to allow his teeth to chatter with the cold, James projected his voice over the wind like a stage actor aiming his soliloquy at the back row. "Now that you mention your nauseating savagery, old man," he said in the snobbiest BBC diction he could muster, "be a sport, unmuzzle your wisdom. What have you got in mind for us tonight? Or should I say for *her*." James pointed at Lupe and sniffed. "Masefield's been so tight-lipped about the details of your, what did you call it, 'MO'?"

Mitch scratched the side of his bald head with the tip of his obsidian knife. "Tell you what, Jimmy, you're in for a transgressive limit experience. A 'surfascist spectacle' *à la* Bataille, with a little cathartic chthonic Theater of Cruelty thrown in, *à la* Artaud. Howsabout Act two, scene three of *Titus Andronicus*, with the Dark Lady here in the role of Lavinia? Crikey, when I cut out her tongue, who the hell will know the difference? Or better yet, think of it as the climax of your hallucination, the part your psyche was too squeamish to finish, where the dragon swoops in to strip you of your sword and violate the virgin on the altar of bloody sacrifice."

"But how do you *stage* such a thing?" James persisted, leaning forward as if with eagerness. "I mean the blocking, man, the props, the stage business!"

"Well, first I get hold of them by the neck." Mitch demonstrated his one-handed throat hold on Lupe, who clawed at his huge fingers to no effect. "Then I make them stuff and tape their own mouths. That just drives them fucking nuts, you know, having to tape their own mouths. Then I go to work." With his free hand, the one holding the knife, Mitch reached down before James could even blink, and sliced open a six-inch cut on the inside of Lupe's left thigh. She squirmed and gurgled beneath his huge hands, her mouth twisting in a silent scream as steamy blood flowed onto the platform and puddled between her legs.

Anticipation as well as fear squeezed James's abdomen like a vise: it was now or never. "What's the chalice for?" he said shrilly, pointing at the grail. "Besides a stage prop to furnish my vision, I mean. And what do you do with the Blessed Sacrament?"

Mitch shifted his body from hip to hip, whether from nerves or the cold, or just aroused by the thought of carnage to come, James couldn't tell. "I've been using one host per kill," he said, slipping the knife between Lupe's breasts and slicing upwards, cutting off the buttons of her blouse one by one. "It's my *osculum infame*, my *missa pro defunctis*...my final 'fuck you' to God!" The last button popped off, and Mitch yanked open her blouse. Sliding the knife under her bra between her breasts, he bisected the undergarment with one yank of his wrist. "To paraphrase the divine Crowley, after I rave and I rape and I rip and I rend, everlasting world without end, I gouge out their beating hearts and stuff a consecrated host right—"

"God damn you!" Lupe screamed, cutting him off as a sudden gust of wind from the window snatched the cries right out of her mouth. Then her eyes rolled into the back of her head. James thought she had fainted outright, but suddenly she gave a violent heave and propelled a cascade of vomit all over Mitch's knife hand and leather jacket sleeve.

Cursing wildly, Mitch dropped the slimy knife with the instinctive recoil of a compulsive clean-freak. He worked feverishly to extricate himself from his soiled jacket as James scrambled on all fours across the floor, diving for the knife and yelling for Lupe to get the hell out of there. In the next instant James had the knife in hand.

But the accumulated traumas had done their work. On her hands and knees in a somnambulant daze, Lupe couldn't seem to get to her feet—a lethargy which gave Mitch just enough time to kick out with one of his size thirteen boots and connect with James's face, breaking his nose.

His head exploding with pain, James clutched at his face, his cupped hands catching the blood pouring from his nose. But the other hand grasped the knife.

In two steps Mitch was on his feet and straddling Lupe. Bending over, he grabbed one of her arms and wrenched it back, snapping it like a dry twig. She screamed; then dropped to the cement, face down and unconscious.

Gasping for breath through his mouth because he nasal cavity was filled with blood, James righted himself against the pain and lurched forward, burying the already bloodied knife almost up to the hilt in Mitch's nearest available body part, his side. Mitch roared, spun around, and sent James reeling across the platform with a staggering blow to the side of his head. James slammed into the door frame at the top of the stairs.

Mitch pulled the knife out of his own flesh with a shriek. He limped toward James, the blade flashing in wide, wild, sweeping arcs. Backing into the corner of the landing at the top of the stairs, James threw his hands in front of his face; but one slash still caught him across his naked left arm, while the next caught him under his left ear. James felt a second's worth of new pain, like fire; then a numbing shock.

"*A hit*," Mitch screeched, stepping back to gape at his bloody handiwork, "*a very palpable hit!*"

James's eyes fluttered down to see a trickle of blood oozing from the superficial wound in his arm, but a stream of blood, black in the snowlight, oozing out rapidly on his bare chest, sometimes spurting from the gash on the side of his neck. Steam rose from it as it met the cold air. James swayed, his mind spinning in a burst of electric dizziness. He slumped to the floor, his back propped against the wall at the top of the stairs. Lifting his left hand, he pressed feebly against the wound at his neck, praying in a fog that if he must bleed to death, as he was clearly about to do, God might at least grant him a few extra minutes of stolen life in order to save Lupe's; or if he couldn't save her, at least to spare her the rest of the torture Mitch had promised.

As if reading James's thoughts, Mitch cried out, "I'll finish you in a minute, but first watch this!"

James looked up to see Mitch, arms outstretched, lift his cold head to bay with bright insanity at the half-moon glowing through the rose window above. "*Veni, veni, Mephistophilis*," Mitch cried in ecstasy, "*orientis princeps Belzebub, inferni ardentis monarcha, et Demogorgon, propitiamus vos, ut appareat et surgat Mephistophilis!*" Mitch made an animal sound at the back of his throat and spat a huge wad of phlegm on Lupe's motionless head. "*Maledicat Dominus!*" Then he dragged her unconscious body by the ankles to the middle of the gallery and scooped up a bit of snow to rub in her face, apparently to make certain that she would be awake as he yanked her shirt and bra over her shattered arm.

The obscene sight of Mitch's huge hands on Lupe's naked skin, underscored by her wretched half-conscious screams, elicited in James a spiraling surge of righteous fury so potent that it shook his frame from head to foot. His back against the wall, James heaved himself upright, one hand on his neck, the other on the Guadalupe medal at his throat. "Showalter!" he bellowed.

Mitch gaped, stunned to see James standing on his bare feet.

"Just for the hell of it," James cried, "what say you we try something *really* transgressive?" Holding Mitch's dumbfounded gaze, James punctuated his challenge by unsnapping and unzipping his jeans. He shimmied out of them. Then his briefs. Kicking his clothes down the stairs in front of him, his left hand once again pressed to the wound draining away his life, James leaned against the wall behind him for support, his naked body as bloody as a newborn's, and almost as helpless. He swallowed several times, trying to take increasingly rapid and shallow breaths through his mouth, between his words: "You wouldn't pass...on a limit-experience...that even Richard enjoyed...would you?"

Mitch frowned in concentration, his eyes traveling up and down James's shivering, bloody body, taking the measure of what was being offered him in exchange for Guadalupe Cruz. "*Richard?*" he gasped out.

"Richard," James declared.

His big Adam's apple working up and down, Mitch limped slowly toward James, Lupe's blouse trailing along the floor behind him like a tattered, bloody flag.

As Mitch drew near, James's glanced, just once, at the chalice on the floor, then at Lupe; then let his eyes drift shut a moment, working to set aside his own harrowing imaginings of approaching humiliation and horror and bend them one last time on beauty, on love, on Lupe, and the Dark Virgin of his vision.

When he felt Mitch's hot breath against his forehead, he opened his eyes and watched, almost indifferently, as Mitch wiped his bloodied face with Lupe's shirt; then tied it around his neck in a makeshift dressing. Face to bloodied face, their warm breaths mingling in the winter air, James noticed that Mitch had lost one of his welkin-blue contacts in their struggle, leaving his right eye naked and pale and lifeless as a fish's. Lifting his knife hand, Mitch brushed a lock of hair away from James's clammy forehead. A look of terrible longing swept fleetingly across the big man's mismatched eyes. "Jimmy," he whispered, almost whimpered, "Jimmy...Jimmy..."

For a moment James was moved to a frightening feeling of pity. He had, he realized, seen this look on this man's face before, perhaps many times, but never noticed it. But it was too late now, far too late for pity or regret, and as Mitch took him by the shoulders and turned him around, almost gently, to face the wall at the top of the stairs, the only love James knew compelled him to shove the tardy emotions from his mind.

James waited until he heard the sound of leather crackling as Mitch unzipped and pushed down his leggings. Taking one last shallow gulp of cold air, all he could get in his tightening lungs, James pressed his palms flat against the wall in front of him. When he felt Mitch's hands on his hips and his body pressing against his, his hot breath against the back of his head, James heaved backwards with every remaining ounce of strength he possessed, sure that he was sending himself as well as the giant hurtling down the steep, narrow Tower stairs behind.

But James didn't pitch backwards; instead he felt Mitch tripping behind him, his ankles vised in his own leggings just as James's shoulder struck the doorjamb. Catching hold of it with one hand, James heard the rumble of Mitch's massive body in thundering free-fall down the steep stairs. Then a sharp cry. Then the sound of air hissing out of Mitch's lungs like a punctured balloon. Then midnight silence.

James tired to right himself against the doorjamb, but his limbs had all gone stiff from the cold and shock, he couldn't feel his feet at all, and his waning strength was now completely spent. He crumpled in a heap on the icy landing, his naked body anesthetized with cold, his throat burning with thirst, the brick walls of the Tower whorling around his head in a blue-white fog. He reached out for a handful of snow to drink, to quench the raging thirst, then heard something and looked up, his eyes rolling: Lupe was conscious, was looking at him, was moving, was dragging herself toward him with her good arm, and groaning like an animal with every racking pull.

James turned over and vomited on the floor; then passed out in his own muck. When he came to again—he didn't know how long he had been out—his head was in Lupe's lap, his body covered with his parka. Her good hand pressed against the cloth at his neck. She was rocking back and forth against her own pain, pleading aloud in English and in Spanish and in cries of anguish, pleading with God and the Mother of God not to let him die.

In truth, all James wanted at this moment of exhaustion and relief was to let go, like this, naked and emptied, his head in her lap. If only to please her, however, he tried to right his spinning mind and to hang on a little longer. But it was no good. He couldn't get his breath, the world in his head was heaving, and he just couldn't hold on.

He didn't hear the sound of many pairs of boots on the stairs as his thoughts tumbled one last time; then grew still; then drifted silently into the heart of the inland sea.

Chapter Sixteen:
The Sign of Victory

Then seeke this path, that I to thee presage,
Which after all to heauen shall thee send;
Then peaceably thy painefull pilgrimage
To yonder same Hierusalem do bend,
Where is for thee ordaind a blessed end:
For thou emongst those Saints, whom thou doest see,
Shalt be a Saint, and thine owne nations frend
And Patrone: thou Saint George shalt called bee,
Saint George of mery England, the signe of victoree.

Edmund Spenser, *The Faerie Qveene*

James's eyes fluttered open to a blur of white. He couldn't seem to move his head, which was mildly throbbing; then felt a quiver of astonishment that he could feel anything at all.

Discovering that he could move his eyes at least, he looked around and remembered that he had seen all this before, this white room with its tubes and bottles and strange machinery with blinking lights; had been awake before, several times, in this room, in this bed. He even remembered, after a moment's mental labor, the bandages over his nose and neck, and the men and women in mauve scrubs who kept popping in every few minutes to perform mysterious medical procedures on him, and pester him with absurd questions, and order him about with testy instructions to move this limb or that finger; or peer into his pupils with penlights, or take his blood pressure, or rearrange the plastic tubing that seemed to sprout from his every appendage. Each separate scene of semi-consciousness came to come to him as a new and unimaginably wonderful awakening, and each time there had been only one impatient question on his tongue—"*Lupe?*"—and each time this nurse or that doctor had assured him that Miss Cruz was just fine, and that she was here in the hospital nearby, and would he *please* lie still and cooperate?

And then, most amazing of all, James's eyes fell on the surpassingly beautiful sight, to carry in his mind forever, of a pair of blue-green eyes framed by a nimbus of black hair.

James smiled weakly, and Lupe smiled back.

"Well, now," he whispered, "this can't be hell if you're here."

Laughing a little, though it wasn't a very happy sound, Lupe stretched out one hand to stroke his cheek. Her other arm, he noticed, was wrapped tightly against her body in a sling underneath a shapeless hospital robe. There was a large bandage on her temple, and some sort of brace encircling her neck.

"You all right?" he said, frowning.

She shrugged. "Fracture. Con-concussion. Exposure, c-c-cuts…a helluva stiff neck." She closed her eyes for a moment and looked to be struggling against tears. "Nothing that won't heal, I guess, now that I know you're g-g-going to be all right." She sniffled. "They-they-they figured they'd b-b-better bring me in, you know, to let you see me, or you'd yank out your IVs and c-c-come looking for me."

"Damned right," he agreed. Then, realizing that he could now move one arm, the one that wasn't IV'd, James reached out to wipe her damp cheek with a tingling finger.

Her face trembled beneath his hand. "J-James," she whispered, "I passed out. What did he d-d-do to you?"

He caressed her face. "Nothing that won't heal, my love, now that I know you're all right." He swallowed, a rush of hellish memories slamming like a freight train into his shocky memory. "My God…my God, what you've suffered because of me…"

She clapped her hand over her mouth and drew her face into a pinched expression he could not understand, because it looked like shame. "I was such a coward," she choked out. "I just wanted to d-d-die."

He tried to shake his head, but the bandages prevented it. "None of that, now," he said firmly, sniffling back his own tears, determined to play the strong one, for the moment, for her sake. "You were half his size. Not to mention, half unconscious from sleeping pills and a blow to the head. Trust me, it was an upside-down grace. If you'd really fought him, it would have ended sooner, I suppose, but we'd both be dead."

She looked as if she didn't believe him, but she nodded anyway, perhaps to humor him. "Quit t-t-talking so much," she said at last, reaching for the box of tissues on his bedside table. "You're kind of stitched tog-g-gether." She blew her nose. "They lost c-c-count of how many pints of blood they've had to hose into you."

Chuckling at that, he tried to obey her, if only to humor her as well. But a few seconds later he just had to ask, "Showalter?"

She pocketed the tissue. "His neck is bro-broken. And he lost a kidney to his own knife. They say if he lives at all, he-he-he'll never wa-wa-walk. Oh, G-G-God forgive me, I'm so g-g-glad!"

James closed his eyes, a half-smile of hard satisfaction tracing his lips.

Lupe squeezed his hand as he began to doze off again. "You're fa-fa-famous, you know."

James's eyes rolled open. "Come again?"

"I said you're f-f-famous. A mo-mo-month ago you were prime suspect. Now you're the hero who t-took down D-D-Dropped Dead Fred. For fifteen minutes at least, you're almost as f-f-famous as…"

"I know. Almost as famous as he is."

Abandoning all pretense, Lupe broke down. "Oh, God," she sobbed, "I thought I'd lost you!"

He stroked her hair and let her cry.

A little while later, when she was once again able to talk, she wiped her face some more and told him all the other things that had happened the night before; how Masefield had found out what was happening and phoned her brother Martin, who had rushed to the Tower with a rosary in one hand and a butcher knife in the other, followed hard upon by a dozen other friars in various states of preparation to do battle, including Holy Hill's septuagenarian infirmarian. The infirmarian had tended to James's otherwise almost certainly mortal arterial wound until Masefield's helicopter arrived a few minutes later, and flew them to the nearest trauma center.

"Bo Jeffrey's out on bail," she added. "In fact, he's out in the waiting room, along wi-wi-with Jack and Masefield and the Lancianos, and my-my-my entire family. Even Ramon's eating crow, and v-v-very humbly, too." Finally smiling a little, she glanced through the window that separated his cubicle from the nurses' station. "You're not really supposed to have visitors yet, but I'm sure they'll let your father in when he arrives."

This was more than James could absorb. "Cyril's coming?" he exclaimed, almost sitting up in bed.

"Blast it, lie still! They'll shoo me out of here if they see you g-getting excited! My d-d-dad called him. He's flying in this evening."

"Well, I'll be damned," James said, settling back against his pillow, drained from the brief exertion. "Matt must have told him I was dying for sure to have accomplished that." His eyes drifted shut again in a druggy warmth. Well, he supposed he *had* been dying, or very nearly. "You know," he said sleepily, "I found out who I am up there."

She leaned forward, her lips against his cheek. "I've always known who you are."

But he didn't hear her. "I'm the man," he said, consciousness drifting, "who refused to become…a dra…"

He slipped into a dreamless sleep.

Epilogue:
The Mystery of Things

...Come, let's away to prison:
We two alone will sing like birds i' the cage:
When thou dost ask me blessing, I'll kneel down
And ask of thee forgiveness: So we'll live,
And pray, and sing, and tell old tales, and laugh
At gilded butterflies, and hear poor rogues
Talk of court news; and we'll talk with them too,
Who loses and who wins, who's in, who's out;
And take upon's the mystery of things,
As if we were God's spies: And we'll wear out,
In a wall'd prison, packs and sects of great ones
That ebb and flow by the moon.

Shakespeare, *King Lear*

A narrow shaft of morning sunlight shone in muted turquoise through the Plexiglas cabin window, warming James's suntanned face. Folding one arm behind his head, he smelled the new varnish over the teak paneling above the berth, heard the lazy lapping of lake water around the hull, felt the gentle rocking of the boat under his back, and the coolness of the sheet over his naked body. He seemed to have awakened from a dream he could not now remember, except that the flavor of it, judging by the wash of luminous contentment it had left behind, must have been both refreshing and enchanted. Feeling a special warmth against his side, he turned his eyes on Lupe's sable hair and bare back.

Smiling, he reached out so that his fingers were just an inch from her skin and let his hand float on the air above the curve of her back and hips, marveling a little that, after five months of marriage, the proximity of her naked body could actually bring him comfort and peace, as well as arousal.

Their period of honeymoon was coming to its proper end, of course, but James felt no sadness at its inevitable passing. The important thing—and he was getting good at knowing what were the important things—was that they were together; that he loved and was loved, even as they were still forced to face, on an almost daily basis, the new and terrible world created for them by the hellish imagination of James Mitchell Showalter. It had taken James a while to admit that it hadn't ended that night in the Tower, and he was beginning to realize that in some ways it never would, at least this side of the General Resurrection.

In spite of Milwaukee's famous Speedy Trial system, Mitch Showalter's day in court had been put off until the paralyzed defendant, at great expense to Wisconsin's taxpayers, was deemed sufficiently "rehabilitated"—Lord, what a word—to sit through the legal proceedings in his motor-powered wheelchair. The preliminary hearings were almost complete, after a brief postponement the month before when Mitch, no doubt hoping to prop up his forthcoming insanity defense, had bit off one of his own senseless fingers right there in the hearing room in front of the judge. The trial itself was to begin in a few days in the same ultra-secure courtroom where Jeff Dahmer's public career had come to its legal end. The judge, however, had not yet delivered a final ruling on whether the trial would be televised, and James was still hoping that he and Lupe would be spared that much at least of the ordeal. After all, he thought, no one had yet consulted them, the key witnesses, on whether they were fit to stand trial.

There were a few improvements, however, in this new world James had come to know: while MPD had not yet been able to bring charges relating to the murders of DeBrun or any of the porn dealers, Nick Calabresi and ten of his closest associates had been indicted by a federal grand jury in Chicago on some two dozen counts of racketeering and conspiracy after one of Calabresi's soldiers, a young Potowatomi from Forest County, had agreed to enter the FBI's Witness Protection Program.

Closer to home, SANA had been mothballed, once and for all, even before the jury in Peter Krato's obstruction-of-justice trial turned in a unanimous conviction. The Archdiocese, which had taken some public heat for not trying to close the place sooner, had bought the big house on Newberry Boulevard as a residence for Catholic students. Renamed "Immaculata House," it was being set up to operate under the direction of the Oratorians along the lines originally set down by Lionel Krato.

Even the seemingly invincible Max Heisler had not come out unscathed by last year's events. Heisler continued his generous support of the Institute which bore his name, but had handed over the day-to-day management of the Great Lakes Bank to his daughter, Fran, and the Institute to Franco Lanciano. Heisler, Lanciano had told James sadly, was a broken man, unable to live with the consequences of his own erroneous judgments concerning Barry DeBrun. The once energetic financier now spent the better part of his solitary hours sitting on the beach at his lakeside home in Door County, pursuing some form of penance obscure to all outsiders.

For the very private James Ireton, the notoriety of the last months had proved almost unendurable, even though the world at large looked upon him, for the moment at least, as a hero. The police had released only the sketchiest description of events that night in the Tower, but not only had the Carmelites seen the number of Shrine visitors nearly double in the last few months, pictures of James and Lupe, as well as of Mitch, had been printed in newspapers and magazines across the country, and on scores of television news programs. They were recognized on the street and begged for their autographs like Hollywood celebrities; requests came in almost daily, offering large sums of money for "exclusive" interviews with famous journalists. When a nervy cable television producer showed up at the Institute entrance one afternoon, seeking the rights to their story for a movie-of-the-week, James had deposited him bodily down the front steps, coming within an inch—and an effusive apology from Dr. Franco Lanciano—of being charged with assault and battery. James had on several occasions been tempted to grab Lupe and run to Toronto, or even back to England. And that was desperate.

Watching the gentle movements of his wife's back as she breathed, James reminded himself that, too soon, the world would be disabused of its image of James Ireton as dragonslayer, when the links he had unintentionally forged in Mitch's chain of grisly responsibility were exposed to public view at the trial; but whatever the world's report, James was determined that he would not be run out of his home, here where his fragile roots had begun to dig deep into the sandy soil along the Lake Michigan shoreline. Lupe's family, now his family, was here. His friends were here—Jack, above all, but also Lanciano and Masefield, and even Trisha Perl. The graves of people he had loved—of Lionel and Fr. Bricusse, of Bel and Nadine and Richard—were here. Lupe, moreover, had a long way to go on her PhD, and James figured he might as well make himself useful in the interim by accepting Lanciano's offer of a faculty position in the new English Renaissance Program. James even nourished the tentative but not entirely untenable hope that in his own new-found peace he might be able to supply just a little of that missing grace and humanity, which Arthur Bricusse had once brought to Western Civ. God knows, James thought, Bricusse would have wanted him to try.

In spite of all the publicity, the Cruz family had somehow managed to keep the February wedding, postponed on the demands of sundry physicians, a small and joyous family event. Cyril had not only summoned the grace to serve as Lector at the nuptial Mass, presided over by Fr. Martin Cruz at Holy Hill, he had even had the good sense to fall under the spell of his new daughter-in-law, Mick-Spic-Yank though she was, and a Papist to boot. "You've done much better than I expected," were Cyril's final words to James before departing for his flight back to London.

James chuckled. Well, it was a beginning; a second chance of a sort, and one he could never have foreseen. He was determined to nurture the relationship like a sickly infant.

The sunlight off the lake refracted in shimmering waves on the ceiling and on the sheets. Feeling Lupe stir beside him, James leaned over to brush his lips against her hair. The familiar rosy scent of it moved him to turn his mind away from horrors to the daily beauty of his life.

The honeymoon he had so carefully planned from his hospital bed was a "barefoot" cruise through the West Indies and Grenadines in a three-masted tall ship. James and Lupe took in lush green islands, turquoise seas, and each other. Then they disembarked for a week in Mexico and a pilgrimage to the Shrine of Our Lady of Guadalupe, which Lupe had humorously referred to as "James's wedding gift to G-G-God"; but how true that was. James would never forget the moment when they stepped out of the tour bus in front of the basilica, his mouth agape at the sheer magnitude of the enormous plaza and its swelling sea of pilgrims. Many of the natives among them, unashamed of their own colorful piety, approached the basilica on penitent knees. To the amazement and embarrassment of his Anglo companions, and in gratitude for the gifts of life and love and a second chance, James, too, had knelt and crossed the cobblestone plaza on bruised and torn knees.

James smile folded into a frown — Lupe turned over on her other side — as he remembered their mountaintop excursion the following day to *Teotihuacan*, the eerie and ancient Place-Where-Men-Become-Gods. There was a pyramid up there, the two hundred foot high Pyramid of the Sun, built two thousand years ago over a cave believed by the Aztecs to be the center of the universe. Something unusual had happened that afternoon at the temple, adorned with the Snake of all snakes. Whether it was the strenuous climb, the thin air and high altitude, or the tour guide's too-vivid narrative of heart-extracting human sacrifices performed on the spot with obsidian blades, Lupe had fainted. That night, and off and on ever since, she had suffered wrenching recurring nightmares.

It was as if, in the love and passion and security of their union, Lupe had begun to gather the very nightmares that James had shaken off, since James's own beastly dreams had been inexplicably exorcised in the Tower. For some reason then, mysterious to him, *he* was the stronger one right now, and she the one needing to see the beauty of life through his eyes, as he had once needed to see it through hers. He was no longer the beggar, feeding on her abundance; there was but one heart between them now, and grace came to them, no longer singly, but as a communion of persons in a covenant of love.

Lupe had, in fact, suffered another dream-reunion with terror just last night. They'd gone ashore for a Fourth of July picnic with friends and family in South Shore park, during which time James had extracted a promise from Masefield, who if not three was at least two sheets to the wind from Mexican beer, to somehow lay hands on that myrtlewood chalice once it was released from police custody after the trial. "It's for my son," James had told Masefield, "remember?" After the festivities, unfortunately, they had all had the rotten luck to catch a glimpse on the five-o-clock news of Mitch Showalter on his way to a hearing. It was the killer's first public appearance since his arrest. Though it was reassuring, in a way, to see the once powerful man gone bloated and flabby, with a urine-bag strapped to his wheelchair, and his bottle-thick glasses amplifying his dull eyes until they looked like a frog's, Showalter had, nonetheless, positively mugged for the camera. Lupe had become instantly sick. Afterward, she had awakened James at midnight with her thrashings. He had soothed her with whispered kisses and tenderly made love to her. She had fallen asleep again while he was still inside her.

Lupe stirred once more; then turned over on her back and yawned.

"Wh-what are you gri-gri-grinning about?" she stammered sleepily, her eyes fluttering open as she stretched. She'd been stammering so badly in fact, these last few months, that she'd begun seeing a therapist.

He nudged a strand of hair from her eyes. "Three guesses and the first two don't count."

She chuckled hoarsely. "I'll ha-ha-have to keep drumming up those nightmares, if you insist on p-p-providing all that lovely ph-ph-physical therapy."

"I'm more than happy to provide the physical therapy without the provocation of nightmares, thank you very much."

She smiled at that, but then a familiar shadow darkened her eyes. She pulled the sheet up over her breasts.

He snuggled in close beside her. "Lupe, I was wondering…"

The sound of her name on his lips seemed to dispel the shadow in her eyes. "Yes, beloved?" she said.

"After the trial, what would you say to a short trip back home. I mean to England. I think it might be time." He put his hand underneath the sheet and gently squeezed the small firm knot at her belly, which was growing daily. "I think it's time to start rebuilding the ruined house of Ireton."

Smiling with contentment at the feel of his hand on her body, she closed her eyes and said, "You know I'd go anywhere with you. To hell and b-back."

"We've already been there," he grumbled, "and one trip's quite enough." Bending over her, his hand slipped down between her legs. "I was hoping for a visit to happier realms. My dreary childhood notwithstanding, there's a good deal to be said for the auld sod. And you simply have to see Salisbury Cathedral."

Her cheeks flushing pink, Lupe folded one leg over his hips and moaned with pleasure. "You are inc-c-corrigible!"

"Ain't I though." His lips moved to her breast. "But after five months of torrid conjugality with me," he added into her skin, "I'm amazed you can still blush."

"After f-f-five months of t-t-torrid conjugality with you," she returned in a throaty voice, one hand gripping his hair, the nails of her other hand digging into his back, "I'm not sure this is pregnancy, or if my reproductive system's simply go-gone into sh-shock."

"And what sport it's been, too," he declared, kissing his way down her body until he was stretched out between her legs, his head on her belly. "Let me see, how did that Donne poem go…

> "Licence my roving hands, and let them go
> Before, behind, between, above, below.
> O my America, my new found land,
> My kingdom, safeliest when with one man manned,
> My mine of precious stones, my empery,
> How blessed am I in this discovering thee!
> To enter in these bonds, is to be free;
> Then where my hand is set, my seal shall be!"

She laughed and laughed at that, and tousled his hair with her fingers, and as she laughed, James laid his ear against her womb as if listening for a tiny heartbeat.

"What do you say, *Dieguito*?" he whispered to the mysterious little being curled within. "Let's see if we can do the thing right this time, shall we?"

Acknowledgments

There is an old saying in the writing trade: a novel is never finished, it is abandoned. As the mother of six children, *The Mystery of Things* took me far longer to abandon than it should have, almost fourteen years. I made every mistake a first-time novelist could possibly make. The upside of this otherwise daunting equation was that I learned a lot along that long road, met a number of fascinating people who would have otherwise remained strangers, and now have the pleasure of publicly thanking at least some of them.

First of all and above all, fourteen years is a long time to pursue what Tolkien once called "a mad hobby." I wouldn't have toughed it out without the unflagging support and encouragement of my husband, Daniel, and our children, Rachel, John, Kevin, Luke, Maire, and Liam. The older kids were my first fans and my first (and last) editors. Without their youthful enthusiasm and storytelling expertise, the narrative would have been a good deal more muddled. Without their elvish eyesight the text would have been a good deal less polished.

Two other wonderful "editors" along the way deserve special mention: Fr. Martinus Cawley of Our Lady of Guadalupe Abbey in Lafayette, Oregon, whose expertise I first sought while researching *la Guadalupana*, and whose lovely translation of the *Nican Mopohua* he graciously permitted me to excerpt; also Meredith Phelan, from whom I learned so much about the publishing business, and who labored with this constitutionally wordy first-timer to reduce the original manuscript from half a million words to a more manageable size. Bless you, Mer!

Things, as it turned out, required a surprising amount of research. Thank God for librarians! I owe much to the dauntless staff of the Kenosha (WI), Public Library, the Salem (OR) Public Library, as well as the librarians of

UW-Parkside, UW-Milwaukee, and Willamette University. They answered my many questions and tidied up after my endless raids on their Shakespeare and Wisconsin history stacks, no doubt without ever knowing what sort of mischief I was up to.

I also owe a debt of gratitude to the officers and staff of the Milwaukee Police Department and *The Milwaukee Journal Sentinel*, all of whom were patient and gracious in answering my questions and leading me about their buildings, and none of whom should be held responsible for any points in the story where I may have "got it wrong."

As a writer whose imagination is most often sparked by a sense of place, I owe similar thanks to the staff, clergy, owners, students, and sundry patrons of the many wonderful local venues, which provided me with an abundance of terrific scene and background locations: Oxford University, Salisbury Cathedral and Wilton House in England, and in Wisconsin: Milwaukee City Hall, Mader's, Karl Ratzsch's, the John Hawks Pub, Beans & Barley, the Milwaukee County Department of Parks, Ray Radigan's, Ma Fischer's Diner, the Milwaukee Marina, the Golda Meir Library, the UW-Milwaukee Newman Center, Marquette University, Carthage College, Bradford High School, Prairie School, Kenosha Harbor, the Port of Milwaukee, the Hoan Bridge, the Quadracci Pavilion, the Firstar Building, the Archdiocese of Milwaukee, the Oriental Theatre, and the Milwaukee Repertory Theater…just for starters! Milwaukee is a great town, and southeastern Wisconsin one of the most vibrant, distinctive, and beautiful regions in the country. Without the inspiration this unique place and its people provided, this book would have never been born. *On, Wisconsin!*

Two very special "venue" mentions must be made.

A good deal of my passion for Shakespeare is owed to the actors, directors, and crew of the American Players Theatre in Spring Green. It was their mastery and enthusiasm, which first showed Clan Murphy how thrilling Shakespeare-in-performance could be. Their late (and much-missed) colleague, Stephen Hemming, who was so very generous of his time with this theatre newbie, will forever figure in my mind as the most intelligent, vital, and magnetic Falstaff and Iago I have ever seen or hope to see. The good God, I am persuaded, has an especially glorious place set aside in heaven for actors.

Sixth and lastly, as Dogberry would way, *The Mystery of Things* was conceived one weekend while I was on retreat at Holy Hill, where an excursion to the top of the Scenic Tower convinced me that it was the perfect venue for a climactic confrontation between Good and Evil. I pray the dear Carmelite friars will forgive me for borrowing their exquisite Shrine for my imaginations of mayhem overturned by grace, and that in some small way this book may serve as an invitation to pilgrims to seek out the blessings to be gleaned at Holy Hill, Shrine of Our Lady Help of Christians.

Our Lady of Guadalupe, Dark Virgin of the Americas…*pray for us sinners, now, and at the hour of our death. Amen.*

To order copies of this book, contact your
local bookstore. You can also order online at
http://www.idyllspress.com, or send a check
for $29.95 plus $2.00 shipping for Media
Mail or $4.00 for Priority Mail to:

Idylls Press
PO Box 3566
Salem, OR 97302-3566

E-mail us at: info@idyllspress.com